The Adventures of Sherlock Holmes

Sir Arthur Conan Doyle

The Adventures of Sherlock Holmes

BOOKS LTD.

Printed in the United States of America

Contents

The Life of Sir Arthur Conan Doyle

Arthur Conan Doyle was born in Edinburgh, Scotland, on May 22, 1859. His grandfather, John Doyle, was a caricaturist whose weekly political cartoons were admired and widely circulated. His father, Charles, also an artist, earned most of his meager income from his position as architect-clerk in the civil service. The fact that the family was not well off did not deter his devoted mother, Mary, from seeing that her seven children were properly educated in the Irish Catholic tradition.

A strict schoolmaster made young Arthur's first two school years patently miserable. From age nine through sixteen he attended the preparatory school of Stonyhurst College, after which he spent a year at a more lenient school in Austria, where he did little to distinguish himself as a student of German, but had great fun playing tuba in the school band.

Upon his return from Austria, Doyle entered the medical school of the University of Edinburgh, where he would meet Dr. Joseph Bell, a surgeon at the Edinburgh infirmary. Thin, wiry, a brilliant diagnostician, it was Bell upon whom Doyle would later model his famous protagonist, Mr. Sherlock Holmes.

Doyle's medical studies were interrupted twice, once in 1880 when he spent seven months as ship's surgeon on a whaling vessel in the Arctic, and again in 1881 when he took a berth as medical officer on a cargo ship bound for Africa. During school vacations he worked as a medical assistant to augment the family's income. A passable student, he received his Bachelor of Medicine degree in 1881 and his doctorate in 1885. In 1882, he set up a small and only modestly successful practice in Southsea, England.

Unlike today, a medical degree in late nineteenth century Britain did not virtually assure one of a comfortable life. Still, had young Dr. Doyle seen fit to establish himself as a "Catholic" doctor, as was the custom of the day, he and his new wife,

Louise (née Hawkins), would have been far better off than they were. However, Doyle had by this time abandoned the Catholic faith, believing that "the evils of religion have all come from accepting things which cannot be proved." Thus he could not in good conscience call upon his family's high-placed Catholic friends for support and referrals.

To fill the spare time between appointments, Conan Doyle appeased his literary penchant by writing stories. Throughout the course of his life, he would write many adventure and science fiction stories, historical romances, books on Spiritualism, and objective works, including, *The War in South Africa: Its Cause and Conduct* (a widely circulated pamphlet denying British atrocities in the Boer War, for which he received his knighthood in 1902), but of his many works, none would be so fervently embraced by readers the world over as those that we have the extreme good fortune to be holding in our hands: *The Adventures of Sherlock Holmes*.

In his later years, Sir Arthur Conan Doyle became convinced that the souls of the dead could communicate with the living, and he devoted much time, energy, and a great deal of his money to the furtherance of the Spiritualist cause. Thus, he died in 1930, secure in his belief that, "Life and love go on forever."

—R.L. Fisher

Foreword

If ever a pair of fictional characters can be said to have leapt from the pages of a literary work and taken on lives of their own, those characters are Dr. Watson and Sherlock Holmes. Even today, a century after the publication of the first Sherlock Holmes adventure, one can find dyed-in-the-wool Sherlockians who insist that Holmes and Watson were not only real people, but that they are, in fact, still alive!

Despite all evidence to the contrary, these disciples insist that the stories involving Sherlock Holmes and his stalwart companion, Watson, were not the product of Sir Arthur Conan Doyle's imagination, but that they faithfully represent the true case histories of the "real" Watson and Holmes. The assumption is that Sir Arthur Conan Doyle signed his name to the Sherlock Holmes stories in order to protect the anonymity of the legitimate author, Dr. John Watson—a situation which, of course, reduces Arthur Conan Doyle's participation in the matter to that of literary agent.

Thankfully, the tongues of most of these Holmesian "scholars" are planted firmly in their cheeks when pronouncements such as these are made (and those whose tongues are elsewhere ought to have their heads examined!). Still, the very fact that grown men and women actually take pleasure in such absurd conjecture is a subject that beckons attention.

What is it about Holmes and Watson that makes them live in our minds? Volumes have been devoted to this question. Many elements have been credited for the enduring popularity of Sherlock Holmes: the consummate casting of Watson as a conservative foil for the eccentricity of Holmes; the often ingenious plotting; the lifelike dialogue; the charming late nineteenth-century London setting. But above all we must pay tribute to Sir Arthur Conan Doyle's extraordinary ability to breathe life into his characters, to make them come alive.

In the years prior to his marriage, Conan Doyle augmented

his meager medical income by writing short stories. A number found their way onto the pages of such small publications as *London Society*, and *The Boy's Own Paper*, but the income generated by Doyle's literary efforts never amounted to more than £15 ($75.00) in any given year.

The years from 1885–1890 were more productive, both from a literary standpoint and from a financial one. Three stories, "Habakuk Jephson's Statement," "John Huxford's Hiatus," and "The Ring of Thoth," were published by the prestigious *Cornhill* magazine for the then stupendous sum of £30 ($150.00) apiece. This was a giant step up for a writer whose stories had previously brought no more than £4 or £5. Any acclaim garnered by the stories, however, did not extend to the author himself, as it was the magazine's policy to not give credit to the writers (and thus to protect them, presumably, from the perils and the degradation of fame). Another story, "The Physiologist's Wife," this time with an author's byline, was published by the venerable Scottish magazine, *Blackwoods*. These literary victories, though small compared to what awaited him, greatly bolstered Conan Doyle's confidence in his abilities and made him eager to conquer new literary ground.

Seeking new challenges, Doyle hit upon the idea of trying his hand at detective fiction. Since his youth, he had been a fan of Edgar Allan Poe's detective, C. Auguste Dupin. Still, as much as he admired Dupin, Doyle believed it possible to add something to the genre of detective fiction by creating a character who would "reduce this unorganized business (fictional detection) to something nearer to an exact science."

At the University of Edinburgh, Doyle had been greatly impressed by one of his teachers, Dr. Joseph Bell, because of his uncanny knack for deduction and "eerie trick of spotting details." It occurred to Doyle that no detective, fictional or otherwise, would suffer by possessing similar aptitudes. Thus, Doyle mixed his ingredients: Dr. Bell's remarkable powers of observation; certain idiosyncrasies borrowed from C. Auguste Dupin; and a few of Doyle's own quirks and mannerisms, and came up with the amazing Mr. Sherlock Holmes.

Surprisingly, the first Sherlock Holmes adventure, *A Study in Scarlet*, which was completed in 1886, did not bring its author anything even remotely approaching fame or prosperity. At least five publishers rejected the manuscript outright before it was finally accepted for publication by Ward, Lock & Co, a company specializing in "cheap" fiction. The expression "cheap" was widely used in those days to describe material of a sensational nature, but in this case the term extended to the writer's renumeration. Conan Doyle received for this novel-length manuscript the paltry sum of £25; and although the company published the book in several editions, he never got a penny more. Indeed, Doyle's luck ran no better when *A Study in Scarlet* finally appeared fourteen months later in the "Beton's Christmas Annual" of 1887. Readers and critics alike were at best tepid in their enthusiasm.

The second Sherlock Holmes adventure, *The Sign of Four*, which appeared in Lippencotts's Magazine in 1890, did scarcely better—which is curious to say the least, because today *The Sign of Four* is generally ranked second only to *The Hound of the Baskervilles*, when compared with the other novel-length adventures of Sherlock Holmes.

The third Sherlock Holmes story, however, "A Scandal in Bohemia," which appeared in the July 1891 issue of the Strand magazine, caused a storm of enthusiasm that had readers crying out for more.

And the rest, as they say, is history.

—R.L. Fisher

A Scandal in Bohemia

To Sherlock Holmes she is always *the* woman. I have seldom heard him mention her under any other name. In his eyes she eclipses and predominates the whole of her sex. It was not that he felt any emotion akin to love for Irene Adler. All emotions, and that one particularly, were abhorrent to his cold, precise but admirably balanced mind. He was, I take it, the most perfect reasoning and observing machine that the world has seen, but as a lover he would have placed himself in a false position. He never spoke of the softer passions, save with a gibe and a sneer. They were admirable things for the observer—excellent for drawing the veil from men's motives and actions. But for the trained reasoner to admit such intrusions into his own delicate and finely adjusted temperament was to introduce a distracting factor which might throw a doubt upon all his mental results. Grit in a sensitive instrument, or a crack in one of his own high-power lenses, would not be more disturbing than a strong emotion in a nature such as his. And yet there was but one woman to him, and that woman was the late Irene Adler, of dubious and questionable memory.

I had seen little of Holmes lately. My marriage had drifted us away from each other. My own complete happiness, and the home-centred interests which rise up around the man who first finds himself master of his own establishment, were sufficient to absorb all my attention, while Holmes, who loathed every form of society with his whole Bohemian soul, remained in our lodgings in Baker Street, buried among his old books, and alternating from week to week between cocaine and ambition, the drowsiness of the drug, and the fierce energy of his own keen nature. He was still, as ever, deeply attracted by the study of crime, and occupied his immense faculties and extraordinary powers of observation in following out those clues, and clearing up those mysteries which had been abandoned as hopeless by the official police. From time to time I heard some vague account of his doings: of his summons to Odessa in the case of the Trepoff murder, of his clearing up of the singular tragedy of the Atkinson brothers at Trincomalee, and finally of the mission which he had accomplished so delicately and successfully for the reigning family of Holland. Beyond these signs of his activity, however, which I merely shared with all the readers of the daily press, I knew little of my former friend and companion.

One night—it was on the twentieth of March, 1888—I was returning from a journey to a patient (for I had now returned to civil practice), when my way led me through Baker Street. As I passed the well-remembered door, which must always be associated in my mind with my wooing, and with the dark incidents of the *Study in Scarlet*, I was seized with a keen desire to see Holmes again, and to know how he was employing his extraordinary powers. His rooms were brilliantly lit, and, even as I looked up, I saw his tall, spare figure pass twice in a dark silhouette against the blind. He was pacing the room swiftly, eagerly, with his head sunk upon his chest and his hands clasped behind him. To me, who knew his every mood and habit, his attitude and manner told their own story. He was at work again. He had risen out of his drug-created dreams and was hot upon the scent of some new problem. I rang the bell and was shown up to the chamber which had formerly been in part my own.

His manner was not effusive. It seldom was; but he was glad, I think, to see me. With hardly a word spoken, but with a kindly eye, he waved me to an armchair, threw across his case of cigars, and indicated a spirit case and a gasogene in the corner. Then he stood before the fire and looked me over in his singular introspective fashion.

"Wedlock suits you," he remarked. "I think, Watson, that you have put on seven and a half pounds since I saw you."

"Seven!" I answered.

"Indeed, I should have thought a little more. Just a trifle more, I fancy, Watson. And in practice again, I observe. You did not tell me that you intended to go into harness."

"Then, how do you know?"

"I see it, I deduce it. How do I know that you have been getting yourself very wet lately, and that you have a most clumsy and careless servant girl?"

"My dear Holmes," said I, "this is too much. You would certainly have been burned, had you lived a few centuries ago. It is true that I had a country walk on Thursday and came home in a dreadful mess, but as I have changed my clothes I can't imagine how you deduce it. As to Mary Jane, she is incorrigible, and my wife has given her notice; but there, again, I fail to see how you work it out."

He chuckled to himself and rubbed his long, nervous hands together.

"It is simplicity itself," said he; "my eyes tell me that on the inside of your left shoe, just where the firelight strikes it, the leather is scored by six almost parallel cuts. Obviously they have been caused by someone who has very carelessly scraped round the edges of the sole in order to remove crusted mud from it. Hence, you see, my double deduction that you had been out in vile weather, and that you had a particularly malignant boot-slitting specimen of the London slavey. As to your practice, if a gentleman walks into my rooms smelling of iodoform, with a black mark of nitrate of silver upon his right forefinger, and a bulge on the right side of his top-hat to show where he has secreted his stethoscope, I must be dull, indeed, if I do not pronounce him to be an active member of the medical profession."

I could not help laughing at the ease with which he explained his process of deduction. "When I hear you give your reasons," I remarked, "the thing always appears to me to be so ridiculously simple that I could easily do it myself, though at each successive instance of your reasoning I am baffled until you explain your process. And yet I believe that my eyes are as good as yours."

"Quite so," he answered, lighting a cigarette, and throwing himself down into an armchair. "You see, but you do not observe. The distinction is clear. For example, you have frequently seen the steps which lead up from the hall to this room."

"Frequently."

"How often?"

"Well, some hundreds of times."

"Then how many are there?"

"How many? I don't know."

"Quite so! You have not observed. And yet you have seen. That is just my point. Now, I know that there are seventeen steps, because I have both seen and observed. By the way, since you are interested in these little problems, and since you are good enough to chronicle one or two of my trifling experiences, you may be interested in this." He threw over a sheet of thick, pink-tinted note-paper which had been lying open upon the table. "It came by the last post," said he. "Read it aloud."

The note was undated, and without either signature or address.

> "There will call upon you to-night, at a quarter to eight o'clock [it said], a gentleman who desires to consult you upon a matter of the very deepest moment. Your recent services to one of the royal houses of Europe have shown that you are one who may safely be trusted with matters which are of an importance which can hardly be exaggerated. This account of you we have from all quarters received. Be in your chamber then at that hour, and do not take it amiss if your visitor wear a mask.

"This is indeed a mystery," I remarked. "What do you imagine that it means?"

"I have no data yet. It is a capital mistake to theorize before one has data. Insensibly one begins to twist facts to suit theories, instead of theories to suit facts. But the note itself. What do you deduce from it?"

I carefully examined the writing, and the paper upon which it was written.

"The man who wrote it was presumably well to do," I remarked, endeavouring to imitate my companion's processes. "Such paper could not be bought under half a crown a packet. It is peculiarly strong and stiff."

"Peculiar—that is the very word," said Holmes. "It is not an English paper at all. Hold it up to the light."

I did so, and saw a large "E" with a small "g," a "P," and a large "G" with a small "t" woven into the texture of the paper.

"What do you make of that?" asked Holmes.

"The name of the maker, no doubt; or his monogram, rather."

"Not at all. The 'G' with the small 't' stands for 'Gesellschaft,' which is the German for 'Company.' It is a customary contraction like our 'Co.' 'P,' of course, stands for 'Papier.' Now for the 'Eg.' Let us glance at our Continental Gazetteer." He took down a heavy brown volume from his shelves. "Eglow, Eglonitz—here we are, Egria. It is in a German-speaking country—in Bohemia, not far from Carlsbad. 'Remarkable as being the scene of the death of Wallenstein, and for its numerous glass-factories and paper-mills.' Ha, ha, my boy, what do you make of that?" His eyes sparkled, and he sent up a great blue triumphant cloud from his cigarette.

"The paper was made in Bohemia," I said.

"Precisely. And the man who wrote the note is a German. Do you note the peculiar construction of the sentence—'This account of you we have from all quarters received.' A Frenchman or Russian could not have written that. It is the German who is so uncourteous to his verbs. It only remains, therefore, to discover what is wanted by this German who writes upon Bohemian paper and prefers wearing a mask to showing his face. And here he comes, if I am not mistaken, to resolve all our doubts."

As he spoke there was the sharp sound of horses' hoofs and grating wheels against the curb, followed by a sharp pull at the bell. Holmes whistled.

"A pair, by the sound," said he. "Yes," he continued, glancing out of the window. "A nice little brougham and a pair of beauties. A hundred and fifty guineas apiece. There's money in this case, Watson, if there is nothing else."

"I think that I had better go, Holmes."

"Not a bit, Doctor. Stay where you are. I am lost without my Boswell. And this promises to be interesting. It would be a pity to miss it."

"But your client—"

"Never mind him. I may want your help, and so may he. Here he comes. Sit down in that armchair, Doctor, and give us your best attention."

A slow and heavy step, which had been heard upon the stairs and in the passage, paused immediately outside the door. Then there was a loud and authoritative tap.

"Come in!" said Holmes.

A man entered who could hardly have been less than six feet six inches in height, with the chest and limbs of a Hercules. His dress was rich with a richness which would, in England, be looked upon as akin to bad taste. Heavy bands of astrakhan were slashed across the sleeves and fronts of his double-breasted coat, while the deep blue cloak which was thrown over his shoulders was lined with flame-coloured silk and secured at the neck with a brooch which consisted of a single flaming beryl. Boots which extended halfway up his calves, and which were trimmed at the tops with rich brown fur, completed the impression of barbaric opulence which was suggested by his whole appearance. He carried a broad-brimmed hat in his hand, while he wore across the upper part of his face, extending down past the cheekbones, a black vizard mask, which he had apparently adjusted that very moment, for his hand was still raised to it as he entered. From the lower part of the face he appeared to be a man of strong character, with a thick, hanging lip, and a long, straight chin suggestive of resolution pushed to the length of obstinacy.

"You had my note?" he asked with a deep harsh voice and a strongly marked German accent. "I told you that I would call." He looked from one to the other of us, as if uncertain which to address.

"Pray take a seat," said Holmes. "This is my friend and colleague, Dr. Watson, who is occasionally good enough to help me in my cases. Whom have I the honour to address?"

"You may address me as the Count Von Kramm, a Bohemian nobleman. I understand that this gentleman, your friend, is a man of honour and discretion, whom I may trust with a matter of the most extreme importance. If not, I should much prefer to communicate with you alone."

I rose to go, but Holmes caught me by the wrist and pushed me back into my chair. "It is both, or none," said he. "You may say before this gentleman anything which you may say to me."

The Count shrugged his broad shoulders. "Then I must begin," said he, "by binding you both to absolute secrecy for two years; at the end of that time the matter will be of no importance. At present it is not too much to say that it is not too much to say that it is of such weight it may have an influence upon European history."

"I promise," said Holmes.

"And I."

"You will excuse this mask," continued our strange visitor. "The august person who employs me wishes his agent to be unknown to you, and I may confess at once that the title by which I have just called myself is not exactly my own."

"I was aware of it," said Holmes drily.

"The circumstances are of great delicacy, and every precaution has to be taken to quench what might grow to be an immense scandal and seriously compromise one of the reigning families of Europe. To speak plainly, the matter implicates the great House of Ormstein, hereditary kings of Bohemia."

"I was also aware of that," murmured Holmes, settling himself down in his armchair and closing his eyes.

Our visitor glanced with some apparent surprise at the languid, lounging figure of the man who had been no doubt depicted to him as the most incisive reasoner and most energetic agent in Europe. Holmes slowly reopened his eyes and looked impatiently at his gigantic client.

"If your Majesty would condescend to state your case," he remarked, "I should be better able to advise you."

The man sprang from his chair and paced up and down the room in uncontrollable agitation. Then, with a gesture of desperation, he tore the mask from his face and hurled it upon the ground. "You are right," he cried; "I am the King. Why should I attempt to conceal it?"

"Why, indeed?" murmured Holmes. "Your Majesty had not spoken before I was aware that I was addressing Wilhelm Gottsreich Sigismond von Ormstein, Grand Duke of Cassel-Felstein, and hereditary King of Bohemia."

"But you can understand," said our strange visitor, sitting down once more and passing his hand over his high white forehead, "you can understand that I am not accustomed to doing such business in my own person. Yet the matter was so delicate that I could not confide it to an agent without putting myself in his power. I have come incognito from Prague for the purpose of consulting you."

"Then, pray consult," said Holmes, shutting his eyes once more.

"The facts are briefly these: Some five years ago, during a lengthy visit to Warsaw, I made the acquaintance of the well-known adventuress, Irene Adler. The name is no doubt familiar to you."

"Kindly look her up in my index, Doctor," murmured Holmes without opening his eyes. For many years he had adopted a system of docketing all paragraphs concerning men and things, so that it was difficult to name a subject or a person on which he could not at once furnish information. In this case I found her biography sandwiched in between that of a Hebrew rabbi and that of a staff-commander who had written a monograph upon the deep-sea fishes.

"Let me see!" said Holmes. "Hum! Born in New Jersey in the year 1858. Contralto—hum! La Scala, hum! Prima donna Imperial Opera of Warsaw—yes! Retired from operatic stage—ha! Living in London—quite so! Your Majesty, as I understand, became entangled with this young person, wrote her some compromising letters, and is now desirous of getting those letters back."

"Precisely so. But how—"

"Was there a secret marriage?"

"None."

"No legal papers or certificates?"

"None."

"Then I fail to follow your Majesty. If this young person should produce her letters for blackmailing or other purposes, how is she to prove their authenticity?"

"There is the writing."

"Pooh, pooh! Forgery."

"My private note-paper."

"Stolen."

"My own seal."

"Imitated."

"My photograph."

"Bought."

"We were both in the photograph."

"Oh, dear! That is very bad! Your Majesty has indeed committed an indiscretion."

"I was mad—insane."

"You have compromised yourself seriously."

"I was only Crown Prince then. I was young. I am but thirty now."

"It must be recovered."

"We have tried and failed."

"Your Majesty must pay. It must be bought."

"She will not sell."

"Stolen, then."

"Five attempts have been made. Twice burglars in my pay ransacked her house. Once we diverted her luggage when she travelled. Twice she has been waylaid. There has been no result."

"No sign of it?"

"Absolutely none."

Holmes laughed. "It is quite a pretty little problem," said he.

"But a very serious one to me," returned the King reproachfully.

"Very, indeed. And what does she propose to do with the photograph?"

"To ruin me."

"But how?"

"I am about to be married."

"So I have heard."

"To Clotilde Lothman von Saxe-Meningen, second daughter of the King of Scandinavia. You may know the strict principles of her family. She is herself the very soul of delicacy. A shadow of a doubt as to my conduct would bring the matter to an end."

"And Irene Adler?"

"Threatens to send them the photograph. And she will do it. I know that she will do it. You do not know her, but she has a soul of steel. She has the face of the most beautiful of women, and the mind of the most resolute of men. Rather than I should marry another woman, there are no lengths to which she would not go—none."

"You are sure that she has not sent it yet?"

"I am sure."

"And why?"

"Because she has said that she would send it on the day when the betrothal was publicly proclaimed. That will be next Monday."

"Oh, then we have three days yet," said Holmes with a yawn. "That is very fortunate, as I have one or two matters of importance to look into just at present. Your Majesty will, of course, stay in London for the present?"

"Certainly. You will find me at the Langham under the name of the Count Von Kramm."

"Then I shall drop you a line to let you know how we progress."

"Pray do so. I shall be all anxiety."

"Then, as to money?"

"You have carte blanche."

"Absolutely?"

"I tell you that I would give one of the provinces of my kingdom to have that photograph."

"And for present expenses?"

The King took a heavy chamois leather bag from under his cloak and laid it on the table.

"There are three hundred pounds in gold and seven hundred in notes," he said.

Holmes scribbled a receipt upon a sheet of his note-book and handed it to him.

"And Mademoiselle's address?" he asked.

"Is Briony Lodge, Serpentine Avenue, St. John's Wood."

Holmes took a note of it. "One other question," said he. "Was the photograph a cabinet?"

"It was."

"Then, good-night, your Majesty, and I trust that we shall soon have some good news for you. And good-night, Watson," he added, as the wheels of the royal brougham rolled down the street. "If you will be good enough to call to-morrow afternoon at three o'clock I should like to chat this little matter over with you."

2

At three o'clock precisely I was at Baker Street, but Holmes had not yet returned. The landlady informed me that he had left the house shortly after eight o'clock in the morning. I sat down beside the fire, however, with the intention of awaiting him, however long he might be. I was already deeply interested in his inquiry, for, though it was surrounded by none of the grim and strange features which were associated with the two crimes which I have already recorded, still, the nature of the case and the exalted station of his client gave it a character of its own. Indeed, apart from the nature of the investigation which my friend had on hand, there was something in his masterly grasp of a situation, and his keen, incisive reasoning, which made it a pleasure to me to study his system of work, and to follow the quick, subtle methods by which he disentangled the most inextricable mysteries. So accustomed was I to his invariable success that the very possibility of his failing had ceased to enter into my head.

It was close upon four before the door opened, and a drunken-looking groom, ill-kempt and side-whiskered, with an inflamed face and disreputable clothes, walked into the room. Accustomed as I was to my friend's amazing powers in the use of disguises,

I had to look three times before I was certain that it was indeed he. With a nod he vanished into the bedroom, whence he emerged in five minutes tweed-suited and respectable, as of old. Putting his hands into his pockets, he stretched out his legs in front of the fire and laughed heartily for some minutes.

"Well, really!" he cried, and then he choked and laughed again until he was obliged to lie back, limp and helpless, in the chair.

"What is it?"

"It's quite too funny. I am sure you could never guess how I employed my morning, or what I ended by doing."

"I can't imagine. I suppose that you have been watching the habits, and perhaps the house, of Miss Irene Adler."

"Quite so; but the sequel was rather unusual. I will tell you, however. I left the house a little after eight o'clock this morning in the character of a groom out of work. There is a wonderful sympathy and freemasonry among horsy men. Be one of them, and you will know all that there is to know. I soon found Briony Lodge. It is a *bijou* villa, with a garden at the back, but built out in front right up to the road, two stories. Chubb lock to the door. Large sitting-room on the right side, well furnished, with long windows almost to the floor, and those preposterous English window fasteners which a child could open. Behind there was nothing remarkable, save that the passage window could be reached from the top of the coach-house. I walked round it and examined it closely from every point of view, but without noting anything else of interest.

"I then lounged down the street and found, as I expected, that there was a mews in a lane which runs down by one wall of the garden. I lent the ostlers a hand in rubbing down their horses, and received in exchange twopence, a glass of half and half, two fills of shag tobacco, and as much information as I could desire about Miss Adler, to say nothing of half a dozen other people in the neighbourhood in whom I was not in the least interested, but whose biographies I was compelled to listen to."

"And what of Irene Adler?" I asked.

"Oh, she has turned all the men's heads down in that part. She is the daintiest thing under a bonnet on this planet. So say the Serpentine-mews, to a man. She lives quietly, sings at concerts, drives out at five every day, and returns at seven sharp for dinner. Seldom goes out at other times, except when she sings.

Has only one male visitor, but a good deal of him. He is dark, handsome, and dashing, never calls less than once a day, and often twice. He is a Mr. Godfrey Norton, of the Inner Temple. See the advantages of a cabman as a confidant. They had driven him home a dozen times from Serpentine-mews, and knew all about him. When I had listened to all they had to tell, I began to walk up and down near Briony Lodge once more, and to think over my plan of campaign.

"This Godfrey Norton was evidently an important factor in the matter. He was a lawyer. That sounded ominous. What was the relation between them, and what the object of his repeated visits? Was she his client, his friend, or his mistress? If the former, she had probably transferred the photograph to his keeping. If the latter, it was less likely. On the issue of this question depended whether I should continue my work at Briony Lodge, or turn my attention to the gentleman's chambers in the Temple. It was a delicate point, and it widened the field of my inquiry. I fear that I bore you with these details, but I have to let you see my little difficulties, if you are to understand the situation."

"I am following you closely," I answered.

"I was still balancing the matter in my mind when a hansom cab drove up to Briony Lodge, and a gentleman sprang out. He was a remarkably handsome man, dark, aquiline, and moustached—evidently the man of whom I had heard. He appeared to be in a great hurry, shouted to the cabman to wait, and brushed past the maid who opened the door with the air of a man who was thoroughly at home.

"He was in the house about half an hour, and I could catch glimpses of him in the windows of the sitting-room, pacing up and down, talking excitedly, and waving his arms. Of her I could see nothing. Presently he emerged, looking even more flurried than before. As he stepped up to the cab, he pulled a gold watch from his pocket and looked at it earnestly, 'Drive like the devil,' he shouted, 'first to Gross & Hankey's in Regent Street, and then to the Church of St. Monica in the Edgeware Road. Half a guinea if you do it in twenty minutes!'

"Away they went, and I was just wondering whether I should not do well to follow them when up the lane came a neat little landau, the coachman with his coat only half-buttoned, and his tie under his ear, while all the tags of his harness were sticking out of the buckles. It hadn't pulled up before she shot out of the hall door and into it. I only caught a glimpse of her at the moment, but she was a lovely woman, with a face that a man might die for.

" 'The Church of St. Monica, John,' she cried, 'and half a sovereign if you reach it in twenty minutes.'

"This was quite too good to lose, Watson. I was just balancing whether I should run for it, or whether I should perch behind her landau when a cab came through the street. The driver looked twice at such a shabby fare, but I jumped in before he could object. 'The Church of St. Monica,' said I, 'and half a sovereign if you reach it in twenty minutes.' It was twenty-five minutes to twelve, and of course it was clear enough what was in the wind.

"My cabby drove fast. I don't think I ever drove faster, but the others were there before us. The cab and the landau with their steaming horses were in front of the door when I arrived. I paid the man and hurried into the church. There was not a soul there save the two whom I had followed and a surpliced clergyman, who seemed to be expostulating with them. They were all three standing in a knot in front of the altar. I lounged up the side aisle like any other idler who has dropped into a church. Suddenly, to my surprise, the three at the altar faced round to me, and Godfrey Norton came running as hard as he could towards me.

" 'Thank God,' he cried. 'You'll do. Come! Come!'

" 'What then?' I asked.

" 'Come, man, come, only three minutes, or it won't be legal.'

"I was half-dragged up to the altar, and before I knew where I was I found myself mumbling responses which were whispered in my ear, and vouching for things of which I knew nothing, and generally assisting in the secure tying up of Irene Adler, spinster, to Godfrey Norton, bachelor. It was all done in an instant, and there was the gentleman thanking me on the one side and the lady on the other, while the clergyman beamed on me in front. It was the most preposterous position in which I ever found myself in my life, and it was the thought of it that started me laughing just now. It seems that there had been some informality about their license, that the clergyman absolutely refused to marry them without a witness of some sort, and that my lucky appearance saved the bridegroom from having to sally out into the streets in search of a best man. The bride gave me a sovereign, and I mean to wear it on my watch-chain in memory of the occasion."

"This is a very unexpected turn of affairs," said I; "and what then?"

"Well, I found my plans very seriously menaced. It looked as if the pair might take an immediate departure, and so necessitate very prompt and energetic measures on my part. At the church door, however, they separated, he driving back to the Temple, and she to her own house. 'I shall drive out in the park at five as usual,' she said as she left him. I heard no more. They drove away in different directions, and I went off to make my own arrangements."

"Which are?"

"Some cold beef and a glass of beer," he answered, ringing the bell. "I have been too busy to think of food, and I am likely to be busier still this evening. By the way, Doctor, I shall want your coöperation."

"I shall be delighted."

"You don't mind breaking the law?"

"Not in the least."

"Nor running a chance of arrest?"

"Not in a good cause."

"Oh, the cause is excellent!"

"Then I am your man."

"I was sure that I might rely on you."

"But what is it you wish?"

"When Mrs. Turner has brought in the tray I will make it clear to you. Now," he said as he turned hungrily on the simple fare that our landlady had provided, "I must discuss it while I eat, for I have not much time. It is nearly five now. In two hours we must be on the scene of action. Miss Irene, or Madame rather, returns from her drive at seven. We must be at Briony Lodge to meet her."

"And what then?"

"You must leave that to me. I have already arranged what is to occur. There is only one point on which I must insist. You must not interfere, come what may. You understand?"

"I am to be neutral?"

"To do nothing whatever. There will probably be some small unpleasantness. Do not join in it. It will end in my being conveyed into the house. Four or five minutes afterwards the sitting-room window will open. You are to station yourself close to that open window."

"Yes."

"You are to watch me, for I will be visible to you."

"Yes."

"And when I raise my hand—so—you will throw into the room what I give you to throw, and will, at the same time, raise the cry of fire. You quite follow me?"

"Entirely."

"It is nothing very formidable," he said, taking a long cigar-shaped roll from his pocket. "It is an ordinary plumber's smoke-rocket, fitted with a cap at either end to make it self-lighting. Your task is confined to that. When you raise your cry of fire, it will be taken up by quite a number of people. You may then walk to the end of the street, and I will rejoin you in ten minutes. I hope that I have made myself clear?"

"I am to remain neutral, to get near the window, to watch you, and at the signal to throw in this object, then to raise the cry of fire, and to wait you at the corner of the street."

"Precisely."

"Then you may entirely rely on me."

"That is excellent. I think, perhaps, it is almost time that I prepare for the new rôle I have to play."

He disappeared into his bedroom and returned in a few minutes in the character of an amiable and simple-minded Nonconformist clergyman. His broad black hat, his baggy trousers, his white tie, his sympathetic smile, and general look of peering and benevolent curiosity were such as Mr. John Hare alone could have equalled. It was not merely that Holmes changed his costume. His expression, his manner, his very soul seemed to vary with every fresh part that he assumed. The stage lost a fine actor, even as science lost an acute reasoner, when he became a specialist in crime.

It was a quarter past six when we left Baker Street, and it still wanted ten minutes to the hour when we found ourselves in Serpentine Avenue. It was already dusk, and the lamps were just being lighted as we paced up and down in front of Briony Lodge, waiting for the coming of its occupant. The house was just such as I had pictured it from Sherlock Holmes's succinct description, but the locality appeared to be less private than I expected. On the contrary, for a small street in a quiet neighbourhood, it was remarkably animated. There was a group of shabbily dressed men smoking and laughing in a corner, a scissors-grinder with his wheel, two guardsmen who were flirting with a nurse-girl, and several well-dressed young men who were lounging up and down with cigars in their mouths.

"You see," remarked Holmes, as we paced to and fro in front of the house, "this marriage rather simplifies matters. The photograph becomes a double-edged weapon now. The chances are that she would be as averse to its being seen by Mr. Godfrey Norton, as our client is to its coming to the eyes of his princess. Now the question is, Where are we to find the photograph?"

"Where, indeed?"

"It is most unlikely that she carries it about with her. It is cabinet size. Too large for easy concealment about a woman's dress. She knows that the King is capable of having her waylaid and searched. Two attempts of the sort have already been made. We may take it, then, that she does not carry it about with her."

"Where, then?"

"Her banker or her lawyer. There is that double possibility. But I am inclined to think neither. Women are naturally secretive, and they like to do their own secreting. Why should she hand it over to anyone else? She could trust her own guardianship, but she could not tell what indirect or political influence might be brought to bear upon a business man. Besides, remember that she had resolved to use it within a few days. It must be in her own house."

"But it has twice been burgled."

"Pshaw! They did not know how to look."

"But how will you look?"

"I will not look."

"What then?"

"I will get her to show me."

"But she will refuse."

"She will not be able to. But I hear the rumble of wheels. It is her carriage. Now carry out my orders to the letter."

As he spoke the gleam of the side-lights of a carriage came round the curve of the avenue. It was a smart little landau which rattled up to the door of Briony Lodge. As it pulled up, one of the loafing men at the corner dashed forward to open the door in the hope of earning a copper, but was elbowed away by another loafer, who had rushed up with the same intention. A fierce quarrel broke out, which was increased by the two guardsmen, who took sides with one of the loungers, and by the scissors-grinder, who was equally hot upon the other side. A blow was struck, and in an instant the lady, who had stepped from her carriage, was the centre of a little knot of flushed and struggling men, who struck savagely at each other with their fists and sticks. Holmes dashed into the crowd to protect the lady; but just as he reached her he gave a cry and dropped to the ground, with the blood running freely down his face. At his fall the guardsmen took to their heels in one direction and the loungers in the other, while a number of better-dressed people, who had watched the scuffle without taking part in it, crowded in to help the lady and to attend to the injured man. Irene Adler, as I will still call her, had hurried up the steps; but she stood at the top with her superb figure outlined against the lights of the hall, looking back into the street.

"Is the poor gentleman much hurt?" she asked.

"He is dead," cried several voices.

"No, no, there's life in him!" shouted another. "But he'll be gone before you can get him to hospital."

"He's a brave fellow," said a woman. "They would have had the lady's purse and watch if it hadn't been for him. They were a gang, and a rough one, too. Ah, he's breathing now."

"He can't lie in the street. May we bring him in, marm?"

"Surely. Bring him into the sitting room. There is a comfortable sofa. This way, please!"

Slowly and solemnly he was borne into Briony Lodge and laid out in the principal room, while I still observed the proceedings from my post by the window. The lamps had been lit, but the blinds had not been drawn, so that I could see Holmes as he lay upon the couch. I do not know whether he was seized with compunction at that moment for the part he was playing, but I know that I never felt more heartily ashamed of myself in my life than when I saw the beautiful creature against whom I was conspiring, or the grace and kindliness with which she waited upon the injured man. And yet it would be the blackest treachery to Holmes to draw back now from the part which he had intrusted to me. I hardened my heart, and took the smoke-rocket from under my ulster. After all, I thought, we are not injuring her. We are but preventing her from injuring another.

Holmes had sat up upon the couch, and I saw him motion like

a man who is in need of air. A maid rushed across and threw open the window. At the same instant I saw him raise his hand, and at the signal I tossed my rocket into the room with a cry of "Fire!" The word was no sooner out of my mouth than the whole crowd of spectators, well dressed and ill—gentlemen, ostlers, and servant-maids—joined in a general shriek of "Fire!" Thick clouds of smoke curled through the room and out at the open window. I caught a glimpse of rushing figures, and a moment later the voice of Holmes from within assuring them that it was a false alarm. Slipping through the shouting crowd I made my way to the corner of the street, and in ten minutes was rejoiced to find my friend's arm in mine, and to get away from the scene of uproar. He walked swiftly and in silence for some few minutes until we had turned down one of the quiet streets which lead towards the Edgeware Road.

"You did it very nicely, Doctor," he remarked. "Nothing could have been better. It is all right."

"You have the photograph?"

"I know where it is."

"And how did you find out?"

"She showed me, as I told you she would."

"I am still in the dark."

"I do not wish to make a mystery," said he, laughing. "The matter was perfectly simple. You, of course, saw that everyone in the street was an accomplice. They were all engaged for the evening."

"I guessed as much."

"Then, when the row broke out, I had a little moist red paint in the palm of my hand. I rushed forward, fell down, clapped my hand to my face, and became a piteous spectacle. It is an old trick."

"That also I could fathom."

"Then they carried me in. She was bound to have me in. What else could she do? And into her sitting-room, which was the very room which I suspected. It lay between that and her bedroom, and I was determined to see which. They laid me on a couch, I motioned for air, they were compelled to open the window, and you had your chance."

"How did that help you?"

"It was all-important. When a woman thinks that her house is on fire, her instinct is at once to rush to the thing which she values most. It is a perfectly overpowering impulse, and I have more than once taken advantage of it. In the case of the Darlington substitution scandal it was of use to me, and also in the Arnsworth Castle business. A married woman grabs at her baby; an unmarried one reaches for her jewel-box. Now it was clear to me that our lady of to-day had nothing in the house more precious to her than what we are in quest of. She would rush to secure it. The alarm of fire was admirably done. The smoke and shouting were enough to shake nerves of steel. She responded beautifully. The photograph is in a recess behind a sliding panel just above the right bell-pull. She was there in an instant, and I caught a glimpse of it as she half-drew it out. When I cried out that it was a false alarm, she replaced it, glanced at the rocket, rushed from the room, and I have not seen her since. I rose, and, making my excuses, escaped from the house. I hesitated whether to attempt to secure the photograph at once; but the coachman had come in, and as he was watching me narrowly it seemed safer to wait. A little over-precipitance may ruin all."

"And now?" I asked.

"Our quest is practically finished. I shall call with the King to-morrow, and with you, if you care to come with us. We will be shown into the sitting-room to wait for the lady; but it is probable that when she comes she may find neither us nor the photograph. It might be a satisfaction to his Majesty to regain it with his own hands."

"And when will you call?"

"At eight in the morning. She will not be up, so that we shall have a clear field. Besides, we must be prompt, for this marriage may mean a complete change in her life and habits. I must wire to the King without delay."

We had reached Baker Street and had stopped at the door. He was searching his pockets for the key when someone passing said:

"Good-night, Mister Sherlock Holmes."

There were several people on the pavement at the time, but the greeting appeared to come from a slim youth in an ulster who had hurried by.

"I've heard that voice before," said Holmes, staring down the dimly lit street. "Now, I wonder who the deuce that could have been."

3

I slept at Baker Street that night, and we were engaged upon our toast and coffee in the morning when the King of Bohemia rushed into the room.

"You have really got it!" he cried, grasping Sherlock Holmes by either shoulder and looking eagerly into his face.

"Not yet."

"But you have hopes?"

"I have hopes."

"Then, come. I am all impatience to be gone."

"We must have a cab."

"No, my brougham is waiting."

"Then that will simplify matters." We descended and started off once more for Briony Lodge.

"Irene Adler is married," remarked Holmes.

"Married! When?"

"Yesterday."

"But to whom?"

"To an English lawyer named Norton."

"But she could not love him."

"I am in hopes that she does."

"And why in hopes?"

"Because it would spare your Majesty all fear of future annoyance. If the lady loves her husband, she does not love your Majesty. If she does not love your Majesty, there is no reason why she should interfere with your Majesty's plan."

"It is true. And yet—Well! I wish she had been of my own station! What a queen she would have made!" He relapsed into a moody silence, which was not broken until we drew up in Serpentine Avenue.

The door of Briony Lodge was open, and an elderly woman stood upon the steps. She watched us with a sardonic eye as we stepped from the brougham.

"Mr. Sherlock Holmes, I believe?" said she.

"I am Mr. Holmes," answered my companion, looking at her with a questioning and rather startled gaze.

"Indeed! My mistress told me that you were likely to call. She left this morning with her husband by the 5:15 train from Charing Cross for the Continent."

"What!" Sherlock Holmes staggered back, white with chagrin and surprise. "Do you mean that she has left England?"

"Never to return."

"And the papers?" asked the King hoarsely. "All is lost."

"We shall see." He pushed past the servant and rushed into the drawing-room, followed by the King and myself. The furniture was scattered about in every direction, with dismantled shelves and open drawers, as if the lady had hurriedly ransacked them before her flight. Holmes rushed at the bell-pull, tore back a small sliding shutter, and, plunging in his hand, pulled out a photograph and a letter. The photograph was of Irene Adler herself in evening dress, the letter was superscribed to "Sherlock Holmes, Esq. To be left till called for." My friend tore it open, and we all three read it together. It was dated at midnight of the preceding night and ran in this way:

MY DEAR MR. SHERLOCK HOLMES:

You really did it very well. You took me in completely. Until after the alarm of fire, I had not a suspicion. But then, when I found how I had betrayed myself, I began to think. I had been warned against you months ago. I had been told that if the King employed an agent it would certainly be you. And your address had been given me. Yet, with all this, you made me reveal what you wanted to know. Even after I became suspicious, I found it hard to think evil of such a dear, kind old clergyman. But, you know, I have been trained as an actress myself. Male costume is nothing new to me. I often take advantage of the freedom which it gives. I sent John, the coachman, to watch you, ran upstairs, got into my walking-clothes, as I call them, and came down just as you departed.

Well, I followed you to your door, and so made sure that I was really an object of interest to the celebrated Mr. Sherlock Holmes. Then I, rather imprudently, wished you good-night, and started for the Temple to see my husband.

We both thought the best resource was flight, when pursued by so formidable an antagonist; so you will find the nest empty when you call to-morrow. As to the photograph, your client may rest in peace. I love and am loved by a better man than he. The King may do what he will without hindrance from one whom he has cruelly wronged. I keep it only to safeguard myself, and to preserve a weapon which will always secure me from any steps which he might take in the future. I leave a photograph which he might care to possess; and I remain, dear Mr. Sherlock Holmes,

Very truly yours,
IRENE NORTON, *née* ADLER.

"What a woman—oh, what a woman!" cried the King of Bohemia, when we had all three read this epistle. "Did I not tell you how quick and resolute she was? Would she not have made an admirable queen? Is it not a pity that she was not on my level?"

"From what I have seen of the lady she seems indeed to be on a very different level to your Majesty," said Holmes coldly. "I am sorry that I have not been able to bring your Majesty's business to a more successful conclusion."

"On the contrary, my dear sir," cried the King; "nothing could be more successful. I know that her word is inviolate. The photograph is now as safe as if it were in the fire."

"I am glad to hear your Majesty say so."

"I am immensely indebted to you. Pray tell me in what way I can reward you. This ring—" He slipped an emerald snake ring from his finger and held it out upon the palm of his hand.

"Your Majesty has something which I should value even more highly," said Holmes.

"You have but to name it."

"This photograph!"

The King stared at him in amazement.

"Irene's photograph!" he cried. "Certainly, if you wish it."

"I thank your Majesty. Then there is no more to be done in the matter. I have the honour to wish you a very good-morning." He bowed, and, turning away without observing the hand which the King had stretched out to him, he set off in my company for his chambers.

And that was how a great scandal threatened to affect the kingdom of Bohemia, and how the best plans of Mr. Sherlock Holmes were beaten by a woman's wit. He used to make merry over the cleverness of women, but I have not heard him do it of late. And when he speaks of Irene Adler, or when he refers to her photograph, it is always under the honourable title of *the* woman.

THE RED-HEADED LEAGUE

I HAD CALLED upon my friend, Mr. Sherlock Holmes, one day in the autumn of last year and found him in deep conversation with a very stout, florid-faced, elderly gentleman with fiery red hair. With an apology for my intrusion, I was about to withdraw when Holmes pulled me abruptly into the room and closed the door behind me.

"You could not possibly have come at a better time, my dear Watson," he said cordially.

"I was afraid that you were engaged."

"So I am. Very much so."

"Then I can wait in the next room."

"Not at all. This gentleman, Mr. Wilson, has been my partner and helper in many of my most successful cases, and I have no doubt that he will be of the utmost use to me in yours also."

The stout gentleman half rose from his chair and gave a bob of greeting, with a quick little questioning glance from his small fat-encircled eyes.

"Try the settee," said Holmes, relapsing into his armchair and putting his fingertips together, as was his custom when in judicial moods. "I know, my dear Watson, that you share my love of all that is bizarre and outside the conventions and humdrum routine of everyday life. You have shown your relish for it by the enthusiasm which has prompted you to chronicle, and, if you will excuse my saying so, somewhat to embellish so many of my own little adventures."

"Your cases have indeed been of the greatest interest to me," I observed.

"You will remember that I remarked the other day, just before we went into the very simple problem presented by Miss Mary Sutherland, that for strange effects and extraordinary combinations we must go to life itself, which is always far more daring than any effort of the imagination."

"A proposition which I took the liberty of doubting."

"You did, Doctor, but none the less you must come round to my view, for otherwise I shall keep on piling fact upon fact on you until your reason breaks down under them and acknowledges me to be right. Now, Mr. Jabez Wilson here has been good enough to call upon me this morning, and to begin a narrative which promises to be one of the most singular which I have listened to for some time. You have heard me remark that the strangest and most unique things are very often connected not with the larger but with the smaller crimes, and occasionally, indeed, where there is room for doubt whether any positive crime has been committed. As far as I have heard it is impossible for me to say whether the present case is an instance of crime or not, but the course of events is certainly among the most singular that I have ever listened to. Perhaps, Mr. Wilson, you would have the great kindness to recommence your narrative. I ask you not merely because my friend Dr. Watson has not heard the opening part but also because the peculiar nature of the story makes me anxious to have every possible detail from your lips. As a rule, when I have heard some slight indication of the course of events, I am able to guide myself by the thousands of other similar cases which occur to my memory. In the present instance I am forced to admit that the facts are, to the best of my belief, unique."

The portly client puffed out his chest with an appearance of some little pride and pulled a dirty and wrinkled newspaper from the inside pocket of his greatcoat. As he glanced down the advertisement column, with his head thrust forward and the paper flattened out upon his knee, I took a good look at the man and endeavoured, after the fashion of my companion, to read the indications which might be presented by his dress or appearance.

I did not gain very much, however, by my inspection. Our visitor bore every mark of being an average commonplace British tradesman, obese, pompous, and slow. He wore rather baggy gray shepherd's check trousers, a not over-clean black frockcoat, unbuttoned in the front, and a drab waistcoat with a heavy brassy Albert chain, and a square pierced bit of metal dangling down as an ornament. A frayed top-hat and a faded brown overcoat with a wrinkled velvet collar lay upon a chair beside him. Altogether, look as I would, there was nothing remarkable about the man save his blazing red head, and the expression of extreme chagrin and discontent upon his features.

Sherlock Holmes's quick eye took in my occupation, and he shook his head with a smile as he noticed my questioning glances. "Beyond the obvious facts that he has at some time done manual labour, that he takes snuff, that he is a Freemason, that he has been in China, and that he has done a considerable amount of writing lately, I can deduce nothing else."

Mr. Jabez Wilson started up in his chair, with his forefinger upon the paper, but his eyes upon my companion.

"How, in the name of good-fortune, did you know all that, Mr. Holmes?" he asked. "How did you know, for example, that I did manual labour? It's as true as gospel, for I began as a ship's carpenter."

"Your hands, my dear sir. Your right hand is quite a size larger than your left. You have worked with it, and the muscles are more developed."

"Well, the snuff, then, and the Freemasonry?"

"I won't insult your intelligence by telling you how I read that, especially as, rather against the strict rules of your order, you use an arc-and-compass breastpin."

"Ah, of course, I forgot that. But the writing?"

"What else can be indicated by that right cuff so very shiny for five inches, and the left one with the smooth patch near the elbow where you rest it upon the desk?"

"Well, but China?"

"The fish that you have tattooed immediately above your right wrist could only have been done in China. I have made a small study of tattoo marks and have even contributed to the literature of the subject. That trick of staining the fishes' scales of a delicate pink is quite peculiar to China. When, in addition, I see a Chinese coin hanging from your watch-chain, the matter becomes even more simple."

Mr. Jabez Wilson laughed heavily. "Well, I never!" said he. "I thought at first that you had done something clever, but I see that there was nothing in it, after all."

"I begin to think, Watson," said Holmes, "that I make a mistake in explaining. '*Omne ignotum pro magnifico*,' you know, and my poor little reputation, such as it is, will suffer shipwreck if I am so candid. Can you not find the advertisement, Mr. Wilson?"

"Yes, I have got it now," he answered with his thick red finger planted halfway down the column. "Here it is. This is what began it all. You just read it for yourself, sir."

I took the paper from him and read as follows.

> To the Red-headed League:
>
> On account of the bequest of the late Ezekiah Hopkins, of Lebanon, Pennsylvania, U. S. A., there is now another vacancy open which entitles a member of the League to a salary of £4 a week for purely nominal services. All red-headed men who are sound in body and mind, and above the age of twenty-one years, are eligible. Apply in person on Monday, at eleven o'clock, to Duncan Ross, at the offices of the League, 7 Pope's Court, Fleet Street.

"What on earth does this mean?" I ejaculated after I had twice read over the extraordinary announcement.

Holmes chuckled and wriggled in his chair, as was his habit when in high spirits. "It is a little off the beaten track, isn't it?" said he. "And now, Mr. Wilson, off you go at scratch and tell us all about yourself, your household, and the effect which this advertisement had upon your fortunes. You will first make a note, Doctor, of the paper and the date."

"It is *The Morning Chronicle* of April 27, 1890. Just two months ago."

"Very good. Now, Mr. Wilson?"

"Well, it is just as I have been telling you, Mr. Sherlock Holmes," said Jabez Wilson, mopping his forehead; "I have a small pawnbroker's business at Coburg Square, near the City. It's not a very large affair, and of late years it has not done more than just give me a living. I used to be able to keep two assistants, but now I only keep one; and I would have a job to pay him but that he is willing to come for half wages so as to learn the business."

"What is the name of this obliging youth?" asked Sherlock Holmes.

"His name is Vincent Spaulding, and he's not such a youth, either. It's hard to say his age. I should not wish a smarter assistant, Mr. Holmes; and I know very well that he could better himself and earn twice what I am able to give him. But, after, all, if he is satisfied, why should I put ideas in his head?"

"Why, indeed? You seem most fortunate in having an employee who comes under the full market price. It is not a common experience among employers in this age. I don't know that your assistant is not as remarkable as your advertisement."

"Oh, he has his faults, too," said Mr. Wilson. "Never was such a fellow for photography. Snapping away with a camera when he ought to be improving his mind, and then diving down into the cellar like a rabbit into its hole to develop his pictures. That is his main fault, but on the whole he's a good worker. There's no vice in him."

"He is still with you, I presume?"

"Yes, sir. He and a girl of fourteen, who does a bit of simple cooking and keeps the place clean—that's all I have in the house, for I am a widower and never had any family. We live very quietly, sir, the three of us; and we keep a roof over our heads and pay our debts, if we do nothing more.

"The first thing that put us out was that advertisement. Spaulding, he came down into the office just this day eight weeks, with this very paper in his hand, and he says:

" 'I wish to the Lord, Mr. Wilson, that I was a red-headed man.'

" 'Why that?' I asks.

" 'Why,' says he, 'here's another vacancy on the League of the Red-headed Men. It's worth quite a little fortune to any man who gets it, and I understand that there are more vacancies than there are men, so that the trustees are at their wits' end what to do with the money. If my hair would only change colour, here's a nice little crib all ready for me to step into.'

" 'Why, what is it, then?' I asked. You see, Mr. Holmes, I am a very stay-at-home man, and as my business came to me instead of my having to go to it, I was often weeks on end without putting my foot over the door-mat. In that way I didn't know much of what was going on outside, and I was always glad of a bit of news.

" 'Have you never heard of the League of the Red-headed Men?' he asked with his eyes open.

" 'Never.'

" 'Why, I wonder at that, for you are eligible yourself for one of the vancancies.'

" 'And what are they worth?' I asked.

" 'Oh, merely a couple of hundred a year, but the work is

slight, and it need not interfere very much with one's other occupations.'

"Well, you can easily think that that made me prick up my ears, for the business has not been over-good for some years, and an extra couple of hundred would have been very handy.

" 'Tell me about it,' said I.

" 'Well,' said he, showing me the advertisement, 'you can see for yourself that the League has a vacancy, and there is the address where you should apply for particulars. As far as I can make out, the League was founded by an American millionaire, Ezekiah Hopkins, who was very peculiar in his ways. He was himself red-headed, and he had a great sympathy for all red-headed men; so when he died it was found that he had left his enormous fortune in the hands of trustees, with instructions to apply the interest to the providing of easy berths to men whose hair is of that colour. From all I hear it is splendid pay and very little to do.'

" 'But,' said I, 'there would be millions of red-headed men who would apply.'

" 'Not so many as you might think,' he answered. 'You see it is really confined to Londoners, and to grown men. This American had started from London when he was young, and he wanted to do the old town a good turn. Then, again, I have heard it is no use your applying if your hair is light red, or dark red, or anything but real bright, blazing, fiery red. Now, if you cared to apply, Mr. Wilson, you would just walk in; but perhaps it would hardly be worth your while to put yourself out of the way for the sake of a few hundred pounds.'

"Now, it is a fact, gentlemen, as you may see for yourselves, that my hair is of a very full and rich tint, so that it seemed to me that if there was to be any competition in the matter I stood as good a chance as any man that I had ever met. Vincent Spaulding seemed to know so much about it that I thought he might prove useful, so I just ordered him to put up the shutters for the day and to come right away with me. He was very willing to have a holiday, so we shut the business up and started off for the address that was given us in the advertisement.

"I never hope to see such a sight as that again, Mr. Holmes. From north, south, east, and west every man who had a shade of red in his hair had tramped into the city to answer the advertisement. Fleet Street was choked with red-headed folk, and

Pope's Court looked like a coster's orange barrow. I should not have thought there were so many in the whole country as were brought together by that single advertisement. Every shade of colour they were—straw, lemon, orange, brick, Irish-setter, liver, clay; but, as Spaulding said, there were not many who had the real vivid flame-coloured tint. When I saw how many were waiting, I would have given it up in despair; but Spaulding would not hear of it. How he did it I could not imagine, but he pushed and pulled and butted until he got me through the crowd, and right up to the steps which led to the office. There was a double stream upon the stair, some going up in hope, and some coming back dejected; but we wedged in as well as we could and soon found ourselves in the office."

"Your experience has been a most entertaining one," remarked Holmes as his client paused and refreshed his memory with a hugh pinch of snuff. "Pray continue your very interesting statement."

"There was nothing in the office but a couple of wooden chairs and a deal table, behind which sat a small man with a head that was even redder than mine. He said a few words to each candidate as he came up, and then he always managed to find some fault in them which would disqualify them. Getting a vacancy did not seem to be such a very easy matter, after all. However, when our turn came the little man was much more favourable to me than to any of the others, and he closed the door as we entered, so that he might have a private word with us.

" 'This is Mr. Jabez Wilson,' said my assistant, 'and he is willing to fill a vacancy in the League.'

" 'And he is admirably suited for it,' the other answered. 'He has every requirement. I cannot recall when I have seen anything so fine.' He took a step backward, cocked his head on one side, and gazed at my hair until I felt quite bashful. Then suddenly he plunged forward, wrung my hand, and congratulated me warmly on my success.

" 'It would be injustice to hesitate,' said he. 'You will, however, I am sure, excuse me for taking an obvious precaution.' With that he seized my hair in both his hands, and tugged until I yelled with the pain. 'There is water in your eyes,' said he as he released me. 'I perceive that all is as it should be. But we have to be careful, for we have twice been deceived by wigs and once by paint. I could tell you tales of cobbler's wax which would disgust you with human nature.' He stepped over to the window and shouted through it at the top of his voice that the vacancy was filled. A groan of disappointment came up from below, and the folk all trooped away in different directions until there was not a red-head to be seen except my own and that of the manager.

" 'My name,' said he, 'is Mr. Duncan Ross, and I am myself one of the pensioners upon the fund left by our noble benefactor. Are you a married man, Mr. Wilson? Have you a family?'

"I answered that I had not.

"His face fell immediately.

" 'Dear me!' he said gravely, 'that is very serious indeed! I am sorry to hear you say that. The fund was, of course, for the propagation and spread of the red-heads as well as for their maintenance. It is exceedingly unfortunate that you should be a bachelor.'

"My face lengthened at this, Mr. Holmes, for I thought that I was not to have the vacancy after all; but after thinking it over for a few minutes he said that it would be all right.

" 'In the case of another,' said he, 'the objection might be fatal, but we must stretch a point in favour of a man with such a head of hair as yours. When shall you be able to enter upon your new duties?'

" 'Well, it is a little awkward, for I have a business already,' said I.

" 'Oh, never mind about that, Mr. Wilson!' said Vincent Spaulding. 'I should be able to look after that for you.'

" 'What would be the hours?' I asked.

" 'Ten to two.'

"Now a pawnbroker's business is mostly done of an evening, Mr. Holmes, especially Thursday and Friday evening, which is just before pay-day; so it would suit me very well to earn a little in the mornings. Besides, I knew that my assistant was a good man, and that he would see to anything that turned up.

" 'That would suit me very well,' said I. 'And the pay?'

" 'Is £4 a week.'

" 'And the work?'

" 'Is purely nominal.'

" 'What do you call purely nominal?'

" 'Well, you have to be in the office, or at least in the building, the whole time. If you leave, you forfeit your whole position forever. The will is very clear upon that point. You don't comply with the conditions if you budge from the office during that time.'

" 'It's only four hours a day, and I should not think of leaving,' said I.

" 'No excuse will avail,' said Mr. Duncan Ross; 'neither sickness nor business nor anything else. There you must stay, or you lose your billet.'

" 'And the work?'

" 'Is to copy out the Encyclopædia Britannica. There is the first volume of it in that press. You must find your own ink, pens, and blotting-paper, but we provide this table and chair. Will you be ready to-morrow?'

" 'Certainly,' I answered.

" 'Then, good-bye, Mr. Jabez Wilson, and let me congratulate you once more on the important position which you have been fortunate enough to gain.' He bowed me out of the room, and I went home with my assistant, hardly knowing what to say or do, I was so pleased at my own good fortune.

"Well, I thought over the matter all day, and by evening I was in low spirits again; for I had quite persuaded myself that the whole affair must be some great hoax or fraud, though what its object might be I could not imagine. It seemed altogether past belief that anyone could make such a will, or that they would pay such a sum for doing anything so simple as copying out the Encyclopædia Britannica. Vincent Spaulding did what he could to cheer me up, but by bedtime I had reasoned myself out of the whole thing. However, in the morning I determined to have a look at it anyhow, so I bought a penny bottle of ink, and with a quill-pen, and seven sheets of foolscap paper, I started off for Pope's Court.

"Well, to my surprise and delight, everything was as right as possible. The table was set out ready for me, and Mr. Duncan Ross was there to see that I got fairly to work. He started me off upon the letter A, and then he left me; but he would drop in from time to time to see that all was right with me. At two o'clock he bade me good-day, complimented me upon the amount that I had written, and locked the door of the office after me.

"This went on day after day, Mr. Holmes, and on Saturday the manager came in and planked down four golden sovereigns for my week's work. It was the same next week, and the same the week after. Every morning I was there at ten, and every afternoon I left at two. By degrees Mr. Duncan Ross took to coming in only once of a morning, and then, after a time, he did not come in at all. Still, of course, I never dared to leave the room for an instant, for I was not sure when he might come, and the billet was such a good one, and suited me so well, that I would not risk the loss of it.

"Eight weeks passed away like this, and I had written about Abbots and Archery and Armour and Architecture and Attica, and hoped with diligence that I might get on to the B's before very long. It cost me something in foolscap, and I had pretty nearly filled a shelf with my writings. And then suddenly the whole business came to an end."

"To an end?"

"Yes, sir. And no later than this morning. I went to my work as usual at ten o'clock, but the door was shut and locked, with a little square of card-board hammered on to the middle of the panel with a tack. Here it is, and you can read for yourself."

He held up a piece of white card-board about the size of a sheet of note-paper. It read in this fashion:

THE RED-HEADED LEAGUE
IS
DISSOLVED.
October 9, 1890.

Sherlock Holmes and I surveyed this curt announcement and the rueful face behind it, until the comical side of the affair so completely overtopped every other consideration that we both burst out into a roar of laughter.

"I cannot see that there is anything very funny," cried our client, flushing up to the roots of his flaming head. "If you can do nothing better than laugh at me, I can go elsewhere."

"No, no," cried Holmes, shoving him back into the chair from which he had half risen. "I really wouldn't miss your case for the world. It is most refreshingly unusual. But there is, if you will excuse my saying so, something just a little funny about it. Pray what steps did you take when you found the card upon the door?"

"I was staggered, sir. I did not know what to do. Then I called at the offices round, but none of them seemed to know anything about it. Finally, I went to the landlord, who is an accountant living on the ground-floor, and I asked him if he could tell me what had become of the Red-headed League. He said that he had never heard of any such body. Then I asked him who Mr. Duncan Ross was. He answered that the name was new to him.

" 'Well,' said I, 'the gentleman at No. 4.'

" 'What, the red-headed man?'

" 'Yes.'

" 'Oh,' said he, 'his name was William Morris. He was a solicitor and was using my room as a temporary convenience until his new premises were ready. He moved out yesterday.'

" 'Where could I find him?'

" 'Oh, at his new offices. He did tell me the address. Yes, 17 King Edward Street, near St. Paul's.'

"I started off, Mr. Holmes, but when I got to that address it was a manufactory of artificial knee-caps, and no one in it had ever heard of either Mr. William Morris or Mr. Duncan Ross."

"And what did you do then?" asked Holmes.

"I went home to Saxe-Coburg Square, and I took the advice of my assistant. But he could not help me in any way. He could only say that if I waited I should hear by post. But that was not quite good enough, Mr. Holmes. I did not wish to lose such a place without a struggle, so, as I had heard that you were good enough to give advice to poor folk who were in need of it, I came right away to you."

"And you did very wisely," said Holmes. "Your case is an exceedingly remarkable one, and I shall be happy to look into it. From what you have told me I think that it is possible that graver issues hang from it than might at first sight appear."

"Grave enough!" said Mr. Jabez Wilson. "Why, I have lost four pound a week."

"As far as you are personally concerned," remarked Holmes, "I do not see that you have any grievance against this extraordinary league. On the contrary, you are, as I understand, richer by some £30, to say nothing of the minute knowledge which you have gained on every subject which comes under the letter A. You have lost nothing by them."

"No, sir. But I want to find out about them, and who they are, and what their object was in playing this prank—if it was a prank—upon me. It was a pretty expensive joke for them, for it cost them two and thirty pounds."

"We shall endeavour to clear up these points for you. And, first, one or two questions, Mr. Wilson. This assistant of yours who first called your attention to the advertisement—how long had he been with you?"

"About a month then."

"How did he come?"

"In answer to an advertisement."

"Was he the only applicant?"

"No, I had a dozen."

"Why did you pick him?"

"Because he was handy and would come cheap."

"At half-wages, in fact."

"Yes."

"What is he like, this Vincent Spaulding?"

"Small, stout-built, very quick in his ways, no hair on his face, though he's not short of thirty. Has a white splash of acid upon his forehead."

Holmes sat up in his chair in considerable excitement. "I thought as much," said he. "Have you ever observed that his ears are pierced for earrings?"

"Yes, sir. He told me that a gypsy had done it for him when he was a lad."

"Hum!" said Holmes, sinking back in deep thought. "He is still with you?"

"Oh, yes, sir; I have only just left him."

"And has your business been attended to in your absence?"

"Nothing to complain of, sir. There's never very much to do of a morning."

"That will do, Mr. Wilson. I shall be happy to give you an opinion upon the subject in the course of a day or two. To-day is Saturday, and I hope that by Monday we may come to a conclusion."

"Well, Watson," said Holmes when our visitor had left us, "what do you make of it all?"

"I make nothing of it," I answered frankly. "It is a most mysterious business."

"As a rule," said Holmes, "the more bizarre a thing is the less mysterious it proves to be. It is your commonplace, featureless crimes which are really puzzling, just as a commonplace face is the most difficult to identify. But I must be prompt over this matter."

"What are you going to do, then?" I asked.

"To smoke," he answered. "It is quite a three pipe problem, and I beg that you won't speak to me for fifty minutes." He curled himself up in his chair, with his thin knees drawn up to his hawk-like nose, and there he sat with his eyes closed and his black clay pipe thrusting out like the bill of some strange bird. I had come to the conclusion that he had dropped asleep, and indeed was nodding myself, when he suddenly sprang out of his chair with the gesture of a man who has made up his mind and put his pipe down upon the mantelpiece.

"Sarasate plays at the St. James's Hall this afternoon," he remarked. "What do you think, Watson? Could your patients spare you for a few hours?"

"I have nothing to do to-day. My practice is never very absorbing."

"Then put on your hat and come. I am going through the City first, and we can have some lunch on the way. I observe that there is a good deal of German music on the programme, which is rather more to my taste than Italian or French. It is introspective, and I want to introspect. Come along!"

We travelled by the Underground as far as Aldersgate; and a short walk took us to Saxe-Coburg Square, the scene of the singular story which we had listened to in the morning. It was a poky, little, shabby-genteel place, where four lines of dingy two-storied brick houses looked out into a small railed-in enclosure, where a lawn of weedy grass and a few clumps of faded laurel-bushes made a hard fight against a smoke-laden and uncongenial atmosphere. Three gilt balls and a brown board with "JABEZ WILSON" in white letters, upon a corner house, announced the place where our red-headed client carried on his business. Sherlock Holmes stopped in front of it with his head on one side and looked it all over, with his eyes shining brightly between puckered lids. Then he walked slowly up the street, and then down again to the corner, still looking keenly at the houses. Finally he returned to the pawnbroker's, and, having thumped vigorously upon the pavement with his stick two or three times, he went up to the door and knocked. It was instantly opened by a bright-looking, clean-shaven young fellow, who asked him to step in.

"Thank you," said Holmes, "I only wished to ask you how you would go from here to the Strand."

"Third right, fourth left," answered the assistant promptly, closing the door.

"Smart fellow, that," observed Holmes as we walked away. "He is, in my judgement, the fourth smartest man in London, and for daring I am not sure that he has not a claim to be third. I have known something of him before."

"Evidently," said I, "Mr. Wilson's assistant counts for a good deal in this mystery of the Red-headed League. I am sure that you inquired your way merely in order that you might see him."

"Not him."

"What then?"

"The knees of his trousers."

"And what did you see?"

"What I expected to see."

"Why did you beat the pavement?"

"My dear doctor, this is a time for observation, not for talk. We are spies in an enemy's country. We know something of Saxe-Coburg Square. Let us now explore the parts which lie behind it."

The road in which we found ourselves as we turned round the corner from the retired Saxe-Coburg Square presented as great a contrast to it as the front of a picture does to the back. It was one of the main arteries which conveyed the traffic of the City to the north west. The roadway was blocked with the immense stream of commerce flowing in a double tide inward and outward, while the footpaths were black with the hurrying swarm of pedestrians. It was difficult to realize as we looked at the line of fine shops and stately business premises that they really abutted on the other side upon the faded and stagnant square which we had just quitted.

"Let me see," said Holmes, standing at the corner and glancing along the line, "I should like just to remember the order of the houses here. It is a hobby of mine to have an exact knowledge of London. There is Mortimer's, the tobacconist, the little newspaper shop, the Coburg branch of the City and Suburban Bank, the Vegetarian Restaurant, and McFarlane's carriage-building depot. That carries us right on to the other block. And now, Doctor, we've done our work, so it's time we had some play. A sandwich and a cup of coffee, and then off to violin-land, where all is sweetness and delicacy and harmony, and there are no red-headed clients to vex us with their conundrums."

My friend was an enthusiastic musician, being himself not only a very capable performer but a composer of no ordinary merit. All the afternoon he sat in the stalls wrapped in the most perfect happiness, gently waving his long, thin fingers in time to the music, while his gently smiling face and his languid, dreamy eyes were as unlike those of Holmes, the sleuth-hound, Holmes the relentless, keen-witted, ready-handed criminal agent, as it was possible to conceive. In his singular character the dual nature alternately asserted itself, and his extreme exactness and astuteness represented, as I have often thought, the reaction against the poetic and contemplative mood which occasionally predominated in him. The swing of his nature took him from extreme languor to devouring energy; and, as I knew well, he was never so truly formidable as when, for days on end, he had been lounging in his armchair amid his improvisations and his black-letter editions. Then it was that the lust of the chase would suddenly come upon him, and that his brilliant reasoning power would rise to the level of intuition, until those who were unacquainted with his methods would look askance at him as on a man whose knowledge was not that of other mortals. When I saw him that afternoon so enwrapped in the music at St. James's Hall I felt that an evil time might be coming upon those whom he had set himself to hunt down.

"You want to go home, no doubt, Doctor," he remarked as we emerged.

"Yes, it would be as well."

"And I have some business to do which will take some hours. This business at Coburg Square is serious."

"Why serious?"

"A considerable crime is in contemplation. I have every reason to believe that we shall be in time to stop it. But to-day being Saturday rather complicates matters. I shall want your help to-night."

"At what time?"

"Ten will be early enough."

"I shall be at Baker Street at ten."

"Very well. And, I say, Doctor, there may be some little danger, so kindly put your army revolver in your pocket." He waved his hand, turned on his heel, and disappeared in an instant among the crowd.

I trust that I am not more dense than my neighbours, but I was always oppressed with a sense of my own stupidity in my dealings with Sherlock Holmes. Here I had heard what he had heard, I had seen what he had seen, and yet from his words it was evident that he saw clearly not only what had happened but what was about to happen, while to me the whole business was still confused and grotesque. As I drove home to my house in Kensington I thought over it all, from the extraordinary story of the red-headed copier of the Encyclopaedia down to the visit to Saxe-Coburg Square, and the ominous words with which he had parted from me. What was this nocturnal expedition, and why should I go armed? Where were we going, and what were we to do? I had the hint from Holmes that this smooth-faced pawnbroker's assistant was a formidable man—a man who might play a deep game. I tried to puzzle it out, but gave it up in despair and set the matter aside until night should bring an explanation.

It was a quarter-past nine when I started from home and made my way across the Park, and so through Oxford Street to Baker Street. Two hansoms were standing at the door, and as I entered the passage I heard the sound of voices from above. On entering his room I found Holmes in animated conversation with two men, one of whom I recognized as Peter Jones, the official police agent, while the other was a long, thin, sad-faced man, with a very shiny hat and oppressively respectable frock-coat.

"Ha! Our party is complete," said Holmes, buttoning up his pea-jacket and taking his heavy hunting crop from the rack. "Watson, I think you know Mr. Jones, of Scotland Yard? Let me introduce you to Mr. Merryweather, who is to be our companion in to-night's adventure."

"We're hunting in couples again, Doctor, you see," said Jones in his consequential way. "Our friend here is a wonderful man for starting a chase. All he wants is an old dog to help him to do the running down."

"I hope a wild goose may not prove to be the end of our chase," observed Mr. Merryweather gloomily.

"You may place considerable confidence in Mr. Holmes, sir," said the police agent loftily. "He has his own little methods, which are, if he won't mind my saying so, just a little too theoretical and fantastic, but he has the makings of a detective in him. It is not too much to say that once or twice, as in that business of the Sholto murder and the Agra treasure, he has been more nearly correct than the official force."

"Oh, if you say so, Mr. Jones, it is all right," said the stranger with deference. "Still, I confess that I miss my rubber. It is the first Saturday night for seven-and-twenty years that I have not had my rubber."

"I think you will find," said Sherlock Holmes, "that you will play for a higher stake to-night than you have ever done yet, and that the play will be more exciting. For you, Mr. Merryweather, the stake will be some £30,000; and for you, Jones, it will be the man upon whom you wish to lay your hands."

"John Clay, the murderer, thief, smasher, and forger. He's a young man, Mr. Merryweather, but he is at the head of his profession, and I would rather have my bracelets on him than on any criminal in London. He's a remarkable man, is young John Clay. His grandfather was a royal duke, and he himself has been to Eton and Oxford. His brain is as cunning as his fingers, and though we meet signs of him at every turn, we never know where to find the man himself. He'll crack a crib in Scotland one week, and be raising money to build an orphanage in Cornwall the next. I've been on his track for years and have never set eyes on him yet."

"I hope that I may have the pleasure of introducing you to-night. I've had one or two little turns also with Mr. John Clay, and I agree with you that he is at the head of his profession. It is past ten, however, and quite time that we started. If you two will take the first hansom, Watson and I will follow in the second."

Sherlock Holmes was not very communicative during the long drive and lay back in the cab humming the tunes which he had heard in the afternoon. We rattled through an endless labyrinth of gas-lit streets until we emerged into Farrington Street.

"We are close there now," my friend remarked. "This fellow Merryweather is a bank director, and personally interested in the matter. I thought it as well to have Jones with us also. He is not a bad fellow, though an absolute imbecile in his profession. He has one positive virtue. He is as brave as a bulldog and as tenacious as a lobster if he gets his claws upon anyone. Here we are, and they are waiting for us."

We had reached the same crowded thoroughfare in which we had found ourselves in the morning. Our cabs were dismissed, and, following the guidance of Mr. Merryweather, we passed down a narrow passage and through a side door, which he opened for us. Within there was a small corridor, which ended in a very massive iron gate. This also was opened, and led down a flight of winding stone steps, which terminated at another formidable gate. Mr. Merryweather stopped to light a lantern, and then conducted us down a dark, earth-smelling passage, and so, after opening a third door, into a huge vault or cellar, which was piled all round with crates and massive boxes.

"You are not very vulnerable from above," Holmes remarked as he held up the lantern and gazed about him.

"Nor from below," said Mr. Merryweather, striking his stick upon the flags which lined the floor. "Why, dear me, it sounds quite hollow!" he remarked, looking up in surprise.

"I must really ask you to be a little more quiet!" said Holmes severely. "You have already imperilled the whole success of our expedition. Might I beg that you would have the goodness to sit down upon one of those boxes, and not to interfere?"

The solemn Mr. Merryweather perched himself upon a crate, with a very injured expression upon his face, while Holmes fell upon his knees upon the floor and, with the lantern and a magnifying lens, began to examine minutely the cracks between the stones. A few seconds sufficed to satisfy him, for he sprang to his feet again and put his glass in his pocket.

"We have at least an hour before us," he remarked, "for they can hardly take any steps until the good pawnbroker is safely in bed. Then they will not lose a minute, for the sooner they do their work the longer time they will have for their escape. We are at present, Doctor—as no doubt you have divined—in the cellar of the City branch of one of the principal London banks. Mr. Merryweather is the chairman of directors, and he will explain to you that there are reasons why the more daring criminals of London should take a considerable interest in this cellar at present."

"It is our French gold," whispered the director. "We have had several warnings that an attempt might be made upon it."

"Your French gold?"

"Yes. We had occasion some months ago to strengthen our resources and borrowed for that purpose 30,000 napoleons from the Bank of France. It has become known that we have never had occasion to unpack the money, and that it is still lying in our cellar. The crate upon which I sit contains 2,000 napoleons packed between layers of lead foil. Our reserve of bullion is much larger at present than is usually kept in a single branch office, and the directors have had misgivings upon the subject."

"Which were very well justified," observed Holmes. "And now it is time that we arranged our little plans. I expect that within an hour matters will come to a head. In the meantime, Mr. Merryweather, we must put the screen over that dark lantern."

"And sit in the dark?"

"I am afraid so. I had brought a pack of cards in my pocket, and I thought that, as we were a *partie carrée*, you might have your rubber after all. But I see that the enemy's preparations have gone so far that we cannot risk the presence of a light. And, first of all, we must choose our positions. These are daring men, and though we shall take them at a disadvantage, they may do us some harm unless we are careful. I shall stand behind this crate, and do you conceal yourselves behind those. Then, when I flash a light upon them, close in swiftly. If they fire, Watson, have no compunction about shooting them down."

I placed my revolver, cocked, upon the top of the wooden case behind which I crouched. Holmes shot the slide across the front of his lantern and left us in pitch darkness—such an absolute darkness as I have never before experienced. The smell of hot metal remained to assure us that the light was still there, ready to flash out at a moment's notice. To me, with my nerves worked up to a pitch of expectancy, there was something depressing and subduing in the sudden gloom, and in the cold dank air of the vault.

"They have but one retreat," whispered Holmes. "That is back through the house into Saxe-Coburg Square. I hope that you have done what I asked you, Jones?"

"I have an inspector and two officers waiting at the front door."

"Then we have stopped all the holes. And now we must be silent and wait."

What a time it seemed! From comparing notes afterwards it was but an hour and a quarter, yet it appeared to me that the night must have almost gone, and the dawn be breaking above us. My limbs were weary and stiff, for I feared to change my position; yet my nerves were worked up to the highest pitch of tension, and my hearing was so acute that I could not only hear the gentle breathing of my companions, but I could distinguish the deeper, heavier in-breath of the bulky Jones from the thin, sighing note of the bank director. From my position I could look over the case in the direction of the floor. Suddenly my eyes caught the glint of a light.

At first it was but a lurid spark upon the stone pavement. Then it lengthened out until it became a yellow line, and then, without any warning or sound, a gash seemed to open and a hand appeared; a white, almost womanly hand, which felt about in the centre of the little area of light. For a minute or more the hand, with its writhing fingers, protruded out of the floor. Then it was withdrawn as suddenly as it appeared, and all was dark again save the single lurid spark which marked a chink between the stones.

Its disappearance, however, was but momentary. With a rending, tearing sound, one of the broad, white stones turned over upon its side and left a square, gaping hole, through which streamed the light of a lantern. Over the edge there peeped a clean-cut, boyish face, which looked keenly about it, and then, with a hand on either side of the aperture, drew itself shoulder-high and waist-high, until one knee rested upon the edge. In another instant he stood at the side of the hole and was hauling after him a companion, lithe and small like himself, with a pale face and a shock of very red hair.

"It's all clear," he whispered. "Have you the chisel and the bags? Great Scott! Jump, Archie, jump, and I'll swing for it!"

Sherlock Holmes had sprung out and seized the intruder by the collar. The other dived down the hole, and I heard the sound of rending cloth as Jones clutched at his skirts. The light flashed upon the barrel of a revolver, but Holmes's hunting crop came down on the man's wrist, and the pistol clinked upon the stone floor.

"It's no use, John Clay," said Holmes blandly. "You have no chance at all."

"So I see," the other answered with the utmost coolness. "I fancy that my pal is all right, though I see you have got his coat-tails."

"There are three men waiting for him at the door," said Holmes.

"Oh, indeed! You seem to have done the thing very completely. I must compliment you."

"And I you," Holmes answered. "Your red-headed idea was very new and effective."

"You'll see your pal again presently," said Jones. "He's quicker at climbing down holes than I am. Just hold out while I fix the derbies."

"I beg that you will not touch me with your filthy hands," remarked our prisoner as the handcuffs clattered upon his wrists. "You may not be aware that I have royal blood in my veins. Have the goodness, also, when you address me always to say 'sir' and 'please.' "

"All right," said Jones with a stare and a snigger. "Well, would you please, sir, march upstairs, where we can get a cab to carry your Highness to the police-station?"

"That is better," said John Clay serenely. He made a sweeping bow to the three of us and walked quietly off in the custody of the detective.

"Really, Mr. Holmes," said Mr. Merryweather as we followed them from the cellar, "I do not know how the bank can thank you or repay you. There is no doubt that you have detected and defeated in the most complete manner one of the most determined attempts at bank robbery that have ever come within my experience."

"I have had one or two little scores of my own to settle with Mr. John Clay," said Holmes. "I have been at some small expense over this matter, which I shall expect the bank to refund, but beyond that I am amply repaid by having had an experience which is in many ways unique, and by hearing the very remarkable narrative of the Red-headed League."

"You see, Watson," he explained in the early hours of the morning as we sat over a glass of whisky and soda in Baker Street, "it was perfectly obvious from the first that the only possible object of this rather fantastic business of the advertisement of the League, and the copying of the Encyclopaedia, must be to get this not over-bright pawnbroker out of the way for a number of hours every day. It was a curious way of managing it, but, really, it would be difficult to suggest a better. The method was no doubt suggested to Clay's ingenious mind by the colour of his accomplice's hair. The £4 a week was a lure which must draw him, and what was it to them, who were playing for thousands? They put in the advertisement, one rogue has the temporary office, the other rogue incites the man to apply for it, and together they manage to secure his absence every morning in the week. From the time that I heard of the assistant having come for half wages, it was obvious to me that he had some strong motive for securing the situation."

"But how could you guess what the motive was?"

"Had there been women in the house, I should have suspected a mere vulgar intrigue. That, however, was out of the question. The man's business was a small one, and there was nothing in his house which could account for such elaborate preparations, and such an expenditure as they were at. It must, then, be something out of the house. What could it be? I thought of the assistant's fondness for photography, and his trick of vanishing into the cellar. The cellar! There was the end of this tangled clue. Then I made inquires as to this mysterious assistant and found that I had to deal with one of the coolest and most daring criminals in London. He was doing something in the cellar—something which took many hours a day for months on end. What could it be, once more? I could think of nothing save that he was running a tunnel to some other building.

"So far I had got when we went to visit the scene of action. I surprised you by beating upon the pavement with my stick. I was ascertaining whether the cellar stretched out in front or behind. It was not in front. Then I rang the bell, and, as I hoped, the assistant answered it. We have had some skirmishes, but we had never set eyes upon each other before. I hardly looked at his face. His knees were what I wished to see. You must yourself have remarked how worn, wrinkled, and stained they were. They spoke of those hours of burrowing. The only remaining point was what they were burrowing for. I walked round the corner, saw the City and Suburban Bank abutted on our friend's premises, and felt that I had solved my problem. When you drove home after the concert I called upon Scotland Yard and upon the chairman of the bank directors, with the result that you have seen."

"And how could you tell that they would make their attempt to-night?" I asked.

"Well, when they closed their League offices that was a sign that they cared no longer about Mr. Jabez Wilson's presence—in other words, that they had completed their tunnel. But it was essential that they should use it soon, as it might be discovered, or the bullion might be removed. Saturday would suit them better than any other day, as it would give them two days for their escape. For all these reasons I expected them to come to-night."

"You reasoned it out beautifully," I exclaimed in unfeigned admiration "It is so long a chain, and yet every link rings true."

"It saved me from ennui," he answered, yawning. "Alas! I already feel it closing in upon me. My life is spent in one long effort to escape from the commonplaces of existence. These little problems help me to do so."

"And you are a benefactor of the race," said I.

He shrugged his shoulders. "Well, perhaps, after all, it is of some little use," he remarked. " *'L'homme c'est rien—l'oeuvre c'est tout,'* as Gustave Flaubert wrote to George Sand."

A Case of Identity

"My dear fellow," said Sherlock Holmes as we sat on either side of the fire in his lodgings at Baker Street, "life is infinitely stranger than anything which the mind of man could invent. We would not dare to conceive the things which are really mere commonplaces of existence. If we could fly out of that window hand in hand, hover over this great city, gently remove the roofs, and peep in at the queer things which are going on, the strange coincidences, the plannings, the cross-purposes, the wonderful chains of events, working through generation, and leading to the most *outré* results, it would make all fiction with its conventionalities and foreseen conclusions most stale and unprofitable."

"And yet I am not convinced of it," I answered. "The cases which come to light in the papers are, as a rule, bald enough, and vulgar enough. We have in our police reports realism pushed to its extreme limits, and yet the result is, it must be confessed, neither fascinating nor artistic."

"A certain selection and discretion must be used in producing a realistic effect," remarked Holmes. "This is wanting in the police report, where more stress is laid, perhaps, upon the platitudes of the magistrate than upon the details, which to an observer contain the vital essence of the whole matter. Depend upon it, there is nothing so unnatural as the commonplace."

I smiled and shook my head. "I can quite understand your thinking so," I said. "Of course, in your position of unofficial adviser and helper to everybody who is absolutely puzzled, throughout three continents, you are brought in contact with all that is strange and bizarre. But here"—I picked up the morning paper from the ground—"let us put it to a practical test. Here is the first heading upon which I come. 'A husband's cruelty to his wife.' There is half a column of print, but I know without reading it that it is all perfectly familiar to me. There is, of course, the other woman, the drink, the push, the blow, the bruise, the sympathetic sister or landlady. The crudest of writers could invent nothing more crude."

"Indeed, your example is an unfortunate one for your argument," said Holmes, taking the paper and glancing his eye down it. "This is the Dundas separation case, and, as it happens, I was engaged in clearing up some small points in connection with it. The husband was a teetotaler, there was no other woman, and the conduct complained of was that he had drifted into the habit of winding up every meal by taking out his false teeth and hurling them at his wife, which, you will allow, is not an action likely to occur to the imagination of the average story-teller. Take a pinch of snuff, Doctor, and acknowledge that I have scored over you in your example."

He held out his snuffbox of old gold, with a great amethyst in the centre of the lid. Its splendour was in such contrast to his homely ways and simple life that I could not help commenting upon it.

"Ah," said he, "I forgot that I had not seen you for some weeks. It is a little souvenir from the King of Bohemia in return for my assistance in the case of the Irene Adler papers."

"And the ring?" I asked, glancing at a remarkable brilliant which sparkled upon his finger.

"It was from the reigning family of Holland, though the matter in which I served them was of such delicacy that I cannot confide it even to you, who have been good enough to chronicle one or two of my little problems."

"And have you any on hand just now?" I asked with interest.

"Some ten or twelve, but none which present any feature of interest. They are important, you understand, without being interesting. Indeed, I have found that it is usually in unimportant matters that there is a field for the observation, and for the quick analysis of cause and effect which gives the charm to an investigation. The larger crimes are apt to be the simpler, for the bigger the crime the more obvious, as a rule, is the motive. In these cases, save for one rather intricate matter which has been referred to me from Marseilles, there is nothing which presents any features of interest. It is possible, however, that I may have something better before very many minutes are over, for this is one of my clients, or I am much mistaken."

He had risen from his chair and was standing between the parted blinds gazing down into the dull neutral-tinted London street. Looking over his shoulder, I saw that on the pavement opposite there stood a large woman with a heavy fur boa round her neck, and a large curling red feather in a broad-brimmed hat which was tilted in a coquettish Duchess of Devonshire fashion over her ear. From under this great panoply she peeped up in a nervous, hesitating fashion at our windows, while her body oscillated backward and forward, and her fingers fidgeted with her glove buttons. Suddenly, with a plunge, as of the swimmer who leaves the bank, she hurried across the road, and we heard the sharp clang of the bell.

"I have seen those symptoms before," said Holmes, throwing his cigarette into the fire. "Oscillation upon the pavement always means an *affaire de cœur*. She would like advice, but is not sure that the matter is not too delicate for communication. And yet even here we may discriminate. When a woman has been seriously wronged by a man she no longer oscillates, and the usual symptom is a broken bell wire. Here we may take it that there is a love matter, but that the maiden is not so much angry as perplexed, or grieved. But here she comes in person to resolve our doubts."

As he spoke there was a tap at the door, and the boy in buttons entered to announce Miss Mary Sutherland, while the lady herself loomed behind his small black figure like a full-sailed merchantman behind a tiny pilot boat. Sherlock Holmes welcomed her with the easy courtesy for which he was remarkable, and, having closed the door and bowed her into an armchair, he looked her over in the minute and yet abstracted fashion which was peculiar to him.

"Do you not find," he said, "that with your short sight it is a little trying to do so much typewriting?"

"I did at first," she answered, "but now I know where the letters are without looking." Then, suddenly realizing the full purport of his words, she gave a violent start and looked up, with fear and astonishment upon her broad, good-humoured face. "You've heard about me, Mr. Holmes," she cried, "else how could you know all that?"

"Never mind," said Holmes, laughing; "it is my business to know things. Perhaps I have trained myself to see what others overlook. If not, why should you come to consult me?"

"I came to you, sir, because I heard of you from Mrs. Etherege, whose husband you found so easy when the police and everyone had given him up for dead. Oh, Mr. Holmes, I wish you would do as much for me. I'm not rich, but still I have a hundred a year in my own right, besides the little that I make by the machine, and I would give it all to know what has become of Mr. Hosmer Angel."

"Why did you come away to consult me in such a hurry?" asked Sherlock Holmes, with his finger-tips together and his eyes to the ceiling.

Again a startled look came over the somewhat vacuous face of Miss Mary Sutherland. "Yes, I did bang out of the house," she said, "for it made me angry to see the easy way in which Mr. Windibank—that is, my father—took it all. He would not go to the police, and he would not go to you, and so at last, as he would do nothing and kept on saying that there was no harm done, it made me mad, and I just on with my things and came right away to you."

"Your father," said Holmes, "your stepfather, surely, since the name is different."

"Yes, my stepfather. I call him father, though it sounds funny, too, for he is only five years and two months older than myself."

"And your mother is alive?"

"Oh, yes, mother is alive and well. I wasn't best pleased, Mr. Holmes, when she married again so soon after father's death, and a man who was nearly fifteen years younger than herself. Father was a plumber in the Tottenham Court Road, and he left a tidy business behind him, which mother carried on with Mr. Hardy, the foreman; but when Mr. Windibank came he made her sell the business, for he was very superior, being a traveller in wines. They got £4700 for the goodwill and interest, which wasn't near as much as father could have got if he had been alive."

I had expected to see Sherlock Holmes impatient under this rambling and inconsequential narrative, but, on the contrary he had listened with the greatest concentration of attention.

"Your own little income," he asked, "does it come out of the business?"

"Oh, no, sir. It is quite separate and was left me by my uncle Ned in Auckland. It is in New Zealand stock, paying 4½ per cent. Two thousand five hundred pounds was the amount, but I can only touch the interest."

"You interest me extremely," said Holmes. "And since you draw so large a sum as a hundred a year, with what you earn into the bargain, you no doubt travel a little and indulge yourself in every way. I believe that a single lady can get on very nicely upon an income of about £60."

"I could do with much less than that, Mr. Holmes, but you understand that as long as I live at home I don't wish to be a burden to them, and so they have the use of the money just while I am staying with them. Of course, that is only just for the time. Mr. Windibank draws my interest every quarter and pays it over to mother, and I find that I can do pretty well with what I earn at typewriting. It brings me twopence a sheet, and I can often do from fifteen to twenty sheets in a day."

"You have made your position very clear to me," said Holmes. "This is my friend, Dr. Watson, before whom you can speak as freely as before myself. Kindly tell us now all about your connection with Mr. Hosmer Angel."

A flush stole over Miss Sutherland's face, and she picked nervously at the fringe of her jacket. "I met him first at the gasfitters' ball," she said. "They used to send father tickets when he was alive, and then afterwards they remembered us, and sent them to mother. Mr. Windibank did not wish us to go. He never did wish us to go anywhere. He would get quite mad if I wanted so much as to join a Sunday-school treat. But this time I was set on going, and I would go; for what right had he to prevent? He said the folk were not fit for us to know, when all father's friends were to be there. And he said that I had nothing fit to wear, when I had my purple plush that I had never so much as taken out of the drawer. At last, when nothing else would do, he went off to France upon the business of the firm, but we went, mother and I, with Mr. Hardy, who used to be our foreman, and it was there I met Mr. Hosmer Angel."

"I suppose," said Holmes, "that when Mr. Windibank came back from France he was very annoyed at your having gone to the ball."

"Oh, well, he was very good about it. He laughed, I remember, and shrugged his shoulders, and said there was no use denying anything to a woman, for she would have her way."

"I see. Then at the gasfitters' ball you met, as I understand, a gentleman called Mr. Hosmer Angel."

"Yes, sir. I met him that night, and he called next day to ask if we had got home all safe, and after that we met him—that is to say, Mr. Holmes, I met him twice for walks, but after that father came back again, and Mr. Hosmer Angel could not come to the house any more."

"No?"

"Well, you know, father didn't like anything of the sort. He wouldn't have any visitors if he could help it, and he used to say that a woman should be happy in her own family circle. But then, as I used to say to mother, a woman wants her own circle to begin with, and I had not got mine yet."

"But how about Mr. Hosmer Angel? Did he make no attempt to see you?"

"Well, father was going off to France again in a week, and Hosmer wrote and said that it would be safer and better not to see each other until he had gone. We could write in the meantime, and he used to write every day. I took the letters in in the morning, so there was no need for father to know."

"Were you engaged to the gentleman at this time?"

"Oh, yes, Mr. Holmes. We were engaged after the first walk that we took. Hosmer—Mr. Angel—was a cashier in an office in Leadenhall Street—and—"

"What office?"

"That's the worst of it, Mr. Holmes, I don't know."

"Where did he live, then?"

"He slept on the premises."

"And you don't know his address?"

"No—except that it was Leadenhall Street."

"Where did you address your letters, then?"

"To the Leadenhall Street Post-Office, to be left till called for. He said that if they were sent to the office he would be chaffed by all the other clerks about having letters from a lady, so I offered to typewrite them, like he did his, but he wouldn't have that, for he said that when I wrote them they seemed to come from me, but when they were typewritten he always felt that the machine had come between us. That will just show you how fond he was of me, Mr. Holmes, and the little things that he would think of."

"It was most suggestive," said Holmes. "It has long been an axiom of mine that the little things are infinitely the most important. Can you remember any other little things about Mr. Hosmer Angel?"

"He was a very shy man, Mr. Holmes. He would rather walk with me in the evening than in the daylight, for he said that he hated to be conspicuous. Very retiring and gentlemanly he was. Even his voice was gentle. He'd had the quinsy and swollen glands when he was young, he told me, and it had left him with a weak throat, and a hesitating, whispering fashion of speech. He was always well dressed, very neat and plain, but his eyes were weak, just as mine are, and he wore tinted glasses against the glare."

"Well, and what happened when Mr. Windibank, your stepfather, returned to France?"

"Mr. Hosmer Angel came to the house again and proposed that we should marry before father came back. He was in dreadful earnest and made me swear, with my hands on the Testament, that whatever happened I would always be true to him. Mother said he was quite right to make me swear, and that it was a sign of his passion. Mother was all in his favour from the first and was even fonder of him than I was. Then, when they talked of marrying within the week, I began to ask about father; but they both said never to mind about father, but just to tell him afterwards, and mother said she would make it all right with him. I didn't quite like that, Mr. Holmes. It seemed funny that I should ask his leave, as he was only a few years older than me; but I didn't want to do anything on the sly, so I wrote to father at Bordeaux, where the company has its French offices, but the letter came back to me on the very morning of the wedding."

"It missed him, then?"

"Yes, sir; for he had started to England just before it arrived."

"Ha! that was unfortunate. Your wedding was arranged, then, for the Friday. Was it to be in church?"

"Yes, sir, but very quietly. It was to be at St. Saviour's near King's Cross, and we were to have breakfast afterwards at the St. Pancras Hotel. Hosmer came for us in a hansom, but as there were two of us he put us both into it and stepped himself into a four-wheeler, which happened to be the only other cab in the street. We got to the church first, and when the four-wheeler drove up we waited for him to step out, but he never did, and when the cabman got down from the box and looked there was no one there! The cabman said that he could not imagine what had become of him, for he had seen him get in with his own eyes. That was last Friday, Mr. Holmes, and I have never seen or heard anything since then to throw any light upon what became of him."

"It seems to me that you have been very shamefully treated," said Holmes.

"Oh, no, sir! He was too good and kind to leave me so. Why, all the morning he was saying to me that, whatever happened, I was to be true; and that even if something quite unforeseen occurred to separate us, I was always to remember that I was pledged to him, and that he would claim his pledge sooner or later. It seemed strange talk for a wedding-morning, but what has happened since gives a meaning to it."

"Most certainly it does. Your own opinion is, then, that some unforeseen catastrophe has occurred to him?"

"Yes, sir. I believe that he foresaw some danger, or else he would not have talked so. And then I think that what he foresaw happened."

"But you have no notion as to what it could have been?"

"None."

"One more question. How did your mother take the matter?"

"She was angry, and said that I was never to speak of the matter again."

"And your father? Did you tell him?"

"Yes; and he seemed to think, with me, that something had happened, and that I should hear of Hosmer again. As he said, what interest could anyone have in bringing me to the doors of the church, and then leaving me? Now, if he had borrowed my money, or if he had married me and got my money settled on him, there might be some reason, but Hosmer was very independent about money and never would look at a shilling of mine. And yet, what could have happened? And why could he not write? Oh, it drives me half-mad to think of it, and I can't sleep a wink at night." She pulled a little handkerchief out of her muff and began to sob heavily into it.

"I shall glance into the case for you," said Holmes, rising, "and I have no doubt that we shall reach some definite result. Let the weight of the matter rest upon me now, and do not let your mind dwell upon it further. Above all, try to let Mr. Hosmer Angel vanish from your memory, as he has done from your life."

"Then you don't think I'll see him again?"

"I fear not."

"Then what has happened to him?"

"You will leave that question in my hands. I should like an accurate description of him and any letters of his which you can spare."

"I advertised for him in last Saturday's *Chronicle*," said she. "Here is the slip and here are four letters from him."

"Thank you. And your address?"

"No. 31 Lyon Place, Camberwell."

"Mr. Angel's address you never had, I understand. Where is your father's place of business?"

"He travels for Westhouse & Marbank, the great claret importers of Frenchurch Street."

"Thank you. You have made your statement very clearly. You will leave the papers here, and remember the advice which I have given you. Let the whole incident be a sealed book, and do not allow it to affect your life."

"You are very kind, Mr. Holmes, but I cannot do that. I shall be true to Hosmer. He shall find me ready when he comes back."

For all the preposterous hat and the vacuous face, there was something noble in the simple faith of our visitor which compelled our respect. She laid her little bundle of papers upon the table and went her way, with a promise to come again whenever she might be summoned.

Sherlock Holmes sat silent for a few minutes with his fingertips still pressed together, his legs stretched out in front of him, and his gaze directed upward to the ceiling. Then he took down from the rack the old and oily clay pipe, which was to him as a counsellor, and, having lit it, he leaned back in his chair, with the thick blue cloud-wreaths spinning up from him, and a look of infinite languor in his face.

"Quite an interesting study, that maiden," he observed. "I found her more interesting than her little problem, which, by the way, is rather a trite one. You will find parallel cases, if you consult my index, in Andover in '77, and there was something of the sort at The Hague last year. Old as is the idea, however, there were one or two details which were new to me. But the maiden herself was most instructive."

"You appeared to read a good deal upon her which was quite invisible to me," I remarked.

"Not invisible but unnoticed, Watson. You did not know where to look, and so you missed all that was important. I can never bring you to realize the importance of sleeves, the suggestiveness of thumb-nails, or the great issues that may hang from a boot-lace. Now, what did you gather from that woman's appearance? Describe it."

"Well, she had a slate-coloured, broad-brimmed straw hat, with a feather of a brickish red. Her jacket was black, with black beads sewn upon it, and a fringe of little black jet ornaments. Her dress was brown, rather darker than coffee colour, with a little purple plush at the neck and sleeves. Her gloves were grayish and were worn through at the right forefinger. Her boots I didn't observe. She had small round, hanging gold earrings, and a general air of being fairly well-to-do in a vulgar, comfortable, easy-going way."

Sherlock Holmes clapped his hands softly together and chuckled.

"'Pon my word, Watson, you are coming along wonderfully. You have really done very well indeed. It is true that you have missed everything of importance, but you have hit upon the method, and you have a quick eye for colour. Never trust to general impressions, my boy, but concentrate yourself upon details. My first glance is always at a woman's sleeve. In a man it is perhaps better first to take the knee of the trouser. As you observe, this woman had plush upon her sleeves, which is a most useful material for showing traces. The double line a little above the wrist, where the typewritist presses against the table, was beautifully defined. The sewing-machine, of the hand type, leaves a similar mark, but only on the left arm, and on the side of it farthest from the thumb, instead of being right across the broadest part, as this was. I then glanced at her face, and, observing the dint of a pince-nez at either side of her nose, I ventured a remark upon short sight and typewriting, which seemed to surprise her."

"It surprised me."

"But, surely, it was obvious. I was then much surprised and interested on glancing down to observe that, though the boots which she was wearing were not unlike each other, they were really odd ones; the one having a slightly decorated toe-cap, and the other a plain one. One was buttoned only in the two lower buttons out of five, and the other at the first, third, and fifth. Now, when you see that a young lady, otherwise neatly dressed, has come away from home with odd boots, half-buttoned, it is no great deduction to say that she came away in a hurry."

"And what else?" I asked, keenly interested, as I always was, by my friend's incisive reasoning.

"I noted, in passing, that she had written a note before leaving home but after being fully dressed. You observed that her right glove was torn at the forefinger, but you did not apparently see that both glove and finger were stained with violet ink. She had written in a hurry and dipped her pen too deep. It must have been this morning, or the mark would not remain clear upon the finger. All this is amusing, though rather elementary, but I must go back to business, Watson. Would you mind reading me the advertised description of Mr. Hosmer Angel?"

I held the little printed slip to the light.

> "Missing [it said] on the morning of the fourteenth, a gentleman named Hosmer Angel. About five feet seven inches in height; strongly built, sallow complexion, black hair, a little bald in the centre, bushy, black side-whiskers and moustache; tinted glasses, slight infirmity of speech. Was dressed, when last seen, in black frock-coat faced with silk, black waistcoat, gold Albert chain, and gray Harris tweed trousers, with brown gaiters over elastic-sided boots. Known to have been employed in an office in Leadenhall Street. Anybody bringing—"

"That will do," said Holmes. "As to the letters," he continued, glancing over them, "they are very commonplace. Absolutely no clue in them to Mr. Angel, save that he quotes Balzac once. There is one remarkable point, however, which will no doubt strike you."

"They are typewritten," I remarked.

"Not only that, but the signature is typewritten. Look at the neat little 'Hosmer Angel' at the bottom. There is a date, you see, but no superscription except Leadenhall Street, which is rather vague. The point about the signature is very suggestive —in fact, we may call it conclusive."

"Of what?"

"My dear fellow, is it possible you do not see how strongly it bears upon the case?"

"I cannot say that I do unless it were that he wished to be able to deny his signature if an action for breach of promise were instituted."

"No, that was not the point. However, I shall write two letters, which should settle the matter. One is to a firm in the City, the other is to the young lady's stepfather, Mr. Windibank, asking him whether he could meet us here at six o'clock tomorrow evening. It is just as well that we should do business with the male relatives. And now, Doctor, we can do nothing until the answers to those letters come, so we may put our little problem upon the shelf for the interim."

I had had so many reasons to believe in my friend's subtle powers of reasoning and extraordinary energy in action that I felt that he must have some solid grounds for the assured and easy demeanour with which he treated the singular mystery which he had been called upon to fathom. Once only had I known him to fail, in the case of the King of Bohemia and of the Irene Adler photograph; but when I looked back to the weird business of 'The Sign of Four', and the extraordinary circumstances connected with 'A Study in Scarlet', I felt that it would be a strange tangle indeed which he could not unravel.

I left him then, still puffing at his black clay pipe, with the conviction that when I came again on the next evening I would find that he held in his hands all the clues which would lead up to the identity of the disappearing bridegroom of Miss Mary Sutherland.

A professional case of great gravity was engaging my own attention at the time, and the whole of next day I was busy at the bedside of the sufferer. It was not until close upon six o'clock that I found myself free and was able to spring into a hansom and drive to Baker Street, half afraid that I might be too late to assist at the dénouement of the little mystery. I found Sherlock Holmes alone, however, half asleep, with his long, thin form curled up in the recesses of his armchair. A formidable array of bottles and test-tubes, with the pungent cleanly smell of hydrochloric acid, told me that he had spent his day in the chemical work which was so dear to him.

"Well, have you solved it?" I asked as I entered.

"Yes. It was the bisulphate of baryta."

"No, no, the mystery!" I cried.

"Oh, that! I thought of the salt that I have been working upon. There was never any mystery in the matter, though, as I said yesterday, some of the details are of interest. The only drawback is that there is no law, I fear, that can touch the scoundrel."

"Who was he, then, and what was his object in deserting Miss Sutherland?"

The question was hardly out of my mouth, and Holmes had not yet opened his lips to reply, when we heard a heavy footfall in the passage and a tap at the door.

"This is the girl's stepfather, Mr. James Windibank," said Holmes. "He has written to me to say that he would be here at six. Come in!"

The man who entered was a sturdy, middle-sized fellow, some thirty years of age, clean-shaven, and sallow-skinned, with a bland, insinuating manner, and a pair of wonderfully sharp and penetrating gray eyes. He shot a questioning glance at each of us, placed his shiny top-hat upon the sideboard, and with a slight bow sidled down into the nearest chair.

"Good-evening, Mr. James Windibank," said Holmes. "I think that this typewritten letter is from you, in which you made an appointment with me for six o'clock?"

"Yes, sir. I am afraid that I am a little late, but I am not quite my own master, you know. I am sorry that Miss Sutherland has troubled you about this little matter, for I think it is far better not to wash linen of the sort in public. It was quite against my wishes that she came, but she is a very excitable, impulsive girl, as you may have noticed, and she is not easily controlled when she has made up her mind on a point. Of course, I did not mind you so much, as you are not connected with the official police, but it is not pleasant to have a family misfortune like this noised abroad. Besides, it is a useless expense, for how could you possibly find this Hosmer Angel?"

"On the contrary," said Holmes quietly; "I have every reason to believe that I will succeed in discovering Mr. Hosmer Angel."

Mr. Windibank gave a violent start and dropped his gloves. "I am delighted to hear it," he said.

"It is a curious thing," remarked Holmes, "that a typewriter has really quite as much individuality as a man's handwriting. Unless they are quite new, no two of them write exactly alike. Some letters get more worn than others, and some wear only on one side. Now, you remark in this note of yours, Mr. Windibank, that in every case there is some little slurring over of the 'e,' and a slight defect in the tail of the 'r.' There are fourteen other characteristics, but those are the more obvious."

"We do all our correspondence with this machine at the office, and no doubt it is a little worn," our visitor answered, glancing keenly at Holmes with his bright little eyes.

"And now I will show you what is really a very interesting study, Mr. Windibank," Holmes continued. "I think of writing another little monograph some of these days on the typewriter and its relation to crime. It is a subject to which I have devoted some little attention. I have here four letters which purport to come from the missing man. They are all typewritten. In each case, not only are the 'e's' slurred and the 'r's' tailless, but you will observe, if you care to use my magnifying lens, that the fourteen other characteristics to which I have alluded are there as well."

Mr. Windibank sprang out of his chair and picked up his hat. "I cannot waste time over this sort of fantastic talk, Mr. Holmes," he said. "If you can catch the man, catch him, and let me know when you have done it."

"Certainly," said Holmes, stepping over and turning the key in the door. "I let you know, then, that I have caught him!"

"What! where?" shouted Mr. Windibank, turning white to his lips and glancing about him like a rat in a trap.

"Oh, it won't do—really it won't," said Holmes suavely. "There is no possible getting out of it, Mr. Windibank. It is quite too transparent, and it was a very bad compliment when you said that it was impossible for me to solve so simple a question. That's right! Sit down and let us talk it over."

Our visitor collapsed into a chair, with a ghastly face and a glitter of moisture on his brow. "It—it's not actionable," he stammered.

"I am very much afraid that it is not. But between ourselves, Windibank, it was as cruel and selfish and heartless a trick in a petty way as ever came before me. Now, let me just run over the course of events, and you will contradict me if I go wrong."

The man sat huddled up in his chair, with his head sunk upon his breast, like one who is utterly crushed. Holmes stuck his feet up on the corner of the mantelpiece and, leaning back with his hands in his pockets, began talking, rather to himself, as it seemed, than to us.

"The man married a woman very much older than himself for her money," said he, "and he enjoyed the use of the money of the daughter as long as she lived with them. It was a considerable sum, for people in their position, and the loss of it would have made a serious difference. It was worth an effort to preserve it. The daughter was of a good, amiable disposition, but affectionate and warm-hearted in her ways, so that it was evident that with her fair personal advantages, and her little income, she would not be allowed to remain single long. Now her marriage would mean, of course, the loss of a hundred a year, so what does her stepfather do to prevent it? He takes the obvious course of keeping her at home and forbidding her to seek the company of people of her own age. But soon he found that that would not answer forever. She became restive, insisted upon her rights, and finally announced her positive intention of going to a certain ball. What does her clever stepfather do then? He conceives an idea more creditable to his head than to his heart. With the connivance and assistance of his wife he disguised himself, covered those keen eyes with tinted glasses, masked the face with a moustache and a pair of bushy whiskers, sunk that clear voice into an insinuating whisper, and doubly secure on account of the girl's short sight, he appears as Mr. Hosmer Angel, and keeps off other lovers by making love himself."

"It was only a joke at first," groaned our visitor. "We never thought that she would have been so carried away."

"Very likely not. However that may be, the young lady was very decidedly carried away, and, having quite made up her mind that her stepfather was in France, the suspicion of treachery never for an instant entered her mind. She was flattered by the gentleman's attentions, and the effect was increased by the loudly expressed admiration of her mother. Then Mr. Angel began to call, for it was obvious that the matter should be pushed as far as it would go if a real effect were to be produced. There were meetings, and an engagement, which would finally secure the girl's affections from turning towards anyone else. But the deception could not be kept up forever. These pretended journeys to France were rather cumbrous. The thing to do was clearly to bring the business to an end in such a dramatic manner that it would leave a permanent impression upon the young lady's mind and prevent her from looking upon any other suitor for some time to come. Hence those vows of fidelity exacted upon a Testament, and hence also the allusions to a possibility of something happening on the very morning of the wedding. James Windibank wished Miss Sutherland to be so bound to Hosmer Angel, and so uncertain as to his fate, that for ten years to come, at any rate, she would not listen to another man. As far as the church door he brough her, and then, as he could go no farther, he conveniently vanished away by the old trick of stepping in at one door of a four-wheeler and out at the other. I think that was the chain of events, Mr. Windibank!"

Our visitor had recovered something of his assurance while Holmes had been talking, and he rose from his chair now with a cold sneer upon his pale face.

"It may be so, or it may not, Mr. Holmes," said he, "but if you are so very sharp you ought to be sharp enough to know that it is you who are breaking the law now, and not me. I have done nothing actionable from the first, but as long as you keep that door locked you lay yourself open to an action for assault and illegal constraint."

"The law cannot, as you say, touch you," said Holmes, unlocking and throwing open the door, "yet there never was a man who deserved punishment more. If the young lady has a brother or a friend, he ought to lay a whip across your shoulders. By Jove!" he continued, flushing up at the sight of the bitter sneer upon the man's face, "it is not part of my duties to my client, but here's a hunting crop handy, and I think I shall just treat myself to—" He took two swift steps to the whip, but before he could grasp it there was a wild clatter of steps upon the stairs, the heavy hall door banged, and from the window we could see Mr. James Windibank running at the top of his speed down the road.

"There's a cold-blooded scoundrel!" said Holmes, laughing, as he threw himself down into his chair once more. "That fellow will rise from crime to crime until he does something very bad, and ends on a gallows. The case has, in some respects, been not entirely devoid of interest."

"I cannot now entirely see all the steps of your reasoning," I remarked.

"Well, of course it was obvious from the first that this Mr. Hosmer Angel must have some strong object for his curious conduct, and it was equally clear that the only man who really profited by the incident, as far as we could see, was the stepfather. Then the fact that the two men were never together, but that the one always appeared when the other was away, was suggestive. So were the tinted spectacles and the curious voice, which both hinted at a disguise, as did the bushy whiskers. My suspicions were all confirmed by his peculiar action in typewriting his signature, which, of course, inferred that his handwriting was so familiar to her that she would recognize even the smallest sample of it. You see all these isolated facts, together with many minor ones, all pointed in the same direction."

"And how did you verify them?"

"Having once spotted my man, it was easy to get corroboration. I knew the firm for which this man worked. Having taken the printed description, I eliminated everything from it which could be the result of a disguise—the whiskers, the glasses, the voice, and I sent it to the firm, with a request that they would inform me whether it answered to the description of any of their travellers. I had already noticed the peculiarities of the typewriter, and I wrote to the man himself at his business address, asking him if he would come here. As I expected, his reply was typewritten and revealed the same trivial but characteristic defects. The same post brought me a letter from Westhouse & Marbank, of Fenchurch Street, to say that the description tallied in every respect with that of their employee, James Windibank. *Voilà tout*!"

"And Miss Sutherland?"

"If I tell her she will not believe me. You may remember the old Persian saying, 'There is danger for him who taketh the tiger cub, and danger also for whoso snatches a delusion from a woman.' There is as much sense in Hafiz as in Horace, and as much knowledge of the world."

The Boscombe Valley Mystery

We were seated at breakfast one morning, my wife and I, when the maid brought in a telegram. It was from Sherlock Holmes and ran in this way:

> Have you a couple of days to spare? Have just been wired for from the west of England in connection with Boscombe Valley tragedy. Shall be glad if you will come with me. Air and scenery perfect. Leave Paddington by the 11:15.

"What do you say, dear?" said my wife, looking across at me. "Will you go?"

"I really don't know what to say. I have a fairly long list at present."

"Oh, Anstruther would do your work for you. You have been looking a little pale lately. I think that the change would do you good, and you are always so interested in Mr. Sherlock Holmes's cases."

"I should be ungrateful if I were not, seeing what I gained through one of them," I answered. "But if I am to go, I must pack at once, for I have only half an hour."

My experience of camp life in Afghanistan had at least had the effect of making me a prompt and ready traveller. My wants were few and simple, so that in less than the time stated I was in a cab with my valise, rattling away to Paddington Station. Sherlock Holmes was pacing up and down the platform, his tall, gaunt figure made even gaunter and taller by his long gray travelling-cloak and close-fitting cloth cap.

"It is really very good of you to come, Watson," said he. "It makes a considerable difference to me, having someone with me on whom I can thoroughly rely. Local aid is always either worthless or else biassed. If you will keep the two corner seats I shall get the tickets."

We had the carriage to ourselves save for an immense litter of papers which Holmes had brought with him. Among these he rummaged and read, with intervals of note-taking and of meditation, until we were past Reading. Then he suddenly rolled them all into a gigantic ball and tossed them up onto the rack.

"Have you heard anything of the case?" he asked.

"Not a word. I have not seen a paper for some days."

"The London press has not had very full accounts. I have just been looking through all the recent papers in order to master the particulars. It seems, from what I gather, to be one of those simple cases which are so extremely difficult."

"That sounds a little paradoxical."

"But it is profoundly true. Singularity is almost invariably a clue. The more featureless and commonplace a crime is, the more difficult it is to bring it home. In this case, however, they have established a very serious case against the son of the murdered man."

"It is a murder, then?"

"Well, it is conjectured to be so. I shall take nothing for granted until I have the opportunity of looking personally into it. I will explain the state of things to you, as far as I have been able to understand it, in a very few words.

"Boscombe Valley is a country district not very far from Ross, in Herefordshire. The largest landed proprietor in that part is a Mr. John Turner, who made his money in Australia and returned some years ago to the old country. One of the farms which he held, that of Hatherley, was let to Mr. Charles McCarthy, who was also an ex-Australian. The men had known each other in the colonies, so that it was not unnatural that when they came to settle down they should do so as near each other as possible. Turner was apparently the richer man, so McCarthy became his tenant but still remained, it seems, upon terms of perfect equality, as they were frequently together. McCarthy had one son, a lad of eighteen, and Turner had an only daughter of the same age, but neither of them had wives living. They appear to have avoided the society of the neighbouring English families and to have led retired lives, though both the McCarthys were fond of sport and were frequently seen at the race-meetings of the neighbourhood. McCarthy kept two servants—a man and a girl. Turner had a considerable household, some half-dozen at the least. That is as much as I have been able to gather about the families. Now for the facts.

"On June 3rd, that is, on Monday last, McCarthy left his

house at Hatherley about three in the afternoon and walked down to the Boscombe Pool, which is a small lake formed by the spreading out of the stream which runs down the Boscombe Valley. He had been out with his serving-man in the morning at Ross, and he had told the man that he must hurry, as he had an appointment of importance to keep at three. From that appointment he never came back alive.

"From Hatherley Farmhouse to the Boscombe Pool is a quarter of a mile, and two people saw him as he passed over this ground. One was an old woman, whose name is not mentioned, and the other was William Crowder, a game-keeper in the employ of Mr. Turner. Both these witnesses depose that Mr. McCarthy was walking alone. The game-keeper adds that within a few minutes of his seeing Mr. McCarthy pass he had seen his son, Mr. James McCarthy, going the same way with a gun under his arm. To the best of his belief, the father was actually in sight at the time, and the son was following him. He thought no more of the matter until he heard in the evening of the tragedy that had occurred.

"The two McCarthys were seen after the time when William Crowder, the game-keeper, lost sight of them. The Boscombe Pool is thickly wooded round, with just a fringe of grass and of reeds round the edge. A girl of fourteen, Patience Moran, who is the daughter of the lodge-keeper of the Boscombe Valley estate, was in one of the woods picking flowers. She states that while she was there she saw, at the border of the wood and close by the lake, Mr. McCarthy and his son, and that they appeared to be having a violent quarrel. She heard Mr. McCarthy the elder using very strong language to his son, and she saw the latter raise up his hand as if to strike his father. She was so frightened by their violence that she ran away and told her mother when she reached home that she had left the two McCarthys quarrelling near Boscombe Pool, and that she was afraid that they were going to fight. She had hardly said the words when young Mr. McCarthy came running up to the lodge to say that he had found his father dead in the wood, and to ask for the help of the lodge-keeper. He was much excited, without either his gun or his hat, and his right hand and sleeve were observed to be stained with fresh blood. On following him they found the dead body stretched out upon the grass beside the pool. The head had been beaten in by repeated blows of some heavy and blunt weapon. The injuries were such as might very well have been inflicted by the butt-end of his son's gun, which was found lying on the grass within a few paces of the body. Under these circumstances the young man was instantly arrested, and a verdict of 'wilful murder' having been returned at the inquest on Tuesday, he was on Wednesday brought before the magistrates at Ross, who have referred the case to the next Assizes. Those are the main facts of the case as they came out before the coroner and the police-court."

"I could hardly imagine a more damning case," I remarked. "If ever circumstantial evidence pointed to a criminal it does so here."

"Circumstantial evidence is a very tricky thing," answered Holmes thoughtfully. "It may seem to point very straight to one thing, but if you shift your own point of view a little, you may find it pointing in an equally uncompromising manner to something entirely different. It must be confessed, however, that the case looks exceedingly grave against the young man, and it is very possible that he is indeed the culprit. There are several people in the neighbourhood, however, and among them Miss Turner, the daughter of the neighbouring landowner, who believe in his innocence, and who have retained Lestrade, whom you may recollect in connection with 'A Study in Scarlet', to work out the case in his interest. Lestrade, being rather puzzled, has referred the case to me, and hence it is that two middle-aged gentlemen are flying westward at fifty miles an hour instead of quietly digesting their breakfasts at home."

"I am afraid," said I, "that the facts are so obvious that you will find little credit to be gained out of this case."

"There is nothing more deceptive than an obvious fact," he answered, laughing. "Besides, we may chance to hit upon some other obvious facts which may have been by no means obvious to Mr. Lestrade. You know me too well to think that I am boasting when I say that I shall either confirm or destroy his theory by means which he is quite incapable of employing, or even of understanding. To take the first example to hand, I very clearly perceive that in your bedroom the window is upon the right-hand side, and yet I question whether Mr. Lestrade would have noted even so self-evident a thing as that."

"How on earth—"

"My dear fellow, I know you well. I know the military neatness which characterizes you. You shave every morning, and in this season you shave by the sunlight; but since your shaving is less and less complete as we get farther back on the left side, until it becomes positively slovenly as we get round the angle of the jaw, it is surely very clear that that side is less illuminated than the other. I could not imagine a man of your habits looking at himself in an equal light and being satisfied with such a result. I only quote this as a trivial example of observation and inference. Therein lies my *métier*, and it is just possible that it may be of some service in the investigation which lies before us. There are one or two minor points which were brought out in the inquest, and which are worth considering."

"What are they?"

"It appears that his arrest did not take place at once, but after the return to Hatherley Farm. On the inspector of constabulary informing him that he was a prisoner, he remarked that he was not surprised to hear it, and that it was no more than his deserts. This observation of his had the natural effect of removing any traces of doubt which might have remained in the minds of the coroner's jury."

"It was a confession," I ejaculated.

"No, for it was followed by a protestation of innocence."

"Coming on the top of such a damning series of events, it was at least a most suspicious remark."

"On the contrary," said Holmes, "it is the brightest rift which I can at present see in the clouds. However innocent he might be, he could not be such an absolute imbecile as not to see that the circumstances were very black against him. Had he appeared surprised at his own arrest, or feigned indignation at it, I should have looked upon it as highly suspicious, because such surprise or anger would not be natural under the circumstances, and yet might appear to be the best policy to a scheming man. His frank acceptance of the situation marks him as either an innocent man, or else as a man of considerable self-restraint and firmness. As to his remark about his deserts, it was also not unnatural if you consider that he stood beside the dead body of his father, and that there is no doubt that he had that very day so far forgotten his filial duty as to bandy words with him, and even, according to the little girl whose evidence is so important, to raise his hand as if to strike him. The self-reproach and contrition which are displayed in his remark appear to me to be the signs of a healthy mind rather than of a guilty one."

I shook my head. "Many men have been hanged on far slighter evidence," I remarked.

"So they have. And many men have been wrongfully hanged."

"What is the young man's own account of the matter?"

"It is, I am afraid, not very encouraging to his supporters, though there are one or two points in it which are suggestive. You will find it here, and may read it for yourself."

He picked out from his bundle a copy of the local Herefordshire paper, and having turned down the sheet he pointed out the paragraph in which the unfortunate young man had given his own statement of what had occurred. I settled myself down in the corner of the carriage and read it very carefully. It ran in this way:

> Mr. James McCarthy, the only son of the deceased, was then called and gave evidence as follows: "I had been away from home for three days at Bristol, and had only just returned upon the morning of last Monday, the 3d. My father was absent from home at the time of my arrival, and I was informed by the maid that he had driven over to Ross with John Cobb, the groom. Shortly after my return I heard the wheels of his trap in the yard, and, looking out of my window, I saw him get out and walk rapidly out of the yard, though I was not aware in which direction he was going. I then took my gun and strolled out in the direction of the Boscombe Pool, with the intention of visiting the rabbit-warren which is upon the other side. On my way I saw William Crowder, the game-keeper, as he had stated in his evidence; but he is mistaken in thinking that I was following my father. I had no idea that he was in front of me. When about a hundred yards from the pool I heard a cry of 'Cooee!' which was a usual signal between my father and myself. I then hurried forward, and found him standing by the pool. He appeared to be much surprised at seeing me and asked me rather roughly what I was doing there. A conversation ensued which led to high words and almost to blows, for my father was a man of a very violent temper. Seeing that his passion was becoming ungovernable, I left him and returned towards Hatherley Farm. I had not gone more than 150 yards, however, when I heard a hideous outcry behind me, which caused me to run back again. I found my father

expiring upon the ground, with his head terribly injured. I dropped my gun and held him in my arms, but he almost instantly expired. I knelt beside him for some minutes, and then made my way to Mr. Turner's lodge-keeper, his house being the nearest, to ask for assistance. I saw no one near my father when I returned, and I have no idea how he came by his injuries. He was not a popular man, being somewhat cold and forbidding in his manners; but he had, as far as I know, no active enemies. I know nothing further of the matter."

The Coroner: Did your father make any statement to you before he died?

Witness: He mumbled a few words, but I could only catch some allusion to a rat.

The Coroner: What did you understand by that?

Witness: It conveyed no meaning to me. I thought that he was delirious.

The Coroner: What was the point upon which you and your father had this final quarrel?

Witness: I should prefer not to answer.

The Coroner: I am afraid that I must press it.

Witness: It is really impossible for me to tell you. I can assure you that it has nothing to do with the sad tragedy which followed.

The Coroner: That is for the court to decide. I need not point out to you that your refusal to answer will prejudice your case considerably in any future proceedings which may arise.

Witness: I must still refuse.

The Coroner: I understand that the cry of "Cooee" was a common signal between you and your father?

Witness: It was.

The Coroner: How was it, then, that he uttered it before he saw you, and before he even knew that you had returned from Bristol?

Witness (with considerable confusion): I do not know.

A Juryman: Did you see nothing which aroused your suspicions when you returned on hearing the cry and found your father fatally injured?

Witness: Nothing definite.

The Coroner: What do you mean?

Witness: I was so disturbed and excited as I rushed out into the open, that I could think of nothing except of my father. Yet I have a vague impression that as I ran forward something lay upon the ground to the left of me. It seemed to me to be something gray in colour, a coat of some sort, or a plaid perhaps. When I rose from my father I looked round for it, but it was gone.

"Do you mean that it disappeared before you went for help?"

"Yes, it was gone."

"You cannot say what it was?"

"No, I had a feeling something was there."

"How far from the body?"

"A dozen yards or so."

"And how far from the edge of the wood?"

"About the same."

"Then if it was removed it was while you were within a dozen yards of it?"

"Yes, but with my back towards it."

This concluded the examination of the witness.

"I see," said I as I glanced down the column, "that the coroner in his concluding remarks was rather severe upon young McCarthy. He calls attention, and with reason, to the discrepancy about his father having signalled to him before seeing him, also to his refusal to give details of his conversation with his father, and his singular account of his father's dying words. They are all, as he remarks, very much against the son."

Holmes laughed softly to himself and stretched himself out upon the cushioned seat. "Both you and the coroner have been at some pains," said he, "to single out the very strongest points in the young man's favour. Don't you see that you alternately give him credit for having too much imagination and too little? Too little, if he could not invent a cause of quarrel which would give him the sympathy of the jury; too much, if he evolved from his own inner consciousness anything so *outré* as a dying reference to a rat, and the incident of the vanishing cloth. No, sir, I shall approach this case from the point of view that what this young man says is true, and we shall see whither that hypothesis will lead us. And now here is my pocket Petrarch, and not another word shall I say of this case until we are on the scene of action.

We lunch at Swindon, and I see that we shall be there in twenty minutes."

It was nearly four o'clock when we at last, after passing through the beautiful Stroud Valley, and over the broad gleaming Severn, found ourselves at the pretty little country-town of Ross. A lean, ferret-like man, furtive and sly-looking, was waiting for us upon the platform. In spite of the light brown dustcoat and leather-leggings which he wore in deference to his rustic surroundings, I had no difficulty in recognizing Lestrade, of Scotland Yard. With him we drove to the Hereford Arms where a room had already been engaged for us.

"I have ordered a carriage," said Lestrade as we sat over a cup of tea. "I knew your energetic nature, and that you would not be happy until you had been on the scene of the crime."

"It was very nice and complimentary of you," Holmes answered. "It is entirely a question of barometric pressure."

Lestrade looked startled. "I do not quite follow," he said.

"How is the glass? Twenty-nine, I see. No wind, and not a cloud in the sky. I have a caseful of cigarettes here which need smoking, and the sofa is very much superior to the usual country hotel abomination. I do not think that it is probable that I shall use the carriage to-night."

Lestrade laughed indulgently. "You have, no doubt, already formed your conclusions from the newspapers," he said. "The case is as plain as a pikestaff, and the more one goes into it the plainer it becomes. Still, of course, one can't refuse a lady, and such a very positive one, too. She had heard of you, and would have your opinion, though I repeatedly told her that there was nothing which you could do which I had not already done. Why, bless my soul! here is her carriage at the door."

He had hardly spoken before there rushed into the room one of the most lovely young women that I have ever seen in my life. Her violet eyes shining, her lips parted, a pink flush upon her cheeks, all thought of her natural reserve lost in her overpowering excitement and concern.

"Oh, Mr. Sherlock Holmes!" she cried, glancing from one to the other of us, and finally, with a woman's quick intuition, fastening upon my companion, "I am so glad that you have come. I have driven down to tell you so. I know that James didn't do it. I know it, and I want you to start upon your work knowing it, too. Never let yourself doubt upon that point. We have known each other since we were little children, and I know his faults as no one else does; but he is too tenderhearted to hurt a fly. Such a charge is absurd to anyone who really knows him."

"I hope we may clear him, Miss Turner," said Sherlock Holmes. "You may rely upon my doing all that I can."

"But you have read the evidence. You have formed some conclusion? Do you not see some loophole, some flaw? Do you not yourself think that he is innocent?"

"I think that it is very probable."

"There, now!" she cried, throwing back her head and looking defiantly at Lestrade. "You hear! He gives me hopes."

Lestrade shrugged his shoulders. "I am afraid that my colleague has been a little quick in forming his conclusions," he said.

"But he is right. Oh! I know that he is right. James never did it. And about his quarrel with his father, I am sure that the reason why he would not speak about it to the coroner was because I was concerned in it."

"In what way?" asked Holmes.

"It is no time for me to hide anything. James and his father had many disagreements about me. Mr. McCarthy was very anxious that there should be a marriage between us. James and I have always loved each other as brother and sister; but of course he is young and has seen very little of life yet, and—and—well, he naturally did not wish to do anything like that yet. So there were quarrels, and this, I am sure, was one of them."

"And your father?" asked Holmes. "Was he in favour of such a union?"

"No, he was averse to it also. No one but Mr. McCarthy was in favour of it." A quick blush passed over her fresh young face as Holmes shot one of his keen, questioning glances at her.

"Thank you for this information," said he. "May I see your father if I call to-morrow?"

"I am afraid the doctor won't allow it."

"The doctor?"

"Yes, have you not heard? Poor father has never been strong for years back, but this has broken him down completely. He has taken to his bed, and Dr. Willows says that he is a wreck and that his nervous system is shattered. Mr. McCarthy was the only man alive who had known dad in the old days in Victoria."

"Ha! In Victoria! That is important."

"Yes, at the mines."

"Quite so; at the gold-mines, where, as I understand, Mr. Turner made his money."

"Yes, certainly."

"Thank you, Miss Turner. You have been of material assistance to me."

"You will tell me if you have any news to-morrow. No doubt you will go to the prison to see James. Oh, if you do, Mr. Holmes, do tell him that I know him to be innocent."

"I will, Miss Turner."

"I must go home now, for dad is very ill, and he misses me so if I leave him. Good-bye, and God help you in your undertaking." She hurried from the room as impulsively as she had entered, and we heard the wheels of her carriage rattle off down the street.

"I am ashamed of you, Holmes," said Lestrade with dignity after a few minutes' silence. "Why should you raise up hopes which you are bound to disappoint? I am not over-tender of heart, but I call it cruel."

"I think that I see my way to clearing James McCarthy," said Holmes. "Have you an order to see him in prison?"

"Yes, but only for you and me."

"Then I shall reconsider my resolution about going out. We have still time to take a train to Hereford and see him to-night?"

"Ample."

"Then let us do so. Watson, I fear that you will find it very slow, but I shall only be away a couple of hours."

I walked down to the station with them, and then wandered through the streets of the little town, finally returning to the hotel, where I lay upon the sofa and tried to interest myself in a yellow-backed novel. The puny plot of the story was so thin, however, when compared to the deep mystery through which we were groping, and I found my attention wander so continually from the fiction to the fact, that I at last flung it across the room and gave myself up entirely to a consideration of the events of the day. Supposing that this unhappy young man's story were absolutely true, then what hellish thing, what absolutely unforeseen and extraordinary calamity could have occurred between the time when he parted from his father, and the moment when, drawn back by his screams, he rushed into the glade? It was something terrible and deadly. What could it be? Might not the nature of the injuries reveal something to my medical instincts? I rang the bell and called for the weekly county paper, which contained a verbatim account of the inquest. In the surgeon's deposition it was stated that the posterior third of the left parietal bone and the left half of the occipital bone had been shattered by a heavy blow from a blunt weapon. I marked the spot upon my own head. Clearly such a blow must have been struck from behind. That was to some extent in favour of the accused, as when seen quarrelling he was face to face with his father. Still, it did not go for very much, for the older man might have turned his back before the blow fell. Still, it might be worth while to call Holmes's attention to it. Then there was the peculiar dying reference to a rat. What could that mean? It could not be delirium. A man dying from a sudden blow does not commonly become delirious. No, it was more likely to be an attempt to explain how he met his fate. But what could it indicate? I cudgelled my brains to find some possible explanation. And then the incident of the gray cloth seen by young McCarthy. If that were true the murderer must have dropped some part of his dress, presumably his overcoat, in his flight, and must have had the hardihood to return and to carry it away at the instant when the son was kneeling with his back turned not a dozen paces off. What a tissue of mysteries and improbabilities the whole thing was! I did not wonder at Lestrade's opinion, and yet I had so much faith in Sherlock Holmes's insight that I could not lose hope as long as every fresh fact seemed to strengthen his conviction of young McCarthy's innocence.

It was late before Sherlock Holmes returned. He came back alone, for Lestrade was staying in lodgings in the town.

"The glass still keeps very high," he remarked as he sat down. "It is of importance that it should not rain before we are able to go over the ground. On the other hand, a man should be at his very best and keenest for such nice work as that, and I did not wish to do it when fagged by a long journey. I have seen young McCarthy."

"And what did you learn from him?"

"Nothing."

"Could he throw no light?"

"None at all. I was inclined to think at one time that he knew who had done it and was screening him or her, but I am convinced now that he is as puzzled as everyone else. He is not a very quick-witted youth, though comely to look at and, I should think, sound at heart."

"I cannot admire his taste," I remarked, "if it is indeed a fact that he was averse to a marriage with so charming a young lady as this Miss Turner."

"Ah, thereby hangs a rather painful tale. This fellow is madly, insanely, in love with her, but some two years ago, when he was only a lad, and before he really knew her, for she had been away five years at a boarding-school, what does the idiot do but get into the clutches of a barmaid in Bristol and marry her at a registry office? No one knows a word of the matter, but you can imagine how maddening it must be to him to be upbraided for not doing what he would give his very eyes to do, but what he knows to be absolutely impossible. It was sheer frenzy of this sort which made him throw his hands up into the air when his father, at their last interview, was goading him on to propose to Miss Turner. On the other hand, he had no means of supporting himself, and his father, who was by all accounts a very hard man, would have thrown him over utterly had he known the truth. It was with his barmaid wife that he had spent the last three days in Bristol, and his father did not know where he was. Mark that point. It is of importance. Good has come out of evil, however, for the barmaid, finding from the papers that he is in serious trouble and likely to be hanged, has thrown him over utterly and has written to him to say that she has a husband already in the Bermuda Dockyard, so that there is really no tie between them. I think that that bit of news has consoled young McCarthy for all that he has suffered."

"But if he is innocent, who has done it?"

"Ah! who? I would call your attention very particularly to two points. One is that the murdered man had an appointment with someone at the pool, and that the someone could not have been his son, for his son was away, and he did not know when he would return. The second is that the murdered man was heard to cry 'Cooee!' before he knew that his son had returned. Those are the crucial points upon which the case depends. And now let us talk about George Meredith, if you please, and we shall leave all minor matters until to-morrow."

There was no rain, as Holmes had foretold, and the morning broke bright and cloudless. At nine o'clock Lestrade called for us with the carriage, and we set off for Hatherley Farm and the Boscombe Pool.

"There is serious news this morning," Lestrade observed. "It is said that Mr. Turner, of the Hall, is so ill that his life is despaired of."

"An elderly man, I presume?" said Holmes.

"About sixty; but his constitution has been shattered by his life abroad, and he has been in failing health for some time. This business has had a very bad effect upon him. He was an old friend of McCarthy's, and, I may add, a great benefactor to him, for I have learned that he gave him Hatherley Farm rent free."

"Indeed! That is interesting," said Holmes.

"Oh, yes! In a hundred other ways he has helped him. Everybody about here speaks of his kindness to him."

"Really! Does it not strike you as a little singular that this McCarthy, who appears to have had little of his own, and to have been under such obligations to Turner, should still talk of marrying his son to Turner's daughter, who is, presumably, heiress to the estate, and that in such a very cocksure manner, as if it were merely a case of a proposal and all else would follow? It is the more strange, since we know that Turner himself was averse to the idea. The daughter told us as much. Do you not deduce something from that?"

"We have got to the deductions and the inferences," said Lestrade, winking at me. "I find it hard enough to tackle facts, Holmes, without flying away after theories and fancies."

"You are right," said Holmes demurely; "you do find it very hard to tackle the facts."

"Anyhow, I have grasped one fact which you seem to find it difficult to get hold of," replied Lestrade with some warmth.

"And that is—"

"That McCarthy senior met his death from McCarthy junior and that all theories to the contrary are the merest moonshine."

"Well, moonshine is a brighter thing than fog," said Holmes, laughing. "But I am very much mistaken if this is not Hatherley Farm upon the left."

"Yes, that is it." It was a widespread, comfortable-looking building, two-storied, slate-roofed, with great yellow blotches of lichen upon the gray walls. The drawn blinds and the smokeless chimneys, however, gave it a stricken look, as though the weight of this horror still lay heavy upon it. We called at the door, when the maid, at Holmes's request, showed us the boots which her master wore at the time of his death, and also a pair of the son's, though not the pair which he had then had. Having measured these very carefully from seven or eight different points, Holmes desired to be led to the court-yard, from which we all followed the winding track which led to Boscombe Pool.

Sherlock Holmes was transformed when he was hot upon such a scent as this. Men who had only known the quiet thinker and logician of Baker Street would have failed to recognize him. His face flushed and darkened. His brows were drawn into two hard black lines, while his eyes shone out from beneath them with a steely glitter. His face was bent downward, his shoulders bowed, his lips compressed, and the veins stood out like whipcord in his long, sinewy neck. His nostrils seemed to dilate with a purely animal lust for the chase, and his mind was so absolutely concentrated upon the matter before him that a question or remark fell unheeded upon his ears, or, at the most, only provoked a quick, impatient snarl in reply. Swiftly and silently he made his way along the track which ran through the meadows, and so by way of the woods to the Boscombe Pool. It was damp, marshy ground, as is all that district, and there were marks of many feet, both upon the path and amid the short grass which bounded it on either side. Sometimes Holmes would hurry on, sometimes stop dead, and once he made quite a little detour into the meadow. Lestrade and I walked behind him, the detective indifferent and contemptuous, while I watched my friend with the interest which sprang from the conviction that every one of his actions was directed towards a definite end.

The Boscombe Pool, which is a little reed-girt sheet of water some fifty yards across, is situated at the boundary between the Hatherley Farm and the private park of the wealthy Mr. Turner. Above the woods which lined it upon the farther side we could see the red, jutting pinnacles which marked the site of the rich landowner's dwelling. On the Hatherley side of the pool the woods grew very thick, and there was a narrow belt of sodden grass twenty paces across between the edge of the trees and the reeds which lined the lake. Lestrade showed us the exact spot at which the body had been found, and, indeed, so moist was the ground, that I could plainly see the traces which had been left by the fall of the stricken man. To Holmes, as I could see by his eager face and peering eyes, very many other things were to be read upon the trampled grass. He ran round, like a dog who is picking up a scent, and then turned upon my companion.

"What did you go into the pool for?" he asked.

"I fished about with a rake. I thought there might be some weapon or other trace. But how on earth—"

"Oh, tut, tut! I have no time! That left foot of yours with its inward twist is all over the place. A mole could trace it, and there it vanishes among the reeds. Oh, how simple it would all have been had I been here before they came like a herd of buffalo and wallowed all over it. Here is where the party with the lodge-keeper came, and they have covered all tracks for six or eight feet round the body. But here are three separate tracks of the same feet." He drew out a lens and lay down upon his waterproof to have a better view, talking all the time rather to himself than to us. "These are young McCarthy's feet. Twice he was walking, and once he ran swiftly, so that the soles are deeply marked and the heels hardly visible. That bears out his story. He ran when he saw his father on the ground. Then here are the father's feet as he paced up and down. What is this, then? It is the butt-end of the gun as the son stood listening. And this? Ha, ha! What have we here? Tiptoes! tiptoes! Square, too, quite unusual boots! They come, they go, they come again—of course that was for the cloak. Now where did they come from?" He ran up and down, sometimes losing, sometimes finding the track until we were well within the edge of the wood and under the shadow of a great beech, the largest tree in the neighbourhood. Holmes traced his way to the farther side of this and lay down once more upon his face with a little cry of satisfaction. For a long time he remained there, turning over the leaves and dried sticks, gathering up what seemed to me to be dust into an envelope and examining with his lens not only the ground but even the bark of the tree as far as he could reach. A jagged stone was lying among the moss, and this also he carefully examined and retained. Then he followed a pathway through the wood until he came to the high-road, where all traces were lost.

"It has been a case of considerable interest," he remarked, returning to his natural manner. "I fancy that this gray house on the right must be the lodge. I think that I will go in and have a word with Moran, and perhaps write a little note. Having done that, we may drive back to our luncheon. You may walk to the cab, and I shall be with you presently."

It was about ten minutes before we regained our cab and drove back into Ross, Holmes still carrying with him the stone which he had picked up in the wood.

"This may interest you, Lestrade," he remarked, holding it out. "The murder was done with it."

"I see no marks."

"There are none."

"How do you know, then?"

"The grass was growing under it. It had only lain there a few days. There was no sign of a place whence it had been taken. It corresponds with the injuries. There is no sign of any other weapon."

"And the murderer?"

"Is a tall man, left-handed, limps with the right leg, wears thick-soled shooting-boots and a gray cloak, smokes Indian cigars, uses a cigar-holder, and carries a blunt pen-knife in his pocket. There are several other indications, but these may be enough to aid us in our search."

Lestrade laughed. "I am afraid that I am still a sceptic," he said. "Theories are all very well, but we have to deal with a hard-headed British jury."

"*Nous verrons*," answered Holmes calmly. "You work your own method, and I shall work mine. I shall be busy this afternoon, and shall probably return to London by the evening train."

"And leave your case unfinished?"

"No, finished."

"But the mystery?"

"It is solved."

"Who was the criminal, then?"

"The gentleman I describe."

"But who is he?"

"Surely it would not be difficult to find out. This is not such a populous neighbourhood."

Lestrade shrugged his shoulders. "I am a practical man," he said, "and I really cannot undertake to go about the country looking for a left-handed gentleman with a game-leg. I should become the laughing-stock of Scotland Yard."

"All right," said Holmes quietly. "I have given you the

chance. Here are your lodgings. Good-bye. I shall drop you a line before I leave."

Having left Lestrade at his rooms, we drove to our hotel, where we found lunch upon the table. Holmes was silent and buried in thought with a pained expression upon his face, as one who finds himself in a perplexing position.

"Look here, Watson," he said when the cloth was cleared; "just sit down in this chair and let me preach to you for a little. I don't know quite what to do, and I should value your advice. Light a cigar and let me expound."

"Pray do so."

"Well, now, in considering this case there are two points about young McCarthy's narrative which struck us both instantly, although they impressed me in his favour and you against him. One was the fact that his father should, according to his account, cry 'Cooee!' before seeing him. The other was his singular dying reference to a rat. He mumbled several words, you understand, but that was all that caught the son's ear. Now from this double point our research must commence, and we will begin it by presuming that what the lad says is absolutely true."

"What of this 'Cooee!' then?"

"Well, obviously it could not have been meant for the son. The son, as far as he knew, was in Bristol. It was mere chance that he was within earshot. The 'Cooee!' was meant to attract the attention of whoever it was that he had the appointment with. But 'Cooee' is a distinctly Australian cry, and one which is used between Australians. There is a strong presumption that the person whom McCarthy expected to meet him at Boscombe Pool was someone who had been in Australia."

"What of the rat, then?"

Sherlock Holmes took a folded paper from his pocket and flattened it out on the table. "This is a map of the Colony of Victoria," he said. "I wired to Bristol for it last night." He put his hand over part of the map. "What do you read?"

"ARAT," I read.

"And now?" He raised his hand.

"BALLARAT."

"Quite so. That was the word the man uttered, and of which his son only caught the last two syllables. He was trying to utter the name of his murderer. So and so, of Ballarat."

"It is wonderful!" I exclaimed.

"It is obvious. And now, you see, I had narrowed the field down considerably. The possession of a gray garment was a third point which, granting the son's statement to be correct, was a certainty. We have come now out of mere vagueness to the definite conception of an Australian from Ballarat with a gray cloak."

"Certainly."

"And one who was at home in the district, for the pool can only be approached by the farm or by the estate, where strangers could hardly wander."

"Quite so."

"Then comes our expedition of to-day. By an examination of the ground I gained the trifling details which I gave to that imbecile Lestrade, as to the personality of the criminal."

"But how did you gain them?"

"You know my method. It is founded upon the observation of trifles."

"His height I know that you might roughly judge from the length of his stride. His boots, too, might be told from their traces."

"Yes, they were peculiar boots."

"But his lameness?"

"The impression of his right foot was always less distinct than his left. He put less weight upon it. Why? Because he limped—he was lame."

"But his left-handedness."

"You were yourself struck by the nature of the injury as recorded by the surgeon at the inquest. The blow was struck from immediately behind, and yet was upon the left side. Now, how can that be unless it were by a left-handed man? He had stood behind that tree during the interview between the father and son. He had even smoked there. I found the ash of a cigar, which my special knowledge of tobacco ashes enables me to pronounce as an Indian cigar. I have, as you know, devoted some attention to this, and written a little monograph on the ashes of 140 different varieties of pipe, cigar, and cigarette tobacco. Having found the ash, I then looked round and discovered the stump among the moss where he had tossed it. It was an Indian cigar, of the variety which are rolled in Rotterdam."

"And the cigar-holder?"

"I could see that the end had not been in his mouth. Therefore he used a holder. The tip had been cut off, not bitten off, but the cut was not a clean one, so I deduced a blunt pen-knife."

"Holmes," I said, "you have drawn a net round this man from which he cannot escape, and you have saved an innocent human life as truly as if you had cut the cord which was hanging him. I see the direction in which all this points. The culprit is—"

"Mr. John Turner," cried the hotel waiter, opening the door of our sitting-room, and ushering in a visitor.

The man who entered was a strange and impressive figure. His slow, limping step and bowed shoulders gave the appearance of decrepitude, and yet his hard, deep-lined, craggy features, and his enormous limbs showed that he was possessed of unusual strength of body and of character. His tangled beard, grizzled hair, and outstanding, drooping eyebrows combined to give an air of dignity and power to his appearance, but his face was of an ashen white, while his lips and the corners of his nostrils were tinged with a shade of blue. It was clear to me at a glance that he was in the grip of some deadly and chronic disease.

"Pray sit down on the sofa," said Holmes gently. "You had my note?"

"Yes, the lodge-keeper brought it up. You said that you wished to see me here to avoid scandal."

"I thought people would talk if I went to the Hall."

"And why did you wish to see me?" He looked across at my companion with despair in his weary eyes, as though his question was already answered.

"Yes," said Holmes, answering the look rather than the words. "It is so. I know all about McCarthy."

The old man sank his face in his hands. "God help me!" he cried. "But I would not have let the young man come to harm. I give you my word that I would have spoken out if it went against him at the Assizes."

"I am glad to hear you say so," said Holmes gravely.

"I would have spoken now had it not been for my dear girl. It would break her heart—it will break her heart when she hears that I am arrested."

"It may not come to that," said Holmes.

"What?"

"I am no official agent. I understand that it was your daughter who required my presence here, and I am acting in her interests. Young McCarthy must be got off, however."

"I am a dying man," said old Turner. "I have had diabetes for years. My doctor says it is a question whether I shall live a month. Yet I would rather die under my own roof than in a jail."

Holmes rose and sat down at the table with his pen in his hand and a bundle of paper before him. "Just tell us the truth," he said. "I shall jot down the facts. You will sign it, and Watson here can witness it. Then I could produce your confession at the last extremity to save young McCarthy. I promise you that I shall not use it unless it is absolutely needed."

"It's as well," said the old man; "it's a question whether I shall live to the Assizes, so it matters little to me, but I should wish to spare Alice the shock. And now I will make the thing clear to you; it has been a long time in the acting, but will not take me long to tell.

"You didn't know this dead man, McCarthy. He was a devil incarnate. I tell you that. God keep you out of the clutches of such a man as he. His grip has been upon me these twenty years, and he has blasted my life. I'll tell you first how I came to be in his power.

"It was in the early '60's at the diggings. I was a young chap then, hot-blooded and reckless, ready to turn my hand at anything; I got among bad companions, took to drink, had no luck with my claim, took to the bush, and in a word became what you would call over here a highway robber. There were six of us, and we had a wild, free life of it, sticking up a station from time to time, or stopping the wagons on the road to the diggings. Black Jack of Ballarat was the name I went under, and our party is still remembered in the colony as the Ballarat Gang.

"One day a gold convoy came down from Ballarat to Melbourne, and we lay in wait for it and attacked it. There were six troopers and six of us, so it was a close thing, but we emptied four of their saddles at the first volley. Three of our boys were killed, however, before we got the swag. I put my pistol to the head of the wagon-driver, who was this very man McCarthy. I wish to the Lord that I had shot him then, but I spared him, though I saw his wicked little eyes fixed on my face, as though to remember every feature. We got away with the gold, became wealthy men, and made our way over to England without being suspected. There I parted from my old pals and determined to settle down to a quiet and respectable life. I bought this estate, which chanced to be in the market, and I set myself to do a little good with my money, to make up for the way in which I had earned it. I married, too, and though my wife died young she left me my dear little Alice. Even when she was just a baby her wee hand seemed to lead me down the right path as nothing else had ever done. In a word, I turned over a new leaf and did my best to make up for the past. All was going well when McCarthy laid his grip upon me.

"I had gone up to town about an investment, and I met him in Regent Street with hardly a coat to his back or a boot to his foot.

" 'Here we are, Jack,' says he, touching me on the arm; 'we'll be as good as a family to you. There's two of us, me and my son, and you can have the keeping of us. If you don't—it's a fine, law-abiding country is England, and there's always a policeman within hail.'

"Well, down they came to the west country, there was no shaking them off, and there they have lived rent free on my best land ever since. There was no rest for me, no peace, no forgetfulness; turn where I would, there was his cunning, grinning face at my elbow. It grew worse as Alice grew up, for he soon saw I was more afraid of her knowing my past than of the police. Whatever he wanted he must have, and whatever it was I gave him without question, land, money, houses, until at last he asked a thing which I could not give. He asked for Alice.

"His son, you see, had grown up, and so had my girl, and as I was known to be in weak health, it seemed a fine stroke to him that his lad should step into the whole property. But there I was firm. I would not have his cursed stock mixed with mine; not that I had any dislike to the lad, but his blood was in him, and that was enough. I stood firm. McCarthy threatened. I braved him to do his worst. We were to meet at the pool midway between our houses to talk it over.

"When we went down there I found him talking with his son, so I smoked a cigar and waited behind a tree until he should be alone. But as I listened to his talk all that was black and bitter in me seemed to come uppermost. He was urging his son to marry my daughter with as little regard for what she might think as if she were a slut from off the streets. It drove me mad to think that I and all that I held most dear should be in the power of such a man as this. Could I not snap the bond? I was already a dying and desperate man. Though clear of mind and fairly strong of limb, I knew that my own fate was sealed. But my memory and my girl! Both could be saved if I could but silence that foul tongue. I did it, Mr. Holmes. I would do it again. Deeply as I have sinned, I have led a life of martyrdom to atone for it. But that my girl should be entangled in the same meshes which held me was more than I could suffer. I struck him down with no more compunction than if he had been some foul and venomous beast. His cry brought back his son; but I had gained the cover of the wood, though I was forced to go back to fetch the cloak which I had dropped in my flight. That is the true story, gentlemen, of all that occurred."

"Well, it is not for me to judge you," said Holmes as the old man signed the statement which had been drawn out. "I pray that we may never be exposed to such a temptation."

"I pray not, sir. And what do you intend to do?"

"In view of your health, nothing. You are yourself aware that you will soon have to answer for your deed at a higher court than the Assizes. I will keep your confession, and if McCarthy is condemned I shall be forced to use it. If not, it shall never be seen by mortal eye; and your secret, whether you be alive or dead, shall be safe with us."

"Farewell, then," said the old man solemnly. "Your own deathbeds, when they come, will be easier for the thought of the peace which you have given to mine." Tottering and shaking in all his giant frame, he stumbled slowly from the room.

"God help us!" said Holmes after a long silence. "Why does fate play such tricks with poor, helpless worms? I never hear of such a case as this that I do not think of Baxter's words, and say, 'There, but for the grace of God, goes Sherlock Holmes.' "

James McCarthy was acquitted at the Assizes on the strength of a number of objections which had been drawn out by Holmes and submitted to the defending counsel. Old Turner lived for seven months after our interview, but he is now dead; and there is every prospect that the son and daughter may come to live happily together in ignorance of the black cloud which rests upon their past.

The Five Orange Pips

WHEN I GLANCE over my notes and records of the Sherlock Holmes cases between the years '82 and '90, I am faced by so many which present strange and interesting features that it is no easy matter to know which to choose and which to leave. Some, however, have already gained publicity through the papers, and others have not offered a field for those peculiar qualities which my friend possessed in so high a degree, and which it is the object of these papers to illustrate. Some, too, have baffled his analytical skill, and would be, as narratives, beginnings without an ending, while others have been but partially cleared up, and have their explanations founded rather upon conjecture and surmise than on that absolute logical proof which was so dear to him. There is, however, one of these last which was so remarkable in its details and so startling in its results that I am tempted to give some account of it in spite of the fact that there are points in connection with it which never have been, and probably never will be, entirely cleared up.

The year '87 furnished us with a long series of cases of greater or less interest, of which I retain the records. Among my headings under this one twelve months I find an account of the adventure of the Paradol Chamber, of the Amateur Mendicant Society, who held a luxurious club in the lower vault of a furniture warehouse, of the facts connected with the loss of the British bark *Sophy Anderson*, of the singular adventures of the Grice Patersons in the island of Uffa, and finally of the Camberwell poisoning case. In the latter, as may be remembered, Sherlock Holmes was able, by winding up the dead man's watch, to prove that it had been wound up two hours before, and that therefore the deceased had gone to bed within that time—a deduction which was of the greatest importance in clearing up the case. All these I may sketch out at some future date, but none of them present such singular features as the strange train of circumstances which I have now taken up my pen to describe.

It was in the latter days of September, and the equinoctial

gales had set in with exceptional violence. All day the wind had screamed and the rain had beaten against the windows, so that even here in the heart of great, hand-made London we were forced to raise our minds for the instant from the routine of life, and to recognize the presence of those great elemental forces which shriek at mankind through the bars of his civilization, like untamed beasts in a cage. As evening drew in, the storm grew higher and louder, and the wind cried and sobbed like a child in the chimney. Sherlock Holmes sat moodily at one side of the fireplace cross-indexing his records of crime, while I at the other was deep in one of Clark Russell's fine sea-stories until the howl of the gale from without seemed to blend with the text, and the splash of the rain to lengthen out into the long swash of the sea waves. My wife was on a visit to her mother's, and for a few days I was a dweller once more in my old quarters at Baker Street.

"Why," said I, glancing up at my companion, "that was surely the bell. Who could come to-night? Some friend of yours, perhaps?"

"Except yourself I have none," he answered. "I do not encourage visitors."

"A client, then?"

"If so, it is a serious case. Nothing less would bring a man out on such a day and at such an hour. But I take it that it is more likely to be some crony of the landlady's."

Sherlock Holmes was wrong in his conjecture, however, for there came a step in the passage and a tapping at the door. He stretched out his long arm to turn the lamp away from himself and towards the vacant chair upon which a newcomer must sit. "Come in!" said he.

The man who entered was young, some two-and-twenty at the outside, well-groomed and trimly clad, with something of refinement and delicacy in his bearing. The streaming umbrella which he held in his hand, and his long shining waterproof told of the fierce weather through which he had come. He looked about him anxiously in the glare of the lamp, and I could see that his face was pale and his eyes heavy, like those of a man who is weighed down with some great anxiety.

"I owe you an apology," he said, raising his golden pince-nez to his eyes. "I trust that I am not intruding. I fear that I have brought some traces of the storm and rain into your snug chamber."

"Give me your coat and umbrella," said Holmes. "They may rest here on the hook and will be dry presently. You have come up from the south-west, I see."

"Yes, from Horsham."

"That clay and chalk mixture which I see upon your toe caps is quite distinctive."

"I have come for advice."

"That is easily got."

"And help."

"That is not always so easy."

"I have heard of you, Mr. Holmes. I heard from Major Prendergast how you saved him in the Tankerville Club scandal."

"Ah, of course. He was wrongfully accused of cheating at cards."

"He said that you could solve anything."

"He said too much."

"That you are never beaten."

"I have been beaten four times—three times by men, and once by a woman."

"But what is that compared with the number of your successes?"

"It is true that I have been generally successful."

"Then you may be so with me."

"I beg that you will draw your chair up to the fire and favour me with some details as to your case."

"It is no ordinary one."

"None of those which come to me are. I am the last court of appeal."

"And yet I question, sir, whether, in all your experience, you have ever listened to a more mysterious and inexplicable chain of events than those which have happened in my own family."

"You fill me with interest," said Holmes. "Pray give us the essential facts from the commencement, and I can afterwards question you as to those details which seem to me to be most important."

The young man pulled his chair up and pushed his wet feet out towards the blaze.

"My name," said he, "is John Openshaw, but my own affairs

have, as far as I can understand, little to do with this awful business. It is a hereditary matter; so in order to give you an idea of the facts, I must go back to the commencement of the affair.

"You must know that my grandfather had two sons—my uncle Elias and my father Joseph. My father had a small factory at Coventry, which he enlarged at the time of the invention of bicycling. He was a patentee of the Openshaw unbreakable tire, and his business met with such success that he was able to sell it and to retire upon a handsome competence.

"My uncle Elias emigrated to America when he was a young man and became a planter in Florida, where he was reported to have done very well. At the time of the war he fought in Jackson's army, and afterwards under Hood, where he rose to be a colonel. When Lee laid down his arms my uncle returned to his plantation, where he remained for three or four years. About 1869 or 1870 he came back to Europe and took a small estate in Sussex, near Horsham. He had made a very considerable fortune in the States, and his reason for leaving them was his aversion to the negroes, and his dislike of the Republican policy in extending the franchise to them. He was a singular man, fierce and quick-tempered, very foul-mouthed when he was angry, and of a most retiring disposition. During all the years that he lived at Horsham, I doubt if ever he set foot in the town. He had a garden and two or three fields round his house, and there he would take his exercise, though very often for weeks on end he would never leave his room. He drank a great deal of brandy and smoked very heavily, but he would see no society and did not want any friends, not even his own brother.

"He didn't mind me; in fact, he took a fancy to me, for at the time when he saw me first I was a youngster of twelve or so. This would be in the year 1878, after he had been eight or nine years in England. He begged my father to let me live with him, and he was very kind to me in his way. When he was sober he used to be fond of playing backgammon and draughts with me, and he would make me his representative both with the servants and with the tradespeople, so that by the time that I was sixteen I was quite master of the house. I kept all the keys and could go where I liked and do what I liked, so long as I did not disturb him in his privacy. There was one singular exception, however, for he had a single room, a lumber-room up among the attics, which was invariably locked, and which he would never permit either me or anyone else to enter. With a boy's curiosity I have peeped through the keyhole, but I was never able to see more than such a collection of old trunks and bundles as would be expected in such a room.

"One day—it was in March, 1883—a letter with a foreign stamp lay upon the table in front of the colonel's plate. It was not a common thing for him to receive letters, for his bills were all paid in ready money, and he had no friends of any sort. 'From India!' said he as he took it up, 'Pondicherry postmark! What can this be?' Opening it hurriedly, out there jumped five little dried orange pips, which pattered down upon his plate. I began to laugh at this, but the laugh was struck from my lips at the sight of his face. His lip had fallen, his eyes were protruding, his skin the color of putty, and he glared at the envelope which he still held in his trembling hand, 'K. K. K.!' he shrieked, and then, 'My God, my God, my sins have overtaken me!'

" 'What is it, uncle?' I cried.

" 'Death,' said he, and rising from the table he retired to his room, leaving me palpitating with horror. I took up the envelope and saw scrawled in red ink upon the inner flap, just above the gum, the letter K three times repeated. There was nothing else save the five dried pips. What could be the reason of his overpowering terror? I left the breakfast-table, and as I ascended the stair I met him coming down with an old rusty key, which must have belonged to the attic, in one hand, and a small brass box, like a cashbox, in the other.

" 'They may do what they like, but I'll checkmate them still,' said he with an oath. 'Tell Mary that I shall want a fire in my room to-day, and send down to Fordham, the Horsham lawyer.'

"I did as he ordered, and when the lawyer arrived I was asked to step up to the room. The fire was burning brightly, and in the grate there was a mass of black, fluffy ashes, as of burned paper, while the brass box stood open and empty beside it. As I glanced at the box I noticed, with a start, that upon the lid was printed the treble K which I had read in the morning upon the envelope.

" 'I wish you, John,' said my uncle, 'to witness my will. I leave my estate, with all its advantages and all its disadvantages, to my brother, your father, whence it will, no doubt, descend to you. If you can enjoy it in peace, well and good! If you find you cannot, take my advice, my boy, and leave it to your deadliest enemy. I am sorry to give you such a two-edged thing, but I can't say what turn things are going to take. Kindly sign the paper where Mr. Fordham shows you.'

"I signed the paper as directed, and the lawyer took it away with him. The singular incident made, as you may think, the deepest impression upon me, and I pondered over it and turned it every way in my mind without being able to make anything of it. Yet I could not shake off the vague feeling of dread which it left behind, though the sensation grew less keen as the weeks passed, and nothing happened to disturb the usual routine of our lives. I could see a change in my uncle, however. He drank more than ever, and he was less inclined for any sort of society. Most of his time he would spend in his room, with the door locked upon the inside, but sometimes he would emerge in a sort of drunken frenzy and would burst out of the house and tear about the garden with a revolver in his hand, screaming out that he was afraid of no man, and that he was not to be cooped up, like a sheep in a pen, by man or devil. When these hot fits were over, however, he would rush tumultuously in at the door and lock and bar it behind him, like a man who can brazen it out no longer against the terror which lies at the roots of his soul. At such times I have seen his face, even on a cold day, glisten with moisture, as though it were new raised from a basin.

"Well, to come to an end of the matter, Mr. Holmes, and not to abuse your patience, there came a night when he made one of those drunken sallies from which he never came back. We found him, when we went to search for him, face downward in a little green-scummed pool, which lay at the foot of the garden. There was no sign of any violence, and the water was but two feet deep, so that the jury, having regard to his known eccentricity, brought in a verdict of 'suicide.' But I, who knew how he winced from the very thought of death, had much ado to persuade myself that he had gone out of his way to meet it. The matter passed, however, and my father entered into possession of the estate, and of some £14,000, which lay to his credit at the bank."

"One moment," Holmes interposed, "your statement is, I foresee, one of the most remarkable to which I have ever listened. Let me have the date of the reception by your uncle of the letter, and the date of his supposed suicide."

"The letter arrived on March 10, 1883. His death was seven weeks later, upon the night of May 2d."

"Thank you. Pray proceed."

"When my father took over the Horsham property, he, at my request, made a careful examination of the attic, which had been always locked up. We found the brass box there, although its contents had been destroyed. On the inside of the cover was a paper label, with the initials of K. K. K. repeated upon it, and 'Letters, memoranda, receipts, and a register' written beneath. These, we presume, indicated the nature of the papers which had been destroyed by Colonel Openshaw. For the rest, there was nothing of much importance in the attic save a great many scattered papers and note-books bearing upon my uncle's life in America. Some of them were of the war time and showed that he had done his duty well and had borne the repute of a brave soldier. Others were of a date during the reconstruction of the Southern states, and were mostly concerned with politics, for he had evidently taken a strong part in opposing the carpet-bag politicians who had been sent down from the North.

"Well, it was the beginning of '84 when my father came to live at Horsham, and all went as well as possible with us until the January of '85. On the fourth day after the new year I heard my father give a sharp cry of surprise as we sat together at the breakfast-table. There he was, sitting with a newly opened envelope in one hand and five dried orange pips in the outstretched palm of the other one. He had always laughed at what he called my cock-and-bull story about the colonel, but he looked very scared and puzzled now that the same thing had come upon himself.

" 'Why, what on earth does this mean, John?' he stammered.

"My heart had turned to lead. 'It is K. K. K.,' said I.

"He looked inside the envelope. 'So it is,' he cried. 'Here are the very letters. But what is this written above them?'

" 'Put the papers on the sundial,' I read, peeping over his shoulder.

" 'What papers? What sundial?' he asked.

" 'The sundial in the garden. There is no other,' said I; 'but the papers must be those that are destroyed.'

" 'Pooh!' said he, gripping hard at his courage. 'We are in a civilized land here, and we can't have tomfoolery of this kind. Where does the thing come from?'

" 'From Dundee,' I answered, glancing at the postmark.

" 'Some preposterous practical joke,' said he. 'What have I to do with sundials and papers? I shall take no notice of such nonsense.'

" 'I should certainly speak to the police,' I said.

" 'And be laughed at for my pains. Nothing of the sort.'

" 'Then let me do so?'

" 'No, I forbid you. I won't have a fuss made about such nonsense.'

"It was in vain to argue with him, for he was a very obstinate man. I went about, however, with a heart which was full of forebodings.

"On the third day after the coming of the letter my father went from home to visit an old friend of his, Major Freebody, who is in command of one of the forts upon Portsdown Hill. I was glad that he should go, for it seemed to me that he was farther from danger when he was away from home. In that, however, I was in error. Upon the second day of his absence I received a telegram from the major, imploring me to come at once. My father had fallen over one of the deep chalk-pits which abound in the neighbourhood, and was lying senseless, with a shattered skull. I hurried to him, but he passed away without having ever recovered his consciousness. He had, as it appears, been returning from Fareham in the twilight, and as the country was unknown to him, and the chalk-pit unfenced, the jury had no hesitation in bringing in a verdict of 'death from accidental causes.' Carefully as I examined every fact connected with his death, I was unable to find anything which could suggest the idea of murder. There were no signs of violence, no footmarks, no robbery, no record of strangers having been seen upon the roads. And yet I need not tell you that my mind was far from at ease, and that I was well-nigh certain that some foul plot had been woven round him.

"In this sinister way I came into my inheritance. You will ask me why I did not dispose of it? I answer, because I was well convinced that our troubles were in some way dependent upon an incident in my uncle's life, and that the danger would be as pressing in one house as in another.

"It was in January, '85, that my poor father met his end, and two years and eight months have elapsed since then. During that time I have lived happily at Horsham, and I had begun to hope that this curse had passed away from the family, and that it had ended with the last generation. I had begun to take comfort too soon, however; yesterday morning the blow fell in the very shape in which it had come upon my father."

The young man took from his waistcoat a crumpled envelope, and turning to the table he shook out upon it five little dried orange pips.

"This is the envelope," he continued. "The postmark is London—eastern division. Within are the very words which were upon my father's last message: 'K. K. K.'; and then 'Put the papers on the sundial.' "

"What have you done?" asked Holmes.

"Nothing."

"Nothing?"

"To tell the truth"—he sank his face into his thin, white hands—"I have felt helpless. I have felt like one of those poor rabbits when the snake is writhing towards it. I seem to be in the grasp of some resistless, inexorable evil, which no foresight and no precautions can guard against."

"Tut! tut!" cried Sherlock Holmes. "You must act, man, or you are lost. Nothing but energy can save you. This is no time for despair."

"I have seen the police."

"Ah!"

"But they listened to my story with a smile. I am convinced that the inspector has formed the opinion that the letters are all practical jokes, and that the deaths of my relations were really accidents, as the jury stated, and were not to be connected with the warnings."

Holmes shook his clenched hands in the air. "Incredible imbecility!" he cried.

"They have, however, allowed me a policeman, who may remain in the house with me."

"Has he come with you to-night?"

"No. His orders were to stay in the house."

Again Holmes raved in the air.

"Why did you come to me," he cried, "and, above all, why did you not come at once?"

"I did not know. It was only to-day that I spoke to Major Prendergast about my troubles and was advised by him to come to you."

"It is really two days since you had the letter. We should have acted before this. You have no further evidence, I suppose, than that which you have placed before us—no suggestive detail which might help us?"

"There is one thing," said John Openshaw. He rummaged in his coat pocket, and, drawing out a piece of discoloured, blue-tinted paper, he laid it out upon the table. "I have some remembrance," said he, "that on the day when my uncle burned the papers I observed that the small, unburned margins which lay amid the ashes were of this particular colour. I found this single sheet upon the floor of his room, and I am inclined to think that it may be one of the papers which has, perhaps, fluttered out from among the others, and in that way has escaped destruction. Beyond the mention of pips, I do not see that it helps us much. I think myself that it is a page from some private diary. The writing is undoubtedly my uncle's."

Holmes moved the lamp, and we both bent over the sheet of paper, which showed by its ragged edge that it had indeed been torn from a book. It was headed, "March, 1869," and beneath were the following enigmatical notices:

4th. Hudson came. Same old platform.
7th. Set the pips on McCauley, Paramore, and John Swain, of St. Augustine.
9th. McCauley cleared.
10th. John Swain cleared.
12th. Visited Paramore. All well.

"Thank you!" said Holmes, folding up the paper and returning it to our visitor. "And now you must on no account lose another instant. We cannot spare time even to discuss what you have told me. You must get home instantly and act."

"What shall I do?"

"There is but one thing to do. It must be done at once. You must put this piece of paper which you have shown us into the brass box which you have described. You must also put in a note to say that all the other papers were burned by your uncle, and that this is the only one which remains. You must assert that in such words as will carry conviction with them. Having done this, you must at once put the box out upon the sundial, as directed. Do you understand?"

"Entirely."

"Do not think of revenge, or anything of the sort, at present. I think that we may gain that by means of the law; but we have our web to weave, while theirs is already woven. The first consideration is to remove the pressing danger which threatens you. The second is to clear up the mystery and to punish the guilty parties."

"I thank you," said the young man, rising and pulling on his overcoat. "You have given me fresh life and hope. I shall certainly do as you advise."

"Do not lose an instant. And, above all, take care of yourself in the meanwhile, for I do not think that there can be a doubt that you are threatened by a very real and imminent danger. How do you go back?

"By train from Waterloo."

"It is not yet nine. The streets will be crowded, so I trust that you may be in safety. And yet you cannot guard yourself too closely."

"I am armed."

"That is well. To-morrow I shall set to work upon your case."

"I shall see you at Horsham, then?"

"No, your secret lies in London. It is there that I shall seek it."

"Then I shall call upon you in a day, or in two days, with news as to the box and the papers. I shall take your advice in every particular." He shook hands with us and took his leave. Outside the wind still screamed and the rain splashed and pattered against the windows. This strange, wild story seemed to have come to us from amid the mad elements—blown in upon us like a sheet of sea-weed in a gale—and now to have been reabsorbed by them once more.

Sherlock Holmes sat for some time in silence, with his head sunk forward and his eyes bent upon the red glow of the fire. Then he lit his pipe, and leaning back in his chair he watched the blue smoke-rings as they chased each other up to the ceiling.

"I think, Watson," he remarked at last, "that of all our cases we have had none more fantastic than this."

"Save, perhaps, the Sign of Four."

"Well, yes. Save, perhaps, that. And yet this John Openshaw seems to me walking amid even greater perils than did the Sholtos."

"But have you," I asked, "formed any definite conception as to what these perils are?"

"There can be no question as to their nature," he answered.

"Then what are they? Who is this K. K. K., and why does he pursue this unhappy family?"

Sherlock Holmes closed his eyes and placed his elbows upon the arms of his chair, with his finger-tips together. "The ideal reasoner," he remarked, "would, when he had once been shown a single fact in all its bearings, deduce from it not only all the chain of events which led up to it but also all the results which would follow from it. As Cuvier could correctly describe a whole animal by the contemplation of a single bone, so the observer who has thoroughly understood one link in a series of incidents should be able to accurately state all the other ones, both before and after. We have not yet grasped the results which the reason alone can attain to. Problems may be solved in the study which have baffled all those who have sought a solution by the aid of their senses. To carry the art, however, to its highest pitch, it is necessary that the reasoner should be able to utilize all the facts which have come to his knowledge; and this in itself implies, as you will readily see, a possession of all knowledge, which, even in these days of free education and encyclopaedias, is a somewhat rare accomplishment. It is not so impossible, however, that a man should possess all knowledge which is likely to be useful to him in his work, and this I have endeavoured in my case to do. If I remember rightly, you on one occasion, in the early days of our friendship, defined my limits in a very precise fashion."

"Yes," I answered, laughing. "It was a singular document. Philosophy, astronomy, and politics were marked at zero, I remember. Botany variable, geology profound as regards the mud-stains from any region within fifty miles of town, chemistry eccentric, anatomy unsystematic, sensational literature and crime records unique, violin-player, boxer, swordsman, lawyer, and self-poisoner by cocaine and tobacco. Those, I think, were the main points of my analysis."

Holmes grinned at the last item. "Well," he said, "I say now, as I said then, that a man should keep his little brain-attic stocked with all the furniture that he is likely to use, and the rest he can put away in the lumber-room of his library, where he can get it if he wants it. Now, for such a case as the one which has been submitted to us to-night, we need certainly to muster all our resources. Kindly hand me down the letter K of the American Encyclopaedia which stands upon the shelf beside you. Thank you. Now let us consider the situation and see what may be deduced from it. In the first place, we may start with a strong presumption that Colonel Openshaw had some very strong reason for leaving America. Men at his time of life do not change all their habits and exchange willingly the charming climate of Florida for the lonely life of an English provincial town. His extreme love of solitude in England suggests the idea that he was in fear of someone or something, so we may assume as a working hypothesis that it was fear of someone or something which drove him from America. As to what it was he feared, we can only deduce that by considering the formidable letters which were received by himself and his successors. Did you remark the postmarks of those letters?"

"The first was from Pondicherry, the second from Dundee, and the third from London."

"From East London. What do you deduce from that?"

"They are all seaports. That the writer was on board of a ship."

"Excellent. We have already a clue. There can be no doubt that the probability—the strong probability—is that the writer was on board of a ship. And now let us consider another point. In the case of Pondicherry, seven weeks elapsed between the threat and its fulfillment, in Dundee it was only some three or four days. Does that suggest anything?"

"A greater distance to travel."

"But the letter had also a greater distance to come."

"Then I do not see the point."

"There is at least a presumption that the vessel in which the man or men are is a sailing-ship. It looks as if they always sent their singular warning or token before them when starting upon their mission. You see how quickly the deed followed the sign when it came from Dundee. If they had come from Pondicherry in a steamer they would have arrived almost as soon as their letter. But, as a matter of fact, seven weeks elapsed. I think that those seven weeks represented the difference between the mail-boat which brought the letter and the sailing vessel which brought the writer."

"It is possible."

"More than that. It is probable. And now you see the deadly

urgency of this new case, and why I urged young Openshaw to caution. The blow has always fallen at the end of the time which it would take the senders to travel the distance. But this one comes from London, and therefore we cannot count upon delay."

"Good God!" I cried. "What can it mean, this relentless persecution?"

"The papers which Openshaw carried are obviously of vital importance to the person or persons in the sailing-ship. I think that it is quite clear that there must be more than one of them. A single man could not have carried out two deaths in such a way as to deceive a coroner's jury. There must have been several in it, and they must have been men of resource and determination. Their papers they mean to have, be the holder of them who it may. In this way you see K. K. K. ceases to be the initials of an individual and becomes the badge of a society."

"But of what society?"

"Have you never—" said Sherlock Holmes, bending forward and sinking his voice—"have you never heard of the Ku Klux Klan?"

"I never have."

Holmes turned over the leaves of the book upon his knee. "Here it is," said he presently:

> "Ku Klux Klan. A name derived from the fanciful resemblance to the sound produced by cocking a rifle. This terrible secret society was formed by some ex-Confederate soldiers in the Southern states after the Civil War, and it rapidly formed local branches in different parts of the country, notably in Tennessee, Louisiana, the Carolinas, Georgia, and Florida. Its power was used for political purposes, principally for the terrorizing of the negro voters and the murdering and driving from the country of those who were opposed to its views. It outrages were usually preceded by a warning sent to the marked man in some fantastic but generally recognized shape—a sprig of oak-leaves in some parts, melon seeds or orange pips in others. On receiving this the victim might either openly abjure his former ways, or might fly from the country. If he braved the matter out, death would unfailingly come upon him, and usually in some strange and unforeseen manner. So perfect was the organization of the society, and so systematic its methods, that

there is hardly a case upon record where any man succeeded in braving it with impunity, or in which any of its outrages were traced home to the perpetrators. For some years the organization flourished in spite of the efforts of the United States government and of the better classes of the community in the South. Eventually, in the year 1869, the movement rather suddenly collapsed, although there have been sporadic outbreaks of the same sort since that date.

"You will observe," said Holmes, laying down the volume, "that the sudden breaking up of the society was coincident with the disappearance of Openshaw from America with their papers. It may well have been cause and effect. It is no wonder that he and his family have some of the more implacable spirits upon their track. You can understand that this register and diary may implicate some of the first men in the South, and that there may be many who will not sleep easy at night until it is recovered."

"Then the page we have seen——"

"Is such as we might expect. It ran, if I remember right, 'sent the pips to A, B, and C'—that is, sent the society's warning to them. Then there are successive entries that A and B cleared, or left the country, and finally that C was visited, with, I fear, a sinister result for C. Well, I think, Doctor, that we may let some light into this dark place, and I believe that the only chance young Openshaw has in the meantime is to do what I have told him. There is nothing more to be said or to be done to-night, so hand me over my violin and let us try to forget for half an hour the miserable weather and the still more miserable ways of our fellowmen."

It had cleared in the morning, and the sun was shining with a subdued brightness through the dim veil which hangs over the great city. Sherlock Holmes was already at breakfast when I came down.

"You will excuse me for not waiting for you," said he; "I have, I foresee, a very busy day before me in looking into this case of young Openshaw's."

"What steps will you take?" I asked.

"It will very much depend upon the results of my first inquiries. I may have to go down to Horsham, after all."

"You will not go there first?"

"No, I shall commence with the City. Just ring the bell and the maid will bring up your coffee."

As I waited, I lifted the unopened newspaper from the table and glanced my eye over it. It rested upon a heading which sent a chill to my heart.

"Holmes," I cried, "you are too late."

"Ah!" said he, laying down his cup, "I feared as much. How was it done?" He spoke calmly, but I could see that he was deeply moved.

"My eye caught the name Openshaw, and the heading 'Tragedy Near Waterloo Bridge.' Here is the account:

> "Between nine and ten last night Police-Constable Cook, of the H Division, on duty near Waterloo Bridge, heard a cry for help and a splash in the water. The night, however, was extremely dark and stormy, so that, in spite of the help of several passers-by, it was quite impossible to effect a rescue. The alarm, however, was given, and, by the aid of the water-police, the body was eventually recovered. It proved to be that of a young gentleman whose name, as it appears from an envelope which was found in his pocket, was John Openshaw, and whose residence is near Horsham. It is conjectured that he may have been hurrying down to catch the last train from Waterloo Station, and that in his haste and the extreme darkness he missed his path and walked over the edge of one of the small landing-places for river steamboats. The body exhibited no traces of violence, and there can be no doubt that the deceased had been the victim of an unfortunate accident, which should have the effect of calling the attention of the authorities to the condition of the riverside landing-stages."

We sat in silence for some minutes, Holmes more depressed and shaken than I had ever seen him.

"That hurts my pride, Watson," he said at last. "It is a pretty feeling, no doubt, but it hurts my pride. It becomes a personal matter with me now, and, if God sends me health, I shall set my hand upon this gang. That he should come to me for help, and that I should send him away to his death——!" He sprang from his chair and paced about the room in uncontrollable agitation, with a flush upon his sallow cheeks and a nervous clasping and unclasping of his long thin hands.

"They must be cunning devils," he exclaimed at last. "How could they have decoyed him down there? The Embankment is not on the direct line to the station. The bridge, no doubt, was too crowded, even on such a night, for their purpose. Well, Watson, we shall see who will win in the long run. I am going out now!"

"To the police?"

"No; I shall be my own police. When I have spun the web they may take the flies, but not before."

All day I was engaged in my professional work, and it was late in the evening before I returned to Baker Street. Sherlock Holmes had not come back yet. It was nearly ten o'clock before he entered, looking pale and worn. He walked up to the sideboard, and tearing a piece from the loaf he devoured it voraciously, washing it down with a long draught of water.

"You are hungry," I remarked.

"Starving. It had escaped my memory. I have had nothing since breakfast."

"Nothing?"

"Not a bite. I had no time to think of it."

"And how have you succeeded?"

"Well."

"You have a clue?"

"I have them in the hollow of my hand. Young Openshaw shall not long remain unavenged. Why, Watson, let us put their own devilish trade-mark upon them. It is well thought of!"

"What do you mean?"

He took an orange from the cupboard, and tearing it to pieces he squeezed out the pips upon the table. Of these he took five and thrust them into an envelope. On the inside of the flap he wrote "S. H. for J. O." Then he sealed it and addressed it to "Captain James Calhoun, Bark *Lone Star*, Savannah, Georgia."

"That will await him when he enters port," said he, chuckling. "It may give him a sleepless night. He will find it as sure a precursor of his fate as Openshaw did before him."

"And who is this Captain Calhoun?"

"The leader of the gang. I shall have the others, but he first."

"How did you trace it, then?"

He took a large sheet of paper from his pocket, all covered with dates and names.

"I have spent the whole day," said he, "over Lloyd's registers and files of the old papers, following the future career of every vessel which touched at Pondicherry in January and February in '83. There were thirty-six ships of fair tonnage which were reported there during those months. Of these, one, the *Lone Star*, instantly attracted my attention, since, although it was reported as having cleared from London, the name is that which is given to one of the states of the Union."

"Texas, I think."

"I was not and am not sure which; but I knew that the ship must have an American origin."

"What then?"

"I searched the Dundee records, and when I found that the bark *Lone Star* was there in January, '85, my suspicion became a certainty. I then inquired as to the vessels which lay at present in the port of London."

"Yes?"

"The *Lone Star* had arrived here last week. I went down to the Albert Dock and found that she had been taken down the river by the early tide this morning, homeward bound to Savannah. I wired to Gravesend and learned that she had passed some time ago, and as the wind is easterly I have no doubt that she is now past the Goodwins and not very far from the Isle of Wight."

"What will you do, then?"

"Oh, I have my hand upon him. He and the two mates, are, as I learn, the only native-born Americans in the ship. The others are Finns and Germans. I know, also, that they were all three away from the ship last night. I had it from the stevedore who has been loading their cargo. By the time that their sailing-ship reaches Savannah the mail-boat will have carried this letter, and the cable will have informed the police of Savannah that these three gentlemen are badly wanted here upon a charge of murder."

There is ever a flaw, however, in the best laid of human plans, and the murderers of John Openshaw were never to receive the orange pips which would show them that another, as cunning and as resolute as themselves, was upon their track. Very long and very severe were the equinoctial gales that year. We waited long for news of the *Lone Star* of Savannah, but none ever reached us. We did at last hear that somewhere far out in the Atlantic a shattered stern-post of the boat was seen swinging in the trough of a wave, with the letters "L. S." carved upon it, and that is all which we shall ever know of the fate of the *Lone Star*.

The Man with the Twisted Lip

Isa Whitney, brother of the late Elias Whitney, D.D., Principal of the Theological College of St. George's, was much addicted to opium. The habit grew upon him, as I understand, from some foolish freak when he was at college; for having read De Quincey's description of his dreams and sensations, he had drenched his tobacco with laudanum in an attempt to produce the same effects. He found, as so many more have done, that the practice is easier to attain than to get rid of, and for many years he continued to be a slave to the drug, an object of mingled horror and pity to his friends and relatives. I can see him now, with yellow, pasty face, drooping lids, and pin-point pupils, all huddled in a chair, the wreck and ruin of a noble man.

One night—it was in June, '89—there came a ring to my bell, about the hour when a man gives his first yawn and glances at the clock. I sat up in my chair, and my wife laid her needle-work down in her lap and made a little face of disappointment.

"A patient!" said she. "You'll have to go out."

I groaned, for I was newly come back from a weary day.

We heard the door open, a few hurried words, and then quick steps upon the linoleum. Our own door flew open, and a lady, clad in some dark-coloured stuff, with a black veil, entered the room.

"You will excuse my calling so late," she began, and then, suddenly losing her self-control, she ran forward, threw her arms about my wife's neck, and sobbed upon her shoulder. "Oh, I'm in such trouble!" she cried; "I do so want a little help."

"Why," said my wife, pulling up her veil, "it is Kate Whitney. How you startled me, Kate! I had not an idea who you were when you came in."

"I didn't know what to do, so I came straight to you." That was always the way. Folk who were in grief came to my wife like birds to a light-house.

"It was very sweet of you to come. Now, you must have some wine and water, and sit here comfortably and tell us all about it. Or should you rather that I sent James off to bed?"

"Oh, no, no! I want the doctor's advice and help, too. It's about Isa. He has not been home for two days. I am so frightened about him!"

It was not the first time that she had spoken to us of her husband's trouble, to me as a doctor, to my wife as an old friend and school companion. We soothed and comforted her by such words as we could find. Did she know where her husband was? Was it possible that we could bring him back to her?

It seems that it was. She had the surest information that of late he had, when the fit was on him, made use of an opium den in the farthest east of the City. Hitherto his orgies had always been confined to one day, and he had come back, twitching and shattered, in the evening. But now the spell had been upon him eight-and-forty hours, and he lay there, doubtless among the dregs of the docks, breathing in the poison or sleeping off the effects. There he was to be found, she was sure of it, at the Bar of Gold, in Upper Swandam Lane. But what was she to do? How could she, a young and timid woman, make her way into such a place and pluck her husband out from among the ruffians who surrounded him?

There was the case, and of course there was but one way out of it. Might I not escort her to this place? And then, as a second thought, why should she come at all? I was Isa Whitney's medical adviser, and as such I had influence over him. I could manage it better if I were alone. I promised her on my word that I would send him home in a cab within two hours if he were indeed at the address which she had given me. And so in ten minutes I had left my armchair and cheery sitting-room behind me, and was speeding eastward in a hansom on a strange errand, as it seemed to me at the time, though the future only could show how strange it was to be.

But there was no great difficulty in the first stage of my adventure. Upper Swandam Lane is a vile alley lurking behind the high wharves which line the north side of the river to the east of London Bridge. Between a slop-shop and a gin-shop, approached by a steep flight of steps leading down to a black gap like the mouth of a cave, I found the den of which I was in search. Ordering my cab to wait, I passed down the steps, worn hollow in the centre by the ceaseless tread of drunken feet; and by the light of a flickering oil-lamp above the door I found the latch and made my way into a long, low room, thick and heavy with the brown opium smoke, and terraced with wooden berths, like the forecastle of an emigrant ship.

Through the gloom one could dimly catch a glimpse of bodies lying in strange fantastic poses, bowed shoulders, bent knees, heads thrown back, and chins pointing upward, with here and there a dark, lack-lustre eye turned upon the newcomer. Out of the black shadows there glimmered little red circles of light, now bright, now faint, as the burning poison waxed or waned in the bowls of the metal pipes. The most lay silent, but some muttered to themselves, and others talked together in a strange, low, monotonous voice, their conversation coming in gushes, and then suddenly tailing off into silence, each mumbling out his own thoughts and paying little heed to the words of his neighbour. At the farther end was a small brazier of burning charcoal, beside which on a three-legged wooden stool there sat a tall, thin old man, with his jaw resting upon his two fists, and his elbows upon his knees, staring into the fire.

As I entered, a sallow Malay attendant had hurried up with a pipe for me and a supply of the drug, beckoning me to an empty berth.

"Thank you. I have not come to stay," said I. "There is a friend of mine here, Mr. Isa Whitney, and I wish to speak with him."

There was a movement and an exclamation from my right, and peering through the gloom I saw Whitney, pale, haggard, and unkempt, staring out at me.

"My God! It's Watson," said he. He was in a pitiable state of reaction, with every nerve in a twitter. "I say, Watson, what o'clock is it?"

"Nearly eleven."

"Of what day?"

"Of Friday, June 19th."

"Good heavens! I thought it was Wednesday. It *is* Wednesday. What d'you want to frighten the chap for?" He sank his face onto his arms and began to sob in a high treble key.

"I tell you that it is Friday, man. Your wife has been waiting this two days for you. You should be ashamed of yourself!"

"So I am. But you've got mixed, Watson, for I have only been here a few hours, three pipes, four pipes—I forget how many. But I'll go home with you. I wouldn't frighten Kate—poor little Kate. Give me your hand! Have you a cab?"

"Yes, I have one waiting."

"Then I shall go in it. But I must owe something. Find what I owe, Watson. I am all off colour. I can do nothing for myself."

I walked down the narrow passage between the double row of sleepers, holding my breath to keep out the vile, stupefying fumes of the drug, and looking about for the manager. As I passed the tall man who sat by the brazier I felt a sudden pluck at my skirt, and a low voice whispered, "Walk past me, and then look back at me." The words fell quite distinctly upon my ear. I glanced down. They could only have come from the old man at my side, and yet he sat now as absorbed as ever, very thin, very wrinkled, bent with age, an opium pipe dangling down from between his knees, as though it had dropped in sheer lassitude from his fingers. I took two steps forward and looked back. It took all my self-control to prevent me from breaking out into a cry of astonishment. He had turned his back so that none could see him but I. His form had filled out, his wrinkles were gone, the dull eyes had regained their fire, and there, sitting by the fire and grinning at my surprise, was none other than Sherlock Holmes. He made a slight motion to me to approach him, and instantly, as he turned his face half round to the company once more, subsided into a doddering, loose-lipped senility.

"Holmes!" I whispered, "what on earth are you doing in this den?"

"As low as you can," he answered; "I have excellent ears. If you would have the great kindness to get rid of that sottish friend of yours I should be exceedingly glad to have a little talk with you."

"I have a cab outside."

"Then pray send him home in it. You may safely trust him, for he appears to be too limp to get into any mischief. I should recommend you also to send a note by the cabman to your wife to say that you have thrown in your lot with me. If you will wait outside, I shall be with you in five minutes."

It was difficult to refuse any of Sherlock Holmes's requests, for they were always so exceedingly definite, and put forward with such a quiet air of mastery. I felt, however, that when Whitney was once confined in the cab my mission was practically accomplished; and for the rest, I could not wish anything better than to be associated with my friend in one of those singular adventures which were the normal condition of his existence. In a few minutes I had written my note, paid Whitney's bill, led him out to the cab, and seen him driven through the darkness. In a very short time a decrepit figure had emerged from the opium den, and I was walking down the street with Sherlock Holmes. For two streets he shuffled along with a bent back and an uncertain foot. Then, glancing quickly round, he straightened himself out and burst into a hearty fit of laughter.

"I suppose, Watson," said he, "that you imagine that I have added opium-smoking to cocaine injections, and all the other little weaknesses on which you have favoured me with your medical views."

"I was certainly surprised to find you there."

"But not more so than I to find you."

"I came to find a friend."

"And I to find an enemy."

"An enemy?"

"Yes; one of my natural enemies, or, shall I say, my natural prey. Briefly, Watson, I am in the midst of a very remarkable inquiry, and I have hoped to find a clue in the incoherent ramblings of these sots, as I have done before now. Had I been recognized in that den my life would not have been worth an hour's purchase; for I have used it before now for my own purposes, and the rascally lascar who runs it has sworn to have vengeance upon me. There is a trap-door at the back of that building, near the corner of Paul's Wharf, which could tell some strange tales of what has passed through it upon the moonless nights."

"What! You do not mean bodies?"

"Ay, bodies, Watson. We should be rich men if we had £1000 for every poor devil who has been done to death in that den. It is the vilest murder-trap on the whole riverside, and I fear that Neville St. Clair has entered it never to leave it more. But our trap should be here." He put his two forefingers between his teeth and whistled shrilly—a signal which was answered by a similar whistle from the distance, followed shortly by the rattle of wheels and the clink of horses' hoofs.

"Now, Watson," said Holmes, as a tall dog-cart dashed up through the gloom, throwing out two golden tunnels of yellow light from its side lanterns. "You'll come with me, won't you?

"If I can be of use."

"Oh, a trusty comrade is always of use; and a chronicler still more so. My room at The Cedars is a double-bedded one."

"The Cedars?"

"Yes; that is Mr. St. Clair's house. I am staying there while I conduct the inquiry."

"Where is it, then?"

"Near Lee, in Kent. We have a seven-mile drive before us."

"But I am all in the dark."

"Of course you are. You'll know all about it presently. Jump up here. All right, John; we shall not need you. Here's half a crown. Look out for me to-morrow, about eleven. Give her her head. So long, then!"

He flicked the horse with his whip, and we dashed away through the endless succession of sombre and deserted streets, which widened gradually, until we were flying across a broad balustraded bridge, with the murky river flowing sluggishly beneath us. Beyond lay another dull wilderness of bricks and mortar, its silence broken only by the heavy, regular footfall of the policeman, or the songs and shouts of some belated party of revellers. A dull wrack was drifting slowly across the sky, and a star or two twinkled dimly here and there through the rifts of the clouds. Holmes drove in silence, with his head sunk upon his breast, and the air of a man who is lost in thought, while I sat beside him, curious to learn what this new quest might be which seemed to tax his powers so sorely, and yet afraid to break in upon the current of his thoughts. We had driven several miles, and were beginning to get to the fringe of the belt of suburban villas, when he shook himself, shrugged his shoulders, and lit up his pipe with the air of a man who has satisfied himself that he is acting for the best.

"You have a grand gift of silence, Watson," said he. "It makes you quite invaluable as a companion. 'Pon my word, it is a great thing for me to have someone to talk to, for my own thoughts are not over-pleasant. I was wondering what I should say to this dear little woman to-night when she meets me at the door."

"You forget that I know nothing about it."

"I shall just have time to tell you the facts of the case before we get to Lee. It seems absurdly simple, and yet, somehow, I can get nothing to go upon. There's plenty of thread, no doubt, but I can't get the end of it into my hand. Now, I'll state the case clearly and concisely to you, Watson, and maybe you can see a spark where all is dark to me."

"Proceed, then."

"Some years ago—to be definite, in May, 1884—there came to Lee a gentleman, Neville St. Clair by name, who appeared to have plenty of money. He took a large villa, laid out the grounds very nicely, and lived generally in good style. By degrees he made friends in the neighbourhood, and in 1887 he married the daughter of a local brewer, by whom he now has two children. He had no occupation, but was interested in several companies and went into town as a rule in the morning, returning by the 5:14 from Cannon Street every night. Mr. St. Clair is now thirty-seven years of age, is a man of temperate habits, a good husband, a very affectionate father, and a man who is popular with all who know him. I may add that his whole debts at the present moment, as far as we have been able to ascertain, amount to £88 10s., while he has £220 standing to his credit in the Capital and Counties Bank. There is no reason, therefore, to think that money troubles have been weighing upon his mind.

"Last Monday Mr. Neville St. Clair went into town rather earlier than usual, remarking before he started that he had two important commissions to perform, and that he would bring his little boy home a box of bricks. Now, by the merest chance, his wife received a telegram upon this same Monday, very shortly after his departure, to the effect that a small parcel of considerable value which she had been expecting was waiting for her at the offices of the Aberdeen Shipping Company. Now, if you are well up in your London, you will know that the office of the company is in Fresno Street, which branches out of Upper Swandam Lane, where you found me to-night. Mrs. St. Clair had her lunch, started for the City, did some shopping, proceeded to the company's office, got her packet, and found herself at exactly 4:35 walking through Swandam Lane on her way back to the station. Have you followed me so far?"

"It is very clear."

"If you remember, Monday was an exceedingly hot day, and Mrs. St. Clair walked slowly, glancing about in the hope of seeing a cab, as she did not like the neighbourhood in which she found herself. While she was walking in this way down Swandam Lane, she suddenly heard an ejaculation or cry, and was struck cold to see her husband looking down at her and, as it seemed to her, beckoning to her from a second-floor window. The window was open, and she distinctly saw his face, which she describes as being terribly agitated. He waved his hands frantically to her, and then vanished from the window so suddenly that it seemed to her that he had been plucked back by some irrestible force from behind. One singular point which struck her quick feminine eye was that although he wore some dark coat, such as he had started to town in, he had on neither collar nor necktie.

"Convinced that something was amiss with him, she rushed down the steps—for the house was none other than the opium den in which you found me to-night—and running through the front room she attempted to ascend the stairs which led to the first floor. At the foot of the stairs, however, she met this lascar scoundrel of whom I have spoken, who thrust her back and, aided by a Dane, who acts as assistant there, pushed her out into the street. Filled with the most maddening doubts and fears, she rushed down the lane and, by rare good-fortune, met in Fresno Street a number of constables with an inspector, all on their way to their beat. The inspector and two men accompanied her back, and in spite of the continued resistance of the proprietor, they made their way to the room in which Mr. St. Clair had last been seen. There was no sign of him there. In fact, in the whole of that floor there was no one to be found save a crippled wretch of hideous aspect, who, it seems, made his home there. Both he and the lascar stoutly swore that no one else had been in the front room during the afternoon. So determined was their denial that the inspector was staggered, and had almost come to believe that Mrs. St. Clair had been deluded when, with a cry, she sprang at a small deal box which lay upon the table and tore the lid from it. Out there fell a cascade of children's bricks. It was the toy which he had promised to bring home.

"This discovery, and the evident confusion which the cripple showed, made the inspector realize that the matter was serious. The rooms were carefully examined, and results all pointed to an abominable crime. The front room was plainly furnished as a sitting-room and led into a small bedroom, which looked out upon the back of one of the wharves. Between the wharf and the bedroom window is a narrow strip, which is dry at low tide but is covered at high tide with at least four and a half feet of water. The bedroom window was a broad one and opened from below. On examination traces of blood were to be seen upon the windowsill, and several scattered drops were visible upon the wooden floor of the bedroom. Thrust away behind a curtain in the front room were all the clothes of Mr. Neville St. Clair, with the exception of his coat. His boots, his socks, his hat, and his watch—all were there. There were no signs of violence upon any of these garments, and there were no other traces of Mr. Neville St. Clair. Out of the window he must apparently have gone, for no other exit could be discovered, and the ominous bloodstains upon the sill gave little promise that he could save himself by swimming, for the tide was at its very highest at the moment of the tragedy.

"And now as to the villains who seemed to be immediately implicated in the matter. The lascar was known to be a man of the vilest antecedents, but as, by Mrs. St. Clair's story, he was known to have been at the foot of the stair within a very few seconds of her husband's appearance at the window, he could hardly have been more than an accessory to the crime. His defense was one of absolute ignorance, and he protested that he had no knowledge as to the doings of Hugh Boone, his lodger, and that he could not account in any way for the presence of the missing gentleman's clothes.

"So much for the lascar manager. Now for the sinister cripple who lives upon the second floor of the opium den, and who was certainly the last human being whose eyes rested upon Neville St. Clair. His name is Hugh Boone, and his hideous face is one which is familiar to every man who goes much to the City. He is a professional beggar, though in order to avoid the police regulations he pretends to a small trade in wax vestas. Some little distance down Threadneedle Street, upon the left-hand side, there is, as you may have remarked, a small angle in the wall. Here it is that this creature takes his daily seat, cross-legged, with his tiny stock of matches on his lap, and as he is a piteous spectacle a small rain of charity descends into the greasy leather cap which lies upon the pavement beside him. I have watched the fellow more than once before ever I thought of making his professional acquaintance, and I have been surprised at the harvest which he has reaped in a short time. His appearance, you see, is so remarkable that no one can pass him without observing him. A shock of orange hair, a pale face disfigured by a horrible scar, which, by its contraction, has turned up the outer edge of his upper lip, a bulldog chin, and a pair of very penetrating dark eyes, which present a singular contrast to the colour of his hair, all mark him out from amid the common crowd of mendicants, and so, too, does his wit, for he is ever ready with a reply to any piece of chaff which may be thrown at him by the passers-by. This is the man whom we now learn to have been the lodger at the opium den, and to have been the last man to see the gentleman of whom we are in quest."

"But a cripple!" said I. "What could he have done single-handed against a man in the prime of life?"

"He is a cripple in the sense that he walks with a limp; but in other respects he appears to be a powerful and well-nurtured man. Surely your medical experience would tell you, Watson, that weakness in one limb is often compensated for by exceptional strength in the others."

"Pray continue your narrative."

"Mrs. St. Clair had fainted at the sight of the blood upon the window, and she was escorted home in a cab by the police, as her presence could be of no help to them in their investigations. Inspector Barton, who had charge of the case, made a very careful examination of the premises, but without finding anything which threw any light upon the matter. One mistake had been made in not arresting Boone instantly, as he was allowed some few minutes during which he might have communicated with his friend the lascar, but this fault was soon remedied, and he was seized and searched, without anything being found which could incriminate him. There were, it is true, some blood-stains upon his right shirt-sleeve, but he pointed to his ring-finger, which had been cut near the nail, and explained that the bleeding came from there, adding that he had been to the window not long before, and that the stains which had been observed there came doubtless from the same source. He denied strenuously having ever seen Mr. Neville St. Clair and swore that the presence of the clothes in his room was as much a mystery to him as to the police. As to Mrs. St. Clair's assertion that she had actually seen her husband at the window, he declared that she must have been either mad or dreaming. He was removed, loudly protesting, to the police-station, while the inspector remained upon the premises in the hope that the ebbing tide might afford some fresh clue.

"And it did, though they hardly found upon the mud-bank what they had feared to find. It was Neville St. Clair's coat, and not Neville St. Clair, which lay uncovered as the tide receded. And what do you think they found in the pockets?"

"I cannot imagine."

"No, I don't think you would guess. Every pocket stuffed with pennies and half-pennies—421 pennies and 270 half-pennies. It was no wonder that it had not been swept away by the tide. But a human body is a different matter. There is a fierce eddy between the wharf and the house. It seemed likely enough that the weighted coat had remained when the stripped body had been sucked away into the river."

"But I understand that all the other clothes were found in the room. Would the body be dressed in a coat alone?"

"No, sir, but the facts might be met speciously enough. Suppose that this man Boone had thrust Neville St. Clair through the window, there is no human eye which could have seen the deed. What would he do then? It would of course instantly strike him that he must get rid of the tell-tale garments. He would seize the coat, then, and be in the act of throwing it out, when it would occur to him that it would swim and not sink. He has little time, for he has heard the scuffle downstairs when the wife tried to force her way up, and perhaps he has already heard from his lascar confederate that the police are hurrying up the street. There is not an instant to be lost. He rushes to some secret hoard, where he has accumulated the fruits of his beggary, and he stuffs all the coins upon which he can lay his hands into the pockets to make sure of the coat's sinking. He throws it out, and would have done the same with the other garments had not he heard the rush of steps below, and only just had time to close the window when the police appeared."

"It certainly sounds feasible."

"Well, we will take it as a working hypothesis for want of a better. Boone, as I have told you, was arrested and taken to the station, but it could not be shown that there had ever before been anything against him. He had for years been known as a professional beggar, but his life appeared to have been a very quiet and innocent one. There the matter stands at present, and the questions which have to be solved—what Neville St. Clair was doing in the opium den, what happened to him when there, where is he now, and what Hugh Boone had to do with his disappearance—are all as far from a solution as ever. I confess that I cannot recall any case within my experience which looked at the first glance so simple and yet which presented such difficulties."

While Sherlock Holmes had been detailing this singular series of events, we had been whirling through the outskirts of the great town until the last straggling houses had been left behind, and we rattled along with a country hedge upon either side of us. Just as he finished, however, we drove through two scattered villages, where a few lights still glimmered in the windows.

"We are on the outskirts of Lee," said my companion. "We have touched on three English counties in our short drive, starting in Middlesex, passing over an angle of Surrey, and ending in Kent. See that light among the trees? That is The Cedars, and beside that lamp sits a woman whose anxious ears have already, I have little doubt, caught the clink of our horse's feet."

"But why are you not conducting the case from Baker Street?" I asked.

"Because there are many inquiries which must be made out here. Mrs. St. Clair has most kindly put two rooms at my disposal, and you may rest assured that she will have nothing but a welcome for my friend and colleague. I hate to meet her, Watson, when I have no news of her husband. Here we are. Whoa, there, whoa!"

We had pulled up in front of a large villa which stood within its own grounds. A stable-boy had run out to the horse's head, and springing down I followed Holmes up the small, winding gravel-drive which led to the house. As we approached, the door flew open, and a little blonde woman stood in the opening, clad in some sort of light mousseline de soie, with a touch of fluffy pink chiffon at her neck and wrists. She stood with her figure outlined against the flood of light, one hand upon the door, one half-raised in her eagerness, her body slightly bent, her head and face protruded, with eager eyes and parted lips, a standing question.

"Well?" she cried, "well?" And then, seeing that there were two of us, she gave a cry of hope which sank into a groan as she saw that my companion shook his head and shrugged his shoulders.

"No good news?"

"None."

"No bad?"

"No."

"Thank God for that. But come in. You must be weary, for you have had a long day."

"This is my friend, Dr. Watson. He has been of most vital use to me in several of my cases, and a lucky chance has made it possible for me to bring him out and associate him with this investigation."

"I am delighted to see you," said she, pressing my hand warmly. "You will, I am sure, forgive anything that may be wanting in our arrangements, when you consider the blow which has come so suddenly upon us."

"My dear madam," said I, "I am an old campaigner, and if I were not I can very well see that no apology is needed. If I can be of any assistance, either to you or to my friend here, I shall be indeed happy."

"Now, Mr. Sherlock Holmes," said the lady as we entered a well-lit dining-room, upon the table of which a cold supper had been laid out, "I should very much like to ask you one or two plain questions, to which I beg that you will give a plain answer."

"Certainly, madam."

"Do not trouble about my feelings. I am not hysterical, nor given to fainting. I simply wish to hear your real, real opinion."

"Upon what point?"

"In your heart of hearts, do you think that Neville is alive?"

Sherlock Holmes seemed to be embarrassed by the question. "Frankly, now!" she repeated, standing upon the rug and looking keenly down at him as he leaned back in a basket-chair.

"Frankly, then, madam, I do not."

"You think that he is dead?"

"I do."

"Murdered?"

"I don't say that. Perhaps."

"And on what day did he meet his death?"

"On Monday."

"Then perhaps, Mr. Holmes, you will be good enough to explain how it is that I have received a letter from him to-day."

Sherlock Holmes sprang out of his chair as if he had been galvanized.

"What!" he roared.

"Yes, to-day." She stood smiling, holding up a little slip of paper in the air.

"May I see it?"

"Certainly."

He snatched it from her in his eagerness, and smoothing it out upon the table he drew over the lamp and examined it intently. I had left my chair and was gazing at it over his shoulder. The envelope was a very coarse one and was stamped with the Gravesend postmark and with the date of that very day, or rather of the day before, for it was considerably after midnight.

"Coarse writing," murmured Holmes. "Surely this is not your husband's writing, madam."

"No, but the enclosure is."

"I perceive also that whoever addressed the envelope had to go and inquire as to the address."

"How can you tell that?"

"The name, you see, is in perfectly black ink, which has dried itself. The rest is of the grayish colour, which shows that blotting-paper has been used. If it had been written straight off, and then blotted, none would be of a deep black shade. This man has written the name, and there has then been a pause before he wrote the address, which can only mean that he was not familiar with it. It is, of course, a trifle, but there is nothing so important as trifles. Let us now see the letter. Ha! there has been an enclosure here!"

"Yes, there was a ring. His signet-ring."

"And you are sure that this is your husband's hand?"

"One of his hands."

"One?"

"His hand when he wrote hurriedly. It is very unlike his usual writing, and yet I know it well."

"Dearest do not be frightened. All will come well. There is a huge error which it may take some little time to rectify. Wait in patience.

"NEVILLE.

Written in pencil upon the fly-leaf of a book, octavo size, no water-mark. Hum! Posted to-day in Gravesend by a man with a dirty thumb. Ha! And the flap has been gummed, if I am not very much in error, by a person who had been chewing tobacco. And you have no doubt that it is your husband's hand, madam?"

"None. Neville wrote those words."

"And they were posted to-day at Gravesend. Well, Mrs. St. Clair, the clouds lighten, though I should not venture to say that the danger is over."

"But he must be alive, Mr. Holmes."

"Unless this is a clever forgery to put us on the wrong scent. The ring, after all, proves nothing. It may have been taken from him."

"No, no; it is, it is his very own writing!"

"Very well. It may, however, have been written on Monday and only posted to-day."

"That is possible."

"If so, much may have happened between."

"Oh, you must not discourage me, Mr. Holmes. I know that all is well with him. There is so keen a sympathy between us that I should know if evil came upon him. On the very day that I saw him last he cut himself in the bedroom, and yet I in the diningroom rushed upstairs instantly with the utmost certainty that something had happened. Do you think that I would respond to such a trifle and yet be ignorant of his death?"

"I have seen too much not to know that the impression of a woman may be more valuable than the conclusion of an analytical reasoner. And in this letter you certainly have a very strong piece of evidence to corroborate your view. But if your husband is alive and able to write letters, why should he remain away from you?"

"I cannot imagine. It is unthinkable."

"And on Monday he made no remarks before leaving you?"

"No."

"And you were surprised to see him in Swandam Lane?"

"Very much so."

"Was the window open?"

"Yes."

"Then he might have called to you?"

"He might."

"He only, as I understand, gave an inarticulate cry?"

"Yes."

"A call for help, you thought?"

"Yes. He waved his hands."

"But it might have been a cry of surprise. Astonishment at the unexpected sight of you might cause him to throw up his hands?"

"It is possible."

"And you thought he was pulled back?"

"He disappeared so suddenly."

"He might have leaped back. You did not see anyone else in the room?"

"No, but this horrible man confessed to having been there, and the lascar was at the foot of the stairs."

"Quite so. Your husband, as far as you could see, had his ordinary clothes on?"

"But without his collar or tie. I distinctly saw his bare throat."

"Had he ever spoken of Swandam Lane?"

"Never."

"Had he ever showed any signs of having taken opium?"

"Never."

"Thank you, Mrs. St. Clair. Those are the principal points about which I wished to be absolutely clear. We shall now have a little supper and then retire, for we may have a very busy day to-morrow."

A large and comfortable double-bedded room had been placed at our disposal, and I was quickly between the sheets, for I was weary after my night of adventure. Sherlock Holmes was a man, however, who, when he had an unsolved problem upon his mind, would go for days, and even for a week, without rest, turning it over, rearranging his facts, looking at it from every point of view until he had either fathomed it or convinced himself that his data were insufficient. It was soon evident to me that he was now preparing for an all-night sitting. He took off his coat and waistcoat, put on a large blue dressing-gown, and then wandered about the room collecting pillows from his bed and cushions from the sofa and armchairs. With these he constructed a sort of Eastern divan, upon which he perched himself cross-legged, with an ounce of shag tobacco and a box of matches laid out in front of him. In the dim light of the lamp I saw him sitting there, an old briar pipe between his lips, his eyes fixed vacantly upon the corner of the ceiling, the blue smoke curling up from him, silent, motionless, with the light shining upon his strong-set aquiline features. So he sat as I dropped off to sleep, and so he sat when a sudden ejaculation caused me to wake up, and I found the summer sun shining into the apartment. The pipe was still between his lips, the smoke still curled upward, and the room was full of a dense tobacco haze, but nothing remained of the heap of shag which I had seen upon the previous night.

"Awake, Watson?" he asked.

"Yes."

"Game for a morning drive?"

"Certainly."

"Then dress. No one is stirring yet, but I know where the stable-boy sleeps, and we shall soon have the trap out." He chuckled to himself as he spoke, his eyes twinkled, and he seemed a different man to the sombre thinker of the previous night.

As I dressed I glanced at my watch. It was no wonder that no one was stirring. It was twenty-five minutes past four. I had hardly finished when Holmes returned with the news that the boy was putting in the horse.

"I want to test a little theory of mine," said he, pulling on his boots. "I think, Watson, that you are now standing in the presence of one of the most absolute fools in Europe. I deserve to be kicked from here to Charing Cross. But I think I have the key of the affair now."

"And where is it?" I asked, smiling.

"In the bathroom," he answered. "Oh, yes, I am not joking," he continued, seeing my look of incredulity. "I have just been there, and I have taken it out, and I have got it in this Gladstone bag. Come on, my boy, and we shall see whether it will not fit the lock."

We made our way downstairs as quietly as possible, and out into the bright morning sunshine. In the road stood our horse and trap, with the half-clad stable-boy waiting at the head. We both sprang in, and away we dashed down the London Road. A few country carts were stirring, bearing in vegetables to the metropolis, but the lines of villas on either side were as silent and lifeless as some city in a dream.

"It has been in some points in a singular case," said Holmes, flicking the horse on into a gallop. "I confess that I have been as blind as a mole, but it is better to learn wisdom late than never to learn it at all."

In town the earliest risers were just beginning to look sleepily from their windows as we drove through the streets of the Surrey side. Passing down the Waterloo Bridge Road we crossed over the river, and dashing up Wellington Street wheeled sharply to the right and found ourselves in Bow Street. Sherlock Holmes was well known to the force, and the two constables at the door saluted him. One of them held the horse's head while the other led us in.

"Who is on duty?" asked Holmes.

"Inspector Bradstreet, sir."

"Ah, Bradstreet, how are you?" A tall, stout official had come down the stone-flagged passage, in a peaked cap and frogged jacket. "I wish to have a quiet word with you, Bradstreet."

"Certainly, Mr. Holmes. Step into my room here."

It was a small, office-like room, with a huge ledger upon the table, and a telephone projecting from the wall. The inspector sat down at his desk.

"What can I do for you, Mr. Holmes?"

"I called about that beggarman, Boone—the one who was charged with being concerned in the disappearance of Mr. Neville St. Clair, of Lee."

"Yes. He was brought up and remanded for further inquiries."

"So I heard. You have him here?"

"In the cells."

"Is he quiet?"

"Oh, he gives no trouble. But he is a dirty scoundrel."

"Dirty?"

"Yes, it is all we can do to make him wash his hands, and his face is as black as a tinker's. Well, when once his case has been settled, he will have a regular prison bath; and I think, if you saw him, you would agree with me that he needed it."

"I should like to see him very much."

"Would you? That is easily done. Come this way. You can leave your bag."

"No, I think that I'll take it."

"Very good. Come this way, if you please." He led us down a passage, opened a barred door, passed down a winding stair, and brought us to a whitewashed corridor with a line of doors on each side.

"The third on the right is his," said the inspector. "Here it is!" He quietly shot back a panel in the upper part of the door and glanced through.

"He is asleep," said he. "You can see him very well."

We both put our eyes to the grating. The prisoner lay with his face towards us, in a very deep sleep, breathing slowly and heavily. He was a middle-sized man, coarsely clad as became his calling, with a coloured shirt protruding through the rent in his tattered coat. He was, as the inspector had said, extremely dirty, but the grime which covered his face could not conceal its repulsive ugliness. A broad wheal from an old scar ran right across it from eye to chin, and by its contraction had turned up one side of the upper lip, so that three teeth were exposed in a perpetual snarl. A shock of very bright red hair grew low over his eyes and forehead.

"He's a beauty, isn't he?" said the inspector.

"He certainly needs a wash," remarked Holmes. "I had an idea that he might, and I took the liberty of bringing the tools with me." He opened the Gladstone bag as he spoke, and took out, to my astonishment, a very large bath-sponge.

"He! he! You are a funny one," chuckled the inspector.

"Now, if you will have the great goodness to open that door very quietly, we will soon make him cut a much more respectable figure."

"Well, I don't know why not," said the inspector. "He doesn't look a credit to the Bow Street cells, does he?" He slipped his key into the lock, and we all very quietly entered the cell. The sleeper half turned, and then settled down once more into a deep slumber. Holmes stooped to the water-jug, moistened his sponge, and then rubbed it twice vigorously across and down the prisoner's face.

"Let me introduce you," he shouted, "to Mr. Neville St. Clair, of Lee, in the county of Kent."

Never in my life have I seen such a sight. The man's face peeled off under the sponge like the bark from a tree. Gone was the coarse brown tint! Gone, too, was the horrid scar which had seamed it across, and the twisted lip which had given the repulsive sneer to the face! A twitch brought away the tangled red hair, and there, sitting up in his bed, was a pale, sad-faced, refined-looking man, black-haired and smooth-skinned, rubbing his eyes and staring about him with sleepy bewilderment. Then suddenly realizing the exposure, he broke into a scream and threw himself down with his face to the pillow.

"Great heavens!" cried the inspector, "it is, indeed, the missing man. I know him from the photograph."

The prisoner turned with the reckless air of a man who abandons himself to his destiny. "Be it so," said he. "And pray, what am I charged with?"

"With making away with Mr. Neville St.——Oh, come, you can't be charged with that unless they make a case of attempted suicide of it," said the inspector with a grin. "Well, I have been twenty-seven years in the force, but this really takes the cake."

"If I am Mr. Neville St. Clair, then it is obvious that no crime has been committed, and that, therefore, I am illegally detained."

"No crime, but a very great error has been committed," said Holmes. "You would have done better to have trusted your wife."

"It was not the wife; it was the children," groaned the prisoner. "God help me, I would not have them ashamed of their father. My God! What an exposure! What can I do?"

Sherlock Holmes sat down beside him on the couch and patted him kindly on the shoulder.

"If you leave it to a court of law to clear the matter up," said he, "of course you can hardly avoid publicity. On the other hand, if you convince the police authorities that there is no possible case against you, I do not know that there is any reason that the details should find their way into the papers. Inspector Bradstreet would, I am sure, make notes upon anything which you might tell us and submit it to the proper authorities. The case would then never go into court at all."

"God bless you!" cried the prisoner passionately. "I would have endured imprisonment, ay, even execution, rather than have left my miserable secret as a family blot to my children.

"You are the first who have ever heard my story. My father was a school-master in Chesterfield, where I received an excellent education. I travelled in my youth, took to the stage, and finally became a reporter on an evening paper in London. One day my editor wished to have a series of articles upon begging in the metropolis, and I volunteered to supply them. There was the point from which all my adventures started. It was only by trying begging as an amateur that I could get the facts upon which to base my articles. When an actor I had, of course, learned all the secrets of making up, and had been famous in the green-room for my skill. I took advantage now of my attainments. I painted my face, and to make myself as pitiable as possible I made a good scar and fixed one side of my lip in a twist by the aid of a small slip of flesh-coloured plaster. Then with a red head of hair, and an appropriate dress, I took my station in the business part of the city, ostensibly as a match-seller but really as a beggar. For seven hours I plied my trade, and when I returned home in the evening I found to my surprise that I had received no less than 26*s*. 4*d*.

"I wrote my articles and thought little more of the matter until, some time later, I backed a bill for a friend and had a writ served upon me for £25. I was at my wit's end where to get the money, but a sudden idea came to me. I begged a fortnight's grace from the creditor, asked for a holiday from my employers, and spent the time in begging in the City under my disguise. In ten days I had the money and had paid the debt.

"Well, you can imagine how hard it was to settle down to arduous work at £2 a week when I knew that I could earn as much in a day by smearing my face with a little paint, laying my cap on the ground, and sitting still. It was a long fight between my pride and the money, but the dollars won at last, and I threw up reporting and sat day after day in the corner which I had first chosen, inspiring pity by my ghastly face and filling my pockets with coppers. Only one man knew my secret. He was the keeper of a low den in which I used to lodge in Swandam Lane, where I could every morning emerge as a squalid beggar and in the evenings transform myself into a well-dressed man about town. This fellow, a lascar, was well paid by me for his rooms, so that I knew my secret was safe in his possession.

"Well, very soon I found that I was saving considerable sums of money. I do not mean that any beggar in the streets of London could earn £700 a year—which is less than my average takings—but I had exceptional advantages in my power of making up, and also in a facility of repartee, which improved by practice and made me quite a recognized character in the City. All day a stream of pennies, varied by silver, poured in upon me, and it was a very bad day in which I failed to take £2.

"As I grew richer I grew more ambitious, took a house in the country, and eventually married, without anyone having a suspicion as to my real occupation. My dear wife knew that I had business in the City. She little knew what.

"Last Monday I had finished for the day and was dressing in my room above the opium den when I looked out of my window and saw, to my horror and astonishment, that my wife was standing in the street, with her eyes fixed full upon me. I gave a cry of surprise, threw up my arms to cover my face, and, rushing to my confidant, the lascar, entreated him to prevent anyone from coming up to me. I heard her voice downstairs, but I knew that she could not ascend. Swiftly I threw off my clothes, pulled on those of a beggar, and put on my pigments and wig. Even a wife's eyes could not pierce so complete a disguise. But then it occurred to me that there might be a search in the room, and that the clothes might betray me. I threw open the window, reopening by my violence a small cut which I had inflicted upon myself in the bedroom that morning. Then I seized my coat, which was weighted by the coppers which I had just transferred to it from the leather bag in which I carried my takings. I hurled it out of the window, and it disappeared into the Thames. The other clothes would have followed, but at that moment there was a rush of constables up the stair, and a few minutes after I found, rather, I confess, to my relief, that instead of being identified as Mr. Neville St. Clair, I was arrested as his murderer.

"I do not know that there is anything else for me to explain. I was determined to preserve my disguise as long as possible, and hence my preference for a dirty face. Knowing that my wife would be terribly anxious, I slipped off my ring and confided it to the lascar at a moment when no constable was watching me, together with a hurried scrawl, telling her that she had no cause to fear."

"That note only reached her yesterday," said Holmes.

"Good God! What a week she must have spent!"

"The police have watched this lascar," said Inspector Bradstreet, "and I can quite understand that he might find it difficult to post a letter unobserved. Probably he handed it to some sailor customer of his, who forgot all about it for some days."

"That was it," said Holmes, nodding approvingly; "I have no doubt of it. But have you never been prosecuted for begging?"

"Many times; but what was a fine to me?"

"It must stop here, however," said Bradstreet. "If the police are to hush this thing up, there must be no more of Hugh Boone."

"I have sworn it by the most solemn oaths which a man can take."

"In that case I think that it is probable that no further steps may be taken. But if you are found again, then all must come out. I am sure, Mr. Holmes, that we are very much indebted to you for having cleared the matter up. I wish I knew how you reach your results."

"I reached this one," said my friend, "by sitting upon five pillows and consuming an ounce of shag. I think, Watson, that if we drive to Baker Street we shall just be in time for breakfast."

The Adventure of the Blue Carbuncle

I HAD CALLED upon my friend Sherlock Holmes upon the second morning after Christmas, with the intention of wishing him the compliments of the season. He was lounging upon the sofa in a purple dressing-gown, a pipe-rack within his reach upon the right, and a pile of crumpled morning papers, evidently newly studied, near at hand. Beside the couch was a wooden chair, and on the angle of the back hung a very seedy and disreputable hard-felt hat, much the worse for wear, and cracked in several places. A lens and a forceps lying upon the seat of the chair suggested that the hat had been suspended in this manner for the purpose of examination.

"You are engaged," said I; "perhaps I interrupt you."

"Not at all. I am glad to have a friend with whom I can discuss my results. The matter is a perfectly trivial one"—he jerked his thumb in the direction of the old hat—"but there are points in connection with it which are not entirely devoid of interest and even of instruction."

I seated myself in his armchair and warmed my hands before his crackling fire, for a sharp frost had set in, and the windows were thick with the ice crystals. "I suppose," I remarked, "that homely as it looks, this thing has some deadly story linked on to it—that it is the clue which will guide you in the solution of some mystery and the punishment of some crime."

"No, no. No crime," said Sherlock Holmes, laughing. "Only one of those whimsical little incidents which will happen when you have four million human beings all jostling each other within the space of a few square miles. Amid the action and reaction of so dense a swarm of humanity, every possible combination of events may be expected to take place, and many a little problem will be presented which may be striking and bizarre without being criminal. We have already had experience of such."

"So much so," I remarked, "that of the last six cases which I have added to my notes, three have been entirely free of any legal crime."

"Precisely. You allude to my attempt to recover the Irene Adler papers, to the singular case of Miss Mary Sutherland, and to the adventure of the man with the twisted lip. Well, I have no doubt that this small matter will fall into the same innocent category. You know Peterson, the commissionaire?"

"Yes."

"It is to him that this trophy belongs."

"It is his hat."

"No, no; he found it. Its owner is unknown. I beg that you will look upon it not as a battered billycock but as an intellectual problem. And, first, as to how it came here. It arrived upon Christmas morning, in company with a good fat goose, which is, I have no doubt, roasting at this moment in front of Peterson's fire. The facts are these: about four o'clock on Christmas morning, Peterson, who, as you know, is a very honest fellow, was returning from some small jollification and was making his way homeward down Tottenham Court Road. In front of him he saw, in the gaslight, a tallish man, walking with a slight stagger, and carrying a white goose slung over his shoulder. As he reached the corner of Goodge Street, a row broke out between this stranger and a little knot of roughs. One of the latter knocked off the man's hat, on which he raised his stick to defend himself and, swinging it over his head, smashed the shop window behind him. Peterson had rushed forward to protect the stranger from his assailants; but the man, shocked at having broken the window, and seeing an official-looking person in uniform rushing towards him, dropped his goose, took to his heels, and vanished amid the labyrinth of small streets which lie at the back of Tottenham Court Road. The roughs had also fled at the appearance of Peterson, so that he was left in possession of the field of battle, and also of the spoils of victory in the shape of this battered hat and a most unimpeachable Christmas goose."

"Which surely he restored to their owner?"

"My dear fellow, there lies the problem. It is true that 'For Mrs. Henry Baker' was printed upon a small card which was tied to the bird's left leg, and it is also true that the initials 'H. B.' are legible upon the lining of this hat; but as there are some thousands of Bakers, and some hundreds of Henry Bakers in this city of ours, it is not easy to restore lost property to any one of them."

"What, then, did Peterson do?"

"He brought round both hat and goose to me on Christmas morning, knowing that even the smallest problems are of interest to me. The goose we retained until this morning, when there were signs that, in spite of the slight frost, it would be well that it should be eaten without unnecessary delay. Its finder has carried it off, therefore, to fulfil the ultimate destiny of a goose, while I continue to retain the hat of the unknown gentleman who lost his Christmas dinner."

"Did he not advertise?"

"No."

"Then, what clue could you have as to his identity?"

"Only as much as we can deduce."

"From his hat?"

"Precisely."

"But you are joking. What can you gather from this old battered felt?"

"Here is my lens. You know my methods. What can you gather yourself as to the individuality of the man who has worn this article?"

I took the tattered object in my hands and turned it over rather ruefully. It was a very ordinary black hat of the usual round shape, hard and much the worse for wear. The lining had been of red silk, but was a good deal discoloured. There was no maker's name; but as Holmes had remarked, the initials "H. B." were scrawled upon one side. It was pierced in the brim for a hatsecurer, but the elastic was missing. For the rest, it was cracked, exceedingly dusty, and spotted in several places, although there seemed to have been some attempt to hide the discoloured patches by smearing them with ink.

"I can see nothing," said I, handing it back to my friend.

"On the contrary, Watson, you can see everything. You fail, however, to reason from what you see. You are too timid in drawing your inferences."

"Then, pray tell me what it is that you can infer from this hat?"

He picked it up and gazed at it in the peculiar introspective fashion which was characteristic of him. "It is perhaps less suggestive than it might have been," he remarked, "and yet there are a few inferences which are very distinct, and a few others which represent at least a strong balance of probability. That the man was highly intellectual is of course obvious upon the face of it, and also that he was fairly well-to-do within the last three years, although he has now fallen upon evil days. He had foresight, but has less now than formerly, pointing to a moral retrogression, which, when taken with the decline of his fortunes, seems to indicate some evil influence, probably drink, at work upon him. This may account also for the obvious fact that his wife has ceased to love him."

"My dear Holmes!"

"He has, however, retained some degree of self-respect," he continued, disregarding my remonstrance. "He is a man who leads a sedentary life, goes out little, is out of training entirely, is middle-aged, has grizzled hair which he has had cut within the last few days, and which he anoints with lime-cream. These are the more patent facts which are to be deduced from his hat. Also, by the way, that it is extremely improbable that he has gas laid on in his house."

"You are certainly joking, Holmes."

"Not in the least. Is it possible that even now, when I give you these results, you are unable to see how they are attained?"

"I have no doubt that I am very stupid, but I must confess that I am unable to follow you. For example, how did you deduce that this man was intellectual?"

For answer Holmes clapped the hat upon his head. It came right over the forehead and settled upon the bridge of his nose. "It is a question of cubic capacity," said he; "a man with so large a brain must have something in it."

"The decline of his fortunes, then?"

"This hat is three years old. These flat brims curled at the edge came in then. It is a hat of the very best quality. Look at the band of ribbed silk and the excellent lining. If this man could afford to buy so expensive a hat three years ago, and has had no hat since, then he has assuredly gone down in the world."

"Well, that is clear enough, certainly. But how about the foresight and the moral retrogression?"

Sherlock Holmes laughed. "Here is the foresight," said he, putting his finger upon the little disc and loop of the hat-securer. "They are never sold upon hats. If this man ordered one, it is a sign of a certain amount of foresight, since he went out of his way to take this precaution against the wind. But since we see that he has broken the elastic and has not troubled to replace it, it is obvious that he has less foresight now than formerly, which is a distinct proof of a weakening nature. On the other hand, he has endeavoured to conceal some of these stains upon the felt by daubing them with ink, which is a sign that he has not entirely lost his self-respect."

"Your reasoning is certainly plausible."

"The further points, that he is middle-aged, that his hair is grizzled, that it has been recently cut, and that he uses lime-cream, are all to be gathered from a close examination of the lower part of the lining. The lens discloses a large number of hair-ends, clean cut by the scissors of the barber. They all appear to be adhesive, and there is a distinct odour of lime-cream. This dust, you will observe, is not the gritty, gray dust of the street but the fluffy brown dust of the house, showing that it has been hung up indoors most of the time; while the marks of moisture upon the inside are proof positive that the wearer perspired very freely, and could therefore, hardly be in the best of training."

"But his wife—you said that she had ceased to love him."

"This hat has not been brushed for weeks. When I see you, my dear Watson, with a week's accumulation of dust upon your hat, and when your wife allows you to go out in such a state, I shall fear that you also have been unfortunate enough to lose your wife's affection."

"But he might be a bachelor."

"Nay, he was bringing home the goose as a peace-offering to his wife. Remember the card upon the bird's leg."

"You have an answer to everything. But how on earth do you deduce that the gas is not laid on in his house?"

"One tallow stain, or even two, might come by chance; but when I see no less than five, I think that there can be little doubt that the individual must be brought into frequent contact with burning tallow—walks upstairs at night probably with his hat in one hand and a guttering candle in the other. Anyhow, he never got tallow-stains from a gas-jet. Are you satisfied?"

"Well, it is very ingenious," said I, laughing; "but since, as you said just now, there has been no crime committed, and no harm done save the loss of a goose, all this seems to be rather a waste of energy."

Sherlock Holmes had opened his mouth to reply, when the door flew open, and Peterson, the commissionaire, rushed into the apartment with flushed cheeks and the face of a man who is dazed with astonishment.

"The goose, Mr. Holmes! The goose, sir!" he gasped.

"Eh? What of it, then? Has it returned to life and flapped off through the kitchen window?" Holmes twisted himself round upon the sofa to get a fairer view of the man's excited face.

"See here, sir! See what my wife found in its crop!" He held out his hand and displayed upon the centre of the palm a brilliantly scintillating blue stone, rather smaller than a bean in size, but of such purity and radiance that it twinkled like an electric point in the dark hollow of his hand.

Sherlock Holmes sat up with a whistle. "By Jove, Peterson!" said he, "this is treasure trove indeed. I suppose you know what you have got?"

"A diamond, sir? A precious stone. It cuts into glass as though it were putty."

"It's more than a precious stone. It is *the* precious stone."

"Not the Countess of Morcar's blue carbuncle!" I ejaculated.

"Precisely so. I ought to know its size and shape, seeing that I have read the advertisement about it in *The Times* every day lately. It is absolutely unique, and its value can only be conjectured, but the reward offered of £1000 is certainly not within a twentieth part of the market price."

"A thousand pounds! Great Lord of mercy!" The commissionaire plumped down into a chair and stared from one to the other of us.

"That is the reward, and I have reason to know that there are sentimental considerations in the background which would induce the Countess to part with half her fortune if she could but recover the gem."

"It was lost, if I remember aright, at the Hotel Cosmopolitan," I remarked.

"Precisely so, on December 22d, just five days ago. John Horner, a plumber, was accused of having abstracted it from the lady's jewel-case. The evidence against him was so strong that the case has been referred to the Assizes. I have some account of the matter here, I believe." He rummaged amid his newspapers, glancing over the dates, until at last he smoothed one out, doubled it over, and read the following paragraph:

> "Hotel Cosmopolitan Jewel Robbery. John Horner, 26, plumber, was brought up upon the charge of having upon the 22d inst., abstracted from the jewel-case of the Countess of Morcar the valuable gem known as the blue carbuncle. James Ryder, upper-attendant at the hotel, gave his evidence to the effect that he had shown Horner up to the dressing-room of the Countess of Morcar upon the day of the robbery in order that he might solder the second bar of the grate, which was loose. He had remained with Horner some little time, but had finally been called away. On returning, he found that Horner had disappeared, that the bureau had been forced open, and that the small morocco casket in which, as it afterwards transpired, the Countess was accustomed to keep her jewel, was lying empty upon the dressing-table. Ryder instantly gave the alarm, and Horner was arrested the same evening; but the stone could not be found either upon his person or in his rooms. Catherine Cusack, maid to the Countess, deposed to having heard Ryder's cry of dismay on discovering the robbery, and to having rushed into the room, where she found matters as described by the last witness. Inspector Bradstreet, B division, gave evidence as to the arrest of Horner, who struggled frantically, and protested his innocence in the strongest terms. Evidence of a previous conviction for robbery having been given against the prisoner, the magistrate refused to deal summarily with the offence, but referred it to the Assizes. Horner, who had shown signs of intense emotion during the proceedings, fainted away at the conclusion and was carried out of court.

"Hum! So much for the police-court," said Holmes thoughtfully, tossing aside the paper. "The question for us now to solve is the sequence of events leading from a rifled jewel-case at one end to the crop of a goose in Tottenham Court Road at the other. You see, Watson, our little deductions have suddenly assumed a much more important and less innocent aspect. Here is the stone; the stone came from the goose, and the goose came from Mr. Henry Baker, the gentleman with the bad hat and all the other characteristics with which I have bored you. So now we must set ourselves very seriously to finding this gentleman and ascertaining what part he has played in this little mystery. To do this, we must try the simplest means first, and these lie undoubtedly in an advertisement in all the evening papers. If this fail, I shall have recourse to other methods."

"What will you say?"

"Give me a pencil and that slip of paper. Now, then:

> "Found at the corner of Goodge Street, a goose and a black felt hat. Mr. Henry Baker can have the same by applying at 6:30 this evening at 221, Baker Street.

That is clear and concise."

"Very. But will he see it?"

"Well, he is sure to keep an eye on the papers, since, to a poor man, the loss was a heavy one. He was clearly so scared by his mischance in breaking the window and by the approach of Peterson that he thought of nothing but flight, but since then he must have bitterly regretted the impulse which caused him to drop his bird. Then, again, the introduction of his name will cause him to see it, for everyone who knows him will direct his attention to it. Here you are, Peterson, run down to the advertising agency and have this put in the evening papers."

"In which, sir?"

"Oh, in the *Globe, Star, Pall Mall, St. James's, Evening News Standard, Echo*, and any others that occur to you."

"Very well, sir. And this stone?"

"Ah, yes, I shall keep the stone. Thank you. And, I say, Peterson, just buy a goose on your way back and leave it here with me, for we must have one to give to this gentleman in place of the one which your family is now devouring."

When the commissionaire had gone, Holmes took up the stone

and held it against the light. "It's a bonny thing," said he. "Just see how it glints and sparkles. Of course it is a nucleus and focus of crime. Every good stone is. They are the devil's pet baits. In the larger and older jewels every facet may stand for a bloody deed. This stone is not yet twenty years old. It was found in the banks of the Amoy River in southern China and is remarkable in having every characteristic of the carbuncle, save that it is blue in shade instead of ruby red. In spite of its youth, it has already a sinister history. There have been two murders, a vitriol-throwing, a suicide, and several robberies brought about for the sake of this forty-grain weight of crystallized charcoal. Who would think that so pretty a toy would be a purveyor to the gallows and the prison? I'll lock it up in my strong box now and drop a line to the Countess to say that we have it."

"Do you think that this man Horner is innocent?"

"I cannot tell."

"Well, then, do you imagine that this other one, Henry Baker, had anything to do with the matter?"

"It is, I think, much more likely that Henry Baker is an absolutely innocent man, who had no idea that the bird which he was carrying was of considerably more value than if it were made of solid gold. That, however, I shall determine by a very simple test if we have an answer to our advertisement."

"And you can do nothing until then?"

"Nothing."

"In that case I shall continue my professional round. But I shall come back in the evening at the hour you have mentioned, for I should like to see the solution of so tangled a business."

"Very glad to see you. I dine at seven. There is a woodcock, I believe. By the way, in view of recent occurrences, perhaps I ought to ask Mrs. Hudson to examine its crop."

I had been delayed at a case, and it was a little after half-past six when I found myself in Baker Street once more. As I approached the house I saw a tall man in a Scotch bonnet with a coat which was buttoned up to his chin waiting outside in the bright semicircle which was thrown from the fanlight. Just as I arrived the door was opened, and we were shown up together to Holmes's room.

"Mr. Henry Baker, I believe," said he, rising from his armchair and greeting his visitor with the easy air of geniality which he could so readily assume. "Pray take this chair by the fire,

Mr. Baker. It is a cold night, and I observe that your circulation is more adapted for summer than for winter. Ah, Watson, you have just come at the right time. Is that your hat, Mr. Baker?"

"Yes, sir, that is undoubtedly my hat."

He was a large man with rounded shoulders, a massive head, and a broad, intelligent face, sloping down to a pointed beard of grizzled brown. A touch of red in nose and cheeks, with a slight tremor of his extended hand, recalled Holmes's surmise as to his habits. His rusty black frock-coat was buttoned right up in front, with the collar turned up, and his lank wrists protruded from his sleeves without a sign of cuff or shirt. He spoke in a slow staccato fashion, choosing his words with care, and gave the impression generally of a man of learning and letters who had had ill-usage at the hands of fortune.

"We have retained these things for some days," said Holmes, "because we expected to see an advertisement from you giving your address. I am at a loss to know now why you did not advertise."

Our visitor gave a rather shamefaced laugh. "Shillings have not been so plentiful with me as they once were," he remarked. "I had no doubt that the gang of roughs who assaulted me had carried off both my hat and the bird. I did not care to spend more money in a hopeless attempt at recovering them."

"Very naturally. By the way, about the bird, we were compelled to eat it."

"To eat it!" Our visitor half rose from his chair in his excitement.

"Yes, it would have been of no use to anyone had we not done so. But I presume that this other goose upon the sideboard, which is about the same weight and perfectly fresh, will answer your purpose equally well?"

"Oh, certainly, certainly," answered Mr. Baker with a sigh of relief.

"Of course, we still have the feathers, legs, crop, and so on of your own bird, so if you wish——"

The man burst into a hearty laugh. "They might be useful to me as relics of my adventure," said he, "but beyond that I can hardly see what use the *disjecta membra* of my late acquaintance are going to be to me. No, sir, I think that, with your permission, I will confine my attentions to the excellent bird which I perceive upon the sideboard."

Sherlock Holmes glanced sharply across at me with a slight shrug of his shoulders.

"There is your hat, then, and there your bird," said he. "By the way, would it bore you to tell me where you got the other one from? I am somewhat of a fowl fancier, and I have seldom seen a better grown goose."

"Certainly, sir," said Baker, who had risen and tucked his newly gained property under his arm. "There are a few of us who frequent the Alpha Inn, near the Museum—we are to be found in the Museum itself during the day, you understand. This year our good host, Windigate by name, instituted a goose club, by which, on consideration of some few pence every week, we were each to receive a bird at Christmas. My pence were duly paid, and the rest is familiar to you. I am much indebted to you, sir, for a Scotch bonnet is fitted neither to my years nor my gravity." With a comical pomposity of manner he bowed solemnly to both of us and strode off upon his way.

"So much for Mr. Henry Baker," said Holmes when he had closed the door behind him. "It is quite certain that he knows nothing whatever about the matter. Are you hungry, Watson?"

"Not particularly."

"Then I suggest that we turn our dinner into a supper and follow up this clue while it is still hot."

"By all means."

It was a bitter night, so we drew on our ulsters and wrapped cravats about our throats. Outside, the stars were shining coldly in a cloudless sky, and the breath of the passers-by blew out into smoke like so many pistol shots. Our footfalls rang out crisply and loudly as we swung through the doctors' quarter, Wimpole Street, Harley Street, and so through Wigmore Street into Oxford Street. In a quarter of an hour we were in Bloomsbury at the Alpha Inn, which is a small public-house at the corner of one of the streets which runs down into Holborn. Holmes pushed open the door of the private bar and ordered two glasses of beer from the ruddy-faced, white-aproned landlord.

"Your beer should be excellent if it is as good as your geese," said he.

"My geese!" The man seemed surprised.

"Yes. I was speaking only half an hour ago to Mr. Henry Baker, who was a member of your goose club."

"Ah! yes, I see. But you see, sir, them's not *our* geese."

"Indeed! Whose, then?"

"Well, I got the two dozen from a salesman in Covent Garden."

"Indeed? I know some of them. Which was it?"

"Breckinridge is his name."

"Ah! I don't know him. Well, here's your good health, landlord, and prosperity to your house. Good-night.

"Now for Mr. Breckinridge," he continued, buttoning up his coat as we came out into the frosty air. "Remember, Watson, that though we have so homely a thing as a goose at one end of this chain, we have at the other a man who will certainly get seven years' penal servitude unless we can establish his innocence. It is possible that our inquiry may but confirm his guilt; but, in any case, we have a line of investigation which has been missed by the police, and which a singular chance has placed in our hands. Let us follow it out to the bitter end. Faces to the south, then, and quick march!"

We passed across Holborn, down Endell Street, and so through a zigzag of slums to Covent Garden Market. One of the largest stalls bore the name of Breckinridge upon it, and the proprietor, a horsy-looking man, with a sharp face and trim side-whiskers, was helping a boy to put up the shutters.

"Good-evening. It's a cold night," said Holmes.

The salesman nodded and shot a questioning glance at my companion.

"Sold out of geese, I see," continued Holmes, pointing at the bare slabs of marble.

"Let you have five hundred to-morrow morning."

"That's no good."

"Well, there are some on the stall with the gas-flare."

"Ah, but I was recommended to you."

"Who by?"

"The landlord of the Alpha."

"Oh, yes; I sent him a couple of dozen."

"Fine birds they were, too. Now where did you get them from?"

To my surprise the question provoked a burst of anger from the salesman.

"Now, then, mister," said he, with his head cocked and his arms akimbo, "what are you driving at? Let's have it straight, now."

"It is straight enough. I should like to know who sold you the geese which you supplied to the Alpha."

"Well, then, I shan't tell you. So now!"

"Oh, it is a matter of no importance; but I don't know why you should be so warm over such a trifle."

"Warm! You'd be as warm, maybe, if you were as pestered as I am. When I pay good money for a good article there should be an end of the business; but it's 'Where are the geese?' and 'Who did you sell the geese to?' and 'What will you take for the geese?' One would think they were the only geese in the world, to hear the fuss that is made over them."

"Well, I have no connection with any other people who have been making inquiries," said Holmes carelessly. "If you won't tell us the bet is off, that is all. But I'm always ready to back my opinion on a matter of fowls, and I have a fiver on it that the bird I ate is country bred."

"Well, then, you've lost your fiver, for it's town bred," snapped the salesman.

"It's nothing of the kind."

"I say it is."

"I don't believe it."

"D'you think you know more about fowls than I, who have handled them ever since I was a nipper? I tell you, all those birds that went to the Alpha were town bred."

"You'll never persuade me to believe that."

"Will you bet, then?"

"It's merely taking your money, for I know that I am right. But I'll have a sovereign on with you, just to teach you not to be obstinate."

The salesman chuckled grimly. "Bring me the books, Bill," said he.

The small boy brought round a small thin volume and a great greasy-backed one, laying them out together beneath the hanging lamp.

"Now then, Mr. Cocksure," said the salesman, "I thought that I was out of geese, but before I finish you'll find that there is still one left in my shop. You see this little book?"

"Well?"

"That's the list of the folk from whom I buy. D'you see? Well, then, here on this page are the country folk, and the numbers after their names are where their accounts are in the big ledger. Now, then! You see this other page in red ink? Well, that is a list of my town suppliers. Now, look at that third name. Just read it out to me."

"Mrs. Oakshott, 117, Brixton Road—249," read Holmes.

"Quite so. Now turn that up in the ledger."

Holmes turned to the page indicated. "Here you are, 'Mrs. Oakshott, 117, Brixton Road, egg and poultry supplier.' "

"Now, then, what's the last entry?"

" 'December 22d. Twenty-four geese at 7*s*. 6*d*.' "

"Quite so. There you are. And underneath?"

" 'Sold to Mr. Windigate of the Alpha, at 12*s*.' "

"What have you to say now?"

Sherlock Holmes looked deeply chagrined. He drew a sovereign from his pocket and threw it down upon the slab, turning away with the air of a man whose disgust is too deep for words. A few yards off he stopped under a lamp-post and laughed in the hearty, noiseless fashion which was peculiar to him.

"When you see a man with whiskers of that cut and the 'Pink 'un' protruding out of his pocket, you can always draw him by a bet," said he. "I daresay that if I had put £100 down in front of him, that man would not have given me such complete information as was drawn from him by the idea that he was doing me on a wager. Well, Watson, we are, I fancy, nearing the end of our quest, and the only point which remains to be determined is whether we should go on to this Mrs. Oakshott to-night, or whether we should reserve it for to-morrow. It is clear from what that surly fellow said that there are others besides ourselves who are anxious about the matter, and I should——"

His remarks were suddenly cut short by a loud hubbub which broke out from the stall which we had just left. Turning round we saw a little rat-faced fellow standing in the centre of the circle of yellow light which was thrown by the swinging lamp, while Breckinridge, the salesman, framed in the door of his stall, was shaking his fists fiercely at the cringing figure.

"I've had enough of you and your geese," he shouted. "I wish you were all at the devil together. If you come pestering me any more with your silly talk I'll set the dog at you. You bring Mrs. Oakshott here and I'll answer her, but what have you to do with it? Did I buy the geese off you?"

"No; but one of them was mine all the same," whined the little man.

"Well, then, ask Mrs. Oakshott for it."

"She told me to ask you."

"Well, you can ask the King of Proosia, for all I care. I've had enough of it. Get out of this!" He rushed fiercely forward, and the inquirer flitted away into the darkness.

"Ha! this may save us a visit to Brixton Road," whispered Holmes. "Come with me, and we will see what is to be made of this fellow." Striding through the scattered knots of people who lounged round the flaring stalls, my companion speedily overtook the little man and touched him upon the shoulder. He sprang round, and I could see in the gas-light that every vestige of colour had been driven from his face.

"Who are you, then? What do you want?" he asked in a quavering voice.

"You will excuse me," said Holmes blandly, "but I could not help overhearing the questions which you put to the salesman just now. I think that I could be of assistance to you."

"You? Who are you? How could you know anything of the matter?"

"My name is Sherlock Holmes. It is my business to know what other people don't know."

"But you can know nothing of this?"

"Excuse me, I know everything of it. You are endeavouring to trace some geese which were sold by Mrs. Oakshott, of Brixton Road, to a salesman named Breckinridge, by him in turn to Mr. Windigate, of the Alpha, and by him to his club, of which Mr. Henry Baker is a member."

"Oh, sir, you are the very man whom I have longed to meet," cried the little fellow with outstretched hands and quivering fingers. "I can hardly explain to you how interested I am in this matter."

Sherlock Holmes hailed a four-wheeler which was passing. "In that case we had better discuss it in a cosy room rather than in this wind-swept market-place," said he. "But pray tell me, before we go farther, who it is that I have the pleasure of assisting."

The man hesitated for an instant. "My name is John Robinson," he answered with a sidelong glance.

"No, no; the real name," said Holmes sweetly. "It is always awkward doing business with an alias."

A flush sprang to the white cheeks of the stranger. "Well, then," said he, "my real name is James Ryder."

"Precisely so. Head attendant at the Hotel Cosmopolitan. Pray step into the cab, and I shall soon be able to tell you everything which you would wish to know."

The little man stood glancing from one to the other of us with half-frightened, half-hopeful eyes, as one who is not sure whether he is on the verge of a windfall or of a catastrophe. Then he stepped into the cab, and in half an hour we were back in the sitting-room at Baker Street. Nothing had been said during our drive, but the high, thin breathing of our new companion, and the claspings and unclaspings of his hands, spoke of the nervous tension within him.

"Here we are!" said Holmes cheerily as we filed into the room. "The fire looks very seasonable in this weather. You look cold, Mr. Ryder. Pray take the basket-chair. I will just put on my slippers before we settle this little matter of yours. Now, then! You want to know what became of those geese?"

"Yes, sir."

"Or rather, I fancy, of that goose. It was one bird, I imagine, in which you were interested—white, with a black bar across the tail."

Ryder quivered with emotion. "Oh, sir," he cried, "can you tell me where it went to?"

"It came here."

"Here?"

"Yes, and a most remarkable bird it proved. I don't wonder that you should take an interest in it. It laid an egg after it was dead—the bonniest, brightest little blue egg that ever was seen. I have it here in my museum."

Our visitor staggered to his feet and clutched the mantelpiece with his right hand. Holmes unlocked his strong-box and held up the blue carbuncle, which shone out like a star, with a cold, brilliant, many-pointed radiance. Ryder stood glaring with a drawn face, uncertain whether to claim or to disown it.

"The game's up, Ryder," said Holmes quietly. "Hold up, man, or you'll be into the fire! Give him an arm back into his chair, Watson. He's not got blood enough to go in for felony with impunity. Give him a dash of brandy. So! Now he looks a little more human. What a shrimp it is, to be sure!"

For a moment he had staggered and nearly fallen, but the

brandy brought a tinge of colour into his cheeks, and he sat staring with frightened eyes at his accuser.

"I have almost every link in my hands, and all the proofs which I could possibly need, so there is little which you need tell me. Still, that little may as well be cleared up to make the case complete. You had heard, Ryder, of this blue stone of the Countess of Morcar's?"

"It was Catherine Cusack who told me of it," said he in a crackling voice.

"I see—her ladyship's waiting-maid. Well, the temptation of sudden wealth so easily acquired was too much for you, as it has been for better men before you; but you were not very scrupulous in the means you used. It seems to me, Ryder, that there is the making of a very pretty villain in you. You knew that this man Horner, the plumber, had been concerned in some such matter before, and that suspicion would rest the more readily upon him. What did you do, then? You made some small job in my lady's room—you and your confederate Cusack—and you managed that he should be the man sent for. Then, when he had left, you rifled the jewel-case, raised the alarm, and had this unfortunate man arrested. You then——"

Ryder threw himself down suddenly upon the rug and clutched at my companion's knees. "For God's sake, have mercy!" he shrieked. 'Think of my father! of my mother! It would break their hearts. I never went wrong before! I never will again. I swear it. I'll swear it on a Bible. Oh, don't bring it into court! For Christ's sake, don't!"

"Get back into your chair!" said Holmes sternly. "It is very well to cringe and crawl now, but you thought little enough of this poor Horner in the dock for a crime of which he knew nothing."

"I will fly, Mr. Holmes. I will leave the country, sir. Then the charge against him will break down."

"Hum! We will talk about that. And now let us hear a true account of the next act. How came the stone into the goose, and how came the goose into the open market? Tell us the truth, for there lies your only hope of safety."

Ryder passed his tongue over his parched lips. "I will tell you it just as it happened, sir," said he. "When Horner had been arrested, it seemed to me that it would be best for me to get away with the stone at once, for I did not know at what moment the police might not take it into their heads to search me and my room. There was no place about the hotel where it would be safe. I went out, as if on some commission, and I made for my sister's house. She had married a man named Oakshott, and lived in Brixton Road, where she fattened fowls for the market. All the way there every man I met seemed to me to be a policeman or a detective; and, for all that it was a cold night, the sweat was pouring down my face before I came to the Brixton Road. My sister asked me what was the matter, and why I was so pale; but I told her that I had been upset by the jewel robbery at the hotel. Then I went into the back yard and smoked a pipe, and wondered what it would be best to do.

"I had a friend once called Maudsley, who went to the bad, and had just been serving his time in Pentonville. One day he had met me, and fell into talk about the ways of thieves, and how they could get rid of what they stole. I knew that he would be true to me, for I knew one or two things about him; so I made up my mind to go right on to Kilburn, where he lived, and take him into my confidence. He would show me how to turn the stone into money. But how to get to him in safety? I thought of the agonies I had gone through in coming from the hotel. I might at any moment be seized and searched, and there would be the stone in my waistcoat pocket. I was leaning against the wall at the time and looking at the geese which were waddling about round my feet, and suddenly an idea came into my head which showed me how I could beat the best detective that ever lived.

"My sister had told me some weeks before that I might have the pick of her geese for a Christmas present, and I knew that she was always as good as her word. I would take my goose now, and in it I would carry my stone to Kilburn. There was a little shed in the yard, and behind this I drove one of the birds —a fine big one, white, with a barred tail. I caught it, and, prying its bill open, I thrust the stone down its throat as far as my finger could reach. The bird gave a gulp, and I felt the stone pass along its gullet and down into its crop. But the creature flapped and struggled, and out came my sister to know what was the matter. As I turned to speak to her the brute broke loose and fluttered off among the others.

" 'Whatever were you doing with that bird, Jem?' says she.

" 'Well,' said I, 'you said you'd give me one for Christmas, and I was feeling which was the fattest.'

" 'Oh,' says she, 'we've set yours aside for you—Jem's bird, we call it. It's the big white one over yonder. There's twenty-six of them, which makes one for you, and one for us, and two dozen for the market.'

" 'Thank you, Maggie,' says I; 'but if it is all the same to you, I'd rather have that one I was handling just now.'

" 'The other is a good three pound heavier,' said she, 'and we fattened it expressly for you.'

" 'Never mind. I'll have the other, and I'll take it now,' said I.

" 'Oh, just as you like,' said she, a little huffed. 'Which is it you want, then?'

" 'That white one with the barred tail, right in the middle of the flock.'

" 'Oh, very well. Kill it and take it with you.'

"Well, I did what she said, Mr. Holmes, and I carried the bird all the way to Kilburn. I told my pal what I had done, for he was a man that it was easy to tell a thing like that to. He laughed until he choked, and we got a knife and opened the goose. My heart turned to water, for there was no sign of the stone, and I knew that some terrible mistake had occurred. I left the bird, rushed back to my sister's, and hurried into the back yard. There was not a bird to be seen there.

" 'Where are they all, Maggie?' I cried.

" 'Gone to the dealer's, Jem.'

" 'Which dealer's?'

" 'Breckinridge, of Covent Garden.'

" 'But was there another with a barred tail?' I asked, 'the same as the one I chose?'

" 'Yes, Jem; there were two barred-tailed ones, and I could never tell them apart.'

"Well, then, of course I saw it all, and I ran off as hard as my feet would carry me to this man Breckinridge; but he had sold the lot at once, and not one word would he tell me as to where they had gone. You heard him yourselves to-night. Well, he has always answered me like that. My sister thinks that I am going mad. Sometimes I think that I am myself. And now—and now I am myself a branded thief, without ever having touched the wealth for which I sold my character. God help me! God help me!" He burst into convulsive sobbing, with his face buried in his hands.

There was a long silence, broken only by his heavy breathing, and by the measured tapping of Sherlock Holmes's finger-tips upon the edge of the table. Then my friend rose and threw open the door.

"Get out!" said he.

"What, sir! Oh, Heaven bless you!"

"No more words. Get out!"

And no more words were needed. There was a rush, a clatter upon the stairs, the bang of a door, and the crisp rattle of running footfalls from the street.

"After all, Watson," said Holmes, reaching up his hand for his clay pipe, "I am not retained by the police to supply their deficiencies. If Horner were in danger it would be another thing; but this fellow will not appear against him, and the case must collapse. I suppose that I am commuting a felony, but it is just possible that I am saving a soul. This fellow will not go wrong again; he is too terribly frightened. Send him to jail now, and you make him a jail-bird for life. Besides, it is the season of forgiveness. Chance has put in our way a most singular and whimsical problem, and its solution is its own reward. If you will have the goodness to touch the bell, Doctor, we will begin another investigation, in which, also a bird will be the chief feature."

The Adventure of the Speckled Band

On glancing over my notes of the seventy odd cases in which I have during the last eight years studied the methods of my friend Sherlock Holmes, I find many tragic, some comic, a large number merely strange, but none commonplace; for, working as he did rather for the love of his art than for the acquirement of wealth, he refused to associate himself with any investigation which did not tend towards the unusual, and even the fantastic. Of all these varied cases, however, I cannot recall any which presented more singular features than that which was associated with the well-known Surrey family of the Roylotts of Stoke Moran. The events in question occurred in the early days of my association with Holmes, when we were sharing rooms as bachelors in Baker Street. It is possible that I might have placed them upon record before, but a promise of secrecy was made at the time, from which I have only been freed during the last month by the untimely death of the lady to whom the pledge was given. It is perhaps as well that the facts should now come to light, for I have reasons to know that there are widespread rumours as to the death of Dr. Grimesby Roylott which tend to make the matter even more terrible than the truth.

It was early in April in the year '83 that I woke one morning to find Sherlock Holmes standing, fully dressed, by the side of my bed. He was a late riser, as a rule, and as the clock on the mantelpiece showed me that it was only a quarter-past seven, I blinked up at him in some surprise, and perhaps just a little resentment, for I was myself regular in my habits.

"Very sorry to knock you up, Watson," said he, "but it's the common lot this morning. Mrs. Hudson has been knocked up, she retorted upon me, and I on you."

"What is it, then—a fire?"

"No; a client. It seems that a young lady has arrived in a considerable state of excitement, who insists upon seeing me. She is waiting now in the sitting-room. Now, when young ladies wander about the metropolis at this hour of the morning, and knock sleepy people up out of their beds, I presume that it is something very pressing which they have to communicate. Should it prove to be an interesting case, you would, I am sure, wish to follow it from the outset. I thought, at any rate, that I should call you and give you the chance."

"My dear fellow, I would not miss it for anything."

I had no keener pleasure than in following Holmes in his professional investigations, and in admiring the rapid deductions, as swift as intuitions, and yet always founded on a logical basis, with which he unravelled the problems which were submitted to him. I rapidly threw on my clothes and was ready in a few minutes to accompany my friend down to the sitting-room. A lady dressed in black and heavily veiled, who had been sitting in the window, rose as we entered.

"Good-morning, madam," said Holmes cheerily. "My name is Sherlock Holmes. This is my intimate friend and associate, Dr. Watson, before whom you can speak as freely as before myself. Ha! I am glad to see that Mrs. Hudson has had the good sense to light the fire. Pray draw up to it, and I shall order you a cup of hot coffee, for I observe that you are shivering."

"It is not cold which makes me shiver," said the woman in a low voice, changing her seat as requested.

"What, then?"

"It is fear, Mr. Holmes. It is terror." She raised her veil as she spoke, and we could see that she was indeed in a pitiable state of agitation, her face all drawn and gray, with restless, frightened eyes, like those of some hunted animal. Her features and figure were those of a woman of thirty, but her hair was shot with premature gray, and her expression was weary and haggard. Sherlock Holmes ran her over with one of his quick, all-comprehensive glances.

"You must not fear," said he soothingly, bending forward and patting her forearm. "We shall soon set matters right, I have no doubt. You have come in by train this morning, I see."

"You know me, then?"

"No, but I observe the second half of a return ticket in the palm of your left glove. You must have started early, and yet you had a good drive in a dog-cart, along heavy roads, before you reached the station."

The lady gave a violent start and stared in bewilderment at my companion.

"There is no mystery, my dear madam," said he, smiling. "The left arm of your jacket is spattered with mud in no less than seven places. The marks are perfectly fresh. There is no vehicle save a dog-cart which throws up mud in that way, and then only when you sit on the left-hand side of the driver."

"Whatever your reasons may be, you are perfectly correct," said she. "I started from home before six, reached Leatherhead at twenty past, and came in by the first train to Waterloo. Sir, I can stand this strain no longer; I shall go mad if it continues. I have no one to turn to—none, save only one, who cares for me, and he, poor fellow, can be of little aid. I have heard of you, Mr. Holmes; I have heard of you from Mrs. Farintosh, whom you helped in the hour of her sore need. It was from her that I had your address. Oh, sir, do you not think that you could help me, too, and at least throw a little light through the dense darkness which surrounds me? At present it is out of my power to reward you for your services, but in a month or six weeks I shall be married, with the control of my own income, and then at least you shall not find me ungrateful."

Holmes turned to his desk and, unlocking it, drew out a small case-book, which he consulted.

"Farintosh," said he. "Ah yes, I recall the case; it was concerned with an opal tiara. I think it was before your time, Watson. I can only say, madam, that I shall be happy to devote the same care to your case as I did to that of your friend. As to reward, my profession is its own reward; but you are at liberty to defray whatever expenses I may be put to, at the time which suits you best. And now I beg that you will lay before us everything that may help us in forming an opinion upon the matter."

"Alas!" replied our visitor, "the very horror of my situation lies in the fact that my fears are so vague, and my suspicions depend so entirely upon small points, which might seem trivial to another, that even he to whom of all others I have a right to look for help and advice looks upon all that I tell him about it as the fancies of a nervous woman. He does not say so, but I can read it from his soothing answers and averted eyes. But I have heard, Mr. Holmes, that you can see deeply into the manifold wickedness of the human heart. You may advise me how to walk amid the dangers which encompass me."

"I am all attention, madam."

"My name is Helen Stoner, and I am living with my stepfather, who is the last survivor of one of the oldest Saxon families in England, the Roylotts of Stoke Moran, on the western border of Surrey."

Holmes nodded his head. "The name is familiar to me," said he.

"The family was at one time among the richest in England, and the estates extended over the borders into Berkshire in the north, and Hampshire in the west. In the last century, however, four successive heirs were of a dissolute and wasteful disposition, and the family ruin was eventually completed by a gambler in the days of the Regency. Nothing was left save a few acres of ground, and the two-hundred-year-old house, which is itself crushed under a heavy mortgage. The last squire dragged out his existence there, living the horrible life of an aristocratic pauper; but his only son, my stepfather, seeing that he must adapt himself to the new conditions, obtained an advance from a relative, which enabled him to take a medical degree and went out to Calcutta, where, by his professional skill and his force of character, he established a large practice. In a fit of anger, however, caused by some robberies which had been perpetrated in the house, he beat his native butler to death and narrowly escaped a capital sentence. As it was, he suffered a long term of imprisonment and afterwards returned to England a morose and disappointed man.

"When Dr. Roylott was in India he married my mother, Mrs. Stoner, the young widow of Major-General Stoner, of the Bengal Artillery. My sister Julia and I were twins, and we were only two years old at the time of my mother's re-marriage. She had a considerable sum of money—not less than £1000 a year—and this she bequeathed to Dr. Roylott entirely while we resided with him, with a provision that a certain annual sum should be allowed to each of us in the event of our marriage. Shortly after our return to England my mother died—she was killed eight years ago in a railway accident near Crewe. Dr. Roylott then abandoned his attempts to establish himself in practice in London and took us to live with him in the old ancestral house at Stoke Moran. The money which my mother had left was enough for all our wants, and there seemed to be no obstacle to our happiness.

"But a terrible change came over our stepfather about this time. Instead of making friends and exchanging visits with our neighbours, who had at first been overjoyed to see a Roylott of Stoke Moran back in the old family seat, he shut himself up in his house and seldom came out save to indulge in ferocious quarrels with whoever might cross his path. Violence of temper approaching to mania has been hereditary in the men of the family, and in my stepfather's case it had, I believe, been intensified by his long residence in the tropics. A series of disgraceful brawls took place, two of which ended in the police-court, until at last he became the terror of the village, and the folks would fly at his approach, for he is a man of immense strength, and absolutely uncontrollable in his anger.

"Last week he hurled the local blacksmith over a parapet into a stream, and it was only by paying over all the money which I could gather together that I was able to avert another public exposure. He had no friends at all save the wandering gypsies, and he would give these vagabonds leave to encamp upon the few acres of bramble-covered land which represent the family estate, and would accept in return the hospitality of their tents, wandering away with them sometimes for weeks on end. He has a passion also for Indian animals, which are sent over to him by a correspondent, and he has at this moment a cheetah and a baboon, which wander freely over his grounds and are feared by the villagers almost as much as their master.

"You can imagine from what I say that my poor sister Julia and I had no great pleasure in our lives. No servant would stay with us, and for a long time we did all the work of the house. She was but thirty at the time of her death, and yet her hair had already begun to whiten, even as mine has."

"Your sister is dead, then?"

"She died just two years ago, and it is of her death that I wish to speak to you. You can understand that, living the life which I have described, we were little likely to see anyone of our own age and position. We had, however, an aunt, my mother's maiden sister, Miss Honoria Westphail, who lives near Harrow, and we were occasionally allowed to pay short visits at this lady's house. Julia went there at Christmas two years ago, and met there a half-pay major of marines, to whom she became engaged. My stepfather learned of the engagement when my sister returned and offered no objection to the marriage; but within a fortnight of the day which had been fixed for the wedding, the terrible event occurred which has deprived me of my only companion."

Sherlock Holmes had been leaning back in his chair with his eyes closed and his head sunk in a cushion, but he half opened his lids now and glanced across at his visitor.

"Pray be precise as to details," said he.

"It is easy for me to be so, for every event of that dreadful time is seared into my memory. The manor-house is, as I have already said, very old, and only one wing is now inhabited. The bedrooms in this wing are on the ground floor, the sitting-rooms being in the central block of the buildings. Of these bedrooms the first is Dr. Roylott's, the second my sister's, and the third my own. There is no communication between them, but they all open out into the same corridor. Do I make myself plain?"

"Perfectly so."

"The windows of the three rooms open out upon the lawn. That fatal night Dr. Roylott had gone to his room early, though we knew that he had not retired to rest, for my sister was troubled by the smell of the strong Indian cigars which it was his custom to smoke. She left her room, therefore, and came into mine, where she sat for some time, chatting about her approaching wedding. At eleven o'clock she rose to leave me, but she paused at the door and looked back.

" 'Tell me, Helen,' said she, 'have you ever heard anyone whistle in the dead of the night?'

" 'Never,' said I.

" 'I suppose that you could not possibly whistle, yourself, in your sleep?'

" 'Certainly not. But why?'

" 'Because during the last few nights I have always, about three in the morning, heard a low, clear whistle. I am a light sleeper, and it has awakened me. I cannot tell where it came from—perhaps from the next room, perhaps from the lawn. I thought that I would just ask you whether you had heard it.'

" 'No, I have not. It must be those wretched gypsies in the plantation.'

" 'Very likely. And yet if it were on the lawn, I wonder that you did not hear it also.'

" 'Ah, but I sleep more heavily than you.'

" 'Well, it is of no great consequence, at any rate.' She smiled back at me, closed my door, and a few moments later I heard her key turn in the lock."

"Indeed," said Holmes. "Was it your custom always to lock yourselves in at night?"

"Always."

"And why?"

"I think that I mentioned to you that the doctor kept a cheetah and a baboon. We had no feeling of security unless our doors were locked."

"Quite so. Pray proceed with your statement."

"I could not sleep that night. A vague feeling of impending misfortune impressed me. My sister and I, you will recollect, were twins, and you know how subtle are the links which bind two souls which are so closely allied. It was a wild night. The wind was howling outside, and the rain was beating and splashing against the windows. Suddenly, amid all the hubbub of the gale, there burst forth the wild scream of a terrified woman. I knew that it was my sister's voice. I sprang from my bed, wrapped a shawl round me, and rushed into the corridor. As I opened my door I seemed to hear a low whistle, such as my sister described, and a few moments later a clanging sound, as if a mass of metal had fallen. As I ran down the passage, my sister's door was unlocked, and revolved slowly upon its hinges. I stared at it horror-stricken, not knowing what was about to issue from it. By the light of the corridor-lamp I saw my sister appear at the opening, her face blanched with terror, her hands groping for help, her whole figure swaying to and fro like that of a drunkard. I ran to her and threw my arms round her, but at that moment her knees seemed to give way and she fell to the ground. She writhed as one who is in terrible pain, and her limbs were dreadfully convulsed. At first I thought that she had not recognized me, but as I bent over her she suddenly shrieked out in a voice which I shall never forget, 'Oh, my God! Helen! It was the band! The speckled band! There was something else which she would fain have said, and she stabbed with her finger into the air in the direction of the doctor's room, but a fresh convulsion seized her and choked her words. I rushed out, calling loudly for my stepfather, and I met him hastening from his room in his dressing-gown. When he reached my sister's side she was unconscious, and though he poured brandy down her throat and sent for medical aid from the village, all efforts were in vain, for she slowly sank and died without having recovered her consciousness. Such was the dreadful end of my beloved sister."

"One moment," said Holmes; "are you sure about this whistle and metallic sound? Could you swear to it?"

"That was what the county coroner asked me at the inquiry. It is my strong impression that I heard it, and yet, among the crash of the gale and the creaking of an old house, I may possibly have been deceived."

"Was your sister dressed?"

"No, she was in her night-dress. In her right hand was found the charred stump of a match, and in her left a match-box."

"Showing that she had struck a light and looked about her when the alarm took place. That is important. And what conclusions did the coroner come to?"

"He investigated the case with great care, for Dr. Roylott's conduct had long been notorious in the county, but he was unable to find any satisfactory cause of death. My evidence showed that the door had been fastened upon the inner side, and the windows were blocked by old-fashioned shutters with broad iron bars, which were secured every night. The walls were carefully sounded, and were shown to be quite solid all round, and the flooring was also thoroughly examined, with the same result. The chimney is wide, but is barred up by four large staples. It is certain, therefore, that my sister was quite alone when she met her end. Besides, there were no marks of any violence upon her."

"How about poison?"

"The doctors examined her for it, but without success."

"What do you think that this unfortunate lady died of, then?"

"It is my belief that she died of pure fear and nervous shock, though what it was that frightened her I cannot imagine."

"Were there gypsies in the plantation at the time?"

"Yes, there are nearly always some there."

"Ah, and what did you gather from this allusion to a band—a speckled band?"

"Sometimes I have thought that it was merely the wild talk of delirium, sometimes that it may have referred to some band of people, perhaps to these very gypsies in the plantation. I do not know whether the spotted handkerchiefs which so many of them wear over their heads might have suggested the strange adjective which she used."

Holmes shook his head like a man who is far from being satisfied.

"These are very deep waters," said he; "pray go on with your narrative."

"Two years have passed since then, and my life has been until lately lonelier than ever. A month ago, however, a dear friend, whom I have known for many years, has done me the honour to ask my hand in marriage. His name is Armitage—Percy Armitage—the second son of Mr. Armitage, of Crane Water, near Reading. My stepfather has offered no opposition to the match, and we are to be married in the course of the spring. Two days ago some repairs were started in the west wing of the building, and my bedroom wall has been pierced, so that I have had to move into the chamber in which my sister died, and to sleep in the very bed in which she slept. Imagine, then, my thrill of terror when last night, as I lay awake, thinking over her terrible fate, I suddenly heard in the silence of the night the low whistle which had been the herald of her own death. I sprang up and lit the lamp, but nothing was to be seen in the room. I was too shaken to go to bed again, however, so I dressed, and as soon as it was daylight I slipped down, got a dog-cart at the Crown

Inn, which is opposite, and drove to Leatherhead, from whence I have come on this morning with the one object of seeing you and asking your advice."

"You have done wisely," said my friend. "But have you told me all?"

"Yes, all."

"Miss Roylott, you have not. You are screening your stepfather."

"Why, what do you mean?"

For answer Holmes pushed back the frill of black lace which fringed the hand that lay upon our visitor's knee. Five little livid spots, the marks of four fingers and a thumb, were printed upon the white wrist.

"You have been cruelly used," said Holmes.

The lady coloured deeply and covered over her injured wrist. "He is a hard man," she said, "and perhaps he hardly knows his own strength."

There was a long silence, during which Holmes leaned his chin upon his hands and stared into the crackling fire.

"This is a very deep business," he said at last. "There are a thousand details which I should desire to know before I decide upon our course of action. Yet we have not a moment to lose. If we were to come to Stoke Moran to-day, would it be possible for us to see over these rooms without the knowledge of your stepfather?"

"As it happens, he spoke of coming into town to-day upon some most important business. It is probable that he will be away all day, and that there would be nothing to disturb you. We have a housekeeper now, but she is old and foolish, and I could easily get her out of the way."

"Excellent. You are not averse to this trip, Watson?"

"By no means."

"Then we shall both come. What are you going to do yourself?"

"I have one or two things which I would wish to do now that I am in town. But I shall return by the twelve o'clock train, so as to be there in time for your coming."

"And you may expect us early in the afternoon. I have myself some small business matters to attend to. Will you not wait and breakfast?"

"No, I must go. My heart is lightened already since I have

confided my trouble to you. I shall look forward to seeing you again this afternoon." She dropped her thick black veil over her face and glided from the room.

"And what do you think of it all, Watson?" asked Sherlock Holmes, leaning back in his chair.

"It seems to me to be a most dark and sinister business."

"Dark enough and sinister enough."

"Yet if the lady is correct in saying that the flooring and walls are sound, and that the door, window, and chimney are impassable, then her sister must have been undoubtedly alone when she met her mysterious end."

"What becomes, then, of these nocturnal whistles, and what of the very peculiar words of the dying woman?"

"I cannot think."

"When you combine the ideas of whistles at night, the presence of a band of gypsies who are on intimate terms with this old doctor, the fact that we have every reason to believe that the doctor has an interest in preventing his stepdaughter's marriage, the dying allusion to a band, and, finally, the fact that Miss Helen Stoner heard a metallic clang, which might have been caused by one of those metal bars that secured the shutters falling back into its place, I think that there is good ground to think that the mystery may be cleared along those lines."

"But what, then, did the gypsies do?"

"I cannot imagine."

"I see many objections to any such theory."

"And so do I. It is precisely for that reason that we are going to Stoke Moran this day. I want to see whether the objections are fatal, of if they may be explained away. But what in the name of the devil!"

The ejaculation had been drawn from my companion by the fact that our door had been suddenly dashed open, and that a huge man had framed himself in the aperture. His costume was a peculiar mixture of the professional and of the agricultural, having a black top-hat, a long frock-coat, and a pair of high gaiters, with a hunting-crop swinging in his hand. So tall was he that his hat actually brushed the cross bar of the doorway, and his breadth seemed to span it across from side to side. A large face, seared with a thousand wrinkles, burned yellow with the sun, and marked with every evil passion, was turned from one to the other of us, while his deep-set, bile-shot eyes, and his high, thin, fleshless nose, gave him somewhat the resemblance to a fierce old bird of prey.

"Which of you is Holmes?" asked this apparition.

"My name, sir; but you have the advantage of me," said my companion quietly.

"I am Dr. Grimesby Roylott, of Stoke Moran."

"Indeed, Doctor," said Holmes blandly. "Pray take a seat."

"I will do nothing of the kind. My stepdaughter has been here. I have traced her. What has she been saying to you?"

"It is a little cold for the time of the year," said Holmes.

"What has she been saying to you?" screamed the old man furiously.

"But I have heard that the crocuses promise well," continued my companion imperturbably.

"Ha! You put me off, do you?" said our new visitor, taking a step forward and shaking his hunting-crop. "I know you, you scoundrel! I have heard of you before. You are Holmes, the meddler."

My friend smiled.

"Holmes, the busybody!"

His smile broadened.

"Holmes, the Scotland Yard Jack-in-office!"

Holmes chuckled heartily. "Your conversation is most entertaining," said he. "When you go out close the door, for there is a decided draught."

"I will go when I have said my say. Don't you dare to meddle with my affairs. I know that Miss Stoner has been here. I traced her! I am a dangerous man to fall foul of! See here." He stepped swiftly forward, seized the poker, and bent it into a curve with his huge brown hands.

"See that you keep yourself out of my grip," he snarled, and hurling the twisted poker into the fireplace he strode out of the room.

"He seems a very amiable person," said Holmes, laughing. "I am not quite so bulky, but if he had remained I might have shown him that my grip was not much more feeble than his own." As he spoke he picked up the steel poker and, with a sudden effort, straightened it out again.

"Fancy his having the insolence to confound me with the official detective force! This incident gives zest to our investigation, however, and I only trust that our little friend will not suffer from her imprudence in allowing this brute to trace her. And now, Watson, we shall order breakfast, and afterwards I shall walk down to Doctors' Commons, where I hope to get some data which may help us in this matter."

It was nearly one o'clock when Sherlock Holmes returned from his excursion. He held in his hand a sheet of blue paper, scrawled over with notes and figures.

"I have seen the will of the deceased wife," said he. "To determine its exact meaning I have been obliged to work out the present prices of the investments with which it is concerned. The total income, which at the time of the wife's death was little short of £1100, is now, through the fall in agricultural prices, not more than £750. Each daughter can claim an income of £250, in case of marriage. It is evident, therefore, that if both girls had married, this beauty would have had a mere pittance, while even one of them would cripple him to a very serious extent. My morning's work has not been wasted, since it has proved that he has the very strongest motives for standing in the way of anything of the sort. And now, Watson, this is too serious for dawdling, especially as the old man is aware that we are interesting ourselves in his affairs; so if you are ready, we shall call a cab and drive to Waterloo. I should be very much obliged if you would slip your revolver into your pocket. An Eley's No. 2 is an excellent argument with gentlemen who can twist steel pokers into knots. That and a tooth-brush are, I think, all that we need."

At Waterloo we were fortunate in catching a train for Leatherhead, where we hired a trap at the station inn and drove for four or five miles through the lovely Surrey lanes. It was a perfect day, with a bright sun and a few fleecy clouds in the heavens. The trees and wayside hedges were just throwing out their first green shoots, and the air was full of the pleasant smell of the moist earth. To me at least there was a strange contrast between the sweet promise of the spring and this sinister quest upon which we were engaged. My companion sat in the front of the trap, his arms folded, his hat pulled down over his eyes, and his chin sunk upon his breast, buried in the deepest thought. Suddenly, however, he started, tapped me on the shoulder, and pointed over the meadows.

"Look there!" said he.

A heavily timbered park stretched up in a gentle slope, thickening into a grove at the highest point. From amid the branches there jutted out the gray gables and high roof-tree of a very old mansion.

"Stoke Moran?" said he.

"Yes, sir, that be the house of Dr. Grimesby Roylott," remarked the driver.

"There is some building going on there," said Holmes; "that is where we are going."

"There's the village," said the driver, pointing to a cluster of roofs some distance to the left; "but if you want to get to the house, you'll find it shorter to get over this stile, and so by the foot-path over the fields. There it is, where the lady is walking."

"And the lady, I fancy, is Miss Stoner," observed Holmes, shading his eyes. "Yes, I think we had better do as you suggest."

We got off, paid our fare, and the trap rattled back on its way to Leatherhead.

"I thought it as well," said Holmes as we climbed the stile, "that this fellow should think we had come here as architects, or on some definite business. It may stop his gossip. Good-afternoon, Miss Stoner. You see that we have been as good as our word."

Our client of the morning had hurried forward to meet us with a face which spoke her joy. "I have been waiting so eagerly for you," she cried, shaking hands with us warmly. "All has turned out splendidly. Dr. Roylott has gone to town, and it is unlikely that he will be back before evening."

"We have had the pleasure of making the doctor's acquaintance," said Holmes, and in a few words he sketched out what had occurred. Miss Stoner turned white to the lips as she listened.

"Good heavens!" she cried, "he has followed me, then."

"So it appears."

"He is so cunning that I never know when I am safe from him. What will he say when he returns?"

"He must guard himself, for he may find that there is someone more cunning than himself upon his track. You must lock yourself up from him to-night. If he is violent, we shall take you away to your aunt's at Harrow. Now, we must make the best use of our time, so kindly take us at once to the rooms which we are to examine."

The building was of gray, lichen-blotched stone, with a high central portion and two curving wings, like the claws of a crab, thrown out on each side. In one of these wings the windows were broken and blocked with wooden boards, while the roof was partly caved in, a picture of ruin. The central portion was in little better repair, but the right-hand block was comparatively modern, and the blinds in the windows, with the blue smoke curling up from the chimneys, showed that this was where the family resided. Some scaffolding had been erected against the end wall, and the stone-work had been broken into, but there were no signs of any workmen at the moment of our visit. Holmes walked slowly up and down the ill-trimmed lawn and examined with deep attention the outsides of the windows.

"This, I take it, belongs to the room in which you used to sleep, the centre one to your sister's, and the one next to the main building to Dr. Roylott's chamber?"

"Exactly so. But I am now sleeping in the middle one."

"Pending the alterations, as I understand. By the way, there does not seem to be any very pressing need for repairs at that end wall."

"There were none. I believe that it was an excuse to move me from my room."

"Ah! that is suggestive. Now, on the other side of this narrow wing runs the corridor from which these three rooms open. There are windows in it, of course?"

"Yes, but very small ones. Too narrow for anyone to pass through."

"As you both locked your doors at night, your rooms were unapproachable from that side. Now, would you have the kindness to go into your room and bar your shutters?"

Miss Stoner did so, and Holmes, after a careful examination through the open window, endeavoured in every way to force the shutter open, but without success. There was no slit through which a knife could be passed to raise the bar. Then with his lens he tested the hinges, but they were of solid iron, built firmly into the massive masonry. "Hum!" said he, scratching his chin in some perplexity, "my theory certainly presents some difficulties. No one could pass these shutters if they were bolted. Well, we shall see if the inside throws any light upon the matter."

A small side door led into the whitewashed corridor from which the three bedrooms opened. Holmes refused to examine the third chamber, so we passed at once to the second, that in which Miss Stoner was now sleeping, and in which her sister had met with her fate. It was a homely little room, with a low ceiling and a gaping fireplace, after the fashion of old country-houses. A brown chest of drawers stood in one corner, a narrow white-counterpaned bed in another, and a dressing-table on the left-hand side of the window. These articles, with two small wicker-work chairs, made up all the furniture in the room save for a square of Wilton carpet in the centre. The boards round and the panelling of the walls were of brown, worm-eaten oak, so old and discoloured that it may have dated from the original building of the house. Holmes drew one of the chairs into a corner and sat silent, while his eyes travelled round and round and up and down, taking in every detail of the apartment.

"Where does that bell communicate with?" he asked at last, pointing to a thick bell-rope which hung down beside the bed, the tassel actually lying upon the pillow.

"It goes to the housekeeper's room."

"It looks newer than the other things?"

"Yes, it was only put there a couple of years ago."

"Your sister asked for it, I suppose?"

"No, I never heard of her using it. We used always to get what we wanted for ourselves."

"Indeed, it seemed unnecessary to put so nice a bell-pull there. You will excuse me for a few minutes while I satisfy myself as to this floor." He threw himself down upon his face with his lens in his hand and crawled swiftly backward and forward, examining minutely the cracks between the boards. Then he did the same with the wood-work with which the chamber was panelled. Finally he walked over to the bed and spent some time in staring at it and in running his eye up and down the wall. Finally he took the bell-rope in his hand and gave it a brisk tug.

"Why, it's a dummy," said he.

"Won't it ring?"

"No, it is not even attached to a wire. This is very interesting. You can see now that it is fastened to a hook just above where the little opening for the ventilator is."

"How very absurd! I never noticed that before."

"Very strange!" muttered Holmes, pulling at the rope. "There are one or two very singular points about this room. For example, what a fool a builder must be to open a ventilator into another room, when, with the same trouble, he might have communicated with the outside air!"

"That is also quite modern," said the lady.

"Done about the same time as the bell-rope?" remarked Holmes.

"Yes, there were several little changes carried out about that time."

"They seem to have been of a most interesting character—dummy bell-ropes, and ventilators which do not ventilate. With your permission, Miss Stoner, we shall now carry our researches into the inner apartment."

Dr. Grimesby Roylott's chamber was larger than that of his stepdaughter, but was as plainly furnished. A camp-bed, a small wooden shelf full of books, mostly of a technical character, an armchair beside the bed, a plain wooden chair against the wall, a round table, and a large iron safe were the principal things which met the eye. Holmes walked slowly round and examined each and all of them with the keenest interest.

"What's in here?" he asked, tapping the safe.

"My stepfather's business papers."

"Oh! you have seen inside, then?"

"Only once, some years ago. I remember that it was full of papers."

"There isn't a cat in it, for example?"

"No. What a strange idea!"

"Well, look at this!" He took up a small saucer of milk which stood on the top of it.

"No; we don't keep a cat. But there is a cheetah and a baboon."

"Ah, yes, of course! Well, a cheetah is just a big cat, and yet a saucer of milk does not go very far in satisfying its wants, I daresay. There is one point which I should wish to determine." He squatted down in front of the wooden chair and examined the seat of it with the greatest attention.

"Thank you. That is quite settled," said he, rising and putting his lens in his pocket. "Hello! Here is something interesting!"

The object which had caught his eye was a small dog lash hung on one corner of the bed. The lash, however, was curled upon itself and tied so as to make a loop of whipcord.

"What do you make of that, Watson?"

"It's a common enough lash. But I don't know why it should be tied."

"That is not quite so common, is it? Ah, me! it's a wicked world, and when a clever man turns his brains to crime it is the worst of all. I think that I have seen enough now, Miss Stoner, and with your permission we shall walk out upon the lawn."

I had never seen my friend's face so grim or his brow so dark as it was when we turned from the scene of this investigation. We had walked several times up and down the lawn, neither Miss Stoner nor myself liking to break in upon his thoughts before he roused himself from his reverie.

"It is very essential, Miss Stoner," said he, "that you should absolutely follow my advice in every respect."

"I shall most certainly do so."

"The matter is too serious for any hesitation. Your life may depend upon your compliance."

"I assure you that I am in your hands."

"In the first place, both my friend and I must spend the night in your room."

Both Miss Stoner and I gazed at him in astonishment.

"Yes, it must be so. Let me explain. I believe that that is the village inn over there?"

"Yes, that is the Crown."

"Very good. Your windows would be visible from there?"

"Certainly."

"You must confine yourself to your room, on pretence of a headache, when your stepfather comes back. Then when you hear him retire for the night, you must open the shutters of your window, undo the hasp, put your lamp there as a signal to us, and then withdraw quietly with everything which you are likely to want into the room which you used to occupy. I have no doubt that, in spite of the repairs, you could manage there for one night."

"Oh, yes, easily."

"The rest you will leave in our hands."

"But what will you do?"

"We shall spend the night in your room, and we shall investigate the cause of this noise which has disturbed you."

"I believe, Mr. Holmes, that you have already made up your mind," said Miss Stoner, laying her hand upon my companion's sleeve.

"Perhaps I have."

"Then, for pity's sake, tell me what was the cause of my sister's death."

"I should prefer to have clearer proofs before I speak."

"You can at least tell me whether my own thought is correct, and if she died from some sudden fright."

"No, I do not think so. I think that there was probably some more tangible cause. And now, Miss Stoner, we must leave you, for if Dr. Roylott returned and saw us our journey would be in vain. Good-bye, and be brave, for if you will do what I have told you you may rest assured that we shall soon drive away the dangers that threaten you."

Sherlock Holmes and I had no difficulty in engaging a bedroom and sitting-room at the Crown Inn. They were on the upper floor, and from our window we could command a view of the avenue gate, and of the inhabited wing of Stoke Moran Manor House. At dusk we saw Dr. Grimesby Roylott drive past, his huge form looming up beside the little figure of the lad who drove him. The boy had some slight difficulty in undoing the heavy iron gates, and we heard the hoarse roar of the doctor's voice and saw the fury with which he shook his clinched fists at him. The trap drove on, and a few minutes later we saw a sudden light spring up among the trees as the lamp was lit in one of the sitting-rooms.

"Do you know, Watson," said Holmes as we sat together in the gathering darkness, "I have really some scruples as to taking you to-night. There is a distinct element of danger."

"Can I be of assistance?"

"Your presence might be invaluable."

"Then I shall certainly come."

"It is very kind of you."

"You speak of danger. You have evidently seen more in these rooms than was visible to me."

"No, but I fancy that I may have deduced a little more. I imagine that you saw all that I did."

"I saw nothing remarkable save the bell-rope, and what purpose that could answer I confess is more than I can imagine."

"You saw the ventilator, too?"

"Yes, but I do not think that it is such a very unusual thing to have a small opening between two rooms. It was so small that a rat could hardly pass through."

"I knew that we should find a ventilator before ever we came to Stoke Moran."

"My dear Holmes!"

"Oh, yes, I did. You remember in her statement she said that her sister could smell Dr. Roylott's cigar. Now, of course that suggested at once that there must be a communication between the two rooms. It could only be a small one, or it would have been remarked upon at the coroner's inquiry. I deduced a ventilator."

"But what harm can there be in that?"

"Well, there is at least a curious coincidence of dates. A ventilator is made, a cord is hung, and a lady who sleeps in the bed dies. Does not that strike you?"

"I cannot as yet see any connection."

"Did you observe anything very peculiar about that bed?"

"No."

"It was clamped to the floor. Did you ever see a bed fastened like that before?"

"I cannot say that I have."

"The lady could not move her bed. It must always be in the same relative position to the ventilator and to the rope—or so we may call it, since it was clearly never meant for a bell-pull."

"Holmes," I cried, "I seem to see dimly what you are hinting at. We are only just in time to prevent some subtle and horrible crime."

"Subtle enough and horrible enough. When a doctor does go wrong he is the first of criminals. He has nerve and he has knowledge. Palmer and Pritchard were among the heads of their profession. This man strikes even deeper, but I think, Watson, that we shall be able to strike deeper still. But we shall have horrors enough before the night is over; for goodness' sake let us have a quiet pipe and turn our minds for a few hours to something more cheerful."

About nine o'clock the light among the trees was extinguished, and all was dark in the direction of the Manor House. Two hours passed slowly away, and then, suddenly, just at the stroke of eleven, a single bright light shone out right in front of us.

"That is our signal," said Holmes, springing to his feet; "it comes from the middle window."

As we passed out he exchanged a few words with the landlord, explaining that we were going on a late visit to an acquaintance, and that it was possible that we might spend the night there. A moment later we were out on the dark road, a chill wind blowing in our faces, and one yellow light twinkling in front of us through the gloom to guide us on our sombre errand.

There was little difficulty in entering the grounds, for unrepaired breaches gaped in the old park wall. Making our way among the trees, we reached the lawn, crossed it, and were about to enter through the window when out from a clump of laurel bushes there darted what seemed to be a hideous and distorted child, who threw itself upon the grass with writhing limbs and then ran swiftly across the lawn into the darkness.

"My God!" I whispered; "did you see it?"

Holmes was for the moment as startled as I. His hand closed like a vise upon my wrist in his agitation. Then he broke into a low laugh and put his lips to my ear.

"It is a nice household," he murmured. "That is the baboon."

I had forgotten the strange pets which the doctor affected. There was a cheetah, too; perhaps we might find it upon our shoulders at any moment. I confess that I felt easier in my mind when, after following Holmes's example and slipping off my shoes, I found myself inside the bedroom. My companion noiselessly closed the shutters, moved the lamp onto the table, and cast his eyes round the room. All was as we had seen it in the daytime. Then creeping up to me and making a trumpet of his hand, he whispered into my ear again so gently that it was all that I could do to distinguish the words:

"The least sound would be fatal to our plans."

I nodded to show that I had heard.

"We must sit without light. He would see it through the ventilator."

I nodded again.

"Do not go asleep; your very life may depend upon it. Have your pistol ready in case we should need it. I will sit on the side of the bed, and you in that chair."

I took out my revolver and laid it on the corner of the table.

Holmes had brought up a long thin cane, and this he placed upon the bed beside him. By it he laid the box of matches and the stump of a candle. Then he turned down the lamp, and we were left in darkness.

How shall I ever forget that dreadful vigil? I could not hear a sound, not even the drawing of a breath, and yet I knew that my companion sat open-eyed, within a few feet of me, in the same state of nervous tension in which I was myself. The shutters cut off the least ray of light, and we waited in absolute darkness. From outside came the occasional cry of a night-bird, and once at our very window a long drawn catlike whine, which told us that the cheetah was indeed at liberty. Far away we could hear the deep tones of the parish clock, which boomed out every quarter of an hour. How long they seemed, those quarters! Twelve struck, and one and two and three, and still we sat waiting silently for whatever might befall.

Suddenly there was the momentary gleam of a light up in the direction of the ventilator, which vanished immediately, but was succeeded by a strong smell of burning oil and heated metal. Someone in the next room had lit a dark-lantern. I heard a gentle sound of movement, and then all was silent once more, though the smell grew stronger. For half an hour I sat with straining ears. Then suddenly another sound became audible—a very gentle, soothing sound, like that of a small jet of steam escaping continually from a kettle. The instant that we heard it, Holmes sprang from the bed, struck a match, and lashed furiously with his cane at the bell-pull.

"You see it, Watson?" he yelled. "You see it?"

But I saw nothing. At the moment when Holmes struck the light I heard a low, clear whistle, but the sudden glare flashing into my weary eyes made it impossible for me to tell what it was at which my friend lashed so savagely. I could, however, see that his face was deadly pale and filled with horror and loathing.

He had ceased to strike and was gazing up at the ventilator when suddenly there broke from the silence of the night the most horrible cry to which I have ever listened. It swelled up louder and louder, a hoarse yell of pain and fear and anger all mingled in the one dreadful shriek. They say that away down in the village, and even in the distant parsonage, that cry raised the sleepers from their beds. It struck cold to our hearts, and I stood gazing at Holmes, and he at me, until the last echoes of it had died away into the silence from which it rose.

"What can it mean?" I gasped.

"It means that it is all over," Holmes answered. "And perhaps, after all, it is for the best. Take your pistol, and we will enter Dr. Roylott's room."

With a grave face he lit the lamp and led the way down the corridor. Twice he struck at the chamber door without any reply from within. Then he turned the handle and entered, I at his heels, with the cocked pistol in my hand.

It was a singular sight which met our eyes. On the table stood a dark-lantern with the shutter half open, throwing a brilliant beam of light upon the iron safe, the door of which was ajar. Beside this table, on the wooden chair, sat Dr. Grimesby Roylott, clad in a long gray dressing-gown, his bare ankles protruding beneath, and his feet thrust into red heelless Turkish slippers. Across his lap lay the short stock with the long lash which we had noticed during the day. His chin was cocked upward and his eyes were fixed in a dreadful, rigid stare at the corner of the ceiling. Round his brow he had a peculiar yellow band, with brownish speckles, which seemed to be bound tightly round his head. As we entered he made neither sound nor motion.

"The band! the speckled band!" whispered Holmes.

I took a step forward. In an instant his strange headgear began to move, and there reared itself from among his hair the squat diamond-shaped head and puffed neck of a loathsome serpent.

"It is a swamp adder!" cried Holmes; "the deadliest snake in India. He had died within ten seconds of being bitten. Violence does, in truth, recoil upon the violent, and the schemer falls into the pit which he digs for another. Let us thrust this creature back into its den, and we can then remove Miss Stoner to some place of shelter and let the county police know what has happened."

As he spoke he drew the dog-whip swiftly from the dead man's lap, and throwing the noose round the reptile's neck he drew it from its horrid perch and, carrying it at arm's length, threw it into the iron safe, which he closed upon it.

Such are the true facts of the death of Dr. Grimesby Roylott, of Stoke Moran. It is not necessary that I should prolong a narrative which has already run to too great a length by telling how we broke the sad news to the terrified girl, how we conveyed her by the morning train to the care of her good aunt at Harrow, of how the slow process of official inquiry came to the conclusion that the doctor met his fate while indiscreetly playing with a dangerous pet. The little which I had yet to learn of the case was told me by Sherlock Holmes as we travelled back next day.

"I had," said he, "come to an entirely erroneous conclusion which shows, my dear Watson, how dangerous it always is to reason from insufficient data. The presence of the gypsies, and the use of the word 'band,' which was used by the poor girl, no doubt to explain the appearance which she had caught a hurried glimpse of by the light of her match, were sufficient to put me upon an entirely wrong scent. I can only claim the merit that I instantly reconsidered my position when, however, it became clear to me that whatever danger threatened an occupant of the room could not come either from the window or the door. My attention was speedily drawn, as I have already remarked to you, to this ventilator, and to the bell-rope which hung down to the bed. The discovery that this was a dummy, and that the bed was clamped to the floor, instantly gave rise to the suspicion that the rope was there as a bridge for something passing through the hole and coming to the bed. The idea of a snake instantly occurred to me, and when I coupled it with my knowledge that the doctor was furnished with a supply of creatures from India, I felt that I was probably on the right track. The idea of using a form of poison which could not possibly be discovered by any chemical test was just such a one as would occur to a clever and ruthless man who had had an Eastern training. The rapidity with which such a poison would take effect would also, from his point of view, be an advantage. It would be a sharp-eyed coroner, indeed, who could distinguish the two little dark punctures which would show where the poison fangs had done their work. Then I thought of the whistle. Of course he must recall the snake before the morning light revealed it to the victim. He had trained it, probably by the use of the milk which we saw, to return to him when summoned. He would put it through this ventilator at the hour that he thought best, with the certainty that it would crawl down the rope and land on the bed. It might or might not bite the occupant, perhaps she might escape every night for a week, but sooner or later she must fall a victim.

"I had come to these conclusions before ever I had entered his room. An inspection of his chair showed me that he had been in the habit of standing on it, which of course would be necessary in order that he should reach the ventilator. The sight of the safe, the saucer of milk, and the loop of whipcord were enough to finally dispel any doubts which may have remained. The metallic clang heard by Miss Stoner was obviously caused by her step-father hastily closing the door of his safe upon its terrible occupant. Having once made up my mind, you know the steps which I took in order to put the matter to the proof. I heard the creature hiss as I have no doubt that you did also, and I instantly lit the light and attacked it."

"With the result of driving it through the ventilator."

"And also with the result of causing it to turn upon its master at the other side. Some of the blows of my cane came home and roused its snakish temper, so that it flew upon the first person it saw. In this way I am no doubt indirectly responsible for Dr. Grimesby Roylott's death, and I cannot say that it is likely to weigh very heavily upon my conscience."

THE ADVENTURE OF THE ENGINEER'S THUMB

OF ALL THE problems which have been submitted to my friend, Mr. Sherlock Holmes, for solution during the years of our intimacy, there were only two which I was the means of introducing to his notice—that of Mr. Hatherley's thumb, and that of Colonel Warburton's madness. Of these the latter may have afforded a finer field for an acute and original observer, but the other was so strange in its inception and so dramatic in its details that it may be the more worthy of being placed upon record, even if it gave my friend fewer openings for those deductive methods of reasoning by which he achieved such remarkable results. The story has, I believe, been told more than once in the newspapers, but, like all such narratives, its effect is much less striking when set forth *en bloc* in a single half-column of print than when the facts slowly evolve before your own eyes, and the mystery clears gradually away as each new discovery furnishes a step which leads on to the complete truth. At the time the circumstances made a deep impression upon me, and the lapse of two years has hardly served to weaken the effect.

It was in the summer of '89, not long after my marriage, that the events occurred which I am now about to summarize. I had returned to civil practice and had finally abandoned Holmes in his Baker Street rooms, although I continually visited him and occasionally even persuaded him to forgo his Bohemian habits so far as to come and visit us. My practice had steadily increased, and as I happened to live at no very great distance from Paddington Station, I got a few patients from among the officials. One of these, whom I had cured of a painful and lingering disease, was never weary of advertising my virtues and of endeavouring to send me on every sufferer over whom he might have any influence.

One morning, at a little before seven o'clock, I was awakened by the maid tapping at the door to announce that two men had come from Paddington and were waiting in the consulting-room. I dressed hurriedly, for I knew by experience that railway cases were seldom trivial, and hastened downstairs. As I descended, my old ally, the guard, came out of the room and closed the door tightly behind him.

"I've got him here," he whispered, jerking his thumb over his shoulder; "he's all right."

"What is it, then?" I asked, for his manner suggested that it was some strange creature which he had caged up in my room.

"It's a new patient," he whispered. "I thought I'd bring him round myself; then he couldn't slip away. There he is, all safe and sound. I must go now, Doctor; I have my dooties, just the same as you." And off he went, this trusty tout, without even giving me time to thank him.

I entered my consulting-room and found a gentleman seated by the table. He was quietly dressed in a suit of heather tweed, with a soft cloth cap which he had laid down upon my books. Round one of his hands he had a handkerchief wrapped, which was mottled all over with bloodstains. He was young, not more than five-and-twenty, I should say, with a strong, masculine face; but he was exceedingly pale and gave me the impression of a man who was suffering from strong agitation, which it took all his strength of mind to control.

"I am sorry to knock you up so early, Doctor," said he, "but I have had a very serious accident during the night. I came in by train this morning, and on inquiring at Paddington as to where I might find a doctor, a worthy fellow very kindly escorted me here. I gave the maid a card, but I see that she has left it upon the side-table."

I took it up and glanced at it. "Mr. Victor Hatherley, hydraulic engineer, 16A, Victoria Street (3rd floor)." That was the name, style, and abode of my morning visitor. "I regret that I have kept you waiting," said I, sitting down in my library-chair. "You are fresh from a night journey, I understand, which is in itself a monotonous occupation."

"Oh, my night could not be called monotonous," said he, and laughed. He laughed very heartily, with a high, ringing note, leaning back in his chair and shaking his sides. All my medical instincts rose up against that laugh.

"Stop it!" I cried; "pull yourself together!" and I poured out some water from a carafe.

It was useless, however. He was off in one of those hysterical outbursts which come upon a strong nature when some great crisis is over and gone. Presently he came to himself once more, very weary and pale-looking.

"I have been making a fool of myself," he gasped.

"Not at all. Drink this." I dashed some brandy into the water, and the colour began to come back to his bloodless cheeks.

"That's better!" said he. "And now, Doctor, perhaps you would kindly attend to my thumb, or rather to the place where my thumb used to be."

He unwound the handkerchief and held out his hand. It gave even my hardened nerves a shudder to look at it. There were four protruding fingers and a horrid red, spongy surface where the thumb should have been. It had been hacked or torn right out from the roots.

"Good heavens!" I cried, "this is a terrible injury. It must have bled considerably."

"Yes, it did. I fainted when it was done, and I think that I must have been senseless for a long time. When I came to I found that it was still bleeding, so I tied one end of my handkerchief very tightly round the wrist and braced it up with a twig."

"Excellent! You should have been a surgeon."

"It is a question of hydraulics, you see, and came within my own province."

"This has been done," said I, examining the wound, "by a very heavy and sharp instrument."

"A thing like a cleaver," said he.

"An accident, I presume?"

"By no means."

"What! a murderous attack?"

"Very murderous indeed."

"You horrify me."

I sponged the wound, cleaned it, dressed it, and finally covered it over with cotton wadding and carbolized bandages. He lay back without wincing, though he bit his lip from time to time.

"How is that?" I asked when I had finished.

"Capital! Between your brandy and your bandage, I feel a new man. I was very weak, but I have had a good deal to go through."

"Perhaps you had better not speak of the matter. It is evidently trying to your nerves."

"Oh, no, not now. I shall have to tell my tale to the police; but, between ourselves, if it were not for the convincing evidence of this wound of mine, I should be surprised if they believed my statement; for it is a very extraordinary one, and I have not much in the way of proof with which to back it up; and, even if they believe me, the clues which I can give them are so vague that it is a question whether justice will be done."

"Ha!" cried I, "if it is anything in the nature of a problem which you desire to see solved, I should strongly recommend you to come to my friend, Mr. Sherlock Holmes, before you go to the official police."

"Oh, I have heard of that fellow," answered my visitor, "and I should be very glad if he would take the matter up, though of course I must use the official police as well. Would you give me an introduction to him?"

"I'll do better. I'll take you round to him myself."

"I should be immensely obliged to you."

"We'll call a cab and go together. We shall just be in time to have a little breakfast with him. Do you feel equal to it?"

"Yes; I shall not feel easy until I have told my story."

"Then my servant will call a cab, and I shall be with you in an instant." I rushed upstairs, explained the matter shortly to my wife, and in five minutes was inside a hansom, driving with my new acquaintance to Baker Street.

Sherlock Holmes was, as I expected, lounging about his sitting-room in his dressing-gown, reading the agony column of *The Times* and smoking his before-breakfast pipe, which was composed of all the plugs and dottles left from his smokes of the day before, all carefully dried and collected on the corner of the mantelpiece. He received us in his quietly genial fashion, ordered fresh rashers and eggs, and joined us in a hearty meal.

When it was concluded he settled our new acquaintance upon the sofa, placed a pillow beneath his head, and laid a glass of brandy and water within his reach.

"It is easy to see that your experience has been no common one, Mr. Hatherley," said he. "Pray, lie down there and make yourself absolutely at home. Tell us what you can, but stop when you are tired and keep up your strength with a little stimulant."

"Thank you," said my patient, "but I have felt another man since the doctor bandaged me, and I think that your breakfast has completed the cure. I shall take up as little of your valuable time as possible, so I shall start at once upon my peculiar experiences."

Holmes sat in his big armchair with the weary, heavy-lidded expression which veiled his keen and eager nature, while I sat opposite to him, and we listened in silence to the strange story which our visitor detailed to us.

"You must know," said he, "that I am an orphan and a bachelor, residing alone in lodgings in London. By profession I am a hydraulic engineer, and I have had considerable experience of my work during the seven years that I was apprenticed to Venner & Matheson, the well-known firm, of Greenwich. Two years ago, having served my time, and having also come into a fair sum of money through my poor father's death, I determined to start in business for myself and took professional chambers in Victoria Street.

"I suppose that everyone finds his first independent start in business a dreary experience. To me it has been exceptionally so. During two years I have had three consultations and one small job, and that is absolutely all that my profession has brought me. My gross takings amount to £27 10*s*. Every day, from nine in the morning until four in the afternoon, I waited in my little den, until at last my heart began to sink, and I came to believe that I should never have any practice at all.

"Yesterday, however, just as I was thinking of leaving the office, my clerk entered to say there was a gentleman waiting who wished to see me upon business. He brought up a card, too, with the name of 'Colonel Lysander Stark' engraved upon it. Close at his heels came the colonel himself, a man rather over the middle size, but of an exceeding thinness. I do not think that I have ever seen so thin a man. His whole face sharpened away into nose and chin, and the skin of his cheeks was drawn quite tense over his outstanding bones. Yet this emaciation seemed to be his natural habit, and due to no disease, for his eye was bright, his step brisk, and his bearing assured. He was plainly but neatly dressed, and his age, I should judge, would be nearer forty than thirty.

" 'Mr. Hatherley?' said he, with something of a German accent. 'You have been recommended to me, Mr. Hatherley, as being a man who is not only proficient in his profession but is also discreet and capable of preserving a secret.'

"I bowed, feeling as flattered as any young man would at such an address. 'May I ask who it was who gave me so good a character?'

" 'Well, perhaps it is better that I should not tell you that just at this moment. I have it from the same source that you are both an orphan and a bachelor and are residing alone in London.'

" 'That is quite correct,' I answered; 'but you will excuse me if I say that I cannot see how all this bears upon my professional qualifications. I understand that it was on a professional matter that you wished to speak to me?'

" 'Undoubtedly so. But you will find that all I say is really to the point. I have a professional commission for you, but absolute secrecy is quite essential—*absolute* secrecy, you understand, and of course we may expect that more from a man who is alone than from one who lives in the bosom of his family.'

" 'If I promise to keep a secret,' said I, 'you may absolutely depend upon my doing so.'

"He looked very hard at me as I spoke, and it seemed to me that I had never seen so suspicious and questioning an eye.

" 'Do you promise, then?' said he at last.

" 'Yes, I promise.'

" 'Absolute and complete silence before, during, and after? No reference to the matter at all, either in word or writing?'

" 'I have already given you my word.'

" 'Very good.' He suddenly sprang up, and darting like lightning across the room he flung open the door. The passage outside was empty.

" 'That's all right,' said he, coming back. 'I know the clerks are sometimes curious as to their master's affairs. Now we can talk in safety.' He drew up his chair very close to mine and began to stare at me again with the same questioning and thoughtful look.

"A feeling of repulsion, and of something akin to fear had begun to rise within me at the strange antics of this fleshless man. Even my dread of losing a client could not restrain me from showing my impatience.

" 'I beg that you will state your business, sir,' said I; 'my time is of value.' Heaven forgive me for that last sentence, but the words came to my lips.

" 'How would fifty guineas for a night's work suit you?' he asked.

" 'Most admirably.'

" 'I say a night's work, but an hour's would be nearer the mark. I simply want your opinion about a hydraulic stamping machine which has got out of gear. If you show us what is wrong we shall soon set it right ourselves. What do you think of such a commission as that?'

" 'The work appears to be light and the pay munificent.'

" 'Precisely so. We shall want you to come to-night by the last train.'

" 'Where to?'

" 'To Eyford, in Berkshire. It is a little place near the borders of Oxfordshire, and within seven miles of Reading. There is a train from Paddington which would bring you there at about 11:15.'

" 'Very good.'

" 'I shall come down in a carriage to meet you.'

" 'There is a drive, then?'

" 'Yes, our little place is quite out in the country. It is a good seven miles from Eyford Station.'

" 'Then we can hardly get there before midnight. I suppose there would be no chance of a train back. I should be compelled to stop the night.'

" 'Yes, we could easily give you a shake-down.'

" 'That is very awkward. Could I not come at some more convenient hour?'

" 'We have judged it best that you should come late. It is to recompense you for any inconvenience that we are paying to you, a young and unknown man, a fee which would buy an opinion from the very heads of your profession. Still, of course, if you would like to draw out of the business, there is plenty of time to do so.'

"I thought of the fifty guineas, and of how very useful they would be to me. 'Not at all,' said I, 'I shall be very happy to accommodate myself to your wishes. I should like, however, to understand a little more clearly what it is that you wish me to do.'

" 'Quite so. It is very natural that the pledge of secrecy which we have exacted from you should have aroused your curiosity. I have no wish to commit you to anything without your having it all laid before you. I suppose that we are absolutely safe from eavesdroppers?'

" 'Entirely.'

" 'Then the matter stands thus. You are probably aware that fuller's-earth is a valuable product, and that it is only found in one or two places in England?'

" 'I have heard so.'

" 'Some little time ago I bought a small place—a very small place—within ten miles of Reading. I was fortunate enough to discover that there was a deposit of fuller's-earth in one of my fields. On examining it, however, I found that this deposit was a comparatively small one, and that it formed a link between two very much larger ones upon the right and left—both of them, however, in the grounds of my neighbours. These good people were absolutely ignorant that their land contained that which was quite as valuable as a gold-mine. Naturally, it was to my interest to buy their land before they discovered its true value, but unfortunately I had no capital by which I could do this. I took a few of my friends into the secret, however, and they suggested that we should quietly and secretly work our own little deposit, and that in this way we should earn the money which would enable us to buy the neighbouring fields. This we have now been doing for some time, and in order to help us in our operations we erected a hydraulic press. This press, as I have already explained, has got out of order, and we wish your advice upon the subject. We guard our secret very jealously, however, and if it once became known that we had hydraulic engineers coming to our little house, it would soon rouse inquiry, and then, if the facts came out, it would be good-bye to any chance of getting these fields and carrying out our plans. That is why I have made you promise me that you will not tell a human being that you are going to Eyford to-night. I hope that I make it all plain?'

" 'I quite follow you,' said I. 'The only point which I could not quite understand was what use you could make of a hydraulic press in excavating fuller's-earth, which, as I understand, is dug out like gravel from a pit.'

" 'Ah!' said he carelessly, 'we have our own process. We compress the earth into bricks, so as to remove them without revealing what they are. But that is a mere detail. I have taken you fully into my confidence now, Mr. Hatherley, and I have shown you how I trust you.' He rose as he spoke. 'I shall expect you, then, at Eyford at 11:15.'

" 'I shall certainly be there.'

" 'And not a word to a soul.' He looked at me with a last, long, questioning gaze, and then, pressing my hand in a cold, dank grasp, he hurried from the room.

"Well, when I came to think it all over in cool blood I was very much astonished, as you may both think, at this sudden commission which had been intrusted to me. On the one hand, of course, I was glad, for the fee was at least tenfold what I should have asked had I set a price upon my own services, and it was possible that this order might lead to other ones. On the other hand, the face and manner of my patron had made an unpleasant impression upon me, and I could not think that his explanation of the fuller's-earth was sufficient to explain the necessity for my coming at midnight, and his extreme anxiety lest I should tell anyone of my errand. However, I threw all fears to the winds, ate a hearty supper, drove to Paddington, and started off, having obeyed to the letter the injunction as to holding my tongue.

"At Reading I had to change not only my carriage but my station. However, I was in time for the last train to Eyford, and I reached the little dim-lit station after eleven o'clock. I was the only passenger who got out there, and there was no one upon the platform save a single sleepy porter with a lantern. As I passed out through the wicket gate, however, I found my acquaintance of the morning waiting in the shadow upon the other side. Without a word he grasped my arm and hurried me into a carriage, the door of which was standing open. He drew up the windows on either side, tapped on the wood-work, and away we went as fast as the horse could go."

"One horse?" interjected Holmes.

"Yes, only one."

"Did you observe the colour?"

"Yes, I saw it by the side-lights when I was stepping into the carriage. It was a chestnut."

"Tired-looking or fresh?"

"Oh, fresh and glossy."

"Thank you. I am sorry to have interrupted you. Pray continue your most interesting statement."

"Away we went then, and we drove for at least an hour. Colonel Lysander Stark had said that it was only seven miles, but I should think, from the rate that we seemed to go, and from the time that we took, that it must have been nearer twelve. He sat at my side in silence all the time, and I was aware, more than once when I glanced in his direction, that he was looking at me with great intensity. The country roads seem to be not very good in that part of the world, for we lurched and jolted terribly. I tried to look out of the windows to see something of where we were, but they were made of frosted glass, and I could make out nothing save the occasional bright blur of a passing light. Now and then I hazarded some remark to break the monotony of the journey, but the colonel answered only in monosyllables, and the conversation soon flagged. At last, however, the bumping of the road was exchanged for the crisp smoothness of a gravel-drive, and the carriage came to a stand. Colonel Lysander Stark sprang out, and, as I followed after him, pulled me swiftly into a porch which gaped in front of us. We stepped, as it were, right out of the carriage and into the hall, so that I failed to catch the most fleeting glance of the front of the house. The instant that I had crossed the threshold the door slammed heavily behind us, and I heard faintly the rattle of the wheels as the carriage drove away.

"It was pitch dark inside the house, and the colonel fumbled about looking for matches and muttering under his breath. Suddenly a door opened at the other end of the passage, and a long, golden bar of light shot out in our direction. It grew broader, and a woman appeared with a lamp in her hand, which she held above her head, pushing her face forward and peering at us. I could see that she was pretty, and from the gloss with which the light shone upon her dark dress I knew that it was a rich material. She spoke a few words in a foreign tongue in a tone as though asking a question, and when my companion answered in a gruff monosyllable she gave such a start that the lamp nearly fell from her hand. Colonel Stark went up to her, whispered something in her ear, and then, pushing her back into the room from whence she had come, he walked towards me again with the lamp in his hand.

" 'Perhaps you will have the kindness to wait in this room for a few minutes,' said he, throwing open another door. It was a quiet, little, plainly furnished room, with a round table in the centre, on which several German books were scattered. Colonel Stark laid down the lamp on the top of a harmonium beside the door. 'I shall not keep you waiting an instant,' said he, and vanished into the darkness.

"I glanced at the books upon the table, and in spite of my ignorance of German I could see that two of them were treatises on science, the others being volumes of poetry. Then I walked across to the window, hoping that I might catch some glimpse of the country-side, but an oak shutter, heavily barred, was folded across it. It was a wonderfully silent house. There was an old clock ticking loudly somewhere in the passage, but otherwise everything was deadly still. A vague feeling of uneasiness began to steal over me. Who were these German people, and what were they doing living in this strange, out-of-the-way place? And where was the place? I was ten miles or so from Eyford, that was all I knew, but whether north, south, east, or west I had no idea. For that matter, Reading, and possibly other large towns, were within that radius, so the place might not be so secluded, after all. Yet it was quite certain, from the absolute stillness, that we were in the country. I paced up and down the room, humming a tune under my breath to keep up my spirits and feeling that I was thoroughly earning my fifty-guinea fee.

"Suddenly, without any preliminary sound in the midst of the utter stillness, the door of my room swung slowly open. The woman was standing in the aperture, the darkness of the hall behind her, the yellow light from the lamp beating upon her eager and beautiful face. I could see at a glance that she was sick with fear, and the sight sent a chill to my own heart. She held up one shaking finger to warn me to be silent, and she shot a few whispered words of broken English at me, her eyes glancing back, like those of a frightened horse, into the gloom behind her.

" 'I would go,' said she, trying hard, as it seemed to me, to speak calmly; 'I would go. I should not stay here. There is no good for you to do.'

" 'But, madam,' said I, 'I have not yet done what I came for. I cannot possibly leave until I have seen the machine.'

" 'It is not worth your while to wait,' she went on. 'You can pass through the door; no one hinders.' And then, seeing that I smiled and shook my head, she suddenly threw aside her constraint and made a step forward, with her hands wrung together. 'For the love of Heaven!' she whispered, 'get away from here before it is too late!'

"But I am somewhat headstrong by nature, and the more ready to engage in an affair when there is some obstacle in the way. I thought of my fifty-guinea fee, of my wearisome journey, and of the unpleasant night which seemed to be before me. Was it all to go for nothing? Why should I slink away without having carried out my commission, and without the payment which was my due? This woman might, for all I knew, be a monomaniac. With a stout bearing, therefore, though her manner had shaken me more than I cared to confess, I still shook my head and declared my intention of remaining where I was. She was about to renew her entreaties when a door slammed overhead, and the sound of several footsteps was heard upon the stairs. She listened for an instant, threw up her hands with a despairing gesture, and vanished as suddenly and as noiselessly as she had come.

"The newcomers were Colonel Lysander Stark and a short thick man with a chinchilla beard growing out of the creases of his double chin, who was introduced to me as Mr. Ferguson.

" 'This is my secretary and manager,' said the colonel. 'By the way, I was under the impression that I left this door shut just now. I fear that you have felt the draught.'

" 'On the contrary,' said I, 'I opened the door myself because I felt the room to be a little close.'

"He shot one of his suspicious looks at me. 'Perhaps we had better proceed to business, then,' said he. 'Mr. Ferguson and I will take you up to see the machine.'

" 'I had better put my hat on, I suppose.'

" 'Oh, no, it is in the house.'

" 'What, you dig fuller's-earth in the house?'

" 'No, no. This is only where we compress it. But never mind that. All we wish you to do is to examine the machine and to let us know what is wrong with it.'

"We went upstairs together, the colonel first with the lamp, the fat manager and I behind him. It was a labyrinth of an old house, with corridors, passages, narrow winding staircases, and little low doors, the thresholds of which were hollowed out by the generations who had crossed them. There were no carpets and no signs of any furniture above the ground floor, while the plaster was peeling off the walls, and the damp was breaking through in green, unhealthy blotches. I tried to put on as unconcerned an air as possible, but I had not forgotten the warnings of the lady, even though I disregarded them, and I kept a keen eye upon my two companions. Ferguson appeared to be a morose and silent man, but I could see from the little that he said that he was at least a fellow-countryman.

"Colonel Lysander Stark stopped at last before a low door, which he unlocked. Within was a small, square room, in which the three of us could hardly get at one time. Ferguson remained outside, and the colonel ushered me in.

" 'We are now,' said he, 'actually within the hydraulic press, and it would be a particularly unpleasant thing for us if anyone were to turn it on. The ceiling of this small chamber is really the end of the descending piston, and it comes down with the force of many tons upon this metal floor. There are small lateral columns of water outside which receive the force, and which transmit and multiply it in the manner which is familiar to you. The machine goes readily enough, but there is some stiffness in the working of it, and it has lost a little of its force. Perhaps you will have the goodness to look it over and show us how we can set it right.'

"I took the lamp from him, and I examined the machine very thoroughly. It was indeed a gigantic one, and capable of exercising enormous pressure. When I passed outside, however, and pressed down the levers which controlled it, I knew at once by the whishing sound that there was a slight leakage, which allowed a regurgitation of water through one of the side cylinders. An examination showed that one of the india-rubber bands which was round the head of a driving-rod had shrunk so as not quite to fill the socket along which it worked. This was clearly the cause of the loss of power, and I pointed it out to my companions, who followed my remarks very carefully and asked several practical questions as to how they should proceed to set it right. When I had made it clear to them, I returned to the main chamber of the machine and took a good look at it to satisfy my own curiosity. It was obvious at a glance that the story of the fuller's-earth was the merest fabrication, for it would be absurd to suppose that so powerful an engine could be designed for so inadequate a purpose. The walls were of wood, but the floor consisted of a large iron trough, and when I came to examine it I could see a crust of metallic deposit all over it. I had stopped and was scraping at this to see exactly what it was when I heard a muttered exclamation in German and saw the cadaverous face of the colonel looking down at me.

" 'What are you doing there?' he asked.

"I felt angry at having been tricked by so elaborate a story as that which he had told me. 'I was admiring your fuller's-earth,' said I; 'I think that I should be better able to advise you as to your machine if I knew what the exact purpose was for which it was used.'

"The instant that I uttered the words I regretted the rashness of my speech. His face set hard, and a baleful light sprang up in his gray eyes.

" 'Very well,' said he, 'you shall know all about the machine.' He took a step backward, slammed the little door, and turned the key in the lock. I rushed towards it and pulled at the handle, but it was quite secure, and did not give in the least to my kicks and shoves. 'Hello!' I yelled. 'Hello! Colonel! Let me out!'

"And then suddenly in the silence I heard a sound which sent my heart into my mouth. It was the clank of the levers and the swish of the leaking cylinder. He had set the engine at work. The lamp still stood upon the floor where I had placed it when examining the trough. By its light I saw that the black ceiling was coming down upon me, slowly, jerkily, but, as none knew better than myself, with a force which must within a minute grind me to a shapeless pulp. I threw myself, screaming, against the door, and dragged with my nails at the lock. I implored the colonel to let me out, but the remorseless clanking of the levers drowned my cries. The ceiling was only a foot or two above my head, and with my hand upraised I could feel its hard, rough surface. Then it flashed through my mind that the pain of my death would depend very much upon the position in which I met it. If I lay on my face the weight would come upon my spine, and I shuddered to think of that dreadful snap. Easier the other way, perhaps; and yet, had I the nerve to lie and look up at that deadly black shadow wavering down upon me? Already I was unable to stand erect, when my eye caught something which brought a gush of hope back to my heart.

"I have said that though the floor and ceiling were of iron, the walls were of wood. As I gave a last hurried glance around, I saw a thin line of yellow light between two of the boards, which broadened and broadened as a small panel was pushed backward. For an instant I could hardly believe that here was indeed a door which led away from death. The next instant I threw myself through, and lay half-fainting upon the other side. The panel had closed again behind me, but the crash of the lamp, and a few moments afterwards the clang of the two slabs of metal, told me how narrow had been my escape.

"I was recalled to myself by a frantic plucking at my wrist, and I found myself lying upon the stone floor of a narrow corridor, while a woman bent over me and tugged at me with her left hand, while she held a candle in her right. It was the same good friend whose warning I had so foolishly rejected.

" 'Good! come!' she cried breathlessly. 'They will be here in a moment. They will see that you are not there. Oh, do not waste the so-precious time, but come!'

"This time, at least, I did not scorn her advice. I staggered to my feet and ran with her along the corridor and down a winding stair. The latter led to another broad passage, and just as we reached it we heard the sound of running feet and the shouting of two voices, one answering the other from the floor on which we were and from the one beneath. My guide stopped and looked about her like one who is at her wit's end. Then she threw open a door which led into a bedroom, through the window of which the moon was shining brightly.

" 'It is your only chance,' said she. 'It is high, but it may be that you can jump it.'

"As she spoke a light sprang into view at the further end of the passage, and I saw the lean figure of Colonel Lysander Stark rushing forward with a lantern in one hand and a weapon like a butcher's cleaver in the other. I rushed across the bedroom, flung open the window, and looked out. How quiet and sweet and wholesome the garden looked in the moonlight, and it could not be more than thirty feet down. I clambered out upon the sill, but I hesitated to jump until I should have heard what passed between my saviour and the ruffian who pursued me. If she were ill-used, then at any risks I was determined to go back to her assistance. The thought had hardly flashed through my mind before he was at the door, pushing his way past her; but she threw her arms round him and tried to hold him back.

" 'Fritz! Fritz!' she cried in English, 'remember your promise after the last time. You said it should not be again. He will be silent! Oh, he will be silent!'

" 'You are mad, Elise!' he shouted, struggling to break away from her. 'You will be the ruin of us. He has seen too much. Let me pass, I say!' He dashed her to one side, and, rushing to the window, cut at me with his heavy weapon. I had let myself go, and was hanging by the hands to the sill, when his blow fell. I was conscious of a dull pain, my grip loosened, and I fell into the garden below.

"I was shaken but not hurt by the fall; so I picked myself up and rushed off among the bushes as hard as I could run, for I understood that I was far from being out of danger yet. Suddenly, however, as I ran, a deadly dizziness and sickness came over me. I glanced down at my hand, which was throbbing painfully, and then, for the first time, saw that my thumb had been cut off and that the blood was pouring from my wound. I endeavoured to tie my handkerchief round it, but there came a sudden buzzing in my ears, and next moment I fell in a dead faint among the rose-bushes.

"How long I remained unconscious I cannot tell. It must have been a very long time, for the moon had sunk, and a bright morning was breaking when I came to myself. My clothes were all sodden with dew, and my coat-sleeve was drenched with blood from my wounded thumb. The smarting of it recalled in an instant all the particulars of my night's adventure, and I sprang to my feet with the feeling that I might hardly yet be safe from my pursuers. But to my astonishment, when I came to look round me, neither house nor garden were to be seen. I had been lying in an angle of the hedge close by the highroad, and just a little lower down was a long building, which proved, upon my approaching it, to be the very station at which I had arrived upon the previous night. Were it not for the ugly wound upon my hand, all that had passed during those dreadful hours might have been an evil dream.

"Half dazed, I went into the station and asked about the morning train. There would be one to Reading in less than an hour. The same porter was on duty, I found, as had been there when I arrived. I inquired of him whether he had ever heard of Colonel Lysander Stark. The name was strange to him. Had he observed a carriage the night before waiting for me? No, he had not. Was there a police-station anywhere near? There was one about three miles off.

"It was too far for me to go, weak and ill as I was. I determined to wait until I got back to town before telling my story to the police. It was a little past six when I arrived, so I went first to have my wound dressed, and then the doctor was kind enough to bring me along here. I put the case into your hands and shall do exactly what you advise."

We both sat in silence for some little time after listening to this extraordinary narrative. Then Sherlock Holmes pulled down from the shelf one of the ponderous commonplace books in which he placed his cuttings.

"Here is an advertisement which will interest you," said he. "It appeared in all the papers about a year ago. Listen to this:

> "Lost, on the 9th inst., Mr. Jeremiah Hayling, aged twenty-six, a hydraulic engineer. Left his lodgings at ten o'clock at night, and has not been heard of since. Was dressed in—

etc., etc. Ha! That represents the last time that the colonel needed to have his machine overhauled, I fancy."

"Good heavens!" cried my patient. "Then that explains what the girl said."

"Undoubtedly. It is quite clear that the colonel was a cool and desperate man, who was absolutely determined that nothing should stand in the way of his little game, like those out-and-out pirates who will leave no survivor from a captured ship. Well, every moment now is precious, so if you feel equal to it we shall go down to Scotland Yard at once as a preliminary to starting for Eyford."

Some three hours or so afterwards we were all in the train together, bound from Reading to the little Berkshire village. There were Sherlock Holmes, the hydraulic engineer, Inspector Bradstreet, of Scotland Yard, a plain-clothes man, and myself. Bradstreet had spread an ordnance map of the county out upon the seat and was busy with his compasses drawing a circle with Eyford for its centre.

"There you are," said he. "That circle is drawn at a radius of ten miles from the village. The place we want must be somewhere near that line. You said ten miles, I think, sir."

"It was an hour's good drive."

"And you think that they brought you back all that way when you were unconscious?"

"They must have done so. I have a confused memory, too, of having been lifted and conveyed somewhere."

"What I cannot understand," said I, "is why they should have spared you when they found you lying fainting in the garden. Perhaps the villain was softened by the woman's entreaties."

"I hardly think that likely. I never saw a more inexorable face in my life."

"Oh, we shall soon clear up all that," said Bradstreet. "Well, I have drawn my circle, and I only wish I knew at what point upon it the folk that we are in search of are to be found."

"I think I could lay my finger on it," said Holmes quietly.

"Really, now!" cried the inspector, "you have formed your opinion! Come, now, we shall see who agrees with you. I say it is south, for the country is more deserted there."

"And I say east," said my patient.

"I am for west," remarked the plain-clothes man. "There are several quiet little villages up there."

"And I am for north," said I, "because there are no hills there, and our friend says that he did not notice the carriage go up any."

"Come," cried the inspector, laughing; "it's a very pretty diversity of opinion. We have boxed the compass among us. Who do you give your casting vote to?"

"You are all wrong."

"But we can't *all* be."

"Oh, yes, you can. This is my point." He placed his finger in the centre of the circle. "This is where we shall find them."

"But the twelve-mile drive?" gasped Hatherley.

"Six out and six back. Nothing simpler. You say yourself that the horse was fresh and glossy when you got in. How could it be that if it had gone twelve miles over heavy roads?"

"Indeed, it is a likely ruse enough," observed Bradstreet thoughtfully. "Of course there can be no doubt as to the nature of this gang."

"None at all," said Holmes. "They are coiners on a large

scale, and have used the machine to form the amalgam which has taken the place of silver."

"We have known for some time that a clever gang was at work," said the inspector. "They have been turning out half-crowns by the thousand. We even traced them as far as Reading, but could get no farther, for they had covered their traces in a way that showed that they were very old hands. But now, thanks to this lucky chance, I think that we have got them right enough."

But the inspector was mistaken, for those criminals were not destined to fall into the hands of justice. As we rolled into Eyford Station we saw a gigantic column of smoke which streamed up from behind a small clump of trees in the neighbourhood and hung like an immense ostrich feather over the landscape.

"A house on fire?" asked Bradstreet as the train steamed off again on its way.

"Yes, sir!" said the station-master.

"When did it break out?"

"I hear that it was during the night, sir, but it has got worse, and the whole place is in a blaze."

"Whose house is it?"

"Dr. Becher's."

"Tell me," broke in the engineer, "is Dr. Becher a German, very thin, with a long, sharp nose?"

The station-master laughed heartily. "No, sir, Dr. Becher is an Englishman, and there isn't a man in the parish who has a better-lined waistcoat. But he has a gentleman staying with him, a patient, as I understand, who is a foreigner, and he looks as if a little good Berkshire beef would do him no harm."

The station-master had not finished his speech before we were all hastening in the direction of the fire. The road topped a low hill, and there was a great widespread whitewashed building in front of us, spouting fire at every chink and window, while in the garden in front three fire-engines were vainly striving to keep the flames under.

"That's it!" cried Hatherley, in intense excitement. "There is the gravel-drive, and there are the rose-bushes where I lay. That second window is the one that I jumped from."

"Well, at least," said Holmes, "you have had your revenge upon them. There can be no question that it was your oil-lamp which, when it was crushed in the press, set fire to the wooden walls, though no doubt they were too excited in the chase after you to observe it at the time. Now keep your eyes open in this crowd for your friends of last night, though I very much fear that they are a good hundred miles off by now."

And Holmes's fears came to be realized, for from that day to this no word has ever been heard either of the beautiful woman, the sinister German, or the morose Englishman. Early that morning a peasant had met a cart containing several people and some very bulky boxes driving rapidly in the direction of Reading, but there all traces of the fugitives disappeared, and even Holmes's ingenuity failed ever to discover the least clue as to their whereabouts.

The firemen had been much perturbed at the strange arrangements which they had found within, and still more so by discovering a newly severed human thumb upon a window-sill of the second floor. About sunset, however, their efforts were at last successful, and they subdued the flames, but not before the roof had fallen in, and the whole place been reduced to such absolute ruin that, save some twisted cylinders and iron piping, not a trace remained of the machinery which had cost our unfortunate acquaintance so dearly. Large masses of nickel and of tin were discovered stored in an out-house, but no coins were to be found, which may have explained the presence of those bulky boxes which have been already referred to.

How our hydraulic engineer had been conveyed from the garden to the spot where he recovered his senses might have remained forever a mystery were it not for the soft mould, which told us a very plain tale. He had evidently been carried down by two persons, one of whom had remarkably small feet and the other unusually large ones. On the whole, it was most probable that the silent Englishman, being less bold or less murderous than his companion, had assisted the woman to bear the unconscious man out of the way of danger.

"Well," said our engineer ruefully as we took our seats to return once more to London, "it has been a pretty business for me! I have lost my thumb and I have lost a fifty-guinea fee, and what have I gained?"

"Experience," said Holmes, laughing. "Indirectly it may be of value, you know; you have only to put it into words to gain the reputation of being excellent company for the remainder of your existence."

The Adventure of the Noble Bachelor

The Lord St. Simon marriage, and its curious termination, have long ceased to be a subject of interest in those exalted circles in which the unfortunate bridegroom moves. Fresh scandals have eclipsed it, and their more piquant details have drawn the gossips away from this four-year-old drama. As I have reason to believe, however, that the full facts have never been revealed to the general public, and as my friend Sherlock Holmes had a considerable share in clearing the matter up, I feel that no memoir of him would be complete without some little sketch of this remarkable episode.

It was a few weeks before my own marriage, during the days when I was still sharing rooms with Holmes in Baker Street, that he came home from an afternoon stroll to find a letter on the table waiting for him. I had remained indoors all day, for the weather had taken a sudden turn to rain, with high autumnal winds, and the Jezail bullet which I had brought back in one of my limbs as a relic of my Afghan campaign throbbed with dull persistence. With my body in one easy-chair and my legs upon another, I had surrounded myself with a cloud of newspapers until at last, saturated with the news of the day, I tossed them all aside and lay listless, watching the huge crest and monogram upon the envelope upon the table and wondering lazily who my friend's noble correspondent could be.

"Here is a very fashionable epistle," I remarked as he entered. "Your morning letters, if I remember right, were from a fishmonger and a tide-waiter."

"Yes, my correspondence has certainly the charm of variety," he answered, smiling, "and the humbler are usually the more interesting. This looks like one of those unwelcome social summonses which call upon a man either to be bored or to lie."

He broke the seal and glanced over the contents.

"Oh, come, it may prove to be something of interest, after all."

"Not social, then?"

"No, distinctly professional."

"And from a noble client?"

"One of the highest in England."

"My dear fellow, I congratulate you."

"I assure you, Watson, without affectation, that the status of my client is a matter of less moment to me than the interest of his case. It is just possible, however, that that also may not be wanting in this new investigation. You have been reading the papers diligently of late, have you not?"

"It looks like it," said I ruefully, pointing to a huge bundle in the corner. "I have had nothing else to do."

"It is fortunate, for you will perhaps be able to post me up. I read nothing except the criminal news and the agony column. The latter is always instructive. But if you have followed recent events so closely you must have read about Lord St. Simon and his wedding?"

"Oh, yes, with the deepest interest."

"That is well. The letter which I hold in my hand is from Lord St. Simon. I will read it to you, and in return you must turn over these papers and let me have whatever bears upon the matter. This is what he says:

"MY DEAR MR. SHERLOCK HOLMES:

"Lord Backwater tells me that I may place implicit reliance upon your judgement and discretion. I have determined, therefore, to call upon you and to consult you in reference to the very painful event which has occurred in connection with my wedding. Mr. Lestrade, of Scotland Yard, is acting already in the matter, but he assures me that he sees no objection to your coöperation, and that he even thinks that it might be of some assistance. I will call at four o'clock in the afternoon, and, should you have any other engagement at that time, I hope that you will postpone it, as this matter is of paramount importance.

"Yours faithfully,

"ST. SIMON.

"It is dated from Grosvenor Mansions, written with a quill pen, and the noble lord has had the misfortune to get a smear of ink upon the outer side of his right little finger," remarked Holmes as he folded up the epistle.

"He says four o'clock. It is three now. He will be here in an hour."

"Then I have just time, with your assistance, to get clear upon the subject. Turn over those papers and arrange the extracts in their order of time, while I take a glance as to who our client is." He picked a red-covered volume from a line of books of reference beside the mantelpiece. "Here he is," said he, sitting down and flattening it out upon his knee. "Lord Robert Walsingham de Vere St. Simon, second son of the Duke of Balmoral. Hum! Arms: Azure, three caltrops in chief over a fess sable. Born in 1846. He's forty-one years of age, which is mature for marriage. Was Under-Secretary for the colonies in a late administration. The Duke, his father, was at one time Secretary for Foreign Affairs. They inherit Plantagenet blood by direct descent, and Tudor on the distaff side. Ha! Well, there is nothing very instructive in all this. I think that I must turn to you, Watson, for something more solid."

"I have very little difficulty in finding what I want," said I, "for the facts are quite recent, and the matter struck me as remarkable. I feared to refer them to you, however, as I knew that you had an inquiry on hand and that you disliked the intrusion of other matters."

"Oh, you mean the little problem of the Grosvenor Square furniture van. That is quite cleared up now—though, indeed, it was obvious from the first. Pray give me the results of your newspaper selections."

"Here is the first notice which I can find. It is in the personal column of the *Morning Post*, and dates, as you see, some weeks back:

> "A marriage has been arranged [it says] and will, if rumour is correct, very shortly take place, between Lord Robert St. Simon, second son of the Duke of Balmoral, and Miss Hatty Doran, the only daughter of Aloysius Doran, Esq., of San Francisco, Cal., U. S. A.

That is all."

"Terse and to the point," remarked Holmes, stretching his long, thin legs towards the fire.

"There was a paragraph amplifying this in one of the society papers of the same week. Ah, here it is:

"There will soon be a call for protection in the marriage market, for the present free-trade principle appears to tell heavily against our home product. One by one the management of the noble houses of Great Britain is passing into the hands of our fair cousins from across the Atlantic. An important addition has been made during the last week to the list of the prizes which have been borne away by these charming invaders. Lord St. Simon, who has shown himself for over twenty years proof against the little god's arrows, has now definitely announced his approaching marriage with Miss Hatty Doran, the fascinating daughter of a California millionaire. Miss Doran, whose graceful figure and striking face attracted much attention at the Westbury House festivities, is an only child, and it is currently reported that her dowry will run to considerably over the six figures, with expectancies for the future. As it is an open secret that the Duke of Balmoral has been compelled to sell his pictures within the last few years, and as Lord St. Simon has no property of his own save the small estate of Birchmoor, it is obvious that the Californian heiress is not the only gainer by an alliance which will enable her to make the easy and common transition from a Republican lady to a British peeress."

"Anything else?" asked Holmes, yawning.

"Oh, yes; plenty. Then there is another note in the *Morning Post* to say that the marriage would be an absolutely quiet one, that it would be at St. George's, Hanover Square, that only half a dozen intimate friends would be invited, and that the party would return to the furnished house at Lancaster Gate which has been taken by Mr. Aloysius Doran. Two days later—that is, on Wednesday last—there is a curt announcement that the wedding had taken place, and that the honeymoon would be passed at Lord Backwater's place, near Petersfield. Those are all the notices which appeared before the disappearance of the bride."

"Before the what?" asked Holmes with a start.

"The vanishing of the lady."

"When did she vanish, then?"

"At the wedding breakfast."

"Indeed. This is more interesting than it promised to be; quite dramatic, in fact."

"Yes; it struck me as being a little out of the common."

"They often vanish before the ceremony, and occasionally during the honeymoon; but I cannot call to mind anything quite so prompt as this. Pray let me have the details."

"I warn you that they are very incomplete."

"Perhaps we may make them less so."

"Such as they are, they are set forth in a single article of a morning paper of yesterday, which I will read to you. It is headed, 'Singular Occurrence at a Fashionable Wedding':

> "The family of Lord Robert St. Simon has been thrown into the greatest consternation by the strange and painful episodes which have taken place in connection with his wedding. The ceremony, as shortly announced in the papers of yesterday, occurred on the previous morning; but it is only now that it has been possible to confirm the strange rumours which have been so persistently floating about. In spite of the attempts of the friends to hush the matter up, so much public attention has now been drawn to it that no good purpose can be served by affecting to disregard what is a common subject for conversation.
>
> "The ceremony, which was performed at St. George's, Hanover Square, was a very quiet one, no one being present save the father of the bride, Mr. Aloysius Doran, the Duchess of Balmoral, Lord Backwater, Lord Eustace, and Lady Clara St. Simon (the younger brother and sister of the bridegroom), and Lady Alicia Whittington. The whole party proceeded afterwards to the house of Mr. Aloysius Doran, at Lancaster Gate, where breakfast had been prepared. It appears that some little trouble was caused by a woman, whose name has not been ascertained, who endeavoured to force her way into the house after the bridal party, alleging that she had some claim upon Lord St. Simon. It was only after a painful and prolonged scene that she was ejected by the butler and the footman. The bride, who had fortunately entered the house before this unpleasant interruption, had sat down to breakfast with the rest, when she complained

of a sudden indisposition and retired to her room. Her prolonged absence having caused some comment, her father followed her, but learned from her maid that she had only come up to her chamber for an instant, caught up an ulster and bonnet, and hurried down to the passage. One of the footmen declared that he had seen a lady leave the house thus apparelled, but had refused to credit that it was his mistress, believing her to be with the company. On ascertaining that his daughter had disappeared, Mr. Aloysius Doran, in conjunction with the bridegroom, instantly put themselves in communication with the police, and very energetic inquiries are being made, which will probably result in a speedy clearing up of this very singular business. Up to a late hour last night, however, nothing had transpired as to the whereabouts of the missing lady. There are rumours of foul play in the matter, and it is said that the police have caused the arrest of the woman who had caused the original disturbance, in the belief that, from jealousy or some other motive, she may have been concerned in the strange disappearance of the bride.''

''And is that all?''

''Only one little item in another of the morning papers, but it is a suggestive one.''

''And it is—''

''That Miss Flora Millar, the lady who had caused the disturbance, has actually been arrested. It appears that she was formerly a *danseuse* at the Allegro, and that she has known the bridegroom for some years. There are no further particulars, and the whole case is in your hands now—so far as it has been set forth in the public press.''

''And an exceedingly interesting case it appears to be. I would not have missed it for worlds. But there is a ring at the bell, Watson, and as the clock makes it a few minutes after four, I have no doubt that this will prove to be our noble client. Do not dream of going, Watson, for I very much prefer having a witness, if only as a check to my own memory.''

''Lord Robert St. Simon,'' announced our page-boy, throwing open the door. A gentleman entered, with a pleasant, cultured face, high-nosed and pale, with something perhaps of petulance about the mouth, and with the steady, well-opened eye of a man whose pleasant lot it had ever been to command and to be obeyed. His manner was brisk, and yet his general appearance gave an undue impression of age, for he had a slight forward stoop and a little bend of the knees as he walked. His hair, too, as he swept off his very curly-brimmed hat, was grizzled round the edges and thin upon the top. As to his dress, it was careful to the verge of foppishness, with high collar, black frock-coat, white waistcoat, yellow gloves, patent-leather shoes, and light-coloured gaiters. He advanced slowly into the room, turning his head from left to right, and swinging in his right hand the cord which held his golden eyeglasses.

"Goodday, Lord St. Simon," said Holmes, rising and bowing. "Pray take the basket-chair. This is my friend and colleague, Dr. Watson. Draw up a little to the fire, and we will talk this matter over."

"A most painful matter to me, as you can most readily imagine, Mr. Holmes. I have been cut to the quick. I understand that you have already managed several delicate cases of this sort, sir, though I presume that they were hardly from the same class of society."

"No, I am descending."

"I beg pardon."

"My last client of the sort was a king."

"Oh, really! I had no idea. And which king?"

"The King of Scandinavia."

"What! Had he lost his wife?"

"You can understand," said Holmes suavely, "that I extend to the affairs of my other clients the same secrecy which I promise to you in yours."

"Of course! Very right! very right! I'm sure I beg pardon. As to my own case, I am ready to give you any information which may assist you in forming an opinion."

"Thank you. I have already learned all that is in the public prints, nothing more. I presume that I may take it as correct—this article, for example, as to the disappearance of the bride."

Lord St. Simon glanced over it. "Yes, it is correct, as far as it goes."

"But it needs a great deal of supplementing before anyone could offer an opinion. I think that I may arrive at my facts most directly by questioning you."

"Pray do so."

"When did you first meet Miss Hatty Doran?"

"In San Francisco, a year ago."

"You were travelling in the States?"

"Yes."

"Did you become engaged then?"

"No."

"But you were on a friendly footing?"

"I was amused by her society, and she could see that I was amused."

"Her father is very rich?"

"He is said to be the richest man on the Pacific slope."

"And how did he make his money?"

"In mining. He had nothing a few years ago. Then he struck gold, invested it, and came up by leaps and bounds."

"Now, what is your own impression as to the young lady's—your wife's character?"

The nobleman swung his glasses a little faster and stared down into the fire. "You see, Mr. Holmes," said he, "my wife was twenty before her father became a rich man. During that time she ran free in a mining camp and wandered through woods or mountains, so that her education has come from Nature rather than from the schoolmaster. She is what we call in England a tomboy, with a strong nature, wild and free, unfettered by any sort of traditions. She is impetuous—volcanic, I was about to say. She is swift in making up her mind and fearless in carrying out her resolutions. On the other hand, I would not have given her the name which I have the honour to bear"—he gave a little stately cough—"had not I thought her to be at bottom a noble woman. I believe that she is capable of heroic self-sacrifice and that anything dishonourable would be repugnant to her."

"Have you her photograph?"

"I brought this with me." He opened a locket and showed us the full face of a very lovely woman. It was not a photograph but an ivory miniature, and the artist had brought out the full effect of the lustrous black hair, the large dark eyes, and the exquisite mouth. Holmes gazed long and earnestly at it. Then he closed the locket and handed it back to Lord St. Simon.

"The young lady came to London, then, and you renewed your acquaintance?"

"Yes, her father brought her over for this last London season. I met her several times, became engaged to her, and have now married her."

"She brought, I understand, a considerable dowry?"

"A fair dowry. Not more than is usual in my family."

"And this, of course, remains to you, since the marriage is a *fait accompli?*"

"I really have made no inquiries on the subject."

"Very naturally not. Did you see Miss Doran on the day before the wedding?"

"Yes."

"Was she in good spirits?"

"Never better. She kept talking of what we should do in our future lives."

"Indeed! That is very interesting. And on the morning of the wedding?"

"She was as bright as possible—at least until after the ceremony."

"And did you observe any change in her then?"

"Well, to tell the truth, I saw then the first signs that I had ever seen that her temper was just a little sharp. The incident, however, was too trivial to relate and can have no possible bearing upon the case."

"Pray let us have it, for all that."

"Oh, it is childish. She dropped her bouquet as we went towards the vestry. She was passing the front pew at the time, and it fell over into the pew. There was a moment's delay, but the gentleman in the pew handed it up to her again, and it did not appear to be the worse for the fall. Yet when I spoke to her of the matter, she answered me abruptly; and in the carriage, on our way home, she seemed absurdly agitated over this trifling cause."

"Indeed! You say that there was a gentleman in the pew. Some of the general public were present, then?"

"Oh, yes. It is impossible to exclude them when the church is open."

"This gentleman was not one of your wife's friends?"

"No, no; I call him a gentleman by courtesy, but he was quite a common-looking person. I hardly noticed his appearance. But really I think that we are wandering rather far from the point."

"Lady St. Simon, then, returned from the wedding in a less

cheerful frame of mind than she had gone to it. What did she do on reëntering her father's house?"

"I saw her in conversation with her maid."

"And who is her maid?"

"Alice is her name. She is an American and came from California with her."

"A confidential servant?"

"A little too much so. It seemed to me that her mistress allowed her to take great liberties. Still, of course, in America they look upon these things in a different way."

"How long did she speak to this Alice?"

"Oh, a few minutes. I had something else to think of."

"You did not overhear what they said?"

"Lady St. Simon said something about 'jumping a claim.' She was accustomed to use slang of the kind. I have no idea what she meant."

"American slang is very expressive sometimes. And what did your wife do when she finished speaking to her maid?"

"She walked into the breakfast-room."

"On your arm?"

"No, alone. She was very independent in little matters like that. Then, after we had sat down for ten minutes or so, she rose hurriedly, muttered some words of apology, and left the room. She never came back."

"But this maid, Alice, as I understand, deposes that she went to her room, covered her bride's dress with a long ulster, put on a bonnet, and went out."

"Quite so. And she was afterwards seen walking into Hyde Park in company with Flora Millar, a woman who is now in custody, and who had already made a disturbance at Mr. Doran's house that morning."

"Ah, yes. I should like a few particulars as to this young lady, and your relations to her."

Lord St. Simon shrugged his shoulders and raised his eyebrows. "We have been on a friendly footing for some years—I may say on a *very* friendly footing. She used to be at the Allegro. I have not treated her ungenerously, and she had no just cause of complaint against me, but you know what women are, Mr. Holmes. Flora was a dear little thing, but exceedingly hot-headed and devotedly attached to me. She wrote me dreadful letters when she heard that I was about to be married, and, to tell the truth, the reason why I had the marriage celebrated so quietly was that I feared lest there might be a scandal in the church. She came to Mr. Doran's door just after we returned, and she endeavoured to push her way in, uttering very abusive expressions towards my wife, and even threatening her, but I had foreseen the possibility of something of the sort, and I had two police fellows there in private clothes, who soon pushed her out again. She was quiet when she saw that there was no good in making a row."

"Did your wife hear all this?"

"No, thank goodness, she did not."

"And she was seen walking with this very woman afterwards?"

"Yes. That is what Mr. Lestrade, of Scotland Yard, looks upon as so serious. It is thought that Flora decoyed my wife out and laid some terrible trap for her."

"Well, it is a possible supposition."

"You think so, too?"

"I did not say a probable one. But you do not yourself look upon this as likely?"

"I do not think Flora would hurt a fly."

"Still, jealousy is a strange transformer of characters. Pray what is your own theory as to what took place?"

"Well, really, I came to seek a theory, not to propound one. I have given you all the facts. Since you ask me, however, I may say that it has occurred to me as possible that the excitement of this affair, the consciousness that she had made so immense a social stride, had the effect of causing some little nervous disturbance in my wife."

"In short, that she had become suddenly deranged?"

"Well, really, when I consider that she has turned her back —I will not say upon me, but upon so much that many have aspired to without success—I can hardly explain it in any other fashion."

"Well, certainly that is also a conceivable hypothesis," said Holmes, smiling. "And now, Lord St. Simon, I think that I have nearly all my data. May I ask whether you were seated at the breakfast-table so that you could see out of the window?"

"We could see the other side of the road and the Park."

"Quite so. Then I do not think that I need to detain you longer. I shall communicate with you."

"Should you be fortunate enough to solve this problem," said our client, rising.

"I have solved it."

"Eh? What was that?"

"I say that I have solved it."

"Where, then, is my wife?"

"That is a detail which I shall speedily supply."

Lord St. Simon shook his head. "I am afraid that it will take wiser heads than yours or mine," he remarked, and bowing in a stately, old-fashioned manner he departed.

"It is very good of Lord St. Simon to honour my head by putting it on a level with his own," said Sherlock Holmes, laughing. "I think that I shall have a whisky and soda and a cigar after all this cross-questioning. I had formed my conclusions as to the case before our client came into the room.

"My dear Holmes!"

"I have notes of several similar cases, though none, as I remarked before, which were quite as prompt. My whole examination served to turn my conjecture into a certainty. Circumstantial evidence is occasionally very convincing, as when you find a trout in the milk, to quote Thoreau's example."

"But I have heard all that you have heard."

"Without, however, the knowledge of preëxisting cases which serves me so well. There was a parallel instance in Aberdeen some years back, and something on very much the same lines at Munich the year after the Franco-Prussian War. It is one of these cases—but, hello, here is Lestrade! Good-afternoon, Lestrade! You will find an extra tumbler upon the sideboard, and there are cigars in the box."

The official detective was attired in a pea-jacket and cravat, which gave him a decidedly nautical appearance, and he carried a black canvas bag in his hand. With a short greeting he seated himself and lit the cigar which had been offered to him.

"What's up, then?" asked Holmes with a twinkle in his eye. "You look dissatisfied."

"And I feel dissatisfied. It is this infernal St. Simon marriage case. I can make neither head nor tail of the business."

"Really! You surprise me."

"Who ever heard of such a mixed affair? Every clue seems to slip through my fingers. I have been at work upon it all day."

"And very wet it seems to have made you," said Holmes, laying his hand upon the arm of the pea-jacket.

"Yes, I have been dragging the Serpentine."

"In heaven's name, what for?"

"In search of the body of Lady St. Simon."

Sherlock Holmes leaned back in his chair and laughed heartily. "Have you dragged the basin of Trafalgar Square fountain?" he asked.

"Why? What do you mean?"

"Because you have just as good a chance of finding this lady in the one as in the other."

Lestrade shot an angry glance at my companion. "I suppose you know all about it," he snarled.

"Well, I have only just heard the facts, but my mind is made up."

"Oh, indeed! Then you think that the Serpentine plays no part in the matter?"

"I think it very unlikely."

"Then perhaps you will kindly explain how it is that we found this in it?" He opened his bag as he spoke, and tumbled onto the floor a wedding-dress of watered silk, a pair of white satin shoes, and a bride's wreath and veil, all discoloured and soaked in water. "There," said he, putting a new wedding-ring upon the top of the pile. "There is a little nut for you to crack, Master Holmes."

"Oh, indeed!" said my friend, blowing blue rings into the air. "You dragged them from the Serpentine?"

"No. They were found floating near the margin by a park-keeper. They have been identified as her clothes, and it seemed to me that if the clothes were there the body would not be far off."

"By the same brilliant reasoning, every man's body is to be found in the neighbourhood of his wardrobe. And pray what did you hope to arrive at through this?"

"At some evidence implicating Flora Millar in the disappearance."

"I am afraid that you will find it difficult."

"Are you, indeed, now?" cried Lestrade with some bitterness. "I am afraid, Holmes, that you are not very practical with your deductions and your inferences. You have made two blunders in as many minutes. This dress does implicate Miss Flora Millar."

"And how?"

"In the dress is a pocket. In the pocket is a card-case. In the card-case is a note. And here is the very note." He slapped it down upon the table in front of him. "Listen to this:

"You will see me when all is ready. Come at once.

"F. H. M.

Now my theory all along has been that Lady St. Simon was decoyed away by Flora Millar, and that she, with confederates, no doubt, was responsible for her disappearance. Here, signed with her initials, is the very note which was no doubt quietly slipped into her hand at the door and which lured her within their reach."

"Very good, Lestrade," said Holmes, laughing. "You really are very fine indeed. Let me see it." He took up the paper in a listless way, but his attention instantly became riveted, and he gave a little cry of satisfaction. "This is indeed important," said he.

"Ha! you find it so?"

"Extremely so. I congratulate you warmly."

Lestrade rose in his triumph and bent his head to look. "Why," he shrieked, "you're looking at the wrong side!"

"On the contrary, this is the right side."

"The right side? You're mad! Here is the note written in pencil over here."

"And over here is what appears to be the fragment of a hotel bill, which interests me deeply."

"There's nothing in it. I looked at it before," said Lestrade.

"Oct. 4th, rooms 8*s*., breakfast 2*s*. 6*d*., cocktail 1*s*., lunch 2*s*. 6*d*., glass sherry, 8*d*.

I see nothing in that."

"Very likely not. It is most important, all the same. As to the note, it is important also, or at least the initials are, so I congratulate you again."

"I've wasted time enough," said Lestrade, rising. "I believe in hard work and not in sitting by the fire spinning fine theories. Good-day, Mr. Holmes, and we shall see which gets to the bottom of the matter first.'' He gathered up the garments, thrust them into the bag, and made for the door.

''Just one hint to you, Lestrade,'' drawled Holmes before his rival vanished; ''I will tell you the true solution of the matter. Lady St. Simon is a myth. There is not, and there never has been, any such person.''

Lestrade looked sadly at my companion. Then he turned to me, tapped his forehead three times, shook his head solemnly, and hurried away.

He had hardly shut the door behind him when Holmes rose to put on his overcoat. ''There is something in what the fellow says about outdoor work,'' he remarked, ''so I think, Watson, that I must leave you to your papers for a little.''

It was after five o'clock when Sherlock Holmes left me, but I had no time to be lonely, for within an hour there arrived a confectioner's man with a very large flat box. This he unpacked with the help of a youth whom he had brought with him, and presently, to my very great astonishment, a quite epicurean little cold supper began to be laid out upon our humble lodging-house mahogany. There were a couple of brace of cold woodcock, a pheasant, a *pâté de foie gras* pie with a group of ancient and cobwebby bottles. Having laid out all these luxuries, my two visitors vanished away, like the genii of the Arabian Nights, with no explanation save that the things had been paid for and were ordered to this address.

Just before nine o'clock Sherlock Holmes stepped briskly into the room. His features were gravely set, but there was a light in his eye which made me think that he had not been disappointed in his conclusions.

''They have laid the supper, then,'' he said, rubbing his hands.

''You seem to expect company. They have laid for five.''

''Yes, I fancy we may have some company dropping in,'' said he. ''I am surprised that Lord St. Simon has not already arrived. Ha! I fancy that I hear his step now upon the stairs.''

It was indeed our visitor of the afternoon who came bustling in, dangling his glasses more vigorously than ever, and with a very perturbed expression upon his aristocratic features.

''My messenger reached you, then?'' asked Holmes.

''Yes, and I confess that the contents startled me beyond measure. Have you good authority for what you say?''

''The best possible.''

Lord St. Simon sank into a chair and passed his hand over his forehead.

"What will the Duke say," he murmured, "when he hears that one of the family has been subjected to such humiliation?"

"It is the purest accident. I cannot allow that there is any humiliation."

"Ah, you look on these things from another standpoint."

"I fail to see that anyone is to blame. I can hardly see how the lady could have acted otherwise, though her abrupt method of doing it was undoubtedly to be regretted. Having no mother, she had no one to advise her at such a crisis."

"It was a slight, sir, a public slight," said Lord St. Simon, tapping his fingers upon the table.

"You must make allowance for this poor girl, placed in so unprecedented a position."

"I will make no allowance. I am very angry indeed, and I have been shamefully used."

"I think that I heard a ring," said Holmes. "Yes, there are steps on the landing. If I cannot persuade you to take a lenient view of the matter, Lord St. Simon, I have brought an advocate here who may be more successful." He opened the door and ushered in a lady and gentleman. "Lord St. Simon," said he, "allow me to introduce you to Mr. and Mrs. Francis Hay Moulton. The lady, I think, you have already met."

At the sight of these newcomers our client had sprung from his seat and stood very erect, with his eyes cast down and his hand thrust into the breast of his frock-coat, a picture of offended dignity. The lady had taken a quick step forward and had held out her hand to him, but he still refused to raise his eyes. It was as well for his resolution, perhaps, for her pleading face was one which it was hard to resist.

"You're angry, Robert," said she. "Well, I guess you have every cause to be."

"Pray make no apology to me," said Lord St. Simon bitterly.

"Oh, yes, I know that I have treated you real bad and that I should have spoken to you before I went; but I was kind of rattled, and from the time when I saw Frank here again I just didn't know what I was doing or saying. I only wonder I didn't fall down and do a faint right there before the altar."

"Perhaps, Mrs. Moulton, you would like my friend and me to leave the room while you explain this matter?"

"If I may give an opinion," remarked the strange gentleman, "we've had just a little too much secrecy over this business already. For my part, I should like all Europe and America to hear the rights of it." He was a small, wiry, sunburnt man, clean-shaven, with a sharp face and alert manner.

"Then I'll tell our story right away," said the lady. "Frank here and I met in '84, in McQuire's camp, near the Rockies, where pa was working a claim. We were engaged to each other, Frank and I; but then one day father struck a rich pocket and made a pile, while poor Frank here had a claim that petered out and came to nothing. The richer pa grew the poorer was Frank; so at last pa wouldn't hear of our engagement lasting any longer, and he took me away to 'Frisco. Frank wouldn't throw up his hand, though; so he followed me there, and he saw me without pa knowing anything about it. It would only have made him mad to know, so we just fixed it all up for ourselves. Frank said that he would go and make his pile, too, and never come back to claim me until he had as much as pa. So then I promised to wait for him to the end of time and pledged myself not to marry anyone else while he lived. 'Why shouldn't we be married right away, then,' said he, 'and then I will feel sure of you; and I won't claim to be your husband until I come back?' Well, we talked it over, and he had fixed it all up so nicely, with a clergyman all ready in waiting, that we just did it right there; and then Frank went off to seek his fortune, and I went back to pa.

"The next I heard of Frank was that he was in Montana, and then he went prospecting in Arizona, and then I heard of him from New Mexico. After that came a long newspaper story about how a miners' camp had been attacked by Apache Indians, and there was my Frank's name among the killed. I fainted dead away, and I was very sick for months after. Pa thought I had a decline and took me to half the doctors in 'Frisco. Not a word of news came for a year and more, so that I never doubted that Frank was really dead. Then Lord St. Simon came to 'Frisco, and we came to London, and a marriage was arranged, and pa was very pleased, but I felt all the time that no man on this earth would ever take the place in my heart that had been given to my poor Frank.

"Still, if I had married Lord St. Simon, of course I'd have done my duty by him. We can't command our love, but we can our actions. I went to the altar with him with the intention to make him just as good a wife as it was in me to be. But you may imagine what I felt when, just as I came to the altar rails, I glanced back and saw Frank standing and looking at me out of the first pew. I thought it was his ghost at first; but when I looked again there he was still, with a kind of question in his eyes, as if to ask me whether I were glad or sorry to see him. I wonder I didn't drop. I know that everything was turning round, and the words of the clergyman were just like the buzz of a bee in my ear. I didn't know what to do. Should I stop the service and make a scene in the church? I glanced at him again, and he seemed to know what I was thinking, for he raised his finger to his lips to tell me to be still. Then I saw him scribble on a piece of paper, and I knew that he was writing me a note. As I passed his pew on the way out I dropped my bouquet over to him, and he slipped the note into my hand when he returned me the flowers. It was only a line asking me to join him when he made the sign to me to do so. Of course I never doubted for a moment that my first duty was now to him, and I determined to do just whatever he might direct.

"When I got back I told my maid, who had known him in California, and had always been his friend. I ordered her to say nothing, but to get a few things packed and my ulster ready. I know I ought to have spoken to Lord St. Simon, but it was dreadful hard before his mother and all those great people. I just made up my mind to run away and explain afterwards. I hadn't been at the table ten minutes before I saw Frank out of the window at the other side of the road. He beckoned to me and then began walking into the Park. I slipped out, put on my things, and followed him. Some woman came talking something or other about Lord St. Simon to me—seemed to me from the little I heard as if he had a little secret of his own before marriage also—but I managed to get away from her and soon overtook Frank. We got into a cab together, and away we drove to some lodgings he had taken in Gordon Square, and that was my true wedding after all those years of waiting. Frank had been a prisoner among the Apaches, had escaped, came on to 'Frisco, found that I had given him up for dead and had gone to England, followed me there, and had come upon me at last on the very morning of my second wedding."

"I saw it in a paper," explained the American. "It gave the name and the church but not where the lady lived."

"Then we had a talk as to what we should do, and Frank was all for openness, but I was so ashamed of it all that I felt as if I should like to vanish away and never see any of them again—just sending a line to pa, perhaps, to show him that I was alive. It was awful to me to think of all those lords and ladies sitting round that breakfast-table and waiting for me to come back. So Frank took my wedding-clothes and things and made a bundle of them, so that I should not be traced, and dropped them away somewhere where no one could find them. It is likely that we should have gone on to Paris to-morrow, only that this good gentleman, Mr. Holmes, came round to us this evening, though how he found us is more than I can think, and he showed us very clearly and kindly that I was wrong and that Frank was right, and that we should be putting ourselves in the wrong if we were so secret. Then he offered to give us a chance of talking to Lord St. Simon alone, and so we came right away round to his rooms at once. Now, Robert, you have heard it all, and I am very sorry if I have given you pain, and I hope that you do not think very meanly of me."

Lord St. Simon had by no means relaxed his rigid attitude, but had listened with a frowning brow and a compressed lip to this long narrative.

"Excuse me," he said, "but it is not my custom to discuss my most intimate personal affairs in this public manner."

"Then you won't forgive me? You won't shake hands before I go?"

"Oh, certainly, if it would give you any pleasure." He put out his hand and coldly grasped that which she extended to him.

"I had hoped," suggested Holmes, "that you would have joined us in a friendly supper."

"I think that there you ask a little too much," responded his Lordship. "I may be forced to acquiesce in these recent developments, but I can hardly be expected to make merry over them. I think that with your permission I will now wish you all a very good-night." He included us all in a sweeping bow and stalked out of the room.

"Then I trust that you at least will honour me with your company," said Sherlock Holmes. "It is always a joy to meet an American, Mr. Moulton, for I am one of those who believe that the folly of a monarch and the blundering of a minister in far-gone years will not prevent our children from being some day citizens of the same world-wide country under a flag which shall be a quartering of the Union Jack with the Stars and Stripes."

"The case has been an interesting one," remarked Holmes when our visitors had left us, "because it serves to show very clearly how simple the explanation may be of an affair which at first sight seems to be almost inexplicable. Nothing could be more natural than the sequence of events as narrated by this lady, and nothing stranger than the result when viewed, for instance, by Mr. Lestrade, of Scotland Yard."

"You were not yourself at fault at all, then?"

"From the first, two facts were very obvious to me, the one that the lady had been quite willing to undergo the wedding ceremony, the other that she had repented of it within a few minutes of returning home. Obviously something had occurred during the morning, then, to cause her to change her mind. What could that something be? She could not have spoken to anyone when she was out, for she had been in the company of the bridegroom. Had she seen someone, then? If she had, it must be someone from America because she had spent so short a time in this country that she could hardly have allowed anyone to acquire so deep an influence over her that the mere sight of him would induce her to change her plans so completely. You see we have already arrived, by a process of exclusion, at the idea that she might have seen an American. Then who could this American be, and why should he possess so much influence over her? It might be a lover; it might be a husband. Her young womanhood had, I knew, been spent in rough scenes and under strange conditions. So far I had got before I ever heard Lord St. Simon's narrative. When he told us of a man in a pew, of the change in the bride's manner, of so transparent a device for obtaining a note as the dropping of a bouquet, of her resort to her confidential maid, and of her very significant allusion to claim-jumping—which in miners' parlance means taking possession of that which another person has a prior claim to—the whole situation became absolutely clear. She had gone off with a man, and the man was either a lover or was a previous husband—the chances being in favour of the latter."

"And how in the world did you find them?"

"It might have been difficult, but friend Lestrade held information in his hands the value of which he did not himself know.

The initials were, of course, of the highest importance, but more valuable still was it to know that within a week he had settled his bill at one of the most select London hotels."

"How did you deduce the select?"

"By the select prices. Eight shillings for a bed and eightpence for a glass of sherry pointed to one of the most expensive hotels. There are not many in London which charge at that rate. In the second one which I visited in Northumberland Avenue, I learned by an inspection of the book that Francis H. Moulton, an American gentleman, had left only the day before, and on looking over the entries against him, I came upon the very items which I had seen in the duplicate bill. His letters were to be forwarded to 226 Gordon Square; so thither I travelled, and being fortunate enough to find the loving couple at home, I ventured to give them some paternal advice and to point out to them that it would be better in every way that they should make their position a little clearer both to the general public and to Lord St. Simon in particular. I invited them to meet him here, and, as you see, I made him keep the appointment."

"But with no very good result," I remarked. "His conduct was certainly not very gracious."

"Ah, Watson," said Holmes, smiling, "perhaps you would not be very gracious either, if, after all the trouble of wooing and wedding, you found yourself deprived in an instant of wife and of fortune. I think that we may judge Lord St. Simon very mercifully and thank our stars that we are never likely to find ourselves in the same position. Draw your chair up and hand me my violin, for the only problem we have still to solve is how to while away these bleak autumnal evenings."

THE ADVENTURE OF THE BERYL CORONET

"HOLMES," SAID I as I stood one morning in our bow-window looking down the street, "here is a madman coming along. It seems rather sad that his relatives should allow him to come out alone."

My friend rose lazily from his armchair and stood with his hands in the pockets of his dressing-gown, looking over my shoulder. It was a bright, crisp February morning, and the snow of the day before still lay deep upon the ground, shimmering brightly in the wintry sun. Down the centre of Baker Street it had been ploughed into a brown crumbly band by the traffic, but at either side and on the heaped-up edges of the foot-paths it still lay as white as when it fell. The gray pavement had been cleaned and scraped, but was still dangerously slippery, so that there were fewer passengers than usual. Indeed, from the direction of the Metropolitan Station no one was coming save the single gentleman whose eccentric conduct had drawn my attention.

He was a man of about fifty, tall, portly, and imposing, with a massive, strongly marked face and a commanding figure. He was dressed in a sombre yet rich style, in black frock-coat, shining hat, neat brown gaiters, and well-cut pearl-gray trousers. Yet his actions were in absurd contrast to the dignity of his dress and features, for he was running hard, with occasional little springs, such as a weary man gives who is little accustomed to set any tax upon his legs. As he ran he jerked his hands up and down, waggled his head, and writhed his face into the most extraordinary contortions.

"What on earth can be the matter with him?" I asked. "He is looking up at the numbers of the houses."

"I believe that he is coming here," said Holmes, rubbing his hands.

"Here?"

"Yes; I rather think he is coming to consult me professionally. I think that I recognize the symptoms. Ha! did I not tell you?" As he spoke, the man, puffing and blowing, rushed at our door and pulled at our bell until the whole house resounded with the clanging.

A few moments later he was in our room, still puffing, still gesticulating, but with so fixed a look of grief and despair in his eyes that our smiles were turned in an instant to horror and pity. For a while he could not get his words out, but swayed his body and plucked at his hair like one who has been driven to the extreme limits of his reason. Then, suddenly springing to his feet, he beat his head against the wall with such force that we both rushed upon him and tore him away to the centre of the room. Sherlock Holmes pushed him down into the easy-chair and, sitting beside him, patted his hand and chatted with him in the easy, soothing tones which he knew so well how to employ.

"You have come to me to tell your story, have you not?" said he. "You are fatigued with your haste. Pray wait until you have recovered yourself, and then I shall be most happy to look into any little problem which you may submit to me."

The man sat for a minute or more with a heaving chest, fighting against his emotion. Then he passed his handkerchief over his brow, set his lips tight, and turned his face towards us.

"No doubt you think me mad?" said he.

"I see that you have had some great trouble," responded Holmes.

"God knows I have!—a trouble which is enough to unseat my reason, so sudden and so terrible is it. Public disgrace I might have faced, although I am a man whose character has never yet borne a stain. Private affliction also is the lot of every man; but the two coming together, and in so frightful a form, have been enough to shake my very soul. Besides, it is not I alone. The very noblest in the land may suffer unless some way be found out of this horrible affair."

"Pray compose yourself, sir," said Holmes, "and let me have a clear account of who you are and what it is that has befallen you."

"My name," answered our visitor, "is probably familiar to your ears. I am Alexander Holder, of the banking firm of Holder & Stevenson, of Threadneedle Street."

The name was indeed well known to us as belonging to the senior partner in the second largest private banking concern in the City of London. What could have happened, then, to bring one of the foremost citizens of London to this most pitiable pass? We waited, all curiosity, until with another effort he braced himself to tell his story.

"I feel that time is of value," said he; "that is why I hastened here when the police inspector suggested that I should secure your coöperation. I came to Baker Street by the Underground and hurried from there on foot, for the cabs go slowly through this snow. That is why I was so out of breath, for I am a man who takes very little exercise. I feel better now, and I will put the facts before you as shortly and yet as clearly as I can.

"It is, of course, well known to you that in a successful

banking business as much depends upon our being able to find remunerative investments for our funds as upon our increasing our connection and the number of our depositors. One of our most lucrative means of laying out money is in the shape of loans, where the security is unimpeachable. We have done a good deal in this direction during the last few years, and there are many noble families to whom we have advanced large sums upon the security of their pictures, libraries, or plate.

"Yesterday morning I was seated in my office at the bank when a card was brought in to me by one of the clerks. I started when I saw the name, for it was that of none other than—well, perhaps even to you I had better say no more than that it was a name which is a household word all over the earth—one of the highest, noblest, most exalted names in England. I was overwhelmed by the honour and attempted, when he entered, to say so, but he plunged at once into business with the air of a man who wishes to hurry quickly through a disagreeable task.

" 'Mr. Holder,' said he, 'I have been informed that you are in the habit of advancing money.'

" 'The firm does so when the security is good,' I answered.

" 'It is absolutely essential to me,' said he, 'that I should have £50,000 at once. I could, of course, borrow so trifling a sum ten times over from my friends, but I much prefer to make it a matter of business and to carry out that business myself. In my position you can readily understand that it is unwise to place one's self under obligations.'

" 'For how long, may I ask, do you want this sum?' I asked.

" 'Next Monday I have a large sum due to me, and I shall then most certainly repay what you advance, with whatever interest you think it right to charge. But it is very essential to me that the money should be paid at once.'

' "I should be happy to advance it without further parley from my own private purse,' said I, 'were it not that the strain would be rather more than it could bear. If, on the other hand, I am to do it in the name of the firm, then in justice to my partner I must insist that, even in your case, every businesslike precaution should be taken.'

" 'I should much prefer to have it so,' said he, raising up a square, black morocco case which he had laid beside his chair. 'You have doubtless heard of the Beryl Coronet?'

" 'One of the most precious public possessions of the empire,' said I.

" 'Precisely.' He opened the case, and there, imbedded in soft, flesh-coloured velvet, lay the magnificent piece of jewellery which he had named. 'There are thirty-nine enormous beryls,' said he, 'and the price of the gold chasing is incalculable. The lowest estimate would put the worth of the coronet at double the sum which I have asked. I am prepared to leave it with you as my security.'

"I took the precious case into my hands and looked in some perplexity from it to my illustrious client.

" 'You doubt its value?' he asked.

" 'Not at all. I only doubt—'

" 'The propriety of my leaving it. You may set your mind at rest about that. I should not dream of doing so were it not absolutely certain that I should be able in four days to reclaim it. It is a pure matter of form. Is the security sufficient?'

" 'Ample.'

" 'You understand, Mr. Holder, that I am giving you a strong proof of the confidence which I have in you, founded upon all that I have heard of you. I rely upon you not only to be discreet and to refrain from all gossip upon the matter but, above all, to preserve this coronet with every possible precaution because I need not say that a great public scandal would be caused if any harm were to befall it. Any injury to it would be almost as serious as its complete loss, for there are no beryls in the world to match these, and it would be impossible to replace them. I leave it with you, however, with every confidence, and I shall call for it in person on Monday morning.'

"Seeing that my client was anxious to leave, I said no more; but, calling for my cashier, I ordered him to pay over fifty £1000 notes. When I was alone once more, however, with the precious case lying upon the table in front of me, I could not but think with some misgivings of the immense responsibility which it entailed upon me. There could be no doubt that, as it was a national possession, a horrible scandal would ensue if any misfortune should occur to it. I already regretted having ever consented to take charge of it. However, it was too late to alter the matter now, so I locked it up in my private safe and turned once more to my work.

"When evening came I felt that it would be an imprudence

to leave so precious a thing in the office behind me. Bankers' safes had been forced before now, and why should not mine be? If so, how terrible would be the position in which I should find myself! I determined, therefore, that for the next few days I would always carry the case backward and forward with me, so that it might never be really out of my reach. With this intention, I called a cab and drove out to my house at Streatham, carrying the jewel with me. I did not breathe freely until I had taken it upstairs and locked it in the bureau of my dressing-room.

"And now a word as to my household, Mr. Holmes, for I wish you to thoroughly understand the situation. My groom and my page sleep out of the house, and may be set aside altogether. I have three maid-servants who have been with me a number of years and whose absolute reliability is quite above suspicion. Another, Lucy Parr, the second waiting-maid, has only been in my service a few months. She came with an excellent character, however, and has always given me satisfaction. She is a very pretty girl and has attracted admirers who have occasionally hung about the place. That is the only drawback which we have found to her, but we believe her to be a thoroughly good girl in every way.

"So much for the servants. My family itself is so small that it will not take me long to describe it. I am a widower and have an only son, Arthur. He has been a disappointment to me, Mr. Holmes—a grievous disappointment. I have no doubt that I am myself to blame. People tell me that I have spoiled him. Very likely I have. When my dear wife died I felt that he was all I had to love. I could not bear to see the smile fade even for a moment from his face. I have never denied him a wish. Perhaps it would have been better for both of us had I been sterner, but I meant it for the best.

"It was naturally my intention that he should succeed me in my business, but he was not of a business turn. He was wild, wayward, and, to speak the truth, I could not trust him in the handling of large sums of money. When he was young he became a member of an aristocratic club, and there, having charming manners, he was soon the intimate of a number of men with long purses and expensive habits. He learned to play heavily at cards and to squander money on the turf, until he had again and again to come to me and implore me to give him an advance upon his allowance, that he might settle his debts of honour. He tried more than once to break away from the dangerous company which he was keeping, but each time the influence of his friend, Sir George Burnwell, was enough to draw him back again.

"And, indeed, I could not wonder that such a man as Sir George Burnwell should gain an influence over him, for he has frequently brought him to my house, and I have found myself that I could hardly resist the fascination of his manner. He is older than Arthur, a man of the world to his finger-tips, one who had been everywhere, seen everything, a brilliant talker, and a man of great personal beauty. Yet when I think of him in cold blood, far away from the glamour of his presence, I am convinced from his cynical speech and the look which I have caught in his eyes that he is one who should be deeply distrusted. So I think, and so, too, thinks my little Mary, who has a woman's quick insight into character.

"And now there is only she to be described. She is my niece; but when my brother died five years ago and left her alone in the world I adopted her, and have looked upon her ever since as my daughter. She is a sunbeam in my house—sweet, loving, beautiful, a wonderful manager and housekeeper, yet as tender and quiet and gentle as a woman could be. She is my right hand. I do not know what I could do without her. In only one matter has she ever gone against my wishes. Twice my boy has asked her to marry him, for he loves her devotedly, but each time she has refused him. I think that if anyone could have drawn him into the right path it would have been she, and that his marriage might have changed his whole life; but now, alas! it is too late —forever too late!

"Now, Mr. Holmes, you know the people who live under my roof, and I shall continue with my miserable story.

"When we were taking coffee in the drawing-room that night after dinner, I told Arthur and Mary my experience, and of the precious treasure which we had under our roof, suppressing only the name of my client. Lucy Parr, who had brought in the coffee, had, I am sure, left the room; but I cannot swear that the door was closed. Mary and Arthur were much interested and wished to see the famous coronet, but I thought it better not to disturb it.

" 'Where have you put it?' asked Arthur.

" 'In my own bureau.'

" 'Well, I hope to goodness the house won't be burgled during the night,' said he.

" 'It is locked up,' I answered.

" 'Oh, any old key will fit that bureau. When I was a youngster I have opened it myself with the key of the box-room cupboard.'

"He often had a wild way of talking, so that I thought little of what he said. He followed me to my room, however, that night with a very grave face.

" 'Look here, dad,' said he with his eyes cast down, 'can you let me have £200?'

" 'No, I cannot!' I answered sharply. 'I have been far too generous with you in money matters.'

" 'You have been very kind,' said he, 'but I must have this money, or else I can never show my face inside the club again.'

" 'And a very good thing, too!' I cried.

" 'Yes, but you would not have me leave it a dishonoured man,' said he. 'I could not bear the disgrace. I must raise the money in some way, and if you will not let me have it, then I must try other means.'

"I was very angry, for this was the third demand during the month. 'You shall not have a farthing from me,' I cried, on which he bowed and left the room without another word.

"When he was gone I unlocked my bureau, made sure that my treasure was safe, and locked it again. Then I started to go round the house to see that all was secure—a duty which I usually leave to Mary but which I thought it well to perform myself that night. As I came down the stairs I saw Mary herself at the side window of the hall, which she closed and fastened as I approached.

" 'Tell me, dad,' said she, looking, I thought, a little disturbed, 'did you give Lucy, the maid, leave to go out to-night?'

" 'Certainly not.'

" 'She came in just now by the back door. I have no doubt that she has only been to the side gate to see someone, but I think that it is hardly safe and should be stopped.'

" 'You must speak to her in the morning, or I will if you prefer it. Are you sure that everything is fastened?'

" 'Quite sure, dad.'

" 'Then, good-night.' I kissed her and went up to my bedroom again, where I was soon asleep.

"I am endeavouring to tell you everything, Mr. Holmes, which may have any bearing upon the case, but I beg that you will question me upon any point which I do not make clear."

"On the contrary, your statement is singularly lucid."

"I come to a part of my story now in which I should wish to be particularly so. I am not a very heavy sleeper, and the anxiety in my mind tended, no doubt, to make me even less so than usual. About two in the morning, then, I was awakened by some sound in the house. It had ceased ere I was wide awake, but it had left an impression behind it as though a window had gently closed somewhere. I lay listening with all my ears. Suddenly, to my horror, there was a distinct sound of footsteps moving softly in the next room. I slipped out of bed, all palpitating with fear, and peeped round the corner of my dressing-room door.

" 'Arthur!' I screamed, 'you villain! you thief! How dare you touch that coronet?'

"The gas was half up, as I had left it, and my unhappy boy, dressed only in his shirt and trousers, was standing beside the light, holding the coronet in his hands. He appeared to be wrenching at it, or bending it with all his strength. At my cry he dropped it from his grasp and turned as pale as death. I snatched it up and examined it. One of the gold corners, with three of the beryls in it, was missing.

" 'You blackguard!' I shouted, beside myself with rage. 'You have destroyed it! You have dishonoured me forever! Where are the jewels which you have stolen?'

" 'Stolen!' he cried.

" 'Yes, thief!' I roared, shaking him by the shoulder.

" 'There are none missing. There cannot be any missing,' said he.

" 'There are three missing. And you know where they are. Must I call you a liar as well as a thief? Did I not see you trying to tear off another piece?'

" 'You have called me names enough,' said he; 'I will not stand it any longer. I shall not say another word about this business, since you have chosen to insult me. I will leave your house in the morning and make my own way in the world.'

" 'You shall leave it in the hands of the police!' I cried, half-mad with grief and rage. 'I shall have this matter probed to the bottom.'

" 'You shall learn nothing from me,' said he with a passion such as I should not have thought was in his nature. 'If you choose to call the police, let the police find what they can.'

"By this time the whole house was astir, for I had raised my voice in my anger. Mary was the first to rush into my room, and, at the sight of the coronet and of Arthur's face, she read the whole story and, with a scream, fell down senseless on the ground. I sent the house-maid for the police and put the investigation into their hands at once. When the inspector and a constable entered the house, Arthur, who had stood sullenly with his arms folded, asked me whether it was my intention to charge him with theft. I answered that it had ceased to be a private matter, but had become a public one, since the ruined coronet was national property. I was determined that the law should have its way in everything.

" 'At least,' said he, 'you will not have me arrested at once. It would be to your advantage as well as mine if I might leave the house for five minutes.'

" 'That you may get away, or perhaps that you may conceal what you have stolen,' said I. And then, realizing the dreadful position in which I was placed, I implored him to remember that not only my honour but that of one who was far greater than I was at stake; and that he threatened to raise a scandal which would convulse the nation. He might avert it all if he would but tell me what he had done with the three missing stones.

" 'You may as well face the matter,' said I; 'you have been caught in the act, and no confession could make your guilt more heinous. If you but make such reparation as is in your power, by telling us where the beryls are, all shall be forgiven and forgotten.'

" 'Keep your forgiveness for those who ask for it,' he answered, turning away from me with a sneer. I saw that he was too hardened for any words of mine to influence him. There was but one way for it. I called in the inspector and gave him into custody. A search was made at once not only of his person but of his room and of every portion of the house where he could possibly have concealed the gems; but no trace of them could be found, nor would the wretched boy open his mouth for all our persuasions and our threats. This morning he was removed to a cell, and I, after going through all the police formalities, have hurried round to you to implore you to use your skill in unravelling the matter. The police have openly confessed that they can at present make nothing of it. You may go to any expense which you think necessary. I have already offered a reward of £1000. My God, what shall I do! I have lost my honour, my gems, and my son in one night. Oh, what shall I do!"

He put a hand on either side of his head and rocked himself to and fro, droning to himself like a child whose grief has got beyond words.

Sherlock Holmes sat silent for some few minutes, with his brows knitted and his eyes fixed upon the fire.

"Do you receive much company?" he asked.

"None save my partner with his family and an occasional friend of Arthur's. Sir George Burnwell has been several times lately. No one else, I think."

"Do you go out much in society?"

"Arthur does. Mary and I stay at home. We neither of us care for it."

"That is unusual in a young girl."

"She is of a quiet nature. Besides, she is not so very young. She is four-and-twenty."

"This matter, from what you say, seems to have been a shock to her also."

"Terrible! She is even more affected than I."

"You have neither of you any doubt as to your son's guilt?"

"How can we have when I saw him with my own eyes with the coronet in his hands."

"I hardly consider that a conclusive proof. Was the remainder of the coronet at all injured?"

"Yes, it was twisted."

"Do you not think, then, that he might have been trying to straighten it?"

"God bless you! You are doing what you can for him and for me. But it is too heavy a task. What was he doing there at all? If his purpose were innocent, why did he not say so?"

"Precisely. And if it were guilty, why did he not invent a lie? His silence appears to me to cut both ways. There are several singular points about the case. What did the police think of the noise which awoke you from your sleep?"

"They considered that it might be caused by Arthur's closing his bedroom door."

"A likely story! As if a man bent on felony would slam his door so as to wake a household. What did they say, then, of the disappearance of these gems?"

"They are still sounding the planking and probing the furniture in the hope of finding them."

"Have they thought of looking outside the house?"

"Yes, they have shown extraordinary energy. The whole garden has already been minutely examined."

"Now, my dear sir," said Holmes, "is it not obvious to you now that this matter really strikes very much deeper than either you or the police were at first inclined to think? It appeared to you to be a simple case; to me it seems exceedingly complex. Consider what is involved by your theory. You suppose that your son came down from his bed, went, at great risk, to your dressing-room, opened your bureau, took out your coronet, broke off by main force a small portion of it, went off to some other place, concealed three gems out of the thirty-nine, with such skill that nobody can find them, and then returned with the other thirty-six into the room in which he exposed himself to the greatest danger of being discovered. I ask you now, is such a theory tenable?"

"But what other is there?" cried the banker with a gesture of despair. "If his motives were innocent, why does he not explain them?"

"It is our task to find that out," replied Holmes; "so now, if you please, Mr. Holder, we will set off for Streatham together, and devote an hour to glancing a little more closely into details."

My friend insisted upon my accompanying them in their expedition, which I was eager enough to do, for my curiosity and sympathy were deeply stirred by the story to which we had listened. I confess that the guilt of the banker's son appeared to me to be as obvious as it did to his unhappy father, but still I had such faith in Holmes's judgment that I felt that there must be some grounds for hope as long as he was dissatisfied with the accepted explanation. He hardly spoke a word the whole way out to the southern suburb, but sat with his chin upon his breast and his hat drawn over his eyes, sunk in the deepest thought. Our client appeared to have taken fresh heart at the little glimpse of hope which had been presented to him, and he even broke into a desultory chat with me over his business affairs. A short railway journey and a shorter walk brought us to Fairbank, the modest residence of the great financier.

Fairbank was a good-sized square house of white stone, standing back a little from the road. A double carriage-sweep, with a snow-clad lawn, stretched down in front to two large iron gates which closed the entrance. On the right side was a small wooden thicket, which led into a narrow path between two neat hedges stretching from the road to the kitchen door, and forming the tradesmen's entrance. On the left ran a lane which led to the stables, and was not itself within the grounds at all, being a public, though little used, thoroughfare. Holmes left us standing at the door and walked slowly all round the house, across the front, down the tradesmen's path, and so round by the garden behind into the stable lane. So long was he that Mr. Holder and I went into the dining-room and waited by the fire until he should return. We were sitting there in silence when the door opened and a young lady came in. She was rather above the middle height, slim, with dark hair and eyes, which seemed the darker against the absolute pallor of her skin. I do not think that I have ever seen such deadly paleness in a woman's face. Her lips, too, were bloodless, but her eyes were flushed with crying. As she swept silently into the room she impressed me with a greater sense of grief than the banker had done in the morning, and it was the more striking in her as she was evidently a woman of strong character, with immense capacity for self-restraint. Disregarding my presence, she went straight to her uncle and passed her hand over his head with a sweet womanly caress.

"You have given orders that Arthur should be liberated, have you not, dad?" she asked.

"No, no, my girl, the matter must be probed to the bottom."

"But I am so sure that he is innocent. You know what woman's instincts are. I know that he has done no harm and that you will be sorry for having acted so harshly."

"Why is he silent, then, if he is innocent?"

"Who knows? Perhaps because he was so angry that you should suspect him."

"How could I help suspecting him, when I actually saw him with the coronet in his hand?"

"Oh, but he had only picked it up to look at it. Oh, do, do take my word for it that he is innocent. Let the matter drop and say no more. It is so dreadful to think of our dear Arthur in prison!"

"I shall never let it drop until the gems are found—never, Mary! Your affection for Arthur blinds you as to the awful consequences to me. Far from hushing the thing up, I have brought a gentleman down from London to inquire more deeply into it."

"This gentleman?" she asked, facing round to me.

"No, his friend. He wished us to leave him alone. He is round in the stable lane now."

"The stable lane?" She raised her dark eyebrows. "What can he hope to find there? Ah! this, I suppose, is he. I trust, sir, that you will succeed in proving, what I feel sure is the truth, that my cousin Arthur is innocent of this crime."

"I fully share your opinion, and I trust, with you, that we may prove it," returned Holmes, going back to the mat to knock the snow from his shoes. "I believe I have the honour of addressing Miss Mary Holder. Might I ask you a question or two?"

"Pray do, sir, if it may help to clear this horrible affair up."

"You heard nothing yourself last night?"

"Nothing, until my uncle here began to speak loudly. I heard that, and I came down."

"You shut up the windows and doors the night before. Did you fasten all the windows?"

"Yes."

"Were they all fastened this morning?"

"Yes."

"You have a maid who has a sweetheart? I think that you remarked to your uncle last night that she had been out to see him?"

"Yes, and she was the girl who waited in the drawing-room, and who may have heard uncle's remarks about the coronet."

"I see. You infer that she may have gone out to tell her sweetheart, and that the two may have planned the robbery."

"But what is the good of all these vague theories," cried the banker impatiently, "when I have told you that I saw Arthur with the coronet in his hands?"

"Wait a little, Mr. Holder. We must come back to that. About this girl, Miss Holder. You saw her return by the kitchen door, I presume?"

"Yes; when I went to see if the door was fastened for the night I met her slipping in. I saw the man, too, in the gloom."

"Do you know him?"

"Oh, yes! he is the green-grocer who brings our vegetables round. His name is Francis Prosper."

"He stood," said Holmes, "to the left of the door—that is to say, farther up the path than is necessary to reach the door?"

"Yes, he did."

"And he is a man with a wooden leg?"

Something like fear sprang up in the young lady's expressive black eyes. "Why, you are like a magician," said she. "How do you know that?" She smiled, but there was no answering smile in Holmes's thin, eager face.

"I should be very glad now to go upstairs," said he. "I shall probably wish to go over the outside of the house again. Perhaps I had better take a look at the lower windows before I go up."

He walked swiftly round from one to the other, pausing only at the large one which looked from the hall onto the stable lane. This he opened and made a very careful examination of the sill with his powerful magnifying lens. "Now we shall go upstairs," said he at last.

The banker's dressing-room was a plainly furnished little chamber, with a gray carpet, a large bureau, and a long mirror. Holmes went to the bureau first and looked hard at the lock.

"Which key was used to open it?" he asked.

"That which my son himself indicated—that of the cupboard of the lumber-room."

"Have you it here?"

"That is it on the dressing-table."

Sherlock Holmes took it up and opened the bureau.

"It is a noiseless lock," said he. "It is no wonder that it did not wake you. This case, I presume, contains the coronet. We must have a look at it." He opened the case, and taking out the diadem he laid it upon the table. It was a magnificent specimen of the jeweller's art, and the thirty-six stones were the finest that I have ever seen. At one side of the coronet was a cracked edge, where a corner holding three gems had been torn away.

"Now, Mr. Holder," said Holmes, "here is the corner which corresponds to that which has been so unfortunately lost. Might I beg that you will break it off."

The banker recoiled in horror. "I should not dream of trying," said he.

"Then I will." Holmes suddenly bent his strength upon it, but without result. "I feel it give a little," said he; "but, though I am exceptionally strong in the fingers, it would take me all my time to break it. An ordinary man could not do it. Now, what do you think would happen if I did break it, Mr. Holder? There would be a noise like a pistol shot. Do you tell me that all this happened within a few yards of your bed and that you heard nothing of it?"

"I do not know what to think. It is all dark to me."

"But perhaps it may grow lighter as we go. What do you think, Miss Holder?"

"I confess that I still share my uncle's perplexity."

"Your son had no shoes or slippers on when you saw him?"

"He had nothing on save only his trousers and shirt."

"Thank you. We have certainly been favoured with extraordinary luck during this inquiry, and it will be entirely our own fault if we do not succeed in clearing the matter up. With your permission, Mr. Holder, I shall now continue my investigations outside."

He went alone, at his own request, for he explained that any unnecessary footmarks might make his task more difficult. For an hour or more he was at work, returning at last with his feet heavy with snow and his features as inscrutable as ever.

"I think that I have seen now all that there is to see, Mr. Holder," said he; "I can serve you best by returning to my rooms."

"But the gems, Mr. Holmes. Where are they?"

"I cannot tell."

The banker wrung his hands. "I shall never see them again!" he cried. "And my son? You give me hopes?"

"My opinion is in no way altered."

"Then, for God's sake, what was this dark business which was acted in my house last night?"

"If you can call upon me at my Baker Street rooms to-morrow morning between nine and ten I shall be happy to do what I can to make it clearer. I understand that you give me carte blanche to act for you, provided only that I get back the gems, and that you place no limit on the sum I may draw."

"I would give my fortune to have them back."

"Very good. I shall look into the matter between this and then. Good-bye; it is just possible that I may have to come over here again before evening."

It was obvious to me that my companion's mind was now made up about the case, although what his conclusions were was more than I could even dimly imagine. Several times during our homeward journey I endeavoured to sound him upon the point, but he always glided away to some other topic, until at last I gave it over in despair. It was not yet three when we found ourselves in our rooms once more. He hurried to his chamber, and was down again in a few minutes dressed as a common loafer. With his collar turned up, his shiny, seedy coat, his red cravat, and his worn boots, he was a perfect sample of the class.

"I think that this should do," said he, glancing into the glass above the fireplace. "I only wish that you could come with me, Watson, but I fear that it won't do. I may be on the trail in this matter, or I may be following a will-o'-the-wisp, but I shall soon know which it is. I hope that I may be back in a few hours." He cut a slice of beef from the joint upon the sideboard, sandwiched it between two rounds of bread, and thrusting this rude meal into his pocket he started off upon his expedition.

I had just finished my tea when he returned, evidently in excellent spirits, swinging an old elastic-sided boot in his hand. He chucked it down into a corner and helped himself to a cup of tea.

"I only looked in as I passed," said he. "I am going right on."

"Where to?"

"Oh, to the other side of the West End. It may be some time before I get back. Don't wait up for me in case I should be late."

"How are you getting on?"

"Oh, so so. Nothing to complain of. I have been out to Streatham since I saw you last, but I did not call at the house. It is a very sweet little problem, and I would not have missed it for a good deal. However, I must not sit gossiping here, but must get these disreputable clothes off and return to my highly respectable self."

I could see by his manner that he had stronger reasons for satisfaction than his words alone would imply. His eyes twinkled, and there was even a touch of colour upon his sallow cheeks. He hastened upstairs, and a few minutes later I heard the slam of the hall door, which told me that he was off once more upon his congenial hunt.

I waited until midnight, but there was no sign of his return, so I retired to my room. It was no uncommon thing for him to be away for days and nights on end when he was hot upon a scent, so that his lateness caused me no surprise. I do not know at what hour he came in, but when I came down to breakfast in the morning there he was with a cup of coffee in one hand and the paper in the other, as fresh and trim as possible.

"You will excuse my beginning without you, Watson," said he, "but you remember that our client has rather an early appointment this morning."

"Why, it is after nine now," I answered. "I should not be surprised if that were he. I thought I heard a ring."

It was, indeed, our friend the financier. I was shocked by the change which had come over him, for his face which was naturally of a broad and massive mould, was now pinched and fallen in, while his hair seemed to me at least a shade whiter. He entered with a weariness and lethargy which was even more painful than his violence of the morning before, and he dropped heavily into the armchair which I pushed forward for him.

"I do not know what I have done to be so severely tried," said he. "Only two days ago I was a happy and prosperous man, without a care in the world. Now I am left to a lonely and dishonoured age. One sorrow comes close upon the heels of another. My niece, Mary, has deserted me."

"Deserted you?"

"Yes. Her bed this morning had not been slept in, her room was empty, and a note for me lay upon the hall table. I had said to her last night, in sorrow and not in anger, that if she had married my boy all might have been well with him. Perhaps it was thoughtless of me to say so. It is to that remark that she refers in this note:

"My Dearest Uncle:

"I feel that I have brought trouble upon you, and that if I had acted differently this terrible misfortune might never have occured. I cannot, with this thought in my mind, ever again be happy under your roof, and I feel that I must leave you forever. Do not worry about my future, for that is provided for; and, above all, do not search for me, for it will be fruitless labour and an ill-service to me. In life or in death, I am ever

"Your loving
"Mary.

"What could she mean by that note, Mr. Holmes? Do you think it points to suicide?"

"No, no, nothing of the kind. It is perhaps the best possible solution. I trust, Mr. Holder, that you are nearing the end of your troubles."

"Ha! You say so! You have heard something, Mr. Holmes; you have learned something! Where are the gems?"

"You would not think £1000 apiece an excessive sum for them?"

"I would pay ten."

"That would be unnecessary. Three thousand will cover the matter. And there is a little reward, I fancy. Have you your check-book? Here is a pen. Better make it out for £4000."

With a dazed face the banker made out the required check. Holmes walked over to his desk, took out a little triangular piece of gold with three gems in it, and threw it down upon the table.

With a shriek of joy our client clutched it up.

"You have it!" he gasped. "I am saved! I am saved!"

The reaction of joy was as passionate as his grief had been, and he hugged his recovered gems to his bosom.

"There is one other thing you owe, Mr. Holder," said Sherlock Holmes rather sternly.

"Owe!" He caught up a pen. "Name the sum, and I will pay it "

"No, the debt is not to me. You owe a very humble apology to that noble lad, your son, who has carried himself in this matter as I should be proud to see my own son do, should I ever chance to have one."

"Then it was not Arthur who took them?"

"I told you yesterday, and I repeat to-day, that it was not."

"You are sure of it! Then let us hurry to him at once to let him know that the truth is known."

"He knows it already. When I had cleared it all up I had an interview with him, and finding that he would not tell me the story, I told it to him, on which he had to confess that I was right and to add the very few details which were not yet quite clear to me. Your news of this morning, however, may open his lips."

"For heaven's sake, tell me, then, what is this extraordinary mystery!"

"I will do so, and I will show you the steps by which I reached it. And let me say to you, first, that which it is hardest for me to say and for you to hear: there has been an understanding between Sir George Burnwell and your niece Mary. They have now fled together."

"My Mary? Impossible!"

"It is unfortunately more than possible; it is certain. Neither you nor your son knew the true character of this man when you admitted him into your family circle. He is one of the most dangerous men in England—a ruined gambler, an absolutely desperate villain, a man without heart or conscience. Your niece knew nothing of such men. When he breathed his vows to her, as he had done to a hundred before her, she flattered herself that she alone had touched his heart. The devil knows best what he said, but at least she became his tool and was in the habit of seeing him nearly every evening."

"I cannot, and I will not, believe it!" cried the banker with an ashen face.

"I will tell you, then, what occurred in your house last night. Your niece, when you had, as she thought, gone to your room, slipped down and talked to her lover through the window which leads into the stable lane. His footmarks had pressed right through the snow, so long had he stood there. She told him of the coronet. His wicked lust for gold kindled at the news, and he bent her to his will. I have no doubt that she loved you, but there are women in whom the love of a lover extinguishes all other loves, and I think that she must have been one. She had hardly listened to his instructions when she saw you coming downstairs, on which she closed the window rapidly and told you about one of the servants' escapade with her wooden-legged lover, which was all perfectly true.

"Your boy, Arthur, went to bed after his interview with you, but he slept badly on account of his uneasiness about his club debts. In the middle of the night he heard a soft tread pass his door, so he rose and, looking out, was surprised to see his cousin walking very stealthily along the passage until she disappeared into your dressing-room. Petrified with astonishment, the lad slipped on some clothes and waited there in the dark to see what would come of this strange affair. Presently she emerged from the room again, and in the light of the passage-lamp your son saw that she carried the precious coronet in her hands. She passed down the stairs, and he, thrilling with horror, ran along and slipped behind the curtain near your door, whence he could see what passed in the hall beneath. He saw her stealthily open the window, hand out the coronet to someone in the gloom, and then closing it once more hurry back to her room, passing quite close to where he stood hid behind the curtain.

"As long as she was on the scene he could not take any action without a horrible exposure of the woman whom he loved. But the instant that she was gone he realized how crushing a misfortune this would be for you, and how all-important it was to set it right. He rushed down, just as he was, in his bare feet, opened the window, sprang out into the snow, and ran down the lane, where he could see a dark figure in the moonlight. Sir George Burnwell tried to get away, but Arthur caught him, and there was a struggle between them, your lad tugging at one side of the coronet, and his opponent at the other. In the scuffle, your son struck Sir George and cut him over the eye. Then something suddenly snapped, and your son, finding that he had the coronet in his hands, rushed back, closed the window, ascended to your room, and had just observed that the coronet had been twisted in the struggle and was endeavouring to straighten it when you appeared upon the scene."

"Is it possible?" gasped the banker.

"You then roused his anger by calling him names at a moment when he felt that he had deserved your warmest thanks. He could not explain the true state of affairs without betraying one who certainly deserved little enough consideration at his hands. He took the more chivalrous view, however, and preserved her secret."

"And that was why she shrieked and fainted when she saw the coronet," cried Mr. Holder. "Oh, my God! what a blind fool I have been! And his asking to be allowed to go out for five minutes! The dear fellow wanted to see if the missing piece were at the scene of the struggle. How cruelly I have misjudged him!"

"When I arrived at the house," continued Holmes, "I at once went very carefully round it to observe if there were any traces in the snow which might help me. I knew that none had fallen since the evening before, and also that there had been a strong frost to preserve impressions. I passed along the tradesmen's path, but found it all trampled down and indistinguishable. Just beyond it, however, at the far side of the kitchen door, a woman had stood and talked with a man, whose round impressions on one side showed that he had a wooden leg. I could even tell that they had been disturbed, for the woman had run back swiftly to the door, as was shown by the deep toe and light heel marks, while Wooden-leg had waited a little, and then had gone away. I thought at the time that this might be the maid and her sweetheart, of whom you had already spoken to me, and inquiry showed it was so. I passed round the garden without seeing anything more than random tracks, which I took to be the police; but when I got into the stable lane a very long and complex story was written in the snow in front of me.

"There was a double line of tracks of a booted man, and a second double line which I saw with delight belonged to a man with naked feet. I was at once convinced from what you had told me that the latter was your son. The first had walked both ways, but the other had run swiftly, and as his tread was marked in places over the depression of the boot, it was obvious that he had passed after the other. I followed them up and found they led to the hall window, where Boots had worn all the snow away while waiting. Then I walked to the other end, which was a hundred yards or more down the lane. I saw where Boots had faced round, where the snow was cut up as though there had been a struggle, and, finally, where a few drops of blood had fallen, to show me that I was not mistaken. Boots had then run down the lane, and another little smudge of blood showed that it was he who had been hurt. When he came to the highroad at the other end, I found that the pavement had been cleared, so there was an end to that clue.

"On entering the house, however, I examined, as you remember, the sill and framework of the hall window with my lens, and I could at once see that someone had passed out. I could distinguish the outline of an instep where the wet foot had been placed in coming in. I was then beginning to be able to form an opinion as to what had occurred. A man had waited outside the window; someone had brought the gems; the deed had been overseen by your son; he had pursued the thief; had struggled with him; they had each tugged at the coronet, their united strength causing injuries which neither alone could have effected. He had returned with the prize, but had left a fragment in the grasp of his opponent. So far I was clear. The question now was, who was the man and who was it brought him the coronet?

"It is an old maxim of mine that when you have excluded the impossible, whatever remains, however improbable, must be the truth. Now, I knew that it was not you who had brought it down, so there only remained your niece and the maids. But if it were the maids, why should your son allow himself to be accused in their place? There could be no possible reason. As he loved his cousin, however, there was an excellent explanation why he should retain her secret—the more so as the secret was a disgraceful one. When I remembered that you had seen her at that window, and how she had fainted on seeing the coronet again, my conjecture became a certainty.

"And who could it be who was her confederate? A lover evidently, for who else could outweigh the love and gratitude which she must feel to you? I knew that you went out little, and that your circle of friends was a very limited one. But among them was Sir George Burnwell. I had heard of him before as being a man of evil reputation among women. It must have been he who wore those boots and retained the missing gems. Even though he knew that Arthur had discovered him, he might still flatter himself that he was safe, for the lad could not say a word without compromising his own family.

"Well, your own good sense will suggest what measures I took next. I went in the shape of a loafer to Sir George's house, managed to pick up an acquaintance with his valet, learned that his master had cut his head the night before, and, finally, at the expense of six shillings, made all sure by buying a pair of his cast-off shoes. With these I journeyed down to Streatham and saw that they exactly fitted the tracks."

"I saw an ill-dressed vagabond in the lane yesterday evening," said Mr. Holder.

"Precisely. It was I. I found that I had my man, so I came home and changed my clothes. It was a delicate part which I had to play then, for I saw that a prosecution must be avoided to avert scandal, and I knew that so astute a villain would see that our hands were tied in the matter. I went and saw him. At first, of course, he denied everything. But when I gave him every particular that had occurred, he tried to bluster and took down a life-preserver from the wall. I knew my man, however, and I clapped a pistol to his head before he could strike. Then he became a little more reasonable. I told him that we would give him a price for the stones he held—£1000 apiece. That brought out the first signs of grief that he had shown. 'Why, dash it all!' said he, 'I've let them go at six hundred for the three!' I soon managed to get the address of the receiver who had them, on promising him that there would be no prosecution. Off I set to him, and after much chaffering I got our stones at £1000 apiece. Then I looked in upon your son, told him that all was right, and eventually got to my bed about two o'clock, after what I may call a really hard day's work."

"A day which has saved England from a great public scandal," said the banker, rising. "Sir, I cannot find words to thank you, but you shall not find me ungrateful for what you have done. Your skill has indeed exceeded all that I have heard of it. And now I must fly to my dear boy to apologize to him for the wrong which I have done him. As to what you tell me of poor Mary, it goes to my very heart. Not even your skill can inform me where she is now."

"I think that we may safely say," returned Holmes, "that she is wherever Sir George Burnwell is. It is equally certain, too, that whatever her sins are, they will soon receive a more than sufficient punishment."

The Adventure of the Copper Beeches

"To the man who loves art for its own sake," remarked Sherlock Holmes, tossing aside the advertisement sheet of the *Daily Telegraph*, "it is frequently in its least important and lowliest manifestations that the keenest pleasure is to be derived. It is pleasant to me to observe, Watson, that you have so far grasped this truth that in these little records of our cases which you have been good enough to draw up, and, I am bound to say, occasionally to embellish, you have given prominence not so much to the many *causes célèbres* and sensational trials in which I have figured but rather to those incidents which may have been trivial in themselves, but which have given room for those faculties of deduction and of logical synthesis which I have made my special province."

"And yet," said I, smiling, "I cannot quite hold myself absolved from the charge of sensationalism which has been urged against my records."

"You have erred, perhaps," he observed, taking up a glowing cinder with the tongs and lighting with it the long cherry-wood pipe which was wont to replace his clay when he was in a disputatious rather than a meditative mood—"you have erred perhaps in attempting to put colour and life into each of your statements instead of confining yourself to the task of placing upon record that severe reasoning from cause to effect which is really the only notable feature about the thing."

"It seems to me that I have done you full justice in the matter," I remarked with some coldness, for I was repelled by the egotism which I had more than once observed to be a strong factor in my friend's singular character.

"No, it is not selfishness or conceit," said he, answering, as was his wont, my thoughts rather than my words. "If I claim full justice for my art, it is because it is an impersonal thing—a thing beyond myself. Crime is common. Logic is rare. Therefore it is upon the logic rather than upon the crime that you should dwell. You have degraded what should have been a course of lectures into a series of tales."

It was a cold morning of the early spring, and we sat after breakfast on either side of a cheery fire in the old room at Baker Street. A thick fog rolled down between the lines of dun-coloured houses, and the opposing windows loomed like dark, shapeless blurs through the heavy yellow wreaths. Our gas was lit and shone on the white cloth and glimmer of china and metal, for the table had not been cleared yet. Sherlock Holmes had been silent all the morning, dipping continuously into the advertisement columns of a succession of papers until at last, having apparently given up his search, he had emerged in no very sweet temper to lecture me upon my literary shortcomings.

"At the same time," he remarked after a pause, during which he had sat puffing at his long pipe and gazing down into the fire, "you can hardly be open to a charge of sensationalism, for out of these cases which you have been so kind as to interest yourself in, a fair proportion do not treat of crime, in its legal sense, at all. The small matter in which I endeavoured to help the King of Bohemia, the singular experience of Miss Mary Sutherland, the problem connected with the man with the twisted lip, and the incident of the noble bachelor, were all matters which are outside the pale of the law. But in avoiding the sensational, I fear that you may have bordered on the trivial."

"The end may have been so," I answered, "but the methods I hold to have been novel and of interest."

"Pshaw, my dear fellow, what do the public, the great unobservant public, who could hardly tell a weaver by his tooth or a compositor by his left thumb, care about the finer shades of analysis and deduction! But, indeed, if you are trivial, I cannot blame you, for the days of the great cases are past. Man, or at least criminal man, has lost all enterprise and originality. As to my own little practice, it seems to be degenerating into an agency for recovering lost lead pencils and giving advice to young ladies from boarding-schools. I think that I have touched bottom at last, however. This note I had this morning marks my zero-point, I fancy. Read it!" He tossed a crumpled letter across to me.

It was dated from Montague Place upon the preceding evening, and ran thus:

DEAR MR. HOLMES:

I am very anxious to consult you as to whether I should or should not accept a situation which has been offered to me as governess. I shall call at half-past ten to-morrow if I do not inconvenience you.

Yours faithfully,
VIOLET HUNTER.

"Do you know the young lady?' I asked.

"Not I."

"It is half-past ten now."

"Yes, and I have no doubt that is her ring."

"It may turn out to be of more interest than you think. You remember that the affair of the blue carbuncle, which appeared to be a mere whim at first, developed into a serious investigation. It may be so in this case, also."

"Well, let us hope so. But our doubts will very soon be solved, for here, unless I am much mistaken, is the person in question."

As he spoke the door opened and a young lady entered the room. She was plainly but neatly dressed, with a bright, quick face, freckled like a plover's egg, and with the brisk manner of a woman who has had her own way to make in the world.

"You will excuse my troubling you, I am sure," said she, as

my companion rose to greet her, "but I have had a very strange experience, and as I have no parents or relations of any sort from whom I could ask advice, I thought that perhaps you would be kind enough to tell me what I should do."

"Pray take a seat, Miss Hunter. I shall be happy to do anything that I can to serve you."

I could see that Holmes was favourably impressed by the manner and speech of his new client. He looked her over in his searching fashion, and then composed himself, with his lids drooping and his finger-tips together, to listen to her story.

"I have been a governess for five years," said she, "in the family of Colonel Spence Munro, but two months ago the colonel received an appointment at Halifax, in Nova Scotia, and took his children over to America with him, so that I found myself without a situation. I advertised, and I answered advertisements, but without success. At last the little money which I had saved began to run short, and I was at my wit's end as to what I should do.

"There is a well-known agency for governesses in the West End called Westaway's, and there I used to call about once a week in order to see whether anything had turned up which might suit me. Westaway was the name of the founder of the business, but it is really managed by Miss Stoper. She sits in her own little office, and the ladies who are seeking employment wait in an anteroom, and are then shown in one by one, when she consults her ledgers and sees whether she has anything which would suit them.

"Well, when I called last week I was shown into the little office as usual, but I found that Miss Stoper was not alone. A prodigiously stout man with a very smiling face and a great heavy chin which rolled down in fold upon fold over his throat sat at her elbow with a pair of glasses on his nose, looking very earnestly at the ladies who entered. As I came in he gave quite a jump in his chair and turned quickly to Miss Stoper.

" 'That will do,' said he; 'I could not ask for anything better. Capital! capital!' He seemed quite enthusiastic and rubbed his hands together in the most genial fashion. He was such a comfortable-looking man that it was quite a pleasure to look at him.

" 'You are looking for a situation, miss?' he asked.

" 'Yes, sir.'

" 'As governess?'

" 'Yes, sir'

" 'And what salary do you ask?'

" 'I had £4 a month in my last place with Colonel Spence Munro.'

" 'Oh, tut, tut! sweating—rank sweating!' he cried, throwing his fat hands out into the air like a man who is in a boiling passion. 'How could anyone offer so pitiful a sum to a lady with such attractions and accomplishments?'

" 'My accomplishments, sir, may be less than you imagine,' said I. 'A little French, a little German, music, and drawing—'

" 'Tut, tut!' he cried. 'This is all quite beside the question. The point is, have you or have you not the bearing and deportment of a lady? There it is in a nutshell. If you have not, you are not fitted for the rearing of a child who may some day play a considerable part in the history of the country. But if you have, why, then, how could any gentleman ask you to condescend to accept anything under the three figures? Your salary with me, madam, would commence at £100 a year.'

"You may imagine, Mr. Holmes, that to me, destitute as I was, such an offer seemed almost too good to be true. The gentleman, however, seeing perhaps the look of incredulity upon my face, opened a pocket-book and took out a note.

" 'It is also my custom,' said he, smiling in the most pleasant fashion until his eyes were just two little shining slits amid the white creases of his face, 'to advance to my young ladies half their salary beforehand, so that they may meet any little expenses of their journey and their wardrobe.'

"It seemed to me that I had never met so fascinating and so thoughtful a man. As I was already in debt to my tradesmen, the advance was a great convenience, and yet there was something unnatural about the whole transaction which made me wish to know a little more before I quite committed myself.

" 'May I ask where you live, sir?' said I.

" 'Hampshire. Charming rural place. The Copper Beeches, five miles on the far side of Winchester. It is the most lovely country, my dear young lady, and the dearest old country-house.'

" 'And my duties, sir? I should be glad to know what they would be.'

" 'One child—one dear little romper just six years old. Oh,

if you could see him killing cockroaches with a slipper! Smack! smack! smack! Three gone before you could wink!' He leaned back in his chair and laughed his eyes into his head again.

"I was a little startled at the nature of the child's amusement, but the father's laughter made me think that perhaps he was joking.

" 'My sole duties, then,' I asked, 'are to take charge of a single child?'

" 'No, no, not the sole, not the sole, my dear young lady,' he cried. 'Your duty would be, as I am sure your good sense would suggest, to obey any little commands my wife might give, provided always that they were such commands as a lady might with propriety obey. You see no difficulty, heh?'

" 'I should be happy to make myself useful.'

" 'Quite so. In dress now, for example. We are faddy people, you know—faddy but kind-hearted. If you were asked to wear any dress which we might give you, you would not object to our little whim. Heh?'

" 'No,' said I, considerably astonished at his words.

" 'Or to sit here, or sit there, that would not be offensive to you?'

" 'Oh, no.'

" 'Or to cut your hair quite short before you come to us?'

"I could hardly believe my ears. As you may observe, Mr. Holmes, my hair is somewhat luxuriant, and of a rather peculiar tint of chestnut. It has been considered artistic. I could not dream of sacrificing it in this offhand fashion.

" 'I am afraid that that is quite impossible,' said I. He had been watching me eagerly out of his small eyes, and I could see a shadow pass over his face as I spoke.

" 'I am afraid that it is quite essential,' said he. 'It is a little fancy of my wife's, and ladies' fancies, you know, madam, ladies' fancies must be consulted. And so you won't cut your hair?'

" 'No, sir, I really could not,' I answered firmly.

" 'Ah, very well; then that quite settles the matter. It is a pity, because in other respects you would really have done very nicely. In that case, Miss Stoper, I had best inspect a few more of your young ladies.'

"The manageress had sat all this while busy with her papers without a word to either of us, but she glanced at me now with so much annoyance upon her face that I could not help suspecting that she had lost a handsome commission through my refusal.

" 'Do you desire your name to be kept upon the books?' she asked.

" 'If you please, Miss Stoper.'

" 'Well, really, it seems rather useless, since you refuse the most excellent offers in this fashion,' said she sharply. 'You can hardly expect us to exert ourselves to find another such opening for you. Good-day to you, Miss Hunter.' She struck a gong upon the table, and I was shown out by the page.

"Well, Mr. Holmes, when I got back to my lodgings and found little enough in the cupboard, and two or three bills upon the table, I began to ask myself whether I had not done a very foolish thing. After all, if these people had strange fads and expected obedience on the most extraordinary matters, they were at least ready to pay for their eccentricity. Very few governesses in England are getting £100 a year. Besides, what use was my hair to me? Many people are improved by wearing it short, and perhaps I should be among the number. Next day I was inclined to think that I had made a mistake, and by the day after I was sure of it. I had almost overcome my pride so far as to go back to the agency and inquire whether the place was still open when I received this letter from the gentleman himself. I have it here, and I will read it to you:

"The Copper Beeches, near Winchester.

"Dear Miss Hunter:

"Miss Stoper has very kindly given me your address, and I write from here to ask you whether you have reconsidered your decision. My wife is very anxious that you should come, for she has been much attracted by my description of you. We are willing to give £30 a quarter, or £120 a year, so as to recompense you for any little inconvenience which our fads may cause you. They are not very exacting, after all. My wife is fond of a particular shade of electric blue, and would like you to wear such a dress indoors in the morning. You need not, however, go to the expense of purchasing one, as we have one belonging to my dear daughter Alice (now in Philadelphia), which would, I should think, fit you very well. Then, as to sitting here or there, or amusing yourself in any manner indicated, that need cause you no inconvenience. As regards your hair, it is no doubt a pity, especially as I could not help remarking its beauty during our short interview, but I am afraid that I must remain firm upon this point, and I only hope that the increased salary may recompense you for the loss. Your duties, as far as the child is concerned, are very light. Now do try to come, and I shall meet you with the dog-cart at Winchester. Let me know your train.

"Yours faithfully,
"JEPHRO RUCASTLE.

"That is the letter which I have just received, Mr. Holmes, and my mind is made up that I will accept it. I thought, however, that before taking the final step I should like to submit the whole matter to your consideration."

"Well, Miss Hunter, if your mind is made up, that settles the question," said Holmes, smiling.

"But you would not advise me to refuse?"

"I confess that it is not the situation which I should like to see a sister of mine apply for."

"What is the meaning of it all, Mr. Holmes?"

"Ah, I have no data. I cannot tell. Perhaps you have yourself formed some opinion?"

"Well, there seems to me to be only one possible solution. Mr. Rucastle seemed to be a very kind, good-natured man. Is it not possible that his wife is a lunatic, that he desires to keep the matter quiet for fear she should be taken to an asylum, and that he humours her fancies in every way in order to prevent an outbreak?"

"That is a possible solution—in fact, as matters stand, it is the most probable one. But in any case it does not seem to be a nice household for a young lady."

"But the money, Mr. Holmes, the money!"

"Well, yes, of course the pay is good—too good. That is what makes me uneasy. Why should they give you £120 a year, when they could have their pick for £40? There must be some strong reason behind."

"I thought that if I told you the circumstances you would understand afterwards if I wanted your help. I should feel so much stronger if I felt that you were at the back of me."

"Oh, you may carry that feeling away with you. I assure you that your little problem promises to be the most interesting which has come my way for some months. There is something distinctly novel about some of the features. If you should find yourself in doubt or in danger—"

"Danger! What danger do you foresee?"

Holmes shook his head gravely. "It would cease to be a danger if we could define it," said he. "But at any time, day or night, a telegram would bring me down to your help."

"That is enough." She rose briskly from her chair with the anxiety all swept from her face. "I shall go down to Hampshire quite easy in my mind now. I shall write to Mr. Rucastle at once, sacrifice my poor hair to-night, and start for Winchester to-morrow." With a few grateful words to Holmes she bade us both good-night and bustled off upon her way.

"At least," said I as we heard her quick, firm steps descending the stairs, "she seems to be a young lady who is very well able to take care of herself."

"And she would need to be," said Holmes gravely. "I am much mistaken if we do not hear from her before many days are past."

It was not very long before my friend's prediction was fulfilled. A fortnight went by, during which I frequently found my thoughts turning in her direction and wondering what strange side-alley of human experience this lonely woman had strayed into. The unusual salary, the curious conditions, the light duties, all pointed to something abnormal, though whether a fad or a plot, or whether the man were a philanthropist or a villain, it was quite beyond my powers to determine. As to Holmes, I observed that he sat frequently for half an hour on end, with knitted brows and an abstracted air, but he swept the matter away with a wave of his hand when I mentioned it. "Data! data! data!" he cried impatiently. "I can't make bricks without clay." And yet he would always wind up by muttering that no sister of his should ever have accepted such a situation.

The telegram which we eventually received came late one night just as I was thinking of turning in and Holmes was settling down to one of those all-night chemical researches which he frequently indulged in, when I would leave him stooping over a retort and a test-tube at night and find him in the same position when I came down to breakfast in the morning. He opened the yellow envelope, and then, glancing at the message, threw it across to me.

"Just look up the trains in Bradshaw," said he, and turned back to his chemical studies.

The summons was a brief and urgent one.

> Please be at the Black Swan Hotel at Winchester at mid-day to-morrow [it said]. Do come! I am at my wit's end.
>
> HUNTER.

"Will you come with me?" asked Holmes, glancing up.

"I should wish to."

"Just look it up, then."

"There is a train at half-past nine," said I, glancing over my Bradshaw. "It is due at Winchester at 11:30."

"That will do very nicely. Then perhaps I had better postpone my analysis of the acetones, as we may need to be at our best in the morning."

By eleven o'clock the next day we were well upon our way to the old English capital. Holmes had been buried in the morning papers all the way down, but after we had passed the Hampshire border he threw them down and began to admire the scenery. It was an ideal spring day, a light blue sky, flecked with little fleecy white clouds drifting across from west to east. The sun was shining very brightly, and yet there was an exhilarating nip in the air, which set an edge to a man's energy. All over the countryside, away to the rolling hills around Aldershot, the little red and gray roofs of the farm-steadings peeped out from amid the light green of the new foliage.

"Are they not fresh and beautiful?" I cried with all the enthusiasm of a man fresh from the fogs of Baker Street.

But Holmes shook his head gravely.

"Do you know, Watson," said he, "that it is one of the curses of a mind with a turn like mine that I must look at everything with reference to my own special subject. You look at these scattered houses, and you are impressed by their beauty. I look at them, and the only thought which comes to me is a feeling of their isolation and of the impunity with which crime may be committed there."

"Good heavens!" I cried. "Who would associate crime with these dear old homesteads?"

"They always fill me with a certain horror. It is my belief, Watson, founded upon my experience, that the lowest and vilest alleys in London do not present a more dreadful record of sin than does the smiling and beautiful countryside."

"You horrify me!"

"But the reason is very obvious. The pressure of public opinion can do in the town what the law cannot accomplish. There is no lane so vile that the scream of a tortured child, or the thud of a drunkard's blow, does not beget sympathy and indignation among the neighbours, and then the whole machinery of justice is ever so close that a word of complaint can set it going, and there is but a step between the crime and the dock. But look at these lonely houses, each in its own fields, filled for the most part with poor ignorant folk who know little of the law. Think of the deeds of hellish cruelty, the hidden wickedness which may go on, year in, year out, in such places, and none the wiser. Had this lady who appeals to us for help gone to live in Winchester, I should never have had a fear for her. It is the five miles of country which makes the danger. Still, it is clear that she is not personally threatened."

"No. If she can come to Winchester to meet us she can get away."

"Quite so. She has her freedom."

"What *can* be the matter, then? Can you suggest no explanation?"

"I have devised seven separate explanations, each of which would cover the facts as far as we know them. But which of these is correct can only be determined by the fresh information which we shall no doubt find waiting for us. Well, there is the tower of the cathedral, and we shall soon learn all that Miss Hunter has to tell."

The Black Swan is an inn of repute in the High Street, at no distance from the station, and there we found the young lady waiting for us. She had engaged a sitting-room, and our lunch awaited us upon the table.

"I am so delighted that you have come," she said earnestly. "It is so very kind of you both; but indeed I do not know what I should do. Your advice will be altogether invaluable to me."

"Pray tell us what has happened to you."

"I will do so, and I must be quick, for I have promised Mr. Rucastle to be back before three. I got his leave to come into town this morning, though he little knew for what purpose."

"Let us have everything in its due order." Holmes thrust his long thin legs out towards the fire and composed himself to listen.

"In the first place, I may say that I have met, on the whole, with no actual ill-treatment from Mr. and Mrs. Rucastle. It is only fair to them to say that. But I cannot understand them, and I am not easy in my mind about them."

"What can you not understand?"

"Their reasons for their conduct. But you shall have it all just as it occurred. When I came down, Mr. Rucastle met me here and drove me in his dog-cart to the Copper Beeches. It is, as he said, beautifully situated, but it is not beautiful in itself, for it is a large square block of a house, whitewashed, but all stained and streaked with damp and bad weather. There are grounds round it, woods on three sides, and on the fourth a field which slopes down to the Southampton highroad, which curves past about a hundred yards from the front door. This ground in front belongs to the house, but the woods all round are part of Lord Southerton's preserves. A clump of copper beeches immediately in front of the hall door has given its name to the place.

"I was driven over by my employer, who was as amiable as ever, and was introduced by him that evening to his wife and the child. There was no truth, Mr. Holmes, in the conjecture which seemed to us to be probable in your rooms at Baker Street. Mrs. Rucastle is not mad. I found her to be a silent, pale-faced woman, much younger than her husband, not more than thirty, I should think, while he can hardly be less than forty-five. From their conversation I have gathered that they have been married about seven years, that he was a widower, and that his only child by the first wife was the daughter who has gone to Philadelphia. Mr. Rucastle told me in private that the reason why she had left them was that she had an unreasoning aversion to her stepmother. As the daughter could not have been less than twenty, I can quite imagine that her position must have been uncomfortable with her father's young wife.

"Mrs. Rucastle seemed to me to be colourless in mind as well as in feature. She impressed me neither favourably nor the reverse. She was a nonentity. It was easy to see that she was passionately devoted both to her husband and to her little son.

Her light gray eyes wandered continually from one to the other, noting every little want and forestalling it if possible. He was kind to her also in his bluff, boisterous fashion, and on the whole they seemed to be a happy couple. And yet she had some secret sorrow, this woman. She would often be lost in deep thought, with the saddest look upon her face. More than once I have surprised her in tears. I have thought sometimes that it was the disposition of her child which weighed upon her mind, for I have never met so utterly spoiled and so ill-natured a little creature. He is small for his age, with a head which is quite disproportionately large. His whole life appears to be spent in an alternation between savage fits of passion and gloomy intervals of sulking. Giving pain to any creature weaker than himself seems to be his one idea of amusement, and he shows quite remarkable talent in planning the capture of mice, little birds, and insects. But I would rather not talk about the creature, Mr. Holmes, and, indeed, he has little to do with my story."

"I am glad of all details," remarked my friend, "whether they seem to you to be relevant or not."

"I shall try not to miss anything of importance. The one unpleasant thing about the house, which struck me at once, was the appearance and conduct of the servants. There are only two, a man and his wife. Toller, for that is his name, is a rough, uncouth man, with grizzled hair and whiskers, and a perpetual smell of drink. Twice since I have been with them he has been quite drunk, and yet Mr. Rucastle seemed to take no notice of it. His wife is a very tall and strong woman with a sour face, as silent as Mrs. Rucastle and much less amiable. They are a most unpleasant couple, but fortunately I spend most of my time in the nursery and my own room, which are next to each other in one corner of the building.

"For two days after my arrival at the Copper Beeches my life was very quiet; on the third, Mrs. Rucastle came down just after breakfast and whispered something to her husband.

" 'Oh, yes,' said he, turning to me, 'we are very much obliged to you, Miss Hunter, for falling in with our whims so far as to cut your hair. I assure you that it has not detracted in the tiniest iota from your appearance. We shall now see how the electric-blue dress will become you. You will find it laid out upon the bed in your room, and if you would be so good as to put it on we should both be extremely obliged.'

"The dress which I found waiting for me was of a peculiar shade of blue. It was of excellent material, a sort of beige, but it bore unmistakable signs of having been worn before. It could not have been a better fit if I had been measured for it. Both Mr. and Mrs. Rucastle expressed a delight at the look of it, which seemed quite exaggerated in its vehemence. They were waiting for me in the drawing-room, which is a very large room, stretching along the entire front of the house, with three long windows reaching down to the floor. A chair had been placed close to the central window, with its back turned towards it. In this I was asked to sit, and then Mr. Rucastle, walking up and down on the other side of the room, began to tell me a series of the funniest stories that I have ever listened to. You cannot imagine how comical he was, and I laughed until I was quite weary. Mrs. Rucastle, however, who has evidently no sense of humour, never so much as smiled, but sat with her hands in her lap, and a sad, anxious look upon her face. After an hour or so, Mr. Rucastle suddenly remarked that it was time to commence the duties of the day, and that I might change my dress and go to little Edward in the nursery.

"Two days later this same performance was gone through under exactly similar circumstances. Again I changed my dress, again I sat in the window, and again I laughed very heartily at the funny stories of which my employer had an immense repertoire, and which he told inimitably. Then he handed me a yellow-backed novel, and moving my chair a little sideways, that my own shadow might not fall upon the page, he begged me to read aloud to him. I read for about ten minutes, beginning in the heart of a chapter, and then suddenly, in the middle of a sentence, he ordered me to cease and to change my dress.

"You can easily imagine, Mr. Holmes, how curious I became as to what the meaning of this extraordinary performance could possibly be. They were always very careful, I observed, to turn my face away from the window, so that I became consumed with the desire to see what was going on behind my back. At first it seemed to be impossible, but I soon devised a means. My hand-mirror had been broken, so a happy thought seized me, and I concealed a piece of the glass in my handkerchief. On the next occasion, in the midst of my laughter, I put my handkerchief up to my eyes, and was able with a little management to see all that there was behind me. I confess that I was disappointed. There was nothing. At least that was my first impression. At the second glance, however, I perceived that there was a man standing in the Southampton Road, a small bearded man in a gray suit, who seemed to be looking in my direction. The road is an important highway, and there are usually people there. This man, however, was leaning against the railings which bordered our field and was looking earnestly up. I lowered my handkerchief and glanced at Mrs. Rucastle to find her eyes fixed upon me with a most searching gaze. She said nothing, but I am convinced that she had divined that I had a mirror in my hand and had seen what was behind me. She rose at once.

" 'Jephro,' said she, 'there is an impertinent fellow upon the road there who stares up at Miss Hunter.'

" 'No friend of yours, Miss Hunter?' he asked.

' "No, I know no one in these parts.'

" 'Dear me! How very impertinent! Kindly turn round and motion to him to go away.'

" 'Surely it would be better to take no notice.'

" 'No, no, we should have him loitering here always. Kindly turn round and wave him away like that.'

"I did as I was told, and at the same instant Mrs. Rucastle drew down the blind. That was a week ago, and from that time I have not sat again in the window, nor have I worn the blue dress, nor seen the man in the road."

"Pray continue," said Holmes. "Your narrative promises to be a most interesting one."

"You will find it rather disconnected, I fear, and there may prove to be little relation between the different incidents of which I speak. On the very first day that I was at the Copper Beeches, Mr. Rucastle took me to a small outhouse which stands near the kitchen door. As we approached it I heard the sharp rattling of a chain, and the sound as of a large animal moving about.

" 'Look in here!' said Mr. Rucastle, showing me a slit between two planks. 'Is he not a beauty?'

"I looked through and was conscious of two glowing eyes, and of a vague figure huddled up in the darkness.

" 'Don't be frightened,' said my employer, laughing at the start which I had given. 'It's only Carlo, my mastiff. I call him mine, but really old Toller, my groom, is the only man who can do anything with him. We feed him once a day, and not too much then, so that he is always as keen as mustard. Toller lets him loose every night, and God help the trespasser whom he lays his fangs upon. For goodness' sake don't you ever on any pretext set your foot over the threshold at night, for it's as much as your life is worth.'

"The warning was no idle one, for two nights later I happened to look out of my bedroom window about two o'clock in the morning. It was a beautiful moonlight night, and the lawn in front of the house was silvered over and almost as bright as day. I was standing, rapt in the peaceful beauty of the scene, when I was aware that something was moving under the shadow of the copper beeches. As it emerged into the moonshine I saw what it was. It was a giant dog, as large as a calf, tawny tinted, with hanging jowl, black muzzle, and huge projecting bones. It walked slowly across the lawn and vanished into the shadow upon the other side. That dreadful sentinel sent a chill to my heart which I do not think that any burglar could have done.

"And now I have a very strange experience to tell you. I had, as you know, cut off my hair in London, and I had placed it in a great coil at the bottom of my trunk. One evening, after the child was in bed, I began to amuse myself by examining the furniture of my room and by rearranging my own little things. There was an old chest of drawers in the room, the two upper ones empty and open, the lower one locked. I had filled the first two with my linen, and as I had still much to pack away I was naturally annoyed at not having the use of the third drawer. It struck me that it might have been fastened by a mere oversight, so I took out my bunch of keys and tried to open it. The very first key fitted to perfection, and I drew the drawer open it. There was only one thing in it, but I am sure that you would never guess what it was. It was my coil of hair.

"I took it up and examined it. It was of the same peculiar tint, and the same thickness. But then the impossibility of the thing obtruded itself upon me. How *could* my hair have been locked in the drawer? With trembling hands I undid my trunk, turned out the contents, and drew from the bottom my own hair. I laid the two tresses together, and I assure you that they were identical. Was it not extraordinary? Puzzle as I would, I could make nothing at all of what it meant. I returned the strange hair to the drawer, and I said nothing of the matter to the Rucastles as I felt that I had put myself in the wrong by opening a drawer which they had locked.

"I am naturally observant, as you may have remarked, Mr. Holmes, and I soon had a pretty good plan of the whole house in my head. There was one wing, however, which appeared not to be inhabited at all. A door which faced that which led into the quarters of the Tollers opened into this suite, but it was invariably locked. One day, however, as I ascended the stair, I met Mr. Rucastle coming out through this door, his keys in his hand, and a look on his face which made him a very different person to the round, jovial man to whom I was accustomed. His cheeks were red, his brow was all crinkled with anger, and the veins stood out at his temples with passion. He locked the door and hurried past me without a word or a look.

"This aroused my curiosity; so when I went out for a walk in the grounds with my charge, I strolled round to the side from which I could see the windows of this part of the house. There were four of them in a row, three of which were simply dirty, while the fourth was shuttered up. They were evidently all deserted. As I strolled up and down, glancing at them occasionally, Mr. Rucastle came out to me, looking as merry and jovial as ever.

" 'Ah!' said he, 'you must not think me rude if I passed you without a word, my dear young lady. I was preoccupied with business matters.'

"I assured him that I was not offended. 'By the way,' said I, 'you seem to have quite a suite of spare rooms up there, and one of them has the shutters up.'

"He looked surprised and, as it seemed to me, a little startled at my remark.

" 'Photography is one of my hobbies,' said he. 'I have made my dark room up there. But, dear me! what an observant young lady we have come upon. Who would have believed it? Who would have ever believed it?' He spoke in a jesting tone, but there was no jest in his eyes as he looked at me. I read suspicion there and annoyance, but no jest.

"Well, Mr. Holmes, from the moment that I understood that there was something about that suite of rooms which I was not to know, I was all on fire to go over them. It was not mere curiosity, though I have my share of that. It was more a feeling of duty—a feeling that some good might come from my penetrating to this place. They talk of woman's instinct; perhaps it was woman's instinct which gave me that feeling. At any rate, it was there, and I was keenly on the lookout for any chance to pass the forbidden door.

"It was only yesterday that the chance came. I may tell you that, besides Mr. Rucastle, both Toller and his wife find something to do in these deserted rooms, and I once saw him carrying a large black linen bag with him through the door. Recently he has been drinking hard, and yesterday evening he was very drunk; and when I came upstairs there was the key in the door. I have no doubt at all that he had left it there. Mr. and Mrs. Rucastle were both downstairs, and the child was with them, so that I had an admirable opportunity. I turned the key gently in the lock, opened the door, and slipped through.

"There was a little passage in front of me, unpapered and uncarpeted, which turned at a right angle at the farther end. Round this corner were three doors in a line, the first and third of which were open. They each led into an empty room, dusty and cheerless, with two windows in the one and one in the other, so thick with dirt that the evening light glimmered dimly through them. The centre door was closed, and across the outside of it had been fastened one of the broad bars of an iron bed, padlocked at one end to a ring in the wall, and fastened at the other with stout cord. The door itself was locked as well, and the key was not there. This barricaded door corresponded clearly with the shuttered window outside, and yet I could see by the glimmer from beneath it that the room was not in darkness. Evidently there was a skylight which let in light from above. As I stood in the passage gazing at the sinister door and wondering what secret it might veil, I suddenly heard the sound of steps within the room and saw a shadow pass backward and forward against the little slit of dim light which shone out from under the door. A mad, unreasoning terror rose up in me at the sight, Mr. Holmes. My overstrung nerves failed me suddenly, and I turned and ran—ran as though some dreadful hand were behind me clutching at the skirt of my dress. I rushed down the passage, through the door, and straight into the arms of Mr. Rucastle, who was waiting outside.

" 'So,' said he, smiling, 'it was you, then. I thought that it must be when I saw the door open.'

" 'Oh, I am so frightened!' I panted.

" 'My dear young lady! my dear young lady!'—you cannot

think how caressing and soothing his manner was—'and what has frightened you, my dear young lady?'

"But his voice was just a little too coaxing. He overdid it. I was keenly on my guard against him.

" 'I was foolish enough to go into the empty wing,' I answered. 'But it is so lonely and eerie in this dim light that I was frightened and ran out again. Oh, it is so dreadfully still in there!'

" 'Only that?' said he, looking at me keenly.

" 'Why, what did you think?' I asked.

" 'Why do you think that I lock this door?'

" 'I am sure that I do not know.'

" 'It is to keep people out who have no business there. Do you see?' He was still smiling in the most amiable manner.

" 'I am sure if I had known—'

" 'Well, then, you know now. And if you ever put your foot over that threshold again'—here in an instant the smile hardened into a grin of rage, and he glared down at me with the face of a demon—'I'll throw you to the mastiff.'

"I was so terrified that I do not know what I did. I suppose that I must have rushed past him into my room. I remember nothing until I found myself lying on my bed trembling all over. Then I thought of you, Mr. Holmes. I could not live there longer without some advice. I was frightened of the house, of the man, of the woman, of the servants, even of the child. They were all horrible to me. If I could only bring you down all would be well. Of course I might have fled from the house, but my curiosity was almost as strong as my fears. My mind was soon made up. I would send you a wire. I put on my hat and cloak, went down to the office, which is about half a mile from the house, and then returned, feeling very much easier. A horrible doubt came into my mind as I approached the door lest the dog might be loose, but I remembered that Toller had drunk himself into a state of insensibility that evening, and I knew that he was the only one in the household who had any influence with the savage creature, or who would venture to set him free. I slipped in in safety and lay awake half the night in my joy at the thought of seeing you. I had no difficulty in getting leave to come into Winchester this morning, but I must be back before three o'clock, for Mr. and Mrs. Rucastle are going on a visit, and will be away all the evening, so that I must look after the child. Now I have told you all my adventures, Mr. Holmes, and I should be very glad if you could tell me what it all means, and, above all, what I should do."

Holmes and I had listened spellbound to this extraordinary story. My friend rose now and paced up and down the room, his hands in his pockets, and an expression of the most profound gravity upon his face.

"Is Toller still drunk?" he asked.

"Yes. I heard his wife tell Mrs. Rucastle that she could do nothing with him."

"That is well. And the Rucastles go out to-night?"

"Yes."

"Is there a cellar with a good strong lock?"

"Yes, the wine-cellar."

"You seem to me to have acted all through this matter like a very brave and sensible girl, Miss Hunter. Do you think that you could perform one more feat? I should not ask it of you if I did not think you a quite exceptional woman."

"I will try. What is it?"

"We shall be at the Copper Beeches by seven o'clock, my friend and I. The Rucastles will be gone by that time, and Toller will, we hope, be incapable. There only remains Mrs. Toller, who might give the alarm. If you could send her into the cellar on some errand, and then turn the key upon her, you would facilitate matters immensely."

"I will do it."

"Excellent! We shall then look thoroughly into the affair. Of course there is only one feasible explanation. You have been brought there to personate someone, and the real person is imprisoned in this chamber. That is obvious. As to who this prisoner is, I have no doubt that it is the daughter, Miss Alice Rucastle, if I remember right, who was said to have gone to America. You were chosen, doubtless, as resembling her in height, figure, and the colour of your hair. Hers had been cut off, very possibly in some illness through which she has passed, and so, of course, yours had to be sacrificed also. By a curious chance you came upon her tresses. The man in the road was undoubtedly some friend of hers—possibly her fiancé—and no doubt, as you wore the girl's dress and were so like her, he was convinced from your laughter, whenever he saw you, and afterwards from your gesture, that Miss Rucastle was perfectly happy, and that she no longer desired his attentions. The dog is let loose at night to prevent him from endeavouring to communicate with her. So much is fairly clear. The most serious point in the case is the disposition of the child."

"What on earth has that to do with it?" I ejaculated.

"My dear Watson, you as a medical man are continually gaining light as to the tendencies of a child by the study of the parents. Don't you see that the converse is equally valid. I have frequently gained my first real insight into the character of parents by studying their children. This child's disposition is abnormally cruel, merely for cruelty's sake, and whether he derives this from his smiling father, as I should suspect, or from his mother, it bodes evil for the poor girl who is in their power."

"I am sure that you are right, Mr. Holmes," cried our client. "A thousand things come back to me which make me certain that you have hit it. Oh, let us lose not an instant in bringing help to this poor creature."

"We must be circumspect, for we are dealing with a very cunning man. We can do nothing until seven o'clock. At that hour we shall be with you, and it will not be long before we solve the mystery."

We were as good as our word, for it was just seven when we reached the Copper Beeches, having put up our trap at a wayside public-house. The group of trees, with their dark leaves shining like burnished metal in the light of the setting sun, were sufficient to mark the house even had Miss Hunter not been standing smiling on the door-step.

"Have you managed it?" asked Holmes.

A loud thudding noise came from somewhere downstairs. "That is Mrs. Toller in the cellar," said she. "Her husband lies snoring on the kitchen rug. Here are his keys, which are the duplicates of Mr. Rucastle's."

"You have done well indeed!" cried Holmes with enthusiasm. "Now lead the way, and we shall soon see the end of this black business."

We passed up the stair, unlocked the door, followed on down a passage, and found ourselves in front of the barricade which Miss Hunter had described. Holmes cut the cord and removed the transverse bar. Then he tried the various keys in the lock, but without success. No sound came from within, and at the silence Holmes's face clouded over.

"I trust that we are not too late," said he. "I think, Miss Hunter, that we had better go in without you. Now, Watson, put your shoulder to it, and we shall see whether we cannot make our way in."

It was an old rickety door and gave at once before our united strength. Together we rushed into the room. It was empty. There was no furniture save a little pallet bed, a small table, and a basketful of linen. The skylight above was open, and the prisoner gone.

"There has been some villainy here," said Holmes; "this beauty has guessed Miss Hunter's intentions and has carried his victim off."

"But how?"

"Through the skylight. We shall soon see how he managed it." He swung himself up onto the roof. "Ah, yes," he cried, "here's the end of a long light ladder against the eaves. That is how he did it."

"But it is impossible," said Miss Hunter; "the ladder was not there when the Rucastles went away."

"He has come back and done it. I tell you that he is a clever and dangerous man. I should not be very much surprised if this were he whose step I hear now upon the stair. I think, Watson, that it would be as well for you to have your pistol ready."

The words were hardly out of his mouth before a man appeared at the door of the room, a very fat and burly man, with a heavy stick in his hand. Miss Hunter screamed and shrunk against the wall at the sight of him, but Sherlock Holmes sprang forward and confronted him.

"You villain!" said he, "where's your daughter?"

The fat man cast his eyes round, and then up at the open skylight.

"It is for me to ask you that," he shrieked, "you thieves! Spies and thieves! I have caught you, have I? You are in my power. I'll serve you!" He turned and clattered down the stairs as hard as he could go.

"He's gone for the dog!" cried Miss Hunter..

"I have my revolver," said I.

"Better close the front door," cried Holmes, and we all rushed down the stairs together. We had hardly reached the hall when we heard the baying of a hound, and then a scream of agony, with a horrible worrying sound which it was dreadful to listen to. An elderly man with a red face and shaking limbs came staggering out at a side door.

"My God!" he cried. "Someone has loosed the dog. It's not been fed for two days. Quick, quick, or it'll be too late!"

Holmes and I rushed out and round the angle of the house, with Toller hurrying behind us. There was the huge famished brute, its black muzzle buried in Rucastle's throat, while he writhed and screamed upon the ground. Running up, I blew its brains out, and it fell over with its keen white teeth still meeting in the great creases of his neck. With much labour we separated them and carried him, living but horribly mangled, into the house. We laid him upon the drawing-room sofa, and having dispatched the sobered Toller to bear the news to his wife, I did what I could to relieve his pain. We were all assembled round him when the door opened, and a tall, gaunt woman entered the room.

"Mrs. Toller!" cried Miss Hunter.

"Yes, miss. Mr. Rucastle let me out when he came back before he went up to you. Ah, miss, it is a pity you didn't let me know what you were planning, for I would have told you that your pains were wasted."

"Ha!" said Holmes, looking keenly at her. "It is clear that Mrs. Toller knows more about this matter than anyone else."

"Yes, sir, I do, and I am ready enough to tell what I know."

"Then, pray, sit down, and let us hear it, for there are several points on which I must confess that I am still in the dark."

"I will soon make it clear to you," said she; "and I'd have done so before now if I could ha' got out from the cellar. If there's police-court business over this, you'll remember that I was the one that stood your friend, and that I was Miss Alice's friend too.

"She was never happy at home, Miss Alice wasn't, from the time that her father married again. She was slighted like and had no say in anything, but it never really became bad for her until after she met Mr. Fowler at a friend's house. As well as I could learn, Miss Alice had rights of her own by will, but she was so quiet and patient, she was, that she never said a word about them, but just left everything in Mr. Rucastle's hands. He knew he was safe with her; but when there was a chance of a husband coming forward, who would ask for all that the law would give him, then her father thought it time to put a stop on it. He wanted her to sign a paper, so that whether she married or not, he could use her money. When she wouldn't do it, he kept on worrying her until she got brain-fever, and for six weeks was at death's door. Then she got better at last, all worn to a shadow, and with her beautiful hair cut off; but that didn't make no change in her young man, and he stuck to her as true as man could be."

Ah," said Holmes, "I think that what you have been good enough to tell us makes the matter fairly clear, and that I can deduce all that remains. Mr. Rucastle then, I presume, took to this system of imprisonment?"

"Yes, sir."

"And brought Miss Hunter down from London in order to get rid of the disagreeable persistence of Mr. Fowler."

"That was it, sir."

"But Mr. Fowler being a persevering man, as a good seaman should be, blockaded the house, and having met you succeeded by certain arguments, metallic or otherwise, in convincing you that your interests were the same as his."

"Mr. Fowler was a very kind-spoken, free-handed gentleman," said Mrs. Toller serenely.

"And in this way he managed that your good man should have no want of drink, and that a ladder should be ready at the moment when your master had gone out."

"You have it, sir, just as it happened."

"I am sure we owe you an apology, Mrs. Toller," said Holmes, "for you have certainly cleared up everything which puzzled us. And here comes the country surgeon and Mrs. Rucastle, so I think, Watson, that we had best escort Miss Hunter back to Winchester, as it seems to me that our *locus standi* now is rather a questionable one."

And thus was solved the mystery of the sinister house with the copper beeches in front of the door. Mr. Rucastle survived, but was always a broken man, kept alive solely through the care of his devoted wife. They still live with their old servants, who probably know so much of Rucastle's past life that he finds it difficult to part from them. Mr. Fowler and Miss Rucastle were married, by special license, in Southampton the day after their flight, and he is now the holder of a government appointment in the island of Mauritius. As to Miss Violet Hunter, my friend Holmes, rather to my disappointment, manifested no further interest in her when once she had ceased to be the centre of one of his problems, and she is now the head of a private school at Walsall, where I believe that she has met with considerable success.

Afterword

Sir Arthur Conan Doyle came to resent his celebrated protagonist, Mr. Sherlock Holmes. The trouble was that the writing of the Holmes adventures was taking far too much time away from what he considered his "more important" work. Indeed, even as early as 1891, Doyle was entertaining dark, brooding thoughts of "slaying Holmes and winding him up for good."

Of course, from the perspective of any avid Sherlock Holmes enthusiast, Conan Doyle's attitude was quite beyond comprehension.

More important than Sherlock Holmes? Impossible!

Yet, for better or for worse, Doyle had opted to make his literary mark not in the area of "cheap" detective fiction, as it was known in his day, but in his meticulously researched historical romances, including *Micah Clarke, The Refugees*, and *The White Company*; his science fiction, most notably *The Lost World* and his objective works, such as *the War in South Africa, Its Cause and Conduct*, in which he attempted (quite successfully it seems) to discredit many of the allegations of atrocity that had been levelled at Britain as a result of her participation in the Boer War.

A cartoon by Sir Bernard Partridge was one of many that poked fun at the strain in the relationship between Conan Doyle and Sherlock Holmes. Pictured is Conan Doyle, manacled to a chair, his head wreathed in smoke, while beside him stands Sherlock Holmes, ruminating intensely, smoking a pipe. Doyle himself, however, was apparently not amused by the situation. In fact, it is said that he seriously considered refusing an offer of knighthood because there was some question as to whether it was being tendered in honor of his Sherlock Holmes stories or for the valuable service he had performed for the empire by writing and arranging for the publication of *The War in South*

Africa. Convinced it was for the latter, Doyle accepted the knighthood in 1903.

Doyle attempted to impede Holmes' progress by placing a higher price on each new collection of stories, but, to his increasing consternation, the publishers were only too willing to meet his demands. Unable to resist the temptation of higher earnings, he was obliged to continue writing Sherlock Holmes adventures, albeit he did so with less and less enthusiasm. The last straw came in 1892 when Doyle asked for and received the then fantastic sum of £1000 ($5,000) for the twelve stories which comprise *The Memoirs of Sherlock Holmes* (1894).

Doyle knew then that Sherlock Holmes would have to die. He performed the dastardly deed (or so he thought) in "The Final Problem," which appeared in the December, 1893 issue of *The Strand*. The story ends with Holmes and his archenemy, Moriarty, plunging from a towering cliff to their apparent deaths in a "dreadful cauldron of swirling water and seething foam."

In his diary, Doyle wrote: *Killed Holmes*.

He should have been so lucky!

The "death" of Sherlock Holmes caused a storm of protest. Torrents of correspondence poured into the offices of Conan Doyle's publishers, threatening, cajoling, *demanding* that Sherlock Holmes be reanimated. Mourners donned black armbands to commemorate their fallen hero. Grown men and women are said to have wept.

But, alas, it was all to no avail. Doyle stood firm in his decision, and indeed it is rumored that our dear friend Holmes might have remained on ice forever had it not been for allegations that Conan Doyle had lost his touch at writing detective fiction. As it was, it would be eight years before Sherlock Holmes would resurface in perhaps the best of all the novel-length adventures. *The Hound of the Baskervilles* (1902). Yet even here, Doyle demonstrated his reluctance to bring Holmes fully back to life by writing the book in the form of a reminiscence rather than as a first-hand narrative.

In 1903, Conan Doyle at last agreed to revitalize Holmes in a series of stories under the title, *The Return of Sherlock Holmes*. The price he received for these thirteen stories was $65,000 (and this for the American rights alone). So great was the public's excitement over the publication of the first installment. "The Adventure of the Empty House," that eager readers waited in line to purchase it and the printers had to work overtime to meet the demand.

A decade would pass before Sherlock Holmes would solve another crime. In the intervening years, Conan Doyle traveled extensively, made two unsuccessful bids for Parliament (in 1900 and 1905), and was himself instrumental in solving a number of crimes. In hopes of establishing a reputation as a science fiction writer that would equal his standing in detective fiction, Doyle wrote *The Lost World* (1912), a book inspired by, and yet quite distinct from, Jules Verne's *A Journey to the Center of the Earth. The Lost World* was published in installments in *The Strand* and met with great success. In 1913, he followed with *The Poison Belt* featuring the same protagonist, Professor George Edward Challenger (Doyle's science fiction counterpart of Sherlock Holmes), whom he is said to have loved above all of his literary creations. This book was also well received.

Sir Arthur Conan Doyle's later years were devoted almost exclusively to investigating and furthering the cause and understanding of Spiritualism. He wrote extensively on the subject and, by his own account, lectured throughout the world before at least a quarter million people. Still, he occasionally found time to write more Sherlock Holmes adventures, including *The Valley of Fear* (1915), and two more collections of short stories, *His Last Bow* (1917), and *The Case-Book of Sherlock Holmes* (1927), which included the last of Doyle's Sherlock Holmes adventures, "Shoscombe Old Place."

Of course, this was not the last we would hear from Mr. Sherlock Holmes. Hundreds, if not thousands, of copies, spoofs, takeoffs and imitations would follow, and, luckily for Sherlock Holmes fans everywhere, it is safe to say that many more are yet to come.

—R.L. Fisher

ALPHONSE JENNY

MÉTHODE 90
ALLEMAND

Collection dirigée par
Jacques Donvez

LE LIVRE DE POCHE

Dans la même collection :
dirigée par Jacques Donvez

MÉTHODE 90 ANGLAIS.
MÉTHODE 90 ESPAGNOL.
MÉTHODE 90 ITALIEN.
MÉTHODE 90 RUSSE.

REMERCIEMENTS

Nous exprimons notre vive reconnaissance aux auteurs, aux journaux et revues, aux maisons d'édition qui ont bien voulu mettre à notre disposition des textes pour le présent ouvrage :

Annabelle – *Burda Moden* – *Das Ideale Heim* – *Deutscher Fremdenverkehrsverband* (en particulier pour le texte de Michael Schiff) – *Die Welt* – *Die Weltwoche* (en particulier pour le texte de Joseph Wechsberg) – *Die Zeit* (en particulier pour le texte de Peter Westphal) – *Frankfurter Allgemeine Zeitung* – *Gmünder Tagespost* – *Kristall* – *Langenscheidts Sprachillustrierte* – *Rheinischer Merkur* (en particulier pour le texte de H. Rieker) – *Schweizer Illustrierte* – *Stern.*
Verlag der Arche, Zürich, pour un texte de Werner Bergengruen – *Verlag Kurt Desch, München, éditions Flammarion, Paris,* et *Calmann-Levy, Paris,* pour des textes de Theodor Plievier et Ernst Wiechert – *Goldmann Verlag, München,* pour un texte de Heinrich Heine – *Verlag Kiepenheuer u. Witsch, Köln,* pour un texte de Heinrich Böll – *Verlag Joseph Knecht, Frankfurt a/Main,* pour un texte de Herbert Kranz – *Piper u. C° Verlag, München,* pour un texte de Heinrich Spoerl – *Schwabenverlag, Stuttgart,* pour un texte d'Eva Rechlin.

Mme G. Thouvenot et Melle Trude Dürr ont bien voulu nous fournir maints conseils et suggestions heureuses. Nous les assurons de toute notre gratitude.

TABLE DES MATIÈRES

Présentation

I. Plan de l'ouvrage

■ ***90 leçons réparties en 3 séries***

leçons 1 à 25 : **éléments de base** (prononciation et grammaire).
leçons 26 à 75 : **situations pratiques** (vocabulaire nouveau).
leçons 76 à 90 : **choix de textes** (langue des journaux, du théâtre et des romans).

■ ***7 leçons de révision*** (10 *bis*, 20 *bis*, 30 *bis*, 40 *bis*, 50 *bis*, 60 *bis*, 70 *bis*).
Exercices de contrôle.

■ ***Mémento grammatical*** (conjugaisons, verbes irréguliers, etc.).

Au total, 2 500 mots du vocabulaire le plus courant.

II. Comment utiliser ce livre

Les leçons 1 à 25 sont conçues pour des débutants qui devront en respecter la progression. Les lecteurs possédant déjà les bases de la langue peuvent revoir ces leçons plus rapidement.

■ ***Cadre de travail :*** Les leçons 1 à 75 comportent 4 pages :
- 1re page (gauche) : texte allemand + prononciation des mots nouveaux.
- 2e page (droite) : traduction du texte allemand + explication de prononciation + vocabulaire.
- 3e page (gauche) : explications de grammaire (parfois précédées de vocabulaire).
- 4e page (droite) : exercice + corrigé (+ parfois texte d'illustration avec sa traduction; dans ce cas, les exercices figurent souvent en 3e page).

■ *Méthode de travail*

- **lire** le texte allemand — le plus souvent possible à haute voix en consultant la page 2 de la leçon.
- **se reporter** au bas de la page 1 pour la **prononciation** des mots signalés par un astérisque (*) ainsi qu'aux notes de la page 2.
- **relire** le texte à la lumière des explications de **grammaire** page 3 (et éventuellement des renvois au Mémento).
- **apprendre,** au fur et à mesure, le **vocabulaire** nouveau de chaque leçon; les noms doivent être retenus avec l'article défini et le pluriel, les verbes irréguliers avec leurs temps primitifs; ne pas oublier qu'un mot isolé n'a pas d'existence. Donc apprendre le vocabulaire avec les phrases correspondantes du texte de la page 1 ou des exercices de la page 4.
- **faire les exercices** de la page 4 et des leçons *bis* (par écrit ou oralement) pour fixer et contrôler les acquisitions.
- **faire** de nombreux **retours en arrière** pour consolider les connaissances; les textes de la page 1 doivent peu à peu être assimilés; ne plus trop se soucier de la traduction.

III. Comment prononcer l'allemand

■ *L'accentuation*

En allemand, dans les mots de plus d'une syllabe on met une syllabe en relief; elle est prononcée avec plus de force (et dite **accentuée** ou **tonique**) au détriment des autres dites **inaccentuées** mais qui ne sont jamais muettes.
C'est la syllabe radicale qui porte l'accent tonique; le plus souvent cette syllabe radicale est la première du mot.
Dans les mots composés et dans les verbes à particules séparables, un premier accent tonique (principal) porte sur le radical du premier élément, tandis que le radical du second élément porte un accent secondaire, moins fort.
A l'accentuation des mots se superpose l'intonation et la mélodie de la phrase tout aussi importantes que la bonne accentuation des éléments isolés. Tout comme en grammaire il s'agit moins de considérer des éléments isolés, mais bien plutôt des structures complètes et des groupes de souffle.

■ *Les sons*

En règle générale **toutes les lettres se prononcent** (exception : *h* après une voyelle et *e* après *i; h* et *e* sont, dans ce cas, des signes d'allongement de la voyelle précédente).
L'allemand marque très nettement la différence entre les voyelles brèves et les voyelles longues; il faut particulièrement veiller à **allonger les longues** (dans les mots nouveaux elles seront indiquées par une **flèche**).
Les voyelles sont **brèves** quand elles sont suivies d'une consonne double ou quand elles sont suivies de plusieurs consonnes (à part quelques exceptions indiquées).
Inversement elles sont **longues** quand elles sont suivies d'une seule consonne ou d'un *h,* qui marque l'allongement. Pour indiquer qu'un *i* est long, on le fait suivre d'un *e.*
Il est important de **ne pas faire de liaison entre les mots,** même entre les différents éléments d'un mot composé.
On lira avec beaucoup d'attention les explications données en page 2 de chaque leçon ou dans le Mémento § 1. Une prononciation correcte est à la portée de tous, mais il faut en avoir le souci constant et s'entraîner régulièrement à haute voix. Une faute de prononciation devra être évitée avec autant de vigilance qu'une faute d'orthographe dans la langue écrite.

Note : Les traductions proposées ont pour principal objectif la compréhension aisée, dans le détail, des textes et formes à étudier.

LEÇONS

Leçon

1 Er lernt im Park

1 Der P**a**rk ist gr**o**ß.
Die T**a**nne ist gr**ü**n.
Das Gr**a**s ist **au**ch gr**ü**n.
— Wie ist der Park? — Er ist groß.
— Wie ist die T**a**nne? — Sie ist grün.
— Wie ist das Gras? — Es ist auch grün.

2 Paul Dumont ist im P**a**rk.
— Was l**e**rnt Paul Dumont?
— Er l**e**rnt D**eu**tsch.
— Ist es schw**e**r?
— Nein; er lernt j**e**den T**a**g eine Lekti**o**n.

3 — Ist der Park groß? — Ja, der Park ist groß.
— Ist das Gras grün? — Ja, das Gras ist grün.
— Ist die T**a**nne auch grün? — Ja, die T**a**nne ist auch grün.

1 [dér p**a**rk içt gr**o**ç — di t**a**ne içt gr**u**n — daç gr**a**ç içt **ao**r grun — vi içt dér p**a**rk — vi içt di t**a**ne — vi içt daç gr**a**ç].

2 [Paul Dumont içt im p**a**rk — vaç lèrnt Paul Dumont — ér lèrnt d**o**eutch — içt èç chv**é**r — n**a**én, ér lèrnt y**é**den' tak **a**éne lèktçi**o**n].

3 [ya].

EILE MIT WEILE

Traduction

Il apprend dans le parc

1 Le parc est grand. Le sapin est vert. L'herbe est également verte. — Comment est le parc? — Il est grand. — Comment est le sapin? — Il est vert. — Comment est l'herbe? — Elle est également verte.

2 Paul Dumont est dans le parc. — Qu'apprend Paul Dumont? — Il apprend l'allemand. — Est-ce difficile? — Non; il apprend chaque jour une leçon.

3 — Le parc est-il grand? — Oui, le parc est grand. — L'herbe est-elle verte? — Oui, l'herbe est verte. — Le sapin est-il vert également? Oui, le sapin est également vert.

Prononciation

Au-dessous de chaque texte vous trouverez, entre crochets, une transcription vous permettant de prononcer correctement.

Les voyelles accentuées sont en caractères gras.

Les voyelles allongées sont soulignées d'une flèche.

Reportez-vous fréquemment au mémento grammatical, où le § 1 est consacré à la prononciation.
Retenez :
La lettre ß se prononce comme le s français dans « grosse »
sch comme le français ch
ü comme le français u
w comme le français v
s au début d'un mot se prononce z
im se prononce comme dans « lime ».

2. Toutes les lettres se prononcent, en particulier le *e* à la fin d'un mot (par exemple : *Tanne*). Mais dans *sie* [zi], le *e* allonge le *i*, et ne se prononce pas. Le *h* dans *sehr* [zér] allonge également le [**é**].

Hâte-toi lentement (Hâte-toi avec loisir).

3. *ch,* dans *auch,* ne se prononce pas comme en français; c'est, ici, un son guttural (râclement au fond de la gorge). Nous représentons ce son par [ṛ]; donc : *auch* se prononce [**a**oṛ].

Vocabulaire

der Park, *le parc*
der Tag, *le jour*
die T**a**nne, *le sapin*
das Gras, *l'herbe*
l**e**rnen, *apprendre*

Grammaire

■ ***Der Park — die Tanne — das Gras.***
Le nom — Le genre.
L'allemand a trois genres, caractérisés par l'article défini : *der* (masculin), *die* (féminin), *das* (neutre). Il est très important d'apprendre les noms avec leur article défini, pour en connaître le genre. En effet, celui-ci ne correspond pas d'une langue à l'autre. Exemple : *die Tanne* (féminin), le sapin (masculin). Au pluriel, ces articles ont une seule forme : *die,* les. Les noms s'écrivent tous avec une majuscule.

■ ***Der Park ist groß.***
Le verbe être : ***sein.***

ich bin, *je suis*
er ist, *il est*
sie ist, *elle est*
es ist, *il est, c'est*
wir sind, *nous sommes*
sie sind, *ils sont*
Sie sind, *vous êtes* (forme de politesse)

● ***Er ist groß — Sie ist grün — Es ist auch grün.***
Aux trois genres correspondent au singulier les trois pronoms de la 3e personne : *er* (masculin), *sie* (féminin), *es* (neutre). Au pluriel, ce pronom est *sie* pour les trois genres. Exemple : *Sie sind grün* : ils sont verts.

■ ***Die Tanne ist grün; das Gras ist auch grün.***
L'adjectif attribut (*grün*), introduit par des verbes comme « être », *sein,* « sembler, devenir, etc. », est invariable en allemand.

Exercices

A *Compléter par l'article défini, puis traduire :*
1. Ist d.. Gras grün? 2. Wie ist d.. Tanne? 3. D.. Park ist auch grün.

B *Traduire en français :*
4. Ich bin groß. 5. Es ist groß. 6. Lernt er im Park? 7. Ist es schwer?

C *Poser deux questions; a) avec* was? (= *que, quoi?*) *b) avec* wie? (= *comment?*)
8. Er lernt Deutsch. 9. Die Tanne ist groß. 10. Das Gras ist grün.

D *Traduire en allemand :*
11. Qu'apprend Paul Dumont? 12. Comment est le parc? 13. Êtes-vous (forme de politesse) dans le (*im*) parc? 14. Le sapin est grand; il est dans le parc.

Corrigé :

A 1. das. 2. die. 3. der. Traduction 1. L'herbe est-elle verte? 2. Comment est le sapin? 3. Le parc aussi est vert.

B 4. Je suis grand[e]. 5. C'est grand. 6. Apprend-il dans le parc? 7. Est-ce difficile?

C 8. a) Was lernt er? b) Wie lernt er? 9. Was ist groß. b) Wie ist die Tanne? 10 a) Was ist grün? b) Wie ist das Gras?

D 11. Was lernt Paul Dumont? 12. Wie ist der Park? 13. Sind Sie im Park? 14. Die Tanne ist groß. sie ist im Park.

2 Der Kongreß in Köln

1 Der Park ist in Köln – Köln ist eine Stadt.
– Wohnt Paul Dumont in Köln?
– Nein, er wohnt in Par**i**s. Aber er ist hier auf einem Kongr**eß**.
– Wie **l**a**n**ge d**au**ert der Kongr**eß**?
– Er d**au**ert eine W**o**che.

2 Paul Dumont **a**rbeitet in Par**is**.
Seine F**i**rma kauft oft Art**i**kel in D**eu**tschland.
– Wo **a**rbeitet Paul Dumont?
– Er **a**rbeitet in Par**is** – Arbeitet er in Köln auch?
– Ja, er arbeitet hier auch.

3 Herr M**ü**ller ist ein Freund; er wohnt in Köln.
Köln ist eine große Stadt.
Das Hot**e**l ist mod**e**rn.

1 [dér p**a**rk içt in' k**eu**ln – k**eu**ln içt **a**éne cht**a**t – v**o**n't Paul Dumont in k**eu**ln – na**é**n ér v**o**n't in' par**i**ç – **a**ber ér içt h**i**r **a**of **a**énem kon'gr**è**ç – v**i** l**a**^{ng}e d**a**oert dér kon'gr**è**ç – ér d**a**oert **a**éne v**o**re].

2 [Paul Dumont **a**rbaétet in' par**i**ç – z**a**éne f**i**rma k**a**oft oft art**i**kel in d**o**eutchlant...]

3 [hèr m**u**ler içt **a**én fr**o**eun't – ér f**u**rt Paul Dumont in' di cht**a**t-k**eu**ln içt **a**éne gr**o**çe chtat – ... – daç hot**è**l içt mod**è**rn].

WIE DIE ARBEIT, SO DER LOHN

Traduction

Le congrès à Cologne

1 Le parc est à Cologne – Cologne est une ville. – Paul Dumont habite-t-il à Cologne? – Non, il habite à Paris. Mais il est ici à (= sur) un congrès. – Combien de temps (mot à mot : combien longtemps) dure le congrès? – Il dure une semaine.

2 Paul Dumont travaille à Paris. Sa firme achète souvent des articles en Allemagne. – Où Paul Dumont travaille-t-il? – Il travaille à Paris – Travaille-t-il à Cologne également? – Oui, ici, il travaille également.

3 Monsieur Müller est un ami; il habite à Cologne. Il conduit Paul Dumont dans un hôtel. Cologne est une grande ville. L'hôtel est moderne.

Prononciation

1 *Wohnen Sie...* . L' « s » de *Sie* est sonore, comme dans « rose »; mais dans *große, Kongreß,* le signe *ß* représente un « s » dur, sourd.

2 *ö* se prononce « eu »; ainsi : *Köln* [keuln].

3 Il est essentiel de toujours prononcer le « h » en début de mot (soufflez, comme pour couvrir une vitre de buée). Par exemple : *hier* [h**i**r]; *Herr* [h**è**r]; *Hotel* [hot**è**l]. On distinguera nettement la prononciation de *Herr,* [h**è**r] (monsieur), de celle de *er* [ér] (il).

4 Nous trouvons ici plusieurs diphtongues : *eine* [**a**éne]; *auf* [**a**of]; *dauert* [d**a**oert]; *arbeitet* [**a**rb**a**étet]; *kauft* [k**a**oft] *Deutschland* [d**o**eutchlant]. Il faut les prononcer brièvement, en une seule émission de voix, et en accentuant la première voyelle.

5 Lisez les textes à haute voix, toujours; marquez fortement les accents (voyelles imprimées en gras); articulez bien les consonnes, par exemple dans *Freund,* [fr**o**eunt].

A chacun selon ses mérites (mot à mot : Comme le travail, ainsi le salaire)

Vocabulaire

der Artikel, *l'article*	die Woche, *la semaine*
der Freund, *l'ami*	das Hotel, *l'hôtel*
der Herr, *le monsieur*	arbeiten, *travailler*
der Kongreß, *le congrès*	führen, *conduire*
die Firma, *la firme*	kaufen, *acheter*
die Stadt, *la ville*	wohnen, *habiter*

Grammaire

■ **Köln ist eine Stadt,** Cologne est une ville.
L'article indéfini.
der Freund, ein Freund, un ami – *die Stadt, eine Stadt,* une ville – *das Hotel, ein Hotel,* un hôtel.
Les articles indéfinis sont *ein* (masculin), *eine* (féminin), *ein* (neutre); ils correspondent à *der, die, das.*

■ **Er wohnt in Köln,** il habite Cologne.
Le verbe régulier (ou « faible »).
Exemple : *wohnen,* habiter – Radical : *wohn*

ich wohn-e, j'habite	*wir wohn-en,* nous habitons
er wohn-t, il habite	*sie wohn-en,* ils habitent
sie wohn-t, elle habite	*Sie wohn-en,* vous habitez (forme de politesse).
es wohn-t, il habite (neutre)	

Ich wohne und ich arbeite in Köln. Er wohnt und er arbeitet in Köln.

Remarque : on ne pourrait avoir *arbeitt,* aussi on intercale un *e* entre les deux *t* (entre celui du radical et celui de la terminaison). C'est ce qu'on fait régulièrement lorsque le radical d'un verbe régulier se termine par *t, d,* ou par un groupe de consonnes difficiles à prononcer.

■ **Ist er in Köln? – Ist Paul in Köln?**
Est-il à Cologne? – Paul est-il à Cologne?
L'interrogation directe.
Notez que le verbe, dans l'interrogation directe, est en première place. Autre exemple :

Kauft seine Firma oft Artikel in Deutschland?
Est-ce que sa firme achète souvent des articles en Allemagne?

■ **Wo arbeiten Sie?** Où travaillez-vous?
La forme de politesse.
C'est la 3e personne du pluriel qui sert de forme de politesse, et non la 2e, comme en français. Le pronom sujet s'écrit alors avec une majuscule : *Sie,* vous.

Exercices

A *Remplacer l'article défini par l'article indéfini :* (Exemple : *der Park, ein Park.*)
1. der Artikel. 2. das Hotel. 3. die Stadt. 4. der Freund. 5. die Firma. 6. das Gras.

B *Ajouter les terminaisons aux verbes et traduire :*
7. Ich lern... 8. Lotte wohn... in Berlin. 9. Wir arbeit... jetzt. 10. Arbeit... er auch? 11. Wo wohn... Sie? 12. Lern... sie oft?

C *L'interrogation directe. Poser les questions correspondant aux phrases suivantes, puis traduire :*
13. Ja, er wohnt in Köln. 14. Ja, Paul Dumont arbeitet in Paris. 15. Ja, Herr Müller führt Paul Dumont in die Stadt. 16. Ja, das Hotel ist modern.

D *Traduire :*
17. Il travaille aussi à Cologne. 18. Est-ce que Cologne est une ville? 19. Où habitez-vous? (*forme de politesse*). 20. Apprend-elle aussi l'allemand?

Corrigé :

A 1. ein Artikel. 2. ein Hotel. 3. eine Stadt. 4. ein Freund. 5. eine Firma. 6. ein Gras.

B 7. ich lerne, *j'apprends.* 8. Lotte wohnt..., *Charlotte habite à Berlin.* 9. Wir arbeiten... *Nous travaillons maintenant.* 10. Arbeitet er..., *travaille-t-il aussi?* 11. Wo wohnen Sie? *Où habitez-vous?* 12. Lernen sie oft? *Étudient-ils souvent?*

C 13. Wohnt er in Köln? *habite-t-il à Cologne?* 14. Arbeitet Paul Dumont in Paris? *Paul Dumont travaille-t-il à Paris?* 15. Führt Herr Müller Paul Dumont in die Stadt? *Est-ce que Monsieur Müller conduit Paul Dumont à travers la ville?* 16. Ist das Hotel modern? *L'hôtel est-il moderne?*

D 17. Er arbeitet auch in Köln. 18. Ist Köln eine Stadt? 19. Wo wohnen Sie? 20. Lernt sie auch Deutsch?

Leçon

3

Das Hotel

1 Paul Dumont hat ein r**u**higes Z**i**mmer.
Das Hot**e**l liegt nicht in der Stadt; es liegt in der V**o**rstadt.
Es hat **ei**nen G**a**rten, **a**ber k**ei**ne Gar**a**ge.
Es hat auch eine sch**ö**ne **Au**ssicht auf den Rhein.

2 — Wo liegt das Hot**e**l? — Es liegt in der V**o**rstadt.
— Hat es eine Gar**a**ge? — Nein, es hat k**ei**ne Gar**a**ge.
— Wie ist das Z**i**mmer? — Es ist r**u**hig.
— H**a**ben Sie eine sch**ö**ne **Au**ssicht? — O ja!

3 — Ich h**a**be kein **Au**to in Köln; es ist in Par**i**s.
— Ich bin ja nur für eine W**o**che hier.
— Aber ich h**a**be keinen G**a**rten in Par**i**s, und der G**a**rten hier ist sehr schön!
Man ist so r**u**hig hier!

1 [Paul Dumont h**a**t aén' r**ou**igeç tç**i**mer — daç hot**è**l l**i**kt in' dér f**o**rchtat — èç h**a**t **a**énen' g**a**rten', **a**ber k**a**éne gar**a**je — èç hat aor **a**éne ch**eu**ne **a**oç/zicht **a**of dén' r**a**én'].

2 [vo l**i**kt daç hot**è**l — èç l**i**kt in' dér f**o**rchtat — hat èç **a**éne gar**a**je — naén', èç hat k**a**éne gar**a**je — vi içt daç tç**i**mer — èç içt r**ou**ich — h**a**ben' zi **a**éne ch**eu**ne **a**oç/zicht — o ya].

3 [ich h**a**be k**a**én' **a**oto in' k**eu**ln'; èç içt in' par**i**ç — ich bin' ya nour fur **a**éne v**o**re hir — **a**ber ich h**a**be k**a**énen' g**a**rten' in' par**i**ç, oun't dér g**a**rten' hir içt zér ch**eu**n' — man' içt zo r**ou**ich hir].

ÜBUNG MACHT DEN MEISTER

Traduction

L'Hôtel

1 Paul Dumont a une chambre calme. L'hôtel ne se trouve pas dans la ville, il se trouve dans le faubourg. Il a un jardin, mais pas de garage. Il a également une belle vue sur le Rhin.

2 — Où l'hôtel se trouve-t-il? — Il se trouve dans la banlieue. — A-t-il un garage? — Non, il n'a pas de garage. — Comment la chambre est-elle? — Elle est calme. — Avez-vous une belle vue? — Ah! oui!

3 Je n'ai pas de voiture à Cologne; elle est à Paris. Je suis (en effet) seulement pour une semaine ici. Mais à Paris, je n'ai pas de jardin; et ce jardin-ci (mot à mot : le jardin ici) est très beau! On est si tranquille ici!

Prononciation

1 Nous trouvons dans cette leçon les mots *nicht, Aussicht, ich,* dans lesquels le « ch » ne se prononce pas comme dans *auch,* mais d'une façon plus chuintée (prononcez « si », laissez les lèvres, les dents et la langue dans cette position, puis soufflez doucement). Nous représentons ce son par [cḫ]. On prononce de même la terminaison *-ig,* par exemple dans *ruhig* [**rou**-icḫ].

2 Dans *ruhiges,* le « h » ne se prononce pas; il indique la longueur de la voyelle qui le précède. Articulez bien le « **g** » comme dans « gare », car il ne s'agit plus, maintenant, d'une terminaison.

3 Le « **z** », comme dans *Zimmer,* équivaut toujours à un t-s (la mouche « tsé-tsé »). Dans ce mot, le double « m » indique que le « i » est bref; prononcez très faiblement la dernière syllabe : [tç**i**-mer].

Vocabulaire

der G**a**rten, *le jardin*
der Rhein, *le Rhin*
die **Au**ssicht, *la vue*
die Gar**a**ge, *le garage*
die V**o**rstadt, *le faubourg*

das **Au**to, *la voiture*
das Z**i**mmer, *la chambre*
h**a**ben, *avoir*
l**ie**gen, *être couché*

C'est en forgeant qu'on devient forgeron (mot à mot : l'exercice fait le maître).

Grammaire

■ **Das Hotel liegt nicht in der Stadt.**
La négation verbale est *nicht.* Elle correspond à notre « ne... pas ».

■ **Das Hotel hat keine Garage.**
L'article négatif *kein* est la négation de *ein.* Cet article signifie « ne pas ... un, ne pas ... une, ne pas ... de ». Il prend les mêmes formes que l'article indéfini *ein,* mais il existe aussi au pluriel.

Masculin :
Das ist ein Garten, c'est un jardin
Das ist kein Garten, ce n'est pas un jardin
Féminin :
Köln ist eine Stadt, Cologne est une ville
Mudau ist keine Stadt, Mudau n'est pas une ville
Neutre :
Hier ist ein Hotel, ici, il y a un hôtel
Hier ist kein Hotel, ici, il n'y a pas d'hôtel
Pluriel :
Das sind Tannen, ce sont des sapins
Das sind keine Tannen, ce ne sont pas des sapins.

■ **Das Hotel hat einen Garten.**
Einen Garten est le complément d'objet direct du verbe. Ce complément prend une forme qu'on appelle l'accusatif. Peu de noms ont une forme particulière à l'accusatif. Pour les articles, seul l'accusatif masculin diffère du nominatif (cas du sujet, habituellement indiqué).

● L'article défini :

	Masculin	Féminin	Neutre	Pluriel
Nominatif	*der Garten*	*die Tanne*	*das Gras*	*die Zimmer*
Accusatif	***den** Garten*	*die Tanne*	*das Gras*	*die Zimmer*

● L'article indéfini :

Accusatif	***einen** Garten*	*eine Tanne*	*ein Gras*	*Zimmer* (sans article)

■ **Ich habe kein Auto hier.**
Le verbe *haben* (avoir) est suivi de l'accusatif :

ich habe einen Freund — *wir haben eine Garage*
er (sie, es) hat ein Auto — *sie (Sie) haben den Park.*

Notez la forme irrégulière : *er hat.* Prononcez le « h »!

Exercices

A *Remplacez les articles par des articles négatifs :*
1. ein Freund. 2. die Tanne. 3. ein Hotel. 4. der Kongreß. 5. eine Vorstadt. 6. das Zimmer.

B *Formez l'accusatif, puis traduisez (version) :*
7. Herr Malk hat ei... Hotel und ei... Garage. 8. Kauft er d... Artikel? 9. Die Stadt hat ein... Park. 10. Herr Müller führt d... Freund. 11. Haben Sie kei... Garten?

C *Traduisez en allemand (thème) :*
12. Nous avons un jardin. 13. Où se trouve le parc? 14. Avez-vous (forme de politesse) un garage? 15. Je n'ai pas de chambre. 16. Monsieur Müller n'a-t-il pas d'ami ici?

D *Traduisez en allemand, puis répondez par la forme négative :*
17. Monsieur Dumont habite-t-il à (in) Lyon? 18. La voiture est-elle verte? 19. Le congrès dure-t-il longtemps (lange)? 20. Achète-t-il une voiture?

Corrigé :

A 1. kein Freund. 2. keine Tanne. 3. kein Hotel. 4. kein Kongreß. 5. keine Vorstadt. 6. kein Zimmer.

B 7. ein Hotel; eine Garage. *Monsieur Malk a un hôtel et un garage.* 8. den Artikel. *Achète-t-il l'article?* 9. einen Park. *La ville a un parc.* 10. den Freund. *Monsieur Müller conduit l'ami.* 11. keinen Garten. *N'avez-vous pas de jardin?*

C 12. Wir haben einen Garten. 13. Wo liegt der Park? 14. Haben Sie eine Garage? 15. Ich habe kein Zimmer. 16. Hat Herr Müller keinen Freund hier?

D 17. Wohnt Herr Dumont in Lyon? — Nein, er wohnt nicht in Lyon. 18. Ist das Auto grün? — Nein, das Auto ist nicht grün. 19. Dauert der Kongreß lange? — Nein, der Kongreß dauert nicht lange. 20. Kauft er ein Auto? — Nein, er kauft kein Auto.

Leçon

4 Briefe an die Freunde

1 Eine Woche ist nicht lang; aber Paul Dumont schreibt doch an die Freunde in Paris.
Er schreibt zwei Briefe und einige Postkarten.
Er ruft den Pförtner.

2 — Herr Möll, fahren Sie in die Stadt?
— Ja, ich fahre jeden Tag in die Stadt.
— Tragen Sie die Briefe hier auf die Post, bitte?
— Ja, gern; ich fahre mit Hans und Dieter.
— Wer ist das? — Es sind meine zwei Söhne.

3 — Wo ist Hans? — Er ist im Garten. Er läuft schnell, er ist noch jung.
— Wen ruft er? — Er ruft Dieter.
Herr Möll fährt in die Stadt. Er kauft einige Postkarten und zwei Hefte. Er trägt die Briefe auf die Post.

1 [aéne vore içt nicht la^{gn}; aber Paul Dumont chraébt dor dén' froeun'den' in' pariç — ér chraébt tçvaé brife oun't aénige poçtkarten' — ér rouft dén' pfeurtner].

2 [hèr meul, faren' zi in di chtat — ya, ich fare yéden' tak in' di chtat — tragen' zi di brife hir aof di poçt, bite — ya, gèrn; ich fare mit han'ç oun't diter — vér içt daç-èç zin't maéne zeune].

3 [vo içt han'ç — ér içt im' garten'. ér loeuft chnèl; ér içt nor you^{ng} — vén' rouft ér — ér rouft diter — hèr meul fèrt in' di chtat, ér kaoft aénige poçt-karten oun't tçvaé hèfte; ér trèkt di brife aof di poçt].

LIEBER SPÄT ALS NIE

Traduction

Des lettres aux amis

1 Une semaine, (ce) n'est pas long; mais Paul Dumont écrit quand même aux (à ses) amis à Paris. Il écrit deux lettres et quelques cartes postales. Il appelle le concierge.

2 — Monsieur Möll, allez-vous (sous-entendu : en véhicule) en ville? — Oui, je vais chaque jour en ville. — Porterez-vous ces lettres-ci à la poste, s'il-vous-plaît? — Oui, volontiers; j' (y) vais avec Jean et Didier. — Qui est-ce? — Ce sont mes deux fils.

3 — Où est Jean? — Il est au jardin. Il court vite, il est encore jeune. — Qui appelle-t-il? — Il appelle Didier. Monsieur Möll va en ville. Il achète quelques cartes postales et deux cahiers. Il porte les lettres à la poste.

Prononciation

Une caractéristique de la prononciation allemande, c'est l'accumulation de consonnes. Exercez-vous à bien prononcer les mots *Pförtner, schreibt.* En lisant à haute voix, ne vous arrêtez pas au milieu d'un groupe de mots constituant une unité de sens. Par exemple, dans la première phrase du § 2, considérez qu'il n'y a que trois mots : *« Herr M**ö**ll — f**a**hren Sie — in die St**a**dt? »*

Vocabulaire

der Brief, *la lettre*
der Sohn, *le fils*
der Tag, *le jour*
die Post, *la poste*
die P**o**stk**a**rte, *la carte postale*
das Heft, *le cahier*

r**u**fen, *appeler*
*f**a**hren (ä) (irrégulier) *rouler*
*l**au**fen (äu) (irrégulier) *courir*
schr**ei**ben (irrégulier) *écrire*
tr**a**gen (ä) (irrégulier) *porter*

Remarque : Les verbes précédés d'un astérisque (*) prennent au passé composé l'auxiliaire *sein* (être).

Mieux (vaut) tard que jamais

■ Er hat zwei Söhne.

Le pluriel des noms masculins et neutres :

Masculins :

der Sohn, le fils	*die Söhne,* les fils
der Park, le parc	*die Parke,* les parcs
der Mann, l'homme	*die Männer,* les hommes
der Garten, le jardin	*die Gärten,* les jardins
der Pförtner, le concierge	*die Pförtner,* les concierges
der Schlüssel, la clé	*die Schlüssel,* les clés
Neutres :	
das Jahr, l'année	*die Jahre,* les années
das Gras, l'herbe	*die Gräser,* les herbes
das Zimmer, la chambre	*die Zimmer,* les chambres

La marque du pluriel peut être *-e, -er, -en.* Les masculins ou neutres terminés en *-el, -en, -er* font leur pluriel sans terminaison. (Ex : *Garten, Schlüssel, Zimmer*). Certains noms prennent au pluriel l'inflexion, c'est-à-dire que la voyelle de leur radical se prononcera autrement : *a* devient *ä* [è], *o* devient *ö* [eu], *u* devient *ü* [u]. (Ex : *Sohn, Mann, Garten, Gras*) (Voyez dans le Mémento, les n° 5 à 14).

Nota :

- Il est indispensable d'apprendre, en même temps que le singulier et l'article défini, le pluriel de tous les noms étudiés.
- Pour abréger, nous indiquons, entre parenthèses, après chaque nom, la terminaison du pluriel et, éventuellement, l'inflexion à placer sur le radical. Exemple : *der Sohn* (¨ e) veut dire que le pluriel de *Sohn* est *die Söhne.*
- Au pluriel, le nominatif et l'accusatif sont toujours semblables.

■ Er fährt in die Stadt und trägt den Brief auf die Post.

Le verbe irrégulier (ou « fort ») au présent.
La voyelle radicale de certains verbes subit des modifications dans la conjugaison. Ces verbes sont appelés irréguliers (ou « forts »).

Ex :	*tragen,* porter	*laufen,* courir
	ich trag-e	*ich lauf-e*
	er (sie, es) trägt	*er (sie, es)* ***läuf****-t*
	wir trag-en	*wir lauf-en*
	sie (Sie) trag-en	*sie (Sie) laufen*

Note : Apprenez toujours : *tragen, er trägt; laufen, er läuft.*

■ **Wer ist das? — Wen ruft er?**

Le pronom interrogatif.

● Pour les personnes, on emploie *Wer?* qui? au nominatif, et *wen?* qui? à l'accusatif.

Wer ruft? Qui appelle? *Hans ruft.* (C'est) Jean (qui) appelle.
Wen ruft er? Qui appelle-t-il? *Er ruft Dieter.* Il appelle Didier.

● Pour les choses, on emploie *was,* que, quoi, pour les deux cas :

Was ist grün? Qu'est-ce qui est vert?
Was schreibt Paul Dumont? Qu'écrit Paul Dumont?

Exercices

A *Mettez les phrases au pluriel, puis traduisez :*
1. Er schreibt einen Brief. 2. Ich rufe den Pförtner. 3. Der Sohn trägt den Brief (auf die Post). 4. Das Gras ist grün. 5. Er fährt schnell.

B *Complétez les questions en employant, selon le cas, wer? wen? ou was? — puis traduisez :*
6. Paul ruft den Pförtner. a) ... ruft den Pförtner? b) ... ruft er? 7. Hans trägt den Brief. a) ... trägt Hans? b) ... trägt den Brief? 8. Sie haben einen Garten. a) ... haben Sie? b) ... hat einen Garten? 9. Herr Müller führt Paul Dumont durch die Stadt. a) ... führt Herr Müller durch die Stadt? b) ... führt Paul Dumont durch die Stadt?

C *Traduisez (thème) :*
10. J'écris une carte postale et une lettre. 11. Porte-t-il les lettres à (= sur, *auf*) la poste? 12. Les fils sont-ils encore jeunes? (construction, voir leçon 3). 13. Les jardins sont-ils calmes? 14. Qui appelle Didier? 15. Qui Didier appelle-t-il?

Corrigé :

A 1. Sie schreiben Briefe. *Ils écrivent des lettres.* 2. Wir rufen die Pförtner. *Nous appelons les concierges.* 3. Die Söhne tragen die Briefe auf die Post. *Les fils portent les lettres à la poste.* 4. Die Gräser sind grün. *Les herbes sont vertes.* 5. Sie fahren schnell. *Ils roulent vite.*

B 6. a) Wer? *Qui appelle le concierge?* b) Wen? *Qui appelle-t-il?* 7. a) Was? *Que porte Jean?* b) Wer? *Qui porte la lettre?* 8. a) Was? *Qu'ont-ils?* b) Wer? *Qui a un jardin?* 9. a) Wen? *Qui Monsieur Müller conduit-il à travers la ville?* b) Wer? *Qui conduit Paul Dumont à travers la ville?*

C 10. Ich schreibe eine Postkarte und einen Brief. 11. Trägt er die Briefe auf die Post? 12. Sind die Söhne noch jung? 13. Sind die Gärten ruhig? 14. Wer ruft Dieter? (sujet : Qui? donc *wer,* nominatif). 15. Wen ruft Dieter? (sujet du verbe : Dieter; il appelle qui? donc *wen,* complément d'objet direct, accusatif).

Leçon

5 Herr Beckmann, der Dolmetscher

1 — H**a**ben Sie viel **A**rbeit in Köln, Herr Dumont?
— Ja, **a**ber d**ie**ser Kongr**e**ß ist sehr interess**a**nt.
Wir h**a**ben einen D**o**lmetscher.
Er spricht gut Franz**ö**sisch.

2 Der D**o**lmetscher heißt Herr B**e**ckmann.
Er spricht m**e**hrere Spr**a**chen : Franz**ö**sisch, **E**nglisch, Sp**a**nisch.
Er kennt v**ie**le St**ä**dte in Eur**o**pa und liest viel.
J**e**der D**o**lmetscher liest viel.

3 Herr B**e**ckmann : — Guten T**a**g, Herr Dumont. Spr**e**chen Sie jetzt ein w**e**nig Deutsch?
Paul Dumont : — Ein w**e**nig nur, Herr B**e**ckmann. **A**ber ich k**e**nne jetzt Köln. Diese Stadt ist so schön!
Ich g**e**he oft an den Rhein.

1 [hèr bèkman', dér dolmètcher — 1. haben' zi fil arbaét in' keuln', hèr Dumont? — naén', aber dizer kon/grèç içt zér intèrèçan't — vir haben' aénen' dolmètcher — ér chpricht gout fran'tseuzich].

2 [dér dolmètcher haéçt hèr bèkman' — ér chpricht mérere chpraren', fran'tçeuzich, è[ng]lich, chpanich — ér kèn't file chtète in' Oeuropa oun't liçt fil — yéder dolmètcher liçt fil].

3 [hèr bèkman' — gouten' tak. hèr Dumont. Chprèchen' zi yètçt aén' vénich doeutch? — Paul Dumont : aén vénich nour, hèr Bekman' — aber ich kène yètçt keuln' — dize chtat içt zo cheun' — ich gée oft an' dén' raén'].

ROM IST NICHT AN EINEM TAG ERBAUT WORDEN

Traduction

Monsieur Beckmann, l'interprète

1 — Avez-vous beaucoup de travail à Cologne, Monsieur Dumont? — Oui, mais ce congrès est très intéressant. Nous avons un interprète. Il parle bien le français.

2 L'interprète s'appelle Monsieur Beckmann. Il parle plusieurs langues : le français, l'anglais, l'espagnol. Il connaît beaucoup de villes en Europe et lit beaucoup. Chaque interprète lit beaucoup.

3 Monsieur Beckmann : — Bonjour, Monsieur Dumont. Parlez-vous maintenant un peu l'allemand? Paul Dumont : — Un peu seulement, Monsieur Beckmann. Mais je connais maintenant Cologne. Cette ville est si belle! Je vais souvent au (bord du) Rhin.

Prononciation

Les nasales n'existent pas en allemand; dans *interessant,* on prononce donc *an,* comme dans le français « Anne »; bien sûr, le *t* final se prononce aussi. L'*r* final est très faible et sourd; ne prononcez pas la dernière syllabe de *« aber, Dolmetscher, dieser »* comme « eur » dans notre mot « beurre », mais très faiblement; l'*r* doit tout juste être perceptible. Enfin, l'*s* est sonore dans *Sie, dieser, sehr, Französisch, so;* nous le représentons par [z] comme dans « zèbre ».

Vocabulaire

der D**o**lmetscher (—), *l'interprète*
die **A**rbeit (-en), *le travail*
die Spr**a**che (n), *la langue*
Eur**o**pa, *l'Europe*

*g**e**hen, *aller*
h**ei**ßen, *s'appeler*
k**e**nnen, *connaître*
l**e**sen (er liest), *lire*
spr**e**chen (er spricht), *parler*

Rome ne s'est pas faite en un jour
(m. à m. : n'a pas été construite...)

Grammaire

■ **Er spricht mehrere Sprachen und kennt viele Städte.**
Le pluriel des noms : les féminins.

● La plupart des noms féminins prennent au pluriel la terminaison *-en* (ou *-n* s'ils sont déjà terminés par *-e*), et pas d'inflexion :

Die Sprache, die Sprachen — die Arbeit, die Arbeiten — die Woche, die Wochen.

● Certains féminins prennent la terminaison *-e* et l'inflexion sur le radical :

Die Stadt, die Städte — die Hand, die Hände, la main.

■ **Er spricht gut Französisch.**
Le verbe irrégulier (ou « fort »).
Les verbes irréguliers dont la voyelle radicale est *-e-* changent au présent cet *-e-* en *-i-* aux deuxième et troisième personnes du singulier.

Ich sprech-e, je parle	*wir sprechen,* nous parlons
er (sie, es) sprich-t, il parle	*sie (Sie) sprechen,* ils parlent, vous parlez.

Dans certains verbes, cette voyelle *-i-* est longue et s'écrit *-ie-*.

Lesen, er liest (lire)
Sehen, er sieht (voir).

Remarquez cependant cette exception : *gehen, er geht* (aller).

■ **Dieser Kongreß ist sehr interessant.**
Les déterminatifs.
dieser, ce; cette; ce...ci; celui-ci; *jeder,* chaque, chacun, *welcher,* quel? lequel?, *einige,* quelques; quelques-uns; *mehrere,* plusieurs, ont les mêmes terminaisons que l'article défini *der, die, das.* Ils peuvent être adjectifs (placés devant le nom) ou pronoms (remplaçant le nom). Exemples :

a) Masculin : *dieser Brief, jeder Brief, welcher Brief? einige Briefe* (pluriel) *mehrere Briefe* (pluriel).
b) féminin : *diese Stadt, jede Stadt,* etc.
c) neutre : *dieses Hotel, jedes Hotel,* etc.
d) pluriel (commun) : *diese Briefe, welche Städte?*

A l'accusatif masculin (article : *den*), nous aurons donc :
diesen Brief, jeden Brief, welchen Brief, einige Briefe (pluriel), *mehrere Briefe* (pluriel).

Exercices

A *Mettez les phrases au pluriel, puis traduisez :*
1. Diese Sprache ist nicht schwer. 2. Welche Stadt ist schön? 3. Sie spricht gut Deutsch. 4. Die Tanne ist grün. 5. Liest er schnell?

B *Faites accorder le verbe avec son sujet, puis traduisez :*
6. Ich (lesen) viel. 7. Sie (schreiben) einen Brief (sing.). 8. Hans (sprechen) Deutsch; er (wohnen) in Köln. 9. Wir (kennen) diese Stadt nicht. 10. Er (lesen) auch viel. 11. Sie (sprechen) nur Englisch.

C *12. Conjuguez le verbe « lesen » (lire), au présent de l'indicatif.*

D *Traduisez (thème) :*
13. Nous avons beaucoup de travail, mais ce travail est intéressant. 14. Ils n'ont pas d'interprète; ils parlent (l')espagnol. 15. Quelle langue est difficile? 16. Laquelle apprenez-vous (fòrme de politesse)? 17. Ces villes sont belles. 18. Celle-ci est très calme.

Corrigé :

A 1. Diese Sprachen sind nicht schwer. *Ces langues ne sont pas difficiles.* 2. Welche Städte sind schön? *Quelles villes sont belles?* 3. Sie sprechen gut Deutsch. *Elles parlent bien l'allemand.* 4. Die Tannen sind grün. *Les sapins sont verts.* 5. Lesen sie schnell? *Lisent-ils vite?*

B 6. Ich lese... *Je lis beaucoup.* 7. Sie schreibt... *Elle écrit une lettre.* 8. Hans spricht... er wohnt... *Jean parle l'allemand; il habite à Cologne.* 9. Wir kennen... *Nous ne connaissons pas cette ville.* 10. Er liest... *Il lit beaucoup également.* 11. Sie sprechen... *Ils ne parlent que l'anglais.*

C Ich lese, er (sie, es) liest, wir lesen, sie (Sie) lesen.

D 13. Wir haben viel Arbeit, aber diese Arbeit ist interessant. 14. Sie haben keinen Dolmetscher; sie sprechen Spanisch. 15. Welche Sprache ist schwer? 16. Welche lernen Sie? 17. Diese Städte sind schön. 18. Diese ist sehr ruhig.

Leçon

6

Diese Sprache ist international

1 Paul Dumont sitzt gern im G**a**rten.
H**eu**te liest er seine Post.
Pl**ö**tzlich hört er **et**was.
Ich bin nicht all**ei**n, denkt er.

2 Da k**o**mmen D**ie**ter und sein Kamer**a**d.
Oft sp**ie**len die J**u**ngen im G**a**rten.
— Hörst du nichts, D**ie**ter? Was ist das? fragt Paul Dumont.
— Ich s**e**he nichts und h**ö**re nichts, Herr Dumont.

3 D**ie**ter ruft s**ei**nen Kamer**a**den.
Jetzt hört man : — Krah! krah!
Ach, das ist ein R**a**be, sagt der J**u**nge.
Ja! d**ie**se Spr**a**che ist internation**a**l, sagt Paul Dumont und lacht.

1 [d**i**ze chpr**a**re içt in'ternatçion**a**l — Paul Dumont zitçt gérn im' g**a**rten' — h**oeu**te l**i**çt ér zaéne post — pl**eu**tçlich heurt ér **è**tvaç — ich bin' nicht al**aé**n dé^ng^kt ér].

2 [da k**o**men' d**i**ter oun't zaén' kamér**a**t — oft chp**i**len' di y**ou**^ng^en' im' g**a**rten' — heurçt dou nichtç, d**i**ter, vaç içt daç? frakt Paul Dumont — ich z**é**e nichtç oun't h**eu**re nichtç, hèr Dumont].

3 [d**i**ter r**ou**ft za**é**nen' kamér**a**den' — yètçt heurt man' ... — ar, daç içt aén' r**a**be, zakt dér y**ou**^ng^e — ya, d**i**ze chpr**a**re içt in'ternatçion**a**l, zakt Paul Dumont oun't lart].

DIE SPRACHE EINES VOLKES IST SEINE SEELE (Fichte).

Traduction

Ce langage est international

1 Paul Dumont aime bien être assis dans le jardin (mot à mot : est assis volontiers...). Aujourd'hui il lit son courrier. Soudain, il entend quelque chose. Je ne suis pas seul, pense-t-il.

2 Voilà qu'arrivent (mot à mot : là arrivent) Didier et son camarade. Les garçons jouent souvent dans le jardin. — N'entends-tu rien, Didier? Qu'est-ce que c'est? demande Paul Dumont. — Je ne vois rien et n'entends rien, Monsieur Dumont.

3 Didier appelle son camarade. Maintenant l'on entend : — crôa, crôa! Ah, c'est un corbeau, dit le garçon. Oh oui, ce langage est international, dit Paul Dumont en riant (mot à mot : et rit).

Prononciation

Au début d'un mot, *sp* se prononcent [chp] et *st* se prononcent [cht]. C'est le cas dans *Sprache, spielen, Stadt.*
b, d, g, sont explosifs en fin de syllabe, ainsi dans : *Kamerad, und, sagt.* Mais dans *Kameraden,* le *d,* qui n'est plus en fin de syllabe, est sonore, comme dans « donner ».
Prononcez donc : [kamér**at** — oun**t** — z**ak**t], mais le nom au pluriel : [kamér**ad**en'].
Dans les leçons précédentes, nous avons vu :

der Tag, *le jour* [dér t**ak**]
der Freund, *l'ami* [dér fr**o**eunt]
Deutschland, *l'Allemagne* [d**o**eutchlan't]

Cependant, le pluriel die Tage, *les jours,* garde le g sonore : [di t**age**].

Vocabulaire

der J**u**nge (n), *le garçon*
der R**a**be (n), *le corbeau*
die Post, *le courrier*
d**e**nken, *penser*
fr**a**gen, *demander*
h**ö**ren, *entendre*
*k**o**mmen, *venir*
l**a**chen, *rire*
s**a**gen, *dire*
s**i**tzen, *être assis*
sp**ie**len, *jouer*

La langue d'un peuple, c'est son âme.

Grammaire

■ **Die Jungen spielen oft im Garten.**
Singulier : *Der Junge spielt oft...*
Le pluriel des noms : les masculins dits faibles.
Certains masculins font leur pluriel en *-en* ou *-n.* Ils prennent cette terminaison à tous les cas, au singulier et au pluriel, sauf au nominatif singulier. On les appelle masculins faibles; ils désignent généralement un être animé. Exemples :

Der Junge ist groß (Nominatif singulier)
Ich rufe den Jungen (Accusatif singulier)
Die Jungen sind groß (Nominatif pluriel)
Ich rufe die Jungen (Accusatif pluriel).

Autres masculins faibles : *der Rabe (n) — der Kamerad (en).*

■ a) *Die Jungen spielen oft im Garten,* les garçons jouent souvent au jardin.
b) *Oft spielen die Jungen im Garten,* souvent, les garçons jouent au jardin.
a) *Der Pförtner hat zwei Söhne,* le concierge a deux fils.
b) *Zwei Söhne hat der Pförtner,* il a deux fils, le concierge.

Dans ces quatre propositions indépendantes, le verbe est à la deuxième place. A la première place, on peut avoir le sujet (exemple a). Cette place peut également être occupée par un terme autre que le sujet (exemple b); dans ce cas, le sujet se place après le verbe (inversion). La construction de la proposition, en allemand, repose avant tout sur la place du verbe.
Autres exemples d'inversion :

Da kommt Dieter, voilà Didier qui arrive.
Im Garten ist ein Rabe, au jardin, il y a (est) un corbeau.
An die Freunde in Paris schreibt er diese Briefe, (c'est) aux amis à Paris (qu') il écrit ces lettres.

Le verbe en deuxième place ne veut pas dire que le verbe doit être le deuxième mot. Devant le verbe, on peut avoir plusieurs mots, à condition qu'ils représentent une seule idée.

Remarque : Nous avons déjà rencontré l'inversion interrogative, dans la leçon 2 :

Wohnt Herr Müller in Köln? Monsieur Müller habite-t-il à Cologne?

Exercices

A *a) Complétez, puis traduisez :*
1. D... Junge... sieht ei... Rab.... 2. Hat er ei... Kamerad...? 3. Ich hör... d... Junge...; er lauf... (im Garten).
b) Mettez les phrases 1 à 3 au pluriel.

B *Changez la construction des phrases suivantes en commençant par le complément mis entre parenthèses, puis traduisez :*
4. Paul liest (oft) im Garten. 5. Paul liest oft (im Garten). 6. Er lernt (jetzt) Deutsch. 7. Er lernt jetzt (Deutsch). 8. Er kauft eine Postkarte (für seinen Freund).

C *Traduisez (thème) :*
9. Karl n'a pas de camarade. 10. Souvent, nous entendons des corbeaux au (*im*) jardin. 11. Appelez-vous les garçons? 12. Paul Dumont connaît-il ce langage? 13. Quel langage est international? 14. Elle achète quelque chose. 15. Aujourd'hui, je ne lis pas beaucoup. 16. Souvent, il n'apprend rien.

Corrigé :

A a) 1. Der Junge sieht einen Raben. *Le garçon voit un corbeau.* 2. Hat er einen Kameraden? *A-t-il un camarade?* 3. Ich höre den Jungen; er läuft im Garten. *J'entends le garçon; il court au jardin.* b) 1. Die Jungen sehen Raben. 2. Haben sie Kameraden? 3. Wir hören die Jungen; sie laufen im Garten.

B 4. Oft liest Paul im Garten. *Souvent, Paul lit au jardin.* 5. Im Garten liest Paul oft. *C'est au jardin que Paul lit souvent.* 6. Jetzt lernt er Deutsch. *Maintenant (ou : c'est maintenant qu') il apprend l'allemand.* 7. Deutsch lernt er jetzt. *C'est l'allemand qu'il apprend maintenant.* 8. Für seinen Freund kauft er eine Postkarte. *C'est pour son ami qu'il achète une carte postale.*

C 9. Karl hat keinen Kameraden. 10. Oft hören wir Raben im Garten. 11. Rufen Sie die Jungen? 12. Kennt Paul Dumont diese Sprache? 14. Sie kauft etwas. 15. Heute lese ich nicht viel. 16. Oft lernt er nichts.

Leçon

7

Im Kongreßsaal

1 Im Kongr**e**ßsaal hat Paul Dumont einen mod**e**rnen Schr**ei**btisch. Auf dem Tisch l**ie**gen seine Dokum**e**nte, seine B**ü**cher und sein K**u**gelschr**ei**ber.
Herr M**ü**ller, sein Freund, ist schon da.

2 Auch Frau K**e**llen hat ihren Schr**ei**btisch hier.
Sie kommt **i**mmer p**ü**nktlich an.
Sie zieht ihren M**a**ntel aus und hört zu.
Ihr M**a**ntel ist kar**ie**rt; ihr Kleid ist sehr schick.

3 – Wo ist denn meine Br**i**lle, Herr M**ü**ller?
– Sie liegt auf **I**hrem Tisch, Frau K**e**llen.
– Ach ja! D**a**nke! Und hier ist auch mein K**u**gelschr**ei**ber.
Ich schr**ei**be schnell **ei**nige Adr**e**ssen ab.

1 [im kon'gr**è**çzal – 1. im' Kon'gr**è**çzal hat Paul Dumont **a**énen' mod**è**rnen' chr**a**éptich – aof dém' t**i**ch l**i**gen' z**a**éne dokoum**e**n'te, z**a**éne b**u**cher oun't z**a**én k**ou**gelchr**a**éber – hèr m**u**ler, z**a**én fr**o**eun't, ist chon **da**].

2 [fr**a**o k**è**len' hat **a**or iren' chr**a**éptich hir – zi k**o**m't **i**mer p**u**^{ng}ktlich an' – zi tçit iren' m**a**n'tel **a**oç oun't h**eu**rt tç**ou** – ir m**a**n'tel içt karirt – ir kl**a**ét içt zer chik].

3 [vo içt dèn m**a**éne br**i**le, hèr m**u**ler ... ar ya, da^{ng}ke – oun't hir içt aor maén' k**ou**gelchr**a**éber – ich chr**a**ébe chnèl **a**énige adr**è**çen' ap].

SCHÖNHEIT VERGEHT, TUGEND BESTEHT

Traduction

Dans la salle de congrès

1 Dans la salle de congrès, Paul Dumont a un bureau moderne. Sur sa table, il y a (mot à mot : sont posés) ses documents, ses livres et son crayon à bille. Monsieur Müller, son ami, est déjà là.

2 Madame Kellen a également, ici, un bureau à elle (mot à mot : son bureau). Elle arrive toujours, à l'heure. Elle enlève son manteau et écoute. Son manteau est à carreaux; sa robe est très chic.

3 Où donc sont mes lunettes, Monsieur Müller? (mot à mot : est ma lunette). Elles sont (posées) sur votre table, Madame Kellen. — Ah oui! Merci! Et voici (ici est) également mon crayon à bille. Je copie vite quelques adresses.

Prononciation

Les voyelles suivies de deux consonnes sont brèves. Ainsi dans *Müller, Kellen, immer, pünktlich, schick, denn, Brille, Herr, schnell.*
La diphtongue *au* se prononce [ao]. Elle est brève et prononcée en une seule émission de voix. Il faut accentuer le *a.* Lisez à haute voix : *Paul, auf, Frau, aus, auch.*

Vocabulaire

der K**u**gelschr**ei**ber (-), *le crayon à bille*
der M**a**ntel (¨), *le manteau*
der Saal (die Säle), *la salle*
der Schr**ei**btisch (-e), *le bureau*
der Tisch (-e), *la table*
die Adr**e**sse (n), *l'adresse*
die Br**i**lle (n), *les lunettes*
die Frau (en), *la femme; madame*
die K**u**gel (n), *la bille, la boule*
das Buch (¨er), *le livre.*
das Dokum**e**nt (e), *le document*
ab/schr**ei**ben, *copier*
*****a**n/k**o**mmen, *arriver*
aus/z**ie**hen, *ôter; déshabiller*
d**a**nke, *merci*
zu/h**ö**ren, *écouter*

La beauté passe, la vertu demeure

Grammaire

■ **Er schreibt einige Adressen ab.**
La particule verbale séparable.
Avec le verbe *schreiben* (écrire) et la particule *ab,* on forme le verbe composé *abschreiben* (copier). Autres exemples :

kommen (venir)	*ankommen* (arriver)
hören (entendre)	*zuhören* (écouter)

● De nombreuses particules (une trentaine) peuvent former ainsi des verbes composés, qui tirent leur véritable sens de la particule.
Ces particules se séparent du verbe dans la proposition principale, au présent, au prétérit et à l'impératif.
Dans la prononciation, les particules séparables portent l'accent principal. Exemples :

ankommen : Sie kommt pünktlich an, elle arrive à l'heure.
zuhören : Hört er gut zu? Écoute-t-il bien?
abschreiben : Jetzt schreiben wir eine Adresse ab.
Maintenant, nous copions une adresse.

● ***Remarque très importante :*** dans les leçons suivantes, sous la rubrique « Vocabulaire », un verbe écrit avec une particule séparable accentuée (voyelle en caractère gras) sera donc un verbe à particule séparable.

■ **Wo ist mein Kugelschreiber?**
L'adjectif possessif.

Possesseur sing.		Masc.	Fém.	Ntre	Plur.
1re pers.	mon	*mein*	*meine*	*mein*	*meine*
2e pers.	ton	*dein*	*deine*	*dein*	*deine*
3e pers.	son (à lui)	*sein*	*seine*	*sein*	*seine*
	son (à elle)	*ihr*	*ihre*	*ihr*	*ihre*
Possesseur pluriel					
1re pers.	notre	*unser*	*unsere*	*unser*	*unsere*
2e pers.	votre	*euer*	*eure*	*euer*	*eure*
3e pers.	leur	*ihr*	*ihre*	*ihr*	*ihre*
f. polit.	votre	*Ihr*	*Ihre*	*Ihr*	*Ihre*

Remarques : 1) L'adjectif possessif se décline comme l'article indéfini *ein.* L'accusatif masculin est donc : *meinen, deinen,* etc. Exemple :

Ich höre meinen Freund.

2) A la 3e personne du singulier, on emploie *sein* quand le possesseur est masculin ou neutre, *ihr* quand le possesseur est féminin. Exemple :

Paul Dumont hat seinen Schreibtisch. Frau Kellen hat ihren Schreibtisch.

Exercices

A *Faites accorder les verbes entre parenthèses en veillant à la place de la particule, puis traduisez :*
1. Wir (ausziehen) unseren Mantel. 2. Mein Freund (ankommen) in Köln. 3. Sie (abschreiben) diesen Brief. 4. (zuhören) wir immer gut? 5. Was (ausziehen) er?

B a) *Complétez par un possessif, puis traduisez :*
6. Ich habe ... Kugelschreiber. 7. Es hat ... Postkarte. 8. Er hat ... Zimmer. 9. Sie hat ... Arbeit.
b) *Mettez ces phrases au pluriel,* (*sauf :* Arbeit).

Corrigé :

A 1. Wir ziehen unseren Mantel aus. *Nous ôtons notre manteau.* 2. Mein Freund kommt in Köln an. *Mon ami arrive à Cologne.* 3. Sie schreibt diesen Brief ab. *Elle copie cette lettre.* 4. Hören wir immer gut zu? *Écoutons-nous toujours bien?* 5. Was zieht er aus? *Qu'est-ce qu'il enlève?*

B a) 6. meinen (Accusatif masculin singulier). *J'ai mon crayon à bille.* 7. seine (Accusatif féminin singulier). *Il a sa carte postale.* 8. sein (Accusatif neutre singulier). *Il a sa chambre.* 9. ihre (Accusatif féminin singulier; possesseur féminin). *Elle a son travail.*

b) 6. Wir haben unsere Kugelschreiber (Accusatif pluriel). 7. Sie haben ihre Postkarten. 8. Sie haben ihre Zimmer. 9. Sie haben ihre Arbeit.

Leçon

8 Ein Tag in Köln

1 Morgens ißt man gut in Deutschland.
Aber Paul Dumont trinkt nur ein wenig Kaffee.
Der Vormittag ist dann für die Arbeit im Kongreß.
Mittags geht er in ein Gasthaus.

2 Nachmittags arbeitet er nicht immer.
Oft geht er den Rhein entlang oder durch die Stadt.
Er wird so schnell nicht müde; er geht gern zu Fuß.
Er wird auch aufs Land fahren.
So lernt er Land und Leute kennen.

3 Heute abend wird er ins Kino gehen.
Dann wird er noch einen Brief schreiben.
Es wird ein langer Tag werden.
Aber nachts schläft man ruhig in der Vorstadt.

1 [aén′ tak in keuln′] morgenç içt man′ gout in doeutchlan′t – aber Paul Dumont tri^{ng}kt nour aén′ vénich kafé – dér formitak içt dan′ fur di arbaét im′ kon′/grèç – am′ mitak gét ér in′ aén′ gaçthaoç.]

2 [narmitakç arbaétet ér nicht imer – oft gét ér dén′ raén′ èntlan^{ng} oder dourch di chtat – ér virt nicht zo chnèl mude – ér gét gèrn tçou fouç.]

3 [hoeute aben′t virt ér in′ç kino géen′ – dan′ virt ér nor aénen′ brif chraében′ – èç virt aén la^{ng}er tak – aber nartç chlèft man′ rouich in′ dér forchtat.]

ALLES ZU SEINER ZEIT

Traduction

Une journée à Cologne

1 Le matin, on mange bien en Allemagne. Mais Paul Dumont ne boit qu'un peu de café. Ensuite, la matinée est pour le travail au congrès. A midi il va dans un restaurant.

2 L'après-midi, il ne travaille pas toujours. Souvent, il longe le Rhin (mot à mot : il va le long du...) ou bien il passe par la ville (mot à mot : il va à travers...). Il ne se fatigue pas si vite (mot à mot : il ne devient pas si vite fatigué); il aime la marche à pied (mot à mot : il va volontiers à pied). Il ira aussi (en véhicule) à la campagne. Ainsi, il apprend à connaître (le) pays et (ses) habitants.

3 Ce soir, il ira au cinéma (mot à mot : aujourd'hui soir...). Ensuite il écrira encore une lettre. Ce sera une longue journée (m. à m. : deviendra). Mais la nuit, on dort paisiblement, en banlieue.

Prononciation

Er geht gern zu Fuß. En tête de mot, **g** a toujours un son guttural dur, comme dans « guérir, guêtre ». Rappelez-vous que dans l'orthographe phonétique, nous le marquons par [g], quelle que soit la voyelle suivante.
ißt, Kongreß, Fuß : la lettre ß [èçtçèt'] correspond toujours à notre « s » dur de laisser.

Vocabulaire

der **A**bend (-e), *le soir*
der Fuß (¨e), *le pied*
der K**a**ffee, *le café*
der M**i**ttag (e), *le midi*
der M**o**rgen (-), *le matin*
der N**a**chmittag (-e), *l'après-midi*
der Tag (-e), *le jour*

die L**eu**te (plur.) *les gens*
die Nacht (¨e), *la nuit*
das G**a**sthaus (¨er), *le restaurant*
das K**i**no (s), *le cinéma*
das Land (¨er), *le pays*
*g**e**hen, *aller*
tr**i**nken, *boire*
essen (er ißt), *manger*

Chaque chose en son temps.

Grammaire

■ Er geht durch die Stadt oder den Rhein entlang.
Prépositions suivies de l'accusatif.
Les prépositions suivantes sont toujours suivies de l'accusatif : *durch,* par, à travers; *für,* pour; *gegen,* contre, vers, envers; *ohne,* sans; *um,* autour de; *entlang,* le long de. (Cette dernière préposition est placée après le complément).
Exemples :

Er kauft es für seinen Freund, il l'achète pour son ami.
Sein Zimmer liegt gegen die Stadt, sa chambre donne (se trouve) vers la ville.
Sie gehen um das Hotel, ils vont autour (font le tour) de l'hôtel.

■ Morgens ißt man gut hier.
Adverbes et compléments de temps.

● A partir du nom *der Morgen,* le matin, on forme l'adverbe de temps *morgens,* le, au matin. De même, *der Vormittag,* donne *vormittags,* dans la matinée.

● Cependant, on peut aussi employer un complément avec préposition : *morgens* ou *am Morgen,* le matin; *mittags* ou *am Mittag,* à midi; *nachmittags* ou *am Nachmittag,* (dans) l'après-midi; *abends* ou *am Abend,* le soir.

Exception : *nachts* ou *in der Nacht,* la nuit.
Notez que les adverbes sont d'un emploi plus fréquent, et qu'ils ne prennent pas de majuscule.

■ Er wird so schnell nicht müde.
L'auxiliaire *werden,* devenir.

ich werde, je deviens	*wir werden,* nous devenons
er (sie, es) wird, il devient	*sie werden,* ils deviennent

Remarquez la forme irrégulière : *er wird.*

■ Er wird ins Kino gehen.
Le futur se forme avec *werden* et l'infinitif du verbe à conjuguer; cet infinitif se place à la fin de la proposition principale ou indépendante.

Ich werde eine Karte kaufen, j'achèterai une carte.
Diese Tanne wird groß werden, ce sapin deviendra grand.
Mittags werden wir gut essen, à midi, nous mangerons bien.
Abends werden sie (Sie) müde sein, le soir ils seront (vous serez) fatigués.

Exercices

A *Complétez puis traduisez :*
1. Sie kommt nicht ohne ihr... Bruder. 2. Wir gehen durch d... Stadt. 3. Er kauft dies... Buch für sein... Söhne. 4. Er geht um d... Auto. 5. Sie gehen d... Garten entlang.

B *Complétez a) par un complément de temps b) par un adverbe de temps, puis traduisez :*
6. Wir arbeiten (der Morgen) und (der Nachmittag). 7. Er schreibt (der Abend) einige Briefe. 8. (die Nacht) schlafe ich gut.

C *Mettez les phrases au futur, puis traduisez :*
9. Er ruft seinen Freund. 10. Ich ziehe den Mantel aus. 11. Wir trinken Kaffee. 12. Ist sie müde? 13. Ich schreibe diese Adresse ab. 14. Sie sitzen im Park.

D *Traduisez (thème) :*
15. Le matin, je ne mange pas beaucoup. 16. Je mangerai bien à midi. 17. J'achèterai une carte postale pour mon ami. 18. La nuit, le faubourg est tranquille. 19. Il viendra sans livres et sans documents.

Corrigé :

A 1. ihren. *Elle ne vient pas sans son frère.* 2. die. *Nous traversons la ville.* 3. dieses; seine. *Il achète ce livre pour ses fils.* 4. das. *Il fait le tour de la voiture (va autour de).* 5. den. *Ils longent le jardin.*

B 6 a) am Morgen und am Nachmittag. b) morgens und nachmittags. *Nous travaillons le matin et l'après-midi.* 7 a) am Abend. b) abends. *Le soir, il écrit quelques lettres.* 8. a) in der Nacht. b) nachts. *La nuit je dors bien.*

C 9. Er wird seinen Freund rufen. *Il appellera son ami.* 10. Ich werde den Mantel ausziehen. *J'ôterai mon manteau.* 11. Wir werden Kaffee trinken. *Nous prendrons du café.* 12. Wird sie müde sein? *Sera-t-elle fatiguée?* 13. Ich werde diese Adresse abschreiben. *Je copierai cette adresse.* 14. Sie werden im Park sitzen. *Ils seront assis dans le parc (Vous serez...).*

D 15. Morgens esse ich nicht viel. 16. Ich werde mittags gut essen. 17. Ich werde eine Postkarte für meinen Freund kaufen. 18. Nachts ist die Vorstadt ruhig. 19. Er wird ohne Bücher und ohne Dokumente kommen.

Leçon

9 Bei der Familie Müller (1)

1 Paul Dumont ist Gast bei der Fam**i**lie M**ü**ller.
Herr Müller hat eine *W**o**hnung in der *M**o**zartstr**a**ße.
Das *Haus geh**ö**rt der F**i**rma IMEX.

2 Der Gast bringt Frau M**ü**ller Bl**u**men.
Den K**i**ndern gibt er *Schokol**a**de.
Herr M**ü**ller zeigt s**ei**nem Freund die W**o**hnung.
Sie ist groß und sehr mod**e**rn.

3 Jetzt tr**i**nken sie *K**a**ffee und essen *K**u**chen.
Sie spr**e**chen von Köln, vom Rhein, von *D**eu**tschland.
Paul Dumont *erz**ä**hlt seinen *G**a**stg**e**bern von *Par**i**s und von s**ei**ner **A**rbeit.

4 In w**e**lcher Str**a**ße hat Herr M**ü**ller eine W**o**hnung?
Wie ist diese W**o**hnung?
Wem geh**ö**rt das Haus?
Wem br**i**ngen Sie Bl**u**men?
Wem g**e**ben Sie d**ie**se Schokol**a**de?

Prononciation des mots précédés du signe *.

1 [v**o**nou[gn]] - [m**o**tçart] - [chtr**a**çe] - [h**a**oç]

2 [chokol**a**de]

3 [kaf**é**] - [k**ou**ren'] - [d**oe**utchlan't] - [èrtç**ê**lt] - [g**a**çtg**é**bern] - [par**i**ç].

JEDER IST HERR IN SEINEM HAUSE

Traduction

Dans la famille Müller (1)

1 Paul Dumont est invité (mot à mot : hôte) dans la famille Müller. Monsieur Müller a un appartement dans la rue Mozart. L'immeuble (la maison) appartient à la firme IMEX.

2 L'hôte apporte des fleurs à Madame Müller. Il donne du chocolat aux enfants. Monsieur Müller montre l'appartement à son ami. Il est grand et très moderne.

3 A présent, ils boivent du café et mangent du gâteau. Ils parlent de Cologne, du Rhin, de l'Allemagne. Paul Dumont parle (mot à mot : raconte) à ses hôtes de Paris et de son travail.

4 Dans quelle rue Monsieur Müller a-t-il un appartement? Comment est cet appartement? A qui la maison appartient-elle? A qui apportez-vous (forme de politesse) des fleurs? A qui donnez-vous ce chocolat?

Prononciation

Les verbes *gehören* et *erzählen* ont un préfixe non accentué (atone) : *ge-* et *er-*. Prononcez cette syllabe faiblement. *Schokolade, modern* ne sont pas d'origine germanique et conservent l'accent tonique original. Cependant, prononcez faiblement l'*e* final de *Schokolade;* n'oubliez pas non plus de prononcer l'*s* finale dans « Paris ».
Le nom composé *G**a**stg**e**ber* a deux accents : un accent tonique sur *Gast,* et un accent moins fort (accent secondaire) sur *-geber.*

Vocabulaire

der Gast (¨e), *l'hôte qui est reçu*
der G**a**stg**e**ber (-), *l'hôte (qui reçoit)*
der K**u**chen (-), *le gâteau*
Die Bl**u**me (n), *la fleur*
die Fam**i**lie (n), *la famille*
die Schokol**a**de, *le chocolat*

die Str**a**ße (n), *la rue*
die W**o**hnung (-en), *l'appartement*
D**eu**tschland, *l'Allemagne*
das Haus (¨er), *la maison*
erz**ä**hlen, *raconter*
z**ei**gen, *montrer*
br**i**ngen (irrégulier), *apporter*
g**e**ben (er gibt), *donner*

Charbonnier est maître chez lui (m. à m. : Chacun est maître dans sa maison).

das Kind _ die Kinder

↳ L'ENFANT

Grammaire

■ Er zeigt seinem Gast die Wohnung.
Le datif.

● *Seinem Gast* est le complément d'attribution. Ce complément se met au datif. En général, le nom complément d'attribution *(seinem Gast)* se place avant le nom complément d'objet direct (*die Wohnung,* accusatif).

● La plupart des noms ne changent pas au datif singulier. Mais au datif pluriel, ils sont tous terminés par *-n,* sauf s'ils finissent au pluriel par s *(den Autos).*

Er zeigt den Gästen die Wohnung, il montre l'appartement aux hôtes.

● C'est l'article ou tout autre déterminatif qui marque le datif.
Singulier :
Masculin : *dem (einem, keinem) Gast,* à l'hôte (à un..., ne pas à un...).
Féminin : *der (einer, keiner) Firma,* à la firme (à une..., ne pas à une...).
Neutre : *dem (einem, keinem) Kind,* à l'enfant (à un..., ne pas à un...).

Pluriel commun aux trois genres :
den Gästen, aux hôtes — *den Firmen,* aux firmes, — *den Kindern,* aux enfants.

● Pour interroger, on emploie *wem* (à qui?).

■ Bei der Familie Müller.

Le datif est également demandé par certaines prépositions :

aus, hors de, en.
Er kommt aus der Stadt, il vient (hors) de la ville.

bei, auprès de, chez (quand il y a état).
Er ist bei seinem Freund, il est chez son ami.

mit, avec.
Er spricht mit einer Dame, il parle avec une dame.

nach, après, vers.
Nach dem Essen trinkt er Kaffee, après le repas, il boit du café.

seit, depuis.
Er ist seit einer Woche in Köln, il est depuis une semaine à Cologne.

von, de.
Sie sprechen von ihrem Hotel, ils parlent de leur hôtel.

zu, à, chez (quand il y a direction).
Er geht zu seinem Freund, il va chez son ami.

Exercices

A *Complétez les terminaisons, et traduisez :*
A. (datif) — 1. Paul schreibt sein... Freund. 2. Er bringt d... Dame ihren Mantel. 3. Er erzählt d... Kinder... von Paris. 4. Er kauft dies... Junge... (singulier) Schokolade. 5. Das Auto gehört unser... Dolmetscher.
B. (datif et accusatif) — 6. Ich bringe d... Pförtner ein... Kugelschreiber. 7. Sie gibt d... Junge... (pluriel) dies... Kuchen.
C. (prépositions + datif) — 8. Er wohnt bei sein... Onkel. 9. Wir sprechen von ihr... Familie. 10. Hans läuft zu sein... Kamerad... (singulier). 11. Nach d... Arbeit gehen sie ins Kino. 12. Er kommt mit ein... Dame.

B *Posez trois questions sur chacune des phrases suivantes, en employant :* A) *Wer?* (= qui?) B) *Wem?* (= à qui?) C) *Was?* (= que? quoi?). 13. Herr Müller zeigt dem Freund die Wohnung. 14. Paul bringt Frau Müller Blumen.

C *Traduisez en allemand (thème) :*
15. Nous montrerons l'hôtel à nos amis. 16. A qui donnez-vous (forme de politesse) ces livres? 17. Il écrira une lettre à son camarade. 18. Cette voiture *(das Auto)* n'appartient pas au portier. 19. Madame Müller apportera un gâteau à vos enfants (forme de politesse).

Corrigé :

A A. 1. seinem. *Paul écrit à son ami.* 2. der. *Il apporte son manteau à la dame.* 3. den Kindern. *Il parle de Paris aux enfants.* 4. diesem. *Il achète du chocolat à ce garçon.* 5. Unserem. *La voiture appartient à notre interprète.*
B. 6. dem; einen. *J'apporte un crayon à bille au concierge.* 7. den Jungen; diesen. *Elle donne ce gâteau aux garçons.*
C. 8. bei seinem. *Il habite chez son oncle.* 9. von ihrer. *Nous parlons de sa famille (à elle, ou bien : de leur famille).* 10. zu seinem Kameraden. *Jean court chez son camarade.* 11. Nach der. *Après le travail, ils vont au cinéma.* 12. Mit einer. *Il viendra (ou : vient) avec une dame.*

B 13. A. Wer zeigt dem Freund die Wohnung? B. Wem zeigt Herr Müller die Wohnung? C. Was zeigt Herr Müller dem Freund? 14. A. Wer bringt Frau Müller Blumen? B. Wem bringt Paul Blumen? C. Was bringt Paul Frau Müller?

C 15. Wir werden unseren Freunden *(datif pluriel)* das Hotel zeigen. 16. Wem geben Sie diese Bücher? 17. Er wird seinem Kameraden *(masculin faible, voir leçon 6)* einen Brief schreiben. 18. Dieses Auto gehört dem Pförtner nicht. 19. Frau Müller wird Ihren Kindern einen Kuchen bringen.

Leçon

10 Bei der Familie Müller (2)

1 — Kommen Sie ein wenig auf die *Terrasse, Herr Dumont!
— Ja, gern. Es ist *angenehm hier.
— Man hört *wohl den *Lärm der Straße. Aber man gewöhnt sich schnell daran.

2 — *Wessen Terrasse ist das?
— Es ist die Terrasse *meines Nachbars.
Seine Frau hat Blumen sehr gern.
*Die Farben ihrer Rosen leuchten in dieser Steinwelt.

3 — Ihre Kinder sind wohl oft *hier?
— Ja; das ist Karls Auto und das sind *Heddys Puppen.
Karl, *komm her!
*Zeige unserem Gast die schöne Aussicht auf den Rhein!

4 — Wessen Frau hat Blumen sehr gern?
— Wessen Kinder sind oft auf der Terrasse?
— Wessen Puppen liegen auf dem Tisch?
— Wessen Auto ist das?

1 [di tèraçe — angeném' — vol — dén' lèrm' —]

2 [vèçen' — maéneç narbarç — di farben' irer rozen' loeuchten' in dizer chtaén'vèlt].

3 [hir — hèdiç poupen' — kom' hér — tçaége oun'serem' gaçt di cheune aoçzicht aof dén' raén'].

KEINE ROSE OHNE DORNEN

Traduction

Chez la famille Müller (2)

1 – Venez un peu sur la terrasse, Monsieur Dumont! – Oui, avec plaisir. C'est agréable ici. – On entend certes les bruits (mot à mot : le bruit) de la rue. Mais on s'y habitue vite.

2 – C'est la terrasse de qui? – C'est la terrasse de notre voisin. Sa femme aime beaucoup (les) fleurs (mot à mot : a les fleurs très volontiers). Les couleurs de ses roses brillent dans ce monde de pierre.

3 – Sans doute vos enfants sont-ils souvent ici? – Oui; voici (c'est) l'auto de Charles, et voici les poupées de Heddy. Charles, viens (par ici)! Montre à notre hôte la belle vue sur le Rhin!

4 – L'épouse de qui aime beaucoup (les) fleurs? – Les enfants de qui sont souvent sur la terrasse? – Les poupées de qui sont (posées) sur la table? – C'est la voiture de qui? (= à qui appartient cette voiture?)

Prononciation

● L'**e** final n'est pas muet en allemand; il se prononce comme [eu] assourdi, sans accent, en laissant tomber la voix. Exercez-vous à le prononcer dans *Fam**i**lie* – *Terr**a**sse* – *Str**a**ße* – ***sei**ne* – ***i**hre* – *P**u**ppe* – ***zei**ge.*
● p, t, k sont explosifs, c'est-à-dire suivis d'un souffle. Ainsi : ***ko**mmen* – *Terr**a**sse* – *K**i**nder* – *Karl* – *P**u**ppe.*

Vocabulaire

der Lärm (plur. inusité), *le bruit*
der N**a**chbar (s, n), *le voisin*
der Stein (-e), *la pierre*
die F**a**rbe (n), *la couleur*
die P**u**ppe (n), *la poupée*
die R**o**se(n), *la rose*
die Terr**a**sse (n), *la terrasse*
die Welt (-en), *le monde*
g**e**rn haben, *aimer bien*
gew**ö**hnen, *habituer*
leuchten, *luire, briller*
verg**e**ssen (er vergißt), *oublier*

Pas de roses sans épines

Grammaire

■ Die Terrasse des Nachbars.
Le génitif.

● Le génitif est le cas du complément du nom : *des Nachbars,* du voisin. Il est marqué par l'article et, pour tous les noms neutres et pour la plupart des masculins, par la terminaison ***s*** au singulier. Les féminins par contre n'ont pas de terminaison : ils sont invariables au singulier. Au pluriel, seul l'article prend la marque du génitif. Exemples :

Masculin : *des (eines, keines) Nachbars,* du voisin.
Féminin : *der (einer, keiner) Familie,* de la famille.
Neutre : *des (eines, keines) Hotels,* de l'hôtel.
Pluriel : *der (keiner) Gäste,* des (= de les) hôtes.

Note : Pour une raison d'euphonie, on intercale un *e* entre le radical de certains noms et la terminaison *s.* Exemple :
des Hauses, des Kindes.

● Les noms propres, masculins ou féminins, prennent *s* au génitif : *Karls,* de Charles, *Heddys,* de Heddy. Mais parfois, dans la langue courante, on remplace ce génitif par une tournure ressemblant au français :

Das Buch von Hans, le livre de Jean.

● *Das ist Karls Auto.* Le génitif dit « saxon ». Le génitif peut précéder le nom déterminé *(Auto).* Dans ce cas, celui-ci perd son article. Exemple : *die Puppen Heddys,* ou bien : *Heddys Puppen.* Cette tournure est surtout employée avec les noms propres.

● *Wessen Auto ist das?*
Après *wessen?,* de qui? interrogatif au génitif, on place directement le nom, sans article. Exemple :

Wessen Buch? le livre de qui?
Wessen Blumen? les fleurs de qui?

■ Karl, komm her!
L'impératif.

2e pers. du sing. : *zeige!* montre! *Komm(e)!* viens!
2e pers. du plur. : *zeigt!* montrez! *Kommt!* venez!
Forme de politesse : *zeigen Sie!* montrez! *Kommen Sie!* venez!
Remarques : 1) A la 2e personne du singulier, on peut supprimer la terminaison *e* pour les verbes très usuels : *zeig!* montre!
2) les verbes irréguliers en *e* prennent au singulier le radical modifié en *i* : Exemple : *sprechen / sprich!* parle! *geben / gib!* donne!

Exercices

A *Complétez, puis traduisez :*
1. Das ist das Hotel mein... Freund... (génitif singulier). 2. Das ist das Buch sein... Sohn... 3. Das sind die Mäntel dies... Dame... (génitif pluriel). 4. Das ist die Wohnung d... Familie Müller. 5. Das ist Emil... Kugelschreiber.

B *Employez le génitif saxon dans les expressions suivantes, puis traduisez :*
6. der Schreibtisch Pauls. 7. das Haus Antons. 8. die Brille des Dolmetschers. 9. der Garten Marthas.

C *Formez l'impératif* (2e personne du singulier; 2e personne du pluriel; forme de politesse) *pour les verbes suivants :*
10. arbeiten. 11. schlafen. 12. sprechen. 13. zuhören (la particule se sépare).

D *Traduisez.*
14. La maison de mon voisin est grande. 15. Le parc de cette ville est calme. 16. La chambre de Paul est moderne. 17. Les fleurs de Madame Müller sont très belles. 18. C'est la maison de qui?

Corrigé :

A 1. meines Freundes. *Voici (= c'est) l'hôtel de mon ami.* 2. seines Sohns. *Voici le livre de son fils.* 3. dieser Damen. *Voici les manteaux de ces dames.* 4. der Familie. *Voici l'appartement de la famille Müller.* 5. Emils. *Voici le crayon à bille d'Émile.*

B 6. Pauls Schreibtisch. *Le bureau de Paul.* 7. Antons Haus. *La maison d'Antoine.* 8. des Dolmetschers Brille. *Les lunettes de l'interprète.* 9. Marthas Garten. *Le jardin de Marthe.*

C 10. arbeite! arbeitet! arbeiten Sie! 11. schlafe! schlaft! schlafen Sie! 12. sprich! sprecht! sprechen Sie! 13. Hör(e) zu! hört zu! hören Sie zu!

D 14. Das Haus meines Nachbars ist groß. 15. Der Park dieser Stadt ist ruhig. 16. Pauls Zimmer ist modern. 17. Frau Müllers Blumen sind sehr schön. 18. Wessen Haus ist das?

Leçon

10 bis

Contrôle et révisions

A **Mettez au pluriel, puis traduisez :**

1. der Brief. 2. ein Buch. 3. dieses Gasthaus. 4. die Frau. 5. welche Stadt? 6. kein Mantel. 7. das Gras. 8. eine Nacht. 9. mein Zimmer. 10. unser Garten.

B **Voici quelques formes verbales avec *du* tu et *ihr* vous :**

Du bist, *tu es;* ihr seid, *vous êtes.* Du hast, *tu as;* ihr habt, *vous avez.* Du wirst, *tu deviens;* ihr werdet, *vous devenez.* Du fragst, *tu demandes;* ihr fragt, *vous demandez.* Du gibst, *tu donnes;* ihr gebt, *vous donnez.* (Voir Mémento n° 43 à 47.)

Mettez au singulier, puis traduisez :

11. Habt ihr eure Hefte? 12. Ihr seid im Zimmer und ihr schreibt Adressen ab. 13. Wo kauft ihr diese Kugelschreiber? 14. Ihr tragt die Briefe auf die Post und ihr sprecht mit Georg.

C **Complétez les adjectifs possessifs, puis traduisez :**

15. Ich suche *(cherche)* mei ... Freund, mei ... Garage, mei ... Hotel, mei ... Mantel.

Mettez cette phrase à la 3e personne du singulier, au masculin (Er...) puis au féminin (Sie...).

D **Transposez les phrases suivantes au présent, puis traduisez :**

16. Er wird eine Brille tragen. 17. Du wirst deinen Freund rufen. 18. Sie werden ihren Mantel ausziehen. 19. Er wird nicht viel essen. 20. Du wirst pünktlich ankommen.

E **Posez quatre questions sur la phrase suivante :**

21. Der Freund des Direktors kauft den Kindern Schokolade.

F **Traduisez les phrases suivantes :**

23. Où est votre hôtel? *(forme de politesse).* 24. Les chambres de cet hôtel sont-elles modernes? 25. A-t-il un garage? 26. Connaissez-vous la ville? 27. N'ôtez-vous pas votre manteau? 28. Paul écrit une lettre à son voisin. 29. Les rues de la ville ne sont pas souvent calmes.

Corrigé :

A 1. die Briefe, *les lettres.* 2. Bücher, *des livres.* 3. Diese Gasthäuser, *ces restaurants.* 4. die Frauen, *les femmes.* 5. welche Städte? *quelles villes?* 6. keine Mäntel, *pas de manteaux.* 7. die Gräser, *les herbes.* 8. Nächte, *des nuits.* 9. meine Zimmer, *mes chambres.* 10. unsere Gärten, *nos jardins.*

B 11. Hast du dein Heft? *As-tu ton cahier?* 12. Du bist im Zimmer und du schreibst eine Adresse ab. *Tu es dans la chambre et tu copies une adresse.* 13. Wo kaufst du diesen Kugelschreiber? *Où achètes-tu ce crayon à bille?* 14. Du trägst den Brief auf die Post und du sprichst mit Georg (verbes irréguliers). *Tu portes la lettre à la poste et tu parles avec Georges.*

C 15. Ich suche meinen Freund, meine Garage, mein Hotel, meinen Mantel. *Je cherche mon ami, mon garage, mon hôtel, mon manteau.* a) Er sucht seinen Freund, seine Garage, sein Hotel, seinen Mantel. b) Sie sucht ihren Freund, ihre Garage, ihr Hotel, ihren Mantel.

D 16. Er trägt eine Brille. *Il porte des* (mot à mot : une) *lunettes.* 17. Du rufst deinen Freund. *Tu appelles ton ami.* 18. Sie ziehen ihren Mantel aus. *Ils ôtent leur manteau.* 19. Er ißt nicht viel. *Il ne mange pas beaucoup.* 20. Du kommst pünktlich an. *Tu arrives à l'heure.*

E 21. *(l'ami du directeur achète du chocolat aux enfants.)* a) Wer kauft den Kindern Schokolade? b) Wessen Freund kauft den Kindern Schokolade? c) Wem kauft der Freund des Direktors Schokolade? d) Was kauft der Freund des Direktors den Kindern?

F 23. Wo ist Ihr Hotel? 24. Sind die Zimmer dieses Hotels modern? 25. Hat es eine Garage? 26. Kennen Sie die Stadt? 27. Ziehen Sie Ihren Mantel nicht aus? 28. Paul schreibt seinem Nachbar einen Brief. 29. Die Straßen der Stadt sind nicht oft ruhig.

Leçon

11 Notizen aus dem Kongreß

1 Paul Dumont kommt aus der Stadt *zur**ü**ck.
Er geht schnell, denn er **a**rbeitet heute auf s**ei**nem Z**i**mmer.
*Er legt s**ei**nen M**a**ntel auf das Bett.
Die Bl**u**men* stellt er an das F**e**nster.

2 Er legt seine Not**i**zen aus dem Kongr**e**ß auf den Tisch.
*Er setzt sich, liest und schreibt.
*Im Hotel ist alles still und Paul Dumont **a**rbeitet schnell.
*Das Th**e**ma seiner **A**rbeit ist internation**a**l.

3 *« V**ie**le St**aa**ten Eur**o**pas h**a**ben eine n**eu**e Agr**a**rpolitik.
Die **A**rbeit *des B**au**ers wird sehr mod**e**rn... »

4 — Wo **a**rbeiten Sie h**eu**te, Herr Dumont?
— Ich **a**rbeite im Hot**e**l, auf m**ei**nem Z**i**mmer.
— Was ist das Th**e**ma **I**hrer **A**rbeit?
— Ich schr**ei**be **ü**ber die Agr**a**rpoliti**k** Eur**o**pas.

1 [not**i**tçen — tçour**u**k — ér l**é**kt — cht**è**lt.]

2 [ér z**è**tçt zicḥ — im' hot**è**l içt **a**leç cht**i**l — daç t**é**ma.]

3 [f**i**le cht**a**ten' **o**eur**o**paç h**a**ben' h**o**eute aéne n**o**eue agr**a**rpoliti**k** — dèç b**a**oerç.]

WIE DIE SAAT, SO DIE ERNTE

Traduction

Notes du congrès

1 Paul Dumont revient de la ville. Il marche vite, car il travaille aujourd'hui dans sa chambre (mot à mot : sur sa chambre). Il pose son manteau sur le lit. Les fleurs, il (les) met à la fenêtre.

2 Il pose ses notes du congrès sur la table. Il s'assied, lit et écrit. Dans l'hôtel, tout est calme et Paul Dumont travaille rapidement. Le sujet de son travail est international.

3 « Beaucoup d'états en Europe (= d'Europe) ont une nouvelle politique agricole. Le travail du paysan se modernise considérablement (mot à mot : devient très moderne)... »

4 – Où travaillez-vous aujourd'hui, Monsieur Dumont? – Je travaille à l'hôtel, dans ma chambre. – Quel est le sujet de votre travail? – J'écris au sujet de la politique agricole de l'Europe.

Prononciation

L'accent d'intonation donne sa vie à la phrase. Dans la troisième phrase du texte, faites ressortir nettement les trois mots accentués : *l**e**gt* – *M**a**ntel* – *B**e**tt.* Prononcez les autres mots de cette phrase faiblement et vite.

Vocabulaire

der B**au**er (s, n), *le paysan*
der Staat (es, en), *l'état*
die Not**i**z (en), *la note*
die Polit**i**k, *la politique*
das Bett (es, en), *le lit*
das F**e**nster (-), *la fenêtre*
das Th**e**ma (plur. die Themen), *le thème, le sujet*
l**e**gen, *poser, mettre (à plat)*
s**e**tzen, *asseoir*
st**e**llen, *poser, mettre (debout)*
*zur**ü**ckk**o**mmen, *revenir*
zur**ü**cktr**a**gen, *rapporter*

● Pour les deux derniers verbes (à particule séparable) voyez la leçon 7 page 3, la remarque très importante.

Exercice sur les mots :

Traduisez : 1. *Reviendra-t-il?* 2. *Les paysans de cet État.* 3. *Le thème de sa politique.*

Corrigé : 1. Wird er zurückkommen? 2. Die Bauern dieses Staates. 3. Das Thema seiner Politik.

On récolte ce qu'on a semé. (m. à m. : Comme les semailles, ainsi la récolte)

■ Viele Staaten Europas.

Les masculins et neutres mixtes.
Quelques noms masculins ou neutres prennent *s* au génitif singulier (= déclinaison forte) et *en* ou *n* à tous les cas du pluriel (ce qui est une caractéristique de la déclinaison dite faible). Exemple :

Sing.	N.	*der Staat,* l'État	Plur.	*die Staaten,* les États
	G.	*des Staates,* de l'État		*der Staaten,* des États
	D.	*dem Staat,* à l'État		*den Staaten,* aux États
	A.	*den Staat,* l'État		*die Staaten,* les États

Suivent cette déclinaison mixte : *der Bauer (s, n),* le paysan – *der Nachbar (s, n),* le voisin – *das Bett (es, en),* le lit – *das Hemd (es, en),* la chemise.
Remarque : Pour ces noms, nous indiquerons entre parenthèses deux terminaisons : la première (*s,* ou *es*) pour le génitif singulier, la deuxième (*n,* ou *en*) pour tous les cas du pluriel.

■ Er stellt die Blumen an das Fenster.

Les verbes dits « factitifs ».
La langue allemande aime exprimer avec précision les modalités d'une action. Ainsi, là où nous employons le verbe « mettre, poser », l'allemand précise si l'objet sera posé « debout, assis, à plat, ou suspendu » : *stellen,* poser, mettre (debout) – *setzen,* asseoir – *legen,* poser, mettre (à plat) – *hängen,* accrocher.
Le complément de lieu de ces verbes est le plus souvent introduit par une préposition suivie de l'accusatif : *auf* (sur), *in* (dans), *an* (à, contre) etc. (Voir leçon 12). Exemple :

Ich lege mein Buch auf den Tisch.

Ce complément répond à la question : *wohin?* (où?)

■ Er geht schnell, denn er arbeitet heute auf seinem Zimmer.

Construction après les conjonctions de coordination.
Denn lie ou coordonne deux propositions indépendantes. Les conjonctions de coordination sont : *aber,* mais; *sondern,* mais au contraire; *allein* (pris parfois dans le sens de « mais »); *denn,* car; *und,* et, oder, *ou.*
Ces conjonctions n'ont aucune influence sur la construction, donc elles n'entraînent pas l'inversion.

Exercices

A *a) Complétez, puis traduisez :*
1. Er spricht (von der Politik) dies... Staat... 2. Der Sohn d... Bauer... kommt zurück. 3. Er leg... d... Hemd auf d... Bett.
b) Mettez les phrases 1 à 3 au pluriel, sauf l'expression entre parenthèses.

B *Complétez en choisissant parmi les quatre verbes factitifs, puis traduisez :*
4. Paul ... den Brief auf sein... Tisch. 5. Der Freund ... einen Tisch in d... Garten. 6. Der Junge ... sein Hemd an d... Fenster. 7. Emma ... ihre Puppe auf ein... Stuhl. 8. Karl ... den Kugelschreiber auf d... Heft.

C *Traduisez :*
9. Il travaille vite, car tout est calme. 10. Mets-tu tes livres et tes notes sur cette table? 11. La femme de mon voisin met la voiture au (= dans le) garage. 12. Mettez mon manteau dans ma chambre! (forme de politesse). 13. Ces chemises sont neuves, mais le manteau est déjà vieux (alt). 14. Les fenêtres de sa maison (à elle) sont-elles vertes? 15. Nous placerons ces chaises dans la salle.

Corrigé :

A a) 1. dieses Staat(e)s. *Il parle de la politique de ce pays.* 2. des Bauers. *Le fils du paysan revient.* 3. Er legt das Hemd auf das Bett. *Il pose la chemise sur le lit.*
b) 1. Sie sprechen von der Politik dieser Staaten. 2. Die Söhne der Bauern kommen zurück. 3. Sie legen die Hemden auf die Betten.

B 4. legt; seinen. *Paul pose la lettre sur sa table.* 5. stellt; den. *L'ami pose (debout) une table dans le jardin.* 6. hängt; das. *Le garçon suspend sa chemise à la fenêtre.* 7. setzt; einen. *Emma assied sa poupée sur une chaise.* 8. legt; das. *Charles pose le crayon à bille sur le cahier.*

C 9. Er arbeitet schnell, denn alles ist still (= ruhig). 10. Legst du deine Hefte und deine Notizen auf diesen Tisch? 11. Die Frau meines Nachbars stellt das Auto in die Garage. 12. Hängen Sie meinen Mantel in mein Zimmer! 13. Diese Hemden sind neu, aber der Mantel ist schon alt. 14. Sind die Fenster ihres Hauses grün? 15. Wir werden diese Stühle in den Saal stellen.

der Stuhl : la chaise

das Heft : le cahier

Leçon
12

Das Warenhaus

1 M**ä**nner, Fr**au**en und K**i**nder g**e**hen im W**a**renh**au**s hin und her.
Sie k**au**fen **o**der *betr**a**chten W**a**ren.
*Hier st**e**hen M**ö**bel, da h**ä**ngen M**ä**ntel, dort l**ie**gen H**e**fte und K**u**gelschr**ei**ber.
Einige D**a**men *bew**u**ndern die n**eu**e M**o**de.

2 — G**u**ten T**a**g. *Was m**ö**chten Sie?
— Ich m**ö**chte ein Hemd.
— *W**e**lche N**u**mmer h**a**ben Sie?
— N**u**mmer *zw**ei**undv**ie**rzig (42).
— Hier ist ein sch**ö**nes und sehr n**eu**es *M**u**ster.
— Ja, es ist sehr schön. *Woh**e**r kommt d**ie**ses M**u**ster?
— Es kommt aus *Italien.
— Gut. Wo ist die *K**a**sse, b**i**tte? — Dort, n**e**ben der *Tr**e**ppe.
— Und wohin führt die Treppe? — In **u**nser Restaur**ant**.
An der Kasse *sitzt eine D**a**me.
Dort *zahlt Herr Dumont.

1 [daç v**a**ren'haoç] 1. [m**è**ner, fr**ao**en' oun't kin'der — bétr**a**rten' w**a**ren' — hir cht**é**en' m**eu**bel — bév**ou**n'dern' di n**o**eue m**o**de]

2 [vaç m**eu**rten' zi? — v**è**lche n**ou**mer — tçva**é**oun'tf**i**rtçich — m**ou**çter — voh**é**r — it**a**lien' — di kaçe — tr**è**pe — zitçt — tç**a**lt.]

KLEIDER MACHEN LEUTE

Traduction

Le grand magasin

1 Des hommes, des femmes et des enfants vont et viennent dans le grand magasin (mot à mot : vont de-ci, de-là). Ils achètent ou bien regardent des marchandises. Ici se trouvent (mot à mot : sont posés debout) des meubles, là sont accrochés des manteaux, là-bas il y a (mot à mot : sont posés à plat) des cahiers et des crayons à bille. Quelques dames admirent la mode nouvelle.

2 — Bonjour, (Monsieur). Que désirez-vous? — Je voudrais une chemise. — Quel est votre numéro? — (C'est le) numéro 42. — Voici un modèle beau et très récent (mot à mot : neuf). — Oui, il est très beau. D'où ce modèle vient-il? — Il vient d'Italie. — Bien. Où est la caisse, s'il-vous-plaît? — Là-bas, à côté de l'escalier. — Et où l'escalier mène-t-il? — A notre restaurant. Une dame est assise à la caisse. (C'est) là-bas (que) Monsieur Dumont paie.

Prononciation

Les voyelles infléchies peuvent être longues ou brèves; nous avons déjà vu que **ä** se prononce [è], **ö** = [eu] et **ü** = [u]. Elles sont longues dans les mots suivants : *M**ö**bel — sch**ö**n — f**ü**hren* (suivies d'une seule consonne ou d'un h), et brèves dans : *M**ä**nner — h**ä**ngen — M**ä**ntel — m**ö**chte* (suivies de deux ou plusieurs consonnes).

Vocabulaire

der Mann (¨er), *l'homme*
die K**a**sse (n), *la caisse*
die M**o**de (n), *la mode*
die N**u**mmer (n), *le numéro*
die Tr**e**ppe (n), *l'escalier*
die W**a**re (n), *la marchandise*
It**a**lien (neutre), *l'Italie*
das M**ö**bel (-), *le meuble*
das M**u**ster (-), *le modèle*
das W**a**renhaus (¨er), *le grand magasin*
betr**a**chten, *contempler, regarder*
bew**u**ndern, *admirer*
ich m**ö**chte, *je voudrais*
z**ah**len, *payer*

L'habit fait le moine (m. à m. : les vêtements font les gens).

Grammaire

■ Hier stehen Möbel, da hängen Mäntel.

Les verbes de position.
Les verbes suivants expriment une position et correspondent aux verbes factitifs étudiés dans la leçon 11.

stehen, être debout	*liegen,* être couché
sitzen, être assis	*hängen,* être accroché

Ces verbes sont irréguliers (forts), alors que les verbes factitifs sont réguliers (faibles). Ils répondent à la question *wo?* (où?)

■ Ich gehe an die Kasse. Eine Dame sitzt an der Kasse.

Les prépositions mixtes.
Neuf prépositions gouvernent l'accusatif *(an die Kasse)* quand le verbe indique un changement de lieu. Elles gouvernent le datif *(an der Kasse)* quand il n'y a pas de direction vers un lieu. Ce sont :

in, dans	*vor,* devant	*unter,* au-dessous de, parmi
an, à, près de	*hinter,* derrière	*neben,* à côté de
auf, sur	*über,* au-dessus de	*zwischen,* entre

Quelquefois, elles se contractent avec l'article défini. Ex. :

in dem = *im* (im Hotel); *in das* = *ins* (ins Hotel).

■ Woher? Wo? Wohin?

- *Woher?* (d'où?) porte sur le lieu d'où l'on vient.

  Woher kommt dieses Muster?

- *Wo?* (où?) porte sur le lieu où l'on est, marque un état.

  Wo ist die Kasse?

- *Wohin?* (où?) porte sur le lieu où l'on va, marque une direction.

  Wohin führt diese Treppe?

Remarque : A la question *wo?* les neuf prépositions mixtes gouvernent le datif; à la question *wohin?* elles gouvernent l'accusatif.

Exercices

A *Formez des questions avec* woher? wo? wohin? *et traduisez :*
1. Die Jungen sitzen im Garten. 2. Herr Müller kommt aus Berlin. 3. Er führt seinen Freund in ein Gasthaus. 4. Dieser Artikel kommt aus Italien. 5. Sie gehen an den Rhein. 6. Er wohnt in Köln.

B *Complétez (Datif? Accusatif?) et traduisez :*
7. Das Auto steht in d... Garage neben d... Hotel. 8. Sie sitzen in d... Park unter ein... Tanne. 9. Wir gehen in d... Stadt, in d... Kino, auf d... Kongreß. 10. Wir sind in d... Stadt, in d... Kino, auf d... Kongreß.

C *Traduisez :*
11. La maison se trouve dans un jardin. 12. Nous irons souvent dans ce jardin. 13. Les enfants sont assis sur la terrasse. 14. Heddy assied sa poupée sur le lit. 15. Je voudrais une chemise, un gâteau, des fleurs, un livre, une carte postale, un crayon à bille.

Corrigé :

A 1. Wo sitzen die Jungen? *Où les garçons sont-ils assis?* 2. Woher kommt Herr Müller? *D'où Monsieur Müller vient-il?* 3. Wohin führt er seinen Freund? *Où conduit-il son ami?* 4. Woher kommt dieser Artikel? *D'où vient cet article?* 5. Wohin gehen sie? *Où vont-ils?* 6. Wo wohnt er? *Où habite-t-il?*

B 7. in der Garage neben dem Hotel. *L'auto est dans le garage, à côté de l'hôtel.* 8. in dem Park (= im) unter einer Tanne. *Ils sont assis dans le parc, sous un sapin.* 9. in die Stadt, in das (= ins) Kino, auf den Kongreß. *Nous allons en (= dans la) ville, au cinéma, au (= sur le) congrès.* 10. in der Stadt, in dem Kino, auf dem Kongreß. *Nous sommes en ville, au cinéma, au congrès.*

C 11. Das Haus steht in einem Garten (position, datif). 12. Wir werden oft in diesen Garten gehen (direction, accusatif). 13. Die Kinder sitzen auf der Terrasse (position, datif). 14. Heddy setzt ihre Puppe auf das Bett (verbe factitif, direction, accusatif). 15. Ich möchte ein Hemd, einen Kuchen, Blumen, ein Buch, eine Postkarte, einen Kugelschreiber.

Leçon

13 Am Morgen im Hotel

1 Nach einem **A**rbeitst**a**g schläft man schnell ein.
M**o**rgens erw**a**cht man *früh und man ist *g**u**ter L**au**ne.
Man *steht auf, man *wäscht sich, k**ä**mmt sich und kl**ei**det sich an Die M**ä**nner ras**ie**ren sich mit einem El**e**ktro-ras**ie**rer.

2 Das *Z**i**mmerm**ä**dchen des Hot**e**ls heißt **E**mma Kr**a**mer.
Emma hat viel **A**rbeit und sie hat es **i**mmer **ei**lig.
J**e**den M**o**rgen bringt sie den *Hot**e**lg**ä**sten **i**hren K**a**ffee oder **i**hren Tee und stellt ihn auf den Tisch.

3 **E**mma ist sehr für ***O**rdnung.
Sie sieht nicht gern **a**llerlei S**a**chen im Z**i**mmer umh**e**rl**ie**gen.
Auch hört man fast j**e**den M**o**rgen d**ie**sen *Dial**o**g :
— Woh**i**n h**ä**nge ich **I**hren M**a**ntel?
— H**ä**ngen Sie ihn h**i**nter die Tür, b**i**tte.
— Woh**i**n l**e**ge ich **I**hre M**a**ppe?
— L**e**gen Sie sie auf d**ie**sen *Stuhl!
— Und d**ie**ses Buch?
— L**e**gen Sie es doch auf den Tisch!

1 [fru — g**ou**ter l**a**one — cht**é**t **a**of — vècht zich].

2 [tç**i**mer m**è**tchen' — hot**è**l g**è**çten']

3 [**o**rdnou^{ng} — dial**o**k — cht**ou**l].

KOMMT ZEIT KOMMT RAT

Traduction

Le matin à l'hôtel

1 Après une journée de travail, on s'endort vite. Le matin, on se réveille de bonne heure et l'on est de bonne humeur. On se lève, on se lave, se coiffe et s'habille. Les hommes se rasent avec un rasoir électrique.

2 La femme de chambre de l'hôtel s'appelle Emma Kramer. Emma a beaucoup de travail et elle est toujours pressée. Chaque matin, elle apporte aux clients (mot à mot : aux hôtes) leur café ou leur thé et le pose sur la table.

3 Emma tient beaucoup à l'ordre. Elle n'aime pas voir toutes sortes de choses traîner (mot à mot : être couchées) dans la chambre. Aussi, (c'est) presque chaque matin (qu')on entend ce dialogue : — Où est-ce que j'accroche votre manteau? — Accrochez-le derrière la porte, je vous prie. — Où est-ce que je pose votre serviette? — Posez-la sur cette chaise! — Et ce livre-ci? — Posez-le donc sur la table!

Prononciation

Ne confondez pas ***sch*** [ch] et ***ch*** [ṛ] ou [cḥ]. Le premier correspond exactement à notre « ch » dans « chemin ». Lisez : *schläft — wäscht — el**e**ktrisch — schr**ei**ben.* Le deuxième est soit guttural *(erw**a**cht; Sachen; B**u**ch),* soit chuinté *(ich, sich; M**ä**dchen).* (Voir Mémento, n° 1 B).

Vocabulaire

der Appar**a**t (-e), *l'appareil*
der Tee, *le thé*
der Stuhl (¨e), *la chaise*
die L**au**ne, *l'humeur*
die **O**rdnung (-en), *l'ordre*
die S**a**che (n), *la chose,*
das M**ä**dchen (-), *la fille,*
ankl**ei**den, *habiller*

***auf**/st**e**hen, *se lever*
eilen, *se hâter*
erw**a**chen, *se réveiller*
h**ei**ßen, *s'appeler*
k**ä**mmen, *peigner*
ras**ie**ren, *raser*
***ei**nschl**a**fen (ä), *s'endormir*
w**a**schen (ä), *laver*

Laissons faire le temps (m. à m. : S'il vient du temps, il vient un conseil).

● Pour les verbes à particule séparable voyez leçon 7.

Grammaire

■ **Hängen Sie ihn hinter die Tür. Paul kämmt sich.**
Le pronom personnel et le pronom réfléchi à l'accusatif.

Herr Müller führt mich in die Stadt, ich freue mich. Monsieur Müller me conduit en ville, je me réjouis.

Er führt dich; du freust dich. Il te conduit, tu te réjouis.
Er führt ihn; er freut sich (masculin)
Er führt sie; sie freut sich (féminin)
Er führt es; es freut sich (neutre)
Er führt uns; wir freuen uns
Er führt euch; ihr freut euch
Er führt sie; sie freuen sich
Er führt Sie; Sie freuen sich (forme de politesse).

Remarques :
a) le pronom complément se place après le verbe conjugué.
b) le pronom réfléchi a les mêmes formes que le pronom personnel complément, sauf à la 3ᵉ personne du singulier et du pluriel, où il est *sich.* (Voir Mémento nº 48).

■ **Er erwacht früh.** Il se réveille de bonne heure.

● Certains verbes réfléchis en français ne le sont pas en allemand. Exemples : s'endormir, *einschlafen;* se hâter, *eilen;* s'appeler, *heißen.*

● Inversement, quelques verbes réfléchis en allemand ne le sont pas en français. Exemples : *sich auf/halten,* séjourner; *sich drehen,* tourner.

■ **Der Arbeitstag. Das Zimmermädchen.**
La journée de travail. La femme de chambre.
Dans les noms composés, l'ordre des termes est l'inverse de celui que nous adopterions en français. Il faut donc traduire d'abord le dernier terme. Le genre du nom composé est celui du dernier terme; c'est celui-ci aussi qui prend la marque du pluriel, et qui se décline. Cependant, l'accent principal est sur le premier élément.

Ex. : *der Stadtgarten,* le jardin municipal, pluriel : *die Stadtgärten.*

Exercices

A *Traduisez, puis remplacez le complément entre parenthèses par un pronom personnel :*
1. Ich rufe (meinen Freund). 2. Er kauft (das Haus). 3. Siehst du (die Terrasse)? 4. Er bringt (die Bücher). 5. Essen Sie (diesen Kuchen) gern?

B *Complétez par le pronom personnel correspondant à la personne indiquée entre parenthèses, puis traduisez :*
6. Hans führt ... (ich) durch Köln. 7. Jetzt kenne ich ... (er) gut. 8. Karl ruft ... (du). 9. Wir führen ... (ihr, 2e personne du pluriel) in die Stadt. 10. Sie hören ... (wir) nicht.

C *Complétez par le pronom réfléchi, puis traduisez :*
11. Wir waschen ... jeden Tag. 12. Die Kinder freuen ... 13. Ihr kämmt ... gut. 14. Kurt kleidet ... schnell an. 15. Aber Heddy kleidet ... langsam (lentement) an.

D *Traduisez :*
16. Connais-tu cet homme? Le connais-tu? 17. Vois-tu ces chaises? Les vois-tu? 18. Entends-tu cette voiture? L'entends-tu? 19. Le matin, je me lève de bonne heure. 20. Je me lave et je m'habille.

Corrigé :

A 1. *J'appelle mon ami.* Ich rufe ihn. 2. *Il achète la maison;* es. 3. *Vois-tu la terrasse?* sie. 4. *Il apporte les livres;* sie. 5. *Aimez-vous (manger) ce gâteau?* ihn.

B 6. mich. *Hans me conduit à travers Cologne.* 7. ihn. *Maintenant je le connais bien.* 8. dich. *Karl t'appelle.* 9. euch. *Nous vous conduisons en ville.* 10. uns. *Ils ne nous entendent pas.*

C 11. uns. *Nous nous lavons chaque jour.* 12. sich. *Les enfants se réjouissent.* 13. euch. *Vous vous coiffez bien.* 14. sich. *Kurt s'habille vite.* 15. sich. *Mais Heddy s'habille lentement.*

D 16. Kennst du diesen Mann? Kennst du ihn? 17. Siehst du diese Stühle? Siehst du sie? 18. Hörst du dieses Auto? Hörst du es? 19. Am Morgen stehe ich früh auf. 20. Ich wasche mich und kleide mich an.

Leçon

14 Ein kleiner Ausflug (1)

1 *Gestern nachmittag machten die *Kollegen aus dem Kongreß einen kleinen Ausflug.
Ein *Bus führte sie nach *Königswinter.
Es ist eine kleine Stadt bei Köln.
Sie liegt am *Fuß des Drachenfels, eines kleinen Berges.

2 Herr Müller zeigte seinen Kollegen die alten Straßen und Häuser.
Er *erzählte ihnen von dem *Leben in den *Kleinstädten Deutschlands.
Alle hörten ihm *aufmerksam *zu.

3 Dann führte er sie in ein altes Gasthaus.
Sie setzten sich um einen Tisch und bestellten *Rheinwein.

4 – Arbeiteten Sie gestern nachmittag, Herr Dumont?
– Nein, wir machten einen schönen Ausflug nach Königswinter.
– Wo liegt denn diese Stadt?
– Sie liegt etwa *fünfundvierzig Kilometer weit von Köln.

1 [aoçflouk]; 1. [gèçtern narmitak] – [kolégen'] – [bouç] – [keunichçvin'ter] – [fouç] – [draren'fèlç]

2 [èrtçèlte] – [lében'] – [klaén'chtèten'] – [aofmèrkçam'] – [tçou]

3 [raén'vaén']

4 [fünfountfirtsich].

GLEICH UND GLEICH GESELLT SICH GERN

Traduction

Une petite excursion (1)

1 Hier après-midi, les collègues du congrès firent une petite excursion. Un autocar les conduisit à Königswinter. C'est une petite ville près de Cologne. Elle se trouve (mot à mot : est posée) au pied du Drachenfels, une petite montagne.

2 Monsieur Müller montra les vieilles rues et maisons à ses collègues. Il leur parla de la vie dans les petites villes d'Allemagne. Tous l'écoutaient attentivement.

3 Ensuite, ils les conduisit dans une vieille auberge. Ils s'assirent autour d'une table et commandèrent du vin du Rhin.

4 – Avez-vous travaillé hier après-midi, Monsieur Dumont? – Non, nous avons fait une belle excursion à Königswinter. – Où donc se trouve cette ville? – Elle est à peu près à quarante cinq kilomètres de Cologne.

Prononciation

La voyelle ***e*** en syllabe accentuée se prononce [é] quand elle est longue, comme dans « léger ». Ainsi : *Koll**e**gen – L**e**ben – **er** – Kilom**e**ter.* Quand elle est brève, elle se prononce [è] comme dans « peste ». C'est le cas dans *g**e**stern – Kongr**e**ß – B**e**rg – s**e**tzen – best**e**llen.*

Vocabulaire

der **Au**sflug (¨-e), *l'excursion*
der Berg (-e), *la montagne*
der Bus (se); der Autobus (se) *l'autocar*
der Dr**a**chenf**e**ls, nom propre, signifie : *le Rocher du Dragon*
der Koll**e**ge (n), *le collègue*
der Reiz (e), *le charme*
der Wein (-e), *le vin*
das L**e**ben (-), *la vie*
best**e**llen, *commander (q.c.)*
l**e**ben, *vivre*

Qui se ressemble s'assemble (pareil et pareil s'associent volontiers)

■ **Er führte sie in ein Gasthaus.**

Le prétérit du verbe régulier (faible).

Er führte est au prétérit. Ce temps correspond à la fois à notre imparfait et à notre passé simple : il conduisait, il conduisit. Il est caractérisé par un *t* devant les terminaisons.

Exemple : Verbe *führen* — Radical : *führ*

Ich führ-t-e	*wir führ-t-en*
du führ-t-est	*ihr führ-t-et*
er (sie, es) führ-t-e	*sie (Sie) führ-t-en*

■ **Er erzählte ihnen von Königswinter. Sie hörten ihm zu.**

● Le pronom personnel au datif. (à qui?)

Er gibt mir ein Buch,	il me donne un livre.
Er gibt dir einen Mantel	il te donne un manteau.
Er gibt ihm eine Karte,	il lui donne une carte.
Er gibt ihr eine Puppe,	il lui donne (à elle) une poupée.
Er gibt ihm einen Ball,	il lui donne un ballon (neutre).
Er gibt uns Bücher,	il nous donne des livres.
Er gibt euch Blumen,	il vous donne des fleurs.
Er gibt ihnen Briefe,	il leur donne des lettres.
Er gibt Ihnen Rosen,	il vous donne des roses (politesse).

● Le pronom réfléchi a les mêmes formes, sauf à la 3e personne du singulier et du pluriel, où il est *sich* (comme à l'accusatif, leçon 13). Exemples :

Ich kaufe mir ein Buch,	je m'achète un livre;
du kaufst dir...,	tu t'achètes...
er kauft sich...,	il s'achète...
sie kauft sich...,	elle s'achète...
es kauft sich...,	il s'achète (neutre)...
wir kaufen uns...,	nous nous achetons...
ihr kauft euch...,	vous vous achetez...
sie kaufen sich...,	ils s'achètent...
Sie kaufen sich...,	vous vous achetez... (forme de politesse).

■ **Sie bestellten Wein.**

Notre article partitif « du, de la, des, de » n'existe pas en allemand : *Kaffee,* du café; *Bier,* de la bière. Mais la forme négative se rend par *kein* : *kein Kaffee,* pas de café; *kein Brot,* pas de pain.

Exercices

A *Mettez les verbes au prétérit, puis traduisez :*
1. Emil kauft eine Postkarte. 2. Du hörst den Lärm nicht. 3. Wir kleiden uns an. 4. Ihr zeigt uns den Rhein. 5. Die Blumen leuchten auf der Terrasse.

B *Remplacer le complément entre parenthèses par le pronom personnel, puis traduisez :*
6. Ich zeige (meinem Kameraden) das Hotel. 7. Paul bringt (den Kindern) Schokolade. 8. Er bringt (der Dame) Blumen. 9. Dieses Auto gehört (dem Kind). 10. Du schreibst (der Familie) einen Brief.

C *Mettez le pronom personnel correspondant au pronom entre parenthèses, puis traduisez :*
11. Karl gibt ... (du) seinen Kugelschreiber. 12. Mein Kollege kommt zu ... (ich). 13. Ich gehe mit ... (ihr, 2ᵉ personne du pluriel) an den Rhein. 14. Emma bringt ... (wir) Kaffee. 15. Peter wohnt bei ... (sie, pluriel).

D *Traduisez :*
16. Nous commandions toujours du café. 17. Tu t'achetais souvent des livres. 18. Ces maisons leur appartenaient. 19. Il s'habilla et il conduisit ses amis dans la ville. 20. Ils s'achetaient du vin.

Corrigé :

A 1. Emil kaufte... *Émile acheta une carte postale.* 2. Du hörtest... *Tu n'entendis pas le bruit.* 3. Wir kleideten... *Nous nous habillâmes.* 4. Ihr zeigtet... *Vous nous avez montré le Rhin.* 5. leuchteten. *Les fleurs brillaient sur la terrasse.*

B 6. ihm. *Je lui montre l'hôtel.* 7. ihnen. *Paul leur apporte du chocolat.* 8. ihr. *Il lui apporte des fleurs.* 9. ihm. *Cette voiture lui appartient.* 10. ihr. *Tu lui écris une lettre.*

C 11. dir. *Charles te donne son crayon à bille.* 12. mir. *Mon collègue vient chez moi.* 13. euch. *Je vais avec vous au Rhin.* 14. uns. *Emma nous apporte du café.* 15. ihnen. *Pierre habite chez eux.*

D 16. Wir bestellten immer Kaffee. 17. Du kauftest dir oft Bücher. 18. Diese Häuser gehörten ihnen. 19. Er kleidete sich an und führte seine Freunde in die Stadt. 20. Sie kauften sich Wein.

Leçon

15 Ein kleiner Ausflug (2)

1 Viele Gäste *saßen im Saal des Gasthofs.
Einige tranken Wein, andere *tranken Bier und aßen ein kaltes Gericht.
An allen Tischen hörte man lachen und erzählen.
Es *herrschte eine *frohe *Stimmung.

2 – Finden Sie unseren Wein so gut wie die französischen Weine? fragte man Paul Dumont.
– Er ist nicht so *stark, aber angenehm zu trinken, antwortete dieser.
Man sprach noch lange von den Weinbergen und Weingärten am Rhein, an der *Mosel, am *Neckar und am *Bodensee, und von ihrem Reiz.

3 Um sieben *Uhr fuhren sie nach Köln *zurück.
Der Bus fuhr schnell; sie kamen bald an.
– Ein schöner Nachmittag, *nicht wahr?
– Ja, ich werde ihn so bald nicht vergessen.

1 [zaçen'] – [tra^ng^ken'] – [hèrchte] – [fro/e] – [chtimou^ng^].

2 [chtark] – [mozel] – [nèkar] – [boden'zé].

3 [our] – [tçouruck] – [nicht var].

DER WEIN ERFREUT DES MENSCHEN HERZ

Traduction

Une petite excursion (2)

1 Beaucoup de clients étaient assis dans la salle du restaurant. Quelques-uns buvaient du vin, d'autres buvaient de la bière et mangeaient un plat froid. A toutes les tables, on entendait rire et raconter. Il régnait une joyeuse ambiance.

2 — Trouvez-vous notre vin aussi bon que les vins français? demanda-t-on à Paul Dumont. — Il n'est pas aussi fort, mais il est agréable à boire, répondit celui-ci. On parla longtemps encore des vignobles et des vignes sur les bords du Rhin, de la Moselle, du Neckar et près du lac de Constance, et de leur charme.

3 A sept heures, ils retournèrent à Cologne. L'autocar roulait vite; ils arrivèrent bientôt. — Une belle après-midi, n'est-ce pas? — Oui, je ne l'oublierai pas de sitôt.

Prononciation

Vous ne confondez plus, maintenant, *ie,* qui est un *i* long [i], et *ei* qui est une diphtongue [**a**é]. Nous rencontrons aujourd'hui ce *i* long dans : *v**ie**le, B**ie**r, w**ie**, d**ie**, d**ie**ser, s**ie**ben.* La diphtongue *ei,* que l'on prononce brièvement, en accentuant le *a,* [**a**é], se trouve dans : *kl**ei**n, **ei**nige, W**ei**n, **ei**n, s**ei**nen, R**ei**z.*

Vocabulaire

der Reiz (-e), *le charme*
die St**i**mmung (-en), *l'ambiance*
die Uhr (-en), *la montre*
das Bier (-e), *la bière*
das Ger**i**cht (-e), *le plat, les mets*
antworten, *répondre*
fr**a**gen (suivi de l'acc. de la personne), *demander*
h**e**rrschen, *régner*
*f**a**hren (er fuhr), *aller (en véhicule)*
f**i**nden (er fand), *trouver*

Exercice sur les mots :
Traduisez : 1. *Le charme de cette ville.* 2. *Tu me demandes.* 3. *Je te répondrai.* 4. *La montre de mon père.*
Corrigé : 1. der Reiz dieser Stadt. 2. Du fragst mich. 3. Ich werde dir antworten. 4. Die Uhr meines Vaters.

Le vin est ami du cœur (Le vin réjouit le cœur de l'homme).

Grammaire

■ Sie tranken Wein oder Bier.

Le prétérit du verbe irrégulier (ou fort).

● Au prétérit, le radical du verbe fort est changé. Le plus souvent, ce changement n'affecte que la voyelle *(trinken > er trank; fahren > er fuhr).* Parfois, les consonnes sont modifiées également *(sitzen > er saß).*

● A la 1re et à la 3e personne du singulier, le verbe fort au prétérit n'a pas de terminaison. Ailleurs, ce sont les mêmes terminaisons qu'au présent.

● Conjugaison du verbe *geben* (donner) au prétérit :

Ich gab, je donnais	*Wir gab-en,* nous donnions
Du gab-st, tu donnais	*Ihr gab-t,* vous donniez
Er (sie, es) gab, il donnait	*sie (Sie) gab-en,* ils donnaient

● Il est nécessaire d'apprendre les verbes forts avec leur prétérit (et, ultérieurement, avec leur participe passé). Voici le prétérit de quelques verbes déjà rencontrés :

schreiben,	*er schrieb*
tragen,	*er trug*
laufen,	*er lief*
sprechen,	*er sprach*
ausziehen,	*er zog aus*
schlafen,	*er schlief*
kommen,	*er kam.*

En cas d'hésitation, recherchez le prétérit dans le Mémento (§ 78).

■ Ist dieser Wein so gut wie die französischen Weine?

La comparaison – Comparatif d'égalité et d'infériorité.

● Le comparatif d'égalité se rend par *so...wie* (aussi...que).

Hans ist so groß wie Karl, Jean est aussi grand que Charles.

● Le comparatif d'infériorité se rend par *nicht so...wie* (pas aussi...que) :

Heddy ist nicht so groß wie Karl, Heddy n'est pas aussi grande que Charles.

■ La numération

1	*eins*	4	*vier*	7	*sieben*	10	*zehn*
2	*zwei*	5	*fünf*	8	*acht*	11	*elf*
3	*drei*	6	*sechs* [zèkç]	9	*neun*	12	*zwölf*

Exercices

A *Mettez les phrases suivantes au prétérit, puis traduisez :*
1. Er trinkt Bier. 2. Ich esse Kuchen. 3. Ihr schreibt einen Brief. 4. Du sprichst gut. 5. Wir kommen früh zurück. 6. Sie fahren nach Paris. 7. Ich gebe dir meine Adresse. 8. Wir ziehen den Mantel an.

B *Formez des phrases avec un comparatif d'égalité, d'après l'exemple suivant :* (Hans — Karl — stark — sein : Hans ist so stark wie Karl, *Hans est aussi fort que Charles.) puis traduisez :*
9. Unser Garten — dieser Park — grün — sein. 10. Helene — Maria — schön — schreiben. 11. Dieser Wein — ein Likör — fast — stark — sein.

C *Traduisez :*

12. Ils trouvaient l'ambiance très gaie. 13. A dix heures, Paul retourna (en voiture) à (= *zu*) l'hôtel. 14. Il enleva son manteau, puis il lut encore un peu. 15. Il dormit aussi bien qu'à *(in)* Paris. 16. Cette bière est très bonne; elle n'est pas aussi forte que le vin.

Corrigé :

A 1. Er trank Bier. *Il but de la bière.* 2. Ich aß Kuchen. *Je mangeai du gâteau.* 3. Ihr schriebt einen Brief. *Vous écriviez une lettre.* 4. Du sprachst gut. *Tu parlais bien.* 5. Wir kamen früh zurück. *Nous retournâmes de bonne heure.* 6. Sie fuhren nach Paris. *Ils allèrent (en véhicule) à Paris.* 7. Ich gab dir meine Adresse. *Je te donnai mon adresse.* 8. Wir zogen den Mantel an. *Nous avons mis (= mîmes) le manteau.*

B 9. Unser Garten ist so grün wie dieser Park. *Notre jardin est aussi vert que ce parc.* 10. Helene schreibt so schön wie Maria. *Hélène écrit aussi bien que Marie.* 11. Dieser Wein ist fast so stark wie ein Likör. *Ce vin est presque aussi fort qu'une liqueur.*

C 12. Sie fanden die Stimmung sehr froh. 13. Um zehn Uhr fuhr Paul zu dem (= zum) Hotel zurück. 14. Er zog seinen Mantel aus, dann las er noch ein wenig. 15. Er schlief so gut wie in Paris. 16. Dieses Bier ist sehr gut; es ist nicht so stark wie der Wein.

Leçon

16 Ein Verkehrsunfall

1 Heute morgen hatte Herr Müller einen Verkehrsunfall mit seinem Auto.
Er fuhr über den Barbarossaplatz.
Da kam ein Lastkraftwagen in *schnellem *Tempo heran.

2 — Mein Wagen fährt schneller als *dieser LKW, sagte sich Herr Müller. Ich komme noch hinüber.
Und er gab noch ein wenig Gas.
Aber schon war ein *Zusammenstoß *unvermeidlich.

3 Beide Wagen bremsten *heftig, doch zu spät.
*Der PKW wurde stark *beschädigt.
Zum Glück gab es nur *Sachschaden.
— Der Klügste gibt nach, sagte sich Herr Müller
Leider denkt man immer zu spät daran.

4 Bald kam auch ein *Verkehrspolizist.
— Wer ist der Fahrer des Lastkraftwagens?
— Wie schnell fuhren Sie?
Er machte sich allerlei Notizen.
Dann *regelte er den Verkehr.

1 [fèrkérçoun'fal] — 1. [chnèlem'] — [tèm'po].

2 [dizer èlkavé] — [tçouzamen'chtoç] — [oun'fèrmaétlich].

3 [hèftich] — [dér pékavé] — [béchèdicht] — [zarchaden'].

4 [fèrkérçpolitçiçt] — [régelte].

DURCH SCHADEN WIRD MAN KLUG

Traduction

Un accident de la circulation

1 Ce matin (mot à mot : aujourd'hui matin) Monsieur Müller eut un accident de la circulation avec sa voiture. Il traversait la place Barbarossa. Voilà qu'un camion s'approcha à grande vitesse.

2 — Ma voiture est plus rapide que ce poids lourd, se dit Monsieur Müller. J'arriverai encore à traverser (mot à mot : je traverse encore). Et il accéléra un peu encore (mot à mot : donna encore un peu de gaz). Mais déjà, un choc était inévitable.

3 Les deux véhicules freinèrent violemment, mais trop tard. La voiture de tourisme fut (mot à mot devint) fortement endommagée. Par bonheur, il n'y eut que des dégâts matériels. — Le plus sage cède, se dit Monsieur Müller (proverbe allemand). Malheureusement, on y pense toujours trop tard.

4 Bientôt arriva également un agent de la circulation. — Qui est le chauffeur du camion? — A quelle vitesse alliez-vous? (mot à mot : combien rapidement rouliez-vous?) Il prit (se fit) toutes sortes de notes. Puis il régla la circulation.

Prononciation

Remarquez l'emploi usuel des abréviations PKW et LKW.
La voyelle accentuée suivie d'une seule consonne est longue : *« W**a**gen-w**e**nig-Sch**a**den-r**e**geln. »*

Vocabulaire

der Pers**o**nenkr**a**ftw**a**gen
der PKW, *la voiture de tourisme*
der Platz (-̈e), *la place*
der Polizi**s**t (-en), *l'agent*
der Sch**a**den (-̈), *le dommage*
der **U**nfall (-̈e), *l'accident*
der Verk**e**hr, *la circulation*
der Zus**a**mmenst**o**ß (-̈e), *le choc*

die Kraft (-̈e), *la force, l'énergie*
die Last (-en), *la charge*
das Glück, *le bonheur, la chance*
besch**ä**digen, *endommager*
br**e**msen, *freiner*
G**a**s g**e**ben, *accélérer*
n**a**chg**e**ben, *céder*
r**e**geln, *régler*
verm**ei**den, *éviter*

Voir page 38 remarque très importante.

On apprend à ses dépens (Par le dommage, on devient avisé)

■ **Er hatte einen Unfall.**
Le prétérit des auxiliaires de temps.

haben	***sein***	***werden***
ich hatte	*ich war*	*ich wurde*
j'avais, j'eus	j'étais, je fus	je devenais, je devins
du hattest	*du warst*	*du wurdest*
er (sie, es) hatte	*er war*	*er wurde*
wir hatten	*wir waren*	*wir wurden*
ihr hattet	*ihr wart*	*ihr wurdet*
sie (Sie) hatten	*sie waren*	*sie wurden*

■ **Mein Wagen fährt schneller als dieser LKW.**
Le comparatif de supériorité se forme en ajoutant **er** à l'adjectif ou à l'adverbe; « que » se traduit par **als.** Exemple :

Dieses Hotel ist moderner als unser Haus, cet Hôtel est plus moderne que notre maison.

■ **Der Klügste gibt nach.**
Le superlatif se forme à l'aide de la terminaison *-ste.* Exemple :

Die schönste Stadt, la plus belle ville.

Pour l'adverbe, on emploie *am -sten.* Exemple :

Dieses Auto fährt am schnellsten, cette voiture roule le plus rapidement.

● La plupart des adjectifs d'une seule syllabe prennent l'inflexion au comparatif et au superlatif. Exemple :

jung, jünger (als), der jüngste, jeune, plus jeune (que), le plus jeune
alt, älter (als), der älteste, âgé, plus âgé (que), le plus âgé.

● Nous étudierons par la suite quelques comparatifs et superlatifs irréguliers. Par exemple :

gut, besser, der beste, bon, meilleur, le meilleur.

■ **La numération.**

13 dr**ei**zehn	16 s**e**chzehn	19 n**eu**nzehn
14 v**ie**rzehn	17 s**ie**bzehn	20 zw**a**nzig
15 f**ü**nfzehn	18 **a**chtzehn	

Exercices

A *Mettez les phrases au prétérit, puis traduisez :*
1. Pierre ist ein Franzose; er hat eine Wohnung in Paris; er fährt nach Deutschland. 2. Wir sind in Köln; wir haben einen Kongreß; unsere Arbeit wird interessant.

B *Formez le comparatif, puis traduisez :*
3. Der Roman war (interessant) als der Film. 4. Die Tanne wurde (groß) und (schön). 5. Frau Kellen war (aufmerksam) als ihr Nachbar.

C *Formez des phrases d'après l'exemple indiqué, puis traduisez :*
(Exemple : jung sein; Dieter; mein Freund; Helga = Dieter ist jung; mein Freund ist jünger; Helga ist die jüngste. *Didier est jeune; mon ami est plus jeune; Helga est la plus jeune*).
6. schnell arbeiten; Emil; diese Dame; Frau Meyer. 7. Lang sein; der Neckar; der Main; der Rhein.

D *Traduisez :*
8. Le camion roulait très vite et l'accident était inévitable. 9. La voiture de tourisme freina trop tard. 10. Qui roulait le plus vite? 11. M. Müller n'était pas plus sage que le conducteur (der Fahrer) du camion. 12. On me montra l'hôtel le plus tranquille de la ville.

Corrigé :

A 1. Pierre war...; er hatte...; er fuhr... *Pierre était un Français; il avait un appartement à Paris; il se rendit en Allemagne.* 2. Wir waren...; wir hatten...; ...wurde. *Nous étions à Cologne; nous avions un congrès; notre travail devint intéressant.*

B 3. interessanter. *Le roman était plus intéressant que le film.* 4. größer; schöner. *Le sapin devenait plus grand et plus beau.* 5. aufmerksamer. *Madame Kellen était plus attentive que son voisin.*

C 6. Emil arbeitet schnell; diese Dame arbeitet schneller; Frau Meyer arbeitet am schnellsten. *Émile travaille vite; cette dame travaille plus vite; Madame Meyer travaille le plus vite.* 7. Der Neckar ist lang; der Main ist länger; der Rhein ist am längsten. *Le Neckar est long; le Main est plus long; le Rhin est le plus long.*

D 8. Der LKW fuhr sehr schnell und der Unfall war unvermeidlich. 9. Der PKW bremste zu spät. 10. Wer fuhr am schnellsten? 11. Herr Müller war nicht klüger als der Fahrer des Lastwagens. 12. Man zeigte mir das ruhigste Hotel der Stadt.

Leçon

17 Ein Gewitter

1 Das *Wetter ist nicht immer angenehm hier.
Gestern hatten wir ein heftiges Gewitter.
Es standen graue Wolken am *Himmel.
Es *blitzte und es donnerte.
Ein starker Regen fiel auf die Stadt.

2 Paul Dumont stand am Fenster und *schaute hinaus.
Nur einige Männer oder Frauen gingen auf der Straße.
Die Kraftwagen fuhren langsamer.

3 – Wie gefällt Ihnen Köln heute, lieber Kollege?
– Nun, bei uns kennen wir dieses Wetter auch.
– Sehen Sie dort, das kleine, blonde Mädchen mit dem großen *Regenschirm?
Sein Nachbar zeigte es ihm.
– Ach wie nett! Es bringt ein wenig *Sonne in die graue, kalte Straße.

4 – Gehen Sie heute auch zu Fuß in Ihr Hotel zurück? Haben Sie einen Regenschirm? Ich fahre Sie gern mit dem Auto zurück.
– *Danke schön! Das ist *sehr lieb von Ihnen.

1 [géviter] – l. [vèter] – [himel] – [blitçte].

2 [chaote].

3 [régen'chirm'] – [zone].

4 [da^{ng}ke cheun'] – [zér lip].

AUF REGEN FOLGT SONNENSCHEIN

Traduction

Un orage

1 Le temps n'est pas toujours agréable ici. Hier nous avions un violent orage. Il y avait des nuages gris dans le ciel. Il faisait des éclairs et il tonnait. Une forte pluie tomba sur la ville.

2 Paul Dumont se tenait à la fenêtre et regardait au-dehors. Quelques hommes ou femmes seulement allaient dans la rue. Les véhicules roulaient plus lentement.

3 — Comment (la ville de) Cologne vous plaît-elle aujourd'hui, cher collègue? — Ma foi, nous connaissons ce temps chez nous également. — Voyez-vous là-bas la petite fille blonde au (avec le) grand parapluie? Son voisin la lui montra. — Que c'est gentil! C'est un peu de soleil dans la rue grise et froide (m. à m. : cela apporte...).

4 — Est-ce que vous rentrerez aujourd'hui également à pied à votre hôtel? Avez-vous un parapluie? Je me fais un plaisir (mot à mot : je vous conduis volontiers...) de vous reconduire en voiture. — Merci bien. Vous êtes très aimable (mot à mot : c'est très aimable de vous).

Prononciation

Dans les mots *Gew**i**tter, gef**ä**llt,* la syllabe *ge* doit être prononcée faiblement, de même que dans *geh**ö**ren, Ger**i**cht.*

Vocabulaire

der H**i**mmel (-), *le ciel*
der R**e**gen, *la pluie*
der R**e**gensch**i**rm (-e), *le parapluie*
die S**o**nne (n), *le soleil*
die W**o**lke (n), *le nuage*
die Zeit (-en), *le temps, l'époque*

das Gew**i**tter (-), *l'orage*
das W**e**tter, *le temps (qu'il fait)*
d**o**nnern, *tonner*
sch**au**en, *regarder*
*f**a**llen (er fällt), *tomber*
gef**a**llen (er gefällt), *plaire*
blitzen, *faire des éclairs*

Après la pluie, le beau temps (A la pluie succède la lumière du soleil)

Grammaire

■ Er stand am Fenster.

Le prétérit des verbes de position et des verbes factitifs.

● Les verbes de position sont irréguliers; au prétérit, ils ont la forme suivante :

stehen > *er stand,* il était debout
sitzen > *er saß,* il était assis
liegen > *er lag,* il était couché
hangen > *er hing,* il était accroché

(Conjugaison : voir leçon 15).

● Les verbes factitifs sont réguliers :

stellen > *er stellte,* il mit ou mettait (debout)
setzen > *er setzte,* il assit
legen > *er legte,* il posa
hängen > *er hängte,* il accrocha

(Conjugaison : voir leçon 14).

■ Sein Nachbar zeigte ihm das Mädchen : er zeigte es ihm.

La place des pronoms compléments.

● Construction habituelle : Le complément d'attribution (datif) précède le complément d'objet direct (accusatif). Exemple :

Der Nachbar zeigte Paul das Mädchen, le voisin montra la fillette à Paul.

● Cependant, le pronom complément se place avant le nom complément. Exemple :

*Er zeigte **es** Paul,* il la montra à Paul.

● Quand il y a deux pronoms compléments, l'accusatif vient avant le datif. Exemple :

*Er zeigte **es ihm,*** il la lui montra.

Notez que le verbe, réclamant la deuxième place, précède les pronoms compléments.

■ Es gab ein Gewitter; es blitzte.

Le pronoms *es* est souvent sujet d'un verbe impersonnel :

Es regnet, il pleut; *es donnert,* il tonne.

On l'emploie également dans des tournures comme : *es gefällt mir,* il (cela) me plaît; *es geht mir gut,* je vais bien; *es gibt* (+ accusatif), il y a (m. à m. : cela donne).

Exercices

A *Mettez les phrases au prétérit, puis traduisez :*
1. Er stellt den Wagen in die Garage und legt die Mappe auf den Tisch. 2. Wir hängen den Mantel an den Haken *(crochet)* und setzen uns. 3. Du liegst im Garten, dein Freund steht neben dir. 4. Sie sitzen am Schreibtisch; eine Uhr hängt vor ihnen.

B *Traduisez les phrases, puis utilisez un pronom personnel pour remplacer a) le complément d'attribution b) le complément direct d'objet c) les deux compléments.* (Ex. : Er zeigt dem Freund das Mädchen; a) er zeigt **ihm** das Mädchen; b) er zeigt **es** dem Freund; c) er zeigt **es ihm.**)
5. Emil bringt seinem Kollegen ein Buch. 6. Wir zeigen dieser Dame den Rhein. 7. Heinz kauft dem Kind eine Uhr.

C *Traduisez :*
8. Hier il faisait des éclairs et il tonnait. 9. C'était un orage; les rues étaient grises. 10. Son parapluie (à elle) était accroché à côté du manteau. 11. Il y a souvent un orage en été *(im Sommer)*. 12. Les enfants étaient assis sur la terrasse et regardaient vers *(nach)* le Rhin.

Corrigé :

A 1. Er stellte... und legte... *Il mit la voiture au garage et posa la serviette sur la table.* 2. Wir hängten... und setzten uns. *Nous accrochions le manteau au crochet (porte-manteau) et nous nous assîmes.* 3. Du lagst..., dein Freund stand... *Tu étais couché au jardin, ton ami se tenait (debout) à côté de toi.* 4. Sie saßen..., eine Uhr hing... *Ils étaient assis au bureau, une pendule était accrochée devant eux.*

B 5. *Émile apporte un livre à son collègue;* a) Emil bringt **ihm** ein Buch; b) Emil bringt **es** seinem Kollegen; c) Emil bringt **es ihm.** 6. *Nous montrons le Rhin à cette dame;* a) wir zeigen **ihr** den Rhein; b) wir zeigen **ihn** der Dame; c) wir zeigen **ihn ihr.** 7. *Heinz achète une montre à l'enfant.* a) Heinz kauft **ihm** eine Uhr; b) Heinz kauft **sie** dem Kind; c) Heinz kauft **sie ihm.**

C 8. Gestern blitzte es (inversion) und es donnerte. 9. Es war ein Gewitter; die Straßen waren grau. 10. Ihr Regenschirm hing neben ihrem Mantel. 11. Es gibt oft ein Gewitter im Sommer. 12. Die Kinder saßen auf der Terrasse und schauten nach dem Rhein.

Leçon

18 Camping

1 Das Camping hat heute viele *Anhänger.
Auch Hans und Werner, die Söhne des Nachbars, wollen einige *Ferientage auf einem *Zeltplatz *verbringen.
Die Jungen haben ein Zelt, einen *Gaskocher, zwei *Luftmatratzen, und alles, was zum Camping gehört.

2 — Wohin fahren wir denn, Hans?
— Möchtest du nicht nach Overath? Es liegt nur 26 (sechsundzwanzig) Kilometer von hier. Dort gibt es einen schönen Zeltplatz.
— Womit fahren wir, mit dem Bus?
— Nein, mit dem *Fahrrad, es ist viel interessanter!

3 Werner will nie sehr weit fahren und der Zeltplatz an der Agger gefällt ihm. Er wird für das Essen sorgen.
Aber Hans mag keine *Konserven.
— Wann werden wir in Overath ankommen?
— Vor Mittag noch, so gegen elf Uhr.
— Nun, da werden wir noch einen angenehmen Platz finden.

1 [anhènger]; [férien'tage]; [tçèltplatç]; [fèrbringen]; [gaçkorer]; [louftmatratçen'].

2 [farrat].

3 [kon'çèrven'].

HUNGER IST DER BESTE KOCH

Traduction

Le camping

1 De nos jours, le camping a beaucoup de partisans. Hans et Werner, les fils du voisin, veulent aussi passer quelques jours de vacances sur un terrain de camping. Les garçons ont une tente, un réchaud à gaz, deux matelas pneumatiques et tout ce qu'il faut pour le camping.

2 — Où donc irons-nous, Hans? (mot à mot : allons-nous). — Ne voudrais-tu pas (aller) à Overath? Ce n'est qu'à 26 kilomètres d'ici. Il y a un beau terrain de camping là-bas. — Comment (y) allons-nous, en autocar? — Non, à bicyclette, c'est beaucoup plus intéressant!

3 Werner ne veut jamais rouler très loin, et le terrain au bord de (mot à mot : à) l'Agger lui plaît. C'est lui qui s'occupera de la nourriture. Mais Hans n'aime pas les conserves. — Quand arriverons-nous à Overath? — Avant midi encore, vers onze heures. — Eh bien, alors, nous trouverons encore une place agréable.

Prononciation

Dans les noms composés, c'est le premier terme qui porte l'accent principal; le deuxième porte l'accent secondaire, moins marqué. Lisez à haute voix : *Z**e**ltpl**a**tz* — *G**a**sk**o**cher* — *L**u**ftmatr**a**tzen.*

Vocabulaire

der **A**nhänger (-), *le partisan*
das C**a**mping, *le camping*
der K**o**cher (-), *le réchaud*
die F**e**rien (plur.), *les vacances*
die Kons**e**rve (n), *la conserve*
die Luft (¨e), *l'air*
die Matr**a**tze (n), *le matelas*
das F**a**hrrad (¨er), *la bicyclette*
das Gas (e), *le gaz*
das Rad (¨er), *la roue*
das Zelt (-e), *la tente*
k**o**chen, *cuire*
s**o**rgen für, *s'occuper de*
verbr**i**ngen, *passer (son temps)*

Il n'est sauce que d'appétit (La faim est le meilleur cuisinier).

Grammaire

■ Werner will nie weit fahren. – Hans mag keine Konserven.

● Les verbes *wollen* et *mögen* signifient « vouloir ». *Wollen* indique une volonté ferme, *mögen* veut dire « vouloir bien, désirer, avoir envie de ».

● Aux trois personnes du présent de l'indicatif, ces deux verbes ont la forme d'un ancien prétérit fort. Au pluriel et au prétérit, ils sont réguliers (avec une exception pour *mögen,* qui fait *ich mochte*).

Wollen		***Mögen***	
Présent	Prétérit	Présent	Prétérit
ich will	*ich wollte*	*ich mag*	*ich mochte*
je veux	je voulais, voulus	je désire	je désirai (s)
du willst	*du wolltest*	*du magst*	*du mochtest*
er(sie, es) will	*er wollte*	*er mag*	*er mochte*
wir wollen	*wir wollten*	*wir mögen*	*wir mochten*
ihr wollt	*ihr wolltet*	*ihr mögt*	*ihr mochtet*
sie, Sie wollen	*sie wollten*	*sie mögen*	*sie mochten*

Remarques : 1. Le verbe *mögen* s'emploie beaucoup au conditionnel :

Ich möchte ein Bier, je voudrais une bière.

2. Il y a 6 verbes comme *wollen* et *mögen,* appelés auxiliaires de mode. Nous étudierons les autres dans les leçons suivantes.

■ Womit fahren wir dorthin?

Les interrogatifs composés.

– *Womit,* avec quoi, correspond à *mit was.* On forme ces interrogatifs avec *wo*?, quoi? suivi de la préposition voulue. Lorsque celle-ci commence par une voyelle, elle est reliée à *wo*? par un *r.* Exemple : *durch, wodurch?* par où? *für, wofür?* pourquoi, dans quel but? *auf, worauf?* sur quoi?

Remarque : Ces interrogatifs composés ne s'emploient que pour des choses.

■ La numération

30, dr**ei**ßig	60, s**e**chzig	90, n**eu**nzig
40, v**ie**rzig	70, s**ie**bzig	100, h**u**ndert
50, f**ü**nfzig	80, **a**chtzig	1000, t**au**send.

Les nombres se forment comme en français, mais l'unité précède la dizaine. Exemple :
45. f**ü**nfundv**ie**rzig; 73. dr**ei**undsi**e**bzig; 629, s**e**chsh**u**ndertn**eu**nundzw**a**nzig.

Exercices

A *Complétez par le verbe indiqué, au présent, puis traduisez :*
1. ich (wollen) Deutsch lernen. 2. Ihr (wollen) ein Buch kaufen. 3. Emil (wollen) früh aufstehen. 4. Du (mögen) diesen Wein nicht. 5. Heddy (mögen) gern Schokolade. 6. Wir (mögen) hier nicht arbeiten.
Mettez ces phrases au prétérit.

B *Posez des questions en employant si possible un interrogatif composé, puis traduisez :*
7. Sie fahren durch die Stadt. 8. Er wohnt bei seinem Onkel. 9. Sie sprachen von Berlin. 10. Er kaufte das Buch für seinen Freund.

C *Traduisez :*
11. N'oubliez pas votre réchaud à gaz et votre matelas pneumatique! (2e pers. plur.) 12. Je n'aime pas ces conserves. 13. Avec qui Hans va-t-il à Overath? 14. De quoi les garçons parleront-ils sous (= dans) la tente? 15. Werner voulait la plus belle bicyclette.

Corrigé :

A 1. will. *Je veux apprendre l'allemand.* 2. wollt. *Vous voulez acheter un livre.* 3. will. *Émile veut se lever de bonne heure.* 4. magst. *Tu n'aimes pas ce vin.* 5. mag. *Heddy aime bien le chocolat.* 6. mögen. *Nous n'avons pas envie de travailler ici.*
1. wollte 2. wolltet 3. wollte 4. mochtest 5. mochte 6. mochten.

B 7. Wodurch fahren Sie? *Par où passez-vous?* 8. Bei wem wohnt er? *Chez qui habite-t-il.* 9. Wovon sprachen sie? *De quoi parlaient-ils?* 10. Für wen kaufte er das Buch? *Pour qui acheta-t-il le livre?*

C 11. Vergeßt euren Gaskocher und eure Luftmatratze nicht! 12. Ich mag diese Konserven nicht. 13. Mit wem fährt Hans nach Overath? 14. Wovon werden die Jungen im Zelt sprechen? 15. Werner wollte das schönste Fahrrad.

Leçon

19 Besichtigung einer Spinnerei

1 Die IMEX ist eine internation**a**le **I**mport-**E**xport-*Ges**e**llschaft.
Sie *l**ie**fert **a**llerl**ei** Masch**i**nen, auch für die *Text**i**lindustr**ie**.
Am Fr**ei**tag n**a**chmittag h**a**ben die Kongr**e**ßt**ei**lnehmer eine Spinner**ei** bes**i**chtigt.
Sie sind mit dem Bus h**i**ngef**a**hren.

2 Ein *Ingeni**eu**r hat **i**hnen die **A**rbeit vom *R**o**hstoff bis zum F**a**den *erkl**ä**rt.
Er hat sie durch die v**ie**len R**äu**me gef**ü**hrt.
Dort h**a**ben sie die mod**e**rnsten Masch**i**nen ges**e**hen.
Sie h**a**ben sich für **a**lles sehr interess**ie**rt.

3 – **U**nsere Fabr**i**k *besch**ä**ftigt 125 (h**u**ndertf**ü**nfunfzw**a**nzig) **A**rbeiter, **A**rbeiter**i**nnen und ***A**ngest**e**llte.
Wir s**o**llten mehr Platz h**a**ben, denn die Masch**i**nen werden **i**mmer gr**ö**ßer.
Nat**ü**rlich muß hier die gr**ö**ßte *S**au**berkeit h**e**rrschen.

4 – Woh**i**n verk**au**fen Sie **I**hre Prod**u**kte?
– Wir verk**au**fen sie in D**eu**tschland, aber auch in ganz Eur**o**pa.
– Und woh**e**r bek**o**mmen Sie die R**o**hst**o**ffe?
– Sie k**o**mmen aus ***A**frika und *Am**e**rika.

1 [bézichtigou^{ng}]; [chpiner**aé**].
[géz**è**lchaft]; [l**i**fert]; [tèkçt**i**lindouçtr**i**].

2 [in'jéni**eu**r]; [r**o**chtof]; [èrkl**è**rt].

3 [béchèfticht]; [**a**n'géchtèlte]; [z**ao**berk**aé**t].

4 [**a**frika]; [am**é**rika].

HANDEL IST DIE MUTTER DES REICHTUMS

Traduction

La visite d'une filature

1 L'IMEX est une société internationale d'importation et d'exportation. Elle fournit toutes sortes de machines, également pour l'industrie textile. Vendredi après-midi, les congressistes (mot à mot : les participants au congrès) ont visité une filature. Ils s'y sont rendus en autocar.

2 Un ingénieur leur a expliqué le travail, depuis la matière première jusqu'au fil. Il les a conduits à travers les nombreuses salles. Là, ils ont vu les machines les plus modernes. Ils se sont beaucoup intéressés à tout cela.

3 – Notre usine occupe 125 ouvriers, ouvrières et employés. Nous devrions avoir plus d'espace, car les machines sont de plus en (mot à mot : deviennent toujours) plus grandes. Naturellement, la plus grande propreté doit régner ici.

4 – Où écoulez-vous (mot à mot : vendez-vous) vos produits? – Nous les vendons en Allemagne, mais aussi dans toute l'Europe. – Et d'où recevez-vous les matières premières? – Elles (nous) arrivent d'Afrique et d'Amérique.

Vocabulaire

der **A**ngest**e**llte (n), *l'employé*
der **A**rbeiter (-), *l'ouvrier*
der F**a**den (¨), *le fil*
der Ingeni**eu**r (- e), *l'ingénieur*
der Raum (¨ e), *l'espace, la salle*
die R**o**hst**o**ffe *(plur.) les matières premières*
die Ges**e**llschaft (-en), *la société*
die S**au**berkeit, *la propreté*
die Spinner**ei** (en), *la filature*
das Prod**u**kt (e), *la production, le produit*
besch**ä**ftigen, *employer*
bes**i**chtigen, *visiter (ville, usine)*
erkl**ä**ren, *expliquer*
sich interess**ie**ren für, *s'intéresser à*
l**ie**fern, *livrer*
t**ei**ln**e**hmen an (+ datif), *participer*
verk**au**fen, *vendre*
n**e**hmen (er nimmt), *prendre*

Le commerce est source (m. à m. : la mère) de richesse.

■ **Er hat sie durch die Räume geführt.**
Le passé composé
De même qu'en français, le passé composé se forme à l'aide de l'auxiliaire *haben* (parfois *sein*) et du participe passé.

● Le verbe faible prend au participe passé le préfixe *ge-* et la terminaison *-t.*
Kaufen > *gekauft,* acheté.

● Le verbe fort (irrégulier) prend le préfixe *ge-* et la terminaison *-en,* mais subit souvent des modifications dans le radical.
Sprechen > *gesprochen,* parlé;
nehmen > *genommen,* pris.

● Le préfixe *ge-* s'intercale entre le verbe et la particule séparable.
Zuhören > *zugehört,* écouté;
abschreiben > *abgeschrieben,* copié.

● Certains verbes ont une particule inséparable; ils ne prennent pas le préfixe *ge-.*
Erklären > *erklärt,* expliqué.
Il en est de même des verbes en *-ieren.*
Interessieren > *interessiert,* intéressé.

● L'auxiliaire du passé composé, *haben* ou *sein,* se met à la deuxième place, tandis que le participe passé se place à la fin de la proposition principale.

■ **Hier muß Sauberkeit herrschen. Wir sollten mehr Platz haben.**
Les verbes *müssen* et *sollen* sont des auxiliaires de mode. Ils ont le sens de « devoir ».

● *müssen,* devoir, être forcé de.
Alle Menschen müssen sterben, tous les hommes doivent mourir.

● *sollen,* devoir, (obligation morale).
Ich soll ihm helfen, je dois l'aider.

Müssen		***Sollen***	
Présent	*Prétérit*	*Présent*	*Prétérit*
ich muß	*ich mußte*	*ich soll*	*ich sollte*
je dois, il faut que je...	je devais, je dus.	je dois	je devais, je dus

Voir Mémento, § 50.

Exercices

A *Formez le participe passé des verbes suivants, et traduisez-le :* a) (*v. faibles*). 1. legen. 2. machen. b) (*v. forts*). 3. trinken (u). 4. sehen (e). c) (*particules séparables*). 5. hinstellen. 6. ankommen d) (*particules inséparables*). 7. bestellen. 8. vergessen. e) (*v. en -ieren*). 9. transportieren. 10. studieren.

B *Mettez les phrases au passé composé, puis traduisez :* 11. Diese Gesellschaft liefert uns Maschinen. 12. Sie bestellt die Maschinen in Holland. 13. Findest du hier diesen Artikel?

C *Complétez en mettant le verbe au présent, puis traduisez :* 14. Emil, du ... ans Telefon kommen (sollen). 15. Er ... diese Maschine noch heute reparieren (müssen).

Mettez ces phrases au prétérit.

D *Traduisez :* 16. Cette filature a acheté ses machines chez *(bei)* IMEX. 17. Avez-vous vendu vos articles en France? 18. Il faut que nous arrivions vers 3 heures (= nous devons arriver).

Corrigé :

A a) 1. gelegt, *posé.* 2. gemacht, *fait.* b) 3. getrunken, *bu*. 4. gesehen, *vu.* c) 5. hingestellt, *disposé.* 6. angekommen, *arrivé.* d) 7. bestellt, *commandé.* 8. vergessen, *oublié.* e) 9. transportiert, *transporté.* 10. studiert, *étudié.*

B 11. ... hat ... geliefert. *Cette société nous a fourni des machines.* 12. Sie hat ... bestellt. *Elle a commandé les machines en Hollande.* 13. Hast du... gefunden? *As-tu trouvé cet article ici?*

C A. 14. sollst. *Émile, tu dois venir au téléphone.* 15. muß. *Il faut qu'il répare cette machine encore aujourd'hui.* B. 14. solltest. 15. mußte.

D 16. Diese Spinnerei hat ihre Maschinen bei IMEX gekauft. 17. Haben Sie Ihre Artikel in Frankreich verkauft? 18. Wir müssen gegen drei Uhr ankommen.

Leçon

20 *Handwerk und Industrie

1 Nach der Besichtigung der Spinnerei sprachen die Herren noch lange vom alten Handwerk und von der modernen Industrie. *Früher spannen viele Familien *selbst ihre Wolle, besonders auf dem Land.
Dann gab es kleine *Werkstätten, in den Dörfern wie in den Städten.

2 Der *Tischler, der *Schneider arbeiteten in ihrer Werkstatt.
Sie hatten sie oft von ihrem Vater übernommen.
Diese Werkstatt war klein und nicht sehr hell.
Die Handwerker durften aber auf ihre Arbeit stolz sein.

3 — Ja, heute arbeiten sie sehr oft in einer Fabrik, sagte Herr Müller.
Ihre Arbeit ist *geregelt, die *Räume sind hell und sauber.
— Aber ihre Produkte sind *anonym, antwortete Herr Neuler; sie machen ihnen weniger Freude.
— Gewiß, sagte Herr Müller. Eine Fabrik kann *jedoch billige Artikel *erzeugen.
Sie kann auch Hunderte von Arbeitern beschäftigen.

1 [han'tvèrk]; [frü/er]; [zèlbçt]; [vèrkchtèten'].

2 [tichler]; [chnaéder].

3 [gérégelt]; [roeume]; [anonum]; [yédor]; [èrtçoeugen'].

HANDWERK HAT GOLDENEN BODEN

Traduction

L'artisanat et l'industrie

1 Après la visite de la filature, les messieurs parlèrent encore longtemps de l'ancien artisanat et de l'industrie moderne. Jadis, beaucoup de familles filaient elles-mêmes leur laine, surtout à la campagne. Puis il y eut de petits ateliers, dans les villages comme dans les villes.

2 L'ébéniste, le tailleur travaillaient dans leur atelier. Ils l'avaient souvent repris de leur père. Cet atelier était exigu et pas très clair. Mais les artisans pouvaient (mot à mot : avaient le droit d') être fiers de (mot à mot : sur) leur travail.

3 — Oui, aujourd'hui, ils travaillent très souvent dans une usine, dit Monsieur Müller. Leur travail est réglementé, les salles sont claires et propres. — Mais leurs produits sont anonymes, répondit Monsieur Neuler, ils leur procurent moins de joie. — Certainement, dit Monsieur Müller. Une usine, cependant, peut produire des articles bon marché. Elle peut aussi employer des centaines d'ouvriers.

Prononciation

La lettre *y*, appelée en allemand [**u**psilọn'], apparaît dans les mots étrangers. Elle se prononce comme la voyelle [u], dans lune, Exemples : *anon**y**m, Hypoth**e**se* [hupot**ẹ**ze]. En tête de mot, elle correspond à notre y dans yeux.

Vocabulaire

der H**a**ndw**e**rker (-), *l'artisan, l'ouvrier*
der Schn**ei**der (-), *le tailleur*
der T**i**schler (-), *l'ébéniste*
die Fr**eu**de (n), *la joie*
Die W**e**rkstatt (e), *l'atelier*
die W**o**lle, *la laine*
das Dorf (¨ er), *le village*
das H**a**ndwerk (-e), *l'artisanat, le métier*
erz**eu**gen, *produire*
übern**e**hmen (a, o, i), *prendre en charge, reprendre*

Tout métier nourrit son homme (m. à m. : Le métier a un fond d'or)

■ **Sie hatten die Werkstatt von ihrem Vater übernommen.**
Le plus-que-parfait se forme à l'aide de l'auxiliaire *haben* (parfois *sein*) au prétérit, et du participe passé du verbe à conjuguer.

Ich hatte eine Fabrik besichtigt, j'avais visité une usine.
Ich war früh gekommen, j'étais venu de bonne heure.

■ **Sie sprachen von Handwerk und Industrie.**
Le radical d'un verbe irrégulier peut s'altérer au prétérit, au participe passé, au présent de l'indicatif (2e et 3e pers. du singulier seulement) et à l'impératif. Nous indiquerons dans cet ordre, après chaque verbe irrégulier, les modifications du radical, et il est indispensable de les apprendre en même temps que l'infinitif. Exemples :

finden (**a, u**), trouver = *er f**a**nd,* il trouva, *er hat... gef**u**nden,* il a trouvé.
*schlafen **(ie, a, ä)**,* dormir = *er schl**ie**f,* il dormit, il dormait, *er hat... geschl**a**fen,* il a dormi, *er schl**ä**ft,* il dort.

■ **Die Fabrik kann billige Artikel erzeugen. Die Handwerker durften stolz sein.**
Les verbes *können* et *dürfen* sont les deux derniers des six auxiliaires de mode. Ils ont le sens général de « pouvoir ».
a) *können :* pouvoir (possibilité matérielle); savoir;
b) *dürfen :* pouvoir (avoir le droit de).

Können		***Dürfen***	
Présent	Prétérit	Présent	Prétérit
Ich kann	*ich konnte*	*ich darf*	*ich durfte*
je peux, sais	je pouvais	je peux	je pouvais
du kannst	*du konntest*	*du darfst*	*du durftest*
er (sie, es) kann	*er konnte*	*er darf*	*er durfte*
wir können	*wir konnten*	*wir dürfen*	*wir durften*
ihr könnt	*ihr konntet*	*ihr dürft*	*ihr durftet*
sie (Sie) können	*sie konnten*	*sie dürfen*	*sie durften*

Exemples :

Ein Blinder kann nicht sehen, un aveugle ne peut pas voir.
Kannst du englisch? sais-tu l'anglais?
Er darf jetzt spielen, il peut jouer maintenant (il en a le droit).

Exercices

A *Mettez au plus-que-parfait, puis traduisez :*
1. Sie sprechen von einer Fabrik. 2. Er verkauft nur gute Produkte. 3. Du wohnst neben einer Tischlerwerkstatt. 4. Ich fahre nach Köln (auxiliaire sein). 5. Sie findet keine Arbeit.

B *Complétez par le verbe au présent, puis traduisez :*
6. Wer ... diesen Koffer tragen? (können). 7. Du ... noch nicht gut italienisch (können). 8. Ihr ... mit diesem Wagen nicht fortfahren (können). 9. ... wir an dieser Besichtigung teilnehmen? (dürfen). 10. Im Kino ... man nicht rauchen, *fumer* (dürfen).

Mettez les phrases 6 à 10 au prétérit.

C *Traduisez :*
11. L'industrie produit souvent des articles bon marché. 12. Tu peux être fier de ta voiture. 13. Ils avaient acheté une usine en (in) Allemagne. 14. Cet ébéniste avait longtemps travaillé en France. 15. Il savait bien (le) français.

Corrigé :

A 1. Sie hatten von einer Fabrik gesprochen. *Ils avaient parlé d'une usine.* 2. Er hatte nur gute Produkte verkauft. *Il n'avait vendu que des produits de qualité.* 3. Du hattest ... gewohnt. *Tu avais habité à côté d'un atelier d'ébénisterie.* 4. Ich war ... gefahren. *J'étais allé à Cologne.* 5. Sie hatte ... gefunden. *Elle n'avait pas trouvé de travail.*

B 6. kann. *Qui peut porter cette malle?* 7. kannst. *Tu ne sais pas bien encore l'italien.* 8. könnt. *Vous ne pouvez pas partir avec cette voiture.* 9. dürfen. *Pouvons-nous (= avons-nous le droit de) participer à cette visite?* 10. darf. *Au cinéma, on ne doit pas (= n'a pas le droit de) fumer.*
6. konnte. 7. konntest. 8. konntet. 9. durften. 10. durfte.

C 11. Die Industrie erzeugt oft billige Artikel. 12. Du darfst stolz auf deinen Wagen sein. 13. Sie hatten eine Fabrik in Deutschland gekauft. 14. Dieser Tischler hatte lange in Frankreich gearbeitet. 15. Er konnte gut französisch.

Leçon

20 bis Contrôle et révisions

A **Complétez les phrases suivantes en employant un verbe factitif (leçon 11) ou un verbe de position (leçon 12) et en mettant les terminaisons, puis traduisez :**

1. Werner l... seine Uhr auf d... Tisch. 2. Jetzt l... die Uhr auf d... Tisch. 3. Emma st... den Stuhl in d... Zimmer. 4. Jetzt st... der Stuhl in d... Zimmer. 5. Heddy s... ihre Puppe auf d... Stuhl. 6. Jetzt s... die Puppe auf d... Stuhl. 7. Ich h... den Regenschirm an d... Tür. 8. Jetzt h... er an d... Tür.

B **Mettez les verbes au prétérit, puis traduisez (pour les verbes réguliers, revoir la leçon 14; pour les verbes irréguliers, la leçon 15) :**

9. Er (lernen) Deutsch. 10. Er (arbeiten) jeden Tag. 11. Du (tragen, u, a; ä) eine Mappe. 12. Wir (finden, a, u) ein gutes Hotel. 13. Ich (erzählen) ihnen von Paris. 14. Alle (zu/hören) mir. 15. Ihr (fahren, u, a; ä) zu schnell. 16. Sie (bestellen) Rheinwein.

C **Mettez les verbes au passé composé, puis traduisez :**

17. Er (schlafen; ie, a, ä) lange. 18. Du (sagen) es mir. 19. Wir (ab/schreiben; ie, ie) es. 20. Ich (zeigen) es ihm. 21. Sie (bewundern) es.

D **Traduisez, puis remplacez les datifs et les accusatifs par des pronoms personnels (veillez à la construction; voir leçons 13, 14, 17) :**

22. Dieser Tischler liefert dem Direktor Möbel. 23. Du verkaufst dem Nachbar dein Auto. 24. Sie bringt der Nachbarin Rosen.

E **Traduisez :**

25. Il veut devenir ingénieur. 26. Elle n'aime pas ce chocolat. 27. Il faut qu'il travaille. (= il doit travailler). 28. Dois-je venir demain (morgen)? 29. Nous ne pouvons pas travailler dans cette pièce. 30. Elle peut (= a le droit de) voir ce film.

Corrigé :

A 1. legt; den. *Werner pose sa montre sur la table.* 2. liegt; dem. *Maintenant, la montre est posée sur la table.* 3. stellt; das. *Emma met la chaise dans la pièce.* 4. steht; dem. *Maintenant, la chaise se trouve (debout) dans la pièce.* 5. setzt; den. *Heddy assied sa poupée sur la chaise.* 6. sitzt; dem. *Maintenant, la poupée est assise sur la chaise.* 7. hänge; die. *J'accroche le parapluie à la porte.* 8. hängt; der. *Maintenant, il est accroché à la porte.*

B 9. lernte. *Il apprenait l'allemand.* 10. arbeitete. *Il travaillait chaque jour.* 11. trugst. *Tu portais une serviette.* 12. fanden. *Nous trouvâmes un bon hôtel.* 13. erzählte. *Je leur parlais de Paris.* 14. Alle hörten mir zu. *Tous m'écoutaient.* 15. fuhrt. *Vous rouliez trop vite.* 16. bestellten. *Ils commandèrent du vin du Rhin.*

C 17. Er hat lange geschlafen. *Il a dormi longtemps.* 18. Du hast es mir gesagt. *Tu me l'as dit.* 19. Wir haben es abgeschrieben. *Nous l'avons copié.* 20. Ich habe es ihm gezeigt. *Je le lui ai montré.* 21. Sie haben es bewundert. *Ils l'ont admiré.*

D 22. *Cet ébéniste fournit des meubles au directeur.* Dieser Tischler liefert sie ihm. 23. *Tu vends ta voiture au (= à ton) voisin.* Du verkaufst es ihm. 24. *Elle apporte des roses à la (= sa) voisine.* Sie bringt sie ihr.

E 25. Er will Ingenieur werden. 26. Sie mag diese Schokolade nicht (*ou :* Sie hat diese Schokolade nicht gern). 27. Er muß arbeiten. 28. Soll ich morgen kommen? 29. In diesem Zimmer können wir nicht arbeiten. 30. Sie darf diesen Film sehen.

Leçon

21 *Erholung zwischen Blumen und *Gemüse

1 In der Vorstadt gibt es viele *Kl**ei**ng**är**tner (oder H**o**bbyg**är**tner).
Ihr Garten ist für sie Freude und Erh**o**lung.
Hier arbeiten sie an den schönen Tagen.
Sie sitzen auch gern in dem *G**a**rtenh**äu**schen, trinken Bier und spielen Karten.
Regen und Sonne, natürlich auch viel Arbeit, haben allerlei Blumen und Gem**ü**se *herv**o**rgebr**a**cht.

2 Herr Möll, der Pförtner, hat auch einen Kl**ei**ng**a**rten.
Seine zwei *Söhne und seine *Tochter Monika helfen ihm oft. Sie pflanzen am liebsten Blumen.
Gestern sind sie alle drei gekommen; sie haben ein wenig gearbeitet. Dann haben sie ihrer Mutter Blumen gebracht.

3 — Wie schön ist diese rote Rose!
Ich möchte nur Rosen in unserem Garten, sagte Monika zu ihren Brüdern. Aber diese lachten über ihre *Schwester.
Sie haben lieber die schönen, gelben *Äpfel, die *saftigen Birnen, die braunen Nüsse.

Attention : Pour les leçons 21 à 25, l'accent tonique ne sera plus marqué par la voyelle en caractère gras lorsqu'il tombera sur la première syllabe du mot. Dans le cas des participes passés, si l'infinitif est accentué sur la première syllabe, le caractère gras ne sera pas employé non plus. Le caractère gras sera employé pour tout mot ayant deux accents (verbe à particule séparable ou mot composé). Dans la prononciation figurée, nous continuerons à employer les caractères gras pour les voyelles toniques.

1 [èrh**o**lou[ng]]; [gem**u**ze]; [kl**a**én'g**è**rtner]; [g**a**rten'h**oe**uç/chen'] [hèrf**o**rgébr**a**rt]. 2 [z**eu**ne]; [t**o**rter]. 3 [chv**è**çter]; [**è**pfel]; [z**a**ftigen'].

WER ZULETZT LACHT, LACHT AM BESTEN

Traduction

Délassement entre les fleurs et les légumes

1 Dans la banlieue, il y a beaucoup de jardiniers amateurs. Leur jardin représente pour eux joie et délassement. Ils travaillent ici par les belles journées. Ils aiment également être assis dans la tonnelle, en buvant de la bière et en jouant aux cartes. La pluie et le soleil, naturellement beaucoup de travail aussi, ont produit toutes sortes de fleurs et de légumes.

2 Monsieur Möll, le portier, a également un petit jardin. Ses deux fils et sa fille Monique l'aident souvent. Ils aiment le plus planter des fleurs. Hier, ils sont venus tous les trois; ils ont travaillé un peu. Ensuite, ils ont porté des fleurs à leur mère.

3 Comme cette rose rouge est belle! Moi, je ne voudrais que des roses dans notre jardin, dit Monique à ses frères. Mais ceux-ci se moquèrent de leur sœur. Ils préfèrent (= aiment mieux) les belles pommes jaunes, les poires juteuses, les noix brunes.

Prononciation

Nous sommes familiarisés maintenant avec cette particularité de prononciation : *u* se dit [ou]. Nous trouvons, dans cette leçon : *Erholung, Blumen, Mutter, unserem.* Cependant, *ü* se prononce [u] comme dans « lune » : *Gemüse, natürlich, Brüdern, Nüsse.*

Vocabulaire

der Apfel (¨), *la pomme*
der Bruder (¨), *le frère*
der Gärtner (-), *le jardinier*
der Saft (¨e), *le jus*
der Sohn (¨e), *le fils*
die Birne (n), *la poire*
die Erh**o**lung, *le délassement*
die Mutter (¨), *la mère*
die Schwester (n), *la sœur*
die Tochter (¨), *la fille*
das Gem**ü**se (sing.), *les légumes*
pflanzen, *planter*
lachen über (+ accusatif), *se moquer de*
helfen (a, o; i) + Datif, *aider*
herv**o**r br**i**ngen (brachte, gebracht), *produire*

Pour ce dernier verbe, leçon 7, 3 remarque très importante.

Rira bien qui rira le dernier (qui rit le dernier, rit le mieux)

Grammaire

■ **Wie schön ist die rote Rose!**
La déclinaison faible de l'adjectif épithète.
L'adjectif épithète se place devant le nom et il prend certaines terminaisons, c'est-à-dire qu'il se décline. Quand il est précédé d'un article défini *(der, die, das; die)* ou d'un déterminatif (*dieser,* etc.; voir leçon 5), il se décline ainsi :

	Masc.	Fém.	Ntre.	Plur. (3 genres)
Nom.	*der gut-e*	*die gut-e*	*das gut-e*	*die gut-en*
Gén.	*des gut-en*	*der gut-en*	*des gut-en*	*der gut-en*
Dat.	*dem gut-en*	*der gut-en*	*dem gut-en*	*den gut-en*
Acc.	*den gut-en*	*die gut-e*	*das gut-e*	*die gut-en*

On appelle cette déclinaison « faible ». Pour bien la retenir, notez que les terminaisons *-en* forment la silhouette d'une clé :

e	*e*	*e*	*en*
en	*en*	*en*	*en*
en	*en*	*en*	*en*
en	*e*	*e*	*en*

■ **Sie sind in den Garten gekommen, und sie haben gearbeitet.**
Emploi des auxiliaires *sein* et *haben.*
Pour former le passé composé ou le plus-que-parfait, on emploie :

● *Sein* a) avec les verbes intransitifs marquant un mouvement *(kommen, gehen)* ou un changement d'état *(erwachen);* b) avec le verbe *sein* lui-même, avec *werden* et *bleiben (ie, ie),* (rester).

Er ist in die Stadt gefahren, il s'est rendu en ville.
Er ist lange dort geblieben, il y est resté longtemps.

● *Haben* a) avec tous les verbes transitifs *(arbeiten, schreiben, nehmen)*
b) avec les verbes réfléchis (voir leçons 13 et 14).

Er hat seinen Kamm genommen, il a pris son peigne.
Er hat sich gekämmt, il s'est coiffé.

■ **Les auxiliaires de temps au passé composé :**
Ich habe... gehabt, du hast... gehabt, j'ai eu, etc.
Ich bin... gewesen, du bist... gewesen, j'ai été, etc.
Ich bin... geworden, du bist... geworden, je suis devenu, etc.

Exercices

A *Complétez les terminaisons des adjectifs, puis traduisez :*
1. Hans legt den rot... Apfel, die saftig... Birne und die braun... Nüsse (plur.) auf den Tisch. 2. Er gab der klein... Schwester diese rot... Rose. 3. Aus den grau... Straßen gingen wir in den ruhig... Park. 4. Welche deutsch... Städte kennst du? 5. Die jung... Dame bewundert die schön... Blumen dieses groß... Gartens.

B *Mettez au passé composé, puis traduisez :*
6. Ich kaufe mir Äpfel. 7. Du gehst in die Stadt. 8. Er pflanzt Gemüse. 9. Wir kleiden uns schnell an. 10. Ihr lauft in den Garten (laufen, ie, au; äu). 11. Sie schlafen lange. 12. Haben Sie diese Birnen gern? 13. Wird er Ingenieur?

C *Traduisez :*
14. Ce grand jardin produit les meilleures pommes et les poires les plus juteuses. 15. Nos voisins ont eu toutes sortes de légumes dans leur jardin. 16. Nous avons commandé cette belle montre pour notre fils. 17. Werner s'est assis dans la voiture neuve de son collègue. 18. L'autocar est arrivé assez *(ziemlich)* tard.

Corrigé :

A 1. roten; saftige; braunen. *Hans pose la pomme rouge, la poire juteuse et les noix brunes sur la table.* 2. kleinen; rote. *Il donna cette rose rouge à la (= sa) petite sœur.* 3. grauen; ruhigen. *Quittant les rues grises (mot à mot : hors des...), nous allâmes dans le parc tranquille.* 4. deutschen. *Quelles villes allemandes connais-tu?* 5. junge; schönen; großen. *La jeune dame admire les belles fleurs de ce grand jardin.*

B 6. Ich habe... gekauft. *Je me suis acheté des pommes.* 7. Du bist... gegangen. *Tu es allé en ville.* 8. Er hat... gepflanzt. *Il a planté des légumes.* 9. Wir haben uns... angekleidet. *Nous nous sommes habillés vite.* 10. Ihr seid... gelaufen. *Vous avez couru au jardin.* 11. Sie haben... geschlafen. *Ils ont dormi longtemps.* 12. Haben Sie... gern gehabt? *Avez-vous aimé ces poires?* 13. Ist er... geworden? *Est-il devenu ingénieur?*

C 14. Dieser große Garten bringt die besten Äpfel und die saftigsten Birnen hervor. 15. Unsere Nachbarn haben allerlei Gemüse in ihrem Garten gehabt. 16. Wir haben diese schöne Uhr für unseren Sohn bestellt. 17. Werner hat sich in den neuen Wagen seines Kollegen gesetzt. 18. Der Bus ist ziemlich spät angekommen.

Leçon

22 Das große *Herbstfest

1 — Einen schönen Pok**a**l haben Sie da, Herr Möll!
— Ja, unser Ver**ei**n hat ihn gewonnen.
Die Kl**ei**ng**ä**rtner geben jedes *Jahr ein großes Herbstfest. *Letztes Jahr fand das Fest am 25. (f**ü**nfundzw**a**nzigsten) *Sept**e**mber statt.
Unser *Ver**e**in stellte seine schönsten Prod**u**kte aus: *Erbsen, Bohnen, Kohl, Kart**o**ffeln.
So bek**a**men wir diesen Pok**a**l.

2 — Es herrschte wohl eine frohe Stimmung?
— Gew**i**ß! Wir haben immer viele Bes**u**cher, weil wir *Mus**i**k, Lieder und Tanz bieten.
Die *älteren Leute lieben die alten Lieder vom Rhein und vom Wein. Die *Jüngeren haben ihre Freude an den mod**e**rnen Tänzen.

3 — War**u**m kommen immer viele Leute?
— Weil sie bei uns eine frohe Stimmung finden.
— Warum kommen die Älteren so gern?
— Weil sie hier ihre alten Lieder hören.
— Und warum kommen auch die Jüngeren?
— Weil wir für sie auch eine moderne Kap**e**lle haben.

1 [h**è**rbçt-f**è**çt]; [y**a**r]; [l**è**tç-teç]; [zèpt**è**m'ber]; [fèr-**a**én']; [**è**rbçen'].
2 [mouz**i**k]; [**è**lteren']; [y**u**^ng^eren'].

FREMDE LÄNDER, FREMDE SITTEN

Traduction

La grande fête d'automne

1 — C'est une belle coupe que vous avez là, Monsieur Möll! — Oui, c'est notre société qui l'a gagnée. Les jardiniers amateurs donnent tous les ans (mot à mot : chaque année) une grande fête d'automne. L'année dernière, la fête eut lieu le 25 septembre. Notre société exposa ses plus beaux produits : des pois, des haricots, des choux, des pommes de terre. C'est ainsi que nous avons reçu (mot à mot : reçûmes) cette coupe.

2 — Il régnait sans doute une joyeuse ambiance? — Que oui! (mot à mot : certainement). Nous avons toujours beaucoup de visiteurs, parce que nous offrons de la musique, des chants et des danses. Les gens d'un certain âge (mot à mot : plus âgés) aiment les vieilles chansons sur le Rhin et sur le vin. Les plus jeunes trouvent leur plaisir aux danses modernes.

3 — Pourquoi y a-t-il toujours beaucoup de monde? (m. à m. : Pourquoi beaucoup de gens viennent-ils toujours?) — Parce qu'ils trouvent chez nous une joyeuse ambiance. — Pourquoi les personnes d'un certain âge aiment-elles tant venir? (mot à mot : viennent-elles si volontiers?) — Parce qu'elles entendent ici leurs vieilles chansons. — Et pourquoi les plus jeunes viennent-ils aussi? — Parce que nous avons, pour eux, également un orchestre moderne.

Vocabulaire

der Herbst, *l'automne*
der Kohl, *le chou*
der Tanz (¨ e), *la danse*
die Bohne (n), *le haricot*
die Erbse (n), *le petit pois*
die Kart**o**ffel (n), *la pomme de terre*
die Leute (plur), *les gens*
die Mus**i**k, *la musique*

das Fest (-e), *la fête*
das Lied (er), *le chant*
das Jahr (-e), *l'année*
ausst**e**llen, *exposer* (Voyez 7,3)
lieben, *aimer*
bieten (o, o), *offrir, présenter*
gew**i**nnen (a, o), *gagner*
st**a**ttf**i**nden (a, u), *avoir lieu*

Autres pays, autres mœurs (pays étrangers, mœurs étrangères)

Grammaire

■ **Weil sie hier ihre alten Lieder hören.**
La proposition subordonnée.

● Dans une proposition subordonnée, introduite par exemple par *weil*, parce que, le verbe conjugué est rejeté à la fin.

● Si le verbe de la subordonnée a une particule séparable, celle-ci reste soudée au verbe. Exemple :

Sie fahren in die Vorstadt, weil dort ein Fest stattfindet, ils vont dans la banlieue parce qu'une fête y a lieu (*m. à m. : parce que là-bas une fête a lieu*).

● Quand le verbe de la subordonnée est à un temps composé (futur, passé composé, plus-que-parfait), c'est l'auxiliaire qui prend la dernière place. Exemple :

Er freut sich, weil er den Pokal gewonnen hat, il se réjouit parce qu'il a remporté la coupe.

● La subordonnée est toujours séparée de la principale par une virgule. *Weil*, parce que, répond à la question *warum?*, pourquoi?

■ **La numération – Le nombre ordinal.**
Pour former les nombres ordinaux, on ajoute au nombre simple la terminaison *-te* jusqu'à 19, et *-ste* à partir de 20. Exemple :

2. *der zweite,* le deuxième. 4. *der vierte,* le quatrième. 19. *der neunzehnte,* le dix-neuvième. 20. *der zwanzigste,* le vingtième. 35. der fünfunddreißigste, le trente-cinquième.

Sont irréguliers :

1. *der erste,* le premier (contraire : *der letzte,* le dernier).
3. *der dritte,* le troisième; *der siebte* (le 7e); *der achte* (le 8e).

■ **Das Fest fand am 25. (fünfundzwanzigsten) September statt.** La date.
Pour indiquer la date, l'allemand emploie le nombre ordinal (le « 25e » septembre, et non le 25), précédé de *am*, contraction de *an dem*.
Pour préciser le jour du mois, on emploie *haben* (+ accusatif) :

Heute haben wir den zehnten Mai. Nous sommes aujourd'hui le 10 mai.

Remarque : Le nombre ordinal est souvent indiqué par un point. Exemple : *der 5.* (= *der fünfte*). Il se décline comme l'adjectif épithète (voir leçon 21).

Exercices

A *Reliez les deux propositions par* weil, *puis traduisez :*
1. Er mag diese Tänze nicht; er ist schon ziemlich alt. 2. Er ist stolz auf seine Wohnung; sie hat eine schöne Terrasse. 3. Sie freuen sich; sie werden bald auf ein Fest gehen. 4. Er fuhr nach München; seine Firma stellte dort Maschinen aus.

B *Traduisez les phrases suivantes, puis posez des questions avec* warum?
5. Diese Fabrik erzeugt billige Artikel, weil sie moderne Maschinen hat. 6. Hans ist nicht zufrieden *(content),* weil er die Konserven nicht liebt.

C *Traduisez :*
7. Les gens sont si gais parce que l'orchestre joue très bien. 8. Ils aiment bien ces chansons parce que leurs pères les ont déjà chantées (singen, a, u). 9. Viendrez-vous le quinze mai? 10. Ces fleurs sont très belles parce que nous avons eu de la pluie et du soleil. 11. Les garçons se moquent de leur sœur parce qu'elle préfère les roses. 12. La société offre toujours de la musique parce que les visiteurs aiment cette ambiance.

Corrigé :

A 1. Er mag..., weil et schon ziemlich alt ist. *Il n'aime pas ces danses parce qu'il est déjà assez âgé.* 2. Er ist stolz..., weil sie eine schöne Terrasse hat. *Il est fier de son appartement parce que celui-ci a une belle terrasse.* 3. Sie..., weil sie bald auf ein Fest gehen werden. *Ils se réjouissent parce qu'ils iront bientôt à une fête.* 4. Er fuhr..., weil seine Firma dort Maschinen ausstellte. *Il se rendit à Münich parce que sa maison y exposait des machines.*

B 5. *Cette usine produit des articles bon marché parce qu'elle a des machines modernes.* Warum erzeugt diese Fabrik billige Artikel? 6. *Hans n'est pas content parce qu'il n'aime pas les conserves.* Warum ist Hans nicht zufrieden?

C 7. Die Leute sind so froh, weil die Kapelle sehr gut spielt. 8. Sie haben diese Lieder gern, weil ihre Väter sie schon gesungen haben. 9. Werden Sie am fünfzehnten Mai kommen? 10. Diese Blumen sind sehr schön, weil wir Regen und Sonne gehabt haben. 11. Die Jungen lachen über ihre Schwester, weil sie die Rosen lieber hat. 12. Der Verein bietet immer Musik, weil die Besucher diese Stimmung lieben (*ou :* gern haben).

Leçon

23 Das *Fernsehen

1 Darf ich Sie heute abend zum F**e**rns**e**hen **ei**nl**a**den?
– Ja, vielen Dank. Was steht auf dem Programm?
– Es ist eine interess**a**nte *Sendung über die Tierwelt im Abendprogramm.
– Da dürfen ihre Kinder wohl auch fernsehen?
– Ja, solche Sendungen sind oft *lehrreich.

2 Lange wollten wir das Fernsehen nicht haben, weil wir nur die Nachteile sahen.
Man sagte uns, daß die Kinder keine Lust zur Arbeit mehr haben. Wir hörten auch, daß das F**e**rns**e**hen das *Gespräch in den Fam**i**lien ***u**nm**ö**glich macht.
Aber wir hatten schon lange ein Radio, später auch ein K**o**fferger**ä**t, und wir sahen, daß wir keine Sklaven der Technik geworden waren.

3 – Eine gew**i**sse *Diszipl**i**n geh**ö**rt aber doch dazu!
– Nat**ü**rlich! Wir *wählen unser Progr**a**mm *sorgfältig aus. Wir erfr**eu**en uns an schönen *The**a**terst**ü**cken oder Filmen. Oft gibt es dann lange Diskussi**o**nen über diese oder jene Sendung.
An m**a**nchen T**a**gen **a**ber m**a**chen wir das Ger**ä**t gar nicht an.
So h**a**ben wir nicht den **Ei**ndruck, daß fr**e**mde St**i**mmen in **u**nserem H**au**se h**e**rrschen.

1 [fèrn'zé/en']; [zèn'dou^{ng}]; [lér/raéch].

2 [n**a**rt**a**éle]; [géchpr**è**ch]; [**oun**'/m**eu**glich]; [çkl**a**fen'];

3 [diçtçipl**i**n]; [v**è**len']; [z**o**rkf**è**ltich]; [té**a**ter/cht**u**ken'].

ERST DIE ARBEIT, DANN DAS SPIEL

Traduction

La télévision

1 — Puis-je vous inviter ce soir à (venir regarder) la télévision? — Oui, merci beaucoup. Qu'y a-t-il au programme? (mot à mot : qu'est-ce qui se trouve sur le programme?) — Au programme de la soirée, il y a une émission intéressante sur le monde des animaux. — Alors vos enfants pourront (mot à mot : ont le droit de) sans doute également (la) regarder? — Oui, de telles émissions sont souvent instructives.

2 Longtemps, nous ne voulions pas (avoir) la télévision, parce que nous ne (= n'en) voyions que les inconvénients. On nous disait que les enfants n'ont plus aucune envie de travailler (mot à mot : envie pour le travail). Nous entendions également que la télévision rend impossible les conversations dans les familles. Mais nous avions déjà longtemps une radio, plus tard également un poste portatif, et nous avons remarqué que nous n'étions pas devenus des esclaves de la technique.

3 — Mais il y faut quand même une certaine discipline! — Bien sûr. Nous choisissons notre programme soigneusement. Nous prenons plaisir à de belles pièces de théâtre ou à de beaux films. Souvent, il y a de longues discussions ensuite sur telle ou telle (mot à mot : celle-ci ou celle-là) émission. Certains jours nous n'allumons même pas l'appareil. Aussi nous n'avons pas l'impression que des voix étrangères règnent dans notre maison.

Vocabulaire

der Eindruck (¨e), *l'impression*
der Koffer (-), *la malle*
der Nachteil (-e), *l'inconvénient*
der Sklave (n), *l'esclave*
der Vorteil (-e), *l'avantage*
die Diskussi**o**n (en), *la discussion*
die Diszipl**i**n, *la discipline*
die Lust, *l'envie, le plaisir*
die Sendung (-en) *l'émission, l'envoi*
die Stimme (n), *la voix*
die Technik, *la technique*
das Fernsehen, *la télévision*
das Gespr**ä**ch (-e), *la conversation*
das Ger**ä**t (-e), *l'appareil*
das Progr**a**mm (-e), *le programme*
das Radio (s), *la radio*
das Stück (-e), *la pièce*
das Tier (-e), *l'animal*
anm**a**chen, *allumer (radio)*
ausm**a**chen, *fermer (radio)*
ausw**ä**hlen, *choisir*
sch**au**en, *regarder*

D'abord le travail, ensuite le jeu.

Prononciation

Le son de notre « j » français (« jouer, jamais ») n'existe pas dans les mots allemands, sauf dans les mots étrangers, comme « *Ingenieur* ». La lettre *j* se prononce comme le « y » dans « yeux ». Vous le prononcerez ainsi dans : *ja, jedes Jahr, die Jüngeren.*

Grammaire

■ **Es gibt oft lange Diskussionen.**
La déclinaison forte de l'adjectif épithète.
Quand l'adjectif épithète n'est pas précédé d'un article ou d'un déterminatif, il prend partout les terminaisons de l'article défini *(der, die, das; die)* sauf au génitif masculin et neutre singulier, où il prend *-en*. Dans ces tournures, l'adjectif remplace en quelque sorte l'article.
Déclinaison :

	Masculin	Féminin	Neutre	Pluriel
N.	*guter*	*gute*	*gutes*	*gute*
G.	*gut**en***	*guter*	*gut**en***	*guter*
D.	*gutem*	*guter*	*gutem*	*guten*
A.	*guten*	*gute*	*gutes*	*gute*

La déclinaison forte s'emploie surtout avec des noms pris dans un sens partitif, ou au pluriel indéfini. Exemples :
Guter Wein (Masc.; nominatif), du bon vin
Frische Luft (Fém.) de l'air frais
Helles Bier (Ntre), de la bière blonde (= claire)
Rote Rosen (plur.) des roses rouges

■ **Wir sahen, daß wir keine Sklaven geworden waren.**
La subordonnée introduite par *daß*, que.
Beaucoup de propositions subordonnées sont introduites par *daß*, que. La construction est la même qu'après *weil*, parce que, et qu'après tout autre terme subordonnant : le verbe est rejeté à la fin de la proposition (voir L. 22).

■ **Temps primitifs des verbes forts** (voir L. 20) :
stehen, être debout — *stand, gestanden*
sitzen, être assis — *saß, gesessen*
liegen, être couché — *lag, gelegen*
hängen, être accroché — *hing, gehangen*

Au passé composé, ces verbes prennent l'auxiliaire *haben*. Ex. :

> *Der Wagen hat lange in der Garage gestanden*, la voiture est restée (mot à mot : a été debout) longtemps au garage.

Exercices

A *Complétez les terminaisons de l'adjectif, puis traduisez :*
1. Sie trinken gut... Wein oder frisch... Bier. 2. Er pflanzte rot... Rosen. 3. Bei schön... Wetter machen wir Camping. 4. Hier standen modern... Koffergeräte. 5. Gelb... Äpfel hingen am Baum *(arbre).*

B *Réunissez les deux propositions par* daß, *en supprimant* es, *puis traduisez :*
6. Er will nach Paris fahren; er sagt es. 7. Werner kommt bald; sie schreibt es. 8. Die Sendung wird interessant sein; er glaubt es *(croire).*

C *Traduisez les phrases suivantes puis mettez-les a) au prétérit, b) au passé-composé :*
9. Das Fernsehgerät steht auf dem Tisch. 10. Das Programm liegt daneben. 11. Ich sitze vor dem Radio.

D *Traduisez :*
12. Les avantages étaient plus grands que les inconvénients. 13. Est-il vrai (wahr) que vous n'ayez pas regardé la pièce de théâtre? 14. Avez-vous l'impression que ce film est vieux?

Corrigé :

A 1. guten; frisches. *Ils boivent du bon vin ou de la bière fraîche.* 2. rote. *Il plantait des roses rouges.* 3. schönem. *Par beau temps nous faisons du camping.* 4. moderne. *Il y avait là (debout) des postes portatifs modernes.* 5. gelbe. *Des pommes jaunes étaient (suspendues) à l'arbre.*

B 6. Er sagt, daß er nach Paris fahren will. *Il dit qu'il veut aller à Paris.* 7. Sie schreibt, daß Werner bald kommt. *Elle écrit que Werner viendra bientôt.* 8. Er glaubt, daß die Sendung interessant sein wird. *Il croit que l'émission sera intéressante.*

C 9. *Le poste de télévision est sur la table* a) Das Fernsehgerät stand... b) Das Fernsehgerät hat... gestanden. 10. *Le programme se trouve à côté* a) Das Programm lag... b) Das Programm hat... gelegen. 11. *Je suis assis devant la radio a) Ich saß... b) Ich habe... gesessen.*

D 12. Die Vorteile waren größer als die Nachteile. 13. Ist es wahr, daß Sie sich das Theaterstück nicht angesehen haben? 14. Haben Sie den Eindruck, daß dieser Film alt ist?

Leçon

24 *Kurznachrichten

1 Herr Müller kauft jeden Morgen seine *Zeitung bei der Z**ei**tungsfr**au**.
Er *erf**ä**hrt so 'allerlei Nachrichten über Politi**k**, Sport, *usw (und so weiter).
Heute morgen las er schnell einige K**u**rzn**a**chrichten.

2 — Bonn — Der britische *Botschafter in der *Bundesrepublik hat die Insel Helgoland als ein *Symb**o**l der *Fr**eu**ndschaft zwischen Gr**o**ßbrit**a**nnien und Deutschland bez**ei**chnet.
Er überr**ei**chte dem B**ü**rgerm**ei**ster zwei Bände mit *Kop**i**en von Dokum**e**nten.
Diese stammen aus der Zeit, wo die Insel unter britischer *Verw**a**ltung stand.

3 Einbruch in der *Hauptstraße. — Gestern gegen 23 Uhr drangen *Diebe in die Wohnung des Herrn *Meyer.
Sie entwendeten *Kleidungsst**ü**cke im Wert von *ca 800 DM (circa **a**chth**u**ndert Deutsche Mark).
Man weiß noch nicht, wie sie in die Wohnung dringen konnten.

1 [k**ou**rtç-narrichten']; [tç**a**étou[ng]]; [èrf**è**rt]; [chport]; [oun't zo v**a**éter].

2 [b**o**tchafter]; [b**ou**ndeçrépoubl**i**k]; [zumb**o**l]; [fr**oe**untchaft]; [gr**o**çbrit**a**ni-en']; [kop**i**-en']; [fèrv**a**ltou[ng]].

3 [h**a**opt-chtr**a**çe]; [d**i**be]; [m**a**yer]; [kl**a**édou[ng]ç-cht**u**ke]; [tç**i**rka].

GELD VERLOREN, NICHTS VERLOREN

Traduction

Nouvelles brèves

1 Monsieur Müller achète chaque matin son journal chez la marchande de journaux. Il apprend ainsi toutes sortes d'informations sur la politique, les sports, etc. Ce matin, il lut rapidement quelques nouvelles brèves.

2 — Bonn — L'ambassadeur britannique en République fédérale a désigné l'île d'Héligoland comme un symbole de l'amitié entre la Grande-Bretagne et l'Allemagne. Il a remis au maire deux volumes avec des copies de documents; ceux-ci datent de l'époque où l'île était placée sous administration britannique.

3 Cambriolage dans la grand'rue. — Hier, vers 23 heures, des voleurs se sont introduits dans l'appartement de Monsieur Meyer. Ils dérobèrent des effets vestimentaires d'une valeur approximative de 800 DM. On ne sait pas encore comment ils ont pu pénétrer dans l'appartement.

Vocabulaire

der Band (¨ e), *le volume*
der B**o**tschafter (-), *l'ambassadeur*
der Bund (¨ e), *l'alliance*
der B**ü**rgermeister (-), *le maire*
der Dieb (e), *le voleur*
der **E**inbruch (¨ e), *le cambriolage*
der Wert (-e), *la valeur*
die Fr**eu**ndschaft (en), *l'amitié*
die **I**nsel (n), *l'île*
die Republ**i**k (en), *la république*

die Kl**ei**dung (en), *l'habillement*
die Kop**i**e (n), *la copie*
die N**a**chricht (-en), *l'information*
die Verw**a**ltung (en), *l'administration*
die Zeit (-en), *le temps, l'époque*
die Z**ei**tung (-en), *le journal*
das Symb**o**l (-e), *le symbole*
bez**ei**chnen, *désigner*
entw**e**nden, *dérober*
st**a**mmen aus, *provenir de*
überr**ei**chen, *remettre*
dr**i**ngen (a, u) in, *pénétrer dans*
erf**a**hren (u, a, ä), *apprendre*

Plaie d'argent n'est pas mortelle (argent perdu, rien perdu)

Grammaire

■ Man weiß es noch nicht.

Le verbe *wissen,* savoir.
La conjugaison de ce verbe ressemble à celle des auxiliaires de mode (voir L. 18 à 20).

Présent		Prétérit
ich weiß, je sais	*wir wissen*	*ich wußte,* je sus, je savais
du weißt	*ihr wißt*	
er (sie, es) weiß	*sie (Sie) wissen*	Participe passé
		gewußt

■ Man weiß noch nicht, wie sie in die Wohnung dringen konnten.

Après *wie,* comme, conjonction de subordination, on fait également le rejet du verbe. Son emploi est plus fréquent qu'en français, surtout après des verbes comme *hören,* entendre, *sehen,* voir, *fühlen,* sentir. Exemples :

> *Ich höre, wie der Wagen abfährt,* j'entends comme la voiture démarre = j'entends la voiture démarrer.
> *Ich sehe, wie er ein Paket bringt,* je vois comme il apporte un colis = je le vois apporter un colis.

■ Gegen 23 Uhr drangen sie in die Wohnung.

L'heure.
Questions : a) *Wieviel Uhr ist es?* Quelle heure est-il? b) *Um wieviel Uhr kam er?* A quelle heure vint-il?

I	II
es ist acht Uhr il est huit heures *es ist zwanzig Uhr* il est vingt heures	*es ist acht Uhr zehn (Minuten)* il est huit heures dix *es ist zehn Minuten nach acht*
III	**IV**
es ist ein Viertel nach acht il est huit heures un quart *es ist acht Uhr fünfzehn* il est 8 heures 15	*es ist halb neun* il est huit heures et demie *es ist zwanzig Uhr dreißig* il est 20 heures 30
V	**VI**
es ist drei Viertel neun il est neuf heures moins le quart *es ist 20 Uhr 45* il est 20 heures 45	*es ist fünf Minuten vor neun* il est neuf heures moins cinq *es ist 20 Uhr 55* il est 20 heures 55

um sechs Uhr, à six heures; *gegen vier Uhr,* vers 4 heures.

Exercices

A a) *Wieviel Uhr ist es? (Donnez les réponses en toutes lettres).* 1. *6 h.* 2. *7 h 1/2.* 3. *9 h 1/4.* 4. *9 h 3/4.* 5. *3 h 10.* 6. *11 h 40.*
b) *Traduisez :* 7. *à 4 h 1/2.* 8. *vers 10 h 3/4.*

B *Reliez les deux propositions par* wie, *comment, en supprimant* es, *puis traduisez :*
9. Sie werden kommen; wir wissen es noch nicht. 10. Es wurde kälter; man fühlte es. 11. Sie arbeiten schnell und sauber; wir sehen es. 12. Die Kinder singen im Garten; wir hören es.

C *Traduisez :*
13. Cette île est un symbole de l'amitié entre deux grands pays. 14. Fritz ne savait pas qu'Héligoland était longtemps placé (verbe *stehen*) sous administration britannique. 15. Heinz lui explique (*erklären*) comment (l')Allemagne a acheté cette île.

Corrigé :

A a) 1. Es ist sechs Uhr. 2. Es ist halb acht. 3. Es ist Viertel nach neun. 4. Es ist drei Viertel zehn. 5. Es ist zehn Minuten nach drei (oder : drei Uhr zehn). 6. Es ist zwanzig Minuten vor zwölf (oder : elf Uhr vierzig). b) 7. um halb fünf. 8. gegen drei Viertel elf.

B 9. Wir wissen noch nicht, wie sie kommen werden. *Nous ne savons pas encore comment ils viendront.* 10. Man fühlte, wie es kälter wurde. *On sentait qu'il faisait (mot à mot : comment il devenait) plus froid.* 11. Wir sehen, wie sie schnell und sauber arbeiten. *Nous les voyons travailler vite et proprement (mot à mot : comment ils travaillent...).* 12. Wir hören, wie die Kinder im Garten singen. *Nous entendons les enfants chanter au jardin.*

C 13. Diese Insel ist ein Symbol der Freundschaft zwischen zwei großen Ländern. 14. Fritz wußte nicht, daß Helgoland lange unter britischer Verwaltung stand. 15. Heinz erklärt ihm, wie Deutschland diese Insel gekauft hat.

Leçon

25 Eine angenehme *Überraschung

1 Die Woche hat sieben Tage. Sie heißen : *Sonntag, Montag, Dienstag, Mittwoch, Donnerstag, Freitag, Samstag.
Heute ist Samstag (man sagt auch : S**o**nn**a**bend) und der Kongreß geht zu Ende.
Morgen soll Paul Dumont nach Paris zur**ü**ckf**a**hren.

2 Aber da bringt Herr Müller ein kurzes Schreiben des *Gener**a**ldir**e**ktors der IMEX :
Das *Zentr**a**lbür**o** in M**ü**nchen braucht einen franz**ö**sischen *M**i**t**a**rbeiter.
Er fragt, ob Paul Dumont diese *Stelle **a**nn**e**hmen möchte.
Paul Dumont ist noch jung und ***u**nverh**ei**ratet.
Mit Freude nimmt er das Angebot an.

3 Er wird noch schnell einige ***A**ngel**e**genheiten in Par**i**s besorgen.
Wenn es möglich ist, wird er schon am Donnerstag nach München **a**bf**a**hren.
Dann wird eine neue *Phase in seinem Leben beg**i**nnen.
Zugl**ei**ch will er meth**o**disch das *Studium der deutschen Sprache *f**o**rts**e**tzen.

1 [uber**a**chou[ng]]; [z**o**n'tak]; [m**o**n'tak]; [d**i**n'çtak]; [m**i**tvor]; [d**o**nerçtak]; [fr**a**étak]; [z**a**m'çtak]; [z**o**n'-aben't].

2 [génér**a**ldir**è**ktorç]; [tçèntr**a**lburo]; [m**i**t-**a**rbaéter]; [cht**è**le]; [**ou**n'fèrh**a**ératet].

3 [**a**n'gél**é**gen'haéten]; [f**a**ze]; [cht**ou**dioum']; [f**o**rt-z**è**tçen'].

FRISCH GEWAGT IST HALB GEWONNEN

Traduction

Une surprise agréable

1 La semaine a sept jours. Ils s'appellent : dimanche, lundi, mardi, mercredi, jeudi, vendredi, samedi. Aujourd'hui, c'est samedi (on dit aussi : « Sonnabend ») et le congrès s'achève. Demain, Paul Dumont doit retourner à Paris.

2 Mais voilà que Monsieur Müller apporte une courte lettre du directeur général de l'IMEX : Le bureau central à Munich a besoin d'un collaborateur français. Il demande si Paul Dumont voudrait accepter ce poste. Paul Dumont est encore jeune et célibataire. C'est avec joie qu'il accepte l'offre.

3 Il réglera rapidement encore quelques affaires à Paris. Si (c'est) possible, il partira dès jeudi pour Munich. Alors commencera une nouvelle phase de sa vie. En même temps, il va poursuivre méthodiquement l'étude de la langue allemande.

Vocabulaire

der Dir**e**ktor (s; en), *le directeur*
der M**i**t**a**rbeiter (-), *le collaborateur*
die **A**ngel**e**genheit (-en), *l'affaire*
die Phase (n), *la phase*
die Stelle (n), *l'endroit*
die Überr**a**schung (-en), *la surprise*
das **A**ngebot (-e), *l'offre*
das Bür**o** (s), *le bureau*
das Ende (s, n), *la fin*
abl**e**hnen, *refuser*
bes**o**rgen, *régler*
brauchen (+ acc.) *avoir besoin de*
h**ei**raten, *épouser*
überr**a**schen, *surprendre*
ann**e**hmen (a, o; i), *accepter* (V. 7,3 : remarque importante)

Exercice sur les mots
Traduisez : 1. *Il me surprend, me surprit, me surprendra, m'a surpris.* 2. *Nous aurons besoin de...* 3. *Un poste, d'un poste, les postes.* 4. *Il est au (= dans le) bureau.* 5. *Il va au bureau.*
Corrigé : 1. Er überrascht mich, überraschte mich, wird mich überraschen, hat mich überrascht. 2. Wir werden... brauchen. 3. Eine Stelle, einer Stelle, die Stellen. 4. Er ist im Büro. 5. Er geht ins Büro.

La fortune sourit aux audacieux (Hardiment osé, à demi gagné).

Grammaire

■ Er bringt ein kurzes Schreiben.

La déclinaison mixte de l'adjectif.

● Quand l'adjectif est précédé de l'article indéfini *ein,* il suit une « déclinaison mixte ».

	Masc.	Fém.	Neutre	Pluriel
N.	*ein gut**er***	*eine gut**e***	*ein gut**es***	*gut**e***
G.	*eines guten*	*einer guten*	*eines guten*	*gut**er***
D.	*einem guten*	*einer guten*	*einem guten*	*gut**en***
A.	*einen gut**en***	*eine gut**e***	*ein gut**es***	*gut**e***

Remarque : Comparez cette déclinaison à la déclinaison faible (L. 21) et à la silhouette de la clé.

● Au singulier, la déclinaison mixte de l'adjectif s'emploie également après les possessifs (*mein, dein,* etc.; voir L. 7) et après l'article négatif (*kein;* voir L. 3).
Au pluriel, après les possessifs (*meine, deine,* etc.) ou l'article négatif (*keine*), on emploie la déclinaison faible. Exemples :

> Singulier : *mein kurzer Brief* (décl. mixte). Pluriel : *meine kurzen Briefe* (décl. faible).

■ Er fragt, ob er diese Stelle annehmen möchte. – Wenn es möglich ist...

Les conjonctions *ob* et *wenn*
Ob traduit notre « si » interrogatif ou dubitatif (je me demande si, je ne sais si...), tandis que *wenn* traduit le « si » conditionnel.

Autres exemples :

> *Weißt du, ob dein Freund kommen wird?* sais-tu, si ton ami viendra?
> *Wenn du kommst, gebe ich dir diesen Brief,* si tu viens, je te donnerai cette lettre.

Ces conjonctions exigent le rejet du verbe.

■ Er besorgt noch einige Angelegenheiten.

Les particules inséparables (cf. L 19, grammaire I).
Besorgen est composé du verbe simple *sorgen* et de la particule inséparable *be-.* Les particules inséparables sont : *be - emp - ent - er - ge - miß - ver - zer.* Ces particules ne sont jamais accentuées; elles restent toujours soudées au verbe; elles entraînent la suppression de *ge* au participe passé.

Exercices

A *Complétez les terminaisons de l'adjectif, puis traduisez :*
1. Man macht ihm ein schön... Angebot. 2. Es ist ein groß... Tag für ihn. 3. Mit einer neu... Stelle beginnt ein neu... Leben. 4. Er besorgt noch eine klein... Angelegenheit. 5. Er hat einen jung... Mitarbeiter.

B *Complétez par* ob *ou* wenn, *puis traduisez :*
6. Ich frage mich, ... diese Stelle interessant ist. 7. Ich nehme das Angebot an, ... Sie mir eine Wohnung geben. 8. Ich möchte wissen, ... München weit von Köln liegt. 9. ... es regnet, werden wir zu Hause bleiben. 10. Ich sehe dich nächstes Jahr wieder, ... du nach Köln kommst.

C *Traduisez :*
11. Si vous avez besoin d'un bon collaborateur, écrivez-moi. 12. Savez-vous, si le congrès s'achève? 13. Pouvez-vous me dire, si ce poste est encore vacant (= *offen*)? 14. Il ne viendra pas, si le temps n'est pas beau.

Corrigé :

A 1. schönes. *On lui fait une belle offre.* 2. großer. *C'est pour lui une grande journée.* 3. neuen; neues. *Avec un poste nouveau, une vie nouvelle commence.* 4. kleine. *Il règle encore une petite affaire.* 5. jungen. *Il a un jeune collaborateur.*

B 6. ob. *Je me demande, si ce poste est intéressant.* 7. wenn. *J'accepte l'offre, si vous me donnez un appartement.* 8. ob. *Je voudrais savoir, si Munich se trouve loin de Cologne.* 9. Wenn. *S'il pleut, nous resterons à la maison.* 10. Wenn. *Je te reverrai (mot à mot : revois) l'année prochaine, si tu viens à Cologne.*

C 11. Wenn Sie einen guten Mitarbeiter brauchen, schreiben Sie mir. 12. Wissen Sie, ob der Kongreß zu Ende geht? 13. Können Sie mir sagen, ob diese Stelle noch offen ist? 14. Er wird nicht kommen (ou : er kommt nicht), wenn das Wetter nicht schön ist.

Leçon

26

Der Wagen

1 Der Fahrer *zieht den *Starter : er läßt den Motor an. Dann kuppelt er aus und drückt auf das Gaspedal (er gibt Gas). Er schaltet den ersten Gang ein und kuppelt langsam ein; der Wagen fährt an. Nach und nach fährt der Wagen schneller. Dann schaltet der Fahrer um, er schaltet in den zweiten Gang ein, dann in den dritten, zuletzt in den vierten.

2 Nun will der Fahrer den Motor abstellen. Er *bremst, kuppelt aus und stellt auf *Leerlauf. Er muß noch den Zündschlüssel drehen und die Handbremse anziehen. Dies alles scheint recht *kompliziert zu sein, aber es ist wirklich nicht schwer, ein Auto zu fahren.

3 Ich persönlich habe die Wagen mit vier Türen am liebsten. Der meine ist ziemlich groß : sechs Personen können darin Platz nehmen. Im Kofferraum, hinten, habe ich immer einen Reservekanister mit Öl, nebst dem *Ersatzrad.
Letzthin habe ich die Räder kreuzweise austauschen lassen : das rechte Vorderrad hat man hinten links angebracht. Aber nun ist das linke Blinklicht außer Betrieb, und die Scheibenwischer quietschen. In der nächsten Autogarage will ich den Wagen abschmieren lassen.

Attention : Des leçons 26 à 75, la voyelle tonique continuera à être marquée en caractère gras pour les mots nouveaux ou pour ceux en ayant deux (verbe à particule séparable, mot composé) à la rubrique vocabulaire seulement. Dans la prononciation figurée, nous continuerons toujours à employer les caractères gras pour les voyelles toniques.

1 [tçit] [cht**a**rter]. **2** [brèm'çt]; [l**é**rl**a**of]; [kom'plitç**i**rt]. **3** [èrz**a**tç-rat].

PROBIEREN GEHT ÜBER STUDIEREN

Traduction

La voiture

1 Le conducteur tire le démarreur; il met le moteur en marche. Puis il débraie et agit sur l'accélérateur. Il met le levier de vitesse en première et embraie lentement : la voiture démarre. Peu à peu, la voiture prend de la vitesse. Alors, le conducteur change de vitesse, il passe en seconde, puis en troisième, enfin en quatrième.

2 A présent, le conducteur veut arrêter le moteur. Il freine, débraie et met au point mort. Il doit encore tourner la clef de contact et mettre (tirer) le frein à main. Tout cela semble bien compliqué, mais il n'est vraiment pas difficile de conduire une voiture.

3 Personnellement je préfère les voitures à quatre portes. La mienne est assez grande : six personnes peuvent y prendre place. Dans la malle arrière, j'ai toujours un bidon d'huile en réserve, avec la roue de secours. Dernièrement, j'ai fait croiser les roues : la roue avant droite est passée roue arrière gauche (m. à m. : on a mis...). Mais maintenant, le clignotant gauche ne marche pas, et les essuie-glaces grincent. Au prochain garage, je ferai graisser la voiture.

Prononciation

Le **v** allemand se prononce [f] : *vier, Vorderrad; Vater; verbringen; viel.* Mais dans les mots étrangers, l'on garde la prononciation [v]. Exemple : *Vase, Violine, November, Reserve.*

Vocabulaire

außer Betr**ie**b, *hors service*
der Ers**a**tz, *le succédané*
der Gang (¨e), *la vitesse*
der Kan**i**ster (-), *le bidon*
der K**o**fferr**au**m, *la malle*
der L**ee**rlauf, *le point mort*
der M**o**tor (s, en) *le moteur*
abst**e**llen, *arrêter (moteur)*
ausk**u**ppeln, *débrayer*
br**e**msen, *freiner*
dr**ü**cken, *presser*
eink**u**ppeln, *embrayer*
einsch**a**lten, *mettre en prise*
umsch**a**lten, *changer de vitesse*
der Sch**ei**benw**i**scher (-), *l'essuie-glace*
der Z**ü**ndschl**ü**ssel (-), *la clef de contact*

Expérience passe science (essayer est supérieur à étudier)

die Br**e**mse (n), *le frein*
die Hand (‥ e), *la main*
das Bl**i**nklicht (-er), *le clignotant*

anlassen (ie, a, ä), *mettre en marche*
anfahren (u, a, ä), *démarrer*
anhalten (ie, a, ä), *s'arrêter*

Grammaire

■ Es ist wirklich nicht schwer, Auto zu fahren.
L'infinitif complément *(fahren)* est précédé de *zu* et se place à la fin de la proposition. Dans les verbes à particule séparable, *zu* s'intercale entre la particule et l'infinitif :

*Er vergißt nicht aus**zu**kuppeln,* il n'oublie pas de débrayer.

On emploie *zu* même après des verbes qui, en français, ont un infinitif complément direct. Exemple :

*Er glaubt, etwas im Motor **zu** hören,* il croit entendre quelque chose dans le moteur.

■ Er muß die Bremse anziehen.
L'infinitif complément n'est pas précédé de *zu* quand il dépend d'un auxiliaire de mode (voir L. 18, 19, 20), ou de l'un des verbes suivants : *lehren,* enseigner — *lernen,* apprendre — *heißen,* ordonner — *helfen,* aider — *sehen,* voir — *hören,* entendre — *lassen,* laisser — *machen,* faire. Exemple :

Er lernt Auto fahren, il apprend à conduire.

Exercices

A *Formez des phrases au présent, puis traduisez :*
1. Er — wollen — der Kofferraum — auf/machen, *ouvrir.* 2. Du — immer vergessen — an/ziehen — die Handbremse. 3. Hier — er — können — fahren — schnell. 4. Es — scheinen, *sembler* — regnen.

B *Traduisez :*
5. Passez-vous souvent en quatrième vitesse? 6. C'est une joie (que) de rouler dans cette voiture neuve. 7. Il voulait s'arrêter, mais il ne pouvait plus freiner. 8. Il espère trouver un garage.

Corrigé :

A Er will den Kofferraum aufmachen. *Il veut ouvrir la malle.* 2. Du vergißt immer, die Handbremse anzuziehen. *Tu oublies toujours de serrer le frein à main.* 3. Hier kann er schnell fahren. *Il peut rouler vite, ici.* 4. Es scheint ***zu*** regnen. *Il semble pleuvoir.*

B 5. Schalten Sie oft den vierten Gang ein? 6. Es ist eine Freude, in diesem neuen Wagen zu fahren. 7. Er wollte anhalten, aber er konnte nicht mehr bremsen. 8. Er hofft, eine Garage zu finden.

Lecture

Appel an die einheimischen Autofahrer

Jetzt in der Urlaubszeit werden die Städte vor fast unlösbare Probleme gestellt. Ortsunkundige Autofahrer suchen im dichten Verkehrsgewühl den richtigen Weg, verirren sich im Labyrinth der Umleitungen, werden nervös und stören so den Verkehr in den Innenstädten.
Der Automobilclub von Deutschland (AvD) appelliert daher an die einheimischen Kraftfahrer, beim Erkennen von fremden Autokennzeichen den ortsunkundigen Fahrern gegenüber Höflichkeit zu üben. Oft genügt schon eine kleine Geste, ein kurzer Zuruf an der Ampel, um sich mit dem Wegsuchenden zu verständigen. Jeder ortsfremde Automobilist wird diesen Kameradschaftsdienst mit großer Dankbarkeit honorieren, und die Stadt, in der ihm diese Hilfe zuteil wurde, in guter Erinnerung behalten.

Aus der Tageszeitung « Gmünder Tagespost »

Appel aux automobilistes de la région

Actuellement, dans la saison des vacances, les villes sont placées devant des problèmes presque insolubles. Des automobilistes ne connaissant pas les lieux cherchent le bon chemin dans la cohue de la circulation, s'égarent dans le labyrinthe des déviations et s'énervent, gênant ainsi la circulation dans le centre des villes.
C'est pourquoi l' « Automobile-Club d'Allemagne » lance un appel aux conducteurs de la région, en les priant — lorsqu'ils reconnaissent une immatriculation étrangère — de faire preuve de courtoisie à l'égard des automobilistes qui ne connaissent pas les lieux. Souvent, il suffit d'un petit geste seulement, d'une brève explication donnée devant les feux, pour se faire entendre de celui qui cherche son chemin. Tout automobiliste étranger à la région se montrera très reconnaissant pour ce service amical et il gardera un bon souvenir de la ville, dans laquelle il a reçu cette aide.

Extrait du quotidien « Gmünder Tagespost »

Leçon
27
An der *Tankstelle

1 — Was nehmen Sie, *gewöhnliches *Benzin oder *Super?
— Super. Volltanken, bitte! Prüfen Sie auch Öl und Reifendruck nach! Wollen Sie bitte die Scheiben reinigen!
— Noch etwas, bitte?
— Das wäre alles für heute. Ich bringe Ihnen den Wagen am nächsten Samstag zum Waschen und auch für den *Ölwechsel. So, und was kostet das?
— Achtundzwanzig Mark fünfzig.
— Hier, bitte.
— Haben Sie kein Kleingeld?
— Nein, ich komme gerade über die *Grenze; ich habe nur diesen Hundert-Mark-Schein.
— Einen Augenblick, bitte!

2 Als Paul nach *Ulm kam, bat er um *Auskunft :
— Ich möchte zum *Verkehrsverein fahren. Welches ist der richtige Weg?
— Fahren Sie geradeaus. Ungefähr hundert Meter von hier kommen Sie an eine Kreuzung. Sie sehen ein Sportgeschäft. Dort biegen Sie nach rechts ein. Sie folgen der Straße, bis sie zur *Einbahnstraße wird. So kommen Sie direkt auf den Münsterplatz und sehen den Verkehrsverein vor sich. Es ist achthundert Meter von hier entfernt.
Paul *besichtigte lange das schöne Ulm.

1 [**ta**^{ng}k-cht**è**le]; [géve**eu**nlicheç]; [bèntç**i**n]; [**zou**per]; [**eu**lvèkçel]; [grèntçe].

2 [oulm']; [**a**oçkoun'ft]; [fèrk**é**rç-fer**a**én']; [**a**én'-ban'-chtr**a**çe]; [bé**zi**chtichte].

WER RASTET DER ROSTET

Traduction

Au poste à essence

1 — Que prenez-vous, de l'essence ordinaire ou du super? — Du super. (Faites) le plein, s'il vous plaît. Vérifiez également l'huile et la pression. Veuillez nettoyer les glaces — Autre chose encore, s'il vous plaît? — C'est (ce serait) tout pour aujourd'hui. Je vous apporterai la voiture samedi prochain, pour le lavage et aussi pour la vidange. Bon, et combien cela fait (coûte)-il? — 28 Mark 50 — Voici, s'il vous plaît — N'avez-vous pas de monnaie? — Non, je viens de passer la frontière; je n'ai que ce billet de 100 marks. — Un instant, s'il vous plaît!

2 Quand Paul arriva à Ulm, il demanda un renseignement :
— Je voudrais me rendre au Syndicat d'Initiative. Quel est le bon chemin? — Suivez (roulez) tout droit. A 100 mètres à peu près d'ici, vous arriverez à un carrefour. Vous verrez un magasin d'articles de sport. Là, vous prendrez (tournerez) à droite. Vous suivrez cette route jusqu'à ce qu'elle devienne à sens unique. Ainsi, vous arriverez directement sur la place de la Cathédrale et vous verrez devant vous le Syndicat d'Initiative. C'est à 800 mètres (distant) d'ici.
Paul visita longtemps la belle ville d'Ulm.

Vocabulaire

der Augenblick (-e), *le clin d'œil, l'instant*
der Druck, *la pression*
der Reifen (-), *le pneu*
der Schein (-e), *la lueur, l'aspect, le billet*
der Verkehr, *la circulation*
der Verk**e**hrsver**e**in (e) *le syndicat d'initiative*
der Weg (-e), *le chemin*
die Bahn (-en), *la voie*
die Bank (¨ e), *le banc*
die Scheibe (n), *la glace*
die T**a**nkst**e**lle (n), *le poste à essence*
die W**i**ndschutzsch**ei**be (n), *le pare-brise*
der Wind (e), *le vent;*
der Schutz, *la protection*
das Geld (er), *l'argent*
das Kl**ei**ngeld, *la monnaie, les pièces*
nachpr**ü**fen, *vérifier*
reinigen, *nettoyer*

Qui s'arrête, se rouille

die **Ei**nbahnstr**a**ße (n), *la voie à sens unique*
die Grenze (n), *la frontière*
die Kreuzung (-en), *le carrefour*
v**o**lltanken, *faire le plein*
wechseln, *changer*
einb**ie**gen (o, o) *tourner dans...*
waschen (u, a, ä), *laver*

Grammaire

■ Als er nach Ulm kam...

Wenn et *als* (quand).
Pour traduire notre « quand » (ou « lorsque »), on emploie :

- *Wenn,* quand le verbe est au présent ou au futur, et au passé pour une action répétée ou durable.
- *Als* pour un verbe au passé, quand il s'agit d'un fait unique.

Remarque : Cette différence se marque en français par le temps du verbe :
Als er kam = quand il vint; fait unique, passé simple.
Wenn er kam = quand il venait, toutes les fois qu'il venait; fait répété, imparfait.
Exemples :

Wenn die Sonne aufgeht..., quand le soleil se lève.
Wenn die Sonne aufgehen wird..., quand le soleil se lèvera.
Wenn die Sonne aufging, schliefen die Kinder noch, quand (toutes les fois que) le soleil se levait, les enfants dormaient encore.
Als die Sonne aufging, waren sie schon zur Abfahrt bereit, quand (= au moment où) le soleil se leva, ils étaient déjà prêts pour le départ.

■ Es ist achthundert Meter von hier entfernt.

C'est à 800 m (distant) d'ici.
L'adjectif *entfernt* (éloigné, distant de) a pour complément *achthundert Meter von hier.* Le complément se place avant l'adjectif. Exemple :

Der Kölner Dom ist 156 m (hundertsechsundfünfzig Meter) hoch, la cathédrale de Cologne est haute de 156 m.

Exercices

A *Transformez la première proposition en subordonnée introduite par* wenn *ou* als, *puis traduisez :*
1. Kurt hatte Zeit; er ging oft spazieren. 2. Er kam um 15 Uhr; der Unfall war schon geschehen *(arrivé).* 3. Es regnet; wir ziehen einen Regenmantel an. 4. Wir sind müde; wir gehen früh zu Bett. 5. Er kam zum ersten Mal nach Köln; er fand die Straße nicht.

B *Traduisez :*
6. Ein sechs Meter langes Auto stand vor dem Hotel. 7. Auf dem Berg sah man einen 120 m hohen Turm. 8. Sein Schwesterchen ist zwei Jahre alt.

C *Traduisez :*
9. Quand vous faites le plein, le pompiste nettoie les glaces. 10. Si vous avez un gros billet, il ira vous chercher de la monnaie. 11. Quand Werner arriva au croisement, il aperçut le Syndicat d'initiative. 12. Avez-vous trouvé son ami, quand vous étiez en Allemagne?

Corrigé :

A 1. Wenn Kurt Zeit hatte, ging er oft spazieren. *Quand Kurt avait le temps, il allait souvent se promener.* 2. Als er um 15 Uhr kam, war der Unfall schon geschehen. *Quand il est venu, à 15 heures, l'accident était déjà arrivé.* 3. Wenn es regnet, ziehen wir einen Regenmantel an. *Quand il pleut, nous mettons un imperméable.* 4. Wenn wir müde sind, gehen wir früh zu Bett. *Quand nous sommes fatigués, nous allons au lit de bonne heure.* 5. Als er zum ersten Mal nach Köln kam, fand er die Straße nicht. *Quand il arriva à Cologne pour la première fois, il ne trouva pas la rue.*

B 6. *Une voiture longue de 6 m se trouvait devant l'hôtel.* 7. *Sur la montagne, on voyait une tour haute de 120 m.* 8. *Sa petite sœur a deux ans (mot à mot : est de deux ans âgée).*

C 9. Wenn Sie volltanken, reinigt der Tankwart die Scheiben. 10. Wenn Sie einen großen Schein haben, holt er Ihnen Kleingeld. 11. Als Werner an die Kreuzung kam, erblickte er den Verkehrsverein. 12. Haben Sie seinen Freund gefunden, als Sie in Deutschland waren?

Leçon

28 Das *Flugzeug

1 Um mit dem Flugzeug zu reisen, muß man einen Flugschein lösen. Diese *Fahrkarte kann für die einfache Fahrt sein.
Man kann aber auch eine Rückfahrkarte kaufen, oder eine *Rundreise-Fahrkarte; dafür bekommt man oft eine *Ermäßigung.

2 Gewöhnlich reserviert man seinen Platz, wenn man die Flugkarte kauft. Jede bedeutende *Fluggesellschaft hat ihr eigenes Büro in den großen Städten.
Aber man kann sich auch an jedes beliebige Reisebüro wenden, denn jedes Reisebüro kann Fahrscheine für alle *Luftlinien beschaffen.

3 Es gibt zwei Klassen : eine Touristenklasse und eine erste Klasse. Gewöhnlich hat man zwanzig oder dreißig Kilo *Freigepäck. Der Tarif für das Übergepäck hängt von der *Entfernung ab. Der Reisende kann sich direkt zum Flughafen begeben, wo er sein Gepäck aufgibt.
Ein Gepäckwagen (oder Gepäckwägelchen) bringt die Koffer zum Flugzeug.

1 [fl**ou**ktç**o**euk]; [f**a**rk**a**rte]; [r**ou**n't-r**a**éze]; [èrm**è**çigou[ng]].

2 [fl**ou**k-gez**è**lchaft]; [l**ou**ft-l**i**nyen'].

3 [fr**a**égép**è**k]; [èn'tf**è**rnou[ng]].

JEDES DING HAT ZWEI SEITEN

Traduction

L'avion

1 Pour voyager par avion, il faut prendre un billet (de vol). Ce billet peut être un aller simple. Mais on peut également acheter un billet aller et retour, ou un billet circulaire; alors (mot à mot : pour cela) on obtient souvent une réduction.

2 En général on réserve sa place quand on achète le billet d'avion. Chaque compagnie d'aviation importante a son bureau particulier dans les grandes villes. Mais on peut s'adresser aussi à n'importe quelle agence de voyage, car toute agence de voyage peut procurer les billets pour n'importe quelle ligne (m. à m. : toutes les lignes).

3 Il existe deux classes : une classe touriste et une première classe. Habituellement, on a une franchise de bagages de 20 à 30 kg. Le tarif pour l'excédent de bagages dépend de la distance. Le voyageur peut se rendre directement à l'aéroport, où il fait enregistrer ses bagages. Un charriot à bagages apporte les valises à l'avion.

Vocabulaire

der Flughafen (¨), *l'aéroport*
der Tar**i**f (-e), *le tarif*
die Entf**e**rnung (-en), *la distance*
die Erm**äß**igung (-en), *la réduction*
die Fahrkarte (n), *le billet*
die Ges**e**llschaft (-en), *la société, la compagnie*
die Hinfahrt (-en), *le voyage aller*
die Linie (n), *la ligne*
die Luft (¨e), *l'air*
die R**ü**ckfahrk**a**rte (n), *le billet aller et retour*
die Rundreise (n), *le voyage circulaire*
das Flugzeug (-e), *l'avion*
das Gep**ä**ck (sing.), *les bagages*
das Wägelchen (-), *la charrette*
best**e**llen, *réserver*
sich wenden an (wandte, gewandt), *s'adresser à*
besch**a**ffen, *procurer*
abh**ä**ngen von (i, a; ä), *dépendre de*
aufg**e**ben (a, e; i), *faire enregistrer*
sich beg**e**ben (a, e; i), *se rendre*
bek**o**mmen (a, o), *recevoir*

Toute médaille a son revers (Chaque chose a deux faces)

Grammaire

■ Um mit dem Flugzeug zu reisen...

La proposition infinitive.
Elle peut avoir les quatre formes suivantes :

● *Er ist glücklich, eine Flugreise zu machen,* il est heureux de faire un voyage en avion (*zu,* de, à, + infinitif).

● *Er nimmt eine Rückfahrkarte, um eine Ermäßigung zu bekommen,* il prend un billet aller et retour, pour obtenir une réduction (*um... zu,* pour + infinitif).

● *Er fuhr weg, ohne Abschied zu nehmen,* il partit sans prendre congé (*ohne... zu,* sans + infinitif).

● *Er wollte den Koffer tragen, anstatt ihn aufzugeben,* il voulut porter la valise, au lieu de la faire enregistrer (*anstatt... zu,* au lieu de + infinitif).

■ Jede bedeutende Fluggesellschaft...

Le participe présent.
Il se forme en ajoutant *-d* à l'infinitif : *lachen* > *lachend,* riant; *springen* > *springend,* sautant. Il s'emploie surtout comme adjectif ou comme adverbe. Exemples :

> *Ein glänzendes Flugzeug,* un avion brillant.
> *Sie kam weinend,* elle vint en pleurant.

Pour la traduction de notre « en + participe présent », voir L. 72.

Exercices

A *Réunissez les deux phrases suivantes en une seule; employez selon le cas,* um... zu, ohne... zu, anstatt... zu, *puis traduisez :*
1. Er besichtigte die Stadt; er sah das Museum nicht. 2. Ich gehe in ein Reisebüro; ich will eine Fahrkarte lösen. 3. Der Tankwart reinigte die Scheiben; er sollte den Reifendruck prüfen.

B *Avec le verbe entre parenthèses, formez un participe présent employé comme épithète, puis traduisez :*
4. Das Kind fiel aus dem (fahren) Auto. 5. (singen) Mädchen gingen an uns vorbei. 6. Man hörte ein (dröhnen, *vrombir)* Flugzeug.

Corrigé :

A 1. Er besichtigte..., ohne das Museum zu sehen. *Il visita la ville, sans voir le musée.* 2. Ich gehe..., um eine Fahrkarte zu lösen. *Je vais dans une agence de voyage, pour acheter un billet.* 3. Der Tankwart..., anstatt den Reifendruck zu prüfen. *Le pompiste nettoya les glaces, au lieu de vérifier la pression des pneus.*

B 4. ... aus dem fahrenden Auto. *L'enfant tomba de la voiture en marche* (m. à m. : *roulante*). 5. Singende Mädchen... *Des jeunes filles qui chantaient, passaient devant nous.* 6. ... ein dröhnendes Flugzeug. *On entendait un avion qui vrombissait.*

Lecture

Unfallversicherung der Fluggäste

In allen deutschen Flughäfen sind Automaten für eine Flugunfallversicherung aufgestellt. Die Mindestgebühr einschließlich der Versicherungssteuer beträgt fünf Mark. Man wirft ein Fünfmarkstück in den Automaten und erhält eine fertige Versicherungspolice für die gewählte Versicherungsart. Der ausgefüllte und unterschriebene Antrag wird in den Automaten geworfen, womit der Versicherungsvertrag abgeschlossen ist. Ein Exemplar der Police behält der Fluggast, ein weiteres, im Postkartenformat, schickt er nach Hause, damit auch dort der Nachweis für den Versicherungsabschluß vorliegt.

(Aus der Wochenzeitung « Die Zeit », Hamburg)

Assurance contre les accidents des passagers

Dans tous les aéroports allemands sont installés des distributeurs automatiques d'assurances contre les accidents aériens. La prime minima se monte à cinq marks, y compris l'impôt sur les assurances. On glisse une pièce de cinq marks dans le distributeur et l'on reçoit une police d'assurance toute faite, correspondant à la nature de l'assurance choisie. La demande remplie et signée est glissée dans le distributeur automatique; là-dessus le contrat d'assurance est conclu.
Le passager conserve un exemplaire de la police et il en envoie un autre, du format d'une carte postale, à son domicile, afin qu'il y existe également la preuve de l'assurance contractée.

Leçon

29 Wir reisen mit dem Flugzeug

1 — Ich möchte mit dem Flugzeug nach München. Können Sie mir bitte die *Startzeiten und Fahrpreise angeben?
— Ja, mein Herr. Wann möchten Sie abreisen?
— Am 15. (fünfzehnten) April — Der 15te April ist ein Samstag. Da haben Sie einen *Abflug morgens um 9 Uhr 30, mit der Lufthansa. Ankunft auf dem Münchener Flughafen um 10 Uhr 55. Nachmittags haben Sie einen zweiten Abflug, um 18 Uhr, mit der SABENA. Landung in München 19 Uhr 30.
Während des Flugs wird Ihnen ein Imbiß gereicht.

2 — Können Sie mir den Tarif angeben?
— Ja, sehr gern. Für die Hinfahrt kostet der Flugschein 190 DM (Deutsche Mark) in der Touristenklasse. Die Hin- und Rückfahrkarte kostet 360 DM. Sie hat zwei Monate *Gültigkeit, mit 20 kg (Kilo) Freigepäck pro Person. In der ersten Klasse kostet die Hinreise 240 DM, die Hin -und Rückreise 456 DM, hier haben Sie 30 kg Freigepäck pro Person. Bevor Sie Ihre Rückreise antreten, müssen Sie die Fluggesellschaft *benachrichtigen.

3 — Die Reisenden nach München, Flug *Nummer 183, werden *gebeten, sich am Durchgang 3 einzufinden. Bitte! Flugkarten vorzeigen!

1 [cht**a**rt-tç**a**éten']; [**a**p-flouk].

2 [g**u**ltichkaét]; [bén**a**rrichtigen'].

3 [n**ou**mer]; [géb**é**ten'].

ZEIT IST GELD

Traduction

Nous voyageons par avion

1 – Je voudrais (aller) à Munich en avion. Pouvez-vous me donner les heures de départ et les prix s'il vous plaît? – Oui, Monsieur. Quand désirez-vous partir? – Le 15 avril – Le 15 avril, c'est un samedi.
Ce jour, vous avez un vol le matin à 9 h 30, par la Lufthansa. Arrivée à l'aéroport de Munich à 10 h 55.
L'après-midi, vous avez un deuxième vol à 18 h, avec la Sabena. Atterrissage à Munich à 19 h 30. Pendant le vol on vous servira une collation.

2 – Pouvez-vous m'indiquer le tarif?
– Oui, avec plaisir. En classe touriste, le billet simple coûte 190 DM; le billet aller-retour fait 360 DM. Il a une validité de 2 mois; franchise de bagages 20 kg par personne. En première classe, c'est 240 DM l'aller simple, aller et retour 456 DM, franchise de bagages 30 kg par personne. Avant d'entreprendre le voyage retour, vous devrez en aviser la compagnie aérienne.

3 – Les voyageurs à destination de Munich, vol numéro 183, sont priés de se présenter à la porte (passage) 3. Présentez les cartes d'embarquement, s'il vous plaît!

Prononciation

Prononcez toujours faiblement, et sans l'allonger, la dernière syllabe contenant un *e* atone, par exemple dans *reisen; München; angeben; morgens; kostet; erster; Nummer.*

Vocabulaire

der Abflug (¨e), *le décollage*
der Durchgang (¨e), *le passage*
der Imbiß (-isse), *le goûter, la collation*
die Ankunft (¨e), *l'arrivée*
der Fahrpreis (-e), *le prix du voyage*
die Startzeit (-en), *l'heure de départ (avion)*
ben**a**chrichtigen, *informer*
ang**e**ben (a, e; i), *indiquer*
eine Reise **a**ntr**e**ten (a, e; i), *commencer un voyage*

Le temps, c'est de l'argent

die Bedingung (-en), *la condition*
die Gültigkeit, *la validité*
die Landung (-en), *l'atterrissage*
die Richtung (-en), *la direction*

auftragen (u, a; ä), *servir*
bitten (bat, gebeten), *prier, demander*
einfinden (a, u), *se présenter*
vorzeigen, *présenter (q. q. c.)*

Exercice sur les mots

Traduisez : 1. *Il m'indique; m'indiqua; m'a indiqué; m'indiquera.* 2. *Le bon goûter, un bon goûter.* 3. *Il me demande mon billet de vol.* Corrigé : 1. Er gibt mir ...an; gab mir ...an; hat mir ...angegeben; wird mir ...angeben. 2. Der gute Imbiß, ein guter Imbiß. 3. Er bittet mich um meinen Flugschein.

Grammaire

■ Bevor Sie Ihre Rückreise antreten...

Les conjonctions de subordination *bevor* et *nachdem.*

Bevor, avant que, ainsi que *nachdem,* après que, doivent toujours être suivis d'un sujet et d'un verbe à un mode personnel. Ces conjonctions n'introduisent jamais un infinitif, comme le font les tournures françaises auxquelles elles correspondent : avant de (+ infinitif), après (+ infinitif passé). Exemples :

Bevor ich den Flugschein löse, möchte ich die Preisbedingungen kennen, avant de prendre (mot à mot : avant que je prenne...) le billet (de vol), je voudrais connaître les conditions (de prix).

Nachdem er die Fluggesellschaft benachrichtigt hatte, trat er die Rückreise an, après avoir avisé la compagnie aérienne (m. à m. : après qu'il eut...), il entreprit le voyage retour.

Remarque : Après *nachdem,* le verbe de la subordonnée est au passé composé (principale au présent) ou au plus-que-parfait (principale au passé).

■ Die Reisenden werden gebeten...

L'adjectif et le participe substantivés.

Un adjectif ou un participe (présent ou passé) peut être employé comme nom. Dans ce cas, il prend une majuscule comme le nom, mais il suit la déclinaison des adjectifs (décl. forte : L. 23; décl. faible : L. 21; décl. mixte : L. 25). Exemples :

blind, aveugle, *der Blinde,* l'aveugle, *ein Blinder,* un aveugle.
reisen, voyager, *der Reisende,* le voyageur, *ein Reisender, die Reisenden* (pluriel)
lehren, enseigner, *der Gelehrte,* le savant.

Exercices

A *Transformez la première proposition en subordonnée introduite, selon le sens, par* nachdem *ou* bevor, *puis traduisez :*
1. Er hat gegessen; er geht spazieren. 2. Wir gehen ins Theater; wir machen unsere Arbeit fertig. 3. Du fuhrst zum Flughafen; du hattest einen Flugschein gelöst. 4. Er war in Ulm angekommen; er besichtigte die Stadt.

B *Mettez les phrases au pluriel, puis traduisez :*
5. Der Blinde trug einen weißen Stock (¨ e) *(canne).* 6. Ein Blinder stand am Ausgang. 7. Er fährt die Kranke *(la malade)* nach Hause.

C *Traduisez :*
8. Je voudrais un billet aller-retour pour Berlin. 9. Un voyageur ne s'était pas présenté à (= sur) l'aéroport. 10. Après avoir freiné, le conducteur débraie. 11. Avant de tirer le frein à main, il coupe le contact. 12. Après avoir regardé en arrière (= *zurück*), il ouvrit la porte.

Corrigé :

A Nachdem er gegessen hat, geht er spazieren. *Après avoir mangé (= après qu'il a ...), il va se promener.* 2. Bevor wir ins Theater gehen, machen wir unsere Arbeit fertig. *Avant d'aller au théâtre (= avant que nous ...), nous terminons notre travail.* 3. Bevor du zum Flughafen fuhrst, hattest du einen Flugschein gelöst. *Avant d'aller à l'aéroport, tu avais pris un billet de vol.* 4. Nachdem er in Ulm angekommen war, besichtigte er die Stadt. *Après être arrivé à Ulm, il visita la ville.*

B 5. Die Blinden trugen weiße Stöcke. *Les aveugles portaient des cannes blanches.* 6. Blinde standen an den Ausgängen. *Des aveugles se tenaient aux sorties.* 7. Sie fahren die Kranken nach Hause. *Ils conduisent les malades à la maison.*

C 8. Ich möchte eine Hin- und Rückfahrkarte nach Berlin. 9. Ein Reisender hatte sich nicht auf dem Flughafen eingefunden. 10. Nachdem er gebremst hat, kuppelt der Fahrer aus. 11. Bevor er die Handbremse anzieht, schaltet er aus. 12. Nachdem er zurückgeschaut hatte, machte er die Tür auf.

(Note : Sur les noms de villes et sur certains noms de provinces, l'on forme des adjectifs en -**er**; ils restent invariables et s'écrivent avec une majuscule. Ex. : der Münchener Flughafen.)

Leçon

30 Die *Eisenbahn

1 Man löst die Fahrkarte *entweder auf dem *Bahnhof oder in einem Reisebüro.
Man kann auch eine Platzkarte lösen.
Für die *Vorortszüge reicht es noch, wenn man seine Karte kurz vor der Abfahrt löst.
Die Rückfahrkarten sind mehrere Tage gültig.
Manche Züge sind *zuschlagspflichtig; gewöhnlich sind es Schnellzüge oder *Luxuszüge.

2 Die Nachtzüge haben gewöhnlich einen oder mehrere Liegewagen (erster oder zweiter Klasse). Manchmal haben sie auch Schlafwagen.
Dort hat jedes *Abteil ein Bett, oder zwei *übereinander gestellte Betten und ein Waschbecken (einen Lav**a**bo).

3 *Jemand fragte den *Schaffner : -Können Sie mir sagen, ob dieser Zug einen *Speisewagen hat?
— Natürlich; die meisten großen Züge haben einen.
In einem Pullmanwagen werden Sie *sogar an Ihrem Platz *bedient.

1 [**a**ézen'ban]; [**è**n'tvéder]; [b**a**n'-h**o**f]; [f**o**r-ortç-tç**u**ge]; [tç**ou**chlakç-pfl**i**ch-tich]; [l**ou**kçouç-tç**u**ge].

2 [**a**ptaél]; [**u**ber-aén**a**n'der]; [gecht**è**lte].

3 [y**é**man't]; [ch**a**fner]; [chp**a**éze-vagen]; [zog**a**r]; [bed**i**nt].

BESSER NEIDER ALS MITLEIDER

Traduction

Le chemin de fer

1 On prend son billet soit à la gare, soit dans une agence; on peut également louer sa place. Pour les trains de banlieue, il suffit (encore) de prendre (m. à m. : si l'on prend) son billet peu de temps avant le départ. Les aller et retour sont valables plusieurs jours. Pour certains trains, il faut payer un supplément; ce sont en général des rapides ou des trains de luxe.

2 Les trains de nuit ont en général une ou plusieurs voitures-couchettes (de 1re ou de 2e classe). Parfois ils ont aussi des wagons-lits. Chaque compartiment comporte alors un lit, ou deux lits superposés, et un lavabo.

3 Quelqu'un demanda au contrôleur : — Pouvez-vous me dire, si ce train a un wagon-restaurant? — Naturellement; la plupart des grands trains en ont un.
Dans une voiture Pullman l'on vous sert même à votre place (m. à m. : vous êtes même servi...)

Prononciation

L'*x* allemand, ainsi que le groupe *chs,* se prononcent |ks|.
Exemples : *der Luxus; die Axt,* la hache; *die Kalbshaxe,* le jarret de veau; *der Ochs,* le bœuf; *der Lachs,* le saumon.

Vocabulaire

der Platz (¨e), *la place*
der V**o**rort (-e), *la banlieue*
der Zug (¨e), *le train*
der Z**u**schlag (¨e), *le supplément*
die **Ei**senb**a**hn (en), *le chemin de fer*
die Pflicht (-en), *le devoir l'obligation*
die Sp**ei**se (n), *l'aliment*
das W**a**schb**e**cken (-), *la cuvette*
bed**ie**nen, *servir (quelqu'un)*
ausst**ei**gen (ie, ie), *descendre de voiture*
einst**ei**gen (ie, ie), *monter en voiture*

Exercice sur les mots.
Traduisez : *1. Un train très long. 2. Je monte en voiture; je suis monté en voiture; je montai en voiture; je monterai en voiture. 3. Une place, d'une place, à une place, les places.* Corrigé : 1. Ein sehr langer Zug. 2. Ich steige ein; ich bin eingestiegen; ich stieg ein; ich werde einsteigen. 3. Ein Platz, eines Platzes, einem Platz, die Plätze.

Il vaut mieux faire envie que pitié

Grammaire

■ **Können Sie mir sagen, ob dieser Zug einen Speisewagen hat?**
La subordonnée interrogative.
Ob, si, (dubitatif ou interrogatif), introduit une subordonnée et entraîne donc le rejet du verbe (voir leçon 25).
Les autres interrogatifs, tels que *wer?,* qui?, *was?* quoi?, *wann?* quand?, *wo?* où?, *womit?* avec quoi? etc. peuvent également introduire une interrogation indirecte, avec rejet du verbe.
Exemples :

Ich weiß nicht, ob ich genug Geld habe, je ne sais pas, si j'ai assez d'argent. *Ich weiß nicht, wann er nach Köln gekommen ist,* je ne sais pas, quand il est venu à Cologne.

■ **Jemand fragte den Schaffner...**
Les pronoms indéfinis :

● *man,* on (au datif : *einem,* à l'accusatif *einen*).

Er sieht einen nicht einmal, il ne vous voit même pas.

● *einer,* un, l'un, *keiner,* aucun, se déclinent sur l'article défini.

Keiner will ihm helfen, aucun ne veut l'aider.

● *jemand,* quelqu'un, *niemand* personne.

● *etwas,* quelque chose, *nichts,* rien.

Exercices

A *Remplacez la proposition interrogative par une subordonnée, puis traduisez :*
1. Ich frage meinen Freund : « Was steht in der Zeitung? » 2. Ich frage Hans : « Hast du deine Fahrkarte gelöst? » 3. « Wo wohnt Rainer jetzt? » « Ich weiß es nicht. »

B *Traduisez :*
4. Je me demande quand ce train partira. 5. Je ne sais plus qui m'avait indiqué cette agence de voyage. 6. Paul ne savait (wußte) pas, si son billet était encore valable. 7. Personne n'a voyagé dans le deuxième wagon-lit. 8. Quelqu'un a-t-il vu mon billet aller-retour?

Corrigé :

A 1. Ich frage meinen Freund, was in der Zeitung steht. *Je demande à mon ami ce qu'il y a dans le journal.* 2. Ich frage Hans, ob er seine Fahrkarte gelöst hat. *Je demande à Hans s'il a pris son billet.* 3. Ich weiß nicht, wo Rainer jetzt wohnt. *Je ne sais pas où Rainer habite maintenant.*

B 4. Ich frage mich, wann dieser Zug abfahren wird. 5. Ich weiß nicht mehr, wer mir dieses Reisebüro angegeben hatte. 6. Paul wußte nicht, ob seine Fahrkarte noch gültig war. 7. Niemand ist im zweiten Schlafwagen gereist. 8. Hat jemand meine Rückfahrkarte gesehen?

Lecture

Frühstück im Sonderzug

Der Speisewagen hält für 1 000 Personen in fünfzehn Wagen das Frühstück bereit. Pagen servieren es den Sonderzuggästen auf Wunsch im Abteil, ebenso andere Mahlzeiten, vorläufig allerdings nur kalte Gerichte, jedoch warme Würstchen und Eierspeisen eingeschlossen. Für später sind auch warme Menüs in der Art des Bordservice in Flugzeugen vorgesehen. Aber der Wagen verfügt auch über 30 Plätze für Gäste, die später frühstücken oder außer der Reihe etwas essen und trinken wollen. Der neue Speisewagentyp ist ein Einfall der Reiseunternehmer, der der Bundesbahn zugute kommen wird, weil er geeignet ist, die Sonderzugreise angenehmer zu machen und dadurch mehr Gäste zu gewinnen.

Aus der Wochenzeitung « Die Zeit », Hamburg.

Le petit déjeûner en train spécial

Au wagon-restaurant, on tient prêt le petit déjeûner pour un millier de personnes dans quinze wagons. Des garçons le servent aux clients du train spécial dans leur compartiment, si ceux-ci le désirent (m. à m. : sur souhait); ils leur servent également d'autres repas, mais pour l'instant des plats froids seulement, ajoutons-y toutefois des saucisses chaudes et des œufs (m. à m. : des mets aux œufs). Pour plus tard, on prévoit aussi (m. à m. : sont prévus) des menus chauds, dans le genre des services à bord des avions. Mais le wagon dispose également de plus de 30 places pour les clients qui veulent prendre leur petit-déjeûner plus tard, ou qui veulent manger et boire quelque chose en dehors du service (m. à m. : du tour, du rang).
Ce nouveau type de wagon-restaurant est une idée des agences de voyages (m. à m. : des entrepreneurs de voyages), qui profitera aux Chemins de Fer Fédéraux, parce qu'elle permet (m. à m. : est propre à) de rendre plus agréable les voyages en train spécial, et ainsi de gagner davantage de clients.

Leçon

30 bis Contrôle et révisions

A **Traduisez, puis formez deux phrases avec weil et denn :**
(voir leçons 11 et 22 pour la construction après weil et denn.)

1. Diebe drangen in die Wohnung ein; die Tür stand offen. 2. Wir gehen zu Bett; die Sendung ist nicht interessant. 3. Er verkauft seinen Wagen; er will einen neuen. 4. Wir haben 30 kg Freigepäck; wir fliegen erster Klasse.

B **Complétez, puis traduisez :**
(Relisez le texte L. 26,4 et voyez le mémento grammatical, nos 24, 25, 26)

5. In einer groß... Stadt ist der Verkehr ein fast unlösbar... Problem. 6. Dies... nervös... Autofahrer sucht den richtig... Weg. 7. Mit gro... Dankbarkeit denke ich an den höflich... Fremden.

C **Reliez les propositions à l'aide de la conjonction indiquée, puis traduisez :** *(Texte L. 30,4; Mémento nos 61, 62)*

8. Sind warme Menüs vorgesehen? sagen Sie es mir (ob). 9. Dieser Wagentyp macht die Reise angenehmer, Georg glaubt es (daß). 10. Der Gast will ein kaltes Gericht; er kann in seinem Abteil bleiben (wenn).

D **Traduisez :**

Wir vermieten Ihnen das Zimmer so billig, weil auf demselben Stock eine kinderreiche Familie wohnt, die ziemlich laut ist. — Das macht nichts aus. Ich bin schwerhörig. — Ach so! Dann kostet das Zimmer zwei Mark mehr.

E **Traduisez :**

— Meine Frau ist eine große Tierfreundin, aber dadurch wird das Leben zu Hause oft ungemütlich. Sie ist ganz verrückt auf Goldfische, Kanarienvögel, Hunde und Katzen. Ihre nicht?
— Es ist nicht ganz dasselbe. Sie hat lieber Nerz, Biber und Hermelin.

Corrigé :

A 1. *Des voleurs ont pénétré dans l'appartement; la porte était ouverte.* a) Diebe drangen in die Wohnung ein, weil die Tür offen stand. b) Diebe drangen in die Wohnung ein, denn die Tür stand offen. 2. *Nous allons au lit; l'émission n'est pas intéressante.* a) Wir gehen zu Bett, weil die Sendung nicht interessant ist. b) Wir ..., denn die Sendung ist nicht interessant. 3. *Il vend sa voiture; il (en) veut une nouvelle.* a) Er verkauft seinen Wagen, weil er einen neuen will. b) Er ..., denn er will einen neuen. 4. *Nous avons une franchise de bagage de 30 kg; nous voyageons (volons) en 1re classe.* a) Wir haben 30 kg Freigepäck, weil wir erster Klasse fliegen. b) Wir ..., denn wir fliegen erster Klasse.

B 5. großen -unlösbares. *Dans une grande ville, la circulation pose un problème presque insoluble.* 6. Dieser nervöse — richtigen. *Cet automobiliste énervé cherche le bon chemin.* 7. großer — höflichen. *C'est avec (une) grande reconnaissance que je pense à l'étranger courtois.*

C 8. Sagen Sie mir, ob warme Menüs vorgesehen sind. *Dites-moi si l'on a prévu des repas chauds.* 9. Georg glaubt, daß dieser Wagentyp die Reise angenehmer macht. *Georg croit que ce type de wagon rend le voyage plus agréable.* 10. Wenn der Gast ein kaltes Gericht will, kann er in seinem Abteil bleiben. *Si le client veut un plat froid, il peut rester dans son compartiment.*

D — Nous vous louons la chambre si bon marché parce qu'au même étage habite une famille nombreuse qui est assez bruyante. — Ça ne fait rien. Je suis dur d'oreille. — Ah! dans ce cas, la chambre coûte deux marks de plus.

E — Ma femme est une grande amie des bêtes, mais de ce fait la vie à la maison est (devient) souvent peu confortable. Elle raffole de poissons rouges, canaris, chiens et chats. La vôtre non? — Ce n'est pas tout à fait pareil. Elle préfère le vison, le castor, l'hermine.

Leçon

31

Sie wollen mit der Eisenbahn fahren

1 — Ich möchte zwei Plätze erster Klasse nach Bonn reservieren. Ich fahre am Donnerstag, am siebenundzwanzigsten Mai, mit dem Zug um zwanzig Uhr ab.
— Was für Plätze wollen sie?
— Einen Eckplatz, Fensterseite, in der Fahrtrichtung, und den Platz daneben.
— Ich bedauere sehr, mein Herr, wir haben keine Fensterplätze mehr. Ich kann Ihnen nur noch einen Eckplatz, Gangseite, geben und zwar gegen die Fahrtrichtung.
— Gut, in Ordnung.

2 — Geben Sie mir eine Fahrkarte erster Klasse nach Remscheid.
— Eine Rückfahrkarte?
— Nein, einfach.
— Das bekommen Sie am Schalter sechs. Nach Remscheid gibt es aber keine erste Klasse; der Zug hat nur zweite.

3 — (Zum Gepäckträger) Für den Zug nach Köln; Wagen Nummer 15; Platznummer 32. Was bin ich Ihnen schuldig?

4 — Wo muß ich nach Remscheid umsteigen?
— In Opladen.
— Habe ich direkten Anschluß?
— Sie müssen zehn Minuten warten.

5 — Um wieviel Uhr kommt der Zug aus Köln an?
— Um acht Uhr fünfundfünfzig. Der Eilzug, der auf Bahnsteig 3 ankommen soll, hat eine Stunde Verspätung.
— Wir werden in der Bahnhofgaststätte oder im Wartesaal warten.

AUS DEN AUGEN, AUS DEM SINN

Traduction

Vous allez prendre le train

1 — Je voudrais réserver deux places de première classe pour Bonn. Je partirai jeudi, 27 mai, par le train de 20 heures. — Quelles places voulez-vous? — Un coin fenêtre, sens de la marche, et la place à côté. — Je regrette beaucoup, Monsieur, nous n'avons plus de coins fenêtres. Je ne puis vous donner qu'un coin couloir, (et) dos tourné à la machine. — Bon, c'est bien.

2 — Donnez-moi un billet de première classe pour Remscheid. — Un aller-retour? — Non, (un aller) simple. — Vous aurez cela au guichet six. Mais pour Remscheid, il n'y a pas de première classe; le train n'a que des secondes.

3 — (Au porteur) Train de Cologne, voiture 15, place 32. Combien vous dois-je?

4 — Pour Remscheid, où dois-je changer? — A Opladen. — Aurai-je la correspondance immédiate? — Il faut attendre 10 minutes.

5 — A quelle heure arrive le train en provenance de Cologne? — A 8 h 55.
Le rapide qui doit arriver sur le quai 3, a une heure de retard. — Nous attendrons au buffet de la gare ou à la salle d'attente.

Vocabulaire

der Anschluß (¨sse), *la correspondance (ch. de fer)*
der Bahnsteig (-e), *le quai*
der Gang (¨e), *le couloir*
der Schalter (-), *le guichet*
der Träger (-), *le porteur*
die Fahrt (en), *le trajet, le parcours*
die Gaststätte (n), *le restaurant, le café*
die Versp**ä**tung (-en), *le retard*
umst**ei**gen (ie, ie), *changer (de train)*

Exercice sur les mots
Traduisez : 1. *Un long trajet, de longs trajets.* 2. *Les fenêtres*

Loin des yeux, loin du cœur (Hors des yeux, hors du cœur)

de ce couloir. 3. *Un vieux porteur; le travail du porteur.* 4. *Il va au (= dans le) restaurant; il est au restaurant.*
Corrigé : 1. Eine lange Fahrt, lange Fahrten. 2. Die Fenster dieses Gangs. 3. Ein alter Gepäckträger; die Arbeit des Gepäckträgers. 4. Er geht in die Gaststätte; er ist in der Gaststätte.

Grammaire

■ **Der Eilzug, der auf Bahnsteig 3 ankommen soll, hat Verspätung.**
La subordonnée relative.

● La proposition subordonnée relative est introduite par un pronom relatif; le verbe est rejeté à la fin de la subordonnée; celle-ci est séparée de la principale par une virgule.

● Les pronoms relatifs au Nominatif et à l'Accusatif sont :

	Masc.	Fém.	Ntre.	Pluriel	
Nom.	*der*	*die*	*das*	*die,*	qui
Acc.	*den*	*die*	*das*	*die,*	que

Exemples :
a) pronoms au nominatif (sujet).

Der Schaffner, ***der*** *die Fahrkarten kontrolliert...,* le contrôleur qui vérifie les billets...
Die Dame, ***die*** *erster Klasse reist...,* la dame qui voyage en 1re classe...
Das Gepäckstück, ***das*** *dort liegt...,* le colis qui est posé là-bas...

b) pronoms relatifs à l'accusatif (complément d'objet direct). Ce pronom est suivi du sujet, puis des compléments, enfin du verbe.

Der Schaffner, ***den*** *ich gestern gerufen hatte,* le contrôleur que j'avais appelé hier...
Die Dame, ***die*** *wir auf dem Bahnsteig sehen...,* la dame que nous voyons sur le quai...
Das Gepäckstück, ***das*** *ich dorthin gelegt habe...,* le colis que j'ai posé là-bas...

■ **Er fährt nach Remscheid. Er muß in Opladen umsteigen.**
Emploi de *in* et de *nach.*
Devant les noms de villes et de pays, l'allemand distingue entre la direction (le mouvement) et l'état (la position, le lieu où l'on est).

● Quand il y a mouvement, on emploie *nach :*

Er fährt nach Bonn, il va à Bonn; *nach England,* en Angleterre; *nach Frankreich,* en France.

● Quand il y a état, on emploie *in :*

Er wohnt in Bonn, il habite à Bonn; *in Deutschland,* en Allemagne.

Exercices

A *Complétez par un pronom relatif, puis traduisez :*
1. Die Fahrkarte, ... ich gekauft habe, ist einfach. 2. Der Platz, ... er reserviert hatte, war ein Eckplatz. 3. Kennst du das Reisebüro, ... in der Mozartstraße liegt? 4. Die Züge, ... Schlafwagen haben, sind Nachtzüge. 5. Die zwei Gepäckträger, ... wir gerufen hatten, kamen schnell.

B *Complétez par* « in » *ou* « nach », *puis traduisez :*
6. Er arbeitet ... München. 7. Seine Schwester lebt ... England. 8. Sie kommt jedes Jahr ... Deutschland. 9. Fährst du bald ... Berlin ab? 10. Er blieb nur eine Woche ... Köln.

C *Traduisez :*
11. Je partirai par le train de huit heures du soir. 12. Les bagages que j'emporte ne sont pas lourds. 13. L'ami qui voyage avec moi, a pris un billet aller-retour. 14. Elle me demande si le prochain train arrivera bientôt. 15. Il habite depuis un an à Mayence *(Mainz).*

Corrigé :

A 1. die. *Le billet que j'ai acheté est un aller simple.* 2. den. *La place qu'il avait réservée était un coin.* 3. das. *Connais-tu l'agence qui se trouve dans la rue Mozart?* 4. die. *Les trains qui ont des wagons-lits, sont des trains de nuit.* 5. die. *Les deux porteurs que nous avions appelés, vinrent vite.*

B 6. in. *Il travaille à Munich.* 7. in. *Sa sœur vit en Angleterre.* 8. nach. *Elle vient tous les ans en Allemagne.* 9. nach. *Pars-tu bientôt pour Berlin?* 10. in. *Il ne resta qu'une semaine à Cologne.*

C 11. Ich werde mit dem Zug um acht Uhr abends wegfahren. 12. Das Gepäck, das ich mitnehme, ist nicht schwer. 13. Der Freund, der mit mir reist, hat eine Rückfahrkarte gelöst. 14. Sie fragt mich, ob der nächste Zug bald ankommt (*ou :* ankommen wird). 15. Er wohnt seit einem Jahr in Mainz.

32 Das Schiff

1 Die Schiffe, wie*z.B. (zum Beispiel) die *Überseedampfer, erlauben uns, angenehme Überfahrten oder Seereisen zu machen. Dies aber unter der Bedingung, daß man nicht leicht seekrank wird. Doch gibt es heutzutage *spezielle Pillen gegen die Seekrankheit.

2 Wenn ein Schiff drei Klassen hat, nimmt die erste Klasse den mittleren Teil ein. Hier findet man die Salons, eine Bar, ein Lesezimmer, einen *geräumigen Speisesaal. Die zweite Klasse oder Touristenklasse liegt hinten, gegen das Heck. Die dritte Klasse liegt vorn, gegen den Bug. Die besten Kabinen sind *diejenigen, die zum Deck hin liegen.

3 Das Leben an *Bord ist angenehm. Einige Fahrgäste (oder *Passagiere) gehen auf dem Deck spazieren. Andere ruhen sich auf einem *Liegestuhl aus. Man braucht keine Langweile zu befürchten, denn es gibt allerlei Veranstaltungen : *Konzerte, Vorträge, Spielfilme. Am letzten Abend einer Kreuzfahrt veranstaltet der Schiffskapitän, dem die Tanzliebhaber sehr dankbar dafür sind, einen Ball.

1 [tçoum b**a**échpil]; [**u**berzé-d**a**m'pfer]; [chpétçy**è**le].

2 [gér**o**eumigen']; [d**i**-y**é**nigen'].

3 [bort]; [paçaj**i**re]; [l**i**ge-cht**ou**l]; [fèr**a**n'chtaltou^{ng}en]; [kontç**è**rte].

STILLE WASSER GRÜNDEN TIEF

Traduction

Le bateau

1 Les bateaux tels que par exemple les transatlantiques nous permettent de faire d'agréables traversées ou voyages en mer. Mais ceci à condition de ne pas être sujet au mal de mer (m. à m. : qu'on ne devienne pas facilement « malade de la mer »). Cependant, il existe de nos jours des pilules spéciales contre le mal de mer.

2 Lorsqu'un bateau a trois classes, la première occupe le centre. On y trouve les salons, un bar, une bibliothèque, une vaste salle à manger. La seconde classe ou classe touriste est à l'arrière vers la poupe. La troisième se trouve à l'avant vers la proue. Les meilleures cabines sont celles qui donnent sur le pont.

3 La vie à bord est agréable. Quelques passagers se promènent sur le pont. D'autres se reposent sur un (fauteuil) transatlantique. On n'a pas à craindre l'ennui, car il y a toutes sortes de manifestations : des concerts, des conférences, des films. La dernière soirée d'une croisière, le commandant (m. à m. : capitaine) — à qui les amateurs de danse sont très reconnaissants (m. à m. : de cela) — organise un bal.

Vocabulaire

der Ball (¨e), *le bal; la balle*
der Bord (e), *le bord*
der Bug (¨e), *la proue*
der Dampfer (-), *le paquebot*
der Fahrgast (¨e), *le passager*
der Liebhaber (-), *l'amateur*
der Liegestuhl (¨e), *la chaise longue*
der Teil (e), *la partie*
die Bar (s), *le bar*
die Brücke (n), *le pont (rivière)*
die Kreuzfahrt (en), *la croisière*
die Langweile, *l'ennui*
die Pille (n), *la pilule*
die See (n), *la mer* (*mais :* der See (s, n), *le lac*)
die Überfahrt (-en), *la traversée*
das Beispiel (e), *l'exemple*
das Deck (e), *le pont (bateau)*
das Heck (e), *la poupe*
das Konz**e**rt (-e), *le concert*
das Schiff (-e), *le bateau*
bef**ü**rchten, *craindre*
erl**au**ben, *permettre*
ver**a**nstalten, *organiser*
einn**e**hmen (a, o; i), *occuper (espace)*

Il n'est pire eau que l'eau qui dort (Les eaux calmes sont profondes)

Grammaire

■ **Der Kapitän, dem die Tanzliebhaber sehr dankbar sind,...**
Le pronom relatif au datif.
Les pronoms relatifs au datif (= à qui) sont :

Masc.	Fém.	Ntre.	Pluriel	
dem	*der*	*dem*	*denen,*	à qui

Der Mann, ***dem*** *dieses Schiff gehört, ist sehr reich,*
l'homme à qui appartient ce bateau, est très riche.

■ **Man braucht keine Langweile zu befürchten.**
Emploi particulier de *brauchen.*
Le verbe *brauchen* signifie : avoir besoin de; utiliser. La tournure *nicht brauchen zu* correspond à la négation du verbe *müssen.*

Er muß einen Brief schreiben, il faut qu'il écrive une lettre.

Négation :

Er braucht keinen Brief zu schreiben, il na pas besoin d'écrire une lettre.

Exercices

A *Faites de la deuxième proposition une subordonnée relative, puis traduisez :*
1. Die Dame dankt uns; wir haben ihr einen Liegestuhl gebracht. 2. Das Kind saß im Lesezimmer; wir wollten ihm die Maschinen zeigen. 3. Der Saal ist sehr groß; wir essen in dem Saal.

B *Mettez les phrases à la forme négative, puis traduisez :*
4. Wir müssen abfahren. 5. Ich muß lange warten.

Corrigé :

A 1. Die Dame, der wir einen Liegestuhl gebracht haben, dankt uns herzlich. *La dame à qui nous avons apporté une chaise-longue, nous remercie cordialement.* 2. Das Kind, dem wir die Maschinen zeigen wollten, saß im Lesezimmer. *L'enfant à qui nous voulions montrer les machines, était assis dans le salon de lecture.* 3. Der Saal, in dem wir essen, ist sehr groß. *La salle, dans laquelle nous mangeons, est très grande.*

B 4. Wir brauchen nicht abzufahren. *Nous n'avons pas besoin de partir.* 5. Ich brauche nicht lange zu warten. *Je n'ai pas besoin d'attendre longtemps.*

Kleine Tips für Studienreisen

Kreuzfahrten sind in den letzten Jahren stark in Mode gekommen. Das Angebot ist riesig. Kreuzfahrten bieten ideale Möglichkeiten, Bildung und Erholung zu verbinden.
Seekrankheit befällt Sie nicht nur auf dem Schiff. Auch im Auto, Flugzeug und in der Eisenbahn. Möglichst nicht bewegten Gegenständen (vorbeifahrenden Zügen oder fahrenden Autos) mit den Augen folgen.
Steuern. Kombinieren Sie ihre Studienreise mit einer berufsbildenden Reise (Fleischer zu den Schlachthöfen von Chicago, Ärzte zu einem Kongreß in Sydney). Dann können Sie einiges von der Steuer absetzen. Verschiedene Unternehmen sind auf solche Reisen spezialisiert.

Aus der Illustrierten « Kristall ».

Petits conseils pour les voyages d'études

Les croisières sont très à la mode, ces dernières années. L'offre (en) est énorme. Les croisières présentent des possibilités idéales pour combiner la culture et la détente.
Le mal de mer ne vous prend pas seulement sur le bateau. Également en voiture, en avion et dans le train. Autant que possible, ne pas suivre du regard des objets mobiles (des trains qui passent ou des voitures en marche).
Impôts. Combinez votre voyage d'études avec un voyage de formation professionnelle (les bouchers iront aux abattoirs de Chicago, les médecins à un congrès à Sydney). Il vous sera alors possible d'obtenir une réduction de vos impôts. Différentes agences sont spécialisées dans ce genre de voyages.

Leçon

33 *Ankunft auf dem Schiff

1 — Fahrscheine vorzeigen, bitte! — Welches ist die Nummer Ihrer *Kajüte? Lassen Sie Ihr Gepäck hier, der Steward wird es Ihnen bringen — Bitte, folgen Sie mir.

2 — Treten Sie bitte ein. Hier ist das Licht für die obere *Koje. Jener Schalter ist für die untere Koje. Wenn Sie rufen wollen, klingeln Sie hier. Da sind Ihre Rettungsringe, deren *Gebrauchsvorschrift Sie lesen sollten. Was die Mahlzeiten anbetrifft, wenden Sie sich an den Steward. Er wird Ihnen einen Platz im Speisesaal anweisen.

3 — Ich möchte *Zigarren.
— Der Verkauf beginnt erst nach dem Auslaufen.
— Mit wieviel Zigaretten darf man das Schiff verlassen?
— Die *Zollbeamten lassen gewöhnlich zweihundert Zigaretten und vierzig Zigarren zu.
— Werden auch andere zollfreie Artikel verkauft?

4 — Ich möchte zwei Liegestühle.
— Backbord oder steuerbord?
— Backbord, bitte, wegen der Sonne.

5 — Könnten Sie mir keine größere Kajüte geben?
— Ich glaube, es wird möglich sein. Ich werde es Ihnen gegen sechs Uhr bestätigen.
— Das ist sehr nett von Ihnen. Besten Dank.

1 [**an**'kounft]; [ka-y**u**te]. 2 [k**o**-ye]; [gébr**a**orç-f**o**rchrift]. 3 [tcig**a**ren]; [tç**o**l-bé-**a**m'ten'].

DIE RATTEN VERLASSEN DAS SINKENDE SCHIFF.

Traduction

L'arrivée à bord

1 — Veuillez présenter vos billets! — Quel numéro de cabine avez-vous? Laissez vos bagages ici, le steward vous les apportera. — Suivez-moi, s'il vous plaît.

2 — Entrez s'il vous plaît. Voici la lumière pour la couchette du haut. Cet interrupteur-là est pour la couchette du bas. Pour appeler, sonnez ici. Voilà vos bouées de sauvetage, dont vous devriez lire les instructions (= le mode d'emploi). Quant aux repas (m. à m. : en ce qui concerne les repas), adressez-vous au steward. C'est lui qui vous placera dans la salle à manger.

3 — Je voudrais des cigares. — La vente commence seulement après l'appareillage. — Avec combien de cigarettes a-t-on le droit de débarquer? — Les douaniers tolèrent en général 200 cigarettes et 40 cigares. — Est-ce qu'on vendra d'autres articles exempts de douane?

4 — Je voudrais deux chaises longues. — A babord ou à tribord? — A babord s'il vous plaît, à cause du soleil.

5 — Est-ce que vous ne pourriez pas me donner une cabine plus grande? — Je crois que ce sera possible. Je vous le confirmerai vers six heures. — C'est très gentil de votre part; je vous remercie beaucoup.

Vocabulaire

der Be**a**mte (n, n), *l'employé, le fonctionnaire*
der Gebr**au**ch (¨e), *l'usage*
der Ring (e), *l'anneau*
der Verk**au**f (¨e), *la vente*
der Zoll, *la douane*
die Kaj**ü**te (n), *la cabine*
die Koje (n), *la couchette*
die Nummer (n), *le numéro*
die Zig**a**rre (n), *le cigare*
die Zigar**e**tte (n), *la cigarette*
best**ä**tigen, *confirmer*
folgen (+ datif), *suivre*
klingeln, *sonner*
retten, *sauver*
ausschi**ff**en, *débarquer (q. q. c.)*
anw**ei**sen (ie, ie), *indiquer*

Quand le navire fait eau, les rats déménagent (Les rats abandonnent le navire qui sombre).

die Rettung (en), *le sauvetage*	**aus**l**au**fen (ie, au; äu), *quitter le port*
die Vorschrift (en), *l'ordre, les instructions*	**zula**ssen (ie, a; ä), *admettre*

Grammaire

■ Die Rettungsringe, deren Gebrauchsvorschrift Sie lesen sollten.

Les pronoms relatifs au génitif sont :

Masc.	Fém.	Ntre.	Pluriel	
dessen	*deren*	*dessen*	*deren*	dont

De même que *wessen* (L. 10), ces génitifs sont directement suivis du nom complété, et celui-ci perd son article.

*Das Schiff, **dessen** Speisesaal so prachtvoll ist, fährt heute aus,* le bateau dont la salle à manger est si luxueuse, appareille aujourd'hui.

*Die Kajüte, **deren** Kojen sehr hübsch sind...,* la cabine, dont les couchettes sont très jolies...

Ce génitif saxon peut être précédé d'une préposition :

*Der Dampfer, **in dessen** Kajüten sie reisten...,* le vapeur, dans les cabines duquel ils voyageaient...

● Remarque générale sur le pronom relatif :
Il a les mêmes formes que l'article défini, sauf au génitif, et au datif pluriel, (voir L. 32).

■ Fahrscheine vorzeigen!

Formes particulières de l'impératif (voir L. 10).
Pour donner un ordre bref et énergique, on peut employer :

● l'infinitif : *Eintreten!* entrez!
● le participe passé : *Eingetreten!* entrez!
● une simple particule séparable : *Herein!* entrez!

La première personne du pluriel se rend ainsi :

● *Treten wir ein!* entrons!
● *Wir wollen eintreten!* entrons!
● *Laßt uns eintreten!* entrons!

Exercices

A *Faites de la 2e proposition une subordonnée relative contenant un pronom relatif au génitif, puis traduisez (le possessif disparaît).*
1. Der Passagier wartet im Büro; sein Fahrschein ist nicht mehr gültig. 2. Die Zigarren kommen aus Brasilien; ihr Verkauf beginnt bald. 3. Der Kapitän ist ein älterer Herr; seine Familie wohnt in Lübeck. 4. Wir helfen der Dame; ihr Koffer ist schwer.

B *Formez l'impératif des verbes suivants :*
5. hinab/gehen (aux différentes formes de la 2e personne du pluriel). 6. arbeiten (1re personne du pluriel).

C *Traduisez :*
7. Quand il arriva à bord, il chercha aussitôt *(= sogleich)* sa cabine. 8. Il demande aux douaniers (*fragen* + accusatif) s'il peut emporter deux cents cigarettes. 9. Le commandant, dont la cabine donne sur le pont, invita (*einladen,* u, a, ä) quelques passagers à sa table. 10. Après avoir loué *(mieten)* une chaise-longue, elle lut son journal.

Corrigé :

A 1. Der Passagier, dessen Fahrschein nicht mehr gültig ist, wartet im Büro. *Le passager dont le billet n'est plus valable, attend au bureau.* 2. Die Zigarren, deren Verkauf bald beginnt, kommen aus Brasilien. *Les cigares, dont la vente commencera bientôt, viennent du Brésil.* 3. Der Kapitän, dessen Familie in Lübeck wohnt, ist ein älterer Herr. *Le commandant (m. à m. : le capitaine) dont la famille habite à Lubeck, est un monsieur assez âgé.* 4. Wir helfen der Dame, deren Koffer schwer ist. *Nous aidons la dame, dont la malle est lourde.*

B 5. geht hinab! hinabgehen! hinabgegangen! hinab! *descendez!*
6. arbeiten wir! wir wollen arbeiten! laßt uns arbeiten! *travaillons!*

C 7. Als er an Bord kam, suchte er sogleich seine Kajüte. 8. Er fragt die Zollbeamten, ob er zweihundert Zigaretten mitnehmen darf. 9. Der Schiffskapitän, dessen Kajüte zu dem Deck hin liegt, lud einige Fahrgäste an seinen Tisch ein. 10. Nachdem sie einen Liegestuhl gemietet hatte, las sie ihre Zeitung.

34 Der Paß

1 Jeder Mensch ist Bürger eines Landes, eines Staates. Paul Dumont ist *Franzose. Welche *Nationalität (oder: Staatsangehörigkeit) haben Sie?
Sind Sie Deutscher? Engländer? *Spanier? Italiener?
Der Paß ist ein Ausweis. Auf einem Ausweis sind Ihr Familienname, Ihre Vornamen, Ihr Geburtsdatum, Ihr *Geburtsort, Ihr *Beruf, Ihr Wohnsitz eingetragen.
Ihre Personalbeschreibung steht auch darauf.
Ihr Paßbild ist auf einer der ersten Seiten.

2 In gewissen Fällen muß man einen *Polizeischein ausfüllen, bevor man über die Grenze geht.
Sobald man eine Grenze überschreitet, muß man der Polizei seinen Paß oder seine Kennkarte vorzeigen.
Für manche Länder muß man außerdem ein *Visum haben.
Aber das Reisen von einem Land in das andere wird immer leichter, und eines Tages werden die Pässe in die *Museen wandern.

3 Für die polizeilichen Nachforschungen wird immer mehr die elektronische Datenverarbeitung eingesetzt. Ja, wenn auch die Pässe allmählich verschwinden, so gibt es bald keinen Winkel mehr auf dieser Erde, wo man ohne Ausweis leben könnte.

1 [cht**a**teç]; [fran'tç**o**ze]; [natçionalit**è**t]; [cht**a**tç-**a**ngéh**eu**richkaét]; [chp**a**nier]; [géb**ou**rtç-ort]; [bér**ou**f].

2 [politç**a**é-ch**a**én']; [v**i**zoum']; [daç mouz**é**-oum', d**i** mouz**é**-en'].

REDEN IST SILBER, SCHWEIGEN IST GOLD

Traduction

Le passeport

1 Tout homme est citoyen d'un pays, d'un État. Paul Dumont est Français. De quelle nationalité êtes-vous? Êtes-vous Allemand? Anglais? Espagnol? Italien? Le passeport est une pièce d'identité. Sur une pièce d'identité sont inscrits votre nom de famille, vos prénoms, votre date de naissance, votre lieu de naissance, votre profession, votre lieu de domicile. Votre signalement s'y trouve aussi. Votre photo d'identité est sur l'une des premières pages.

2 Dans certains cas, il faut remplir une fiche de police avant de passer la frontière. Dès qu'on traverse une frontière, on doit présenter son passeport ou sa carte d'identité à la police. Pour certains pays, il faut en outre avoir un visa. Mais les voyages d'un pays à l'autre deviennent de plus en plus faciles, et un jour, les passeports prendront le chemin des musées.

3 Pour les recherches policières, on utilise de plus en plus le travail des ordinateurs. Certes, même si les passeports disparaissent peu à peu, il n'y aura bientôt plus guère un coin sur cette terre où l'on puisse vivre sans pièce d'identité.

Vocabulaire

der Ausweis (e), *la pièce d'identité*
der Ber**u**f (-e), *la profession, le métier*
der Fall (¨e), *le cas*
der Name (ns, n), *le nom*
der Ort (-e), *le lieu*
der Paß (¨sse), *le passeport*
der Vornamen (-), *le prénom*
der Wohnsitz (-e), *le domicile*

die Nationalität (-en), *la nationalité* (*ou* : die Staatsangehörigkeit, *m. à m. : l'appartenance à un État*)
die Poliz**ei**, *la police*
die Seite (n), *la plage, le côté*
das Datum (plur. die Daten), *la date; la donnée (math.)*
das Mus**e**um (plur. die Museen), *le musée*
das Paßbild (-er), *la photo d'identité*
das Visum (plur. die Visa), *le Visa*
ausf**ü**llen, *remplir*

La parole est d'argent, le silence est d'or

die Geb**u**rt (-en), *la naissance*
die K**e**nnkarte (n), *la carte d'identité*
wandern, *voyager (à pied)*
eintr**a**gen (u, a; ä), *inscrire*
überschr**ei**ten (itt, itt), *franchir*

Grammaire

■ **Sobald man eine Grenze überschreitet,...**
Autres conjonctions de subordination, entraînant toujours le rejet du verbe : *sobald,* dès que; *solange,* tant que; *während,* pendant que.

■ **Das Reisen wird immer leichter.**
L'infinitif substantivé.
Un infinitif peut être employé comme nom. Ce substantif est toujours du neutre; il n'a pas de pluriel et il s'écrit avec une majuscule. Exemples :

essen, das Essen, le repas; *lachen, das Lachen,* le rire.

■ **Eines Tages werden die Pässe in die Museen wandern.**
Le complément de temps.

● Le complément de temps indiquant un moment peu précis se met au génitif ou au datif précédé de *am.* Exemples :

Eines Tages, un jour; *des Morgens,* le matin; *sonntags,* le dimanche.

Ou bien :

Am Tage, le jour; *am Montag,* le lundi; *am Anfang,* au début.

Exception : *In der Nacht* (ou : *nachts*), la nuit.

● Lorsqu'il indique un moment précis ou une durée, il se met à l'accusatif. Exemples :

Jeden Sonntag, chaque dimanche; *nächste Woche,* la semaine prochaine; *den ganzen Tag,* toute la journée.

Exercice

Formez des subordonnées en employant la conjonction indiquée, puis traduisez :
1. Die Reisenden steigen an Bord. Die Polizei prüft ihre Pässe (während). 2. Du bleibst in deinem Land. Du brauchst keinen Paß (solange). 3. Er kam in München an. Er suchte den Verkehrsverein (sobald).

Corrigé :

1. Während die Reisenden an Bord steigen, prüft die Polizei ihre Pässe. *Pendant que les voyageurs montent à bord, la police examine leurs passeports.* 2. Du brauchst keinen Paß, solange du in deinem Land bleibst. *Tu n'as pas besoin de passeport, tant que tu restes dans ton pays.* 3. Sobald er in München ankam, suchte er den Verkehrsverein. *Dès qu'il arriva à Munich, il rechercha le syndicat d'initiative.*

Lecture

Tips für den Umgang mit Zöllnern

Auf die Frage eines Zollbeamten, ob Sie etwas zu verzollen haben, können Sie zweierlei antworten : entweder präzise angeben, was und wieviel Sie bei sich haben – oder aber sagen : « Bitte, sehen Sie nach ». In beiden Fällen haben Sie der Anzeigepflicht genügt. Wenn Sie aber erklären, Sie hätten nichts zu verzollen, und der Beamte findet doch drei Flaschen Kognak in Ihrem Gepäck, zahlen Sie außer dem üblichen Zoll noch einen Zollzuschlag.

Aus der Wochenzeitschrift « Stern »

Conseils pour les rapports avec les douaniers

A la question d'un douanier, si vous avez quelque chose à déclarer, vous pouvez répondre de deux façons : ou bien vous indiquez avec précision la nature et la quantité de ce que vous avez sur vous (mot à mot : quoi et combien...), ou bien, vous dites : « Regardez vous-même, je vous prie ». Dans les deux cas, vous avez accompli votre devoir (mot à mot : ... de déclaration). Mais, si vous affirmez que vous n'avez rien à déclarer et que le douanier (le fonctionnaire) trouve quand même trois bouteilles de cognac dans vos bagages, vous paierez une surtaxe en plus du droit de douane usuel.

35 *Zoll und *Wechselgeschäft

1 An der Grenze können die Zollbeamten Ihr Gepäck untersuchen. Die Waren, die nicht zollfrei sind, müssen Sie verzollen. Die Zollgebühren schwanken sehr. Oft wird ein gewisses *Quantum Zigaretten für den persönlichen Gebrauch zugelassen.

2 — Ihren Paß, bitte! — Welches ist ihr Gepäck?
— Hier, dieser Handkoffer, der kleinere dort, diese Mappe und dieses *Paket. Das ist alles.
— Haben Sie nichts zu verzollen? Keine Zigaretten? Keinen *Alkohol? Kein Parfüm?
— Nein, ich habe nur persönliche Sachen, einige *Reiseandenken und Bücher. Sonst nichts.
— Machen Sie bitte diesen Handkoffer auf! — Gut.
Der Zollbeamte macht ein *Kreidezeichen auf das Gepäck.

3 — Wo befindet sich eine *Wechselstube (= das Wechselbüro)?
— *Jenseits der Brücke, links. Ich glaube, dort ist der *Kurs am günstigsten.
— Ich möchte Geld wechseln. Ich möchte deutsches Geld gegen französisches einwechseln.

1 [tçol]; [v**è**kçel-géch**è**ft]; [kv**a**n'toum'].

2 [pak**é**t]; [**a**lko-hol]; r**a**éze-**a**n'dèn'ken'; [kr**a**éde-tç**a**échen'].

3 v**è**kçel-cht**ou**be]; [y**é**nzaétç]; [kourç].

EINMAL IST KEINMAL

Traduction

Douane et change

1 A la frontière, les douaniers peuvent examiner vos bagages. Vous devez déclarer les marchandises qui ne sont pas exemptes de douane. Les droits de douane sont très variables. Souvent on tolère une certaine quantité de cigarettes, pour sa consommation personnelle.

2 — Votre passeport, s'il-vous-plaît! — Quels sont vos bagages? — Voici : cette valise, la plus petite là-bas, cette serviette et ce paquet. C'est tout. — N'avez-vous rien à déclarer? (m. à m. : à dédouaner). Pas de cigarettes? d'alcools? de parfum? — Non, je n'ai que des affaires personnelles, quelques souvenirs (de voyage) et des livres. Rien d'autre. — Ouvrez s'il vous plaît cette valise! — C'est bien.
Le douanier marque les bagages à la craie (m. à m. : fait une marque à la craie sur les bagages).

3 — Où se trouve un bureau de change? — Au-delà du pont, à gauche. Je crois que le cours est le plus favorable, là-bas. — Je voudrais changer de l'argent. Je voudrais acheter des marks avec de la monnaie française (m. à m. : changer... contre...)

Prononciation

Qu se prononce [kv]. Exemples : *das Quantum; das Quartett* [kvart**è**t], le quatuor; *die Quelle* [kv**è**le], la source.

Vocabulaire

der **A**lkohol (-e), *l'alcool*
der Gebr**au**ch (¨e), *l'usage*
der Kurs (e), *le cours*
der W**e**chsel, *le change*
die Br**ü**cke (n), *le pont*
die Geb**ü**hr (-en), *la taxe*
das Gesch**ä**ft (-e), *l'affaire, le magasin*
das Geld (er), *l'argent*
das Parf**üm** (-e), *le parfum*
das Qu**a**ntum (plur. die Quanten), *la quantité*

Une fois n'est pas coutume (Une fois, c'est jamais)

die Kr**ei**de (n), *la craie*
die Z**o**llgebühren (plur.), *les droits de douane*
das **A**nd**e**nken (-), *le souvenir*
das Z**ei**chen, (-), *le signe*
gl**au**ben, *croire*
schw**a**nken, *être balancé, instable*
unters**u**chen, *examiner*
verz**o**llen, *dédouaner*

Exercices sur les mots.
Traduisez : *1. Il examine mes bagages; examina; a examiné; examinera. 2. L'usage personnel. 3. Une bonne affaire; de bonnes affaires. 4. Il va sur le pont; il est sur le pont.*
Corrigé : 1. Er untersucht mein Gepäck; untersuchte; hat...untersucht; wird...untersuchen. 2. Der persönliche Gebrauch. 3. Ein gutes Geschäft; gute Geschäfte. 4. Er geht auf die Brücke; er steht auf der Brücke.

Grammaire

■ Ich glaube, dort ist der Kurs günstiger.
Daß sous-entendu.
La conjonction *daß* peut être sous-entendue après les verbes qui ont le sens de penser, dire, croire, savoir, craindre (verbes d'opinion). Dans ce cas, la subordonnée non introduite par *daß* se construit comme une proposition principale : son verbe est en deuxième place; à la première place peut se trouver le sujet (construction directe) ou un complément (construction inverse). Cette suppression de *daß* n'est pas possible quand la proposition principale est négative.

Ich denke, daß dieser Artikel zollfrei ist (rejet) ou : *Ich denke, dieser Artikel ist zollfrei* (verbe 2e place), je pense que cet article est exempt de douane.

■ Die Wechselstube liegt jenseits der Brücke.
Prépositions gouvernant le génitif.
Voici les prépositions les plus usitées qui sont toujours suivies du génitif : *trotz,* malgré; *längs,* le long de; *diesseits,* en deçà de; *jenseits,* au-delà de; *wegen,* à cause de; *während,* pendant.

Wegen seines ungültigen Passes, à cause de son passeport non valable.
Während der Reise, pendant le voyage.
Trotz des Regens, malgré la pluie.

Exercices

Supprimez daß, *puis traduisez :*
1. Ich weiß, daß ich meinen Paß vorzeigen muß. 2. Wir glauben, daß dieses Buch nicht zu verzollen ist. 3. Emma schreibt, daß ihre Reise wundervoll ist.

Complétez les terminaisons, puis traduisez :
4. Während d... Winter... (der Winter, *l'hiver*) blieben sie in d... Stadt. 5. Er ging längs d... Rhein... spazieren. 6. Trotz d... hoh... Zollgebühren kauften sie den Wagen. 7. Wegen sein... Beruf... wurde sein Gepäck lange untersucht.

Traduisez :
8. Deux douaniers examinaient ses bagages et sa voiture, mais il n'avait que (= seulement, *nur*) des marchandises exemptes de droits. 9. Ils croyaient qu'il ne voulait pas payer *(bezahlen)* les droits de douane. 10. Ces vêtements sont pour mon usage personnel, dit-il. 11. Les souvenirs de voyage qu'il avait achetés se trouvaient dans la deuxième valise.

Corrigé :

1. Ich weiß, ich muß meinen Paß vorzeigen. *Je sais que je dois présenter mon passeport.* 2. Wir glauben, dieses Buch ist nicht zu verzollen. *Nous croyons que ce livre n'est pas à dédouaner.* 3. Emma schreibt, ihre Reise ist wundervoll. *Emma écrit que son voyage est merveilleux.*

4. des Winters; in der Stadt. *Pendant l'hiver, ils restaient en ville.* 5. des Rheins. *Il allait se promener le long du Rhin.* 6. der hohen. *Malgré les droits de douanes élevés, ils ont acheté la voiture.* 7. Seines Berufs. *C'est à cause de sa profession que ses bagages furent longuement visités.*

8. Zwei Zollbeamte untersuchten sein Gepäck und seinen Wagen, aber er hatte nur zollfreie Waren. 9. Sie glaubten, er wollte keine Zollgebühren bezahlen. 10. Diese Kleider sind für meinen persönlichen Gebrauch, sagte er. 11. Die Reiseandenken, die er gekauft hatte, waren im zweiten Handkoffer.

Leçon

36 Der Gasthof

1 Wenn wir verreist sind und eine Unterkunft suchen, wenden wir uns an den Verkehrsverein. Hier wird uns von einem Angestellten ein *Unterkunftsverzeichnis überreicht. Auf diesem Verzeichnis finden wir Hotels, *Gasthöfe (oder *Gasthäuser) und *Gaststätten.

2 Ein Unternehmen, das in Deutschland als Hotel bezeichnet wird, ist gewöhnlich *luxuriöser als ein Gasthof. Der Gasthof ist ein *gediegenes, gut geführtes Haus; oft wird hier Vollpension angeboten. Das Gasthaus (oder die Gastwirtschaft) ist ein wenig einfacher; aber man kann auch hier *bequeme Zimmer finden und die Küche ist meistens bürgerlich. Die Gaststätte *vermietet keine Zimmer.

3 Die Preise richten sich nach der Zahl der Betten. Hinzu kommt die zehn-, zwölf- oder *fünfzehnprozentige Bedienung. In der *Urlaubszeit ist es ratsam, sein Zimmer im *Voraus zu reservieren. Wenn die Gasthöfe kein freies Zimmer mehr haben, kann man oft ein *Privatquartier finden.

1 [fèrtç**a**éçhniç]; [g**a**çt-heufe]; [g**a**çt-hoeuzer]; [g**a**çt-chtèten'].

2 [loukçouri**eu**zer]; [gédigeneç]; [békvéme]; [fèrmitet].

3 [-protç**è**n'tige]; [**ou**rlaobç-tç**a**ét]; [for-**a**oç]; [privat-kvartir].

EIN SPERLING IN DER HAND IST BESSER ALS ZWEI AUF DEM DACH

Traduction

L'Hôtel

1 Quand nous sommes en voyage et que nous cherchons à nous loger, nous nous adressons au syndicat d'initiative. Là, une liste des hôtels nous est remise par un employé. Sur cette liste, nous trouvons des hôtels, des hôtels-restaurants et des cafés-restaurants.

2 Un établissement désigné en Allemagne comme « hôtel », est en général plus luxueux qu'un « Gasthof ». L'hôtel-restaurant est une maison soignée, bien tenue; souvent on y offre la pension complète. L'auberge est un peu plus simple; mais là aussi, on peut trouver des chambres confortables et la cuisine y est le plus souvent bourgeoise. Le café-restaurant ne loue pas de chambres.

3 Les prix sont calculés d'après le nombre de lits. Le service de 10, 12 ou 15 % s'y ajoute. Pendant la période des vacances, il est prudent de réserver sa chambre à l'avance. Si les hôtels n'ont plus de chambre libre, on peut souvent trouver une chambre chez l'habitant.

Vocabulaire

der Gasthof (¨ e), *l'hôtel-restaurant*
der Preis (-e), *le prix*
der Urlaub (-e), *le congé*
die Bed**ie**nung (-en), *le service*
die Gaststätte (n), *le café le restaurant*
die Küche (n), *la cuisine*

die Unterkunft (¨ e), *le logis, l'abri*
die V**o**llpensi**o**n (-en), *la pension complète*
die Zahl (-en), *le nombre*
das Quart**ie**r (-e), *le logement*
berechnen, *calculer*
verm**ie**ten, *louer*
*verr**ei**sen, *partir en voyage*
anb**ie**ten (o, o), *présenter, offrir.*

Un tien vaut mieux que deux tu l'auras (Un moineau dans la main, c'est mieux que deux sur le toit).

Grammaire

■ **Ein Unterkunftsverzeichnis wird uns von einem Angestellten überreicht.**

● Cette phrase est au passif. Remarquez l'emploi de *wird* (auxiliaire *werden*), alors qu'en français on prend « être ». Le participe passé du verbe à conjuguer *(überreicht)* se met à la fin. Autre exemple :

> *Das Gepäck wird vom Gepäckträger hinaufgetragen,* les bagages sont montés par le porteur = le porteur monte les bagages (Présent).

● Le complément du passif (par...) est introduit généralement par *von.*

> *Von einem Angestellten,* par un employé.

Cependant, quand il ne désigne qu'un instrument, un moyen, ce complément est introduit par *durch.*

> *Der Gasthof wurde durch den Krieg zerstört,* l'hôtel fut détruit par la guerre.

● L'emploi du passif est très fréquent en allemand. Le français préfère la forme active, avec le sujet « on ».

> *Dieses Hotel wurde mir empfohlen,* cet hôtel me fut recommandé = on me recommanda cet hôtel.

● Pour exprimer un état, l'allemand emploie le verbe *sein.*

> *Alle Zimmer sind besetzt,* toutes les chambres sont occupées.

Exercices

A *Mettez au passif, puis traduisez :*
1. Der Dolmetscher zeigte uns das beste Hotel. 2. Frau Anita führt diese Pension gut. 3. Die Gäste trinken guten Wein. 4. Herr Müller bestellte ein Bier.

B *Mettez à la forme active, puis traduisez :*
5. Das Gepäck wird vom Zollbeamten untersucht. 6. Von diesen Reisenden wurde viel Geld gewechselt.

C *Traduisez :*
7. La liste des hôtels qui nous fut remise par l'employé, nous était très utile *(nützlich).* 8. Nous fûmes conduits dans un bon hôtel-restaurant.

Corrigé :

A 1. Das beste Hotel wurde uns vom Dolmetscher gezeigt. *Le meilleur hôtel nous fut montré par l'interprète.* 2. Diese Pension wird von Frau Anita gut geführt. *Cette pension est bien dirigée par Madame Anita.* 3. Guter Wein wird von den Gästen getrunken. *Les clients boivent du bon vin.* 4. Ein Bier wurde von Herrn Müller bestellt. *Une bière fut commandée par M. Müller.*

B 5. Der Zollbeamte untersucht das Gepäck. *Le douanier visite les bagages.* 6. Diese Reisenden wechselten viel Geld. *Ces voyageurs changèrent beaucoup d'argent.*

C 7. Das Unterkunftsverzeichnis, das uns vom Angestellten überreicht wurde, war uns sehr nützlich. 8. Wir wurden in ein gutes Gasthaus geführt.

Lecture

Angeber

Wassersüppchen zu Hause — auf der Urlaubsreise dafür nur echten Kaviar : dies ist das Fazit einer « diskret veranstalteten » Umfrage in zehn italienischen und französischen Luxus-Hotels. Wie finanzieren Sie Ihren Urlaub? Die Antwort : Jeder fünfte Besucher hatte sich die Aufenthaltskosten zusammengespart und erklärte sich nicht abgeneigt, eines « gehobenen Urlaubs » wegen auf Anschaffungen im Haus zu verzichten.

Aus der Wochenzeitung « Die Zeit », Hamburg.

Les hâbleurs

A la maison, une petite soupe maigre (mot à mot : à l'eau) mais comme touriste, uniquement du caviar, et du vrai : voilà le résultat d'une enquête « menée discrètement » dans dix hôtels de luxe italiens et français. Comment financez-vous vos vacances? La réponse : Un estivant sur cinq (mot à mot : chaque cinquième visiteur) avait fait des économies pour le coût du séjour et déclarait n'être pas hostile à l'idée de renoncer à des achats pour la maison, s'il obtient par là des vacances d'une certaine classe (m. à m. : à cause de vacances élevées).

Leçon

37

Wir reservieren ein Zimmer im Hotel

1 **Brieflich :**

Paris, *den 3. Januar

Sehr *geehrter Herr *Geschäftsführer,

Hiermit bitte ich Sie, mir ein *Einzelzimmer mit Bad (ein Doppelzimmer; ein Zimmer mit einem großen Bett; mit einem Kinderbettchen) für den 23. (dreiundzwanzigsten) dieses Monats zu reservieren. Ich möchte ein ruhiges Zimmer, nach der Sonnenseite. Ich werde am Abend gegen sieben Uhr ankommen und bis zum 27. (siebenundzwanzigsten) am Morgen bleiben.

In Erwartung Ihrer *Bestätigung, grüßt Sie freundlichst.

Paul Dumont

2 **Telefonisch :**

— Hallo! Könnte ich ein Zimmer für den 6. (sechsten) nächsten Monats haben?
— Ja, mein Herr. Welches ist Ihr Name, bitte?
— Paul Dumont.
— Um wieviel Uhr kommen Sie bei uns an?
— Spät abends. Was kostet das Zimmer, bitte?
— Zwischen zwanzig und fünfundzwanzig Mark, je nach dem Zimmer.

1 [dén' driten' yanouar]; [gé-érter]; [géchèftç-furer];
[aén'tçel-tçimer]; [béchtètigou[gn]]

VERSCHIEBE NICHT AUF MORGEN, WAS DU HEUTE KANNST BESORGEN

Traduction

Nous réservons une chambre à l'hôtel

A *Par lettre :*

Paris, le 3 Janvier

Monsieur, (mot à mot : très honoré Monsieur le Directeur)
Veuillez me retenir une chambre à un lit avec salle de bain (à deux lits, à un grand lit, avec un lit d'enfant) pour le 23 courant. Je voudrais une chambre tranquille, au midi. J'arriverai dans la soirée vers 7 heures et je resterai jusqu'au 27 au matin.

Dans l'attente de votre confirmation, je vous prie d'agréer, Monsieur, l'expression de mes salutations distinguées.

Paul Dumont

B *Par téléphone :*

— Allo! Pourrais-je avoir une chambre pour le 6 du mois prochain? — Oui, Monsieur. C'est à quel nom? — Paul Dumont. — A quelle heure arriverez-vous chez nous? — Tard dans la soirée. Quel sera le prix de la chambre, s'il vous plaît? — Entre 20 et 25 marks, selon la chambre.

Prononciation

Dans *Hallo,* prononcez le « h » expiré, de même dans *hiermit, Herr.* Cependant, dans les mots *sehr, geehrter, -führer, ruhiges, Uhr, ihrer,* le « h » n'est qu'un signe d'allongement.

Vocabulaire

der Gesch**ä**ftsf**ü**hrer (-), *le gérant, le directeur commercial*

die Best**ä**tigung (-en), *la confirmation*
das Bad (⸚ er), *le bain*
ehren, *honorer*

Quand on s'adresse à une personne à qui l'on veut témoigner du respect, ou quand on ne connaît pas le destinataire, la lettre commence souvent par la formule *Sehr geehrter Herr...,* toujours suivie du nom ou d'un titre.

Ne remets pas au lendemain ce que tu peux faire le jour même (ce dont tu peux t'occuper).

Sehr geehrter Herr Direktor (mot à mot : Très honoré Monsieur le Directeur)
Sehr geehrter Herr Meyer

Cependant, on emploie également le pluriel, sans plus de précision :

Sehr geehrte Herren, ... Messieurs, ...

Grammaire

■ **Wann kommen Sie an?** Quand arriverez-vous?

● Nous avons vu, dans la leçon 8, que le futur se forme à l'aide de l'auxiliaire *werden* et de l'infinitif du verbe à conjuguer (Ne pas confondre avec le passif : auxiliaire *werden* + participe passé.)

Er wird in diesem Hotel ankommen.

● Cependant, le futur est parfois rendu par le simple présent de l'indicatif, surtout quand un adverbe tel que *bald,* bientôt; *morgen,* demain, en précise le sens.

Er kommt bald an, il arrivera bientôt.

Le présent à la place du futur s'emploie habituellement pour les auxiliaires de mode.

Wir werden nach Köln fahren; Hans darf auch mit,
nous irons à Cologne; Hans pourra venir également.

● Notre futur proche « je vais... » se rend en allemand par *wollen.*

Ich will telefonieren, je vais téléphoner.

■ **Wann kommen Sie bei uns an?**

● Quand il y a direction, « chez » se traduit par *zu :*

Er geht zu seinem Freund, il va chez son ami.

● Quand il y a « état », chez se traduit par *bei :*

Er ist bei seinem Freund, il est chez son ami.

Remarque : Pour le verbe *ankommen,* arriver, on considère le résultat de l'action, donc l'état. (Voir L. 9). Revoir aussi la leçon 31, pour *in* et *nach.*

Exercices

A *Mettez au pluriel, puis traduisez :*
1. Dieser Reisende sucht ein luxuriöses Hotel. 2. Er reserviert ein ruhiges Zimmer. 3. Ein alter Pförtner gibt ihm den Schlüssel zu seinem Zimmer.

B *Complétez par* **bei** *ou* **zu,** *puis traduisez :*
4. Führen Sie mich ... dem Geschäftsführer. 5. Er begleitet ihn ... dem Pförtner. 6. Inge wohnt ... ihrem Onkel. 7. Sie fährt jeden Samstag ... ihren Eltern. 8. Sie bleibt den ganzen Sonntag ... ihnen.

C *Traduisez :*
9. Je vais vous montrer votre chambre. 10. Je resterai une semaine seulement. 11. Pourrai-je utiliser *(benützen)* votre garage? 12. La femme de chambre nous apportera le petit déjeuner chaque matin à huit heures. 13. Pourrai-je prendre un bain ce soir? (= aujourd'hui soir).

Corrigé :

A 1. Diese Reisenden suchen luxuriöse Hotels. *Ces voyageurs cherchent des hôtels luxueux.* 2. Sie reservieren ruhige Zimmer. *Ils réservent des chambres calmes.* 3. Alte Pförtner geben ihnen die Schlüssel zu ihren Zimmern. *De vieux concierges leur donnent les clés de leurs chambres.*

B 4. zu. *Conduisez-moi chez le directeur.* 5. zu. *Il l'accompagne chez le concierge.* 6. bei. *Inge habite chez son oncle.* 7. zu. *Elle se rend tous les samedis (mot à mot : chaque samedi) chez ses parents.* 8. bei. *Elle reste chez eux toute la journée du dimanche.*

C 9. Ich will Ihnen Ihr Zimmer zeigen. 10. Ich bleibe nur eine Woche (*ou bien :* Ich werde... bleiben). 11. Darf ich Ihre Garage benützen? 12. Das Zimmermädchen bringt uns das Frühstück jeden Morgen um acht Uhr. 13. Kann ich heute abend ein Bad nehmen?

Leçon

38 Ankunft im Hotel

1 — Vor acht Tagen habe ich ein Zimmer reserviert.
(Der Angestellte sucht im Fremdenbuch nach).
— Ach ja! Sie haben Nummer fünfzig. Es ist ein großes Zimmer mit Bad, im fünften Stock.

2 — Möchten Sie bitte den Meldezettel ausfüllen. Wenn Sie mir Ihren Paß lassen wollen, werde ich es für Sie tun.
— Ist Post für mich da, bitte?
— Ich will nachsehen, aber ich glaube nicht. Nein, es ist nichts da für Sie.

3 (Der Gepäckträger führt den Gast zum Fahrstuhl).
— Wollen Sie bitte einsteigen! Ihr Koffer kommt mit dem Gepäckaufzug nach.
— Es ist schönes Wetter heute, nicht wahr? Das Barometer steht auf schön. Es soll die ganze Woche hindurch so bleiben.
— Hoffentlich!

4 — Hier ist Ihr Zimmer; links ist der Wandschrank und rechts das Badezimmer.
(Der Gepäckträger macht das Licht an und stellt die Handkoffer hin. Der Gast gibt ihm ein Trinkgeld).
— Danke schön. Benötigen Sie etwas, so brauchen Sie nur zu klingeln.

WER DEN PFENNIG NICHT EHRT, IST DES TALERS NICHT WERT.

Traduction

Arrivée à l'hôtel

1 — J'ai réservé une chambre voici huit jours.
(L'employé cherche dans son registre).
— Ah! oui. Vous avez le n° 50. C'est une grande chambre avec salle de bain, au 5ᵉ étage.

2 — Veuillez remplir votre fiche, Monsieur. Si vous voulez bien me laisser votre passeport, je le ferai pour vous.
— Est-ce que j'ai du courrier, s'il vous plaît?
— Je vais voir, mais je ne crois pas. Non, Monsieur, il n'y a rien pour vous.

3 (Le porteur conduit le client à l'ascenseur).
— Prenez la peine d'entrer, Monsieur. Votre malle arrivera (suivra) par le monte-charge.
— Il fait beau aujourd'hui, n'est-ce pas? Le baromètre est au beau fixe. Il paraît que cela va rester ainsi toute la semaine.
— Espérons-le.

4 — Voici votre chambre; le placard est à gauche et la salle de bain à droite.
(Le porteur ouvre l'électricité et dépose les valises. Le client lui donne un pourboire).
— Merci bien. Si vous avez besoin de quelque chose, vous n'avez qu'à sonner.

Vocabulaire

der Aufzug (⸗e), *l'ascenseur*
der Fahrstuhl (⸗e), *l'ascenseur*
der Fremde (n), *l'étranger*
der Schrank (⸗e), *l'armoire*
der Wandschrank (⸗e), *le placard*
die Wand (⸗e), *la cloison*
das Barom**e**ter (-), *le baromètre*
das Fremdenbuch (⸗er), *le registre (des voyageurs)*
das Trinkgeld (er), *le pourboire*
ben**ö**tigen, *avoir besoin de*
melden, *annoncer*

Il n'y a pas de petites économies.
(Celui qui n'honore pas le pfennig ne mérite pas le thaler)

Exercice sur les mots

Traduisez : 1. *L'étrangère; un étranger; une étrangère; des étrangers.* 2. *Il a allumé...* 3. *Il éteindra.* 4. *Un beau pourboire.* 5. *Elle n'a besoin de rien; elle avait besoin de quelque chose.*

Corrigé : 1. Die Fremde; ein Fremder; eine Fremde; Fremde. (C'est la déclinaison de l'adjectif épithète). 2. Er hat... angemacht. 3. Er wird... ausmachen. 4. Ein schönes Trinkgeld. 5. Sie benötigt (= braucht) nichts; sie benötigte (= brauchte) etwas.

Grammaire

■ **Benötigen Sie etwas, so brauchen Sie nur zu klingeln.**

La suppression de *wenn.*

On peut sous-entendre la conjonction *wenn,* quand la proposition surbordonnée précède la principale. Dans ce cas, on fait l'inversion au début de la subordonnée et la principale est introduite par *so* ou *da* qui n'ont pas à être traduits.

Wenn Sie ein Zimmer reservieren, schreiben Sie früh genug = Reservieren Sie ein Zimmer, so schreiben Sie früh genug, si vous réservez une chambre, écrivez assez tôt.

Remarque : Il ne faut pas oublier de rendre ce *wenn* sous-entendu, par « si » ou « quand » dans la traduction.

■ **Es soll die ganze Woche hindurch so bleiben.**

Les nuances du verbe *sollen.*

Le verbe *sollen* marque habituellement une obligation morale. (Voir L. 19). Il peut également exprimer :

- une assertion d'autrui (on dit que, il paraît que).

  Dieses Hotel soll sehr modern sein, on dit que cet hôtel est très moderne.

- un ordre, à la 3e personne.

  Er soll ja nicht kommen! surtout, qu'il ne vienne pas!

- une éventualité (en français : venir à).

  Wenn er sterben sollte,... = Sollte er sterben,..., s'il venait à mourir...

Exercices

A *Supprimez* wenn, *puis traduisez :*
1. Wenn das Zimmer zu kalt ist, stellt er die Zentralheizung an *(chauffage central).* 2. Wenn Sie nicht schlafen können, machen Sie das Fenster zu. 3. Wenn wir nicht zufrieden sind, werden wir den Geschäftsführer rufen.

B *Traduisez en français :*
4. Sollte es regnen, so bleibe ich auf meinem Zimmer. 5. Diese Dame soll sehr reich *(riche)* sein. 6. Er soll langsamer fahren. 7. Soll ich zu dir kommen? 8. Dieser Reisende soll aus Spanien zurückkommen.

C *Traduisez en allemand :*
9. Votre nom ne se trouve pas dans le registre des voyageurs. 10. Si vous voulez une chambre au premier étage, écrivez-le nous, s'il vous plaît. 11. Quand le porteur reviendra, vous lui donnerez ce pourboire. 12. Espérons que le temps restera beau.

Corrigé :

A 1. Ist das Zimmer zu kalt, so stellt er die Zentralheizung an. *Si la chambre est trop froide, il ouvre le chauffage central.* 2. Können Sie nicht schlafen, so machen Sie... *Si vous ne pouvez pas dormir, fermez la fenêtre.* 3. Sind wir nicht zufrieden, so werden wir... *Si nous ne sommes pas satisfaits, nous appellerons le directeur.*

B 4. S'il venait à pleuvoir, je resterai dans ma chambre (Gram. 2 c). 5. On dit que cette dame est très riche (Gram. 2 a). 6. Qu'il conduise plus lentement! (Gram. 2 b) 7. Dois-je venir chez toi? (Gram. Leçon 19) 8. Il paraît que ce voyageur revient d'Espagne (Gram. 2 a).

C 9. Ihr Name steht nicht im Fremdenbuch. 10. Wollen Sie ein Zimmer im ersten Stock, so schreiben Sie es uns, bitte. 11. Wenn der Gepäckträger zurückkommt, geben Sie ihm dieses Trinkgeld *(le présent mis pour le futur, voir L. 37).* 12. Hoffentlich wird das Wetter schön bleiben (*ou* : Hoffentlich bleibt das Wetter schön).

Leçon

39 Die *Mahlzeiten

1 Das Frühstück kann immer im Hotel eingenommen werden. Man kann es auf sein Zimmer bringen lassen; in gewissen Hotels muß man dafür einen Zuschlag zahlen. Manchmal ist der Preis des Frühstücks im Zimmerpreis einbegriffen.

2 Oft geben die Hotels weder Mittag- noch Abendessen, auch kein Vesperbrot. Dann muß man in eine Gastwirtschaft, in einen Gasthof oder in ein Café gehen. Manche Gaststätten haben *Selbstbedienung. Will man Kuchen essen, so geht man in eine Konditorei.

3 Wir essen von einem Teller und trinken aus einem Glas. Mit dem Löffel essen wir die Suppe oder die Sahnespeisen, mit der Gabel die anderen Speisen. Das Fleisch wird mit dem Messer geschnitten. In den Gasthäusern sind die Teller aus Steingut oder aus Porzellan; die Mundtücher (Servietten) sowie die Tischtücher sind aus Lein. Neulich ist Paul zu einem Picknick eingeladen worden. Da benützte man Teller und Gläser aus Pappe und *Papierservietten.

1 [di m**a**l-tç**a**éten']; [tç**ou**chlak].

2 [z**è**lbçt-béd**i**nou[gn]].

3 [pap**i**r-zèrvi**è**ten'].

SALZ UND BROT MACHT DIE WANGEN ROT

Traduction

Les repas

1 Le petit déjeuner peut toujours se prendre à l'hôtel. On peut le faire monter dans sa chambre; dans certains hôtels, il faut alors payer un supplément. Parfois, le prix du petit déjeuner est compris dans celui de la chambre.

2 Souvent les hôtels ne servent ni le déjeuner, ni le dîner, non plus que le goûter. Alors, il faut aller dans une auberge, un restaurant ou un café. Certains restaurants ont un libre-service. Si l'on veut manger des gâteaux, on va dans une pâtisserie.

3 Nous mangeons dans une assiette et nous buvons dans un verre. C'est avec la cuiller que nous mangeons le potage ou les crèmes, avec la fourchette les autres mets. L'on coupe la viande avec le couteau. Dans les restaurants, les assiettes sont en faïence ou en porcelaine; les serviettes ainsi que les nappes sont en toile. Dernièrement Paul a été invité à un pique-nique; on y a utilisé des assiettes et des verres en carton et des serviettes en papier.

Vocabulaire

der Löffel (-), *la cuiller*
der Mund (-e), *la bouche*
der Teller (-), *l'assiette*
der Lein, *le lin*
die Gabel (n), *la fourchette*
die Leinwand (¨ e), *la toile, l'écran*
die Pappe, *le carton*
die Sahne (n), *la crème*
die S**e**lbstbed**ie**nung, *le libre-service*
die Servi**e**tte (n), *la serviette*
die Suppe (n), *la soupe*

das Brot (-e), *le pain*
das Fleisch, *la viande*
das Glas (¨ er), *le verre*
das Messer (-), *le couteau*
das Mundtuch (¨ er), *la serviette (de table)*
das Porzell**a**n (-), *la porcelaine*
das Steingut (¨ er), *la faïence*
das Tischtuch (¨ er), *la nappe*
das Vesperbrot (-e), *le goûter*
schneiden (schnitt, geschnitten), *couper.*

Exercice sur les mots

Traduisez : 1. *Une grande cuiller.* 2. *Un bon couteau.* 3. *Une four-*

Frugalité est mère de santé (Sel et pain font les joues roses) *chette neuve.* 4. *Il a coupé du pain.* 5. *Elle n'aime pas la crème.* Corrigé : 1. Ein großer Löffel. 2. Ein gutes Messer. 3. Eine neue Gabel. 4. Er hat Brot geschnitten. 5. Sie mag die Sahne nicht (= sie ißt nicht gern Sahne).

Grammaire

Neulich ist Paul zu einem Picknick eingeladen worden. Notez cette forme surcomposée du verbe; c'est le passé composé du passif *(ist... eingeladen worden).* Autres exemples :

> *Ich bin in eine Konditorei geführt worden,* j'ai été conduit dans une pâtisserie = on m'a conduit dans une pâtisserie.

En employant *war* au lieu de *ist,* nous formons le plus-que-parfait :

> *Ich war... geführt worden,* j'avais été conduit.
> *Sie war... eingeladen worden,* elle avait été invitée.

Exercices

A *Mettez au passé-composé, puis traduisez :*
1. In diesem Hotel wird kein Mittagessen gegeben. 2. Dieser Kuchen wird in einer Konditorei gekauft. 3. Das Zimmer wird von Emil reserviert.

B *Traduisez :*
4. Le supplément que vous avez payé, n'est pas très élevé *(hoch).* 5. Il voudrait savoir si ce restaurant a un libre-service. 6. Ces serviettes de papier avaient été achetées par sa sœur. 7. Dans cet hôtel-restaurant, le déjeuner est servi à partir de (*ab...*) onze heures et demie. 8. Nous allions toujours dans cette pâtisserie pour manger du gâteau.

Corrigé :

A 1. In diesem Hotel ist kein Mittagessen gegeben worden. *Dans cet hôtel on n'a pas donné de déjeuner* (mot à mot : *n'a pas été donné...).* 2. Dieser Kuchen ist in einer Konditorei gekauft worden. *Ce gâteau a été acheté dans une pâtisserie.* 3. Das Zimmer ist von Emil reserviert worden. *La chambre a été réservée par Émile.*

B 4. Der Zuschlag, den Sie bezahlt haben, ist nicht sehr hoch. 5. Er möchte wissen, ob dieses Gasthaus Selbstbedienung hat. 6. Diese Papierservietten waren von seiner Schwester gekauft worden. 7. In diesem Gasthof wird das Mittagessen ab halb zwölf (Uhr) aufgetragen. 8. Wir gingen immer in diese Konditorei, um Kuchen zu essen.

Lecture

Küchenzettel für April	Menus pour le mois d'avril
Sonntag	*Dimanche*
Kressesalat	Salade de cresson
Schweineschnitzel mit	Escalope de porc
Erbsen und Reis	Petits pois et riz
Obstsalat mit Schlagsahne	Salade de fruits, crème fouettée.
Montag	*Lundi*
Sardinenbrötchen	Canapés aux sardines
Gemüsesuppe mit Würstchen	Soupe de légumes et saucisses
Vanillepudding mit Himbeer-soße	Pudding à la vanille et crème de framboises.
Dienstag	*Mardi*
1 Glas Orangenmilch	1 verre de lait à l'orange
Eierravioli mit grünem Salat	Raviolis aux œufs, salade verte
Ananas mit Sahnetupfen	Ananas (garnis) à la crème
Mittwoch	*Mercredi*
Frühlingssuppe	Potage printanier
Gebratene Leber mit	Foie grillé, haricots verts
grünen Bohnen und Kartoffeln	et pommes de terre
Obsttörtchen	Tartelettes aux fruits
Donnerstag	*Jeudi*
Tomatentoast mit Kräutern	Toasts aux tomates et fines herbes
Sauerkraut mit Schweineripp-chen und Püree	Choucroute, côtelettes de porc et purée
Mirabellenkompott	Compote de mirabelles
Freitag	*Vendredi*
Nudelsuppe mit Zwiebeln	Soupe aux pâtes et aux oignons
Kabeljaufilet mit Kapern,	Filet de cabillaud aux câpres
Salzkartoffeln	pommes vapeur
Rhabarber mit Eisschneehaube	Rhubarbe meringuée
Samstag	*Samedi*
1 Glas Orangensaft	1 verre de jus d'orange
Kalbsnieren mit Kartoffel-bällchen und Spinat	Rognons de veau, croquettes de pommes de terre et épinards
Apfelmus	Compote de pommes

Aus der Zeitschrif « BURDA MODEN »

Leçon

40 Das *Frühstück

1 Gestern abend hatte ich gebeten, daß man uns das Frühstück um acht Uhr aufs Zimmer bringe. Wir haben noch nichts bekommen. Sicherlich ist es *vergessen worden.
— Einen Augenblick, ich verbinde Sie mit dem Restaurant.
— Guten Morgen, mein Herr! Womit kann ich Ihnen dienen?
— Können Sie uns bitte sofort das Frühstück heraufbringen? Wir warten schon zwanzig Minuten darauf. Ich hatte es für acht Uhr bestellt.
— Ach! Entschuldigen Sie, bitte, man hat mir nichts gesagt.

2 — Was möchten Sie?
— Zweimal *Orangensaft, einen Kaffe und einen Tee, mit Brot, Butter und Marmelade.
— Tee mit Milch oder mit *Zitrone?
— Mit Zitrone.
— Wollen Sie *geröstete *Brotschnitten (*Toaste) oder Hörnchen? *Vielleicht auch *Honig?
— Bringen Sie mir bitte *Zwieback und auch etwas Honig.
— Es wird Ihnen sogleich hinaufgebracht, mein Herr.

1 [fr**u**-chtuk]; [fèrg**è**çen'].

2 [or**an**gen' zaft]; tçitr**o**ne; [gér**eu**çtete]; [br**o**t-chn**i**ten']; [t**o**çte]; [fil**a**écht]; [h**o**nich]; [tçv**i**bak].

SPINNE AM MORGEN, KUMMER UND SORGEN

Traduction

Le petit déjeuner

1 J'avais demandé hier au soir qu'on nous monte le petit déjeuner à huit heures. Nous n'avons encore rien reçu. On a certainement oublié. — Un instant, je vous passe le restaurant (mot à mot : je vous relie...). — Bonjour Monsieur. Qu'y a-t-il pour votre service? — Pouvez-vous nous monter le petit déjeuner tout de suite, s'il vous plaît? Voici vingt minutes que nous l'attendons. Je l'avais commandé pour huit heures. — Ah! Excusez, je vous prie, on ne m'a rien dit.

2 — Que désirez-vous? — Deux jus d'orange, un café et un thé avec du pain, du beurre et de la confiture. — Thé au lait ou au citron? — Au citron. — Voulez-vous du pain grillé ou des croissants? Peut-être aussi du miel? — Apportez-moi des biscottes et un peu de miel également. — On vous montera cela tout de suite, Monsieur.

Prononciation

Die Orange et *das Restaurant* se prononcent comme en français. Mais pour les deux mots, il faut articuler la marque du pluriel : *die Orangen — die Restaurants.*

Vocabulaire

der Honig, *le miel*
der Saft (¨ e), *le jus*
der Tee (s), *le thé*
der Zwieback (-e), *la biscotte*
die Marmel**a**de (n), *la confiture*
die Or**a**nge (n), = die Apfelsine (n)
die Schnitte (n) 1. *la tranche de pain.* 2. *la tartine*
die Zitr**o**ne (n), *le citron*
das Hörnchen (-), *le croissant*
dienen, *servir*
rösten, *griller*
verl**a**ngen, *demander, exiger*
verb**i**nden (a, u), *lier, relier*

Araignée du matin, chagrin (et soucis)

■ **Ich hatte verlangt, daß man das Frühstück aufs Zimmer bringe.**
Daß man bringe qui rapporte ici un ordre ou un souhait, est au subjonctif.

Man bediene mich etwas schneller! qu'on me serve un peu plus vite!
Man sagt, er diene als Kellner, on dit qu'il sert comme garçon de café.
Wenn er doch käme! si seulement il venait!
Er tut, als ob er krank sei (ou : *wäre*), il fait comme s'il était malade.

Dans ces exemples, nous constatons que le subjonctif sert à exprimer ce qui est irréel, incertain, douteux. L'allemand dispose de deux subjonctifs (1 et 2), chacun ayant un présent, un passé et un futur. Les trois temps du subjonctif 1 sont formés sur le radical de l'infinitif (infinitif du verbe considéré, ou infinitif de ses auxiliaires de temps). Les trois temps du subjonctif 2 sont formés, eux, sur le radical du passé. Voici la conjugaison de *wohnen,* habiter, verbe régulier, et de *tragen,* porter, verbe irrégulier, au présent du subjonctif 1 :

ich wohne, que j'habite	*ich trage,* que je porte
du wohnest	*du tragest*
er (sie, es) wohne	*er (sie, es) trage*
wir wohnen	*wir tragen*
ihr wohnet	*ihr traget*
sie (Sie) wohnen	*sie (Sie) tragen*

Remarque : Les verbes réguliers et irréguliers ont la même terminaison. La voyelle radicale de ces derniers n'est pas modifiée.

■ a) Le présent du subjonctif 2 des verbes réguliers a la même forme que le prétérit de l'indicatif : *ich wohnte, du wohntest,* (voir Leçon 14).
b) *Wenn er käme...* s'il venait... *Wenn ich trüge...,* si je portais... Le présent du subjonctif 2 des verbes irréguliers se forme sur le radical du passé *(kommen, kam; tragen, trug);* on y ajoute l'inflexion si possible, et les terminaisons du subjonctif présent.

ich käme	*ich trüge*	*wir kämen*	*wir trügen*
je viendrais,	je porterais	*ihr kämet*	*ihr trüget*
du kämest	*du trügest*	*sie (Sie) kämen*	*sie trügen*
er (sie, es) käme	*er trüge*		

Nous verrons ultérieurement les emplois du subjonctif particuliers à l'allemand. Notez que le présent du subjonctif 2 sert souvent de conditionnel.

Exercices

A *Faites des subordonnées interrogatives avec* ob, *si, en mettant le verbe au subjonctif 1 présent, puis traduisez :*
1. Der Gast fragt : « Bringt Emma das Frühstück bald? Kommt der Briefträger heute? Fährt dieses Taxi in die Stadt? »

B *Mettez les phrases au présent du subjonctif 2, puis traduisez (par le conditionnel) :*
2. Emma vergißt das Frühstück. 3. Der Gast ruft an. 4. Man verbindet ihn mit dem Restaurant. 5. Man gibt ihm Honig. 6. Man stellt zwei Teller auf den Tisch.

C *Traduisez :*
7. Mon petit déjeuner a été commandé hier soir à neuf heures. 8. Passez-moi immédiatement *(sofort)* le gérant. 9. On montera du pain et du beurre à ces clients. 10. N'oubliez pas le jus d'orange. 11. Je prendrais du café. 12. Je mangerais des croissants chauds avec de la confiture.

Corrigé :

A 1. Der Gast fragt, ob Emma das Frühstück bald bringe, ob der Briefträger heute komme, ob dieses Taxi in die Stadt fahre. *Le client demande si Emma apportera bientôt le petit déjeuner, si le facteur passe aujourd'hui, si ce taxi va en ville.*

B 2. Emma vergäße das Frühstück. *Emma oublierait le petit déjeuner.* 3. Der Gast riefe an. *Le client téléphonerait.* 4. Man verbände... *On lui passerait le restaurant.* 5. Man gäbe... *On lui donnerait du miel.* 6. Man stellte... *On poserait deux assiettes sur la table.*

C 7. Mein Frühstück ist gestern abend um neun Uhr bestellt worden. 8. Verbinden Sie mich sofort mit dem Geschäftsführer. 9. Man wird diesen Gästen Brot und Butter hinaufbringen. 10. Vergessen Sie den Orangensaft nicht. 11. Ich nähme Kaffee. 12. Ich äße warme Hörnchen mit Marmelade.

Leçon

40 bis — Contrôle et révisions

A **Complétez par le pronom relatif, puis traduisez :**

(Relisez le texte L. 32,4 et voyez le Mémento n° 37).

1. Die Kreuzfahrt, ... ich diesen Sommer machte, dauerte zwei Wochen. 2. Der Tip, ... du mir gabst, war mir sehr nützlich. 3. Der Arzt, ... er den Brief sandte, wohnt in Sydney. 4. Der Fleischer, ... Geschäft geschlossen ist, ist nach Chicago abgefahren. 5. Die Touristen, ... man die Schlachthöfe zeigte, waren meistens Fleischer.

B **Supprimez wenn ou daß dans les phrases suivantes, puis traduisez :**

(Relisez le texte L. 34,4 et voyez le Mémento n° 66 et 67).

6. Ich sage dem Zöllner, daß ich nichts zu verzollen habe. 7. Wenn wir alles präzise angeben, zahlen wir oft keine Zollgebühr. 8. Wenn der Zöllner drei Flaschen Kognak findet, zahlen Sie einen Zuschlag. 9. Sie erklären, daß sie den Apparat nicht in Deutschland gekauft haben.

C **Mettez les phrases suivantes au passif, après les avoir traduites :**

(Texte L. 36,4 et Mémento n° 49).

10. Die Zeitung veranstaltet eine Umfrage. 11. Der Reporter besuchte zehn Hotels. 12. Er hat viele Gäste ausgefragt.

D **Traduisez :**

Blumen und Geschäfte

Die Bedeutung der Blumenzucht hat seit dem zweiten Weltkrieg immer mehr zugenommen. Der Konsum hat andere Schichten der Gesellschaft erreicht. Blumen werden nicht mehr nur bei besonderen Anlässen gekauft. So ist die romantische Handwerkstätigkeit in eine authentische Industrie übergegangen. Italien, der größte Blumenexporteur Europas vor Holland, Frankreich und der Bundesrepublik Deutschland, hat seine Anpflanzungsfläche für Blumen etwa verdreifacht.

Aus der Wochenzeitung « Die Weltwoche », Zürich.

Corrigé :

A 1. die. *La croisière que j'ai faite cet été, a duré deux semaines.* 2. den. *Le conseil (m. à m. tuyau) que tu m'as donné, m'a été très utile.* 3. dem. *Le médecin, à qui il a envoyé la lettre, habite Sydney.* 4. dessen. *Le boucher dont le magasin est fermé, est parti pour Chicago.* 5. denen. *Les touristes auxquels on a montré les abattoirs, étaient pour la plupart des bouchers.*

6. Ich sage dem Zöllner, ich habe nichts zu verzollen. *Je dis au douanier que je n'ai rien à déclarer.* 7. Geben wir alles präzise an, so zahlen wir oft keine Zollgebühr. *Si nous indiquons tout avec précision, souvent nous ne payons pas de droits.* 8. Findet der Zöllner drei Flaschen Kognak, so zahlen Sie einen Zuschlag. *Si le douanier trouve 3 bouteilles de cognac, vous paierez un supplément.* 9. Sie erklären, sie haben den Apparat nicht in Deutschland gekauft. *Ils affirment qu'ils n'ont pas acheté cet appareil en Allemagne.*

10. a) *Le journal organise une enquête.* b) Eine Umfrage wird von der Zeitung veranstaltet. 11. a) *Le reporter a visité (m. à m. : visita) dix hôtels.* b) Zehn Hotels wurden vom Reporter besucht. 12. a) *Il a questionné beaucoup de clients.* b) Viele Gäste sind von ihm ausgefragt worden.

Les fleurs et les affaires.
L'importance de la culture des fleurs n'a cessé d'augmenter, depuis la deuxième guerre mondiale. La consommation a atteint d'autres couches de la société. Ce n'est plus seulement pour des occasions particulières que l'on achète des fleurs. Aussi, la profession romantique à caractère artisanal s'est-elle transformée en une véritable industrie. L'Italie, le plus grand exportateur de fleurs, avant la Hollande, la France et la République Fédérale d'Allemagne, a triplé à peu près la superficie consacrée à la floriculture.
Extrait de l'hebdomadaire « Die Weltwoche » (= La Semaine dans le Monde), Zurich.

41 Mittagessen in aller Eile

(der Herr : H; die Dame : D; der Oberkellner : O)

1 H — Herr Ober, bitte! Zeigen Sie uns die *Speisekarte. Wir haben es eilig. Was haben Sie bereit?
O — Heute gibt es Fisch mit Kapernsoße. Sie müßten aber ein wenig warten, somit geht es nicht.
D — Oh! Doch! Fisch — wir sind am Meer; hier muß er frisch sein.
H — Wir haben keine Zeit. Wir wollen heute abend besser essen.
O — Unter diesen *Umständen schlage ich Ihnen Rinderbraten mit Rosenkohl und Kartoffelbrei vor.
D — Ja, das sagt mir zu.
O — Und womit wollen Sie beginnen?
H — Mit einer Vorspeise : Butter, *Radieschen und geräuchertem *Lachs.

2 O — Möchten Sie etwas trinken?
D — Ja, Mineralwasser.
H — Ein wenig Wein, trotzdem. Eine halbe Flasche Rheinwein.
O — Und als *Nachtisch?
D — Das werden wir nachher sehen.

3 — Ich möchte Brot, bitte.
— Haben Sie Senf, Salz und Pfeffer?
— Bringen Sie den nächsten Gang, bitte.

1 [chp**a**éze-k**a**rte]; [**ou**m'cht**è**n'den']; [rad**i**ç-chen']; [lakç].

2 [nartich].

EINEM LEEREN MAGEN IST NICHT GUT PREDIGEN

Traduction

Un déjeuner expédié

(Le monsieur : M; la dame : D; le garçon : G)

1 M — Garçon, s'il vous plaît, montrez-nous le menu. Nous sommes pressés. Qu'est-ce qu'il y a de prêt? G — Aujourd'hui il y a du poisson avec une sauce aux câpres. Mais vous devriez attendre un peu, aussi cela ne va pas. D — Ah! si, du poisson — nous sommes à la mer; il doit être frais ici. M — Nous n'avons pas le temps. Nous mangerons mieux ce soir. G — Dans ces conditions, je vous propose du rôti de bœuf avec des choux de Bruxelles et de la purée de pomme de terre. D — Oui, cela me convient. G — Et par quoi voulez-vous commencer? M — Par un hors-d'œuvre : du beurre, des radis et du saumon fumé.

2 G — Désirez-vous boire quelque chose? D — Oui, de l'eau minérale. M — Un peu de vin, quand même. Une demi-bouteille de vin du Rhin. G — Et pour le dessert? D — On verra tout à l'heure.

3 — Je voudrais du pain, s'il vous plaît. — Avez-vous de la moutarde, du sel et du poivre? — Vous nous apportez la suite, s'il vous plaît (m. à m. : le service suivant).

Vocabulaire

der Braten (-), *le rôti*
der Brei (-e), *la purée*
der Lachs (-e), *le saumon*
der Nachtisch (-e), das Dessert (s)
der Ober(kellner) (-), *le maître d'hôtel, le garçon*
der Pfeffer, *le poivre*
der Senf, *la moutarde*
der Umstand (¨e), *la circonstance*
die Flasche (n), *la bouteille*
die Kaper (n), *le câpre*
die Soße (n) = die Sauce (n)
die Vorspeise (n), *le hors-d'œuvre*
das Meer (-e), *la mer*
das Rad**ie**schen (-), *le radis*
das Rind (-er), *le bœuf, la génisse*
das Salz (-e), *le sel*
das Wasser (-), *l'eau*
z**u**s**a**gen (+ datif), *accepter, plaire*
v**o**rschl**a**gen (u, a; ä), *proposer*
ich habe es eilig, *je suis pressé*

Ventre affamé n'a pas d'oreilles (Il est malaisé de prêcher un estomac vide).

Grammaire

■ ***Heute gibt es Fisch mit Kapernsoße.***
Notre tournure « il y a », dans le sens de « il existe », est rendue par *es gibt* (+ accusatif).

Es gibt nichts Neues unter der Sonne, il n'y a rien de nouveau sous le soleil.
Es gab Lachs, il y eut du saumon :
Es wird Braten geben, il y aura du rôti.

● *Ein schöner Schrank steht dort,* il y a une belle armoire là-bas. Avec une idée de lieu, de position, « il y a » est rendu par un verbe de position (voir L. 12).

● *Es sind noch drei Flaschen im Kühlschrank,* il y a encore trois bouteilles dans le réfrigérateur.
Pour préciser le nombre, on emploie : *es ist...* ou *es sind....* Le verbe s'accorde avec le sujet réel (drei Flaschen).

● *Ich erfuhr es vor einem Jahr,* je l'ai appris il y a un an.
An sens temporel, « il y a » = *vor* (+ datif) pour une action terminée dans le passé.

● *Ich weiß es seit einem Jahr,* il y a un an que je le sais.
L'action commencée dans le passé, dure encore; « il y a » = *seit* (+ datif).

Exercice

Traduisez :
1. Il y a du bon vin ici. 2. Sur la table, il y avait quelques tasses. 3. Il y a de beaux tableaux (*das Gemälde,-*) dans cette pièce. 4. Il y avait dix personnes à la grande table. 5. Il y a une heure (que) nous attendons. 6. Il y a deux semaines, nous avons mangé au « Weißen Rößl » (= Cheval Blanc).

Corrigé :

1. Es gibt guten Wein hier. 2. Auf dem Tisch standen einige Tassen. 3. Es hängen schöne Gemälde in diesem Zimmer. 4. Es waren zehn Personen am großen Tisch. 5. Seit einer Stunde warten wir. 6. Vor zwei Wochen haben wir im « Weißen Rößl » gegessen.

Lecture

Der Sieger

In einem gutgeleiteten Restaurant bestellte sich Max Reger einen Hummer. Als der Kellner den zehnfüßigen Krebs brachte, fiel dem Komponisten auf, daß der Hummer nur eine Schere hatte. Auf seine Beanstandung erklärte der herbeigeeilte Geschäftsführer indigniert : « Es kommt vor, mein Herr, daß die Hummer miteinander kämpfen, und da reißt der eine dem anderen manchmal eine Schere aus ».
« Also so ist das », lächelte Max Reger freundlich, « nun gut, dann lassen Sie mir bitte den Sieger servieren ».

Aus der Wochenzeitung « Rheinischer Merkur » (Köln).

Le vainqueur

Dans un restaurant bien géré, Max Reger commanda un homard. Lorsque le garçon apporta le crustacé décapode, le compositeur remarqua que le homard n'avait qu'une pince. A la suite de sa réclamation, le gérant accourut et expliqua avec indignation : « Il arrive, Monsieur, que les homards se combattent, et parfois l'un arrache à l'autre une pince ».
« Ah, c'est donc ainsi, dit Max Reger avec un sourire aimable, eh bien, dans ce cas, faites-moi servir le vainqueur, je vous prie. »

Leçon

42

Das Abendessen

(der Oberkellner : O; der Herr : H; die Dame : D).

1 O – Möchten Sie mit einem Aperitif beginnen? mit einem Portwein? einem Fruchtsaft? Was für einen Fruchtsaft möchten Sie? Während Sie Ihren Aperitif trinken, wollen Sie bitte ihr Menü zusammenstellen?

2 H – Ja, recht so; bringen Sie uns die Speisekarte. Nun, was essen Sie gern? Rohkost? Fisch? Abends essen Sie kein Fleisch, nicht wahr? Es gibt hier eine Spezialität : eine Schüsselpastete; sie schmeckt ausgezeichnet. Wählen Sie, was hätten Sie gern?

D – Ich möchte etwas leicht Verdauliches. Die Pastete liegt zu schwer im Magen. Ich nehme Fisch, das ist alles.

H – Nein, nehmen Sie doch noch etwas dazu.

D – Etwas Reis; dann werde ich schon sehen.

3 O – Was für einen Wein darf ich Ihnen bringen?

H – Zeigen Sie uns bitte die Weinkarte. Ich glaube, Weißwein würde besser dazu passen als Rotwein, was meinen Sie?

4 H – Zum Nachtisch gibt es hier eine sehr feine Obsttorte; ich kann sie Ihnen bestens empfehlen.

D – Ach, ich bin wirklich nicht mehr hungrig. Am liebsten würde ich etwas Obst essen.

5 O – Trinken Sie Kaffee?

H – Ja, zwei Tassen, bitte. Das wäre alles.

O – Vielleicht einen Likör zum Abschluß, ein Gläschen Kognak?...

H – Herr Ober, zahlen bitte!

WER DIE WAHL HAT, HAT DIE QUAL

Traduction

Le dîner

(Le garçon : G; Le client : M; La cliente : D).

1 G — Voulez-vous un apéritif pour commencer? un porto, un jus de fruit? Quel jus de fruit désireriez-vous? Pendant que vous prenez l'apéritif, voulez-vous composer votre menu?

2 M — C'est cela; apportez-nous le menu. Voyons, qu'est-ce que vous aimez? des crudités? du poisson? Vous ne prenez pas de viande le soir, n'est-ce pas? Il y a ici une spécialité : un pâté en terrine; il est excellent. Choisissez. Qu'est-ce que vous aimeriez prendre?
D — Je voudrais quelque chose de léger (m. à m. : à digérer). Le pâté c'est trop lourd (m. à m. : à l'estomac). Je vais prendre du poisson, ce sera tout.
M — Non, prenez donc quelque chose avec!
D — Un peu de riz; puis je verrai (déjà).

3 G — Comme vin, qu'est-ce que je vous servirai? M — Montrez-nous la carte des vins, s'il vous plaît. Je pense qu'un vin blanc irait mieux qu'un vin rouge, qu'en pensez-vous?

4 M — Comme dessert, il y a une très bonne tarte aux fruits ici; je vous la conseillerais (m. à m. : je peux vous la conseiller fortement). D — Ah, je n'ai vraiment plus faim. Je préférerais des fruits.

5 G — Prendrez-vous le café? M — Oui, deux tasses s'il vous plaît. Ce sera tout. G — Peut-être une liqueur pour terminer, un cognac? M — Garçon, l'addition s'il vous plaît (m. à m. : payer, s'il vous plaît).

Vocabulaire

der Abschluß (¨ sse), *la conclusion*
der Likör (-e), *la liqueur*
der Nachtisch (e), *le dessert*
der Reis, *le riz*
die Folge (n), *la suite*

die Torte (n), *la tarte*
aufst**e**llen, *établir*
meinen, *penser, être d'avis*
passen (+ zu), *convenir*
schm**e**cken, *goûter, plaire (au goût)*

Quiconque a le choix, a le tourment.

die Pastete (n), *le pâté*
die Rohkost, *le régime cru*
die Schüssel (n), *le plat, la terrine*
die Spezialität (-en), *la spécialité*

verdauen, *digérer*
wählen, *choisir; élire*
raten (ie, a; ä), *conseiller; deviner*

Grammaire

■ Am liebsten hätte ich Obst.

Les verbes *sein, haben, werden,* auxiliaires de temps, prennent les formes suivantes au présent du subjonctif 2 :

sein, être : *ich wäre,* je serais, que je fusse
haben, avoir : *ich hätte,* j'aurais, que j'eusse
werden, devenir : *ich würde,* je deviendrais, que je devinsse

Cette dernière forme sert également d'auxiliaire pour le conditionnel.
Pour la conjugaison, voir Mémento, n° 43 à 45.

■ Weißwein würde besser dazu passen.

Notre conditionnel s'exprime à l'aide de *würde* et de l'infinitif du verbe à conjuguer, placé à la fin de la proposition. Cette forme représente le subjonctif 2 au futur.
Exemples :

Ich würde es bestellen, je le commanderais.
Du würdest es holen, tu irais le chercher.
Er würde es aufmachen, il l'ouvrirait.
Wir würden die Spezialität versuchen, nous goûterions à la spécialité.
Ihr würdet Pastete essen, vous mangeriez du pâté.
Sie würden einen Aperitif trinken, ils boiraient un apéritif.

La forme avec *würde* se remplace souvent par le présent du subjonctif 2 (voir L. 40), surtout pour les verbes irréguliers.

Ich würde dir raten = Ich riete dir, je te conseillerais.
Er würde hungrig sein = Er wäre hungrig, il serait affamé, il aurait faim.
Sie würden eine Spezialität haben = Sie hätten eine Spezialität, ils auraient une spécialité.
Wir würden sofort kommen = Wir kämen sofort, nous viendrions aussitôt.

Exercices

A *Transposez au présent du subjonctif 2, puis traduisez :*
1. Dieser Gasthof hat eine gute Küche. 2. Pastete und Fisch sind seine Spezialitäten. 3. Die Gäste essen auch gern seine Torten. 4. Sie trinken schwarzen Kaffee.

B *Transposez au futur du subjonctif 2, puis traduisez :*
5. Er ißt nach der Karte. 6. Wir speisen nach festem Preis. 7. Sie wählt das Tagesmenü. 8. Diese Torte schmeckt sehr fein.

C *Traduisez :*
9. Cette dame voudrait du poisson, car c'est léger. 10. Le vin rouge n'irait pas avec *(zu)* ce plat *(das Gericht).* 11. Je pense que cette tarte aux fruits serait excellente. 12. Le café que vous nous avez servi, n'était plus chaud. 13. Le pain, le couvert *(das Gedeck, e)* et le service seraient compris.

Corrigé :

A 1. Dieser Gasthof hätte... *Ce restaurant aurait une bonne cuisine.* 2. Pastete und Fisch wären... *Le pâté et le poisson seraient ses spécialités.* 3. Die Gäste äßen... *Les clients aimeraient également ses tartes.* 4. Sie tränken... *Ils prendraient (boiraient) du café noir.*

B 5. Er würde... essen. *Il mangerait à la carte.* 6. Wir würden... speisen. *Nous mangerions à prix fixe.* 7. Sie würde... wählen. *Elle choisirait le plat du jour.* 8. Diese Torte würde... schmecken. *Cette tarte serait très bonne (au goût).*

C 9. Diese Dame möchte Fisch, denn es ist leicht verdaulich. 10. Rotwein würde nicht zu diesem Gericht passen. 11. Ich meine, diese Obsttorte wäre ausgezeichnet *(plutôt que :* würde... sein). 12. Der Kaffee, den Sie uns serviert haben, war nicht mehr warm. 13. (das) Brot, (das) Gedeck und (die) Bedienung wären einbegriffen.

Leçon

43 Der Stadtverkehr

1 Die Landstraßen führen in die Stadt hinein und bilden breite Straßen, die man auch Boulevards oder Alleen nennt. An den Kreuzungen mehrerer Straßen sind Plätze. In die Hauptstraßen münden engere Straßen oder Gassen ein. In den alten Vierteln gibt es oft Sackgassen.

2 Auf manchen Straßen können Fahrzeuge in beiden Fahrtrichtungen verkehren. Andere Straßen dagegen sind Einbahnstraßen. Breite Brücken führen über den Fluß. Um Verkehrstockungen an gewissen Kreuzungen zu vermeiden, muß ein Teil der Fahrzeuge durch einen Tunnel fahren.

3 Die Fußgänger gehen auf dem Bürgersteig. Um über die Straße zu gehen, benützen sie die Fußgängerstreifen, (oder : die Zebrastreifen). Der Verkehr wird durch Verkehrsampeln geregelt : grün, gelb, rot. An den gefährlichen Kreuzungen stehen Verkehrspolizisten.

4 Will man von einem bestimmten Punkt aus zu einem anderen fahren, so kann man die öffentlichen Verkehrsmittel benützen : den Autobus, die Straßenbahn, den Obus, die U-Bahn. Wer es eilig hat, nimmt eine Taxe (eine Droschke). Die Taxen befinden sich besonders auf den Parkplätzen.

1 [cht**a**t-fèrk**é**r]; [al**é**-en']; [kr**o**eutçou^{gn}en']

2 [b**u**rger-cht**a**ék.]

3 [**o**-bouç]; [**ou**-ban].

VORSICHT IST DIE MUTTER DER WEISHEIT

Traduction

Circulation en ville

Les routes pénètrent en ville en formant de larges rues que l'on appelle aussi boulevards ou avenues. Aux croisements de plusieurs rues il y a des places. Sur les rues principales débouchent des rues plus étroites ou des ruelles. Dans les vieux quartiers il y a souvent des impasses.

Dans certaines voies, les véhicules peuvent circuler dans les deux sens. Par contre, d'autres rues sont à sens unique. De larges ponts franchissent la rivière. Pour éviter les encombrements à certains carrefours, une partie des voitures doivent passer par un tunnel.

Les piétons marchent sur le trottoir. Pour traverser la rue, ils empruntent les passages cloutés. La circulation est réglée par des feux : vert, orange, rouge. Aux carrefours dangereux, il y a des agents.

Si l'on veut aller d'un point à l'autre, on peut utiliser les transports en commun : l'autobus, le tramway, le trolleybus, le métro. Celui qui est pressé, prend un taxi. Les taxis se trouvent particulièrement aux lieux de stationnement.

Vocabulaire

der Bürgersteig (-e), *le trottoir*
der Fluß (⸗sse), *la rivière*
der Fußgänger (-), *le piéton*
der Mund (-e), *la bouche*
der Obus (se), *le trolley*
der Polizist (-en), *l'agent*
der Punkt (-e), *le point*
der Streifen (-), *la bande, la raie*
die Droschke (n), *le fiacre, le taxi*
die Gasse (n), *la ruelle*
die Landstraße (n), *la grand'route*
die Sackgasse (n), *l'impasse*
die Stockung (-en), *l'embouteillage*
die Taxe (n), *le taxi; la taxe*
die U-Bahn (en), *le chemin de fer souterrain*
das Viertel (-), *le quartier*

Prudence est mère de (sagesse =) sûreté.

der Tunnel (-), *le tunnel*
die All**ee** (n), *l'allée*
die Ampel (n), *la lampe*

(ein)münden,
déboucher, se jeter dans
regeln, *régler*
verm**ei**den (ie, ie), *éviter*

Grammaire

■ Von einem bestimmten Punkt aus.

Quelques prépositions sont précisées par l'emploi d'une particule placée après le complément. Exemples :

Von Montag ab,
à partir de lundi.
Von Kindheit an,
dès l'enfance.

Von Köln aus,
au départ de Cologne.
Auf den Berg zu,
en direction de la montagne.

■ Die Straße, die Straßen – der Fluß, die Flüsse.

L's dur [ç] ne s'écrit « ss » qu'entre deux voyelles, si la première de celles-ci est brève : *gewisse, die Gasse.* A la fin d'un mot ou d'une syllabe, on écrit toujours *ß : der Fluß – er läßt – das Eßzimmer.* Entre deux voyelles dont la première est longue, on écrit *ß : die Grüße,* les salutations – *heißen,* s'appeler – *die Maße,* les mesures ». (La lettre *ß* s'appelle « s-z ».)

Exercices

A *Traduisez :*
1. Von jetzt ab vermeiden wir diese Kreuzung. 2. Von dieser Brücke aus ist es nicht mehr weit. 3. Fahren Sie immer geradeaus auf diesen Kirchturm zu! 4. Wir werden bis Sonntag hier bleiben.

B *Mettez au pluriel, puis traduisez :*
5. **a)** *voyelles brèves :* ich muß; er ißt; der Bus. **b)** *voyelles longues :* der Fuß; er aß; der Zusammenstoß.

Corrigé :

A 1. A partir de maintenant nous éviterons ce carrefour. 2. Depuis ce pont, ce n'est plus loin. 3. Allez toujours tout droit en direction de ce clocher. 4. Nous resterons ici jusqu'à dimanche.

B 5 **a)** wir müssen, *nous devons*; sie essen, *ils mangent*; die Busse, *les cars.* **b)** die Füße, *les pieds*; sie aßen, *ils mangeaient*; die Zusammenstöße, *les chocs.*

Für den französischen Autofahrer in der Bundesrepublik.

Die Verkehrszeichen entsprechen im allgemeinen der internationalen Verkehrsordnung. Auf der Autobahn darf man nur auf den markierten Parkplätzen anhalten. Nur wer eine Panne hat, darf am Straßenrand parken.
Ein gelbes Nummernschild oder ein auf der Spitze stehendes Quadrat kennzeichnen eine Hauptstraße. Auf diesen Straßen hat man Vorfahrt. Aber an einer Kreuzung mit einer anderen Hauptstraße geht die Vorfahrt verloren : hier hat Vorfahrtsrecht, wer von rechts kommt.
Der Kreisverkehr wird durch drei weiße Pfeiler auf blauem Grund angezeigt. Die Vorfahrt gehört hier demjenigen, der sich schon im Kreisverkehr befindet.
In einer Steigung wird manchmal die äußerste rechte Fahrbahn « Kriechspur » genannt. Langsame Fahrzeuge oder schwere Wohnwagen müssen diese Fahrbahn obligatorisch benutzen.

A l'intention de l'automobiliste français en Allemagne Fédérale

La signalisation routière est en général conforme au code international. Sur l'autoroute, on ne doit s'arrêter qu'aux endroits de stationnement indiqués. En cas de panne seulement, (m. à m. : celui qui a une panne) on a le droit de stationner sur le bas-côté.
Un numéro sur plaque jaune, ou bien un carré posé sur l'angle indiquent une route à grande circulation. Sur ces voies, on a la priorité. Mais au croisement avec une autre route à grande circulation, la priorité est supprimée; dans ce cas, la priorité est à celui qui vient de droite.
Le sens giratoire est indiqué par trois flèches blanches sur fond bleu. La priorité appartient à celui qui est déjà engagé dans le sens giratoire.
Dans une côte, on appelle parfois la bande à l'extrême droite « voie pour véhicules lents » (m. à m. : piste pour ramper). Les véhicules lents ou les caravanes lourdes doivent obligatoirement utiliser cette piste.

Leçon

44 Wie man nach dem Weg fragt

1 — Ich möchte auf die Bank gehen. Könnten Sie mir bitte den Weg weisen?
— Ja, gern. Die Bank liegt ganz in der Nähe. Wenn sie aus Ihrem Hotel kommen, gehen Sie nach links. Dann nehmen Sie die erste Straße zu Ihrer Linken; Sie bleiben also immer auf dieser Seite des Bürgersteigs. Die Bank ist das dritte oder vierte Haus.

2 — Ich möchte das Museum besichtigen; wie komme ich am besten dorthin? Ich bin fremd in dieser Stadt.
— Zu Fuß sind es dreiviertel Stunden von hier aus. Sie können aber mit dem Omnibus hinfahren, denn es ist etwas schwierig, wenn man die Stadt nicht kennt. Wissen Sie, wo der Rathausplatz ist? — Nein — Sehen Sie dort die Verkehrsampel? Dort gehen Sie nach rechts, dann geradeaus; Sie kommen auf einen Platz, wo sich die Haltestelle des Omnibusses befindet. Zum Museum sind es kaum zehn Minuten.

3 — Verzeihen Sie, Herr Schutzmann, wie komme ich zum Hauptbahnhof?
— Sie können mit diesem Obus fahren; der bringt Sie aber nicht direkt dorthin. Fahren Sie bis zum Marktplatz; dort steigen Sie in die Linie 5 um; an der vierten Haltestelle steigen Sie aus und sind direkt am Hauptbahnhof.
— Besten Dank für die Auskunft.
— Herr Schaffner, sagen Sie mir bitte, wann ich aussteigen muß.

AN DEN FEDERN ERKENNT MAN DEN VOGEL

Traduction

Comment demander son chemin

1 – Je voudrais aller à la banque. Pourriez-vous m'indiquer le chemin, s'il vous plaît? – Oui, volontiers. La banque est tout près d'ici. En sortant de l'hôtel, prenez à gauche. Puis vous prenez la première rue à gauche; vous resterez donc toujours sur le trottoir de ce côté-ci. La banque est la troisième ou quatrième maison.

2 – Je voudrais visiter le musée; quelle serait la meilleure façon de m'y rendre? Je suis étranger dans cette ville. – D'ici vous mettrez trois quarts d'heure à pied. Mais vous pouvez prendre l'autobus, car c'est un peu difficile, quand on ne connaît pas la ville. Savez-vous où se trouve la place de l'hôtel de ville? – Non – Voyez-vous là-bas les feux? (mot à mot : la lampe pour la circulation). Vous irez là-bas à droite, puis tout droit; vous arriverez à une place où se trouve la station d'autobus. Jusqu'au musée, il y a à peine dix minutes.

3 – Pardon, Monsieur l'agent, pour aller à la Gare Centrale? – Vous pouvez prendre ce trolley; mais il (celui-ci) ne vous y conduira pas directement. Vous le prendrez jusqu'à la place du Marché; là-bas, vous changerez et prendrez la ligne 5; au quatrième arrêt vous descendrez et vous serez directement à la Gare Centrale. – Merci bien pour le renseignement. – Monsieur le contrôleur, veuillez me dire quand il me faudra (mot à mot : je dois) descendre.

Vocabulaire

der Schaffner (-), *le receveur*
der Schutzmann (plur. die Schutzleute), *le gardien de la paix*
die Auskunft (¨e), *le renseignement*
die Nähe, *la proximité*
die Stelle (n), *l'endroit*
die H**a**ltest**e**lle (n), *la station, l'arrêt*
das Rathaus (¨er), *l'hôtel de ville*
Haupt... (dans les noms composés) *principal*
verz**ei**hen (ie, ie) *pardonner*
weisen (ie, ie) *indiquer*

On reconnaît l'oiseau à son plumage.

■ Es ist schwierig, wenn man die Stadt nicht kennt.

Le verbe *kennen,* connaître, a les terminaisons d'un verbe régulier, mais son radical change au prétérit et au participe passé, comme les verbes irréguliers : *kennen, kannte, gekannt.*

Ich kenne die Stadt gut, je connais bien cette ville.
Ich kannte ihn dem Namen nach, je le connaissais de nom.
Ich habe diese Person nie gekannt, je n'ai jamais connu cette personne.

Les verbes suivants ont les mêmes caractéristiques : *brennen,* brûler; *nennen,* nommer; *rennen,* courir; *senden,* envoyer; *wenden,* tourner.

Das Holz brennt gut, le bois brûle bien.
Das Licht brannte die ganze Nacht hindurch, la lumière brûlait toute la nuit.
Ich habe mich am Motor verbrannt, je me suis brûlé au moteur.
Ich sende ihm einen Brief, je lui envoie une lettre.
Ich sandte ihm oft Postkarten, je lui envoyais souvent des cartes postales.
Ich habe ihm ein Paket gesandt, je lui ai envoyé un paquet.

● ***Remarques :***

1. Les verbes *bringen, brachte, gebracht,* apporter, et *denken, dachte, gedacht,* penser, ont eux aussi les mêmes caractéristiques.

2. Le verbe *rennen* prend l'auxiliaire *sein* au passé composé et au plus-que-parfait.

Er ist in den Garten gerannt, il a couru au jardin.

3. Pour *senden* et *wenden,* on peut également employer les formes du verbe régulier, au prétérit et au participe passé.

Ich sendete (= *sandte*), *ich habe gesendet* (= *gesandt*).
Ich wendete (=*wandte*), je tournais; *ich habe gewendet* (= *gewandt*), j'ai tourné. Voir Mémento, n° 53.

Apprenez les verbes irréguliers avec leurs temps primitifs (infinitif, prétérit, participe passé) tout comme vous apprenez les noms avec leur pluriel. Faites de fréquentes révisions.

Exercices

A *Mettez les phrases au passé composé, puis traduisez :*
1. Sie kennen die Stadt. 2. Ein Junge rennt über die Brücke. 3. Sie senden uns Postkarten. 4. Ich denke an dich. 5. Er bringt einen Stadtplan mit.

B a) *Traduisez les phrases suivantes.* b) *Transformez-les en subordonnées interrogatives, introduites par* Sagen Sie mir bitte, ob..., *Dites-moi s'il-vous-plaît si...*
6. Ist das Postamt weit von hier? 7. Ist das die Beethovenstraße? 8. Muß ich mit der Straßenbahn oder mit dem Autobus hinfahren? 9. Ist es in dieser Richtung? 10. Gibt es hier ein Polizeibüro?

C *Traduisez :*
11. Voyez-vous ce café? L'hôtel se trouve deux rues plus loin. 12. Vous ne pouvez pas y aller à pied, car c'est trop loin. 13. Nous aimerions prendre (= prendrions volontiers) un taxi. 14. Il voulait descendre au troisième arrêt, mais il se trompa *(sich irren).*

Corrigé :

A 1. Sie haben die Stadt gekannt. *Ils ont connu la ville.* 2. Ein Junge ist... gerannt. *Un garçon a franchi le pont en courant.* 3. Sie haben... gesandt (= gesendet). *Ils nous ont envoyé des cartes postales.* 4. Ich habe... gedacht. *J'ai pensé à toi.* 5. Er hat... mitgebracht. *Il a apporté un plan de la ville.*

B 6a) *Le bureau de poste est-il loin d'ici?* 7a) *Est-ce là la rue Beethoven?* 8a) *Dois-je m'y rendre par le tramway ou par l'autobus?* 9a) *Est-ce dans cette direction?* 10a) *Y a-t-il un commissariat ici?*
6b) Sagen Sie mir bitte, ob das Postamt weit von hier liegt. 7b) ..., ob das die Beethovenstraße ist. 8b) ..., ob ich mit der Straßenbahn oder mit dem Autobus hinfahren muß. 9b) ..., ob es in dieser Richtung ist. 10b) ..., ob es hier ein Polizeibüro gibt.

C 11. Sehen Sie dieses Wirtshaus (dieses Café)? Das Hotel liegt zwei Straßen weiter. 12. Sie können nicht zu Fuß hingehen, denn es ist zu weit. 13. Wir würden gern ein Taxi nehmen (= wir nähmen gern...). 14. Er wollte an der dritten Haltestelle aussteigen, aber er irrte sich.

Leçon

45 Die Bank; die Post

1 Wenn man Geld *wechseln will, geht man auf die Bank. Der *Wechselkurs ist immer angeschlagen. Er verändert sich meistens von einem Tag zum andern.
Um einen Scheck einzulösen, wendet man sich an einen anderen Schalter. Ist man nicht bekannt, so muß man einen Personalausweis vorzeigen. *Reiseschecks werden fast überall als Zahlungsmittel angenommen. Man braucht sie nur zu unterschreiben (= unterzeichnen).

2 Einen gekreuzten Scheck kann man nur dann zur *Einziehung überreichen, wenn man selbst ein Bankkonto oder ein Postscheckkonto hat.
Wenn es diese modernen Zahlungsmittel nicht gäbe, wären das Reisen und der Handel oft schwierig.

3 Auch auf dem Postamt kann man Geld absenden oder in Empfang nehmen, und zwar mit gewöhnlicher oder mit telegraphischer Postanweisung. Der Briefträger bringt auch den *Betrag einer *Postanweisung dem *Empfänger ins Haus. In diesem Fall ist es üblich, ihm ein kleines Trinkgeld zu geben.

1 [v**è**kçeln']; [kourç]; [r**a**éze-ch**è**kç].

2 [**a**én'tçi-ou[gn]].

3 [bétr**a**k]; [èm'pf**è**[gn]er]; [p**o**çt-**a**nv**a**ézou[gn]].

DOPPELT GENÄHT HÄLT BESSER

Traduction

La banque; la poste

1 Si l'on veut changer de l'argent, on va à la banque. Le cours du change est toujours affiché. Le plus souvent, il varie d'un jour à l'autre. Pour encaisser un chèque, on s'adresse à un autre guichet. Si l'on n'est pas connu, il faut présenter une pièce d'identité. Les chèques de voyage sont acceptés comme moyen de paiement un peu partout. Il suffit de les signer (m. à m. : on n'a besoin que de les signer).

2 On ne peut remettre à l'encaissement un chèque barré que si l'on a soi-même un compte en banque ou un compte courant postal. Si ces moyens de paiement modernes n'existaient pas, les voyages et le commerce seraient souvent difficiles.

3 Au bureau de poste également, on peut envoyer ou toucher de l'argent, et ce par mandat ordinaire ou par mandat télégraphique. Le facteur règle aussi le montant d'un mandat au domicile du destinataire (m. à m. : apporte au destinataire...). Dans ce cas, il est d'usage de lui donner un petit pourboire.

Vocabulaire

der Betr**a**g, (¨ e), *le montant*
der Briefträger (-), *le facteur*
der Empf**ä**nger (-), *le destinataire*
der Absender (-) *l'expéditeur*
der Handel, *le commerce*
der Scheck (s), *le chèque*
die **Ei**nkass**ie**rung (en), *l'encaissement*
die Einziehung (-en), *idem*

die P**o**st**a**nweisung (-en), *le mandat*
die Zahlung (-en), *le paiement*
das Amt (¨ er), *le bureau, l'office*
das Konto (die Konten), *le compte*
das Mittel (-), *le moyen*
einkass**ie**ren, *encaisser*
kreuzen, *croiser, barrer*
(sich) ver**ä**ndern, *varier*
abs**e**nden (voir L. 44), *expédier*
anschl**a**gen (u, a; ä), *afficher*
empf**a**ngen (i, a; ä), *accueillir*
unterschr**ei**ben (ie, ie), *signer*
unterz**ei**chnen *(idem)*

Deux sûretés valent mieux qu'une. (Doublement cousu tient mieux.)

Grammaire

Wenn es diese Zahlungsmittel nicht gäbe, wäre der Handel schwierig.

Après *wenn*, si (conditionnel), le verbe se met au subjonctif 2 présent. La proposition principale est au subjonctif 2 futur. Cependant, nous avons vu (L. 42) que le subjonctif 2 futur est souvent remplacé par le subjonctif 2 présent. Voici d'autres exemples :

Wenn ich Zeit hätte, würde ich nach Mainz fahren (ou : *führe ich nach Mainz*), si j'avais le temps, j'irais à Mayence.

Wenn meine Freunde kämen, würden wir frohe Lieder singen (ou : *sängen wir frohe Lieder*), si mes amis venaient, nous chanterions de gaies chansons.

Exercices

A *Traduisez en français :*

1. Wenn ich auf die Bank ginge, würde ich deinen Scheck mitnehmen. 2. Wenn Sie kein Bankkonto hätten, könnten Sie diesen gekreuzten Scheck nicht einkassieren. 3. Wenn sie ihre Kennkarte verlöre, würde sie aufs Kommissariat gehen.

B *Traduisez en allemand :*

4. Si je voyais ton ami, je lui donnerais le livre. 5. S'il n'avait pas de voiture, il prendrait un taxi. 6. S'il pleuvait, nous visiterions le musée.

Corrigé :

(Faites également, à partir de ce corrigé, l'exercice inverse).

A 1. Si j'allais à la banque, j'emporterais ton chèque. 2. Si vous n'aviez pas de compte en banque, vous ne pourriez encaisser ce chèque barré. 3. Si elle perdait sa carte d'identité, elle irait au commissariat.

B 4. Wenn ich deinen Freund sähe, würde ich ihm das Buch geben (= gäbe ich...). 5. Wenn er keinen Wagen hätte, würde er eine Taxe nehmen (= nähme er...). 6. Wenn es regnete, würden wir das Museum besichtigen (= besichtigten wir..., *mais pour les verbes faibles, le subjonctif 2 présent ne se distingue pas de l'indicatif, et l'on préfèrera l'emploi de* würde).

Lecture

Mißglückter Banküberfall

Die Kette der Banküberfälle in Baden — Württemberg reißt nicht ab. Nachdem ein unbekannter Mann am Mittwoch in der Filiale X der Volksbank bei einem bewaffneten Überfall 6.000 Mark erbeutet hatte, hieß es am Donnerstag in der Volksbank von Y « Hände hoch ». Am Vormittag gegen elf Uhr drang ein zwischen 20 und 25 Jahre alter Mann in die Bank ein und forderte den Zweigstellenleiter mit vorgehaltener Pistole auf, alles Geld herauszugeben. « Machen Sie keine falsche Bewegung », setzte er hinzu. Der Bankangestellte erkannte jedoch, daß der Räuber ihn mit einer Kinderpistole aus Plastik bluffte. Er löste die Alarmanlage aus und schon beim ersten Heulton der Sirene lief der Räuber davon. Er flüchtete in einem roten Volkswagen, den er vorher in Stuttgart gestohlen hatte. Der Täter trug eine Sonnenbrille und einen schwarzen Schlapphut. Er hat blondes Haar und ist etwa 1,80 Meter groß.

Aus der Zeitung « Gmünder Tagespost »

Agression manquée contre une banque

La série des agressions contre les banques en Bade-Wurtemberg ne cesse pas (m. à m. : la chaîne... ne se rompt pas). Après qu'un inconnu eut enlevé 6.000 Marks lors d'une attaque à main armée, mercredi, dans la filiale X de la Banque Populaire, on entendit, jeudi, dans la Banque Populaire de Y crier « Haut les mains ». Dans la matinée, vers onze heures, un homme âgé de 20 à 25 ans pénétra dans la banque et, pistolet au poing (m. à m. : avec un pistolet tenu devant), il somma le directeur de la filiale de (lui) remettre tout l'argent. « Pas un geste! (m. à m. : pas un mouvement faux, suspect) », ajouta-t-il. Cependant, l'employé de banque reconnut que le bandit (le) bluffait avec un pistolet d'enfant, en matière plastique. Il déclencha le système d'alarme et, dès le premier hurlement de la sirène, le bandit détala. Il s'enfuit dans une « Volkswagen » rouge, qu'il avait volée auparavant à Stuttgart. L'auteur (de l'agression) portait des lunettes de soleil et un chapeau mou noir. Il a les cheveux blonds et mesure (m. à m. : est grand de...) à peu près 1,80 m.

Leçon

46 Auf der Bank

1 — Ich möchte deutsches Geld. Wie ist der Wechselkurs heute?
— Die Mark gilt 1,... F (einen Franc, ... Centimes); mit der Bankprovision macht es 5 Centimes mehr.
— Ach! Sie ist teurer als das letzte Mal, als ich Geld umwechselte.
— Das mag sein. Mit dem Andrang der Touristen steigen die Preise. In einem Monat haben wir wieder den üblichen Kurs.
— Geben Sie mir also 2.000 (zweitausend) Mark, oder geben Sie mir besser deutsches Geld für 3.000 Francs. Wie lange wird es wohl dauern?
— Höchstens fünf Minuten. — Wo löst man bitte die Schecks ein? — Am Schalter 16.

2 — Könnte ich diesen Scheck einlösen, bitte? (Der Angestellte schaut sich den Scheck an und liest den Namen des Zahlungsempfängers) — Sind Sie Herr Dumont? — Ja. — Haben Sie einen Ausweis, bitte, z. B. (zum Beispiel) Ihren Paß? — Unterschreiben Sie bitte auf der Rückseite! Hier ist eine Marke. Wenn Ihre Nummer ausgerufen wird, gehen Sie an die Kasse, Schalter 7.

3 — (Der Kassierer ruft die Nummer auf, die auf der Marke steht) — Was für Scheine wollen Sie, Zehn-, Fünfzig- oder Hundertmarkscheine? — Geben Sie mir bitte Fünfzigmarkscheine, und für fünfzig Mark Kleingeld. — ...und fünfzig macht zweitausend. So, mein Herr. Wollen Sie bitte nachzählen. — Besten Dank, auf Wiedersehen. — Bitte schön!

UNRECHT GUT GEDEIHT NICHT

Traduction

A la banque

1 — Je voudrais acheter des marks (mot à mot : je voudrais de la monnaie allemande). Quel est le cours du change aujourd'hui? — Le mark vaut 1,... F; avec la commission de banque, cela fait 5 centimes de plus. — Tiens! Il est plus cher que la dernière fois où j'ai changé de l'argent. — C'est possible. Avec l'afflux des touristes, les prix montent. D'ici un mois nous aurons de nouveau le cours normal. — Donnez-moi donc 2.000 marks, ou plutôt donnez-moi pour 3.000 francs de marks. Combien de temps cela va-t-il prendre? — Tout au plus cinq minutes. — Où touche-t-on les chèques, s'il vous plaît? — Au guichet 16.

2 Est-ce que je pourrais toucher ce chèque, s'il vous plaît? (L'employé regarde le chèque et lit le nom du bénéficiaire) — Vous êtes Monsieur Dumont? — Oui — Avez-vous une pièce d'identité, s'il vous plaît, votre passeport, par exemple? — Veuillez signer au dos! Voici un jeton. Quand on appellera votre numéro, vous vous présenterez à la caisse, guichet 7.

3 (Le caissier appelle le numéro porté sur le jeton) — Quelle sorte de coupures voulez-vous, des billets de 10, 50 ou 100 marks? — Donnez-moi, s'il vous plaît, des billets de 50 marks, et 50 marks de petite monnaie. — ... et 50 qui font 2.000. Voici, Monsieur; recomptez s'il vous plaît — Merci bien; au revoir — A votre service.

Vocabulaire

der Andrang, *l'affluence*
der Wechselkurs (-e), *le cours du change*
die Banknote (n), *le billet de banque*
die Marke (n), *la marque, le jeton*
die Provision (-en) / die Kommission (-en) } *la commission.*

die Rückseite (n), *le verso*
n**a**chz**ä**hlen, *recompter*
umw**e**chseln, *changer*
gelten (a, o; i), *valoir*
steigen (ie, ie), *monter*
die Mark, *le mark*

Bien mal acquis ne profite jamais.

Grammaire

Ich möchte deutsches Geld.
Könnte ich diesen Scheck einlösen?
Nous avons étudié les six verbes auxiliaires de mode dans les leçons 18, 19, 20. Dans ces deux exemples, *mögen* et *können* sont au présent du subjonctif 2, qui leur sert de conditionnel. Nous nous rappelons qu'au prétérit de l'indicatif, aucun de ces verbes ne gardait l'inflexion (ni, du reste, au participe passé). Cependant, au présent du subjonctif 2, l'inflexion reparaît pour les 4 verbes qui la possèdent à l'infinitif. Exemples :

können : *ich konnte,* je pouvais; *ich könnte,* je pourrais; *(ich habe gekonnt)*

dürfen : *ich durfte,* j'avais le droit de; *ich dürfte,* j'aurais le droit de; *(ich habe gedurft)*

müssen : *ich mußte,* il fallait que je...; *ich müßte,* il faudrait que je...; *(ich habe gemußt)*

mögen : *ich mochte,* je désirais; *ich möchte,* je désirerais; *(ich habe gemocht)*

wollen : *ich wollte,* je voulais; *ich wollte,* je voudrais; *(ich habe gewollt)*

sollen : *ich sollte,* je devais; *ich sollte,* je devrais; *(ich habe gesollt).*

Notez que pour les deux derniers verbes, l'expression du conditionnel ne diffère pas du prétérit de l'indicatif. Seul le contexte en éclaire le sens.
Au présent du subjonctif 2, ces auxiliaires de mode prennent les terminaisons du verbe faible au prétérit (voir leçon 14).

Exercices

A *Mettez les phrases au présent du subjonctif 2, puis traduisez :*
1. Er kann den Namen nicht lesen. 2. Er darf nicht so viel Geld wechseln. 3. Ich muß ein Bankkonto haben. 4. Ich mag diesen alten Schein nicht. 5. Wir sollen immer Kleingeld haben.

B *Commencez les phrases suivantes par* ich möchte, *puis traduisez :*
Exemple : Ich möchte Einkäufe machen. *Je voudrais faire des achats.*
6. Ich gehe auf die Bank. 7. Ich wechsle Geld. 8. Ich frage nach dem Wechselkurs. 9. Ich warte nicht lange. 10. Ich fahre mit dem Taxi zurück.

C *Traduisez :*

11. A quel guichet pouvait-il avoir des marks (= de la monnaie allemande)? 12. Il m'a demandé, à quel guichet il pourrait avoir des marks. 13. Je voulais toucher un chèque. 14. Je lui ai dit que je voudrais toucher un chèque. 15. Après avoir signé le chèque, il attendit devant la caisse.

Corrigé :

A 1. Er könnte den Namen nicht lesen. *Il ne pourrait pas lire le nom.* 2. Er dürfte... *Il ne pourrait pas (= n'aurait pas le droit de) changer autant d'argent.* 3. Ich müßte... *Il faudrait que j'ai (= je devrais avoir) un compte en banque.* 4. Ich möchte... *Je ne voudrais pas ce vieux billet.* 5. Wir sollten... *Nous devrions toujours avoir de la monnaie.*

B 6. Ich möchte auf die Bank gehen. *Je voudrais aller à la banque.* 7. Ich möchte Geld wechseln. *Je voudrais changer de l'argent.* 8. Ich möchte nach dem Wechselkurs fragen. *Je voudrais demander (quel est) le cours du change.* 9. Ich möchte nicht lange warten. *Je ne voudrais pas attendre longtemps.* 10. Ich möchte mit dem Taxi zurückfahren. *Je voudrais retourner en taxi.*

C 11. An welchem Schalter konnte er deutsches Geld haben? 12. Er hat mich gefragt, an welchem Schalter er deutsches Geld haben könnte. 13. Ich wollte einen Scheck einlösen. 14. Ich habe ihm gesagt, daß ich einen Scheck einlösen möchte. 15. Nachdem er den Scheck unterschrieben hatte, wartete er vor der Kasse.

Leçon

47 Auf der Post

1 – Wo ist der Schalter für postlagernde Briefe, bitte?
– Dort hinten rechts.
– Danke schön. (Der Reisende zeigt dem Postbeamten, der sich hinter dem Schalter befindet, seinen Paß; er hat ihn auf der ersten Seite aufgeschlagen).
– Sie sind Herr Dumont?
– Ja, richtig.
– Ich will nachsehen.

2 – Ich möchte diesen Eilbrief einschreiben lassen.
– Am nächsten Schalter, bitte.
– Ich möchte auch drei Briefmarken für Luftpostbriefe nach Schweden und vier Briefmarken für Postkarten mit weniger als fünf Wörtern.
– Was kostet das alles zusammen?
– Wo ist der Briefkasten, bitte?

3 – Wenn ich jetzt ein Telegramm aufgebe, um wieviel Uhr wird es wohl in Paris ausgetragen?
– Vergessen Sie den Namen und die Anschrift des Absenders nicht!

4 – Der Briefträger ist schon vorbeigekommen. Aber es war nichts für Sie da.
– Sonderbar! Nun bin ich schon seit zwei Tagen ohne Post von zu Hause.
– Warten Sie bis auf die Briefausgabe von heute abend. Vielleicht ist dann etwas für Sie da.

LÜGEN HABEN KURZE BEINE

Traduction

A la poste

1 — Où est le guichet de la poste restante, s'il vous plaît? — Au fond à droite. — Merci, Monsieur. (Le voyageur montre son passeport à l'employé qui se trouve derrière le guichet; il l'a ouvert à la première page.) — C'est Monsieur Dumont? — C'est cela. — Je vais voir.

2 — Je voudrais envoyer cette lettre exprès en recommandé. — C'est au guichet suivant, s'il vous plaît. — Je voudrais aussi trois timbres pour des lettres à destination de la Suède, par avion, et quatre timbres pour des cartes postales de moins de cinq mots. — Combien cela fait-il en tout? — Où est la boîte aux lettres, s'il vous plaît?

3 — Si je remets un télégramme maintenant, à quelle heure approximativement sera-t-il distribué à Paris? — N'oubliez pas le nom et l'adresse de l'expéditeur!

4 — Le facteur est déjà passé. Mais il n'y avait rien pour vous. — C'est curieux, je n'ai pas reçu de courrier de chez moi depuis deux jours (m. à m. : maintenant, je suis déjà depuis 2 jours sans courrier...). — Attendez la distribution de ce soir. Peut-être aurez-vous quelque chose.

Vocabulaire

der Absender (-), *l'expéditeur*
der Briefkasten (¨), *la boîte aux lettres*
der Eilbrief (-e), *la lettre exprès*
die Anschrift (-en), = die Adr**e**sse (n), *l'adresse*
die Ausgabe (n), *la distribution; la dépense*
die Briefmarke (n), *le timbre*
die Luftpost, *la poste aérienne*
das Telegr**a**mm (-e), *le télégramme*
aufschl**a**gen (u, a; ä), *ouvrir (livre); augmenter (prix)*
austr**a**gen (u, a; ä), *distribuer (courrier)*
einschr**ei**ben (ie, ie), *inscrire*
n**a**chs**e**hen (a, e; ie) *examiner, suivre des yeux*

Le mensonge ne mène pas loin. (Les mensonges ont les jambes courtes.)

■ **Briefe nach Schweden.**
Des lettres à destination de la Suède.

● Le nom de pays *Schweden* s'emploie sans article. Il en est ainsi de tous les noms de pays, de villes et de continents, ces noms sont du neutre et prennent -s au génitif. Exemples :

Köln liegt in Deutschland, Cologne se trouve en Allemagne.
Amerika ist heutzutage nicht mehr weit, l'Amérique n'est plus loin de nos jours.
Die Produkte Englands (= Englands Produkte), les produits de l'Angleterre.

● L'article *das* reparaît devant ces noms, lorsqu'ils sont précédés d'un adjectif épithète. Exemples :

Das neue Europa, l'Europe nouvelle.
Das sonnige Italien, l'Italie ensoleillée.

● ***Exceptions :*** Les noms de pays suivants sont du féminin et prennent toujours l'article : *die Schweiz,* la Suisse; *die Türkei,* la Turquie; *die Tschechoslowakei,* la Tchécoslovaquie; *die Pfalz,* le Palatinat. D'autre part, le neutre *das Elsaß,* l'Alsace, prend toujours l'article également, ainsi que le pluriel *die Niederlande,* les Pays-Bas.

■ **Er zeigt dem Postbeamten seinen Paß.**
Les terminaisons du mot *Beamte* (employé, fonctionnaire), dépendent de l'article ou du déterminatif qui le précède (voir L. 29 : l'adjectif et le participe substantivés). Exemples :

a) déclinaison faible : *der Beamte, des Beamten, die Beamten.*
b) déclinaison mixte : *ein Beamter, eines Beamten.*
c) déclinaison forte : *Beamte,* des employés.

■ **Auf der Post.**
Observez l'emploi fréquent de *auf,* sur, suivi du datif (lieu, position) ou de l'accusatif (direction vers).

Er lebt auf dem Land, il vit à la campagne.
Sie geht auf den Markt, elle va au marché.
Das Auto steht auf der Straße, la voiture est dans la rue.

Exercices

A *Formez des phrases avec les mots suivants, puis traduisez :*
1. Herr Müller; sonnig; Spanien; fahren nach. 2. Helga; Frankreich; Belgien; und; reisen durch. 3. Rainer; schön; Italien; noch nicht; kennen. 4. Amerika; haben; groß; modern; Städte.

B *Complétez, puis traduisez :*
5. Gestern abend ging Helga auf d... Ball. 6. Sie blieb lange auf d... Ball. 7. Sie fährt oft auf d... Land.

C *Traduisez :*
8. Où est la grande (= principale) poste? 9. Avez-vous du courrier pour moi? 10. Où reçoit-on les lettres en poste-restante? 11. Je voudrais envoyer un télégramme en *(nach)* France. 12. Je voudrais aussi expédier un paquet *(das Paket)* en Suisse.

Corrigé :

A 1. Herr Müller fährt nach dem sonnigen Spanien. *Monsieur Müller part pour la riante Espagne.* 2. Helga reist durch Frankreich und Belgien. *Helga traverse (= voyage à travers) la France et la Belgique.* 3. Rainer kennt das schöne Italien noch nicht. *Rainer ne connaît pas encore la belle Italie.* 4. Amerika hat große moderne Städte. *L'Amérique a de grandes villes modernes.*

B 5. Auf den Ball. *Hier soir, Helga est allée au bal.* 6. Auf dem Ball. *Elle est restée longtemps au bal.* 7. Auf das Land. *Elle va souvent à la campagne.*

C 8. Wo ist die Hauptpost? 9. Haben Sie Post für mich? 10. Wo bekommt man die postlagernden Briefe? 11. Ich möchte ein Telegramm nach Frankreich aufgeben. 12. Ich möchte auch ein Paket in die Schweiz senden.

Leçon

48 Der Fernsprecher

1 — Fräulein, bitte, Nummer 39 59 (neununddreißig neunundfünfzig) in Göppingen.
— Bitte, bleiben Sie am Apparat.
— Unterbrechen Sie nicht! (oder : Nicht trennen!)
— Fräulein, kann ich nach Berlin durchwählen?
— Ja; wählen Sie selbst Ihre Nummer auf der Wählscheibe.
— Die Leitung ist besetzt; hängen Sie bitte ein; ich werde zurückrufen.
— Fräulein, es liegt ein Irrtum vor; ich hatte die Nummer 76 53 verlangt, und Sie haben mir 76 52 gegeben.

2 — Fräulein, wie lange müßte ich wohl warten für ein Telefongespräch nach Belgrad?
— Bitte, geben Sie mir eine R-Verbindung mit Ulm, 22 43 (zwoundzwanzig dreiundvierzig).

3 Hier ist die Auskunftstelle. Sprechen Sie, bitte.
— Ich möchte Herrn Gustav Becher in Stuttgart anrufen. Es ist ein neuer Teilnehmer, der noch nicht im Telefonbuch (= im Teilnehmerverzeichnis) steht.

4 — Hallo! Wer ist am Apparat?
— Hier ist Kurt Bresch. Guten Tag, Frau Müller. Könnte ich Ihren Mann sprechen?
— Er ist leider nicht zu Hause. Soll ich ihm etwas ausrichten?
— Nein, ich möchte persönlich mit ihm sprechen. Um wieviel Uhr wird er wohl zurückkommen?
— Gewöhnlich kommt er gegen sechs Uhr abends nach Hause.
— Besten Dank. Auf Wiedersehen, gnädige Frau.

ZUVIEL SPRECHEN IST VOM ÜBEL

Traduction

Le téléphone

1 — Mademoiselle, voulez-vous me donner, s'il vous plaît, le numéro 39 59 à Göppingen. — Ne quittez pas (m. à m. : restez à l'appareil). — Ne coupez pas.
— Mademoiselle, les communications téléphoniques pour Berlin sont-elles automatiques? (m. à m. : puis-je choisir directement?)
— Oui; composez vous-même votre numéro sur le disque. La ligne est occupée; raccrochez! Je vous rappellerai.
— Mademoiselle, il y a une erreur. Je vous avais demandé le 76 53, et vous m'avez donné 76 52.

2 — Mademoiselle, combien d'attente y a-t-il pour une communication pour Belgrade?
— Mademoiselle, veuillez me donner une communication P. C. V. avec Ulm, 22 43.

3 — (Ici le) Service de renseignements. Parlez, s'il vous plaît.
— Je voudrais téléphoner à Monsieur Gustave Becher, à Stuttgart. C'est un nouvel abonné qui n'est pas encore sur l'annuaire.

4 — Allo! C'est de la part de qui? (m. à m. : qui est à l'appareil?)
— Ici, Kurt Bresch. Bonjour, Madame Müller. Pourrais-je parler à votre mari? — Je regrette, il n'est pas à la maison. Dois-je lui transmettre quelque chose? — Non, je désirerais lui parler personnellement. A quelle heure pensez-vous qu'il reviendra? — Il rentre d'ordinaire vers six heures du soir. — Merci bien. Au revoir, Madame.

Vocabulaire

der Apparat (-e), *l'appareil*
der Irrtum (¨ er), *l'erreur*
der Teilnehmer (-), *le participant*
ici, abréviation pour : der Fernsprechteilnehmer (-), *l'abonné au téléphone*
das Ferngespräch (-e), *la c. interurbaine*
das Fernamt (¨ er), *l'interurbain*
das Verz**ei**chnis (se), *la liste*
anr**u**fen, *appeler (au téléphone)*
ausr**i**chten, *transmettre*
bes**e**tzen, *occuper*

Trop parler nuit (mot à mot : est (de) mal).

die Leitung (-en), *la ligne, la direction*
die Verbindung (-en), *la communication*
einhängen, *raccrocher*
zurückrufen, *rappeler*
unterbrechen (a, o; i), *interrompre*
vorliegen (a, e), *exister*

Grammaire

■ Welches ist Ihre Nummer? Was für einen Apparat haben Sie?
Quel est votre numéro? Quel (= quelle sorte d')appareil avez-vous?
On emploie *welcher,* quel? lequel? quand la question porte sur une personne ou une chose définie; on répond à cette question par un article défini. Cet interrogatif se décline sur *der, die, das.* Avec *was für ein,* quelle sorte de, la question porte d'une façon générale sur une personne ou une chose; on y répond par un article indéfini. Seul *ein* se décline, dans ce groupe.

> *Welches Gespräch dauerte am längsten, das Ortsgespräch oder das Fernsgespräch? — das Ortsgespräch,* quelle communication a duré le plus longtemps, l'urbaine ou l'interurbaine? — C'est la communication urbaine.
> *Was für ein Gespräch hatten Sie? — Ein Ortsgespräch,* quelle (sorte de) communication aviez-vous? — Une communication urbaine.
> *Mit was für einem Wagen fuhr er? — Mit einem Volkswagen (mit + datif),* dans quelle (genre de) voiture a-t-il roulé? — Dans une Volkswagen.

■ Nummer zwoundsiebzig (72).
Au téléphone, il est d'usage de prononcer *zwo* à la place de *zwei,* pour éviter la confusion avec *drei.*

● *Hier Kurt Bresch.*
On a l'habitude en Allemagne d'annoncer son nom au téléphone. Notre formule « j'écoute » est donc inusitée.

● Les mots *Telefon, Foto* peuvent encore s'écrire avec « ph » *Telephon, Photo.*

● *Auf Wiedersehen, gnädige Frau.*
Frau, dame, doit être suivi du nom de famille ou d'un titre :

> *Besten Dank, Frau Müller,* merci bien, madame (Müller).

On peut également le faire précéder de *gnädig* (m. à m. : gracieux), sans ajouter le nom :

> *Vielen Dank, gnädige Frau,* merci beaucoup, madame (style soutenu).

Exercices

A *Traduisez, puis posez une question se rapportant aux mots entre parenthèses :*
1. Er hat den (letzten) Brief noch nicht bekommen. 2. Er trug einen (blauen) Mantel. 3. Er kam mit einem (sehr freundlichen) Herrn. 4. Er brachte uns (interessante) Bücher mit. 5. Er wohnt in der (Mozartstraße).

B *Traduisez :*
6. Nous n'avons pas parlé longtemps; on nous a coupé. 7. Je voudrais le numéro 3.22. 8. Si j'avais l'annuaire, je ne vous demanderais pas le numéro de cet abonné *(fragen + nach).* 9. Croyez-vous qu'il y avait une erreur? 10. Elle ne m'a rien transmis; elle l'a sûrement oublié.

Corrigé :

A 1. *Il n'a pas encore reçu la dernière lettre.* Welchen Brief hat er noch nicht bekommen? 2. *Il portait un manteau bleu.* Was für einen Mantel trug er? 3. *Il est venu avec un monsieur très aimable.* Mit was für einem Herrn ist er gekommen? 4. *Il nous a apporté des livres intéressants.* Was für Bücher brachte er uns mit? (« ein » *disparaît au pluriel*). 5. *Il habite la rue Mozart.* In was für einer Straße wohnt er?

B 6. Wir haben nicht lange gesprochen; man hat uns unterbrochen. 7. Bitte (= ich möchte) Nummer drei – zwoundzwanzig. 8. Wenn ich das Telephonbuch hätte, würde ich Sie nicht nach der Nummer dieses Teilnehmers fragen. 9. Glauben Sie, daß ein Irrtum vorlag? 10. Sie hat mir nichts ausgerichtet; sie hat es sicher vergessen.

Leçon

49 Der *Arzt

1 Wenn wir uns nicht wohl fühlen, können wir uns meistens selbst pflegen. Gegen *Kopfschmerzen nehmen wir eine Tablette.
Haben wir uns erkältet und husten wir, so kaufen wir Hustenbonbons. In allen Apotheken werden Heilmittel gegen Grippe und *Schnupfen verkauft, sowie Thermometer, um das Fieber zu messen.
Gegen Schmerzen oder Rheuma gibt es Flüssigkeiten, mit denen wir uns einreiben können.
Mit Kapseln oder mit Pulver, das im Wasser aufgelöst wird, lindern wir die Magenschmerzen.

2 Wenn wir richtig krank sind, ziehen wir lieber einen Arzt zu Rate, vor allem wenn wir die *Berufstätigkeit unterbrechen müssen. Können wir unsere Wohnung verlassen, so suchen wir den Arzt zu den Sprechzeiten in seiner Praxis auf. Wenn wir aber das Zimmer hüten müssen, bitten wir ihn, zu uns nach Hause zu kommen.

3 Der Arzt verschreibt ein *Rezept. Darauf notiert er die *Arzneien, die wir einnehmen müssen; manchmal müssen wir eine Diät einhalten. Der Apotheker fertigt das Rezept an.

1 [artçt]; [k**o**pf-chm**è**rtçen']; [chn**ou**-pfen']

2 [bér**ou**fç-t**è**tichkaét]

3 [rétç**è**pt]; [artçn**a**é-en'].

MAN SOLL DEN TEUFEL NICHT AN DIE WAND MALEN

Traduction

Le médecin

1 Lorsque nous ne sommes (m. à m. : nous sentons) pas bien, nous sommes le plus souvent capables de nous soigner nous-mêmes. Pour les maux de tête, nous prenons un comprimé. Si nous avons pris froid et que nous toussons, nous achetons des bonbons contre la toux. Dans toutes les pharmacies, on vend des remèdes contre la grippe et le rhume de cerveau, ainsi que des thermomètres pour prendre la fièvre. Pour les douleurs ou les rhumatismes, il existe des liquides et des pommades, avec lesquelles nous pouvons nous frictionner. Avec des cachets et des poudres à dissoudre dans l'eau, nous soulageons les maux d'estomac.

2 Si nous sommes vraiment malades, nous préférons consulter un médecin, surtout si nous devons interrompre nos activités professionnelles. Si nous pouvons nous déplacer, nous allons voir le médecin dans son cabinet aux heures de consultation. Mais si nous devons garder la chambre, nous le prions de venir (nous voir) à domicile.

3 Le médecin rédige une ordonnance. Il y note les médicaments que nous devons prendre; parfois nous devons nous mettre au régime (m. à m. : tenir un régime). C'est le pharmacien qui exécute l'ordonnance.

Vocabulaire

der Apotheker (-), *le pharmacien*
der Arzt (¨e), *le médecin*
der Magen (-), *l'estomac*
der Rat (die Ratschläge) *le conseil (avis)*
der Schmerz (es, en), *la douleur*
der Schnupfen (-), *le rhume de cerveau*
das Heilmittel (-), *le remède*
das Pulver (-), *la poudre*
das Rez**e**pt (-e), *l'ordonnance*
das Rheuma, *le rhumatisme*
das Sprechz**i**mmer (-), *le cabinet de consultation*
das Thermom**e**ter (-), *le thermomètre*

Il ne faut pas tenter le diable
(On ne doit pas peindre le diable au mur).

die Apoth**e**ke (n), *la pharmacie*
die Arzn**ei** (-en), *le médicament*
die Di**ä**t (-en), *le régime*
die Flüssigkeit (-en), *le liquide*
die Grippe, *la grippe*
die Kapsel (n), *le cachet*
die Salbe (n), *la pommade*
die Tätigkeit (-en), *l'activité*
das Bonb**on** (s), *le bonbon*
das Fieber (-), *la fièvre*
anf**e**rtigen, *fabriquer*
aufl**ö**sen, *dissoudre*
sich erk**ä**lten, *prendre froid*
fühlen, *sentir*
hüten, *garder*
husten, *tousser*
lindern, *soulager*
pflegen, *soigner*
verz**ei**chnen, *noter*
einn**e**hmen (a, o; i), *prendre, avaler*
einr**ei**ben (ie, ie), *frictionner*
messen (a, e; i), *mesurer*
unterw**e**rfen (a, o; i), *soumettre*
verl**a**ssen (ie, a; ä), *quitter*
verschr**ei**ben (ie, ie), *prescrire*
(*)ziehen (zog, gezogen), *tirer, tracer; s'en aller.*

Grammaire

Wir ziehen lieber einen Arzt zu Rate.
Nous préférons consulter un médecin (m. à m. : nous prenons plus volontiers conseil d'un médecin).
Lieber, plus volontiers, est le comparatif irrégulier de *gern,* volontiers (voir L. 16). Le superlatif est : *am liebsten,* de préférence. Avec un verbe, *gern, lieber, am liebsten* se traduisent généralement par aimer; aimer mieux; aimer le mieux. Exemples :

Ich esse gern Pflaumen, j'aime (bien) les prunes.
Ich esse lieber Trauben, j'aime mieux le raisin.
Ich esse am liebsten Kirschen, j'aime le mieux = ce que je préfère, ce sont les cerises.

● Autres comparatifs et superlatifs irréguliers :
Viel, mehr, am meisten, beaucoup, plus, le plus.

Hans hat viel Geld (argent).
Fritz hat mehr Geld.
Kurt hat am meisten.

Hoch, höher, am höchsten, haut, plus haut, le plus haut.

Karl springt (saute) *hoch.*
Max springt höher.
Moritz springt am höchsten.

Nach, näher, am nächsten, proche.

Révisez également les degrés de *gut* dans la leçon 16.

Exercices

Traduisez :
1. J'aime boire de l'eau (= je bois volontiers...). 2. J'aime mieux boire de la bière. 3. J'aime le mieux boire du vin. 4. Ce médecin-ci a beaucoup de clients. 5. Celui-là (en) a davantage. 6. Notre médecin de famille (en) a le plus. 7. J'avais pris froid et je toussais.
A partir du corrigé ci-dessous, faites la traduction inverse.

Corrigé :

1. Ich trinke gern Wasser. 2. Ich trinke lieber Bier. 3. Am liebsten trinke ich Wein. 4. Dieser Arzt hat viele Patienten. 5. Jener hat mehr. 6. Unser Familienarzt hat am meisten. 7. Ich hatte mich erkältet und ich hustete.

Lecture

Neuralgie

Ein bekannter Arzt wird zu seinem Verdruß von eingebildeten Kranken aus der sogenannten besten Gesellschaft geradezu überlaufen. Insbesondere belästigt ihn oft eine Dame mit ihren imaginären Leiden.
Eines Tages aber ist sie tatsächlich erkrankt. « Sie haben Neuralgie », stellt der Professor fest. « Ach, wie interessant... Aber woher kommt Neuralgie? » fragt sie, bereits unter der Tür. « Aus dem Griechischen! » knurrt der Arzt und schiebt sie sanft hinaus.

Aus der Schweizer Illustrierten Zeitung.

Neuralgie

A son grand déplaisir, un médecin renommé est littéralement assiégé par des malades imaginaires venant de la soi-disant bonne (m. à m. : meilleure) société. Une dame en particulier l'importune souvent de ses maux imaginaires.
Mais voici qu'un jour elle est réellement tombée malade. « Vous avez de la neuralgie », constate le médecin. « Ah! comme c'est intéressant... Mais d'où vient donc la neuralgie? » demande-t-elle, déjà sur le pas de la porte. « Du grec! » grogne le médecin en la poussant doucement en dehors.

Leçon

50 Beim Arzt – Beim Zahnarzt

1 — Was fehlt Ihnen? Wo haben Sie Schmerzen?
— Ich habe Magenschmerzen; nach dem Mittagessen bin ich schläfrig; ich kann nur mühsam arbeiten. Oft habe ich Migräne.
— Wie alt sind Sie?
— Ich bin vierzig Jahre alt.
— Rauchen Sie? Trinken Sie Alkohol? Verschaffen Sie sich Bewegung? Schlafen Sie gut? Wieviel Stunden? Haben Sie ein geordnetes Leben? Hatten Sie letzten Winter Grippe? Leiden Sie nicht an Verstopfung?

2 — Kleiden Sie sich aus, damit ich Sie untersuche. Legen Sie sich auf dieses Sofa. Tue ich Ihnen weh? Diese Körperstelle ist etwas empfindlich. Gut! Atmen Sie tief. Das Herz ist in Ordnung. Der Blutdruck ist normal.

3 Meiner Meinung nach sind die Leber und die Gallenblase etwas träge. Wir wollen eine Blut- und Harnanalyse vornehmen. Ich werde Sie erst in Behandlung nehmen, wenn wir das Ergebnis kennen. Essen Sie inzwischen leicht verdauliche Kost. Meiden Sie alles, was schwer im Magen liegt und fett ist. Es wird nicht schlimm sein, aber Sie müssen trotzdem aufpassen.

4 (Beim Zahnarzt) — Hallo! Herr Doktor? Könnten Sie mich heute nachmittag empfangen?
— Oh! Das wird leider kaum möglich sein. Bis halb neun, heute abend, sind Patienten vorbestellt. Haben Sie Zahnweh?
— Ja, ich habe seit zwei Stunden rasende Zahnschmerzen. Au!
— Nun gut, dann kommen Sie eben um sechs Uhr.
— Ich danke Ihnen bestens, Herr Doktor. Bis gleich.

DAS ÜBEL KOMMT GERITTEN – UND GEHT WEG MIT SCHRITTEN

Traduction

Chez le médecin – Chez le dentiste

1 — Qu'est-ce qui ne va pas (m. à m. : vous manque)? Où avez-vous mal? — J'ai mal à l'estomac; j'ai sommeil après le déjeuner; je ne puis travailler que difficilement. J'ai des migraines fréquentes. — Quel âge avez-vous? — J'ai quarante ans (mot à mot : je suis de 40 ans âgé). — Est-ce que vous fumez? Buvez-vous de l'alcool? Prenez-vous de l'exercice? Dormez-vous bien? Combien d'heures? Avez-vous une vie régulière? Avez-vous été grippé, l'hiver dernier? N'êtes-vous pas constipé (m. à m. : ne souffrez-vous pas de constipation)?

2 — Déshabillez-vous que je vous examine. Allongez-vous sur ce divan. Je ne vous fais pas mal? Cette région est un peu sensible. Bien! Respirez fort. Le cœur va bien. La tension artérielle est normale.

3 Je pense que le foie et la vésicule biliaire sont un peu paresseux. Nous allons faire une analyse de sang et une analyse d'urine. Je ne vous donnerai votre traitement que lorsque nous aurons le résultat. Entre temps, mangez légèrement (m. à m. : de la nourriture facile à digérer). Évitez tout ce qui est lourd (m. à m. : à l'estomac) et gras. Ce n'est pas grave, sans doute, mais il faut tout de même faire attention.

4 (Chez le dentiste) — Allô Docteur? Est-ce que vous pourriez me prendre cet après-midi? — Oh! Cela va être difficile (m. à m. : cela sera hélas à peine possible). J'ai des rendez-vous jusqu'à 8 h 30 ce soir. Avez-vous mal aux dents? — Oui, j'ai une rage de dents depuis deux heures. Pouh! — Eh bien, dans ce cas, venez donc à six heures. — Je vous en remercie, Docteur. A tout à l'heure!

Vocabulaire

atmen, *respirer.*
aufp**a**ssen (+ auf + accusatif), *faire attention à.*
auskl**ei**den, *déshabiller.*
beh**a**ndeln, *traiter.*
unters**u**chen, *examiner.*
m**ei**den (ie, ie)), *éviter.*
v**o**rn**e**hmen (a, o, i), *entreprendre.*

Le mal vient à cheval – et s'en va à pied.

Grammaire

■ ***Wo haben Sie Schmerzen? – Kommen Sie in einer Woche wieder.***
Le genre et la variabilité des noms est une des difficultés de la langue allemande. Cependant, pour être capable de bien employer un nom, il suffit de connaître son article défini et son pluriel, et, pour certains, le génitif singulier. Les principes généraux suivants doivent nous guider :

1 Tous les neutres prennent *s* au génitif singulier : *des Bluts,* du sang; *des Sofas,* du canapé. (Mémento, n° 11 à 14).

2 La plupart des masculins prennent *s* au génitif singulier : *des Körpers* (du corps); les autres prennent *-n* ou *-en : des Patienten* (du malade). (Mémento, n° 5 à 10).

3 Les noms masculins et neutres qui ajoutent *s* au génitif singulier ne prennent pas de terminaison aux autres cas du singulier : *der Körper,* le corps; *dem Körper,* au corps; *den Körper,* le corps.

4 Tous les féminins sont invariables au singulier : *die Kost,* la nourriture; *der Kost,* de (à) la nourriture. (Mémento n° 15 et 16).

5 Au pluriel, le nominatif, le génitif et l'accusatif sont toujours semblables : *die, der, die Ärzte,* les, des, les médecins.

6 Au datif pluriel, tous les noms ajoutent *-n* à la terminaison du nominatif pluriel : *die Ärzte,* les médecins; *den Ärzten,* aux médecins; *die Kinder,* les enfants; *den Kindern,* aux enfants.
Cependant, si le nom a déjà une terminaison en *-n* ou *-en* au nominatif pluriel, les quatre cas du pluriel sont semblables : *die, der, den, die Schmerzen,* les, des, aux, les douleurs.
On apprendra les noms toujours de la façon suivante : *der Arm, die Arme,* le bras; *der Schmerz, des Schmerzes, die Schmerzen,* la douleur (masculin mixte; voir L. 11).

■ ***Das Herz ist in Ordnung. Aus der Tiefe des Herzens.***
(Le cœur va bien. Du fond du cœur).
Le nom *Herz* (cœur) suit au singulier une déclinaison qui lui est particulière : *das Herz, des Herzens, dem Herzen, das Herz.* Pluriel : *die, der, den, die Herzen.*

Exercices

A *Ajoutez l'article défini au nominatif singulier, au génitif singulier, au nominatif pluriel, puis traduisez.*
1. Flug. 2. Hand. 3. Tag. 4. Straße. 5. Haus. 6. Mensch. 7. Fenster. 8. Mann. 9. Frau. 10. Vater.

B *Traduisez, puis mettez au prétérit.*
11. Wie geht es Ihrem Großvater? 12. Danke, nicht sehr gut; er fühlt sich nicht wohl. 13. Er klagt über (*se plaint de*) Magenschmerzen. 14. Er hat keinen Appetit und atmet schwer. 15. Oft hat er auch Kopfschmerzen (der Kopf (-ë), la tête).

C *Traduisez.*
16. Docteur, voudriez-vous examiner mon fils? 17. Il a pris froid; il a mal à la gorge (*der Hals, -ë*). 18. Ce n'est pas grave (*schlimm*); voici une ordonnance; demain, il ira déjà mieux (= cela va à lui...).

Corrigé :

A 1. der Flug, des Flugs, die Flüge, *le vol.* 2. Die Hand, der Hand, die Hände, *la main.* 3. Der Tag, des Tags, die Tage, *le jour.* 4. Die Straße, der Straße, die Straßen, *la rue.* 5. Das Haus, des Hauses, die Häuser, *la maison.* 6. Der Mensch, des Menschen, die Menschen, *l'être humain.* 7. Das Fenster, des Fensters, die Fenster, *la fenêtre.* 8. Der Mann, des Manns, die Männer, *l'homme.* 9. Die Frau, der Frau, die Frauen, *la femme.* 10. der Vater, des Vaters, die Väter, *le père.*

B 11. *Comment va votre grand-père?* (mot à mot : comment cela va-t-il à ...) Wie ging es... 12. *Merci, pas très bien; il ne se sent pas bien.* Er fühlte ... 13. *Il se plaint de maux d'estomac.* Er klagte über ... 14. *Il n'a pas d'appétit et respire péniblement.* Er hatte... und atmete... 15. *Souvent, il a aussi des maux de tête.* Oft hatte er ...

C 16. Herr Doktor, möchten Sie meinen Sohn untersuchen? 17. Er hat sich erkältet; er hat Halsschmerzen. 18. Es ist nicht schlimm; hier ist ein Rezept; morgen geht es ihm schon besser.

Leçon

50 bis — Contrôle et révisions

A **Relisez le texte L. 43, 4 et la grammaire L. 41, 3 et traduisez :**

1. Il y a beaucoup de voitures sur ce terrain de stationnement. 2. Autrefois *(einst)* il n'y avait pas d'autoroutes. 3. Il y a trois flèches blanches sur ce panneau. 4. Elles indiquent le sens giratoire; y a-t-il longtemps que vous le saviez?

B **Faites des phrases conditionnelles avec « wenn », si, puis traduisez (Lecture L. 45,4; grammaire, L. 45,3).**

5. Er macht eine Bewegung; der Räuber schießt. 6. Er trägt keine Sonnenbrille; ich erkenne ihn. 7. Die Sirene heult; der Räuber läuft davon. 8. Er hat keinen Wagen gestohlen; er kann nicht flüchten.

C **Remplacez les mots entre parenthèses par le comparatif, puis traduisez (Lecture L. 41,4; grammaire, L. 49,3) :**

9. Er ißt (gern) Hummer. 10. Dieses Restaurant hat (viel) Gäste. 11. Nun läuft der Kellner (schnell). 12. Der Geschäftsführer spricht (klug). 13. Aber der Komponist antwortet (gut). 14. Zum Schluß wird er (freundlich).

D *Lecture :*

Forschung und Medizin.

Kupfer besitzt, wie sich bei westdeutschen Versuchen zeigte, eine starke bakterientötende Wirkung, insbesondere gegen Staphylokokken. Deshalb empfehlen die Mediziner der Industrie, Haltegriffe in öffentlichen Verkehrsmitteln sowie Treppengeländer, Türklinken usw. in Krankenhäusern und Schulen nicht mehr aus den rostfreien Metallen — wie Chromnickelstahl, Aluminium und Chrom — herzustellen, sondern wie früher die als Messing bezeichnete Kupfer-Zink-Legierung zu verwenden.

Aus der Wochenzeitung DIE WELTWOCHE, Zürich

E *Humor*

Der Arzt zu seinem Patienten :

— Warum haben Sie mir meinen Brief mit der Rechnung ungeöffnet zurückgeschickt?

— Weil ich doch jede Aufregung vermeiden soll!

Corrigé :

A 1. Es stehen viele Wagen auf diesem Parkplatz. 2. Einst gab es keine Autobahnen. 3. Es sind drei weiße Pfeiler auf diesem Schild. 4. Sie zeigen den Kreisverkehr an; wußten Sie es seit langem?

B 5. Wenn er eine Bewegung machte, würde der Räuber schießen (= schösse der Räuber). *S'il faisait un geste, le bandit tirerait.* 6. Wenn er keine Sonnenbrille trüge, würde ich ihn erkennen. *S'il ne portait pas de lunettes de soleil, je le reconnaîtrais.* 7. Wenn die Sirene heulte, liefe der Räuber davon (würde ... davon laufen). *Si la sirène mugissait, le bandit détalerait.* 8. Wenn er keinen Wagen gestohlen hätte, könnte er nicht flüchten. *S'il n'avait pas volé de voiture, il ne pourrait pas s'enfuir.*

C 9. lieber. *Il aime mieux manger du homard.* 10. mehr. *Ce restaurant a plus de clients.* 11. schneller. *Maintenant, le garçon court plus vite.* 12. klüger. *Le gérant parle avec plus de finesse.* 13. besser. *Mais le compositeur répond mieux.* 14. freundlicher. *Finalement, il devient plus aimable.*

D La recherche et la médecine.

Le cuivre, ainsi que des expériences effectuées en République Fédérale d'Allemagne l'ont démontré, possède un fort pouvoir bactéricide, en particulier contre les staphylocoques. C'est pourquoi les médecins recommandent à l'industrie de ne plus fabriquer en métaux inoxydables — tels que l'acier chromé au nickel, l'aluminium, le chrome — les poignées d'appui dans les véhicules des transports publics, de même que les mains-courantes, les poignées de porte dans les hôpitaux et dans les écoles, mais d'utiliser comme autrefois l'alliage de cuivre et de zinc, appelé laiton.

E *Humour*

Le médecin à son client :

— Pourquoi m'avez-vous retourné, sans l'avoir ouverte, ma lettre contenant la facture?

— Mais (c'est) parce que je dois éviter toute émotion!

Die Denkmäler

1 Traditionsgemäß hat ein Dorf zwei öffentliche Gebäude : das Rathaus und die Kirche. Je bedeutender die Stadt ist, desto größer ist die Zahl der öffentlichen Gebäude.
In den bevölkerten Städten befindet sich auf den Bahnhöfen und in den Kaufhäusern oft eine große Menschenmenge. *Hauptpostamt, Banken, Niederlassungen großer Gesellschaften, wie Versicherungsgesellschaften usw. nehmen ganze Gebäude ein.

2 In einer Landeshauptstadt umfassen die *Dienststellen der verschiedenen Ministerien unzählige Büros. In vielen modernen Städten sind die Verwaltungen an einem Ort, der Stadtverwaltung, zusammengebracht.
Um Raum zu sparen, wird auch in die Höhe gebaut : in manchen Städten werden die alten Türme von Wolkenkratzern überragt.

3 Im Monat August besichtigen viele Touristen die Kunstwerke und andere Sehenswürdigkeiten : Denkmäler, Dome (oder Kathedralen), Kirchen, *Tempel, Kapellen. Oft werden Paläste und Schlösser zu Museen.

4 Die öffentlichen Bibliotheken, die Universitäten, die Gymnasien und Oberschulen, die Theater- und Konzertsäle geben der Stadt ihren geistigen Ruf.

1 [traditçi**o**n'ç-gém**è**ç]; [h**a**opt-poçt-am't]; [fèrz**i**cherou^{gn}ç] — [géz**è**lchaften'].

2 [l**a**n'deç-h**a**opt-chtat]; [d**i**n'çt-cht**è**len'].

3 [z**é**-en'ç-v**u**rdicḥ-kaéten']; [t**è**m'pel].

ES IST NICHT ALLES GOLD WAS GLÄNZT

Traduction

Les monuments

1 Un village a traditionnellement deux édifices publics : la mairie et l'église. Plus la ville est importante, plus le nombre des édifices est grand.
Dans les villes peuplées, une grande foule se trouve souvent dans les gares et dans les grands magasins. La poste centrale, les banques, les sièges de grandes sociétés, telles que les compagnies d'assurance, etc., occupent des immeubles entiers.

2 Dans une capitale d'État, les différents services des ministères occupent d'innombrables bureaux. Dans beaucoup de villes modernes les services administratifs sont groupés à un même endroit : le centre administratif.
On construit aussi en hauteur pour économiser la place : dans plus d'une ville, les vieilles tours sont dominées par des gratte-ciel.

3 Au mois d'août, beaucoup de touristes visitent les œuvres d'art et autres curiosités : les monuments, cathédrales, églises, temples, chapelles. Souvent, les palais et les châteaux sont transformés en musées.

4 Les bibliothèques publiques, les Universités, les lycées et collèges, les théâtres et salles de concerts donnent à la ville sa réputation intellectuelle.

Vocabulaire

der Dienst (– e), *le service*
der Dom (– e), *la cathédrale*
der Pal**a**st (⁼ e), *le palais*
der Ruf (– e), *la réputation*
die Traditi**o**n (– en), *la tradition*
der Tempel (–), *le temple*
die Universit**ä**t (– en), *l'université*
das Denkmal (⁼ er), *le monument*
das Geb**ä**ude (–), *le bâtiment*
das Gymnasium (– ien), *le lycée*
das Kunstwerk (e), *l'œuvre d'art*
das Minister/ium (– ien), *le ministère*

Tout ce qui brille n'est pas or.

der Tour**i**st (– en), *le touriste*
der Wolkenkratzer (–), *le gratte-ciel*
die H**au**ptstadt (⁼̈ e), *la capitale*
die Kirche (n), *l'église*
die Kap**e**lle (n), *la chapelle*
die **O**bersch**u**le (n), *le collège*
die S**e**henswürdigkeit (–en), *chose digne d'être vue*
das Schloß (⁼̈ sser), le château
(die Burg (– en), *le château-fort*)
das The**a**ter (–), *le théâtre*
bev**ö**lkern, *peupler*
überr**a**gen, *surplomber*
verw**a**ndeln, *transformer*
d**a**rbieten (o, o), *présenter*

Grammaire

■ **Die Verwaltungen werden an einem Ort, der Stadtverwaltung, zusammengebracht.**
der Stadtverwaltung est mis en apposition à *Ort,* et se met au même cas que ce dernier, c'est-à-dire au datif, ici. Le nom placé en apposition prend en allemand l'article défini ou indéfini, selon le sens. Exemples :

Wien, die Hauptstadt Österreichs, Vienne, capitale de l'Autriche.

Heidelberg, eine romantische Stadt am Neckar, Heidelberg, ville romantique sur le Neckar.

■ **Im Monat August kommen viele Touristen.**
August, nom propre mis en apposition à *Monat,* n'est pas relié par une préposition, comme en français : au mois d'août. C'est le cas pour tous les noms propres et pour certaines expressions qu'on apprendra par l'usage. Exemples :

Die Stadt Leipzig, la ville de Leipzig.
Im Monat April, au mois d'avril.
Ein Meter Tuch, un mètre de drap.
Ein Pfund Brot, une livre de pain.
Zwei Kilo Birnen, deux kilos de poires.
Ein Glas Apfelsaft, un verre de jus de pomme.

Exercices

Traduisez :
1. Munich, capitale de la Bavière (= *Bayern*), a de grands musées. 2. Paul a visité Ulm, ville ancienne sur le Danube (*die Donau*). 3. (C'est) au mois de mai (que) cette région est la plus belle. 4. Je voudrais un verre de vin. 5. Donnez-moi

s'il vous plaît une livre de viande. 6. Cet édifice est la banque la plus grande de notre ville.
A partir du corrigé ci-dessous, faites la traduction inverse.

Corrigé :

1. München, die Hauptstadt Bayerns, hat große Museen. 2. Paul hat Ulm, eine alte Stadt an der Donau, besichtigt. 3. Im Monat Mai ist diese Gegend am schönsten. 4. Ich möchte ein Glas Wein. 5. Geben Sie mir bitte ein Pfund Fleisch. 6. Dieses Gebäude ist die größte Bank unserer Stadt.

Lecture

Außerhalb der Saison

Schon seit Jahren macht sich die Stadt Salzburg einen Ehrgeiz daraus, sich nicht nur während der sommerlichen Festspielmonate auf ihren größten Sohn zu besinnen. So finden, auch in diesem Jahr wieder, in der Residenz und im Schloß Mirabell von Mai bis Oktober, 175 Kammermusikabende in der Reihe « Salzburger Schloßkonzerte » statt, und unter dem Motto « Musikalischer Frühling » werden vom 15. April bis zum 24. Mai an zehn historischen Plätzen Salzburgs Werke Mozarts und der Wiener Klassiker aufgeführt.

Aus der Wochenzeitung « Die Zeit »

Hors saison

Depuis des années déjà, la ville de Salzbourg se fait un point d'honneur (mot à mot : une ambition) de ne pas limiter aux mois du Festival d'Été l'évocation de son fils le plus illustre (mot à mot : de se souvenir non seulement...)
Ainsi, 175 soirées de musique de chambre seront organisées cette année encore à la Résidence et au Château Mirabell, depuis le mois de mai jusqu'en octobre, dans le cycle des « Concerts aux châteaux de Salzbourg », et — du 15 avril au 20 mai — on présentera des œuvres de Mozart et des classiques viennois dans une dizaine de sites historiques de la ville de Salzbourg, sous la devise « Printemps musical ».

Leçon

52

Im Museum

1 — Ist das Museum heute geöffnet, bitte?
— Ja, das Museum ist jeden Tag, außer Dienstag geöffnet.
— Welches sind die *Besuchszeiten?
— Morgens von zehn bis zwölf und nachmittags von vierzehn bis siebzehn Uhr. Am Mittwoch und am Freitag abend von zwanzig bis zweiundzwanzig Uhr.

2 — Was kostet der Eintritt, bitte? Ich bin Student; habe ich ein Anrecht auf *Preisermäßigung?
— Jawohl. Sie bezahlen den halben Preis, wie die Besuchergruppen.
— Könnten Sie mir sagen, wo sich die Gemälde von Schwind befinden?
— Die Räume, die ihnen gewidmet sind, werden zur Zeit umgebaut. Vorübergehend werden die Gemälde im Untergeschoß ausgestellt. Steigen Sie nach dem Bildersaal der Expressionisten die Treppe hinab; nehmen Sie danach den ersten Gang links; Sie kommen dann in die romanische Skulpturengalerie.

3 — Wo kann man Reproduktionen erstehen?
— Im Erdgeschoß, hinter dem Teesalon, links.
— Ich hätte gern das *Selbstbildnis von Rembrandt. Ich habe es nirgends finden können. Sie haben es hier in weiß und schwarz, ich hätte es aber gern farbig.
— Leider haben wir es nicht farbig, aber wir haben Dias, wenn Sie das wünschen.

1 [béz**ou**chç-tç**a**éten']. **2** [praéç-èrm**è**çigou[gn]]. **3** [z**è**lbçt-b**i**ltniç].

DAS WERK LOBT DEN MEISTER

Traduction

Au musée

1 — Le musée est-il ouvert aujourd'hui, s'il vous plaît?
— Oui, le musée est ouvert tous les jours à l'exception du mardi.
— Quelles sont les heures de visite?
— De 10 h à 12 h le matin et de 14 h à 17 h l'après-midi. Les mercredi et vendredi soirs de 20 h à 22 h.

2 — Quel est le prix d'entrée, s'il vous plaît? Je suis étudiant; ai-je droit à une réduction (de prix)?
— Parfaitement, vous payez demi-tarif, comme les groupes (de visiteurs).
— Pouvez-vous me dire où se trouvent les (tableaux de) Schwind?
— Les salles qui leur sont consacrées sont actuellement en travaux. Les toiles sont temporairement exposées au sous-sol. Descendez l'escalier après la galerie des expressionnistes; prenez ensuite le premier couloir à gauche; vous arrivez alors dans la galerie des sculptures romanes.

3 — Où peut-on se procurer des reproductions?
— Au rez-de-chaussée, à gauche, derrière le salon de thé.
— Je voudrais le portrait de Rembrandt peint par lui-même. Je n'ai pu le trouver nulle part. Vous l'avez ici en noir et blanc, mais je le voudrais en couleur.
— Malheureusement nous ne l'avons pas en couleur, mais si vous le désirez, nous avons des diapositives.

Vocabulaire

der Bes**u**cher (-), *le visiteur*
der Eintritt (-e), *l'entrée*
der Stud**e**nt (-en), *l'étudiant*
die Ausstellung (-en), *l'exposition*
die Erm**ä**ßigung (-en), *la réduction*
das Dia (s), *la diapositive*
das Erdgeschoß (sse), *le rez-de-chaussée*
das Gem**ä**lde (-), *le tableau, la peinture*
das S**e**lbstb**i**ldnis (se), *le portrait du peintre par lui-même*
das **U**ntergeschoß (sse), *le sous-sol*

C'est à l'œuvre qu'on reconnaît l'artisan (l'œuvre loue le maître).

die Gruppe (n), *le groupe*
das Anrecht (-e), (auf), *le droit (à)*
umb**au**en, *transformer (construction)*
widmen, *consacrer*
vor**ü**berg**e**hen (i, a), *passer*

Grammaire

■ Ich habe es nirgends finden können.

Le verbe de cette phrase est au passé composé : *Ich habe... können,* j'ai pu. Or, à la place du participe passé habituel *gekonnt,* auquel nous nous attendrions normalement, nous trouvons ici un participe passé à forme d'infinitif. Cette substitution se fait chaque fois qu'un auxiliaire de mode (L. 18, 19, 20) à un temps composé du passé, a pour complément un infinitif (dans notre exemple, cet infinitif complément est *finden,* trouver).

Er hat das Museum besichtigen wollen, il a voulu visiter le musée.
Helga hat nicht kommen mögen, Helga n'a pas eu envie de venir.
Max hatte lange warten müssen, Max avait dû attendre longtemps.
Er hatte nicht vorgehen dürfen, il n'avait pas eu le droit de passer le premier (m. à m. : devant).

Cette règle du « double infinitif » s'applique aussi au verbe *lassen,* laisser, faire, et, facultativement, à quelques autres verbes comme *sehen,* voir; *hören,* entendre; *helfen,* aider.

Er hat den Wächter kommen lassen, il a fait venir le gardien.
Er hat ihn die Treppe heraufkommen hören (ou *gehört*), il l'a entendu monter l'escalier.

■ Wo sind die Gemälde von Schwind?

● Le complément du nom, *von Schwind,* n'exprime pas, ici, la possession (= génitif), mais l'origine, la provenance. Dans ce cas, on emploie une préposition : *von* (+ Datif), de. Exemples :

Ein Roman von Kafka, un roman de Kafka.
Der Zug von Köln, le train (venant) de Cologne.

● Dans la langue courante, on emploie parfois *von* là où le génitif serait de rigueur. Exemple :
Ein Freund von Karl, un ami de Charles, au lieu de *Ein Freund Karls.*

● Cependant, *von* remplace obligatoirement le génitif pluriel sans article. Exemple :

Der Besuch eines Museums, mais au pluriel : *der Besuch von Museen,* la visite de musées.

Exercices

A *Mettez au passé composé, puis traduisez :*
1. Der Student kann schön malen *(peindre).* 2. Dürfen Sie im Museum rauchen *(fumer)*? 3. Kurt mag nicht ins Untergeschoß gehen. 4. Hilde läßt sich die Dias präsentieren. 5. Wir hören niemand sprechen. 6. Ich will es nicht.

B *Mettez l'expression entre parenthèses au pluriel, puis traduisez :*
7. Der Wert (eines Gemäldes). 8. Der Kauf (eines Führers) *(guide).* 9. Der Bau (eines Domes).

C *Traduisez :*
10. Nous n'avons pu visiter toutes les salles. 11. Ces touristes ont voulu acheter des diapositives en couleur. 12. Avez-vous pu rester longtemps? 13. Si le musée était fermé, nous visiterions la cathédrale. 14. Dans cette salle, il y a de beaux tableaux de Schwind, peintre romantique *(romantisch)* allemand.

Corrigé :

A 1. ... hat ... malen können. *L'étudiant a bien su peindre.* 2. Haben Sie ... rauchen dürfen? *Avez-vous eu le droit de fumer dans le musée?* 3. ... hat ... gehen mögen. *Kurt n'a pas eu envie de descendre au sous-sol.* 4. ... hat sich ... präsentieren lassen. *Hilde s'est fait présenter les diapositives.* 5. ... haben ... sprechen hören. *Nous n'avons entendu parler personne.* 6. Ich habe es nicht gewollt. *Je ne l'ai pas voulu* (pas d'infinitif complément).

9. Der Wert von Gemälden. *La valeur de tableaux.* 8. Der Kauf von Führern. *L'achat de guides.* 7. Der Bau von Domen. *La construction de cathédrales.*

10. Wir haben nicht alle Säle besuchen können. 11. Diese Touristen haben Farbdias kaufen wollen. 12. Haben Sie lange bleiben können? 13. Wenn das Museum geschlossen wäre, würden wir den Dom besichtigen. 14. In diesem Saal gibt es schöne Gemälde von Schwind, einem romantischen deutschen Maler.

Leçon

53 Im Theater

1 — Haben Sie noch Plätze für den « Zerbrochenen Krug »?
— Für nächsten Dienstag also, um zwanzig Uhr fünfundvierzig? Ach! Da ist ja Galaaufführung; ich bedauere, mein Herr alles ist ausverkauft. Vielleicht haben Sie noch Glück an einer Verkaufsstelle in der Stadt. Doch werden die Plätze der vierten Galerie erst dreiviertel Stunden vor dem Aufgehen des Vorhangs verkauft. Am besten kommen Sie gleich um zwanzig Uhr und stellen sich an.

2 — Bleibt Ihnen noch etwas übrig für die nächste Aufführung von « Wilhelm Tell », am Donnerstag nachmittag?
— Ich habe nur noch vier Klappsitze im Balkon, zwei Logenplätze und einige Parkettplätze. Wieviel Plätze wünschen Sie denn?
— Zwei.
— Obgleich unsere Klappsitze auch bequem sind, schlage ich Ihnen die Parkettplätze 130 und 132 vor, vorne rechts. Ich habe nichts anderes, aber es ist ein recht guter Platz.

3 — Wer spielt den Tell in dieser Aufführung? Ist es Karl Schuri?
— Nein, er spielt heute nicht; die Rolle ist doppelt besetzt.
— Ach, schade!
— Nun, mein Herr, wozu entschließen Sie sich?
— Nun, ich will sie trotzdem nehmen.
(In Deutschland ist es nicht üblich, der Platzanweiserin ein Trinkgeld zu geben).

EHRE, DEM EHRE GEBÜHRT

Traduction

Au théâtre

1 — Avez-vous encore des places pour la « Cruche Cassée »?
— Pour mardi prochain donc, à 20 h 45? Ah! c'est soirée de gala; je regrette, Monsieur, tout est pris. Peut-être aurez-vous quelque chance encore (en vous adressant) à une agence en ville. Cependant, les places de quatrième galerie ne sont mises en vente que trois quart d'heure avant le lever du rideau. Le mieux, c'est de venir dès 20 h et de faire la queue.

2 — Vous reste-t-il quelque chose pour la prochaine représentation de « Guillaume Tell », le jeudi après-midi?
— Je n'ai plus que quatre strapontins au balcon, deux fauteuils de loge et quelques fauteuils d'orchestre. Combien de places voudriez-vous donc? — Deux. — Bien que nos strapontins soient confortables (eux) aussi, je vous propose les fauteuils d'orchestre 130 et 132, en avant à droite. C'est tout ce que j'ai, mais c'est une place fort convenable.

3 — Qui est-ce qui fait Tell, dans cette représentation? Est-ce Karl Schuri? — Non, il ne joue pas aujourd'hui; c'est son remplaçant (m. à m. : le rôle est doublé). — Ah! C'est dommage! — Alors, Monsieur, que décidez-vous? — Bah! Je vais les prendre quand même.
(Il n'est pas d'usage, en Allemagne, de donner un pourboire à l'ouvreuse).

Vocabulaire

der Balk**o**n (-e), *le balcon*
der Klappsitz (-e), *le strapontin*
der Park**e**ttplatz (¨e), *le fauteuil d'orchestre*
der Sperrsitz (-e), *idem*
die Loge (n), *la loge*
die Pl**a**tz**a**nweiserin (nen), *l'ouvreuse*
sich **a**n'st**e**llen (ici), *se mettre à la queue*
(die) Schlange stehen, *faire la queue*

A tout seigneur tout honneur (Honneur à qui honneur est dû).

der Stock (die Stockwerke), *l'étage*
der Vorhang (⸗e), *le rideau*
die Aufführung (-en), *la représentation*
die Galer**ie** (n), *la galerie*
die Kontr**o**lle (n), *le contrôle*
ausverk**au**fen, *vendre tout, solder*
bed**au**ern, *regretter*
aufgehen.(ging, gegangen) *s'élever*
sich entschließen (o, o) (+ zu) *se décider (à)*
bleiben (ie, ie), *rester*
übrigbl**ei**ben *(idem)*

Grammaire

■ Obgleich unsere Klappsitze bequem sind,...
Notez que dans cette proposition, le verbe *sind* est à l'indicatif, et non au subjonctif comme en français après « quoique, bien que ». *Obschon, obwohl,* qui ont le même sens (bien que), sont également suivis de l'indicatif. Exemple :

Obwohl der Saal groß ist, ist alles ausverkauft, bien que la salle soit grande, tout est vendu.

L'indicatif s'emploie aussi après *bis,* jusqu'à ce que, et *bevor,* avant que, si le fait rapporté est réel. Exemple :

Ich bleibe an meinem Platz, bis du zurückkommst, je resterai à ma place jusqu'à ce que tu reviennes.

■ Es bleiben nur vier Klappsitze.
Il ne reste que quatre strapontins.
Diese Plätze werden erst morgen verkauft.
Ces places ne seront vendues que demain.
Nur, seulement, ne... que, s'emploie dans le sens de « pas davantage » (restriction simple). *Erst,* seulement, ne... que..., a le sens de « pas encore davantage » (restriction provisoire) ou « pas plus tôt que » (sens temporel). Exemples :

Ein Parkettplatz kostet nur fünf Mark, un fauteuil d'orchestre ne coûte que cinq marks.

Die Aufführung beginnt erst um neun Uhr, la représentation ne commence qu'à neuf heures.

■ Er stellt sich an.
Il se met à la queue (m. à m. : il se place contre).
Dans cette expression, on sous-entend *an die Reihe,* à la file. Autrement, « faire la queue » signifie *Schlange stehen* (*die Schlange (n),* le serpent). Exemple :

Er stand Schlange vor der Theaterkasse, il fit la queue devant la caisse du théâtre.

Exercices

A *Accordez le verbe entre parenthèses, puis traduisez :*
1. Obwohl diese Komödie sehr lustig (sein), gefällt sie nicht allen Zuschauern *(spectateurs).* 2. Paul liest das Programm, bis der Vorhang (aufgehen). 3. Bevor die Aufführung (beginnen), geht das Licht *(lumière)* aus. 4. Schuri hatte nur wenig Erfolg *(succès)* heute, obgleich er wie immer (spielen).

B *Complétez par* nur *ou* erst, *puis traduisez :*
5. Dieses Stück *(pièce)* hat... drei Akte. 6. Wir werden... gegen acht Uhr kommen. 7. Ich kenne dieses Theater... seit kurzer Zeit. 8. Hier werden... gute Stücke gespielt.

C *Traduisez :*
9. Je voudrais deux places seulement. 10. Ils ne sont rentrés qu'à une heure. 11. Nous attendrons jusqu'à ce que nous ayons une bonne place. 12. Bien que la caisse n'ouvre *(öffnen)* qu'à huit heures, Werner vint à sept heures et demie déjà.

Corrigé :

A 1. ist. *Bien que cette comédie soit très gaie, elle ne plaît pas à tous les spectateurs.* 2. aufgeht. *Paul lit son programme, jusqu'à ce que le rideau se lève (jusqu'au lever du rideau).* 3. beginnt. *Avant que la représentation commence, la lumière s'éteint.* 4. gespielt hat. *Schuri n'avait que peu de succès, bien qu'il ait joué comme toujours.*

B 5. nur. *Cette pièce n'a que trois actes.* 6. erst. *Nous n'arriverons que vers huit heures.* 7. erst. *Je connais ce théâtre depuis peu de temps seulement.* 8. nur. *Ici, on ne joue (m. à m. : sont jouées) que de bonnes pièces.*

C 9. Ich möchte nur zwei Plätze. 10. Sie sind erst um ein Uhr nach Hause gekommen. 11. Wir warten, bis wir einen guten Platz bekommen. 12. Obwohl die Kasse erst um acht Uhr öffnet, kam Werner schon um halb acht.

Leçon

54

Münchner Oktoberfest und Rheinischer Karneval

1 – Möchten Sie nicht das alljährlich in München stattfindende Oktoberfest besuchen? Es ist Bayerns berühmtestes Fest. Aus aller Welt kommen die Besucher, um die geliebte Stadt wiederzusehen und einen feuchtfröhlichen Abend zu verleben. Auf der mit Schaubuden und Karussels bedeckten Theresienwiese herrscht ein frohes Treiben. In den riesigen Bierzelten sitzen Tausende von Leuten; die Kellnerinnen bahnen sich einen Weg, mit vier Krügen in jeder Hand. Das frische Bier fließt in Strömen. Überall duftet es nach Brathendeln, nach Weißwurst. Ganze Ochsen werden am Spieß gebraten. Blaskapellen spielen einen Walzer auf. Lustige, von allen Gästen im Chor mitgesungene Trinklieder erklingen im Zelt : « Bier her! Bier her! oder ich fall um! »

2 – Letztes Jahr waren wir auf dem Karneval zu Koblenz. Welch ein tolles Leben in den Straßen der Stadt! Männer, Frauen und Kinder waren verkleidet, sangen, lachten und vergnügten sich. Ich erinnere mich besonders an den Umzug am Rosenmontag. Bekannte Persönlichkeiten wurden auf den in den Straßen vorbeifahrenden Wagen dargestellt; natürlich war alles ein großer Ulk. Prinz Karneval und seine Prinzessin kamen auf dem prunkvollsten aller Wagen daher und ernteten stürmischen Beifall. Man war so richtig in der Stimmung des Rheinischen Karnevals.

MAN MUß DIE FESTE FEIERN WIE SIE FALLEN

Traduction

La Fête d'Octobre à Munich et le carnaval rhénan

1 — Ne voudriez-vous pas aller à la Fête d'Octobre qui a lieu tous les ans (m. à m. : ayant lieu...) à Munich? C'est la fête la plus célèbre de la Bavière. Les visiteurs viennent du monde entier pour revoir la ville qu'ils aiment et pour passer une soirée à boire et à s'amuser (m. à m. : une soirée humide et gaie). Sur la « Prairie de Thérèse », couverte de baraques de foire et de manèges, règne une joyeuse animation. Des milliers de personnes sont assises sous les tentes gigantesques des brasseries (m. à m. : de la bière); les serveuses se frayent un chemin, portant 4 cruches dans chaque main. La bière fraîche coule à flots. Partout l'on sent la bonne odeur des poulets rôtis, des saucisses. Des bœufs entiers sont rôtis à la broche. Des orchestres d'instruments à vent invitent à la valse. De gaies chansons à boire retentissent sous la tente, reprises en chœur par toute l'assistance (par tous les clients) : « De la bière! de la bière! sinon je trépasse (tombe) »!

2 L'an passé, nous étions au carnaval de Coblence. Quelle vie délirante dans les rues de la ville! Les hommes, les femmes et les enfants étaient déguisés et chantaient, riaient et s'amusaient. Je me souviens particulièrement du cortège du Lundi des Roses. Des personnalités connues étaient représentées sur des chars qui passaient dans les rues; bien entendu, tout cela était une grosse bouffonnerie. Le Prince Carnaval et sa Princesse arrivaient sur le plus somptueux de tous les chars et soulevaient (m. à m. : récoltaient) des tonnerres d'applaudissement. On était vraiment dans l'ambiance du Carnaval Rhénan.

Vocabulaire

der Beifall, *les applaudissements.*
der Krug (⸗ e), *la cruche*
der Ochs (en), *le bœuf*
der Strom (⸗ e), *le courant, le fleuve*
der Ulk (-e), *la plaisanterie*
die Wiese (n), *le pré*
die Wurst (⸗ e), *le saucisson*
Bayern (neutre), *la Bavière*
das Hendel (-), (Autriche), *le poulet*
das Treiben, *l'animation*
die Kellnerin (nen), *la serveuse*
die Schau, *la vue, l'exposition*

Il faut prendre le temps comme il vient.
(Il faut célébrer les fêtes comme elles tombent.)

Grammaire

Das alljährlich in München stattfindende Okotoberfest... Auf dem mit Schaubuden bedeckten Gelände...

Dans ces deux expressions, nous trouvons ce qu'on appelle une « proposition qualificative ». Devant le nom qualifié *(Oktoberfest* ou *Gelände)* est placé un adjectif ou, le plus souvent, un participe. Dans notre premier exemple, c'est le participe présent : *stattfindend,* ayant lieu (L. 28); dans le deuxième, le participe passé : *bedeckt,* couvert (L. 19). Ces participes sont devenus de véritables adjectifs et se déclinent comme tels (voir L. 21, 23, 25). En outre, l'adjectif est lui-même précédé de ses compléments *(alljährlich in München* ou *mit Schaubuden).* L'ordre de la proposition qualificative est donc le suivant : article (s'il y en a un) — compléments de l'adjectif — adjectif — nom.

Cette proposition qualificative correspond à une subordonnée relative (voir L. 31). Ex. :

Das Oktoberfest, das alljährlich in München stattfindet.

Elle est fréquente dans les articles de journaux, dans la langue technique, mais lourde et rarement employée dans la langue parlée.

Exercices

Transformez les propositions relatives en qualificatives, puis traduisez :

1. Eine Kellnerin, die mehrere Krüge trug, lächelte uns zu. 2. Das Lied, das von der Kapelle gespielt wurde, war ein Walzer. 3. Alle Menschen, die hier vorbeizogen, trugen Masken. 4. Die Kinder, die vor der Bude standen, waren froh. (Remarque : Avec les verbes de position — L. 12 — on prend toujours le participe présent).

Corrigé :

1. Eine mehrere Krüge tragende Kellnerin lächelte uns zu. *Une serveuse qui portait plusieurs cruches, nous souriait.* 2. Das von der Kapelle gespielte Lied war ein Walzer. *La chanson jouée par l'orchestre était une valse.* 3. Alle hier vorbeiziehenden Menschen trugen Masken. *Tous les gens qui passaient ici portaient des masques.* 4. Die vor der Bude stehenden Kinder waren froh. *Les enfants se trouvant devant la baraque étaient joyeux.*

Lecture

Die Rache

Der bekannte Schauspieler Beckmann hatte in einem Lustspiel ein Huhn zu tranchieren. Er machte dies sehr fachmännisch und verzehrte mit Appetit das ganze Huhn auf offener Bühne.
Als bei der nächsten Vorstellung diese appetitliche Szene wiederkam, war Beckmann nicht wenig überrascht, als ihm ein Ersatzhuhn aus Pappe serviert wurde; er ließ sich aber nicht aus der Fassung bringen und tranchierte auch dieses Huhn, das dem sparsamen Direktor also teuerer zu stehen kam als das gebratene. Der Direktor ließ ihm daher das nächste Mal ein Huhn auftischen, das aus hartem Holz geschnitzt war. Der Komiker, der vorher davon Wind bekommen hatte, ließ sich aber dadurch nicht aus der Ruhe bringen. Er holte eine kleine Holzsäge aus der Tasche und fing unter dem großen Beifall des Publikums an, das Huhn zu zersägen.
Von da an bekam er wieder sein leckeres Brathuhn.

Aus « Langenscheidt's Sprachillustrierte ».

La vengeance

Beckmann, l'acteur bien connu, dut découper un poulet au cours d'une comédie. Il le fit avec beaucoup de compétence et mangea le poulet de (bon) appétit devant le public (m. à m. : sur la scène ouverte).
Quand on en revint à cette scène, lors de la représentation suivante, quel ne fut pas l'étonnement de Beckmann, lorsqu'on lui servit un faux poulet (m. à m. : un poulet de remplacement) en carton. Mais il ne perdit pas contenance (m. à m. : ne se laissa pas décontenancer) et découpa également ce poulet-là, qui revint donc plus cher au directeur économe que le (poulet) rôti.
Aussi, le directeur lui fit-il servir la fois suivante un poulet taillé dans du bois dur. Mais le comédien qui en avait eu vent (plus tôt), ne perdit pas pour autant son sang-froid. Il tira de sa poche une petite scie à bois et se mit à découper le poulet, sous les applaudissements nourris du public.
Depuis ce jour-là, il eut de nouveau son délicieux poulet rôti.

Leçon

55 Höflichkeit

1 — Guten Abend, mein Herr, wie geht es Ihnen?
— Danke, sehr gut, und Ihnen?
— Es freut mich sehr, Sie zu treffen. Darf ich Ihnen meinen Bruder vorstellen? Ihr Gatte kennt ihn recht gut.
— Ich freue mich, Ihre Bekanntschaft zu machen.
— Guten Tag, mein Herr; mein Mann hat mir in der Tat schon viel von Ihnen erzählt.

2 — ... Ich habe noch gar nicht nach Ihren Kindern gefragt; was machen sie denn?
— Danke, es geht allen gut.
— Und wie geht es Ihrem Herrn Vater?
— Nicht besonders gut. Er erholt sich nur langsam von seiner Krankheit.
— Richten Sie ihm bitte viele Grüße aus; ich wünsche ihm eine baldige Genesung.
— Ich will es gern ausrichten.
— Was ich noch sagen wollte, haben Sie Nachricht von Ihrem Freund Setzer?

3 Im Briefverkehr :
a) Lieber Herr Meier! b) Sehr geehrter Herr Direktor! c) Sehr geehrte Herren!
Schlußformeln :
a) Mit freundlichem Gruß, Ihr Peter Lang. b) Mit verbindlichen Empfehlungen, Peter Lang. c) Hochachtungsvoll, Peter Lang.

4 a) Ich wünsche Ihnen ein glückliches neues Jahr.
b) Fröhliche Weihnachten; viel Glück zum neuen Jahr.
c) Wir gratulieren und wünschen dem jungen Paar recht viel Glück. d) Herzliches Beileid.

MIT SANFTMUT KOMMT MAN AUCH ZUM ZIEL

Traduction

Politesse

1 – Bonsoir Monsieur, comment allez-vous? – Merci, très bien, et vous? – Je suis très heureux de vous rencontrer. Permettez-moi de vous présenter mon frère; votre époux le connaît fort bien. – Je suis heureux de faire votre connaissance. – Bonjour Monsieur, en effet mon mari m'a beaucoup parlé de vous.

2 – ... Je ne vous ai pas demandé encore comment allaient vos enfants? (m. à m. : je ne me suis pas informé encore de...). – Merci, ils vont tous bien. – Et Monsieur votre père? – Moyennement. Il ne se remet que lentement de sa maladie. – Vous lui transmettrez mes amitiés et mes vœux de prompt rétablissement (m. à m. : Je lui souhaite ...). – Je n'y manquerai pas (m. à m. : je vais le lui faire savoir volontiers). – A propos, avez-vous des nouvelles de votre ami Setzer?

3 Dans la correspondance :
a) Cher Monsieur Meier, b) Monsieur le Directeur, (m. à m. : Très honoré...) c) Messieurs,
Formules finales :
a) Croyez à mes sentiments très amicaux, votre Peter Lang.
b) Je vous prie d'agréer, Messieurs, l'expression de mes sentiments distingués.
c) Veuillez agréer, Monsieur, l'expression de ma considération distinguée.

4 a) Je vous souhaite une bonne année.
b) Joyeux Noël; meilleurs vœux de bonne année (m. à m. : beaucoup de bonheur pour le nouvel an).
c) Félicitations et vœux de bonheur aux jeunes mariés.
d) Sincères condoléances.

Vocabulaire

der Gatte (n), *l'époux*
der Tod, *la mort*
die Gattin (nen), *l'épouse*
das Glück, *le bonheur, la chance*
gratul**ie**ren, *féliciter*
sich erh**o**len, *se rétablir*

Plus fait douceur que violence. (Avec de la douceur également, on atteint son but.)

die Gen**e**sung (-en), *le rétablissement*
die H**ö**flichkeit (-en), *la politesse*
die Krankheit (-en), *la maladie*
das Leid (-en), *la peine*
das Beileid, *les condoléances*
ver**e**hren, *respecter, vénérer*
v**o**rst**e**llen, *présenter*
z**u**s**e**tzen (+ Datif), *tourmenter*
ausspr**e**chen (a, o, i) *exprimer*
treffen (a, o, i), *atteindre, rencontrer*

Grammaire

Wie geht es Ihnen? – Es freut mich...

Nous avons vu (L. 17) que *es* peut être le sujet d'un verbe impersonnel tel que *es regnet,* il pleut. Nous avons retrouvé *es* sujet de « il y a » : *es gibt, es ist, es steht,* etc. (L. 41). Dans *Wie geht es Ihnen?* Comment allez-vous? – *Es freut mich...* Je suis heureuse... (m. à m. : cela me réjouit), *es* est employé comme sujet de tournures impersonnelles.

Es wundert mich, (accusatif), j'en suis étonné.
Es ärgert mich, j'en suis irrité.
Es langweilt mich, je m'ennuie.
Es hungert mich, j'ai faim.
Es friert mich, j'ai froid *(frieren; o, o).*
Es tut mir (datif) *leid,* j'en suis désolé.
Es schmeckt mir, je trouve cela bon; c'est bon.
Es geht mir gut, je vais bien.
Es scheint mir, als ob, il me semble que *(scheinen; ie, ie).*
Es ist, als ob..., on dirait que (m. à m. : c'est comme si).
Es ist kalt; warm, il fait froid; chaud.
Es klopft, on frappe.

C'est le complément qui nous indique le sujet :

Es freut ihn, il en est heureux.
Es ärgert sie, elle en est irritée.
Es wundert uns, nous en sommes étonnés.
Schmeckt's Ihnen? le trouvez-vous bon? est-ce bon?

Enfin, *es* se trouve souvent au début d'une proposition principale dont le verbe est suivi du sujet réel :

Es kamen zwei Züge an, deux trains arrivèrent.
Es fahren viele Schiffe auf dem Rhein, beaucoup de bateaux naviguent sur le Rhin.

Notez que dans ces phrases, le verbe s'accorde avec le sujet réel.

Exercices

A *Mettez au prétérit, puis traduisez :*
1. Es hungert mich, aber ich habe keinen Durst. 2. Es ärgert uns, aber wir zeigen es nicht. 3. Es wundert mich nicht, daß er so spät kommt. 4. Es langweilt sie, alle wissen es. 5. Es tut ihm leid. 6. Es schmeckt ihr nicht. 7. Es ist kalt, und es wird Nacht. 8. Klopft es? — Ja, es sind unsere Freunde.

B *Traduisez :*
9. Comment va Madame votre mère? 10. Veuillez transmettre mes amitiés à votre collègue. 11. Nous n'avons pas de nouvelles de sa famille. 12. Nous nous réjouissons tous de (= *auf* + *accusatif)* votre visite.

C *Employez les verbes suivants dans une tournure impersonnelle, avec le pronom complément à la 3ᵉ pers. du sing., masc. :*
13. wundern. 14. ärgern. 15. langweilen. 16. hungern. 17. gut gehen. 18. scheinen, als ob... 19. leid tun. 20. frieren.

Corrigé :

A 1. Es hungerte mich, aber ich hatte... *J'avais faim, mais pas soif.* 2. Es ärgerte uns, aber wir zeigten es nicht. *Nous en étions irrités, mais nous ne le montrâmes pas.* 3. Es wunderte mich nicht, daß er so spät kam. *Je n'étais pas étonné de ce qu'il vint si tard.* 4. Es langweilte sie, alle wußten es. *Elle s'ennuyait, tout le monde le savait.* 5. Es tat ihm leid. *Il le regrettait.* 6. Es schmeckte ihr nicht. *Elle ne le trouvait pas bon.* 7. Es war kalt, und es wurde Nacht. *Il faisait froid et la nuit tombait (m. à m. : il devenait nuit).* 8. Klopfte es? — Ja, es waren... *Est-ce qu'on avait frappé? — Oui, c'était nos amis.*

B 9. Wie geht es Ihrer Frau Mutter? 10. Wollen Sie bitte Ihrem Kollegen meine freundlichen Grüße ausrichten (= Richten Sie bitte...). 11. Wir haben keine Nachricht von seiner Familie. 12. Wir freuen uns alle auf Ihren Besuch.

C 13. Es wundert ihn. *Il en est étonné.* 14. Es ärgert ihn. *Il en est irrité.* 15. Es langweilt ihn. *Il s'ennuie.* 16. Es hungert ihn. *Il a faim.* 17. Es geht ihm gut. *Il va bien.* 18. Es scheint ihm, als ob... *Il lui semble que...* 19. Es tut ihm leid. *Il le regrette.* 20. Es friert ihn. *Il a froid.*

56 Wir besuchen gemeinsame Freunde

(Man verabredet sich telefonisch).
— Wir wollen Ihnen von Seiten unserer gemeinsamen Freunde, der Familie Roth, viele Grüße bestellen.
— Ja, eben haben sie uns Ihren Besuch angekündigt. Es freut uns sehr Ihre Bekanntschaft zu machen. Kommen Sie doch einmal nach dem Abendessen vorbei; wir werden Kaffee trinken und miteinander plaudern. Welcher Tag wäre Ihnen am liebsten? Sie wollen sich bestimmt vieles anschauen und Ihre Zeit ist wohl bemessen. Bestimmen Sie also einen Tag, wir werden uns danach richten.
— Wäre Ihnen der Samstag abend gelegen?
— Ach! leider sind wir am Samstag nicht in München. Wir fahren nämlich jeden Samstag weg. Am Sonntag aber kommen wir nicht zu spät nach Hause zurück, um die Verkehrsstockungen zu vermeiden. Wollen Sie also nächsten Sonntag vorbeikommen, nach dem Abendessen, so gegen neun Uhr?
— Ja, es wird wohl möglich sein. Wir haben am Abend eine Verabredung; ich glaube aber, wir können um neun bei Ihnen sein.
— Wo könnte ich Sie erreichen, falls ein unvorhersehbares Hindernis dazwischen kommt?
— Rufen Sie die Nummer achtunddreißig vierzig zwoundsechzig an.
— Ist die Anschrift : Marktplatz, Nummer drei, richtig?
— Ja sie stimmt. Im vierten Stock, dritte Tür rechts, wenn man aus dem Fahrstuhl kommt.
— Schön! Auf baldiges Wiedersehen!

UNVERHOFFT KOMMT OFT

Traduction

Nous rendons visite à des amis communs

(L'on prend rendez-vous par téléphone).
— Nous irons vous saluer de la part de nos amis communs, la famille Roth (m. à m. : Nous allons vous transmettre...) — Oui, justement ils nous ont annoncé votre visite. Nous ferons votre connaissance avec beaucoup de plaisir (m. à m. : cela nous réjouit beaucoup...). Passez donc un jour après dîner, nous prendrons le café et nous bavarderons (ensemble). Quel jour cela vous serait-il le plus agréable? Vous avez certainement beaucoup de choses à voir et votre temps est compté. Donc, fixez un jour. Votre jour sera le nôtre (mot à mot : nous nous y conformerons). — Est-ce que le samedi soir vous conviendrait? — Ah! malheureusement nous ne sommes pas à Münich le samedi. C'est que nous partons tous les samedis. Mais nous rentrerons dimanche, pas trop tard pour éviter les encombrements sur les routes. Voulez-vous passer dimanche prochain après dîner, vers 9 h? — Oui, ce sera sans doute possible. Nous avons un rendez-vous dans la soirée; mais je crois que nous pourrons être chez vous à 9 h. — Où pourrais-je vous toucher si, éventuellement, un empêchement imprévu se présentait? — Appelez le 38.40.62. — Votre adresse, c'est bien 3, place du Marché? — C'est cela (mot à mot : elle est juste). Au 4e étage, 3e porte de droite en sortant de l'ascenseur. — Parfait. A bientôt!

Vocabulaire

die Bek**a**nntschaft (-en), *la connaissance*
die Ver**a**bredung (-en), *le rendez-vous*
ank**ü**ndigen, *annoncer*
best**i**mmen, *déterminer, fixer*
err**ei**chen, *atteindre*
plaudern, *bavarder*
sich richten (nach), *se conformer à*
stimmen, *être juste*
bem**e**ssen (a, e, i), *mesurer*
vorh**e**rs**e**hen (a, e, ie), *prévoir*

L'imprévu arrive souvent.

■ Wir werden uns danach richten

Nous nous y conformerons; nous nous en accommoderons.
Dans cette phrase, le verbe *sich richten nach* (+ datif), se conformer à, aurait pour complément *dem, diesem,* cela :

Wir richten uns nach dem, nous nous conformerons à cela.

Or, le groupe *nach + dem,* se remplace par un démonstratif composé, où la préposition est précédée de *da* (ou *dar,* si elle commence par une voyelle). La plupart des prépositions peuvent se combiner ainsi : *dafür, damit, darauf, darin.* Ces démonstratifs composés correspondent souvent à notre « en », ou « y ».

Denken an, penser à.
Ich denke daran, j'y pense.
Fragen nach, s'informer.
Haben Sie schon danach gefragt?
Vous en êtes-vous déjà informé?
Erzählen von, parler de.
Sein Besuch bei Müllers? Er erzählte mir lange davon, sa visite chez les Müller? Il m'en a parlé longtemps.
Stolz auf, fier de.
Sie hat schöne Blumen; sie ist stolz darauf, elle a de belles fleurs; elle en est fière.
Dankbar für, reconnaissant de.
Ich bin Ihnen sehr dankbar dafür, je vous en suis très reconnaissant.

Cependant, ces démonstratifs ne s'emploient pas pour désigner des personnes :

Ich erzähle von ihm, je parle de lui.
Ich bin stolz auf ihn (et non *darauf),* je suis fier de lui.

■ Ein unvorhersehbares Hindernis

L'adjectif *unvorhersehbar,* imprévisible, vient du verbe *vorher/sehen,* prévoir. Le préfixe *un* indique l'absence, la négation, le contraire. Exemples :

ruhig, calme; *unruhig,* inquiet.
bequem, confortable; *unbequem,* inconfortable.

Ce préfixe sert aussi à former des noms.

das Glück, le bonheur, la chance; *das Unglück,* le malheur, la malchance.

Exercices

A *Traduisez, puis, remplacez le complément entre parenthèses par un démonstratif composé :*
1. Was machst du (mit diesem alten Mantel)? 2. Was haben Sie (für das Kleid) gezahlt? Ich freue mich sehr (auf deinen Besuch). 4. Hat sie Angst (*peur*) (vor dem Gewitter)? 5. Ich werde mich immer (an diesen Tag) erinnern (*souvenir*). 6. Wir warten lange (auf den Obus).

B *Donnez le contraire des adjectifs et noms suivants, puis traduisez :*
7. angenehm. 8. appetitlich. 9. brauchbar. 10. eingeladen. 11. die Aufmerksamkeit. 12. die Ordnung.

C *Traduisez :*
13. Nous avons des amis communs qui habitent à Munich. 14. Connaissez-vous ce poisson? ici, nous en mangeons souvent *(essen von).* 15. J'ai bien reçu votre invitation *(die Einladung);* je vous en remercie beaucoup.

Corrigé :

A 1. *Que fais-tu de ce vieux manteau?* Was machst du damit? 2. *Qu'avez-vous payé pour la robe?* Was haben Sie dafür gezahlt? 3. *Je me réjouis beaucoup de ta visite.* Ich freue mich sehr darauf. 4. *A-t-elle peur de l'orage?* Hat sie Angst davor? 5. *Je me souviendrai toujours de cette journée.* Ich werde mich immer daran erinnern. 6. *Nous attendons longtemps le trolley.* Wir warten lange darauf.

B 7. unangenehm, *désagréable.* 8. unappetitlich, *peu appétissant.* 9. unbrauchbar, *inutilisable.* 10. uneingeladen, *sans être invité.* 11. die Unaufmerksamkeit, *l'inattention.* 12. die Unordnung, *le désordre.*

C 13. Wir haben gemeinsame Freunde, die in München wohnen. 14. Kennen Sie diesen Fisch? Hier essen wir oft davon. 15. Ich habe Ihre Einladung gut erhalten; ich danke Ihnen sehr dafür.

Leçon

57

Auf dem Land

1 Ich mag die Großstadt sehr gern. Aber nach einer Woche muß ich hinaus in die *Natur, in die freie Luft. Manche Leute haben ein Landhaus, wo sie den Sonntag verbringen, oder gar das *Wochenende, wenn sie am Samstag frei haben. Da ich gern wandere, mache ich oft am Wochenende einen Ausflug aufs Land. Dort ist alles so ruhig, so erfrischend.

2 Wie gern habe ich die Wälder mit ihren stillen Pfaden unter hohen Bäumen! Stundenlang kann man dort *spazieren gehen oder reiten. Man kann sich in den Schatten legen und träumen, oder auf einer Lichtung ein Sonnenbad nehmen. Auch Picknick mache ich gern.

3 Obwohl es in unseren Flüssen immer weniger Fische gibt, gehe ich gern angeln. Andere gehen auf die Jagd. Ich jage lieber nach schönen Lichtbildern. Neulich habe ich einen interessanten Film über das Leben auf dem Lande gedreht; es ist mir gelungen, wunderschöne Landschaften aufzunehmen.

1 [nat**ou**r]; [w**o**ren'**è**n'de].

2 [chpatç**i**ren'].

NACH GETANER ARBEIT IST GUT RUHEN

Traduction

A la campagne

1 J'aime beaucoup la grande ville. Mais au bout de huit jours (d'une semaine) il faut que je sorte dans la nature, au grand air (m. à m. : à l'air libre). Certains ont une maison de campagne où ils vont passer le dimanche ou même la fin de la semaine, s'ils ont congé le samedi. Comme j'aime les randonnées, je fais souvent en fin de semaine une excursion à la campagne. Tout y est si calme, si reposant.

2 Que j'aime les forêts avec leurs sentiers silencieux sous de grands arbres! L'on peut s'y promener des heures et des heures, ou monter à cheval. On peut s'étendre à l'ombre et rêver, ou prendre un bain de soleil dans une clairière. J'aime aussi les repas sur l'herbe.

3 Bien qu'il y ait de moins en moins (m. à m. : toujours moins) de poissons dans nos rivières, j'aime bien pêcher à la ligne. D'autres vont à la chasse. Moi, je préfère la chasse aux belles photographies. Dernièrement, j'ai fait un film intéressant sur la vie à la campagne; j'ai réussi à prendre d'admirables paysages.

Vocabulaire

der Jäger (-), *le chasseur*
der Pfad (-e), *le sentier*
der Schatten (-), *l'ombre*
der Wald (‥ er), *la forêt*
die Jagd (-en), *la chasse*
die Lichtung (-en), *la clairière*
die Natur, *la nature*
die Wanderung (-en), *la (grande) marche*
das Lichtbild (-er), *la photo*
das Photo (s), *idem*
das Picknick (s), *le pique-nique*
das Wochenende (n), *la fin de la semaine*
angeln, *pêcher à la ligne*
drehen, *tourner*
fischen, *pêcher*
jagen, *chasser*
träumen, *rêver*
wandern, *voyager (à pied)*
gelingen (a, u), *réussir*
es gelingt mir, *je réussis (à) ...*
*reiten, (ritt, geritten), *monter à cheval*

Quand la tâche est finie, il fait bon se reposer.

Grammaire

■ Wie gern habe ich die Wälder!

Dans la proposition exclamative, la construction est généralement inverse. L'adjectif ou l'adverbe se placent après *wie*, comme.

Wie schön ist diese Lichtung im Sommer! Comme cette clairière est belle, en été.

Cependant, on trouve aussi la construction avec rejet du verbe :

Wie schön diese Lichtung im Sommer ist!

■ Ich muß hinaus.

Notez l'emploi absolu de *hinaus*, qui marque l'idée de sortir (*aus*), de s'éloigner (*hin*). Le verbe de mouvement (par exemple : *gehen* ou *fahren*) est sous-entendu.

■ Da ich gern wandere...

Da peut avoir trois significations :

- Avec rejet du verbe, *da* signifie : puisque, comme.

  Da ich gerne Lichtbilder mache, nehme ich immer meine Kamera mit, comme j'aime prendre des photos, j'emporte toujours mon appareil.

- Autrement, il signifie : là (adverbe de lieu).

  Da fand ich einen stillen Ort, j'ai trouvé là un endroit calme.

- ou bien : alors, (adverbe de temps).

  Es war drei Uhr; da legte ich mich in den Schatten, il était trois heures; alors, je me suis allongé à l'ombre.

Exercices

Traduisez :

1. Comme ces arbres sont hauts! 2. Comme il monte bien à cheval! 3. Comme il aime aller à la chasse! 4. Comme ce film est intéressant! 5. Il avait une maison de campagne; (c'est) là (qu') il passait souvent le dimanche. 6. Comme il aime la nature, il photographie souvent des paysages. 7. Il pleuvait; alors, je suis resté à la maison. 8. J'ai trouvé là un sentier très agréable.

Corrigé :

1. Wie hoch sind diese Bäume! 2. Wie schön reitet er! 3. Wie gern geht er auf die Jagd! 4. Wie interessant ist dieser Film! 5. Er hatte ein Landhaus; da verbrachte er oft den Sonntag. 6. Da er die Natur liebt, nimmt er oft Landschaften auf. 7. Es regnete; da bin ich zu Hause geblieben. 8. Da habe ich einen sehr angenehmen Pfad gefunden.

Lecture

Wanderung bei Innsbruck

Große Omnibusse fahren ins Tal hinein. Ihnen gehört die Landstraße. Die Wanderer nehmen dankbar die Wiesenwege auf halber Höhe und grüßen den Ruetzbach, der ihnen plaudernd entgegenkommt und nur an wenigen Stellen zwischen künstlichen Böschungen dahinschnellt; sonst macht er fröhlich und selig. Was alles unterwegs ist, mit Stadt- oder Wanderschuhen, es trifft mitten in Neustift zusammen, einen Steinwurf von der Kirche entfernt, die ein Pfarrherr im 18. Jahrhundert nach eigenem Gutdünken (wie manch anderes Kirchlein im Tal) entworfen, mit viel Geschmack und geschultem Sinn gebaut hat.

Aus der Tageszeitung « Frankfurter Allgemeine Zeitung »

Une excursion dans la région d'Innsbruck

De grands autocars pénètrent dans la vallée. C'est à eux qu'appartient la grand-route. Les touristes empruntent avec plaisir (m. à m. : reconnaissance) les sentiers à travers champs, (m. à m. : prairies) à mi-pente et saluent le ruisseau, le Ruetzbach, qui vient à leur rencontre tout en bavardant et qui ne précipite (son cours) qu'en peu d'endroits, entre des berges artificielles; ailleurs il est gai et heureux. Tout ce qui est en chemin, tout ce qui porte chaussures de ville ou de route, se réunit dans le centre de Neustift, à un jet de pierre de l'église, dont un curé, au 18e siècle, avait tracé le plan à son idée (comme ce fut le cas pour maintes petites églises de la vallée), et qu'il avait édifiée avec beaucoup de goût et avec un esprit averti.

Leçon

58 Ausflüge

1 — Heute ist das Wetter wirklich schön. Seit zwei Tagen regnet es nicht mehr; die Sonne scheint; der Boden ist wohl trocken. Heute nachmittag können wir ein Picknick im Grünen machen, oder wir werden uns ins « Wirtshaus zur Linde » begeben. Bereiten Sie uns doch ein kaltes *Mahl, einige belegte Brötchen, Obst, Kaffee in einer *Isolierflasche. Wir werden alles in den Rucksack stecken, und Hans wird ihn tragen.

2 — Vergessen Sie Ihre Badehose nicht!
— Leider habe ich keine mitgebracht. Könnten Sie mir eine leihen?
— *Selbstverständlich. Aber fragen Sie doch Hans danach. Er hat ungefähr Ihre Größe.
— Kann man hier tauchen?
— Gewiß! Hier ist der See drei Meter tief.

3 — Können Sie *Schi laufen?
— Ist es schon lange her, daß Sie es gelernt haben?
— Es hat geschneit. Schade, daß ich meine Schistiefel nicht mitgebracht habe. Die Bahn ist prächtig, und der Schilift ist schon in Betrieb!
— Wenn ich das gewußt hätte!

1 [mal]; [izolir-flache].

2 [zèlbçt-fèrchtèn'tlich].

3 [chi].

UNTER DEN BLINDEN IST DER EINÄUGIGE KÖNIG

Traduction

Excursions

1 Aujourd'hui il fait vraiment beau. Depuis deux jours, il ne pleut plus; le soleil brille; le sol doit être sec (m. à m. : est sans doute sec). Cet après-midi, nous pourrons déjeuner sur l'herbe (m. à m. : faire un pique-nique dans la verdure) ou bien nous nous rendrons dans l'« Auberge du Tilleul ». Préparez-nous donc un repas froid, quelques sandwiches, des fruits, du café dans une bouteille Thermos. Nous mettrons tout cela dans le sac à dos et Jean le portera.

2 — N'oubliez pas votre caleçon de bain. — Je n'en ai pas emporté, malheureusement. Pourriez-vous m'en prêter un? — Naturellement. Mais demandez-le donc à Jean. Il a à peu près votre taille. — Est-ce qu'on peut plonger ici? — Certainement. Ici, le lac a une profondeur de trois mètres (m. à m. : est profond de trois mètres).

3 — Est-ce que vous savez skier? — Y a-t-il longtemps que vous l'avez appris? — Il a neigé. C'est dommage que je n'ai pas apporté mes chaussures (m. à m. : bottes) de ski. La piste est magnifique, et le téleski fonctionne déjà! (m. à m. : est déjà en fonction). — Si j'avais su (cela)!

Vocabulaire

der Betr**ie**b (-e), *l'activité*
der Boden (¨), *le sol*
der Rucksack (¨ e), *le sac à dos*
der Schi (-er), *le ski*
der Schilift (e), *le téléski*
der Schnee, *la neige*
der See (s, n), *le lac*
der Stiefel (-), *la botte*
die B**a**deh**o**se (n), *le caleçon de bain*
(der B**a**de**a**nzug (¨ e), *le maillot de bain*

die See (n), *la mer*
das Bad (¨ er), *le bain*
das Mahl (-e), *le repas*
das Obst (sing.), *les fruits*
baden, *(se) baigner*
bel**e**gen, *garnir, couvrir*
ber**ei**ten, *préparer*
schn**ei**en, *neiger*
stecken, *mettre, enfoncer*
untert**au**chen, *plonger*
emp**o**rt**au**chen, *émerger*
leihen (ie, ie), *prêter, emprunter.*

Au royaume des aveugles, les borgnes sont roi
(Parmi les aveugles, le borgne est roi).

Wenn ich das gewußt hätte!
Dans cette phrase, le verbe est au passé du subjonctif 2. Cette forme ressemble au plus-que-parfait de l'indicatif (L. 20), cependant, au lieu de *ich hatte* ou *ich war,* on se sert de *ich hätte* ou *ich wäre* (subjonctif 2).

● Le subjonctif peut s'employer dans une phrase exclamative.
a) Au présent, 2ᵉ forme, il exprime un souhait :

Wenn ich es nur wüßte! si seulement je le savais!
Wenn ich nur meine Badehose hätte! si seulement j'avais mon caleçon de bain!
Wenn ich doch Schi laufen könnte! si seulement je savais faire du ski!

Remarque : Dans ces phrases, on peut également sous-entendre *wenn,* en faisant l'inversion (cf. L. 38).

Wüßte ich es nur! Hätte ich nur meine Badehose!

b) Au passé, 2ᵉ forme, il exprime un regret :

Wenn wir das gewußt hätten! si nous l'avions su!
Wenn das Wetter doch schöner gewesen wäre! ah! si le temps avait été plus beau!
Wenn es nur mehr geschneit hätte! si seulement il avait neigé davantage!

Là aussi, on peut employer l'inversion :

Hätte es nur mehr geschneit!

● Le passé du subjonctif 2 s'emploie aussi dans la phrase conditionnelle au passé (cf. L. 45).

Wenn es nicht geregnet hätte, hätten wir im Freien gegessen, s'il n'avait pas plu, nous aurions mangé en plein air.
Wenn Hans nicht gekommen wäre, hätte Ilse den Rucksack getragen, si Hans n'était pas venu, (c'est) Ilse (qui) aurait porté le sac à dos.
Wenn es geschneit hätte, hätten wir unsere Schier mitgenommen, s'il avait neigé, nous aurions emporté nos skis.
Wenn der Bademeister nicht untergetaucht wäre, wäre der Junge ertrunken, si le maître-nageur n'avait pas plongé, le garçon se serait noyé.

Exercices

A *Exprimez un souhait à l'aide du verbe entre parenthèses, puis traduisez :*
1. Wenn meine Freunde nur schon da (sein)! 2. (Geben) es nur mehr Fische hier! 3. Wenn er mir doch seine Schier (leihen).

B *Exprimez un regret, puis traduisez :*
4. Wenn ich doch meine Kamera nicht (vergessen)! 5. ... wir doch diese Lichtung gleich (finden)! 6. Wenn ich es nur (lernen)!

C *Faites des phrases conditionnelles au passé, puis traduisez :*
7. Ich habe meine Badehose mitgebracht; ich bin im See geschwommen. 8. Der Schilift ist in Betrieb gewesen; ich habe mich gut amüsiert. 9. Sie hat uns ein kaltes Mahl bereitet; wir haben ein Picknick gemacht.

D *Traduire :*
10. Si seulement le sac à dos n'était pas si lourd! 11. Que n'avons-nous acheté cette maison de campagne! (= Si seulement...) 12. Si le lac avait été plus profond, nous aurions plongé.

Corrigé :

A 1. Wenn ... wären. *Si seulement mes amis étaient déjà là!* 2. Gäbe es ... hier! *Ah! s'il y avait davantage de poissons ici!* 3. Wenn er ... liehe! *Si seulement il me prêtait ses skis!*

B 4. Wenn ... nicht vergessen hätte! *Si seulement je n'avais pas oublié mon appareil photographique!* 5. Hätten wir doch ... gefunden! *Que n'avons-nous trouvé cette clairière tout de suite.* 6. Wenn ... gelernt hätte! *Que ne l'ai-je appris!*

C 7. Wenn ich meine Badehose mitgebracht hätte, wäre ich ... geschwommen. *Si j'avais emporté mon caleçon de bain, j'aurais nagé dans le lac.* 8. Wenn der Schilift in Betrieb gewesen wäre, hätte ich ... amüsiert. *Si le téléski avait fonctionné, je me serais bien amusé.* 9. Wenn sie uns ... bereitet hätte, hätten wir ein Picknick gemacht. *Si elle nous avait préparé un repas froid, nous aurions fait un pique-nique.*

D 10. Wenn der Rucksack nur nicht so schwer wäre! 11. Hätten wir doch dieses Landhaus gekauft! 12. Wenn der See tiefer gewesen wäre, wären wir getaucht. (= Wäre der See...)

Leçon

59 Wir kaufen den Freunden Reiseandenken

1 — Was für ein Problem, die Reiseandenken für die Verwandten und Freunde!
— Was würde ihnen Freude bereiten?
— Welche *Summe kann ich für diese Art Einkäufe ausgeben?
— Wieviel wird mir übrigbleiben, wenn alles bezahlt sein wird, das Hotel, die Taxe, der Gepäckträger, der Speisewagen, oder das Benzin für das Auto? Vor meiner Abreise möchte ich nicht noch einmal Geld wechseln.

2 — Zuletzt : lohnt es sich, diesen oder jenen Artikel der Souvenirläden zu kaufen?
— Ist er wirklich *typisch? Wurde er wirklich im Lande selbst hergestellt?

3 — Was könnte ich nur als Reiseandenken mitbringen? Man riet mir, in die Domgasse zu gehen. Dort gibt es einen Laden, wo hübsche Töpferwaren ausgestellt sind. Auch Puppen sah ich im Schaufenster; das ist wohl ein wenig abgedroschen, aber meiner kleinen Nichte würde es Freude machen. Für ihren Bruder könnte ich eine Mundharmonika kaufen. Sie ist hier gewiß billiger als in Paris. Und dann, kommt sie aus Deutschland, so macht es einen guten Eindruck.

1 [z**ou**me]

2 [t**u**pich]

FRIEDE ERNÄHRT, UNFRIEDE VERZEHRT

Traduction

Nous achetons des souvenirs pour nos amis

1 — Quel problème, ces souvenirs de voyage pour les parents et amis! — Qu'est-ce qui leur ferait plaisir? — Quelle somme puis-je consacrer à ce genre d'achats? (m. à m. : dépenser pour...). — Combien (d'argent) me restera-t-il, quand tout sera payé, l'hôtel, le taxi, le porteur, le wagon-restaurant, ou l'essence pour la voiture? Je n'aimerais pas changer encore une fois de l'argent avant mon départ.

2 — Enfin : est-ce que cela vaut la peine d'acheter tel ou tel article des boutiques de souvenirs? — Est-il vraiment typique? A-t-il vraiment été fait dans le pays-même? (m. à m. : fut-il ... fabriqué ...).

3 Que pourrais-je bien rapporter comme souvenir?
On me conseilla d'aller dans la rue de la cathédrale. Là-bas, il y a une boutique où l'on expose de jolies poteries (m. à m. : où sont exposées...). J'ai vu également des poupées, dans la devanture; c'est un peu banal, certes, mais cela ferait plaisir à ma petite nièce. Pour son frère, je pourrais acheter un harmonica. C'est certainement moins cher ici qu'à Paris. Et puis, venant d'Allemagne, cela fera bon effet (m. à m. : s'il vient d'Allemagne).

Vocabulaire

der Neffe (n), *le neveu*
der Topf (¨ e), *le pot*
der Töpfer (-), *le potier*
der Verw**a**ndte (n), *le (proche) parent*
ein Verw**a**ndter, *un (proche) parent*
die Art (-en), *la façon*
die Nichte (n), *la nièce*

die M**u**ndharm**o**nika (s), *l'harmonica*
(die Z**ie**hharm**o**nika, *l'accordéon)*
die Summe (n), *la somme*
das Sch**au**f**e**nster (-), *la devanture*
lohnen, *récompenser*
es lohnt sich, *cela vaut la peine*
herst**e**llen, *fabriquer*
ausg**e**ben (a, e; i), *dépenser*

La paix nourrit, la guerre consume.

Grammaire

■ **Man riet mir, in die Domgasse zu gehen.**
Le verbe *raten,* conseiller, fait au prétérit *riet,* au participe passé *geraten;* au présent : *du rätst, er rät* (voir L. 4 et 20). Les verbes irréguliers suivants ont les mêmes temps primitifs : *blasen,* souffler; *halten,* tenir; *lassen,* laisser; *schlafen,* dormir; *fallen (fiel, gefallen),* tomber.

■ **Der Gepäckträger, der Töpfer.** Le porteur, le potier.
Avec le suffixe *-er* on a formé des noms de personnes désignant soit une activité, soit une habitation. Exemples :

der Fleischer (-), le boucher
der Bäcker, le boulanger
der Arbeiter (-), l'ouvrier
der Kölner (-), l'habitant de Cologne
der Städter (-), le citadin

D'autres noms en *-er* désignent des instruments. Exemples :

der Schläger (-), la raquette (tennis)
der Plattenspieler (-), le tourne-disque

Exercices

A *Traduisez puis mettez : a) au prétérit, b) au passé composé :*
1. Er bläst Trompete. 2. Sie fallen ins Wasser. 3. Sie hält ihr Kind an der Hand. 4. Ich lasse dich in Ruhe. 5. Er schläft tief.

B *Traduisez :*
6. Si seulement je savais quelle sorte de souvenir je dois lui apporter. 7. Comme ces poteries sont fabriquées ici, je vais en emporter plusieurs. 8. Comme cette devanture est belle!

Corrigé :

1. *Il joue de la trompette;* a) Er blies...; b) Er hat... geblasen. 2. *Ils tombent à l'eau;* a) Sie fielen ...; b) Sie sind ... gefallen. 3. *Elle tient son enfant par la main;* a) Sie hielt ...; b) Sie hat ... gehalten. 4. *Je te laisse tranquille;* a) Ich ließ ...; b) Ich habe ... gelassen. 5. *Il dort profondément;* a) Er schlief ... b) Er hat ... geschlafen.

B 6. Wenn ich nur wüßte, was für ein Reiseandenken ich ihm mitbringen soll! 7. Da diese Töpferwaren hier hergestellt werden, will ich mehrere davon mitnehmen. 8. Wie schön ist dieses Schaufenster!

Auch Maharadschas aus Stoff...

(Von unserem Korrespondenten)

Mit dem Wohlstand steigt die Reisewelle, und mit ihr steigt die Souvenirwelle – diese Kausalkette bewirkte, daß in Wiesbaden eine der seltsamsten Messen abgehalten wurde : der « Internationale Salon Souvenir und Geschenk », der an diesem Montag seine Pforten schließt.
Da tickt ein Heer von Andenkenuhren, Schwarzwälder Uhren, Aschenbecheruhren, Uhren mit Muscheln, Uhren mit Musik. Da wogt es von Andenkentüchern, Autokissen, Wimpeln, glitzert und funkelt es von Straß, von mehr oder weniger silbernen Anhängern. Es stapeln sich Trachtengruppen und Whiskyfäßchen, indische Maharadschas aus Stoff und Gartenlämpchen aus Blech, die beliebten Flaschen mit dem Segelschiff im Bauch (made im Odenwald) und die nicht minder beliebten, goldverzierten Täßchen, Gläschen, Thermometerchen, Barometerchen. Ewiger Kitsch – durchsetzt von solidem Kunsthandwerk.

Aus « die Welt »

Même des maharadjas en étoffe...

(De notre correspondant)

Avec la prospérité, la vogue des voyages augmente, et avec celle-ci, la vogue des souvenirs. Cette relation (m. à m. : chaîne) de cause à effet a amené l'organisation, à Wiesbaden, d'une des foires les plus curieuses : le « Salon International du Souvenir et du Cadeau », qui fermera ses portes ce lundi-ci.
On y entend le tic-tac d'une armée de pendulettes-souvenirs, de coucous de la Forêt-Noire, de pendulettes-cendriers, de pendulettes chargées de coquillages, de pendulettes musicales. On y voit une mer de foulards-souvenirs, de coussins pour voitures, de fanions, un scintillement et un flamboiement de strass et de pendeloques plus ou moins en argent. Là s'entassent des séries de poupées en costumes folkloriques et des tonnelets de whisky, des maharadjas hindous en étoffe et de petites lampes de jardin en tôle, les bouteilles si appréciées, (fabriquées dans l'Odenwald) qui ont un voilier dans leur ventre, et les petites tasses, les petits verres, les petits thermomètres, les petits baromètres, ornés de dorures et qui ne sont pas moins appréciés. C'est l'éternel toc – pénétré par le travail sérieux de l'ouvrier d'art (m. à m. : du métier d'art).

Leçon

60 Ein Bummel durch das Geschäftsviertel

1 Heute habe ich nichts einzukaufen. Ich schaue mir nur die Schaufenster der Geschäfte an. Ich habe absichtlich kein Geld mitgenommen. In diesem Viertel befinden sich lauter Luxusgeschäfte. Hier ist alles mit viel Geschmack und Phantasie eingerichtet.

2 Mit besonderer Freude betrachte ich die Schaufenster der Juweliere. Edelsteine und Juwelen, Goldschmiedearbeiten und Tafelbesteck glänzen im Lichte der Scheinwerfer. Wie kunstwoll sind diese Armbänder, Ohrringe, Spangen und Manschettenknöpfe ausgestellt!
Ich verweile gern bei den Buchhändlern; ich nehme ein Buch von einem Regal, blättere darin, stelle es wieder zurück, nehme ein anderes.

3 Ich treffe nicht gern eine zu rasche Entscheidung. Ich denke lieber nach, komme lieber noch einmal zum Schaufenster zurück, um den Gegenstand noch einmal zu betrachten. Ich stelle mir vor, wie er sich bei mir machen würde. Ich frage mich, ob er mir nützen würde. Dann erst denke ich ans Kaufen.

4 In meinem früheren Viertel gab es fast ausschließlich Lebensmittelgeschäfte : Gemüse- und Obsthandlunqen, Fleischerläden, eine Bäckerei und Konditorei im Erdgeschoß unseres Hauses. Gegenüber war ein Feinkosthändler, der gute Einfälle hatte : er verkaufte exotische Produkte und Fertiggerichte.

GLÜCK UND GLAS, WIE BALD BRICHT DAS!

Traduction

En flânant dans le quartier des affaires

1 Aujourd'hui je n'ai pas d'achats à faire. Je regarde simplement les devantures des magasins. Je n'ai pas emporté d'argent, exprès. Dans ce quartier, il n'y a que des magasins de luxe. Tout y est disposé avec beaucoup de goût et d'imagination.

2 C'est avec une joie particulière que je contemple les devantures des bijoutiers. Les pierres précieuses et les bijoux, les orfèvreries et les couverts brillent dans la lumière des projecteurs. Avec quel art ces bracelets, boucles d'oreille, agrafes et boutons de manchettes sont-ils exposés!
J'aime rester chez les libraires; je prends un livre sur un rayon, je le feuillette, je le remets, j'en prends un autre.

3 Je n'aime pas me décider tout de suite (m. à m. : je ne prends pas volontiers une décision trop rapide). Je préfère réfléchir, revenir devant l'étalage pour regarder à nouveau l'objet. Je m'imagine comment il ferait chez moi. Je me demande s'il me rendrait service. C'est alors seulement que je pense à l'achat.

4 Dans mon ancien quartier, il n'y avait guère que (m. à m. : presque exclusivement) des magasins d'alimentation : des magasins de légumes et de fruits, des boucheries, une boulangerie-pâtisserie au bas de chez moi. Un épicier, en face, et qui avait de bonnes idées, vendait des produits exotiques et des plats tout préparés.

Vocabulaire

der Antiquar (-e), *l'antiquaire*
der B**u**chh**ä**ndler (-), *le libraire*
der **E**delst**ei**n (-e), *la pierre précieuse*
der G**e**genst**a**nd (¨e), *l'objet*
der Geist (-er), *l'esprit*
der Geschm**a**ck, *le goût, la saveur*
die Mansch**e**tte (n), *la manchette*
die Phantas**ie**, *l'imagination, la fantaisie*
die Spange (n), *l'agrafe*
das Armband (¨er), *le bracelet*
das Besteck (e), *le couvert*
das Heim, *le chez-soi*
das Juw**e**l (en), *le bijou*
das Reg**a**l (e), *le rayon, l'étagère*

Le bonheur, comme le verre, est fragile
(Bonheur et verre, comme cela se brise vite!)

der Goldschmied (-e), *le bijoutier*
der Juwelier (-e), *l'orfèvre*
der Knopf (⸗e), *le bouton*
der Luxus, *le luxe*
der Ohrring (-e), *la boucle d'oreille*
der Scheinwerfer (-), *le projecteur, le phare*
die Entscheidung (-en), *la décision*
die Lebensmittel (plur.), *l'alimentation*
benützen, *utiliser*
blättern, *feuilleter*
bummeln, *flâner*
glänzen, *briller*
nützen, *profiter, servir*
(aus)schmücken, *décorer*
verweilen, *demeurer*
nachdenken (dachte, gedacht) über, *réfléchir sur*
ich bleibe...stehen, *je m'arrête*

Grammaire

■ Ich treffe eine Entscheidung. Ich nehme ein Buch.

Les verbes *treffen* et *nehmen* appartiennent au même groupe de verbes irréguliers (groupe *e — a — o*). Leurs temps principaux sont :
Treffen, atteindre, rencontrer; *er traf,* il atteignit; *er hat getroffen,* il a atteint; *er trifft,* il atteint.
Nehmen, prendre; *nahm, genommen; er nimmt.*
Autres verbes irréguliers de ce groupe :
brechen (a, o; i), briser, cueillir;
**erschrecken (a, o; i),* s'effrayer;
gelten (a, o; i), valoir;
helfen (a, o; i), (+ datif), aider;
sprechen (a, o; i), parler;
**sterben (a, o; i),* mourir;
werfen (a, o; i), jeter, lancer;
empfehlen (a, o; ie), recommander.

Remarque : Les composés de ces verbes gardent les mêmes formes irrégulières. Exemple : *zerbrechen (a, o; i),* casser.

■ Ich will es daheim lesen.

Daheim, chez moi, à la maison, s'emploie quand on « est » à la maison (lieu, état); dans le même sens, on peut dire aussi *zu Hause.* Exemple :

Er bleibt gern daheim = er bleibt gern zu Hause, il aime rester à la maison (= chez lui).

Pour indiquer que l'on « va » à la maison (direction), il faut employer *heim* ou *nach Hause.* Exemple :

Er kam spät heim = er kam spät nach Hause, il rentra tard (à la maison, chez lui).

Remarque : *heim* se retrouve dans : *das Heim,* le foyer, le chez-soi; *das Altersheim,* l'asile de vieillards; *die Heimat,* le pays natal; *heimlich,* familier, intime; *geheim,* secret.

Exercices

Traduisez puis mettez : a) au prétérit, b) au passé composé :
1. Ich breche eine Rose. 2. Er erschrickt nicht leicht. 3. Dieser Schein gilt 100 Mark. 4. Du hilfst der alten Frau. 5. Sie stirbt. 6. Wir werfen Schneebälle. 7. Sie empfehlen uns das Hotel. 8. Er verspricht allerlei. 9. Sie werfen die Flaschen um.

Complétez par heim (nach Hause) *ou* daheim (zu Hause), *puis traduisez :*
10. Der Goldschmied arbeitet ..., in seinem Atelier. 11. Dietrich bummelt, anstatt ... zu gehen.

Traduisez :
12. Je voudrais une bague en or *(golden).* 13. Combien coûte ce bracelet? 14. Si je voulais décorer ma maison de campagne, j'irais chez cet antiquaire. 15. Bien que ces pierres ne soient pas authentiques *(echt),* elles plairont quand même à ma petite sœur.

Corrigé :

1. *Je cueille une rose.* a) Ich brach ... b) Ich habe ... gebrochen. 2. *Il ne s'effraie pas vite (facilement).* a) Er erschrak ... b) Er ist ... erschrocken. 3. *Ce billet vaut 100 Marks.* a) ... galt ... b) ... hat ... gegolten. 4. *Tu aides la vieille femme.* a) Du halfst ... b) Du hast ... geholfen. 5. *Elle meurt.* a) Sie starb. b) Sie ist gestorben. 6. *Nous lançons des boules de neige.* a) Wir warfen ... b) Wir haben ... geworfen. 7. *Ils nous recommandent l'hôtel.* a) Sie empfahlen ... b) Sie haben ... empfohlen. 8. *Il promet toutes sortes de choses.* a) Er versprach ... b) Er hat ... versprochen. 9. *Ils renversent les bouteilles.* a) Sie warfen ... um. b) Sie haben ... umgeworfen.

10. daheim (zu Hause). *L'orfèvre travaille chez lui, dans son atelier.* 11. heim (nach Hause). *Didier flâne, au lieu de rentrer (à la maison).*

12. Ich möchte einen goldenen Ring. 13. Wieviel kostet dieses Armband? 14. Wenn ich mein Landhaus ausschmücken wollte, ginge ich zu diesem Antiquar. 15. Obwohl diese Steine nicht echt sind, werden sie meiner kleinen Schwester doch gefallen.

Leçon

60 bis Contrôle et révisions

A **Traduisez, puis mettez au passé composé : (Relisez le texte L. 51,4, la grammaire L. 52,3 et voyez le Mémento n° 50, c).**

1. Ich will diese Festspiele besuchen. 2. Ich muß mir ein Abonnement bestellen. 3. Ich kann bis zum 28sten August hier bleiben. 4. Ich lasse mich zum Schloß Mirabell fahren. 5. Ich sehe viele Fremden kommen.

B **Traduisez (Texte L. 57,4; grammaire L 53,3) :**

6. Bien que de grands autocars pénètrent dans la vallée, beaucoup de touristes empruntent les sentiers. 7. Le ruisseau s'élance en peu d'endroits seulement, jusqu'à ce qu'il devienne tout à fait (*ganz*) paisible. 8. Quoiqu'il portât des chaussures de ville, Kurt a marché aussi vite que ses camarades. 9. L'église de Neustift a été construite avec beaucoup de goût, bien que son architecte fût un simple (*einfach*) curé.

C **Transformez les propositions qualificatives en relatives, puis traduisez (Texte L 59,4; grammaire L 54,3) :**

10. Die in diesem Saal tickenden Uhren kommen aus dem Schwarzwald. 11. Das in jener Ecke hängende Gartenlämpchen ist aus Blech. 12. Die von den Touristen gekauften Andenken sind oft Kitsch.

D **Traduisez :**

Signal aus San Diego

Die Geschichte vom Gastwirt, der in seinem Lokal ein Schild aufgehängt hat mit der Aufschrift : « Seien Sie nett zu meinem Personal. Gäste gibt's genug, aber keine Kellner », die Geschichte ist alt. Sie kennzeichnet einen Zustand, an den man sich fast schon gewöhnt hat. Doch dieser Zustand ist noch steigerungsfähig, wie eine Meldung aus Amerika besagt.

Um sein Bedienungspersonal nicht durch unhöfliche Besucher zu verlieren, verspricht Jim Frasers Drugstore in San Diego jedem eine Tasse Kaffee gratis, der die Kellnerin anlächelt. Bisher wurden mehr als 14 000 Tassen kostenlos ausgeschenkt.

Aus der Wochenzeitung « Rheinischer Merkur » (Köln).

Corrigé :

A 1. *Je veux visiter ce festival.* Ich habe ... besuchen wollen. 2. *Il faut que je me fasse réserver un abonnement.* Ich habe mir ... bestellen müssen. 3. *Je peux rester ici jusqu'au 28 Août.* Ich habe bis... hier bleiben können. 4. *Je me fais conduire au Château Mirabell.* Ich habe ... führen lassen. 5. *Je vois venir beaucoup d'étrangers.* Ich habe ... kommen sehen.

B 6. Obwohl große Omnibusse ins Tal hineinfahren, nehmen viele Touristen die Wiesenwege. 7. Der Bach schnellt nur an wenigen Stellen dahin, bis er ganz ruhig wird. 8. Obwohl Kurt Stadtschuhe trug, ist er so schnell wie seine Kameraden gegangen (marschiert). 9. Die Neustifter Kirche ist mit viel Geschmack gebaut worden, obwohl ihr Architekt ein einfacher Pfarrherr war.

C 10. Die Uhren, die in diesem Saal ticken, kommen aus .. *Les montres qui font entendre leur tic-tac dans cette salle, viennent de la Forêt Noire.* 11. Das Gartenlämpchen, das in jener Ecke hängt, ist ... *La lampe de jardin qui est accrochée dans ce coin-là est en tôle.* 12. Die Andenken, die von den Touristen gekauft werden, sind ... *Les souvenirs achetés par les touristes, sont souvent du toc.*

D Un avertissement depuis San Diego
L'histoire de ce restaurateur qui dans son établissement a affiché un écriteau portant l'inscription « Soyez aimables envers mon personnel. Des clients, il y en a suffisamment, mais non des garçons de café », cette histoire est vieille. Elle caractérise une situation à laquelle on s'est presque habitué déjà. Pourtant, cette situation est susceptible de s'aggraver encore, selon une nouvelle provenant d'Amérique (*m. à m. :* comme une annonce venant d'Amérique le mentionne).
Afin de ne pas perdre son personnel de service du fait de clients discourtois, le drugstore de Jim Fraser, à San Diego, promet une tasse de café gratuite à toute personne (*m. à m. :* à chacun) qui sourit à la serveuse. Jusqu'à présent, plus de 14 000 tasses ont été servies gratuitement.

Leçon

61

Einkäufe in einem Lebensmittelgeschäft

1 (In einem Selbstbedienungsladen)
— Wo ist die Käseabteilung, bitte?
— Ganz hinten links, neben den Wurstwaren.
— Ich suche vergebens nach dem Gebäck.
— Schauen Sie bitte auf das blaue Schild, hinter Ihnen!
— Ich sehe den Preis nicht. Er ist wohl nicht angegeben?
— Fragen Sie bitte den Abteilungsleiter.

2 (Beim Kleinhändler)
— Ich möchte Butter, bitte.
— Wieviel?
— Zwei Pfund.
— Ist es recht so? Wünschen Sie sonst noch etwas?
— Nein, das wäre alles.
— Haben Sie ein Einkaufsnetz? Oder darf ich Ihnen mit einer Papiertasche aushelfen?
— Ja, sehr gern. Besten Dank.
— Bitte schön!

3 Ich habe mir alles aufgeschrieben, was ich einzukaufen hatte. Einen Augenblick, ich will nachsehen, ob ich nichts vergessen habe.
— Ach, ich muß zurückkehren. Ich habe den Kaffee und die Schokolade vergessen. Wo kann ich das nur finden?
— In welcher Abteilung sind die Geschirrspülmittel und die Waschmittel?
— Sie finden sie in der Abteilung für Reinigungsmittel.

WIE DER PREIS, SO DIE WARE

Traduction

Achats dans un magasin d'alimentation

1 (Dans un magasin de libre-service).
— Où sont les fromages, s'il vous plaît? (m. à m. : le rayon des fromages). — Tout au fond à gauche, à côté de la charcuterie. — Je cherche en vain (le rayon) des gâteaux. — Veuillez consulter l'écriteau bleu, derrière vous. — Je ne vois pas le prix. Il ne semble pas indiqué. — Demandez s'il vous plaît au chef de rayon.

2 (Chez le détaillant).
— Je voudrais du beurre, s'il vous plaît. — Combien, Madame? — Deux livres. — Est-ce que cela ira comme ceci? (m. à m. : est-ce bien ainsi?) Et avec cela? (m. à m. : voulez-vous autre chose encore?) — Non, c'est tout (m. à m. : ce serait) — Avez-vous un filet (à provisions)? Ou — si cela peut vous rendre service — voulez-vous que je vous donne un sac de papier? (puis-je vous aider...) — Oui, très volontiers. Merci bien. — A votre service.

3 — J'ai tout noté ce qu'il fallait que j'achète. Un instant, je vais voir, si je n'ai rien oublié. — Ah! je suis obligée de retourner. J'ai oublié le café et le chocolat. Où donc pourrai-je trouver cela? — A quel rayon se trouvent les produits pour faire la vaisselle, et les poudres à laver le linge? — Vous les trouverez au rayon des produits d'entretien.

Vocabulaire

der Einkauf (¨e), *l'achat*
der Handel, *le commerce*
der Händler (-), *le commerçant*
der Käse (-), *le fromage*
der Schinken (-), *le jambon*
die Abt**ei**lung, *le service, le rayon*
die S**e**lbstbedi**e**nung (-en) *le libre-service*
die Tasche (n), *la poche, le sac*
die Wäsche (n), *la lessive*
das Geb**ä**ck (sing), *les gâteaux*
das Gesch**i**rr (sing), *la vaisselle*
das Mittel (-), *le moyen*
das Netz (e), *le filet*
das Pfund, *la livre*
das Schild (-er), *l'enseigne*
das W**a**schm**i**ttel (-), *la lessive (poudre)*

Tel prix, telle marchandise

■ Wo ist die Gebäckabteilung? Wo sind die Waschmittel?
Dans *Gebäck* et dans *Waschmittel,* nous retrouvons les verbes *backen* et *waschen,* qui appartiennent au groupe *a — u — a* des verbes irréguliers. Exemples :
Backen, cuire (au four); *er buk,* il cuisait; *er hat ... gebacken,* il a cuit; *er bäckt,* il cuit (au prétérit, également : *er backte*).
Waschen, laver; *er wusch,* il lavait; *er hat ... gewaschen,* il a lavé; *er wäscht,* il lave.
Autres verbes irréguliers de ce groupe :

fahren (u, a; ä), aller (en voiture);
graben (u, a; ä), creuser;
schlagen (u, a; ä), frapper, battre;
tragen (u, a, ä), porter;
wachsen (u, a; ä), pousser, croître;
laden (u, a; er lädt ou *er ladet),* charger, inviter;
schaffen (u, a; er schafft), créer.

Remarques :
a) Au sens de : faire, travailler, *schaffen* est régulier.

b) Les verbes irréguliers en *a* ont tous un participe passé en *a* (voir L. 59).

■ Alles, was ich einzukaufen hatte.
(m. à m. : tout ce que j'avais à acheter.)
Le verbe *haben* employé avec un infinitif complément, exprime une idée de devoir.

Ich habe noch ein Kilo Reis zu kaufen,
il me faut encore acheter un kilo de riz.
Das hat nichts zu sagen, cela ne veut rien dire.

L'idée de devoir peut aussi s'exprimer par *sein* suivi d'un infinitif complément.

Es ist noch Mehl zu kaufen, il faut acheter de la farine encore.

■ Ich möchte zwei Pfund Reis.
Das Pfund, la livre, est invariable après un nombre. Il en est ainsi des noms de mesure masculins ou neutres : *das Kilo; das Liter; das Glas,* le verre; *das Stück,* la pièce; *der Mann,* l'homme (comme « mesure militaire »), etc. Exemples :

Drei Kilo Fleisch, 3 kilos de viande;
Zwei Glas Wasser, 2 verres d'eau;
Seine Kompanie zählte 100 Mann,
sa compagnie avait 100 hommes.

Mais on dira : *3 Flaschen Wein,* 3 bouteilles de vin, en mettant *die Flasche,* nom féminin, au pluriel.

Exercices

A *Traduisez puis mettez : a) au présent, b) au passé composé :*
1. Sie buk guten Kuchen. 2. Ich fuhr ihn nach Hause. 3. Das Gemüse wuchs schön. 4. Der Blitz schlug in den Baum ein. 5. Sie trug die Einkäufe in den Wagen. 6. Sie luden mich zu Tisch ein.

B *Formez des infinitives avec* haben. *Ensuite, traduisez :*
Exemple : Ich muß pünktlich zu Hause sein. Ich habe pünktlich zu Hause zu sein. *Il faut que je sois rentré à l'heure.*
7. Wir müssen heute abend noch Brot kaufen. 8. Er muß seiner Mutter das Netz tragen. 9. Der Händler muß die Preise angeben.

C *Traduisez :*
10. Veuillez m'indiquer le rayon d'alimentation. 11. Quel est le prix de ce jambon? 12. Ces œufs (*das Ei, (-er)* sont-ils frais? 13. Donnez-moi deux livres de boudin (*die Blutwurst*), trois bouteilles de bière et deux kilos de pain bis (= noir). 14. Pourriez-vous me dire à quelle heure le magasin ferme?

Corrigé :

A 1. *Elle faisait du bon gâteau* a) Sie bäckt ... b) Sie hat ... gebacken. 2. *Je le conduisis à la maison.* a) Ich fahre ... b) Ich habe ... gefahren. 3. *Les légumes poussaient bien.* a) ... wächst ... b) ... ist ... gewachsen. 4. *La foudre tomba sur l'arbre.* a) Der Blitz schlägt ... ein. b) Der Blitz hat ... eingeschlagen. 5. *Elle porta ses achats dans la voiture.* a) Sie trägt ... b) Sie hat ... getragen. 6. *Ils m'invitèrent à dîner (= à table).* a) Sie laden ... ein. b) Sie haben ... eingeladen.

B 7. Wir haben heute abend noch Brot zu kaufen. *Il nous faut encore acheter du pain ce soir.* 8. Er hat seiner Mutter das Netz zu tragen. *Il doit porter le filet pour sa mère.* 9. Der Händler hat die Preise anzugeben. *Le marchand doit indiquer ses prix.*

C 10. Bitte, zeigen Sie mir die Abteilung für Lebensmittel (= die Lebensmittelabteilung). 11. Was kostet dieser Schinken? 12. Sind diese Eier frisch? 13. Geben Sie mir zwei Pfund Blutwurst, drei Flaschen Bier und zwei Kilo Schwarzbrot. 14. Könnten Sie mir sagen, wann das Geschäft geschlossen wird?

Leçon

62

Bücher, Papierwaren, Zeitungen

1 — Ich möchte schwarzblaue Tinte für meinen Füller, einen roten Filzschreiber und dann noch eine Patrone für meinen Kugelschreiber. Er hört immer wieder auf zu schreiben!
— Mutti, die Lehrerin hat gesagt, wir brauchen Farbstifte, eine große Schachtel.
— Die Feder meines Füllers ist kaputt. Wie lange würde es dauern, um sie auszuwechseln?
— Ich nehme auch ein Radiergummi mit.

2 — Briefpapier, bitte.
— Welches Format und welche Qualität wünschen Sie? Und was für Briefumschläge? Gewöhnliche oder gefütterte?
— Gewöhnliche. Geben Sie mir auch Luftpostpapier. Einen Block von kleinem Format und ein Päckchen Briefumschläge.
— Ich will Ihnen das alles einwickeln und mit einer Schnur zubinden.

3 — Haben Sie französische Zeitungen?
— Ja, mein Herr. Bedienen Sie sich, bitte.
— Ach, sie sind alle von vorgestern. Um wieviel Uhr kommen sie an?
— Gewöhnlich zwischen zehn und zwölf Uhr.
— Können Sie mir « Le Monde » beiseitelegen? Ich hole sie gegen Mittag ab.
— Selbstverständlich, mein Herr. Ich werde dafür sorgen.
— Besten Dank, Fräulein; das ist sehr freundlich von Ihnen.

EINE HAND WÄSCHT DIE ANDERE

Traduction

Livres, papiers, journaux

1 — Je voudrais de l'encre bleu-noir pour mon stylo, un crayon feutre rouge, et puis encore une recharge pour mon stylo à bille. Il tombe toujours en panne (m. à m. : il cesse toujours d'écrire). — Maman, la maîtresse a dit qu'il nous faut des crayons de couleur, une grande boîte. — La plume de mon stylo est cassée. Combien de temps cela prendrait-il (cela durerait-il) pour la changer? — Je prendrai aussi une gomme.

2 — Du papier à lettres, s'il vous plaît. — Quel format et quelle qualité désirez-vous? Et comme enveloppes? des enveloppes ordinaires ou des enveloppes doublées? — Des enveloppes ordinaires. Donnez-moi aussi du papier pour lettres par avion. Un bloc petit format et un paquet d'enveloppes. — Je vais vous envelopper tout cela et le fermer avec une ficelle.

3 — Avez-vous des journaux français? — Oui, Monsieur. Servez-vous, s'il vous plaît. — Ah! Ils sont tous d'avant-hier. A quelle heure arrivent-ils? — En général entre 10 h et midi. — Pouvez-vous me mettre « Le Monde » de côté? Je passerai le prendre vers midi. — Bien entendu, Monsieur. Je m'en occuperai. — Merci beaucoup, Mademoiselle. Vous êtes très aimable.

Vocabulaire

der (Br**ie**f)**u**mschlag (¨e), *l'enveloppe*
der Farbstift (-e), *le crayon de couleur*
der F**i**lzschr**ei**ber (-), *le crayon feutre*
der Füller (-), *le stylo*
der K**u**gelschr**ei**ber (-), *le stylo (ou crayon) à bille*
die Feder (n), *la plume*
die Flugpost, *la poste aérienne*
die Schachtel (n), *la boîte*
die Schnur (¨e), *le cordon, le fil*
die Tinte (n), *l'encre*
das Gummi, *le caoutchouc*
das Päckchen (-), *le (petit) paquet*
die Patr**o**ne (n), *la cartouche*
die Qualit**ä**t (-en), *la qualité*
die Quantit**ä**t (-en), *la quantité*

Les loups ne se mangent pas entre eux. (Une main lave l'autre).

■ **Geben Sie mir auch Flugpostpapier**

Le verbe irrégulier *geben* fait partie du groupe *e - a - e* (infinitif en *e*, prétérit en *a*, participe passé en *e*). Exemple :

Geben, donner; *er gab*, il donna, il donnait; *er hat gegeben*, il a donné; *er gibt*, il donne.

Autres verbes irréguliers de ce groupe :

essen (aß, gegessen; er ißt), manger;
fressen (a, e; i), manger (en parlant des animaux);
messen (a, e; i) mesurer;
treten (a, e; er tritt), marcher;
vergessen (a, e; i), oublier.

Les trois verbes suivants ont aux 2e et 3e personnes singulier du présent un radical long, en *ie* :

geschehen (a, e, es geschieht), arriver, avoir lieu;
lesen (a, e; ich lese, du liest, er liest), lire;
sehen (a, e; ich sehe, du siehst, er sieht), voir.

Pour la conjugaison de ces verbes, revoyez les leçons 5, 15, 19.

■ **Ich will es mit einer Schnur zubinden.**

Zubinden est le verbe *binden*, lier, composé avec la particule séparable *zu*.

● Ici, cette particule marque la « fermeture ». Nous retrouvons ce sens dans *zu/machen*, fermer; *zu/drücken*, fermer en pressant; *zu/knöpfen*, fermer en boutonnant = boutonner.

Machen Sie die Tür zu! Fermez la porte!

● *Zu* peut également marquer une augmentation : *zu/nehmen*, augmenter; *zu/tun*, (ou : *hinzu/tun*), ajouter. Exemple :

Nun nehmen die Tage zu, à présent, les jours augmentent.

● Enfin, la particule *zu* indique souvent une « direction vers » : *zu/fahren* (+ datif), se diriger vers; *zu/rufen* (+ datif), crier vers quelqu'un; *zu/schauen* (+ datif), regarder, être spectateur. Exemple :

Wir schauten den Arbeitern zu, nous regardions (faire) les ouvriers.

Remarque : Dans la leçon 9, nous avons étudié *zu* en tant que préposition gouvernant le datif, et signifiant « à » (but), « chez ».

Exercices

A *Traduisez, puis mettez a) au présent, b) au passé composé :*
1. Aßen Sie dieses Gericht gern? 2. Er trat ans Fenster. 3. Sie vergaß immer etwas. 4. Es geschah ein Unglück. 5. Ich las es in der Zeitung. 6. Sahst du den Krankenwagen?

B *Mettez au futur, puis traduisez :*
7. Hier nehmen alle Pensionäre zu. 8. Am Samstag bleibt das Büro zu. 9. Er fährt auf das Dorf zu.

E *Traduisez :*
10. Avez-vous des crayons à bille rouges? 11. Enveloppez s'il vous plaît ce papier à lettre et ces enveloppes. 12. Quand les journaux arrivent-ils de (= *aus*) France? 13. Moi, je préfère lire un journal allemand, parce que j'apprends un peu chaque jour.

Corrigé :

A 1. *Aimiez-vous (manger) ce plat?* a) Essen Sie ...? b) Haben Sie ... gegessen? 2. *Il se mit (m. à m. : marcha) à la fenêtre.* a) Er tritt... b) Er ist ... getreten. 3. *Elle oubliait toujours quelque chose.* a) Sie vergißt ... B) Sie hat ... vergessen. 4. *Il est arrivé (m. à m. : arriva) un malheur.* a) Es geschieht ... b) Es ist ... geschehen. 5. *Je l'ai lu dans le journal.* a) Ich lese ... b) Ich habe ... gelesen. 6. *As-tu vu l'ambulance?* a) Siehst du ...? B) Hast du... gesehen?

B 7. Hier werden alle Pensionäre zunehmen. *Ici, tous les pensionnaires prendront du poids.* 8. Am Samstag wird das Büro zubleiben. *Samedi, le bureau restera fermé.* 9. Er wird dem Dorf zufahren. *Il se dirigera vers le village.*

C 10. Haben Sie rote Kugelschreiber? 11. Wickeln Sie bitte dieses Briefpapier und diese (Brief)umschläge ein. 12. Wann treffen die Zeitungen aus Frankreich ein? 13. Ich lese lieber eine deutsche Zeitung, weil ich jeden Tag etwas (= ein wenig) hinzulerne.

Leçon

63 Herrenkleidung

1 Die Herrenkleidung soll einfach und gut geschnitten sein. Die Mode bestimmt gewöhnlich die Farbe des Stoffes und die Form der Jacke; diese kann einreihig oder zweireihig sein. Die Knöpfe können höher oder tiefer sitzen. Die Hosenweite und die Länge verändern sich oft von Jahr zu Jahr. Die Weste ist so ziemlich aus der Mode gekommen; aber wohl oder übel macht ein Anzug ohne Weste immer einen etwas nachlässigen Eindruck.
In der Wahl der Krawatte und in der Art, wie er das Kavaliertuch faltet, kann ein Mann seine Phantasie walten lassen. Oft paßt die Krawatte zu den Socken, was aber nur bei dunklen Farben zu empfehlen ist.

2 Da die jungen Männer noch keine soziale Funktion haben, sind sie freier in ihrer Wahl. Eine gewisse Exzentrizität gehört zu ihrem Alter, doch darf sie den guten Ton nicht verletzen und sollte ihnen gut stehen. Sie tragen gern eine Samthose, ein karriertes Hemd, einen dicken, wollenen Pullover.

3 — Ich möchte mir einen Überzieher anfertigen lassen. Zeigen Sie mir bitte Ihre Muster. Was wird diesen Winter getragen?
— Das hängt von Ihrem Geschmack ab. Soll es ein Sommer- oder ein Übergangsmantel sein, mit Raglanschnitt, ein- oder zweireihig geknöpft? Die Mäntel sind ein wenig kürzer als voriges Jahr. Die Farbtöne hier werden in diesem Jahr bevorzugt. Es ist ein erstklassiges Material.
— Ich habe es sehr eilig. Wann kann ich zur ersten Anprobe kommen?

EINE SCHWALBE MACHT NOCH KEINEN SOMMER

Traduction

Vêtements d'homme

1 Les vêtements d'homme doivent être sobres et bien coupés. Habituellement, la mode fixe la couleur du tissu et la forme du veston; celui-ci peut être droit, ou croisé (m. à m. : à un ou deux rangs). Les boutons peuvent être placés plus ou moins haut. La largeur et la longueur du pantalon varient souvent d'une année à l'autre. Le gilet est à peu près passé de mode; mais, qu'on le veuille ou non (m. à m. : bon gré, mal gré), un complet sans gilet fera toujours une impression quelque peu négligée.
C'est dans le choix de la cravate et dans la manière de plier la pochette qu'un homme peut donner libre cours à (m. à m. : laisser régner) sa fantaisie. Souvent, la cravate va avec les chaussettes, mais cela ne se recommande que dans les tons foncés.

2 Les jeunes gens, n'ayant point encore de fonction sociale (m. à m. : Comme les jeunes...), jouissent de plus de liberté dans leur choix. Une certaine excentricité est de leur âge, cependant elle doit être de bon ton (m. à m. : ne doit pas blesser...) et il faudrait qu'elle leur sied bien. Ils aiment porter un pantalon de velours, une chemise à carreaux, un pull de grosse laine.

3 — Je désire me faire faire un pardessus. Veuillez me montrer vos échantillons. Qu'est-ce qu'on porte cet hiver? — Cela dépend de votre goût. Voulez-vous un pardessus d'été ou de demi-saison, forme (m. à m. : coupe) raglan, droite ou croisée? Les manteaux sont un peu plus courts que l'an passé. Ces tons-ci ont la préférence, cette année. C'est une matière de première qualité. — Je suis très pressé. Quand puis-je passer pour le premier essayage?

Vocabulaire

der Anzug (″e), *le complet*
der Pull(over) (-), *le pull*
der Samt (-e), *le velours*
die Tasche (n), *la poche*
die Wahl (-en), *le choix, l'élection*
die Weste (n), *le gilet*

Une hirondelle ne fait pas le printemps (m. à m. : ne fait pas l'été encore).

der Schnitt (-e), *la coupe*
der Stoff (-e), *l'étoffe*
der Ton (¨e), *le son, le ton*
der Übergang (¨e), *la transition*
der **Ü**berz**ie**her (-), *le pardessus*
die Anprobe (n), *l'essayage*
die Form (en), *la forme*
die Hose (n), *le pantalon la culotte*
(die Kn**ie**h**o**sen (plur.), *les culottes)*

die Wolle, *la laine*
die B**au**mw**o**lle, *le coton*
das Hemd (s, en), *la chemise*
das Kaval**ie**rtuch (¨er), *la pochette*
das Taschentuch (¨er), *le mouchoir*
das Tuch (¨er), *le drap, la toile*
die Jacke (n), *la veste*
die Kraw**a**tte (n), *la cravate*
die Mode (n), *la mode*
die Socke (n), *la chaussette*

Grammaire

Die Herrenkleidung soll gut geschnitten sein.
Geschnitten est le participe passé du verbe *schneiden.* Les verbes irréguliers en *ei* forment deux groupes; l'un prend un *i* bref aux temps du passé *(ei, i, i),* l'autre un *ie,* c'est-à-dire [i] long *(ei, ie, ie).* Voici quelques verbes du premier de ces groupes :

schneiden, couper; *er schnitt,* il coupa; *er hat geschnitten,* il a coupé.
greifen, saisir; *er griff,* il saisit; *er hat gegriffen,* il a saisi.
beißen (iß, issen), mordre;
gleichen (i, i), ressembler;
gleiten (itt, itten), glisser;
leiden (itt, itten), souffrir;
pfeifen (iff, iffen), siffler;
reiten (itt, itten), aller à cheval;
schreiten (itt, itten) marcher;
streichen (i, i), frotter, étendre (du beurre, etc.);
zerreißen (i, i), déchirer.

Exercices

A *Traduisez puis mettez a) au présent, b) au prétérit :*
1. Er hat sich auf die Zunge *(la langue)* gebissen. 2. Sie wird ihrem Vater gleichen. 3. Die Tasse ist mir aus den Händen geglitten. 4. Ich habe meinem Hund gepfiffen. 5. Ich bin spazieren geritten. 6. Wir sind über eine Brücke geschritten.

B *Traduisez :*
7. Pouvez-vous me confectionner un complet avec ce tissu? 8. Il me le faut bientôt, car ma veste est déchirée.

Corrigé :

A 1. *Il s'est mordu la langue.* a) Er beißt... b) Er biß... 2. *Elle ressemblera à son père.* a) Sie gleicht... b) Sie glich... 3. *La tasse m'a glissé des mains.* a) ... gleitet... b) ... glitt... 4. *J'ai sifflé mon chien.* a) Ich pfeife... b) Ich pfiff... 5. *J'ai fait une promenade à cheval.* a) Ich reite spazieren. b) Ich ritt... 6. *Nous avons franchi un pont.* a) Wir schreiten... b) Wir schritten...

B 7. Können Sie mir aus diesem Stoff einen Anzug anfertigen? 8. Ich brauche ihn bald, denn meine Jacke ist zerrissen.

Lecture

Eine Anzeige des Deutschen Krawatten-Instituts, die den französischen Leser wohl überraschen wird :

Hilf ihm, Luise

Er vergißt's doch immer. Immer wieder trägt er die von gestern. Willst Du, daß sie « Krawatten-Muffel » zu ihm sagen? Zu ihm, der Tiere liebt und stets sein Auto pflegt und nichts auf die Familie kommen läßt? Es ist doch wirklich nicht so schwierig : Einfach jeden Morgen eine andere Krawatte — und ab und zu mal eine neue kaufen. Das einzige ist : daran denken. Hilf ihm dabei, Luise — ja?

Kristall

Une annonce de l'Institut allemand de la Cravate, qui surprendra probablement le lecteur français :

Aide-le, Louise

Il oublie toujours (m. à m. : il l'oublie quand même toujours). Sans cesse, il porte celle d'hier. Veux-tu qu'on lui reproche de bouder les cravates (m. à m. : qu'ils lui disent « boudeur de cravates »)? Lui qui aime les animaux et qui prend toujours soin de sa voiture et qui tient tant au bon renom de sa famille (m. à m. : qui ne laisse rien venir sur sa famille)? Pourtant, ce n'est (vraiment) pas difficile : Simplement, mettre une nouvelle cravate chaque matin — et, de temps à autre, en acheter une neuve. Il suffit d'y penser (m. à m. : l'unique chose, c'est...). Tu l'y aideras, Louise — n'est-ce pas?

Leçon

64 Damenkleidung

1 — Ich persönlich habe das klassische Kostüm überhaupt nicht gern. Ich bin zwar nicht dick, aber auch nicht schlank. Außerdem finde ich, daß es männlich wirkt. — Ich bin Ihrer Meinung. Ein gut geschnittenes Kostüm aus schönem Stoff, das läßt sich wohl ab und zu nachmittags tragen. Aber es geht nichts über ein Kleid, nicht wahr? Es gibt viel mehr Variationsmöglichkeiten bei den Kleidern.

2 (In der Konfektionsabteilung)
— Dieses hellgelbe Kleid gefällt mir gut. Kann ich in die Kabine zum Anprobieren?
— Bitte schön!
— Könnten Sie mir einiges abändern? Die Brustabnäher sind nicht lang genug. Das Kleid scheint mir zu lang zu sein : fünf Zentimeter kürzer, bitte! Die Ärmel dagegen sind mir zu kurz. Können diese Änderungen bis Donnerstag fertig sein? — Warten Sie einen Augenblick, bitte, ich werde nachfragen.

3 (Bei der Näherin)
— Gelb wird viel getragen. Hier ein Modell, das nicht zu teuer ist und Sie gut kleiden wird, glaube ich.
— Ich hätte gern ein ärmelloses Kleid. Machen Sie mir bitte einen Ausschnitt, der den Hals ziemlich freilegt. Ich habe nämlich ein sehr schönes Halsband, und ich möchte es hervorheben. Ich habe ziemlich breite Hüften; geben Sie acht auf die Abnäher. Betonen Sie die Taille nicht zu stark; machen Sie sie nicht zu eng.
— Welches Futter? Ein Taft, im selben Ton?
— Ja, bitte sehr.

STETER TROPFEN HÖHLT DEN STEIN

Traduction

Vêtements de femme

1 — Personnellement, je n'aime pas du tout le costume tailleur classique. Sans être forte, je ne suis pas mince (m. à m. : certes, je ne suis pas forte, mais...). Et puis, je trouve que cela fait (m. à m. : agit) masculin.
— Je suis de votre avis. Un tailleur bien coupé et de beau drap, cela peut se porter de temps en temps l'après-midi. Mais rien ne vaut (m. à m. : il ne va rien par-dessus...) une robe, n'est-ce-pas? Il y a beaucoup plus de fantaisie (de possibilités de variations) dans les robes.

2 (Dans le rayon du prêt-à-porter).
— Cette robe jaune clair me plaît bien. Puis-je passer à la cabine pour l'essayage? — Je vous en prie! — Pourriez-vous me faire quelques retouches (m. à m. : me changer certaines choses)? Les pinces de poitrine ne sont pas assez longues. La robe me semble trop longue : 5 cm de moins, s'il vous plaît. Les manches par contre me semblent trop courtes. Est-ce que ces retouches peuvent être faites (m. à m. : prêtes, finies) pour jeudi? — Attendez un instant, je vais demander.

3 (Chez la couturière).
— Le jaune se porte beaucoup (m. à m. : est porté...). Voici un modèle qui ne revient pas trop cher et qui vous ira bien, je crois. — J'aimerais une robe sans manches. Vous me ferez une encolure qui dégage le cou. C'est que j'ai un très beau collier, et je voudrais le mettre en valeur. J'ai les hanches assez fortes; attention aux pinces (de reins). Ne marquez pas trop la taille; laissez-la assez libre (m. à m. : ne la faites pas trop serrée).
— Comme doublure? Un taffetas ton sur ton (m. à m. : dans le même ton)? — Oui, je vous en prie.

Vocabulaire

der **A**bn**ä**her (-), *la pince (couture)*
der Ärmel (-), *la manche*
der Ausschnitt, *la coupe; le décolleté*
das Futter, (-), *la doublure; le fourrage*
das Kleid (-er), *la robe, le vêtement*
das Kost**ü**m (-e), *le tailleur*

La goutte creuse la pierre (goutte incessante...)

■ **Ich möchte das Halsband hervorheben.**
Dans *hervor-heben,* mettre en valeur, souligner, nous trouvons le verbe *heben* du groupe des verbes irréguliers en *e — o — o :*

heben, soulever; *er hob,* il souleva; *er hat gehoben,* il a soulevé; *er hebt,* il soulève.

Les mêmes voyelles se retrouvent dans : *scheren (o,o;e),* tondre; *weben (o,o;e),* tisser. Nous remarquons que dans ces verbes-ci, le radical reste inchangé au présent : *er hebt, er schert, er webt.* Par contre, le radical subit la transformation habituelle en *i* (voir L. 60 et 62) dans les verbes suivants :
dreschen, battre le blé, *drosch, gedroschen, er drischt; quellen (o, o; i),* jaillir; *schmelzen (o, o; i),* fondre; *schwellen (o, o; i),* s'enfler.

Remarques : *weben* peut aussi suivre la conjugaison régulière : *er wob* ou *er webte,* il tissait; *et hat gewoben* ou *er hat gewebt,* il a tissé.
Schmelzen est régulier au sens de « faire fondre » :

Das Eis schmolz an der Sonne (v. irrégulier), la glace fondait au soleil;

mais :

Die Sonne schmelzte das Eis, le soleil fit fondre la glace.

De même, *schwellen* est régulier au sens de « faire gonfler ».

■ **Die Brustabnäher sind nicht lang genug. Sie hat ziemlich breite Hüften.**
Dans ces deux phrases, notre terme « assez » est rendu tantôt par *genug,* tantôt par *ziemlich.*

● On traduit « assez » par *genug,* dans le sens de « suffisamment ».

Ist der Halsausschnitt groß genug? l'encolure est-elle assez grande?

● Dans le sens de « passablement », on le traduit par *ziemlich.*

Ich finde dieses Kleid ziemlich altmodisch, je trouve cette robe assez démodée.

■ **Ein ärmelloses Kleid.**
Le suffixe *los* marque la privation. Exemples :

farblos, sans couleur; *mutlos,* sans courage; *arbeitslos,* sans travail; *ein Arbeitsloser,* un chômeur.

Exercices

A *Traduisez, puis mettez a) au présent, b) au prétérit :*
1. Er hat den Handschuh (*gant*) aufgehoben. 2. Wir werden diesen Rasen (*gazon*) kurz scheren. 3. Hier hat man diesen guten Stoff gewoben. 4. Das Erdöl (= das Petroleum) ist aus dem Boden gequollen. 5. Seine Backe (*joue*) wird bald anschwellen.

B *Complétez par* genug *ou* ziemlich, *puis traduisez :*
6. Dieser Mantel ist zwar... lang, und trotzdem fand sie ihn nicht lang... 7. Hast du ... Geld bei dir, um das Kostüm gleich zu bezahlen? 8. Dieses Muster ist ... teuer.

C *Traduisez :*
9. Montrez-moi vos robes en jersey (*das Strickjersey*). 10. Cette veste de daim (*das Velours-Leder*) me plairait beaucoup; puis-je l'essayer? 11. Avant de l'essayer, je voudrais connaître son prix. 12. La robe de soirée que vous avez dans la vitrine, est très jolie également.

Corrigé :

A 1. *Il a ramassé le gant.* a) Er hebt...auf. b) Er hob... auf. 2. *Nous allons tondre court ce gazon.* a) Wir scheren... b) Wir schoren... 3. *C'est ici qu'on tisse cette bonne étoffe.* a) Hier webt man... b) Hier wob (webte) man... 4. *Le pétrole a jailli du sol.* a) ...quillt... b) ...quoll... 5. *Sa joue enflera bientôt.* a) ... schwillt... b) ...schwoll...

B 6. ziemlich; genug. *Ce manteau, il est vrai, est assez long, et pourtant, elle ne le trouva pas suffisamment long.* 7. genug. *As-tu assez d'argent sur toi pour payer le tailleur tout de suite?* 8. ziemlich. *Ce modèle est assez cher.*

C 9. Zeigen Sie mir Ihre Kleider aus Strickjersey. 10. Diese Jacke aus Velours-Leder würde mir sehr gefallen; kann ich sie anprobieren? 11. Bevor ich sie anprobiere, möchte ich ihren Preis kennen. 12. Das Abendkleid, das Sie im Schaufenster haben, ist auch (ebenfalls) sehr hübsch.

Leçon

Im Schuhgeschäft und beim Schuster

1 — Womit kann ich Ihnen dienen?
— Ich möchte ein Paar schwarze Halbschuhe.
— Haben Sie sich ein Modell im Schaufenster gemerkt?
— Ja. Am besten zeige ich es Ihnen.

2 — Was für eine Schuhgröße haben Sie?
— Einundvierzig; ich habe einen ziemlich breiten Fuß.
(Der Kunde hat den linken Schuh gleich ausgezogen, um Zeit zu gewinnen. Indessen kommt der Verkäufer zurück, mit Pappschachteln beladen).
— Dieser Schuh drückt mich.
— Leider ist es die größte Nummer, die mir von diesem Modell übrigbleibt. Ich will jedoch im Vorrat nachsehen.
— Es tut mir sehr leid, aber ich verfüge nicht mehr über die größere Nummer.
— Nun, probieren wir also dieses andere Modell an!
— O! Es ist mir viel zu weit!
— Dieser Schuh paßt mir besser; ich bin bequem darin.

3 Brauchen Sie sonst noch etwas? Vielleicht ein Schuhpflegemittel : Schuhwichse, Schuhcreme, eine Sprühflasche, eine Schuhbürste? Wir haben auch Socken und Kniestrümpfe in einem ganz neuen Muster. Darf ich sie Ihnen zeigen?
— Nein, danke; ich bin damit versorgt.

4 (Beim Schuster)
— Bitte, besohlen Sie mir diese Schuhe : Absatz und Sohle.
— Wann werden sie fertig sein?
— Freitag abends, gegen sieben Uhr; ist es Ihnen so recht?
— Möchten Sie Leder- oder Gummisohlen?

SCHUSTER, BLEIB' BEI DEINEM LEISTEN

Traduction

Dans le magasin de chaussures et chez le cordonnier

1 — Qu'y a-t-il pour votre service? (m. à m. : avec quoi puis-je vous servir?) — Je voudrais une paire de chaussures basses, noires. — Avez-vous remarqué un modèle en devanture? — Oui. Le mieux est que je vous le montre.

2 — Quelle est votre pointure? — Du 41; j'ai le pied assez large. (Le client a tout de suite ôté sa chaussure de gauche pour gagner du temps. Sur ces entrefaites, le vendeur revient chargé de cartons.)
— Cette chaussure me serre. — Malheureusement c'est la taille la plus grande qui me reste dans ce modèle. Je vais cependant m'en assurer dans la réserve. — Je regrette beaucoup, mais je ne dispose plus de la taille au-dessus. — Eh bien, essayons donc cet autre modèle! Ah! C'est bien trop grand. — Cette chaussure va mieux; j'y suis à l'aise.

3 — Avez-vous besoin d'autre chose? Peut-être un produit d'entretien : cirage, crème, un vaporisateur, une brosse? Nous avons également des chaussettes et des demi-bas d'un modèle très récent. Puis-je vous les montrer? — Non, merci; j'en suis pourvu.

4 (Chez le cordonnier)
— Voulez-vous me ressemeler ces chaussures : talon et semelle. — Quand est-ce qu'elles seront prêtes? — Vendredi soir, vers 7 heures; cela irait? — Voudriez-vous des semelles de cuir ou de caoutchouc?

Vocabulaire

der Absatz (¨ e), *le talon*
der Halbschuh (-e), *la chaussure basse*
der Schuh (-e), *la chaussure*
der Schuster (-), *le cordonnier*
der Strumpf (¨ e), *le bas*
der Verk**äu**fer (-), *le vendeur*
der Vorrat (¨ e), *la réserve*
die Bürste (n), *la brosse*
die Sohle (n), *la semelle*
die Wichse (n), *le cirage*
das Leder (-), *le cuir*
das Knie (-), *le genou*

A chacun son métier (Savetier, reste près de ta forme).

■ **Die größte Nummer, die mir übrigbleibt.**
Übrig/bleiben, être de reste, rester, est un verbe irrégulier du groupe *ei-ie-ie.* Exemple :

bleiben, rester; *er blieb,* il resta; *er ist geblieben,* il est resté.

Appartiennent à ce groupe :

**gedeihen (ie-ie),* prospérer	*schreiben (ie, ie),* écrire
leihen (ie,ie) prêter	*schreien (ie,ie)* crier
meiden (ie,ie) éviter	*schweigen (ie,ie)* se taire
preisen (ie,ie) louer, vanter	**steigen (ie,ie)* monter
reiben (ie,ie) frotter	*treiben (ie,ie)* pousser
**scheiden (ie,ie)* se séparer	*verzeihen (ie,ie)* pardonner
scheinen (ie,ie) luire, sembler	*weisen (ie,ie)* indiquer

Remarques :

● Ces verbes ont un [i] long, écrit *ie,* au prétérit et au participe passé, alors que ceux étudiés dans la leçon 63 ont un [i] bref.

● Le verbe *steigen* est souvent accompagné d'une préposition ou d'une particule qui en précise ou modifie le sens.

Ich steige auf den Turm, je monte sur la tour.
Ich steige den Berg hinab, je descends la montagne.

■ **Es tut mir sehr leid.**
Traduction de « beaucoup »

● *sehr,* beaucoup, très, grandement, exprime l'intensité.

Ich danke Ihnen sehr für Ihre Aufnahme,
je vous remercie beaucoup de votre accueil.

● *viel,* beaucoup, nombre de..., exprime la quantité.

Er hat viel gelesen, il a beaucoup lu.

■ *Das Schuhpflegemittel (-) :* le produit d'entretien pour chaussures.
Notez l'ordre des termes dans les noms composés; nous traduisons en commençant par le dernier : *das Mittel (-),* le moyen, le produit; *die Pflege (n),* les soins (donnés), l'entretien; *der Schuh (e)* la chaussure. Genre et pluriel sont ceux du dernier terme (leçon 13).

Exercices

A *Traduisez puis mettez a) au prétérit, b) au passé composé :*
1. Er leiht mir seine Schuhbürste. 2. Wir reiben diese Schuhe mit einem weichen Lappen. 3. Du schreibst dir den Preis auf. 4. Sie weist mir den Weg. 5. Die Jungen steigen über den Zaun (clôture).

B *Complétez par* sehr *ou* viel, *puis traduisez :*
6. Wir freuen uns ..., Sie kennen zu lernen. 7. Sie haben ... gegessen und ... getrunken. 8. Zwar weiß er ..., doch möcht'er alles wissen. 9. Sie liebt das Reisen...

B *Traduisez :*
10. Ce modèle me plaît beaucoup parce qu'il a un talon assez haut. 11. Si vous aviez des brosses en nylon, j'(en) achèterais bien (= volontiers) quelques-unes. 12. Mon ami préfère (vorziehen) les semelles en caoutchouc.

Corrigé :

A 1. *Il me prête sa brosse à chaussures.* a) Er lieh ... b) Er hat ... geliehen. 2. *Nous frottons ces chaussures avec un chiffon doux.* a) Wir rieben ... b) Wir haben ... gerieben. 3. *Tu (te) notes les prix.* a) Du schreibst ... auf. b) Du hast ... aufgeschrieben. 4. *Elle m'indique le chemin.* a) Sie wies ... b) Sie hat ... gewiesen. 5. *Les garçons passent par-dessus la clôture.* a) ... stiegen ... . b) ... sind ... gestiegen.

B 6. sehr. *Nous sommes très heureux de faire votre connaissance (m. à m. : nous nous réjouissons beaucoup d'apprendre à vous connaître).* 7. viel; viel. *Ils ont beaucoup mangé et beaucoup bu.* 8. viel. *Il sait beaucoup sans doute, mais il voudrait tout savoir.* 9. sehr. *Elle aime beaucoup les voyages.*

C 10. Dieses Modell gefällt mir sehr, weil es einen ziemlich hohen Absatz hat. 11. Wenn Sie Nylonbürsten hätten, würde ich gerne einige kaufen. 12. Mein Freund zieht die Gummisohlen vor.

Leçon

66

Beim Frisör

1 — Wohin gehen Sie?
— Ich gehe zum Frisör. Ich habe mich auf neun Uhr vormerken lassen. Es wird etwa eine halbe Stunde dauern. Ich werde mich auch rasieren lassen; ich komme nicht dazu, es selbst zu machen.

2 — Wer ist an der Reihe?
— Ich bin dran.
— Wie soll ich Ihnen das Haar schneiden?
— Nicht zu kurz, aber auch nicht zu lang. Hauptsächlich im Nacken und an den Seiten.
— Bitte, Haarwaschen, und Kopfmassage.
— Was für ein Haarpflegemittel wünschen Sie? und was für ein Haaröl?
— Soll ich den Scheitel links oder rechts ziehen?

3 (Im Damensalon)
— Möchten Sie ein Shampoon gegen sprödes Haar oder gegen Schuppen und fettes Haar?
— Reichen Sie mir bitte die Haarnadeln. Da steht die Schachtel.
— Setzen Sie sich bitte unter die Trockenhaube.
— Was den Haarschnitt betrifft, möchte ich eine Stirnlocke rechts, und einen Knoten im Nacken. Dauerwellen mag ich nicht. Ich finde, sie eignen sich nicht für mein Haar.
— Brauchen Sie keine Schönheitsmittel? eine Toilettenseife? eine Tages-, Nacht- oder Reinigungscreme? Wir haben auch sehr moderne Lippenstifte und Kölnisches Wasser in Zerstäubern.

BEI NACHT SIND ALLE KATZEN GRAU

Traduction

Chez le coiffeur

1 — Où allez-vous? — Je vais chez le coiffeur. J'ai pris un rendez-vous pour 9 heures. Cela durera une demi-heure à peu près. Je me ferai également raser; je n'arrive pas à le faire moi-même.

2 — A qui le tour? — C'est à moi. — Comment voulez-vous que je vous coupe les cheveux? — Ni trop court, ni trop long non plus. Surtout dans la nuque et aux côtés. — Un shampooing, s'il vous plaît. Ensuite une friction. — Que désirez-vous comme lotion tonique? et comme brillantine? — Dois-je faire la raie à gauche ou à droite?

3 (Au salon de dames) — Désirez-vous un shampooing contre les cheveux secs (m. à m. : cassants) ou contre les pellicules et les cheveux gras? — Voulez-vous me passer les épingles s'il vous plaît? — Voici la boîte. — Placez-vous sous le séchoir, s'il vous plaît. — Pour (ce qui concerne) la coupe, je désirerais une boucle sur le front, à droite, et un chignon dans la nuque. Je n'aime pas la permanente. Je trouve qu'elle ne convient pas à mes cheveux. — Est-ce qu'il ne vous faut pas de produits de beauté? Un savon de toilette? une crème de base, une crème nourrissante ou une crème à nettoyer? Nous avons également des bâtons de rouge à lèvres très modernes, et de l'eau de Cologne en vaporisateur.

Vocabulaire

der Fris**ö**r (e), *le coiffeur*
der Knoten (-), *le nœud*
der Nacken (-), *la nuque*
der Sch**ei**tel (-), *la raie*
der Stift (e), *le crayon*
der Zerst**äu**ber (-), *le vaporisateur*
die Lippe (n), *la lèvre*
die Locke (n), *la boucle*
die Mass**a**ge (n), *le massage, la friction*
die Nadel (n), *l'aiguille*
die Reihe (n), *le rang*
die Reinigung (en), *le nettoyage*
die Schuppe (n), *l'écaille; la pellicule*
die Stirn (en), *le front*
die Welle (n), *la vague; l'ondulation*
das Haar (e), *le cheveu; la chevelure*
das Shamp**oo**n (s), *le shampooing*
ras**ie**ren, *raser*
trocknen, *sécher*

La nuit, tous les chats sont gris.

Grammaire

Ich finde, sie eignen sich nicht für mein Haar.
Le verbe *finden,* trouver, fait au prétérit *fand,* et au participe passé *gefunden.*

Appartiennent au groupe de verbes irréguliers en *i-a-u* :

binden (a, u), lier
**dringen (a, u)* pénétrer
**gelingen (a, u),* réussir
klingen (a, u), résonner
ringen (a, u) lutter
schlingen (a, u) enlacer
schwingen (a, u) brandir
singen (a, u) chanter
**sinken (a, u)* s'enfoncer
**springen (a, u)* sauter
stinken (a, u) puer
trinken (a, u) boire
**verschwinden (a, u)* disparaître
winden (a, u) tordre
zwingen (a, u) forcer

Remarque : *gelingen* s'emploie surtout comme verbe impersonnel, avec le datif.

Es gelingt mir, den Motor zu reparieren; je réussis à réparer le moteur.
Es gelingt dir..., tu réussis...
Es gelingt ihm..., il réussit...

Exercices

A *Traduisez, puis mettez : a) au prétérit; b) au passé composé :*
1. Wir trinken aus einem Kelchglas (coupe). 2. Es gelingt ihnen zu fliehen. 3. Sie bindet ein Band um die Blumen. 4. Das Wasser dringt in das Schiff. 5. Das Schiff versinkt. 6. Das klingt sonderbar.

B *Traduisez :*
7. Voudriez-vous me tailler également la barbe (*der Bart*)? 8. C'est bien ainsi.

Corrigé :

A 1. *Nous buvons dans une coupe;* a) Wir tranken...; b) Wir haben... getrunken. 2. *Ils réussissent à fuir;* a) Es gelang ...; b) Es ist ... gelungen. 3. *Elle noue un ruban autour des fleurs;* a) Sie band ...; b) Sie hat ... gebunden. 4. *L'eau pénètre dans le navire;* a) ... drang ...; b) ... ist ... gedrungen. 5. *Le navire sombre;* a) ... versank; b) ... ist versunken. 6. *Cela paraît (m. à m. : résonne) étrange;* a) Das klang ...; b) Das hat ... geklungen.

B 7. Wollen Sie mir bitte auch den Bart schneiden? 8. Es ist so recht.

Lecture

Wetterbericht

Am Freitag wird die Besserung anhalten. Veränderliches Wetter mit ziemlich schönen Aufheiterungen und vereinzelten örtlichen Schauern. Schwacher Wind aus nord-westlicher Richtung. Höchsttemperaturen zwischen 22 und 26 Grad. Wetteraussichten für das Wochenende : Sommerliches Wetter mit angenehmen Temperaturen. Abflauender Wind.

Humor

Fritz in der Konditorei : « Ich möchte ein Stück Apfelkuchen. » — Nachdem der Konditor ihm den Teller gebracht hat, erklärt Fritz, er zöge eine Tasse Schokolade vor. Er bekommt sie, trinkt sie aus und will den Teeraum verlassen. Der Konditor : « Hallo, bezahlen! » — Fritz : « Was denn? » — « Die Schokolade. » — « Dafür habe ich Ihnen doch den Apfelkuchen gegeben. » — « Den haben Sie auch nicht bezahlt. » — « Ja, hab' ich ihn denn gegessen? »

Bulletin météorologique

L'amélioration se poursuivra vendredi. Temps variable avec d'assez belles éclaircies et rares averses locales. Vent faible de secteur nord-ouest. Températures maximales comprises entre 22° et 26°. Prévision pour la fin de semaine : temps estival s'accompagnant de températures agréables. Vent plus modéré.

Humour

Frédéric dans la pâtisserie : « Je voudrais un morceau de tarte aux pommes. » — Après que le pâtissier lui a apporté l'assiette, Frédéric déclare qu'il préfère une tasse de chocolat. Il la reçoit, la vide et s'apprête à quitter le salon de thé. Le pâtissier : « Hola! il faut payer! » — Frédéric : « Quoi donc? » — « Le chocolat. » — « Mais je vous ai donné en retour la tarte aux pommes. » — « Celle-ci non plus, vous ne l'avez pas payée. » — « Ah mais! l'ai-je donc mangée? »

Leçon

67 Unterhalt, Sauberkeit

1 (In der Parfümerie)
— Ich möchte Zahnpaste, bitte.
— Was für eine Marke? Eine kleine oder eine große Tube?
— Geben Sie mir auch eine Zahnbürste, aber ja keine aus Nylon.
— Ich kann Ihnen einen ausgezeichneten Artikel anbieten. Soll sie hart oder eher weich sein? Je härter sie ist, desto besser putzt sie, meinen viele Käufer.

2 (In der Färberei)
— Hier bringe ich einen Anzug.
— Was ist zu tun?
— Reinigen und bügeln. Von Hand, bitte.
— O! hier sehe ich Flecken. Es sind keine Fettflecken. Wissen Sie, was es ist?
— Ich glaube, es sind Obstflecken. Ich habe nichts damit versucht, aus Angst, ich könnte Schaden anrichten. Ich lasse Ihnen auch ein Paar Handschuhe und einen Schal zum Reinigen zurück. Wollen Sie dann noch diese Hose aufbügeln; achten Sie bitte auf eine gute Bügelfalte. Aber bürsten Sie sie vorher gründlich aus.

3 (Beim Drogisten)
— Ich möchte einen Fleckenreiniger, bitte.
— Eine Creme oder eine Flüssigkeit?
— Eine Creme wäre mir lieber.
— Hier habe ich ein neues Mittel. Ich glaube, es ist sehr wirksam. Die Gebrauchsanweisung liegt bei.
— Was für ein Pflegemittel für Lederwaren haben Sie? Und was für ein Waschmittel für Diolen-Hemden?
— Wo könnte ich meine Wäsche waschen lassen?

NEUE BESEN KEHREN GUT

Traduction

Entretien, propreté

1 (Dans la parfumerie)
— Je voudrais de la pâte dentifrice, s'il vous plaît. — Quelle marque? un petit ou un grand tube? — Donnez-moi également une brosse à dents, mais pas en nylon surtout. — Je puis vous offrir un excellent article. Doit-elle être dure ou plutôt douce? Plus elle est dure, mieux elle nettoie, pensent beaucoup d'acheteurs.

2 (Dans la teinturerie)
— Voici un complet (m. à m. : ici j'apporte...) — Que faut-il faire? — (Le) nettoyer et (le) repasser. A la main, s'il vous plaît. — Ah! je vois ici des taches. Ce ne sont pas des taches de graisse. Savez-vous ce que c'est? — Je crois que ce sont des taches de fruit. Je n'y ai pas touché (m. à m. : je n'ai rien essayé avec) de peur de causer des dégâts (m. à m. : que je puisse causer... (suppression de daß). Je vous laisse aussi une paire de gants et un châle à détacher. Puis, veuillez donner également un coup de fer à ce pantalon; faites attention à bien marquer le pli. Mais auparavant, donnez un bon coup de brosse.

3 (Chez le droguiste)
— Je voudrais un détachant s'il vous plaît. — Une crème ou un liquide? — Je préférerais une crème. — Voici quelque chose de nouveau. Je crois que c'est très efficace. La notice d'emploi est jointe. — Qu'est-ce que vous avez pour entretenir les cuirs? (m. à m. : Quel produit d'entretien pour les cuirs avez-vous?) Et quelle lessive pour chemises de Tergal? — Où pourrais-je faire blanchir mon linge?

Vocabulaire

der Drog**i**st (en, en), *le droguiste*
der Flecken (-), *la tache*
der Handschuh (-e), *le gant*
der Schaden (‥), *le dommage*
die Färber**ei** (en), *la teinturerie*

das Paar (-e), *la paire, le couple*
der Gebr**au**ch (‥ e), *l'usage*
die Anweisung (en), *l'indication*
bügeln, *repasser*
bürsten, *brosser*
zur**ü**ckg**e**ben (a, e, i), *rendre*

Tout nouveau, tout beau (Balais neufs nettoient bien).

■ **Ich kann Ihnen diesen Artikel anbieten.**
An/bieten, bieten, offrir, proposer. Prétérit : *ich bot (an),* j'offris, j'offrais. Passé composé : *ich habe (an)geboten,* j'ai offert.
Appartiennent au groupe de verbes irréguliers en ie-o-o :

biegen (o, o) plier
**fliegen (o, o)* voler
**fliehen (o, o)* fuir
**fließen (o, o)* couler
frieren (o, o) geler
genießen (o, o) jouir
gießen (o, o) verser
**kriechen (o, o)* ramper
riechen (o, o) sentir
schieben (o, o) pousser
schießen (o, o) tirer (arme)
schließen (o, o) fermer
**sprießen (o, o)* bourgeonner
verdrießen (o, o) contrarier
verlieren (o, o) perdre
wiegen (o, o) peser
ziehen (o, o) tirer; s'en aller
betrügen (o, o) tromper
lügen (o, o) mentir

Remarque :

Das Pferd hat den Wagen gezogen, le cheval a tiré la voiture (verbe transitif, auxiliaire *haben*).

Die Schwalben sind nach Süden gezogen, les hirondelles sont parties vers le sud (verbe intransitif de direction : auxiliaire *sein*).

■ **Je härter sie ist, desto besser putzt sie.**
Je... (subordonnée), *desto...* (principale) : plus... plus...

● Après *je..., desto...,* on emploie le comparatif.

Je höher wir stiegen, desto blauer wurde der Himmel plus nous montions, plus le ciel devenait bleu.

Notez le rejet du verbe après *je,* et l'inversion après *desto.*

● Avec un verbe, on emploie *je mehr..., desto mehr...*

Je mehr sie sprach, desto mehr lächelten die Zollbeamten, plus elle parlait, plus les douaniers souriaient.

■ *Die Flüssigkeit,* le liquide.
Avec le suffixe *-keit* (ou : *-heit*) on forme des noms féminins qui marquent un état.

die Dankbarkeit, la reconnaissance; *die Schönheit,* la beauté.

Exercices

A *Traduisez, puis mettez a) au présent, b) au passé composé :* 1. Der Laden schloß um halb sieben. 2. Wir flogen zwei Stunden lang. 3. Ich schoß einen Hasen *(lièvre).* 4. Sie zogen in ferne Länder. 5. Du zogst das Boot an das Ufer *(berge).*

B *Formez une phrase avec* je ...., desto ...., *puis traduisez :* 6. Er wird alt; er wird bescheiden *(modeste).* 7. Die Lampe ist nah; sie leuchtet hell. 8. Die Sonne scheint warm; der Wein wird gut. 9. Er arbeitet; er bekommt Kunden *(clients).*

C *Traduisez :* 10. Où avez-vous perdu votre gant neuf? 11. Quand mon pantalon sera-t-il repassé? 12. Tu m'as beaucoup contrarié, mais je sais que tu n'as pas menti.

Corrigé :

A 1. *Le magasin fermait à 6 h 1/2.* a) Der Laden schließt... b) Der Laden hat ... geschlossen. 2. *Nous avons volé pendant 2 heures.* a) Wir fliegen ... b) Wir sind ... geflogen. 3. *Je tirai un lièvre.* a) Ich schieße... b) Ich habe ... geschossen. 4. *Ils sont partis dans des pays lointains.* a) Sie ziehen ... b) Sie sind ... gezogen. 5. *Tu as tiré la barque sur la berge.* a) Du ziehst ... b) Du hast ... gezogen.

B 6. Je älter er wird, desto bescheidener wird er. *Plus il prend de l'âge, plus il est modeste.* 7. Je näher die Lampe ist, desto heller leuchtet sie. *Plus la lampe est près, plus la lumière est claire (m. à m. : plus clairement elle éclaire).* 8. Je wärmer die Sonne scheint, desto besser wird der Wein. *Plus le soleil est chaud, plus le vin sera bon.* 9. Je mehr er arbeitet, desto mehr Gäste bekommt er. *Plus il travaille, plus il a de clients.*

C 10. Wo haben Sie Ihren neuen Handschuh verloren? 11. Wann wird meine Hose gebügelt werden? *(passif).* 12. Du hast mich sehr verdrossen, aber ich weiß, du hast nicht gelogen.

Leçon

68 Das Landhaus

1 Vor kurzem haben wir auf dem Land ein Haus mit Garten gekauft.

2 Es ist ein alter Bauernhof, den unser Architekt hübsch umgebaut hat. Aus dem Pferdestall haben wir eine Garage gemacht. In der Scheune haben wir einen sehr geräumigen Spiel- und Aufenthaltsraum eingerichtet. In allen Zimmern haben wir Elektrizität. Das Wasser des Brunnens wird durch einen Motor in einen Behälter hinaufgepumpt.

3 Unser Landhaus hat dicke Steinmauern; es ist mit einem roten Ziegeldach bedeckt; ein anderer Teil des Gebäudes ist aus Backstein. Es besteht aus einem Erdgeschoß mit Küche, einem Wohnzimmer und einem kleineren Raum, der als Eßzimmer dient. Im ersten Stock sind drei Schlafzimmer und das Badezimmer. Darüber liegt der Dachboden. Die Treppe ist aus Holz.

4 Der Garten ist ziemlich groß. Vorn haben wir Blumen pflanzen lassen. Wir haben einen Tisch und eine Bank auf den Rasen gestellt. Im Sommer können wir im Freien essen. Wie angenehm ist es im Schatten der Bäume!
Dahinter liegt ein Gemüsegarten. Etwas weiter befindet sich ein See, wo wir im Sommer jeden Tag schwimmen.

EIGNER HERD IST GOLDES WERT

Traduction

La maison de campagne

1 – Nous avons acheté récemment une maison à la campagne avec un jardin.

2 – C'est une ancienne ferme que notre architecte a très joliment transformée. De l'écurie, nous avons fait un garage. Dans la grange nous avons installé une salle de jeux et de réunion très spacieuse. Nous avons l'électricité dans toutes les pièces. L'eau du puits est montée dans un réservoir par un moteur.

3 Notre maison de campagne a d'épais murs de pierre. Elle est couverte d'un toit de tuiles rouges; une autre partie du bâtiment est en briques. Elle comporte un rez-de-chaussée avec la cuisine, la salle de séjour et une pièce plus petite qui sert de salle à manger. Au premier étage il y a trois chambres et la salle de bain. Au-dessus, il y a le grenier. L'escalier est en bois.

4 Le jardin est assez grand. Par devant, nous avons fait planter des fleurs. Nous avons installé une table et un banc sur la pelouse. L'été nous pouvons prendre nos repas en plein air. Que c'est agréable, à l'ombre des arbres! Par derrière, il y a un jardin potager. Un peu plus loin se trouve un lac où nous nageons tous les jours, en été.

Vocabulaire

der B**au**ernh**o**f (¨e), *la ferme*
der Brunnen (-), *la fontaine*
der Rasen (-), *le gazon*
der Stall (¨e), *l'écurie*
die Elektrizit**ä**t, *l'électricité*
die Mauer (n), *le mur*
die Scheune (n), *la grange*
das Dach (¨er), *le toit*

das Freie, *le plein air*
das W**o**hnz**i**mmer (-), *la salle de séjour*
baden, *(se) baigner*
bauen, *construire*
bedecken, *(re)couvrir*
einr**i**chten, *installer*
pumpen, *pomper*
umb**au**en, *transformer*

Rien ne vaut le chez soi (Un foyer à soi vaut de l'or)

Grammaire

Wir schwimmen jeden Tag.
Schwimmen, nager; *er schwamm,* il nagea, il nageait; *er ist geschwommen,* il a nagé.
Les verbes suivants appartiennent au même groupe en i - a - o :

beginnen (a, o), commencer
gewinnen (a, o), gagner
**rinnen (a, o),* ruisseler
sinnen (a, o), songer
spinnen (a, o), filer

Les verbes *glimmen (glomm, geglommen)* brûler (sans flamme) et **klimmen (klomm, geklommen),* grimper, ont un *o* bref tant au prétérit qu'au participe passé.

Exercices

A *Traduisez, puis : mettez a) au futur, b) au passé composé :*
1. Er sinnt über seine Arbeit. 2. Wir erklommen den Gipfel des Berges. 3. Womit beginnen wir? 4. Du gewinnst das große Los *(lot).* 5. Ihre Tränen *(larmes)* rannen.

B *Traduisez :*
6. De combien d'étages se compose votre maison de campagne? 7. Quand fut-elle construite? 8. Il a surtout voulu transformer la vieille grange. 9. Si l'écurie était plus grande, nous pourrions en faire deux garages.

Corrigé :

A 1. *Il songe à son travail.* a) Er wird... sinnen. b) Er hat... gesonnen. 2. *Nous escaladions le sommet de la montagne.* a) Wir werden... erklimmen. b) Wir haben... erklommen. 3. *Par quoi commençons-nous?* a) Womit werden wir beginnen? b) Womit haben wir begonnen? 4. *Tu gagnes le gros lot.* a) Du wirst ... gewinnen b) Du hast ... gewonnen. 5. *Ses larmes coulaient.* a) ... werden rinnen. b) ...sind geronnen.

B 6. Aus wieviel Stockwerken besteht Ihr Landhaus? 7. Wann wurde es gebaut? 8. Er hat besonders die alte Scheune umbauen wollen. 9. Wenn der Pferdestall größer wäre, könnten wir zwei Garagen daraus machen.

Lecture

Unser Haus am Wiesenrand

Wissen Sie es schon? Am Wiesenrand sollen hundert Häuser entstehen. Wissen Sie, dort, wenn man den kleinen Weg weitergeht, geht es zum Schützenplatz. Ein kleines Wäldchen ist da, saftige Wiesen, einsame Feldwege, und viel Weite und Freiheit. Mein Haus wird das letzte sein mit dem Blick auf die grüne Weide. Wissen Sie, kein Nachbar kann mir ins Fenster hineinschauen. Ich werde allein sein mit den Meinen und brauche doch nicht auf Gesellschaft zu verzichten. Denn hundert Häuser werden in unserer Siedlung stehen, eines so schmuck wie das andere. Im Vertrauen gesagt! Vorläufig weiß ich das nur aus dem Modell unserer Baugenossenschaft. Aber ich kann mir unsere Siedlung so recht gut vorstellen. Da werden Anlagen sein, feste Wege und Straßen, die nur die Anlieger mit ihren Fahrzeugen im Vier-Kilometer-Tempo benützen dürfen. Und dann die Spielplätze mit Schaukeln, Rutschbahnen und Sandkisten für unsere Kleinen.

Nach Hans Bahrs
(Aus der Zeitschrift « Das ideale Heim »)

Notre maison en bordure des prés

Le savez-vous déjà? En bordure des prés, on construira une centaine de maisons. Vous savez bien, c'est là-bas : quand on continue le petit chemin, il nous mène au champ de tir. On y trouve un petit bois, de grasses prairies, des chemins ruraux déserts, et beaucoup d'espace et de liberté. Ma maison sera la dernière avec vue sur les pâturages verts. Vous savez, aucun voisin ne pourra regarder par ma fenêtre. Je serai seul avec les miens, et pourtant il ne me faudra pas renoncer à la société, car il y aura dans notre lotissement une centaine de maisons, l'une aussi coquette que l'autre. Soit dit entre nous : pour le moment, je ne le sais que d'après le modèle de notre coopérative de construction. Mais je peux si bien me représenter notre lotissement. Il y aura des jardins, et des chemins et des routes carrossables (m. à m. : solides) que seuls les riverains pourront utiliser avec leurs voitures à une vitesse de quatre kilomètres à l'heure. Et puis il y aura les terrains de jeux avec des balançoires, des toboggans et des bacs à sable pour nos petits.

(Extrait de la revue « Le foyer idéal »)

Leçon

69 Die Wohnung

1 Mit meinen Freunden aus dem Büro habe ich kürzlich über das Wohnen in einer Großstadt gesprochen.
— « Wir haben eine ganz kleine Wohnung in der Nähe der Stadtmitte », sagte Uwe. « Sie liegt im 4. (vierten) Stock eines modernen Mietshauses. Es ist unmöglich, einen Schrank zu stellen. Wir müssen uns mit dem Allernotwendigsten an Möbeln begnügen. Es ist ausgeschlossen, einen Wohnzimmerschrank oder Anbaumöbel unterzubringen. Zum Glück konnten wir im Flur Wandschränke einbauen lassen; wir räumen viele Sachen hinein. »

2 Er sagte noch, daß in ihrem Wohnzimmer gerade Platz genug für einen Tisch, vier Stühle und zwei Sessel sei. Ihr Fernsehapparat stehe in einer Ecke, auf einem ganz kleinen Tischchen. Im Schlafzimmer hätten sie außer dem Wandschrank nur das Bett und ein Wandregal über dem Heizkörper. Seine Frau hätte gleich am ersten Tag allerlei Nippsachen darauf gestellt.

3 — « In der Küche hingegen ist alles bei der Hand », unterbrach ihn da seine junge Gemahlin. « Es ist ein leichtes, sich vom Spülstein nach dem elektrischen Kühlschrank zu drehen, und vom Kühlschrank nach dem Gasherd. Allerdings muß man schlank sein! »

4 Es sei nur eine provisorische Lösung, sagte mein Freund. Sie seien damals recht froh gewesen, eine solche Wohnung zu finden. Natürlich würden sie sich in ein paar Jahren eine eigene Wohnung kaufen. Sie würden dann selber stolze Hausbesitzer sein, fügte er lächelnd hinzu.

WIE MAN SICH BETTET, SO SCHLÄFT MAN

Traduction

L'appartement

1 J'ai discuté récemment, avec mes amis du bureau (des problèmes) du logement dans une grande ville.
— « Nous occupons un tout petit appartement près du centre de la ville », dit Uwe. « Il se trouve au 4e étage d'une maison de rapport moderne. Impossible d'y loger une armoire. Nous devons nous contenter du minimum de meubles indispensables. Il n'est pas question de faire entrer un buffet ou des meubles par éléments. Heureusement, dans l'entrée, nous avons pu faire mettre (m. à m. : encastrer) des placards; nous y rangeons beaucoup de choses. »

2 Il dit encore que dans leur salle commune, il y avait juste assez de place pour une table, quatre chaises et deux fauteuils. Leur poste de télévision, dit-il, se trouvait dans un coin, sur un guéridon minuscule. Il ajouta que dans la chambre à coucher, outre le placard, ils n'avaient que le lit et une étagère au-dessus du radiateur. Sa femme, poursuivit-il, y avait posé dès le premier jour toutes sortes de bibelots.

3 — « Dans la cuisine par contre on a tout sous la main », dit alors sa jeune épouse, lui coupant la parole. « C'est chose facile de se tourner de l'évier vers le réfrigérateur, et du réfrigérateur vers la cuisinière à gaz. Il est vrai qu'il faut être mince! »

4 Mon ami dit que ce n'était qu'une solution d'attente et qu'ils avaient été très heureux, à l'époque, de trouver un tel appartement. Naturellement, ils achèteraient dans quelques années un appartement à eux, déclara-t-il. Il ajouta en souriant qu'ils seraient eux-mêmes, alors, de fiers propriétaires.

Vocabulaire

der Besitzer (-), *le propriétaire*
der Flur (-e), *l'entrée, le vestibule*
der Heizkörper (-), *le radiateur*
der Herd (-e), *le foyer*
der Schrank (¨ e), *l'armoire*
die Nippsache (n), *le bibelot*
die Wand (¨ e), *la cloison, le mur*
das Mietshaus (¨ er), *la maison de rapport*
der Mieter, *le locataire*
die **A**nbaum**ö**bel (plur.), *les meubles par éléments*

Comme on fait son lit, on dort.

der Kühlschrank (⸚e), *le réfrigérateur*
der Sessel (-), *le fauteuil*
der Spülstein (-e), *l'évier*
die Ecke (n), *le coin*
die Gem**a**hlin (nen), *l'épouse*
der Gem**a**hl (-e), *l'époux*
die Heizung (-en), *le chauffage*

die Lösung (-en), *la solution*
aufr**äu**men, *ranger*
(sich) begn**ü**gen (mit), *(se) contenter (de)*
einb**au**en, *encastrer*
hinz**u**f**ü**gen, *ajouter*
unterbr**i**ngen (brachte, gebracht), *mettre à l'abri, caser*
(sich) unterh**a**lten (ie, a; ä), *(s') entretenir*

Grammaire

Ihr Fernsehapparat stehe in einer Ecke.
Le style indirect.

● Dans cette phrase, comme dans tout le § 2 et dans le § 4, on cite les paroles d'un interlocuteur, sans le faire parler directement. On dit que ces passages sont au « style indirect »; celui-ci consiste à rapporter les paroles ou pensées d'autrui.

● Les verbes *sei, stehe, hätte,* etc. sont au subjonctif; l'emploi de ce mode indique que le narrateur se borne à rapporter certaines affirmations, sans les tenir pour vrai ni les contester. Le subjonctif est le mode habituel du style indirect. Cependant, le narrateur peut employer l'indicatif s'il veut indiquer qu'il considère comme certain le fait rapporté.

Mein Freund sagte, daß er glücklich ist, mon ami dit qu'il était heureux (on prend parti).

Mais :

Mein Freund sagte, daß er glücklich sei, mon ami dit qu'il était heureux (on ne se prononce pas).

● Souvent, on supprime *daß* (Mémento, n° 67); les subordonnées au style indirect prennent alors l'allure de propositions principales. Seul, le verbe au subjonctif indique qu'il s'agit de paroles rapportées (texte, §§ 2 et 4).

● Le temps dans le style indirect. Voici le § 4 transposé dans le style direct : *Mein Freund sagte : « Es ist nur eine... Wir sind damals... gewesen, eine... zu finden. Natürlich werden wir uns... kaufen. » Er fügte lächelnd hinzu : « Wir werden dann... sein. »*

Ainsi, le subjonctif 1 présent correspond au présent de l'indicatif, le subjonctif 1 passé correspond aux temps passés de l'indicatif, et le subjonctif 1 futur remplace le futur du style direct. On emploïe aussi des formes de remplacement. V. Mémento, § 73.

Exercices

A *Transposez le § 2 du texte au style direct.*

B *Traduisez puis transposez au style direct :*
1. Er sagt, diese Kommode komme von seinem Großvater; sie habe lange auf dem Speicher gestanden. 2. Inge schreibt, daß es dort schöne alte Möbel gäbe; sie sei gestern in ein Geschäft gegangen; man würde ihr einen Stilsessel reservieren.

C *Traduisez, puis transposez au style indirect :*
3. Karl erklärt : « Eine solche Wohnung gefällt mir. Ich suchte schon lange eine größere. Ich werde sie mieten. Wir werden nächsten Monat umziehen. »

Corrigé :

A Er sagte noch : « In *unserem* Wohnzimmer *ist... Unser* Fernsehapparat *steht...* Im Schlafzimmer *haben wir... Meine* Frau *hat... gestellt* ».

B 1. *Il dit que cette commode vient de son grand-père et qu'elle avait été longtemps au grenier.* Er sagt : « Diese K... *kommt* von *meinem* G...; sie *stand* lange... ». 2. *Inge écrit qu'il y a là-bas de beaux meubles anciens, qu'elle est allée la veille dans un magasin, qu'on lui réservera un fauteuil de style.* B. Inge schreibt : « Es *gibt...; ich bin... gegangen;* man *wird mir... reservieren* ».

C 3. *Charles déclare : « Un tel appartement me plaît. Depuis longtemps déjà j'en cherchais un plus grand. Je le louerai. Nous déménagerons le mois prochain ».* Karl erklärt, eine s. W. *gefalle (gefiele)* ihm; er *habe (hätte)... gesucht;* er *würde (werde)* sie *mieten; sie würden (werden)* nächsten Monat *umziehen.*

Leçon

70 Freunde stellen Ihnen die Wohnung zur Verfügung

1 — Hören Sie mal, liebe Freunde! Während der Urlaubszeit steht unsere Wohnung leer. Wir schlagen Ihnen vor, wenn Ihnen das recht ist, sie zu benützen.
— Wir möchten Ihnen aber keine Umstände machen.
— Unter uns kann man doch nicht von Umständen sprechen! Sie wissen, wie die Wohnung aussieht. Sie ist nicht luxuriös, aber doch bequem und angenehm.

2 — Hier sind die Schlüssel. Der kleinere ist für die Haustür, der größere für die Wohnungstür. Sie ist ein wenig schwer zu öffnen. Im Flur werden wir einen Wandschrank frei lassen, mit einigen Kleiderbügeln. Sie können Ihre Sachen in die Schubladen einräumen. Wird Ihnen das wohl ausreichen? — Gewiß. Wenn wir verreisen, nehmen wir immer nur das Nötigste mit.

3 — Selbstverständlich verfügen Sie ganz nach Belieben über die Küche. Ich empfehle Ihnen, den Gashahn gut zuzudrehen.
— Im Badezimmer finden Sie eine Steckdose über dem Waschtisch. Wir haben zweihundertzwanzig Volt.

4 — Könnten Sie mir sagen, wo die Decken, die Bettücher und die Handtücher aufgeräumt sind?
— Ich bitte Sie : genieren Sie sich nicht! Benutzen Sie alles, was Sie brauchen. Tun Sie, als ob Sie zu Hause wären.

EIN MANN, EIN WORT

Traduction

Des amis mettent leur appartement à votre disposition

1 — Écoutez, chers amis, pendant les vacances (m. à m. : la période des vacances) notre appartement est vide. Nous vous proposons — si cela vous convient — de vous y installer (m. à m. : de l'utiliser). — Mais nous ne voudrions pas vous déranger. — Mais on ne peut parler de dérangement entre nous. Vous savez comment est (m. à m. : paraît) l'appartement. Il n'est pas luxueux, mais cependant, commode et agréable.

2 — Voici les clés. La plus petite ouvre la porte sur la rue; la plus grande est pour la porte d'entrée. Elle est un peu dure à ouvrir. Nous laisserons dans le vestibule un placard libre avec quelques cintres. Vous pourrez ranger vos affaires dans les tiroirs. Est-ce que cela vous suffira? — Certainement. Quand nous partons en voyage, nous n'emportons toujours que le strict nécessaire.

3 — Naturellement, vous disposerez comme vous l'entendez de la cuisine. Je vous recommande de bien fermer le robinet à gaz. — Dans la salle de bain, vous trouverez une prise de courant au-dessus du lavabo. Nous avons du 220 volts.

4 — Pourriez-vous me dire où sont rangés les couvertures, les draps et les serviettes de toilette?
— Je vous en prie : ne vous gênez pas! Servez-vous de tout ce qu'il vous faut. Faites comme chez vous (m. à m. : comme si vous étiez à la maison).

Vocabulaire

der Kl**ei**derb**ü**gel (-) *le cintre*
der Schlüssel (-), *la clé*
Die Decke (n), *la couverture, le plafond*
die Sache (n), *la chose*
die Sch**u**bl**a**de (n), *le tiroir*
die St**e**ckd**o**se (n), *la prise de courant*
das Bettuch (¨er), *le drap*
das Handtuch (¨er), *la serviette de toilette*
(sich), gen**ie**ren, *(se) gêner*
z**u**dr**e**hen, *fermer (en tournant)*
auss**e**hen (a, e; ie), *avoir l'air de*
schließen (o, o), *fermer*

Chose promise, chose due
(Un homme d'honneur n'a qu'une parole).

Grammaire

■ Tun Sie, als ob...

Faites, comme si...

Tun, faire, verbe irrégulier, devient au prétérit *er tat* il faisait, il fit, au participe passé *getan,* fait. Ce verbe n'entre dans aucune des séries étudiées dans les leçons précédentes. Il en est de même des verbes suivants :

*gehen	*ging*	*gegangen*	aller
hauen	*hieb*	*gehauen*	frapper; couper
heißen	*hieß*	*geheißen*	s'appeler; dire de
*kommen	*kam*	*gekommen*	venir
rufen	*rief*	*gerufen*	appeler; s'écrier
stehen	*stand*	*gestanden*	être debout
stoßen	*stieß*	*gestoßen*	heurter, pousser

■ ... als ob Sie zu Hause wären.

... comme si vous étiez chez vous.

● *Als ob, als wenn,* comme si, sont suivis du subjonctif et entraînent le rejet du verbe. Ex. :

Er tut, als ob (als wenn) er keine Zeit hätte, il fait comme s'il n'avait pas le temps.

● *Ob* et *wenn* peuvent être supprimés. On fait alors l'inversion après *als.* Ex. :

Er tut, als hätte er keine Zeit, il fait comme s'il n'avait pas le temps.

■ Genieren Sie sich nicht!

● *Sich,* pronom réfléchi de la 3e personne singulier et pluriel (leçons 13 et 14) désigne la même personne que le sujet. Ex. :

Sie kaufen sich Souvenirs, ils s'achètent des souvenirs (à eux-mêmes).

● Quand l'action est réciproque, il faut employer le pronom *einander,* l'un l'autre, qui est invariable. Ex. :

Sie kaufen einander Souvenirs, ils s'achètent des souvenirs (les uns aux autres).

Sie genieren einander, ils se gênent (mutuellement).

Formes composées : *miteinander,* l'un avec l'autre; *gegeneinander,* l'un contre l'autre, etc.

Exercices

A *Traduisez puis : mettez a) au prétérit, b) au plus-que-parfait :* 1. Die Mutter geht in die Küche. 2. Sie kommt aus dem Eßzimmer. 3. Sie ruft ihre Tochter. 4. Sie stößt den Tisch an die Wand. 5. Sie heißt ihre Tochter essen.

B *Mettez le verbe entre parenthèses à la forme voulue, puis : a) traduisez, b) supprimez* wenn *ou* ob.
6. Er tut, als ob er fest (schlafen). 7. Es scheint, als wenn der Baum (umfallen). 8. Sie benehmen sich, als ob sie allein im Gasthaus (sein). 9. Sie geht vorbei, als wenn sie uns nicht (sehen).

C *Traduisez :*
10. Tous les voyageurs se parlaient (= les uns avec les autres). 11. Ils s'entraidaient, comme s'ils étaient de vieux amis. 12. Ils posèrent les valises les unes à côté des autres. 13. Kurt dispose de l'appartement comme s'il était chez lui. 14. Dans le tiroir, les serviettes et les draps sont posés les uns sur les autres.

Corrigé :

A 1. *Maman va dans la cuisine.* a) ... ging ... b) ... war ... gegangen. 2. *Elle sort de la salle à manger.* a) Sie kam ... b) Sie war ... gekommen. 3. *Elle appelle sa fille.* a) Sie rief ... b) Sie hatte ... gerufen. 4. *Elle pousse la table contre le mur.* a) Sie stieß ... b) Sie hatte ... gestoßen. 5. *Elle dit à sa fille de manger.* a) Sie hieß ... b) Sie hatte ihre Tochter essen heißen *(double infinitif, facultatif avec* heißen) *ou :* ... essen *ge*heißen.

B 6. schliefe. a) *Il fait comme s'il dormait profondément.* b) Er tut, als schliefe er ... 7. umfiele. a) *On dirait que l'arbre va tomber (m. à m. : il semble).* b) Es scheint, als fiele ... um. 8. wären. a) *Ils se comportent comme s'ils étaient seuls au restaurant.* b) Sie ..., als wären sie ... 9. sähe. a) *Elle passe, comme si elle ne vous voyait pas.* b) Sie ..., als sähe sie ...

C 10. Alle Reisenden sprachen miteinander. 11. Sie halfen einander, als wären sie alte Freunde. 12. Sie stellten die Handkoffer nebeneinander. 13. Kurt verfügt über die Wohnung, als ob er zu Hause wäre. 14. In der Schublade liegen die Handtücher und die Bettücher aufeinander.

Leçon

70 bis Contrôle et révisions

A **Traduisez puis mettez a) au passé composé; b) au prétérit (Relisez L. 63, 4) :**

1. Luise wird ihrem Mann helfen. 2. Er wird es nie mehr vergessen. 3. Werden Sie oft solche Anzeigen lesen? 4. Finden Sie den Stil lebendig? 5. Entspricht er *(correspondre)* dem Stil unserer Werbung (= Publizität)?

B **Complétez par « ziemlich » (Lecture L. 66,4; grammaire L. 64, 3) ou « genug », puis traduisez :**

6. Das Wetter war ... warm, aber nicht warm ... um zu baden. 7. Die Prognose war ... optimistisch. 8. Der Wind war stark ... und die Segelboote *(voiliers)* konnten ausfahren.

C **Traduisez puis transposez au style indirect (Lecture L. 68,4; grammaire L. 69,3) :**

9. Mein Freund schrieb uns : « Ich habe einen Bauplatz gekauft. Er liegt am Wiesenrand. Dort gibt es viel Weite. Wir werden sehr glücklich sein und kein Nachbar wird uns stören *(déranger)* ».

D **Traduisez :**

Schule und Fortschritt

Man hat festgestellt, daß der Leistungsdurchschnitt bei Schulprüfungen in den heißen Gegenden des australischen Bundeslandes Victoria wesentlich niedriger ist als in seinen kühleren Gebieten. Deswegen will man die Prüfungsräume in 47 Schulen mit fahrbaren Klimaanlagen ausstatten.

(Die Weltwoche)

E **Traduisez :**

Humor

Herr Zechbeck prahlt gern. Indem er mit seinem Freund an einem Schloß vorbeifährt, sagt er : « Dieses Schloß ist von meinen Ahnen erbaut worden. » — « So, waren sie Maurer? » fragt der Freund, schlagfertig.

Corrigé :

A 1. *Louise aidera son mari.* a) hat ... geholfen. b) half. 2. *Il ne l'oubliera plus jamais.* a) hat ... vergessen. b) vergaß. 3. *Lirez-vous souvent de telles annonces?* a) Haben Sie ... gelesen? b) Lasen Sie ...? 4. *Trouvez-vous ce style vivant?* a) Haben Sie ... gefunden? b) Fanden Sie ... ? 5. *Est-ce qu'il correspond au style de notre publicité?* a) Hat er ... entsprochen? b) Entsprach er ... ?

B 6. ziemlich; genug. *Le temps était assez chaud, mais pas assez pour se baigner.* 7. ziemlich. *Les pronostics étaient assez optimistes.* 8. genug. *Le vent était assez fort et les voiliers ont pu sortir (du port).*

C 9. *Mon ami nous a écrit : « J'ai acheté un terrain de construction. Il se trouve en bordure des prés. Là-bas, il y a beaucoup d'espace. Nous serons très heureux et aucun voisin ne nous dérangera. »* Mein Freund schrieb uns, er habe (hätte) einen Bauplatz gekauft; dieser liege (läge) am Wiesenrand; dort gebe (gäbe) es viel Weite. Sie würden sehr glücklich sein und kein Nachbar würde sie stören.

D École et progrès

On a constaté que la moyenne des réussites aux examens scolaires est sensiblement plus basse dans les contrées chaudes de Victoria, État fédéral d'Australie, que dans ses régions plus fraîches. Aussi, on a l'intention d'équiper les salles d'examen dans 47 écoles d'appareils de climatisation mobiles.

E Humour

Monsieur Zechbeck aime bien se vanter. En passant avec son ami près d'un château, il dit : « Ce château a été construit par mes ancêtres. » – « Tiens! Est-ce qu'ils étaient maçons? » demande son ami, du tac au tac.

Leçon

71

Die Familie

1 Wir heirateten, als wir zwanzig waren. Nun ist es schon neununddreißig Jahre her.
Wir bekamen drei Kinder. Das älteste, eine Tochter, hat einen Elektroingenieur geheiratet. Sie sind glücklich. Wir sind Großeltern. Unsere beiden Enkelkinder, ein Junge und ein Mädchen, sind sechs, beziehungsweise vier Jahre alt. Sie leben auf dem Land, bei den Schwiegereltern unserer Tochter. Es ist in der Nähe der Fabrik, in der unser Schwiegersohn arbeitet.

2 Unser zweites Kind, ein Junge, ist zweiundzwanzig Jahre alt. Er ist noch ledig, aber er wird bald heiraten, sobald er seine Studien absolviert hat. Er ist M**u**siker und unsere zukünftige Schwiegertochter schwärmt auch Mus**i**k. Wir hoffen, daß auch sie ein glückliches Ehepaar werden.

3 Sowohl von der Seite meiner Frau als auch von meiner Seite haben wir zahlreiche Verwandte : Onkel, Tanten, Vettern, Kusinen.. Oft kennen wir uns darin nicht aus.
Ab und zu gibt es ein Familienfest, eine Taufe oder eine Hochzeit; dann kommen wir alle zusammen. Auch bei einem Begräbnis treffen wir entfernte Verwandte.

ALTE LIEBE ROSTET NICHT

Traduction

La Famille

1 Nous nous sommes mariés quand nous avions vingt ans. Cela remonte déjà à trente-neuf ans.
Nous avons eu trois enfants. L'aînée, une fille, a épousé un ingénieur électricien. Ils sont heureux. Nous sommes grands-parents. Nos deux petits-enfants, un garçon et une fille, ont respectivement six ans et quatre ans. Ils vivent à la campagne, chez les beaux-parents de notre fille. C'est près de l'usine où travaille notre gendre.

2 Notre deuxième enfant, un garçon, a vingt-deux ans. Il est encore célibataire, mais il va bientôt se marier, dès qu'il aura terminé ses études. Il est musicien et notre future bru raffole également de musique. Nous espérons qu'ils feront eux aussi un ménage heureux.

3 Tant du côté de ma femme que du mien, nous avons une nombreuse parenté : oncles, tantes, cousins, cousines. Nous nous y perdons souvent (m. à m. : souvent nous ne nous y connaissons pas).
De temps à autre il y a une fête de famille, un baptême ou un mariage; alors nous nous retrouvons tous. Lors d'un enterrement également, nous rencontrons des parents éloignés.

Vocabulaire

der Musiker (-), *le musicien*
der Vetter (s, n), *le cousin*
die Kus**i**ne (n), *la cousine*
das Ehepaar (-e), *les (2) époux*
die **E**nkelk**i**nder (plur.), *les (arrière)-petits-enfants*
das Studium (die Studien), *l'étude*
die Schw**ie**ger**e**ltern (plur.) *les beaux-parents*
der Schw**ie**gers**o**hn (¨e), *le gendre*
die Schw**ie**gert**o**chter (¨), *la bru*
absolv**ie**ren, *absoudre; terminer*
heiraten, *se marier; épouser*
hoffen (auf), *espérer*
schwärmen (für), *se passionner de*

On revient toujours à ses premières amours
(Viel amour ne rouille pas).

Grammaire

■ Es ist schon neununddreißig Jahre her.

Her marque ici le temps dont on parle, avec une nuance de « point de départ ». Le plus souvent, *her* exprime le rapprochement par rapport à la personne qui parle (leçon 54 : *« Bier her! Bier her!* de la bière! apportez de la bière!) L'éloignement par rapport à la personne qui parle s'exprime par *hin* (leçon 12). Avec une deuxième particule, on ajoute une nouvelle précision : *herauf,* rapprochement + montée; *herab,* rapprochement + descente; *hinauf,* éloignement + montée, etc.

■ Er hat seine Studien absolviert.

Dans cette phrase au passé composé, nous remarquons que le participe passé du verbe *absolvieren* ne prend pas le préfixe *ge-;* c'est le cas pour tous les verbes en *ieren.* Ex. :

> *studieren,* étudier; *er studierte,* il étudiait; *er hat... studiert,* il a étudié;
> *probieren,* essayer; *er probierte,* il essayait; *er hat es probiert,* il l'a essayé (leçon 19).

Exercices

Traduire :

1. A-t-il terminé ses études? 2. Il avait tout essayé, mais sans trouver de solution. 3. Après avoir transporté les livres et le linge, ils emballèrent (ein/packen) la vaisselle. 4. La voiture descendit la rue et s'arrêta devant notre maison. 5. Moi, je regardais par la fenêtre.

Corrigé :

1. Hat er seine Studien absolviert? 2. Er hatte alles probiert, ohne eine Lösung zu finden. 3. Nachdem sie die Bücher und die Wäsche abtransportiert hatten, packten sie das Geschirr ein. 4. Der Wagen fuhr die Straße herab und hielt vor unserem Haus. 5. Ich schaute zum Fenster hinaus.

Wenn der Haushalt zur Eheklippe wird

Für die immer größer werdende Zahl der berufstätigen Hausfrauen bedeutet der Haushalt eine zusätzliche Belastung. Beruf und Ehe sind wahrhaftig genug, um Kopf, Herz, Hände und die 24 Stunden des Tages einer Frau auszufüllen : der Haushalt dazu ist zu viel. Hat sie keine gute Haushalthilfe? Dann muß sie alle hundert kleinen Dinge selber erledigen, Betten machen, planen, einkaufen, kochen, Tisch decken, abwaschen, die Wäsche in Ordnung halten, die Kleider zur Reinigung bringen und abholen, die Zimmerpflanzen gießen, Hund oder Katze versorgen, abgerissene Knöpfe annähen. Ihre Sonntagsruhe benützt sie dann vermutlich dazu, ihren Böden Glanz zu verleihen, notwendige Reparaturen auszuführen — und einmal in der Woche richtig zu kochen! Die Kette auch nur des Allernotwendigsten reißt nie ab, und immer ist im Hintergrund das unbehagliche Gefühl, daß der Haushalt da und dort bedenklich knarre und eben nicht tadellos sei, nicht so wie der mütterliche oder — der schwiegermütterliche.

Aus der Zeitschrift «Annabelle» (Zürich)

Quand les travaux ménagers deviennent un écueil pour le couple

Pour les femmes de plus en plus nombreuses qui exercent un métier, le ménage représente une charge supplémentaire. Métier et mariage sont largement suffisants pour occuper l'esprit, le cœur, les mains et les 24 heures de la journée d'une femme : ajoutez à cela, le ménage, c'en est trop. Et si la maîtresse de maison n'a pas d'aide ménagère convenable? Alors, il faut qu'elle s'occupe elle-même d'une centaine de petits détails : les lits, un plan de travail, les achats, la cuisine, le couvert, essuyer (la table), tenir son linge en ordre, apporter les vêtements au nettoyage et les (y) reprendre, arroser les plantes d'appartement, prendre soin du chien et du chat, recoudre les boutons arrachés. Son repos dominical, elle l'emploiera alors probablement à faire briller ses parquets (m. à m. : à conférer un éclat à ses sols), à effectuer des réparations nécessaires — et à faire de la vraie cuisine, une fois par semaine! La série des occupations absolument indispensables ne cesse jamais (m. à m. : la chaîne... ne se brise pas) et constamment est présent, à l'arrière-plan, ce sentiment de malaise : le ménage laisse parfois à désirer de façon inquiétante (m. à m. : grince...) et n'est pas impeccable, comme celui de la mère, ou — de la belle-mère.

Leçon
72 Kinder und Schule

1 Unser Sohn Hans wird nächstens elf Jahre alt. Seit fünf Jahren, von seinem sechsten Lebensjahr an, geht er in die Schule. Als er sechs Jahre alt war, hatte er schon ein Jahr lang den Kindergarten besucht. Dort hatte er seine ersten Lieder gelernt, seine ersten Zeichnungen gemacht. Er war bei fröhlichem Spiel an Ordnung gewöhnt worden. Den Nachmittag hatte er damit verbracht, mit seinen kleinen Kameraden herumzuspringen.

2 Seither hat er lesen und schreiben gelernt. Man hat ihn in Erdkunde und Geschichte unterrichtet. Er kann zusammenzählen, abziehen, vervielfachen und teilen. Er macht Rechenaufgaben und Aufsätze. Er hat einige Kenntisse in Naturkunde. Auch mit dem Erlernen einer Fremdsprache hat er bereits begonnen. Zu dem, was ihn seine Lehrer in der Schule lehren, muß er noch nachmittags zu Hause arbeiten. Er muß seine Lektionen lernen und seine Aufgaben machen.

3 Er geht gern in die Schule. Während der ersten Ferientage wird ihm die Zeit lang und er sehnt sich nach seinen Kameraden. Aber danach fahren wir ans Meer, manchmal auch aufs Land. Dort macht er neue Bekanntschaften. Er spielt, er läuft und springt den ganzen Tag hin und her. Er verbringt die Regentage, indem er Abenteuerromane liest. Jeden Tag übt er mindestens eine halbe Stunde lang Klavier.

AUS KINDERN WERDEN LEUTE

Traduction

Les enfants et l'école

1 Notre fils Jean aura prochainement onze ans. Il va à l'école depuis cinq ans, depuis l'âge de six ans. A cet âge, il avait fréquenté l'école maternelle depuis un an déjà. Il y avait appris ses premiers chants, (il y avait) fait ses premiers dessins. Il avait été habitué à l'ordre, tout en jouant gaiement. Il avait passé les après-midis à s'ébattre avec ses petits camarades.

2 Depuis, il a appris à lire et à écrire. On lui a enseigné la géographie, l'histoire. Il sait faire des additions, des soustractions, des multiplications et des divisions (m. à m. : il sait additionner, soustraire,...). Il fait des problèmes et des rédactions. Il a quelques connaissances en science naturelle. Il a également commencé déjà l'étude d'une langue (vivante) étrangère. En plus de ce que ses maîtres lui apprennent à l'école, il doit travailler encore l'après-midi, chez nous. Il faut qu'il apprenne ses leçons et qu'il fasse ses devoirs.

3 Il aime aller en classe. Pendant les premiers jours de vacances, il trouve le temps long et s'ennuie de ses camarades. Mais ensuite, nous allons au bord de la mer, parfois aussi à la campagne. Là, il se fait de nouvelles connaissances. Il joue, court, saute à longueur de journée (de-ci, de-là). Il passe les journées de pluie en lisant des romans d'aventures. Tous les jours, il étudie son piano pendant une demi-heure au moins.

Vocabulaire

der Aufsatz (⸚ e), *la rédaction*
die **Au**fg**a**be (n), *le devoir*
der **E**rdk**u**nde, *la géographie*
die Gesch**i**chte (n), *l'histoire*
die Kenntnis (se), *la connaissance*
die Schule (n), *l'école*
die Übung (en), *l'exercice*
die Zeichnung (en), *le dessin*
das Klav**ie**r (e), *le piano*
das Spiel (e), *le jeu*
gew**ö**hnen (an), *habituer (à)*
lehren (+ acc.), *apprendre enseigner*
rechnen, *calculer*
sich sehnen (nach), *désirer ardemment*
unterr**i**chten, *enseigner*
beg**i**nnen (a, o) (mit), *commencer*
springen (a, u), *sauter*

Petit poisson deviendra grand
(Les enfants deviendront de grandes personnes).

■ **Bei fröhlichem Spiel – Indem er Romane liest.**
(En jouant gaiement. – En lisant des romans.)
Notre participe présent (jouant, lisant) est rendu différemment en allemand.

● En chantant, *beim Singen;* en mangeant, *beim Essen.*

Donc, *beim (bei dem)* + infinitif substantivé (leçon 34), si l'infinitif n'a pas de complément.

● En chantant un air populaire, il... *Indem er eine Volksweise singt,...*

En mangeant des fruits, nous... *Indem* (ou : *wenn,* ou *während*) wir Obst essen,...

Quand notre participe présent a un complément, on forme le plus souvent une subordonnée introduite par la conjonction qui convient selon le sens : *indem,* tandis que; *während,* pendant que; *wenn,* quand; *als,* quand; *da,* puisque, etc.

Arrivant en retard, il ne trouva plus de place, *da er zu spät kam, fand er keinen Platz mehr.*

● Nous avons vu, dans la leçon 28, que le participe présent allemand s'emploie surtout comme adjectif ou comme adverbe :

Ein lachendes Kind, un enfant riant.
Es kommt lachend, il vient en riant.

■ **Zu dem, was...**
Le pronom relatif *was,* ce qui, ce que, s'emploie pour désigner une chose; *wer,* celui qui, une personne.

Was schön ist, (das) bewundert man immer, ce qui est beau, on l'admire toujours.
Wer heute kauft, (der) kauft billig; celui qui (quiconque) achète aujourd'hui, achète avantageusement (m. à m. : à bas prix).

Les pronoms *das* ou *der* peuvent être employés comme corrélatifs.

■ Notez le régime des verbes suivants :

Er lehrt ihn Deutsch, il lui apprend l'allemand.
Es beginnt mit Musik, cela commence par de la musique.
Er gewöhnt sich an das Wetter, il s'habitue au temps.
Er unterrichtet sie in Erdkunde, il leur enseigne la géographie.

(Mémento, n° 74 à 77).

Exercices

A *Traduisez :*

1. Wahrend er zeichnete, dachte er an sein Vaterhaus. 2. Indem er auf dem Hof herumsprang, fiel er auf den Rücken. 3. Wenn du eine Fremdsprache lernst, wirst du mehr Erfolg haben. 4. Als ich nach Hause kam, fand ich deinen Brief. 5. Da er seine Rechenaufgabe vergessen hatte, wurde er bestraft.

B *Transformez les phrases en employant* wer *ou* was, *puis traduisez :*
6. Wenn einer es wagt, so gewinnt er. 7. Wenn einer den andern eine Grube *(fosse)* gräbt, fällt er selbst hinein. 8. Ich weiß es nicht; es macht mich nicht heiß. 9. Es neckt sich; es liebt sich.

C *Traduisez :*
10. Il nous avait enseigné l'histoire en nous montrant des centaines de gravures. 11. En faisant attention, tu t'habitueras vite au froid.

Corrigé :

A 1. En dessinant, il pensait à sa maison paternelle. 2. En s'ébattant dans la cour, il tomba à la renverse (= sur le dos). 3. En apprenant une langue étrangère, tu auras plus de succès. 4. En rentrant, j'ai trouvé ta lettre. 5. Ayant oublié son problème, il fut puni.

B 6. Wer wagt, gewinnt (*proverbe*). *Celui qui ose, gagne.* (*La fortune sourit aux audacieux*). 7. Wer andern eine Grube gräbt, (der) fällt selbst hinein (*prov.*). *Quiconque creuse une fosse pour les autres, y tombe lui-même. (Tel est pris qui croyait prendre).* 8. Was ich nicht weiß, macht mich nicht heiß (*prov.*). *Ce que je ne sais pas, ne me touche pas (m. à m. : ne m'échaude pas).* 9. Was sich neckt, das liebt sich (*prov.*). *Ce qui se taquine (bien) s'aime (bien).*

C 10. Er hatte uns Geschichte gelehrt (*ou* : in G. unterrichtet), indem er uns hunderte von Bildern zeigte. 11. Wenn du aufpaßt, gewöhnst du dich schnell an die Kälte.

Leçon

73 Der menschliche Körper

1 Meine Kinder verschaffen sich gern Bewegung. Sie fürchten weder Kälte, noch Hitze. Sie spielen im Regen, laufen bei Wind und Wetter mit entblößtem Oberkörper umher; dennoch haben sie sich noch nie einen Schnupfen geholt. Ihre Glieder werden gekräftigt und ihr Körper wird geschmeidig, wenn sie so im Freien klettern, springen, den Hügel hinauf- und hinablaufen. Es schläft sich viel besser unter freiem Himmel, und der Schlaf ist erquickender, weil man eine reine und gesunde Luft atmet.

2 Abends, wenn ich nach der Aufregung des Tages nach Hause komme, entspanne ich mich. Im Dunklen und in aller Stille lege ich mich auf den Teppich. Ich schließe die Augen, ich höre auf nichts. Ich hebe den rechten Arm und lasse ihn wieder schwer hinunterfallen, so schlaff, als wäre er leblos. Dann drehe ich den Kopf nach rechts, nach links. Danach ist die Reihe am linken Bein, dann am rechten; ich beuge sie nacheinander und lasse sie wieder erschlaffen. Ich richte mich auf; ich stelle mir vor, meine Wirbelsäule wäre geschmeidig wie ein Blumenstiel. Ich biege sie nach allen Richtungen, mit eingezogenem Bauch, nach hinten fallenden Schultern, dann mit vorgestrecktem Rumpf. Ich strecke meine Finger aus.

3 Der Mensch ist ein gefühlvolles, kluges, mutiges und leidenschaftliches Wesen. Genau wie die Tiere, kann er Leid oder Wohlbehagen empfinden. Nur der Mensch aber lacht oder weint.
Mancher hat einen sehr tiefen, angeborenen Sinn für Rhythmus. Dadurch vielleicht hat der Mensch an der Ewigkeit teil.

DER MENSCH DENKT, GOTT LENKT

Traduction

Le corps humain

1 Mes enfants aiment se donner du mouvement. Ils ne craignent ni le froid, ni la chaleur. Ils jouent sous la pluie, ils courent par tous les temps (m. à m. : par vent et tempête), torse nu; pourtant ils ne se sont jamais enrhumés. Leurs membres se musclent et leur corps s'assouplit à grimper et à sauter au grand air, à monter et à descendre la colline.
L'on dort beaucoup mieux à la belle étoile et le sommeil est plus reposant parce qu'on respire un air pur et sain.

2 Le soir, en rentrant, après l'énervement de la journée, je me relaxe. Dans l'obscurité et dans le plus grand silence, je m'allonge sur le tapis. Je ferme les yeux, je n'écoute rien. Je lève le bras droit et je le laisse retomber lourdement, mou comme s'il était mort. Puis je porte (tourne) la tête à droite, à gauche. Ensuite vient le tour de la jambe gauche, puis de la droite; je les plie l'une après l'autre pour les laisser ensuite se détendre. Je me mets debout; je m'imagine que ma colonne vertébrale est flexible comme la tige d'une fleur. Je la plie dans tous les sens, le ventre bien rentré, les épaules tombant en arrière, puis le tronc en avant. J'étire mes doigts.

3 L'homme est un être sensible, intelligent, courageux et passionné. Tout comme les animaux, il peut ressentir la douleur ou le bien-être. Mais il n'y a que l'homme qui rie ou pleure.
Certains ont un sens inné très profond du rythme. C'est peut-être par là que l'homme rejoint l'éternité.

Vocabulaire

der Arm (-e), *le bras*
der Rumpf (¨e), *le tronc, le torse*
der **O**berk**ö**rper (-), *le buste*
der Schlaf, *le sommeil*
der Sinn (-e), *le sens*
die Ewigkeit (en), *l'éternité*
die Schulter (n), *l'épaule*
die W**i**rbels**äu**le (n), *la colonne vertébrale*
das Bein (-e), *la jambe*
das Gef**ü**hl (-e), *la sensation*
das Glied (-er), *le membre*
das Wesen (-), *l'être; l'essence*

L'homme propose, Dieu dispose (l'homme pense, Dieu dirige).

Grammaire

■ Sie fürchten weder Kälte, noch Hitze.

● *weder... noch...,* ni..., ni... exprime une alternative négative.
Sie war weder reich noch schön, elle n'était ni riche, ni belle.

● Pour exprimer une alternative positive, on emploie *entweder... oder...,* ou..., ou...
Er kommt entweder heute abend oder morgen früh, il viendra ou ce soir, ou demain matin.

■ So schlaff, als wäre er leblos.

Traduction de *als.*

● Dans cet exemple, *als* se traduit par : comme si, *ob* étant sous-entendu (leçon 70).

● *als* = quand.
Als die Polizisten kamen, randalierte eben der junge Mann, quand les agents arrivèrent, le jeune homme était en train de faire du tapage. (leçon 20).

● *als* = que (après un comparatif de supériorité).
Dort fühlen Sie sich wohler als in der Kneipe,
là-bas, vous vous sentirez mieux qu'au bistrot (leçon 16).

● *als* = que (après *nichts,* rien; *niemand,* personne).
Nun trinkt er nichts anderes als Wasser,
maintenant, il ne boit rien d'autre que de l'eau.
Niemand anders als er kann uns helfen.
personne d'autre que lui ne pourra nous aider.

● *als* = comme, en qualité de.
Als Musiker verdient er kaum sein Brot,
comme musicien, il gagne à peine son pain.

Exercices

Traduisez :
1. Je n'ai ni le temps, ni l'argent pour rester plus longtemps ici. 2. Ou bien tu prends le train, ou bien tu fais de l'auto-stop. 3. Tu pourras travailler comme garçon de café. 4. Il n'est rien moins que riche.

Corrigé :

1. Ich habe weder Zeit noch Geld, um länger hier zu bleiben. 2. Entweder fährst du mit dem Zug, oder (du fährst) per Anhalter. 3. Du kannst als Kellner arbeiten (*ou :* wirst... können). 4. Er ist nichts weniger als reich.

Lecture

Das Urteil

« Im Namen des Volkes... » hat ein Amtsrichter ein Urteil gesprochen, das schnell über die Grenzen der norddeutschen Stadt Bad Oldesloe hinaus bekannt wurde. Der Mann in der schwarzen Robe hat einen jungen Mann dazu verurteilt, Sport zu treiben...
Weil er in einer Gaststätte randaliert und später einen Polizisten angegriffen hatte, saß der 23 jährige Bäcker Gerd C. auf der Anklagebank. « Ich weiß nicht, wie das alles passiert ist », sagte er, « ich kann mich an nichts mehr erinnern, denn ich war stark betrunken ».
Das Oldesloer Schöffengericht sprach das Urteil : 450 Mark Geldstrafe! Und innerhalb von vier Wochen muß der junge Bäcker einem Sportverein beitreten und dem Gericht mitteilen, welche Sportart er sich ausgewählt hat! Was sich der Richter dabei gedacht hat, wurde aus der Urteilsbegründung erkennbar : « Durch den Sport werden Sie sich hoffentlich das Trinken abgewöhnen. Auf dem Sportplatz werden Sie sich sehr schnell wohler fühlen als in der Kneipe ».

W. A. R.

(Aus der Wochenzeitung « Rheinischer Merkur »)

La sentence

« Au nom du peuple... », un magistrat a rendu un jugement qui fut rapidement connu au-delà des limites de la ville de Bad Oldesloe, en Allemagne du Nord. L'homme en toge noire a condamné un jeune homme... à la pratique du sport.
C'est parce qu'il avait fait du tapage dans un café et attaqué par la suite un agent de police, que Gerd C., boulanger, (âgé de) 23 ans, se trouvait sur le banc des accusés. « Je ne sais comment tout cela s'est passé », dit-il, « je ne me souviens plus de rien (m. à m. : je ne peux plus me souvenir), car j'étais passablement ivre! »
Le jury d'Oldesloe a prononcé la sentence (suivante) : une amende de 450 marks! Et dans un délai de quatre semaines, le jeune boulanger doit adhérer à une association sportive et faire connaître au tribunal le sport qu'il a choisi! On comprit les intentions du juge à l'exposé des motifs du jugement : (m. à m. : ce que le juge a pensé alors, devint reconnaissable...)
« Grâce au sport — nous l'espérons — vous vous corrigerez de l'habitude de boire. Sur le stade, vous vous sentirez très vite plus à l'aise (m. à m. : mieux) qu'au bistrot ».

Leçon

74

Was lesen Sie gerne?

1 Mein Beruf erlaubt es mir nicht, der Lektüre so viel Zeit zu widmen, wie ich es gerne täte. Wenn ich einen freien Augenblick habe, blättere ich in einer Zeitschrift oder in einer Illustrierten. Genau wie die Kinder schaue ich mir zuerst die Bilder an. Manche Reportagen sind recht gut abgefaßt. Manche Zeitungsartikel sind sogar ziemlich objektiv. Aber die Presse befaßt sich fast ausschließlich mit dem Zeitgeschehen.

2 Was die Romane und die Erzählungen anbetrifft, so lasse ich mich gerne vom Leitfaden einer Geschichte führen, auch wenn die Charaktere konventionell und willkürlich sind. Ich stelle mir nämlich vor, daß das Zuspitzen der Handlung und die Lösung des Knotens, die vom Verfasser ersonnen wurden, anders sein könnten. Jedoch lasse ich mich gerne vom Dichter und seinem Stil verleiten. Wie oft bemächtigen sie sich meiner!

3 Ich habe die Kl**a**ssiker lieber als die Rom**a**ntiker. Ich bin eher klassisch als romantisch veranlagt. Viele neuere und sogar moderne Werke scheinen mir überholt zu sein. Es kommt auch vor, daß ich meine Ansicht ändere, daß ich das, was ich gestern anbetete, gleichsam verbrenne.

4 Dagegen bin ich ein immer größerer Liebhaber der Geschichte. Es ist schwierig, die Ereignisse aus dem Altertum und aus dem Mittelalter wieder vor die Augen zu führen. Doch ist es ein spannendes Studium. Die namhaftesten Helden bleiben uns vielleicht fremd.
Ich habe auch eine kleine Schwäche für Reiseberichte. Ich kann mehrere Sprachen lesen, brauche aber ein Wörterbuch dazu.

JEDEM NARREN GEFÄLLT SEINE KAPPE

Traduction

Qu'aimez-vous lire?

1 – Mon métier ne me permet pas de consacrer à la lecture autant de temps que je le voudrais. Lorsque j'ai une minute (m. à m. : un moment libre), je feuillette une revue ou un illustré. Tout comme les enfants, je regarde d'abord les images. Certains reportages sont fort bien rédigés. Certains articles de journaux sont même assez objectifs. Mais la presse ne s'intéresse (m. à m. : ne s'occupe... de) guère qu'à l'actualité.

2 Pour ce qui est des romans et des récits, j'aime me laisser guider par le fil (conducteur) d'une histoire, même si les caractères sont conventionnels ou arbitraires. Je me représente, en effet, que l'action et le dénouement imaginés par leur auteur pourraient être différents. Mais je me laisse volontiers séduire par l'auteur (m. à m. : poète) et par son style. Que de fois ils me captivent (m. à m. : s'emparent de moi)!

3 – Je préfère les classiques aux romantiques. Je suis (m. à m. : de don) classique plutôt que romantique. Beaucoup d'œuvres plus récentes et même modernes me semblent dépassées. Il m'arrive aussi de changer d'idée, pour ainsi dire de brûler ce que j'ai adoré hier.

4 Par contre j'aime de plus en plus l'histoire (m. à m. : je suis un amateur toujours plus grand...). Il est difficile de retracer les événements de l'Antiquité et du Moyen âge. Pourtant, c'est là une étude passionnante. Les héros les plus considérables nous restent peut-être inconnus.
J'ai un faible pour les récits de voyages. Je peux lire dans plusieurs langues, mais il me faut un dictionnaire (m. à m. : pour cela).

Vocabulaire

der Be**r**icht (e), *le rapport*
der Chara**k**ter (e), *le caractère*
der Held (en), *le héros*
die Aktualit**ä**t (en), *l'actualité*
das Altertum (⸚ er), *l'antiquité*

Chaque fou a sa marotte (m. à m. : A chaque fou plaît sa coiffe).

das Bild (-er), *l'image*
das Ereignis (se), *l'événement*
das Märchen (-), *le conte*
der Klassiker (-), *le classique*
der Leitfaden (⁼̈), *le fil conducteur*
der Romantiker (-), *le romantique*
der Stil (e), *le style*
der Verfasser (-), *l'auteur*
die Erzählung (-en), *le récit*
die Handlung (-en), *l'action*
die Illustrierte (n), *l'illustré*
die Presse, *la presse*
die Reportage (n), *le reportage*
die Schwäche (n), *la faiblesse, le faible*
das Mittelalter, *le Moyen âge*
das Werk (e), *l'œuvre*
das Wörterbuch (⁼̈ er), *le dictionnaire*
abfassen, *rédiger*
anbelangen, *concerner*
anbeten, *adorer*
sich befassen mit, *s'occuper de*
überholen, *dépasser*
veranlagen, *douer*
verleiten, *séduire*
ersinnen (a, o), *imaginer*
verbrennen (mixte), *brûler*
vorkommen (a, o), *arriver, se passer*

Grammaire

■ Wie oft bemächtigen sie sich meiner!

Le verbe *sich bemächtigen* se construit avec le génitif (*meiner,* de moi). Les verbes gouvernant le génitif ne sont guère nombreux et s'emploient peu dans la langue parlée. En voici quelques-uns :

bedürfen, avoir besoin de (a)
berauben, dépouiller de
sich bedienen, se servir de (b)
sich erbarmen, avoir pitié de (c)
sich erinnern, se souvenir de (d)
sich erfreuen, jouir de
gedenken, se souvenir (e)
sich rühmen, se vanter de
sich schämen, avoir honte de

Er erbarmt sich des Bettlers, il a pitié du mendiant.
Sie erfreut sich einer guten Gesundheit, elle jouit d'une bonne santé.

Remarques : On emploie plus couramment a) *brauchen* (+ accus.). b) *benutzen* (+ accus.). c) *Mitleid haben (mit).* d) et e) *sich erinnern an* (+ accus.).

■ **Le pronom personnel au génitif :**

Er bedarf meiner, il a besoin de moi.
Er erinnert sich deiner, il se souvient de toi.
Ich gedenke seiner, je me souviens de lui.
— — *ihrer,* — — d'elle.
— — *seiner* (neutre), — de lui.
Bedarf er unser? A-t-il besoin de nous?
Wir erbarmen uns euer, nous avons pitié de vous.
Ich gedenke ihrer (Ihrer), je me souviens d'eux (de vous) (3e pers. du plur. et forme de politesse).

Exercices

A *Complétez, puis traduisez :*
1. Es bedarf nur ein... Wort... 2. Wer bediente sich mein... neu... Wagen...? 3. Sie gedenkt gern jen... still... Stunden. 4. Oft rühmt er sich sein... Reichtum... 5. Das Geschäft erfreut sich ein... gut... Ruf... 6. Er schämt sich nicht einmal sein... bös... Handlung.

B *Traduisez :*
7. Je voudrais un dictionnaire allemand-français. 8. Pourriez-vous m'indiquer un bon roman en langue allemande? 9. Voici un ouvrage très intéressant sur l'histoire de notre ville. 10. Quels hebdomadaires pourriez-vous me recommander? 11. En Allemagne, je lis souvent *Die Zeit* et *Rheinischer Merkur*; en Suisse, *Die Weltwoche.* 12. Je vais aussi m'abonner à ce quotidien; c'est une excellente façon d'apprendre la langue.

Corrigé :

A 1. eines Wortes. *Il suffit de (dire) un mot.* 2. meines neuen Wagens. *Qui s'est servi de ma voiture neuve?* 3. jener stillen Stunden. *Elle aime à se souvenir de ces heures paisibles.* 4. seines Reichtums. *Souvent, il tire vanité de sa fortune.* 5. eines guten Ruf(e)s. *L'affaire jouit d'une bonne réputation.* 6. seiner bösen Handlung. *Il n'a même pas honte de sa mauvaise action.*

B 7. Ich möchte ein deutsch-französisches Wörterbuch. 8. Könnten Sie mir einen guten Roman in deutscher Sprache angeben? 9. Hier ist ein sehr interessantes Buch über die Geschichte unserer Stadt. 10. Was für Wochenzeitungen könnten Sie mir empfehlen? 11. In Deutschland lese ich oft « Die Zeit » und den « Rheinischen Merkur »; in der Schweiz, « Die Weltwoche ». 12. Ich will auch diese Tageszeitung abonnieren; es ist eine vortreffliche Art, die Sprache zu erlernen.

Leçon

75

Was sehen Sie gerne? Was hören Sie gerne?

1 — Ich bewundere die mittelalterliche Baukunst, sei es die romanische oder die gotische. Ich kann mich nicht satt sehen an den Kirchen und Domen in Europa, die Gottes Größe verherrlichen.
Haben Sie den Stephansdom zu Wien bei schönem Wetter gesehen? Seine Fenster und Bildsäulen, seine Portale und Bildwerke, sein wunderbares Hauptschiff und sein himmelstrebender Turm verbinden mehrere Stile zu einer harmonischen Einheit.

2 — In der Malerei schwärme ich für die Werke aus dem XV. Jh. Die Primitiven verlocken mich durch ihre Freimütigkeit und ihre Verfeinerung.
— Verstehen Sie etwas von abstrakter Kunst? Ich werde nicht klug daraus.
— Aber, mein Lieber, warum soll denn der Maler die Wirklichkeit nachbilden? Der Photograph, der über eine gute Kamera, einen guten Film verfügt, ist viel genauer.

3 — Seitdem ich einen Fernsehapparat habe, gehe ich weder ins Kino, noch ins Konzert. Es werden ausgezeichnete Filme gegeben und viele Sinfoniekonzerte übertragen. Zudem habe ich einen Plattenspieler, um mir die Musik anzuhören, die mir gefällt.
— Vielleicht haben Sie doch nicht recht. Gestern z. B. (zum Beispiel) haben Sie den Liederàbend der Wiener Sängerknaben versäumt. Es war einfach großartig. Und außerdem, meine Liebe, werden alle Ihre Apparate niemals das Vergnügen ersetzen, Musik selbst zu spielen.

WAS LANGE WÄHRT, WIRD GUT

Traduction

Qu'aimez-vous voir? Qu'aimez-vous entendre?

1 — J'admire l'architecture médiévale, qu'elle soit romane ou gothique. Je ne me lasse pas (m. à m. : je ne peux pas me rassasier) de voir les églises et les cathédrales d'Europe qui illustrent la grandeur de Dieu.
Avez-vous vu par beau temps la cathédrale Saint-Étienne, à Vienne? Ses vitraux et statues, ses portails et sculptures, sa merveilleuse nef principale et sa tour qui s'élance vers les cieux, combinent plusieurs styles pour en faire une unité harmonieuse.

2 — En peinture, j'ai un fort penchant pour le xve siècle. Les primitifs me séduisent par leur sincérité et leur raffinement.
— Vous comprenez quelque chose à l'art abstrait, vous? Moi, je n'y comprends rien.
— Mais, mon cher, pourquoi voulez-vous que le peintre imite le réel? Le photographe, disposant d'un bon appareil, d'une bonne pellicule, est beaucoup plus exact.

3 — Depuis que j'ai la télévision, je ne vais ni au cinéma, ni au concert. On donne d'excellents films et beaucoup de concerts symphoniques sont retransmis. Et puis, j'ai un électrophone pour écouter la musique qui me plaît.
— Vous n'avez peut-être pas raison. Hier par exemple, vous avez manqué le récital (m. à m. : soirée de chants) des Petits Chanteurs de Vienne. C'était tout simplement magnifique. Et d'ailleurs, ma chère, tous vos appareils ne remplaceront jamais le plaisir de faire soi-même de la musique.

Vocabulaire

der Bau (e), *la construction*
(der) Gott (¨ er), *Dieu*
das Hauptschiff (e), *la nef principale*
das Jahrh**u**ndert (-), *le siècle*
das Leiden (-), *la souffrance*

Tout vient à point pour qui sait attendre.
(Ce qui dure longtemps, réussit).

der Maler (-), *le peintre*
der Pl**a**ttenspi**e**ler (-), *l'électrophone*
der Sänger (-), *le chanteur*
der Turm (¨ e), *la tour*
die B**i**lds**ä**ule (n), *la statue*
die Einheit (en), *l'unité*
die Kamera(s), *l'appareil photographique*
die Kunst (¨ e), *l'art*
die Maler**ei**, *la peinture*
die Mus**i**k, *la musique*
die (Schall)platte (n), *le disque*
die Seele (n), *l'âme*
das Hauptschiff (e), *la nef principale*
das Port**a**l (e), *le portail*
das Portr**ä**t (e), *le portrait*
das Werk (e), *l'œuvre*
anh**ö**ren, *écouter*
beschw**ö**ren, *évoquer*
ers**e**tzen, *remplacer*
n**a**chb**i**lden, *imiter*
streben (nach), *tendre (vers)*
verh**e**rrlichen, *magnifier*
verl**o**cken, *séduire*
vers**äu**men, *manquer, perdre*
v**o**rf**ü**hren, *représenter*
übertr**a**gen (u, a), *(re)transmettre*

Grammaire

■ Ich kann mich nicht satt sehen...

Dans cette tournure particulière à la langue allemande (germanisme), nous trouvons le verbe *sehen* à la forme réfléchie (*mich*), accompagné d'un adjectif (*satt*), qui indique le résultat vers lequel tend l'action.

Ich lache mich tot, je meurs de rire.
Du lachtest dich krumm, tu te tordais de rire.
Er aß sich nie satt, il ne mangeait jamais à satiété.
Sie hat sich fast blind geweint, elle a pleuré à en être presque aveugle.

■ ...die Gottes Größe verherrlichen.

(m. à m. : ...qui de Dieu (la) grandeur illustrent).
Remarquez ce génitif saxon (leçon 10), qui est d'un emploi courant avec les noms propres, les prénoms ou les proverbes. Autre construction : ... *die die Größe Gottes verherrlichen* (m. à m. : ... qui la grandeur de Dieu illustrent).

■ Ich bewundere... Ich betrachte...

La particule *be-*, inséparable, entre dans la formation de nombreux verbes, presque tous transitifs.

- Parfois, elle marque un renforcement du sens du verbe simple : Ex. : *decken, bedecken,* couvrir; *grüßen, begrüßen,* saluer.

● Elle sert surtout à former des verbes transitifs :

ruhig, calme; *beruhigen,* calmer
das Wasser, l'eau; *bewässern,* arroser
das Wunder, la merveille; *bewundern,* admirer
antworten + auf (+ accus.) = *beantworten* (+ acc.), répondre à

Ich antworte auf seinen Brief

ou :

Ich beantworte seinen Brief, je réponds à sa lettre.

De même : *wohnen in (einem Haus) = bewohnen,* habiter.

● Elle peut aussi modifier le sens d'un verbe : *schwören,* jurer, prêter serment; *beschwören,* évoquer.

Exercices

A *Employez des verbes avec* be-, *puis traduisez :*
1. Die Eltern machen ihren Kindern Geschenke (*cadeaux*). 2. Dieser Film macht die Zuschauer lustig. 3. Der Schnee bildet eine Decke auf dem Land. 4. Sie weint um ihr verstorbenes (*mort*) Kind. 5. Der Arzt kämpft (*lutte*) gegen die Krankheiten. 6. Ein Wald bildet die Grenze unseres Gartens.

B *Traduisez :*
7. Irez-vous au cinéma, ce soir? 8. Aimez-vous les dessins animés (der Trickfilm)? 9. Après le dîner, j'écouterai quelques disques. 10. Si nous avions la télévision, nous irions moins souvent au concert. 11. Bien qu'elle ait toutes sortes d'appareils modernes, elle aime mieux faire elle-même de la musique. 12. Que (c'est) magnifique!

Corrigé :

A 1. Die Eltern beschenken ihre Kinder. *Les parents font des cadeaux à leurs enfants.* 2. Dieser Film belustigt die Zuschauer. *Ce film amuse les spectateurs.* 3. Der Schnee bedeckt das Land. *La neige recouvre la campagne.* 4. Sie beweint ihr verstorbenes Kind. *Elle pleure son enfant mort.* 5. Der Arzt bekämpft die Krankheiten. *Le médecin combat les maladies.* 6. Ein Wald begrenzt unseren Garten. *Une forêt borne notre jardin.*

B 7. Gehen Sie heute abend ins Kino? 8. Sehen Sie gerne (die) Trickfilme? 9. Nach dem Abendessen werde ich mir einige Schallplatten anhören. 10. Wenn wir das Fernsehen hätten, gingen wir weniger oft ins Konzert. 11. Obwohl sie allerlei moderne Apparate hat, spielt sie lieber selbst Musik. 12. Wie großartig!

Leçon

76 Urlaub in Deutschland

1 Kommen Sie vom Süden her, aus Norden oder Westen...? Oder landen Sie vielleicht nach langem Flug im Herzen des Landes? Stets wird ihr erster Eindruck anders sein. Altes verbindet sich mit Neuem[1], Historie mit Gegenwart. Und genauso wechselvoll ist die Landschaft :
Im Süden sind es die Alpen, sind es die Seen und die Höhen der Schwarzwaldausläufer[2]. Im Westen beherrschen der Rhein und seine Nebenflüsse das Bild. Auch dies wechselvoll : Niederungen mit weiten Wiesen, gewaltige Industrielandschaften und Weinberge an hohen, burggekrönten[3] Ufern. Im Norden die Küste, Marschland und traditionsreiche Hafenstädte. Dahinter die Heide, die Mittelgebirge, das malerische Bild kleiner Städte und Dörfer.
So werden Sie sich als Gast nicht nur erholen. Sie werden auch Eindrücke gewinnen, die in ihrer Vielfalt sehr stark sind.

2 Abseits der großen Straßen – da ist das romantische Deutschland! Da sind Städte, Burgen und Landschaften, um die sich Sagen und Märchen ranken[4] und die bis zum heutigen Tage ihren verträumten Charakter nicht verloren haben. Hier ist die Tradition wachgeblieben[5] und läßt in farbenfrohen Festen die Vergangenheit lebendig werden. Jeder Urlaubstag bringt neue Überraschungen : Fahrten mit der Kutsche, Besuche in geheimnisvollen Tropfsteinhöhlen[6] oder Ausflüge in einsame Naturschutzgebiete.
Abseits der großen Straßen lernen Sie Deutschland kennen. Hier kann man noch auf Entdeckungsreisen gehen, stille Täler und abgelegene Badeseen kennen lernen, und ist doch immer

1. *Altes... mit Neuem :* adjectifs substantivés, déclinaison forte (Précis, n° 25).
2. *aus/laufen,* sortir; *der Ausläufer* (-), le garçon de course; le prolongement; le contrefort.
3. *krönen,* couronner vient de *die Krone* (n), la couronne. – *die Burg (-en),* le château fort; *das Schloß (¨ sser),* le château, le manoir.
4. m. à m. : entourer de leurs vrilles – *die Ranke,* la vrille, le sarment – *umranken,* grimper autour de...
5. m. à m. : ...est resté éveillée. – *wach,* éveillé; *wachen,* veiller; *wach/rufen,* évoquer.
6. *der Tropfstein (-e),* la stalactite ou la stalagmite.

Vacances en Allemagne

1 Venez-vous du Sud, du Nord ou de l'Ouest...? Ou peut-être allez-vous atterrir en plein cœur du pays après un long trajet en avion (m. à m. : vol)? Toujours, votre première impression sera différente. L'ancien et le nouveau, le passé et le présent s'entremêlent. Et le paysage est tout aussi divers :
Au Sud, ce sont les Alpes, ce sont les lacs et les collines des contreforts de la Forêt-Noire. A l'Ouest, le Rhin et ses affluents dominent le tableau. Cela aussi plein de diversité : les fonds de vallées avec de vastes prairies, les régions aux puissantes industries, les vignobles sur des rivages escarpés, couronnés de châteaux forts. Au Nord, c'est le littoral, le « Marschland » (m. à m. : contrée marécageuse) et les ports riches en traditions. Vers l'intérieur du pays, la lande, les montagnes moyennes, le tableau pittoresque des petites villes et des villages.
Ainsi, comme visiteur, vous pourrez non seulement vous détendre, vous recueillerez également des impressions très fortes dans leur variété.

2 A l'écart des grandes routes — voici l'Allemagne romantique. Voici des villes, des châteaux et des paysages autour desquels se sont accumulés légendes et contes et qui, jusque de nos jours, n'ont rien perdu de leur caractère rêveur. Ici, la tradition est restée vivante et, à travers des fêtes aux couleurs gaies, elle fait renaître le passé. Chaque jour de vacances apporte des surprises nouvelles : promenades en calèche, visites de mystérieuses grottes de stalagmites, ou bien excursions au milieu de sites solitaires et protégés.
C'est à l'écart des grandes routes que vous apprendrez à connaître l'Allemagne. Ici, l'on peut encore partir à la découverte, apprendre à connaître des vallées silencieuses, des lacs retirés

wieder behaglich aufgehoben[7] : Gutgeführte Hotels und bei[8] aller Romantik modern eingerichtete Gaststätten findet man überall. Es fehlt also nicht an den Annehmlichkeiten, auf die man heute — auch im Urlaub — nur ungern verzichtet.

3 Es ist nicht jedermanns Sache[9], Museen zu besuchen. Mancher liebt mehr die Kunst dort, wo sie sich im täglichen Leben darbietet : auf den Straßen und Plätzen, auf den Anhöhen, an den Flüssen.

In Deutschland sind sich die Kulturen Europas begegnet. Hier haben Bildschnitzer, Baumeister, Maler aus dem ganzen Abendland neben einheimischen Künstlern ihre Spuren hinterlassen. Sie werden Kirchen, Schlössern, Rathäusern, aber auch Wohnbauten, Theatern und Opernhäusern der verschiedensten Stile begegnen[10]. Strenge Gotik, überwältigende Renaissance, verspieltes Barock. Dann Dokumente aus vorchristlicher Zeit, römische Amphitheater, Reste des Limes[11] und Kirchen aus unserer Zeit, Plastiken zeitgenössischer Bildhauer in Grünanlagen, auf Plätzen oder an Brunnen.

So ist die Kunst aller Epochen in Deutschland lebendig geblieben — es wird Ihnen viel Freude machen, diese Schätze aufzustöbern.

MICHAEL SCHIFF, (Deutschland)
Deutscher Fremdenverkehrsverband, Frankfurt/Main

7. *auf/heben (o, o),* (ici) : mettre de côté, conserver : *er ist gut aufgehoben,* il est en bonnes mains, on prend soin de lui.
8. *bei* exprime ici une idée de restriction : malgré, en dépit de.
9. *jedermanns Sache :* génétif saxon (Leçon 10, n° 1 c).
10. *begegnen,* rencontrer, gouverne le datif; ses compléments, ici au datif pluriel, ont tous la terminaison *-n.* (Précis, n° 74).
11. Le « limes » était la frontière fortifiée de l'Empire romain; il s'étendait depuis Rheinbrohl, au Nord de Coblence, jusqu'à Lorch, sur le Danube.

qui invitent à la baignade, et pourtant, l'on est toujours assuré d'avoir un gîte confortable : des hôtels bien tenus et des restaurants qui, malgré tout leur romantisme, ont des installations modernes, on en trouve partout.
En somme, rien ne manque de ces commodités auxquelles aujourd'hui — même en vacances — on ne renonce pas volontiers.

3 Ce n'est pas l'affaire de tout le monde que de visiter des musées. Il en est qui aiment davantage l'art, là où il se présente dans la vie quotidienne : dans les rues et sur les places, sur les collines, au bord des rivières.
En Allemagne, les cultures européennes se sont rencontrées. Ici, sculpteurs, architectes, peintres venus de tout l'Occident ont laissé leurs empreintes, sans compter les artistes locaux. Vous trouverez des églises, des châteaux, des hôtels de ville, mais aussi des résidences, des théâtres et des opéras des styles les plus divers. Gothique sévère, Renaissance grandiose, baroque enjoué. Ensuite, des témoignages de l'époque pré-chrétienne, des amphithéâtres romains, des restes du « limes », et des églises de notre temps, des sculptures d'artistes contemporains, dans des parcs, sur des places ou près des fontaines.
Ainsi, l'art de toutes les époques est resté vivant en Allemagne — cela vous fera un grand plaisir que de dénicher ces trésors.

Leçon

77 Stadt und Land

1 Im Weinkeller[1] eines alten Rathauses funkelt der Wein im Glas. An den Wänden hängen die Bilder weitgereister Kaufleute und ehrbarer Zunftmeister, die hier einst zu Rat gesessen haben. Heute sitzen Sie hier, umgeben von[2] den Nachfahren jener Herren mit weißer Krause und goldener Kette. Draußen aber herrscht modernes Leben. Neben dem alten Rathaus ein kühner Glaspalast; dahinter der Markt, kaum anders als früher. Grobes Pflaster, farbige Schirme[3] und eine bunte Vielfalt von Fischen, von Obst, Gemüse und den frischen Beeren[4] aus Wald und Heide. Inmitten ein Brunnen, jahrhundertealt, von einer Skulptur überragt.
Und dann ein Wechsel : moderne Großstadt! Breite Straßen, die neue Oper, schnelle Verkehrsmittel und eine Atmosphäre ganz eigener Art : Internationalität. Vielleicht zeigt man gerade eine große Ausstellung. Vielleicht bildet ein künstlerisches Ereignis ersten Ranges den Anziehungspunkt für alle.

2 Viele deutsche Volkslieder singen von der Gastlichkeit. Und das mit Recht! Wer Gaumen und Magen nicht mit auf Reisen schicken möchte, wer bei seinen heimischen Gerichten bleiben will, der findet sie auch in Deutschland. Auf den Speisenkarten der großen Hotels wie im Angebot der vielen Spezialitäten-Restaurants.
Wer richtig zu reisen versteht, der will aber die Ferne auch auf der Zunge schmecken. Dazu geht man in die kleinen Gasthöfe – oft abseits der großen Straße. Man kann auch dort wohnen. Man wird überalll saubere, freundliche Zimmer finden.
Sie werden auch von den heimischen Getränken kosten[5], die nirgends so gut schmecken wie dort, wo sie zu Hause sind : Wein – und zwar nicht nur am Rhein –, Bier, klare Schnäpse, Obstbranntweine[6]. Vielleicht haben Sie diese Getränke schon in

1. *der Weinkeller* (-), m. à m. : la cave à vin, le cellier.
2. *umgeben von...* La particule *um* est ici inséparable. Ex. : *Ein Garten umgibt das Haus,* un jardin entoure la maison.
3. *der Schirm (-e),* la défense, l'abri; *der Regenschirm,* le parapluie; *der Sonnenschirm,* l'ombrelle.
4. *die Beere (n),* la baie, le grain. *Die Heidelbeere,* la myrtille; *die Himbeere,* la framboise; *die Brombeere,* la mûre; *die Erdbeere,* la fraise; *die Johannisbeere,* la groseille.
5. *kosten :* 1. coûter. 2. goûter, déguster.
6. *der Branntwein (-e),* l'eau-de-vie; *brennen (brannte, gebrannt),* brûler, distiller.

La ville et la campagne

1 Dans le caveau d'un vieil hôtel de ville, le vin scintille dans les verres. Aux murs sont accrochés les portraits de commerçants qui ont parcouru le monde, et de vénérables maîtres de corporation qui jadis, ici-même, ont assisté au conseil. Aujourd'hui, c'est vous qui êtes assis à cette même place, entouré par les descendants de ces personnages au jabot blanc et à la chaîne d'or. Mais, dehors, règne la vie moderne. Près de l'ancien hôtel de ville, un audacieux palais de verre; derrière, le marché, à peine différent de ce qu'il était autrefois. Du gros pavé, des parasols multicolores et une abondance pittoresque de poissons, de fruits, de légumes, et des baies fraîches de la forêt ou de la lande. Au centre, une fontaine vieille de plusieurs siècles, surmontée d'une sculpture.
Et puis, un changement : la grande cité moderne! Les rues larges, le nouvel opéra, les moyens de transport rapides et une atmosphère tout à fait particulière : l'atmosphère internationale. Peut-être présente-t-on justement une grande exposition. C'est peut-être un événement artistique de premier ordre qui constitue pour tout le monde le centre d'attraction.

2 De nombreuses chansons populaires allemandes célèbrent l'hospitalité. Et ceci avec juste raison! Celui qui ne désire pas faire participer palais et estomac à ses voyages, celui qui veut s'en tenir aux plats de chez lui, il les trouvera en Allemagne également. Sur les menus des grands hôtels; comme dans les suggestions des nombreux restaurants à spécialités.
Mais qui s'y entend en voyages, voudra goûter aussi le dépaysement sur sa langue. A cet effet, on va dans les petites auberges — souvent à l'écart de la grand'route. On peut aussi y loger. On trouvera partout des chambres nettes et accueillantes.
Vous goûterez également les boissons locales qui nulle part n'ont autant de saveur que là où elles sont chez elles : le vin et cela pas seulement sur le Rhin —, la bière, les alcools limpides, les eaux-de-vie de fruits. Vous avez peut-être déjà goûté ces boissons

Ihrer Heimat probiert – gewiß aber nicht die Speisen. Die vielfältigen Gemüse, dit Fischgerichte... und nicht zuletzt die mächtigen Braten mit großen runden Knödeln[7] oder die Würstchen, eigenartig gewürzt und mit ungewohnten Beigaben versehen.

3 Die schönsten Feste, die man hierzulande feiert, stehen kaum im Kalender. Ihr Dasein, ihre Kraft und ihre jährliche Wiederkehr verdanken sie der Tradition. Hier ist es jener Brauch, dort ein anderer. Jede Stadt – ja jedes Dorf – hat seine eigenen überlieferten Feste. Alte Masken und Trachten, geheimnisvolle Tänze und seltsame Klänge aus sonst kaum bekannten Instrumenten.
Man begrüßt den Frühling oder vertreibt den Winter. In bunten Umzügen feiert man Ernte und Weinlese, begrüßt Märzenbier und Maibock, begeht[8] die Feste der Fischer und Holzfäller, der Almhirten[9] und Jäger.

4 Entfernungen sagen heute gar nichts. Kilometer und Meile können lang und kurz sein. Entscheidend ist die Qualität der Verkehrswege. Die Deutsche Bundesbahn ist für ihre Pünktlichkeit bekannt. Schnell sind viele deutsche Straßen, voran die Autobahnen, deren Netz ständig wächst. Gemächlicher sind die Reisen mit den Fluß- und Seeschiffen. Zahlreiche Busse erschließen jene Gebiete, in die kein Schienenstrang[10] führt. So gibt es keinen Winkel dieses Landes, den Sie nicht erreichen könnten.

MICHAEL SCHIFF, (Deutschland)
Deutscher Fremdenverkehrsverband, Frankfurt/Main

7. *der Knödel (-),* la boulette, la quenelle; *Leberknödel,* quenelles de foie.
8. *ein Fest begehen,* célébrer une fête. Autres sens de *begehen :* 1. passer sur, parcourir. 2. commettre : *Er hat einen Fehler begangen,* il a commis une faute.
9. *der Hirt (en),* le pâtre; *die Alm (en),* le pâturage alpestre.
10. *der Strang (¨ e),* la corde, la voie – *die Schiene (n),* le rail.

chez vous — mais sûrement pas les mets. Les nombreuses variétés de légumes, les plats de poissons... et — ce ne sont pas les derniers de la liste (m. à m. : non en dernier) — les rôtis imposants (servis) avec de grandes quenelles rondes, ou les saucisses épicées d'une manière particulière, accompagnées de garnitures inhabituelles.

3 Les plus belles fêtes que l'on célèbre dans ce pays sont à peine mentionnées sur le calendrier. Leur existence, leur vigueur et leur retour annuel, elles le doivent à la tradition. Ici, c'est telle coutume, là, c'est telle autre. Chaque ville — chaque village même — a ses fêtes propres, traditionnelles. Masques et costumes anciens, danses au caractère mystérieux et airs étranges, joués sur des instruments à peine connus ailleurs.
On salue le printemps ou bien l'on déloge l'hiver. En cortèges aux vives couleurs, on célèbre la moisson ou les vendanges, on salue la bière de mars ou le bock de mai, on fête les pêcheurs et les bûcherons, les pâtres des montagnes et les chasseurs.

4 Les distances aujourd'hui ne signifient rien du tout. Les kilomètres et les lieues peuvent être longs et courts. Ce qui est décisif, c'est la qualité des voies de communication. Les chemins de fer Fédéraux sont connus pour leur exactitude. Beaucoup de routes allemandes permettent de faire de la vitesse (m. à m. : sont rapides) — en tête, les autoroutes, dont le réseau s'étend constamment. Les voyages en bateau sur les fleuves et les lacs présentent, eux, plus de confort. De nombreux autobus permettent l'accès de ces régions où aucune voie ferrée ne pénètre. Ainsi, il n'y a pas un seul endroit (m. à m. : coin) de ce pays, que vous ne puissiez atteindre.

78 Der Gevatter Tod

Es[1] hatte ein armer Mann zwölf Kinder und mußte Tag und Nacht arbeiten, damit er ihnen nur Brot geben konnte. Als nun das dreizehnte zur Welt kam, wußte er sich in seiner Not nicht zu helfen, lief hinaus auf die große Landstraße und wollte den ersten, der ihm begegnete, zu Gevatter[2] bitten. Der erste, der ihm begegnete, das war der liebe Gott; der wußte schon, was er auf dem Herzen hatte, und sprach zu ihm :
— Armer Mann, du dauerst mich, ich will dein Kind aus der Taufe heben, will für es sorgen und es glücklich machen auf Erden.
Der Mann sprach :
— Wer bist du?
— Ich bin der liebe Gott.
— So begehr ich dich nicht zum Gevatter, sagte der Mann, du gibst den Reichen und lässest den Armen hungern.
Das sprach der Mann, weil er nicht wußte, wie weislich Gott Reichtum und Armut verteilt. Also wendete[3] er sich von dem Herrn und ging weiter. Da trat der Teufel zu ihm und sprach :
— Was suchst du? Willst du mich zum Paten deines Kindes nehmen, so will ich ihm Gold die Hülle und Fülle[4] und alle Lust der Welt dazu geben.
Der Mann fragte :
— Wer bist du?
— Ich bin der Teufel.
— So begehr ich dich nicht zum Gevatter, sprach der Mann, du betrügst und verführst die Menschen.
Er ging weiter, da kam der dürrbeinige Tod auf ihn zugeschritten und sprach :

1. *Es,* sujet apparent de *hatte* ne se traduit pas. C'est une tournure fréquente. Ex. : *Es glaubten alle, daß...* tous croyaient que... (Leçon 17).
2. *der Gevatter* (-), le parrain. Termes plus fréquents : *der Taufzeuge (n, n)* (m. à m. : le témoin au baptême), ou : *der Pate (n, n); die Patin (nen),* la marraine.
3. Notez le prétérit régulier de *wenden*. On dit également : *wandte* (voir leçon 44, remarque 3).
4. *die Hülle und Fülle,* ou *in Hülle und Fülle,* en abondance, à foison. L'allemand a une prédilection pour ces expressions binaires. Nous trouvons plus loin : *weit und breit,* partout à la ronde.

La Mort marraine

Un pauvre homme avait douze enfants et il devait travailler jour et nuit afin de pouvoir leur procurer seulement du pain! Or, quand le treizième vint au monde il ne sut, dans sa détresse, comment se tirer d'affaire (m. à m. : s'aider); il sortit en courant sur la grand'route dans l'intention de prier le premier qui le croiserait d'être le parrain. Le premier à le croiser, ce fut le bon Dieu, qui savait déjà ce qu'il avait sur le cœur et lui dit :
– Pauvre homme, tu me fais de la peine; je veux bien tenir ton enfant sur les fonts baptismaux, je veux bien prendre soin de lui et le rendre heureux sur terre.
L'homme dit :
– Qui es-tu?
– Je suis le bon Dieu.
– Alors, je ne veux pas de toi pour parrain, dit l'homme, tu donnes aux riches et tu laisses le pauvre souffrir de la faim. L'homme disait cela, parce qu'il ne savait pas combien sagement Dieu répartit la richesse et la pauvreté. Ainsi donc, il se détourna du Seigneur et continua son chemin. Alors, le diable s'approcha de lui et dit :
– Que cherches-tu? Si tu veux bien de moi pour parrain de ton enfant, je lui prodiguerai de l'or en abondance et en plus tous les plaisirs de ce monde.
L'homme demanda :
– Qui es-tu?
– Je suis le diable.
– Dans ce cas, je ne veux pas de toi pour parrain, dit l'homme, tu trompes et tu pervertis les hommes.
Il continua son chemin, lorsqu'il vit venir à lui la Mort aux jambes décharnées; elle lui dit :

— Nimm mich zu Gevatter.
Der Mann fragte :
— Wer bist du?
— Ich bin der Tod, der alle gleich macht. Da sprach der Mann :
— Du bist der Rechte, du holst den Reichen wie den Armen ohne Unterschied, du sollst mein Gevattersmann sein.
Der Tod antwortete :
— Ich will dein Kind reich und berühmt machen, denn wer mich zum Freunde hat, dem kann's nicht fehlen.
Der Mann sprach :
— Künftigen Sonntag ist die Taufe, da stelle dich zur rechten Zeit ein.
Der Tod erschien, wie er versprochen hatte, und stand ganz ordentlich Gevatter.
Als der Knabe zu Jahren gekommen war, trat zu einer Zeit der Pate ein und hieß ihn mitgehen. Er führte ihn hinaus in den Wald, zeigte ihm ein Kraut, das da wuchs, und sprach :
— Jetzt sollst[5] du dein Patengeschenk empfangen. Ich mache dich zu einem berühmten Arzt. Wenn du zu einem Kranken gerufen wirst, so will ich dir jedesmal erscheinen. Steh ich zu Häupten des Kranken, so kannst du keck sprechen, du wolltest ihn wieder gesund machen, und gibst du ihm dann von jenem Kraut ein, so wird er genesen. Steh ich aber zu Füßen des Kranken, so ist er mein, und du mußt sagen, alle Hilfe sei[6] umsonst und kein Arzt in der Welt könne[6] ihn retten. Aber hüte dich, daß du das Kraut nicht gegen meinen Willen gebrauchst, es könnte dir schlimm ergehen.
Es dauerte nicht lange, so war der Jüngling der berühmteste Arzt auf der ganzen Welt. « Er braucht nur den Kranken anzusehen, so weiß er schon, wie es steht, ob er wieder gesund wird oder ob er sterben muß », so hieß es von ihm. Weit und breit kamen die Leute herbei, holten ihn zu den Kranken und gaben ihm so viel Gold, daß er bald ein reicher Mann war. Nun trug es sich zu, daß der Konig erkrankte; der Arzt ward[7] berufen und sollte sagen, ob Genesung möglich wäre. Wie er aber zu dem Bette trat, so stand der Tod zu den Füßen des Kranken, und da war für ihn kein Kraut mehr gewachsen.

(Fortsetzung folgt)

5. *Sollen* est employé ici comme auxiliaire du futur, avec une nuance d'impératif. Nous le trouvons dans le même sens un peu plus haut : Sois le parrain, ou : tu seras le parrain (Mémento n° 51).
6. Ces deux verbes sont au subjonctif (voyez le style indirect, Mémento n° 73).
7. *ward* est une forme ancienne du prétérit de *werden;* on dit aujourd'hui : *er wurde,* il devint, il fut (Mémento n° 45).

— Prends-moi pour marraine.
L'homme lui demanda :
— Qui es-tu?
— Je suis la Mort, qui rend tous égaux.
Alors, l'homme lui dit :
— Toi, tu es équitable, tu viens chercher le riche tout comme le pauvre, sans distinction; sois la marraine (de mon enfant).
La Mort répondit :
— Je rendrai ton enfant riche et illustre, car celui qui a mon amitié ne manquera de rien (m. à m. : ... qui m'a comme amie, à celui il ne peut manquer).
L'homme dit :
— Dimanche prochain, ce sera le baptême; tâche de venir à temps!
La mort apparut comme elle l'avait promis et elle remplit très bien son rôle de marraine (m. à m. : et se tenait tout à fait convenablement comme marraine).
Quand l'enfant fut devenu grand, sa marraine se présenta et lui dit de le suivre. Elle le conduisit dans la forêt, lui montra une herbe qui y poussait, et dit :
— Maintenant, tu recevras ton cadeau de baptême. Je ferai de toi un médecin célèbre. Chaque fois que tu seras appelé chez un malade, je t'apparaîtrai. Lorsque je me tiendrai à la tête du malade, tu pourras dire hardiment que tu le guériras; et si tu lui fais prendre cette herbe (comme remède), il recouvrera la santé. Mais lorsque je me tiendrai aux pieds du malade, celui-ci m'appartiendra, et tu devras dire que tous les soins seront inutiles et qu'aucun médecin au monde ne pourra le sauver. Mais prends garde de te servir de cette herbe contre ma volonté; il pourrait t'arriver malheur (m. à m. : cela pourrait aller mal pour toi).
Le jeune homme ne tarda pas (m. à m. : cela ne dura pas longtemps) à devenir le médecin le plus célèbre du monde entier. « Il n'a qu'à regarder le malade pour savoir aussitôt ce qu'il en est, s'il se rétablira ou s'il doit mourir », voilà ce qu'on disait de lui. De partout les gens arrivaient, le faisaient venir chez les malades et lui donnaient tant d'or qu'il fut bientôt un homme riche. Or, il advint que le roi tomba malade; on appela le médecin et il devait se prononcer sur la possibilité d'une guérison (m. à m. : si la guérison était possible). Mais comme il s'approcha du lit, la Mort se tenait aux pieds du malade, et plus aucune herbe ne pouvait le sauver (m. à m. : n'avait poussé pour lui).

(à suivre)

Leçon

79 Der Gevatter Tod

(Forsetzung und Schluß)

Wenn ich doch einmal den Tod überlisten könnte, dachte der Arzt, er wird's freilich übelnehmen, aber da[1] ich sein bin, so drückt er wohl ein Auge zu : ich will's wagen. Er faßte also den Kranken und legte ihn verkehrt, so daß der Tod zu Häupten desselben[2] zu stehen kam. Dann gab er ihm von dem Kraute ein, und der König erholte sich und ward wieder gesund. Der Tod aber kam zu dem Arzte, machte ein böses Gesicht, drohte mit dem Finger und sagte :

– Du hast mich hinter das Licht geführt. Diesmal will ich dir's nachsehen, weil du mein Patenkind bist; aber wagst du das noch einmal, so geht dir's an den Kragen, und ich nehme dich selbst mit fort.

Bald hernach verfiel die Tochter des Königs in eine schwere Krankheit. Sie war sein einziges Kind, und er weinte Tag und Nacht, daß ihm die Augen erblindeten. Er ließ bekanntmachen, wer sie vom Tode errettete, der sollte ihr Gemahl werden und die Krone erben. Der Arzt, als er zu dem Bett der Kranken kam, erblickte den Tod zu ihren Füßen. Er hätte sich der Warnung seines Paten erinnern sollen, aber die große Schönheit der Königstochter und das Glück, ihr Gemahl zu werden, betörten ihn so, daß er alle Gedanken in den Wind schlug[3]. Er sah nicht, daß der Tod ihm zornige Blicke zuwarf, die Hand in die Höhe hob und mit der dürren Faust drohte; et hob die Kranke auf und legte ihr Haupt dahin, wo die Füße gelegen hatten. Dann gab er ihr das Kraut ein, und alsbald röteten sich ihre Wangen, und das Leben regte sich von neuem.

Der Tod, als er sich zum zweitenmal um sein Eigentum betrogen sah, ging mit langen Schritten auf den Arzt zu und sprach :

– Es ist aus mit dir, und die Reihe kommt nun an dich,

packte ihn mit seiner eiskalten Hand so hart, daß er nicht widerstehen[4] konnte, und führte ihn in eine unterirdische Höhle. Da sah

1. *Da,* avec rejet du verbe signifie puisque, comme (Leçon 57).
2. *desselben,* génitif de *derselbe,* le même; ce pronom se décline comme *der gute* (précis, n° 24) mais s'écrit en un seul mot. Fém. : *dieselbe;* ntre : *dasselbe.*
3. *etwas in den Wind schlagen,* jeter au vent, ne tenir aucun compte de quelque chose.
4. *widerstehen,* résister, *wider,* contre, opposé à, anti... ne doit pas être confondu avec *wieder,* de nouveau.

La mort marraine *(suite)*

Si seulement je pouvais pour une fois duper la mort, pensa le médecin; certes, elle le prendra en mauvaise partie, mais comme je suis son filleul, elle fera semblant de ne pas voir (m. à m. : fermera un œil) : je vais m'y hasarder. Il saisit donc le malade et le retourna (m. à m. : le coucha à l'envers) de sorte que la Mort se trouvât placée du côté de sa tête. Ensuite il lui fit prendre de cette herbe, et le roi se rétablit et recouvra la santé. Mais la Mort vint chez le médecin, prit un air fâché, menaça du doigt et dit :

— Tu m'as dupé (m. à m. : mené derrière la lumière). Pour cette fois, je veux bien te le pardonner parce que tu es mon filleul, mais si tu t'y hasardes encore, c'en est fait de toi (m. à m. : cela ira à ton col), et c'est toi-même que j'enlèverai.

A quelque temps de là, la fille du roi tomba gravement malade. Elle était son unique enfant et il pleurait nuit et jour, à en devenir aveugle. Il fit publier que celui qui la guérirait, deviendrait son époux et qu'il hériterait de la couronne. Quand le médecin s'approcha du lit de la malade, il vit la Mort se tenir à ses pieds. Il aurait dû se souvenir de l'avertissement de sa marraine, mais la grande beauté de la princesse et la chance de devenir son époux le fascinaient tellement qu'il écarta toute réflexion. Il ne vit pas que la Mort lui lançait des regards courroucés, qu'elle levait la main et le menaçait de son poing décharné; il souleva la malade et lui mit la tête à l'endroit où ses pieds avaient reposé. Puis il donna de cette herbe et bientôt, ses joues reprirent couleur (m. à m. : rougirent) et la vie s'éveilla de nouveau (en elle).

Quand la Mort se vit frustrée de son bien pour la deuxième fois, elle se rendit à grands pas chez le médecin et dit :

— C'en est fait de toi; maintenant, ton tour est arrivé.

Elle le saisit si rudement de sa main glacée qu'il ne put résister et elle le conduisit dans une caverne (m. à m. : sous terre). Là, il vit

er, wie tausend und tausend Lichter in unübersehbaren Reihen brannten, einige groß, andere halbgroß, andere klein. Jeden Augenblick verloschen einige, und andere brannten wieder auf, also daß die Flämmchen[5] in beständigem Wechsel hin und her zu hüpfen schienen.
— Siehst du, sprach der Tod, das sind die Lebenslichter der Menschen. Die großen gehören Kindern, die halbgroßen Eheleuten in ihren besten Jahren, die kleinen gehören Greisen. Doch auch Kinder und junge Leute haben oft nur ein kleines Lichtchen.
— Zeige mir mein Lebenslicht, sagte der Arzt und meinte, es wäre noch recht groß.
Der Tod deutete auf ein kleines Endchen, das eben auszugehen drohte, und sagte :
— Siehst du, da ist es.
— Ach, lieber Pate, sagte der erschrockene Arzt, zündet[6] mir ein neues an, tut[6] mir's zuliebe, damit ich mein Leben genießen kann, König werde und Gemahl der schönen Königstochter.
— Ich kann nicht, antwortete der Tod, erst muß eins verlöschen, ehe ein neues anbrennt.
— So setzt das alte auf ein neues, das gleich fortbrennt, wenn jenes zu Ende ist, bat der Arzt.
Der Tod stellte sich, als ob er seinen Wunsch erfüllen wollte und holte ein frisches Licht herbei. Aber da er sich rächen wollte, versah er's beim Umstecken absichtlich, und das Stückchen fiel um und verlosch. Alsbald sank der Arzt zu Boden und war nun selbst in die Hand des Todes geraten.

Brüder GRIMM

5. *die Flamme,* la flamme; *das Flämmchen* (-), la petite flamme. Nous trouvons plus loin d'autres diminutifs : *das Lichtchen,* la petite lumière; *das Endchen,* le petit bout; *das Stückchen,* le petit morceau (voir leçon 28).
6. La 2e pers. du pluriel comme forme de politesse est un usage ancien et poétique, qui se rapproche du français. On dit aujourd'hui : *zünden Sie... an, tun Sie...*

brûler des milliers de torches en rangées qui s'étendaient à perte de vue, quelques-unes grandes, d'autres moyennes, d'autres petites. A chaque instant il s'en éteignait quelques-unes, et d'autres par contre s'allumaient, de sorte que les flammes paraissaient sautiller, de-ci de-là, en un changement perpétuel.

— Tu vois, dit la Mort, ce sont les lumières de vie des hommes. Les grandes sont celles des enfants, les moyennes celles des époux dans la fleur de l'âge, les petites celles des vieillards. Cependant, les enfants et les jeunes gens n'ont souvent, eux aussi, qu'une toute petite lumière.

— Montre-moi ma lumière de vie, dit le médecin, pensant qu'elle devait être bien grande encore.

La Mort lui montra un tout petit bout (de torche), qui menaçait justement de s'éteindre, et dit :

— Tu vois, elle est là.

— Ah, chère marraine, dit le médecin épouvanté, allumez-m'en une nouvelle, faites-le par amitié pour moi, afin que je puisse jouir de ma vie, devenir roi et époux de la belle princesse.

— Je ne peux pas, répondit la mort, il faut d'abord que l'une s'éteigne avant qu'une autre s'allume.

— Placez donc l'ancienne sur une nouvelle qui continuera à brûler aussitôt, quand celle-là s'éteindra, supplia le médecin.

La Mort fit semblant d'exaucer son souhait et alla chercher une torche nouvelle. Mais comme elle voulait se venger, elle se fourvoya intentionnellement en changeant (la torche) et le petit bout se renversa et s'éteignit. Aussitôt, le médecin s'affaissa et il était maintenant tombé à son tour dans la main de la Mort.

D'après les frères Grimm

Leçon

80 Ein Held, ein ganz großer Held

Dann erzählte Schuster Bombe aus seinem Leben. Seine Erzählungen übertrafen alle Berichte und Geschichten, sogar die Bilder an seinen Wänden. Dabei wußte man nicht einmal genau, ob es überhaupt die Wahrheit war, was er sagte.
Er sagte etwa[1] :
— Einmal in China, ich hatte nur mein Taschenmesser bei mir und ging gerade ganz versunken[2] durch einen Bambuswald; da, mit einmal höre ich es im Bambus knacken. Verdutzt bleibe ich stehen. Ich horche. Was war das? Ein leises Fauchen[3]! Und dann rieche ich es auch schon : der scharfe Dunst eines Raubtieres! Zum Überlegen war keine Zeit mehr, in der nächsten Sekunde war die Bestie nach einem gewaltigen Sprung vor meinen Füßen. Ein Tiger! So lang wie ein Pferd, mit Augen wie Fahrradlampen...
Tina und Kai brachten kein Wort mehr heraus, wenn Bombe mit solchen Geschichten anfing. Sie hingen mit den Augen an seinen Lippen. Manchmal hielt er zwischen den Zähnen ein halbes Dutzend Nägel, die er mit der Zeit verarbeiten mußte, aber er erzählte trotzdem, mit eigenartiger Aussprache, und das machte die Sache nur noch aufregender. Tina und Kai fürchteten dauernd, er könnte die Nägel verschlucken. Nur bei den spannendsten Stellen seiner Abenteuer vergaßen sie vor Erregung, daran zu denken. Oder er erzählte :
— Ich war noch ziemlich jung, als die Sache mit dem Haifisch passierte. Ich war über Bord gefallen. Die See ging hoch, wie mein Dach ist. Das heißt : ich war nicht eigenmächtig[4] in den Ozean gefallen, er selbst hatte mich in seinen schäumenden Schlund gerissen! Ich sage euch, der Ozean ist gierig wie das Mörderpack, das in ihm haust[5], gierig wie seine Haifische. Ich

1. *Etwa,* à peu près (synonyme de : *ungefähr*), ou : peut-être, par hasard.
2. *Versunken,* participe passé de *versinken* (a, u), (s') enfoncer, couler à fond; être absorbé.
3. *fauchen,* feuler, cracher est employé ici comme nom. De même un peu plus loin : *überlegen,* réfléchir, *das Überlegen,* la réflexion.
4. *eigenmächtig* a) autoritaire b) de sa propre autorité; *mächtig,* puissant; *eigen,* à soi, personnel, propre.
5. *hausen,* habiter (*das Haus,* la maison). Ce verbe a une nuance péjorative ou inquiétante : avoir son repaire.

Un héros, un très grand héros

Alors « Bombe », le cordonnier, racontait ses aventures (m. à m. : ... de sa vie). Ses récits l'emportaient sur tous les reportages et sur toutes les histoires, même sur les gravures de ses murs. Avec cela, on ne savait même pas exactement si ce qu'il disait était bien la vérité.

Il disait par exemple :

– Un jour, en Chine, je n'avais que mon couteau de poche sur moi et tout en rêvant je traversais une forêt de bambous, voilà que, tout à coup, j'entends un craquement dans les bambous. Je m'arrête, au comble de la surprise. Je tends l'oreille. Qu'était-ce? Un feulement, très léger! Et déjà, je perçois l'odeur : l'odeur âcre d'un félin! Je n'avais plus le temps de réfléchir, la seconde d'après, la bête féroce, après un bond prodigieux, se trouvait devant moi (m. à m. mes pieds). Un tigre! Aussi long qu'un cheval, des yeux comme des projecteurs de bicyclette... »

Tina et Kai ne pouvaient plus proférer un seul mot, quand « Bombe » entamait de telles histoires. Leurs regards étaient suspendus à ses lèvres. Parfois, il tenait entre ses dents une douzaine de pointes que peu à peu il allait utiliser dans son travail, mais il parlait quand même, avec une prononciation singulière, et cela rendait l'affaire encore plus palpitante.

Tina et Kai craignaient sans cesse qu'il n'avalât (m. à m. : qu'il pût avaler) ses pointes. Ce n'est qu'aux passages les plus passionnants de ses aventures que, dans leur excitation, ils oubliaient d'y penser. Ou bien, il racontait (l'histoire suivante) :

– J'étais encore passablement jeune quand il m'arriva l'affaire du requin. J'étais tombé par-dessus bord. La mer montait aussi haut que mon toit. A vrai dire (m. à m. : c'est-à-dire) : je n'étais pas tombé de mon chef dans l'océan, c'est lui-même qui m'avait tiré dans ses abîmes écumants. Je vous le dis : l'océan est vorace comme cette racaille d'assassins qui l'habitent, vorace comme

knallte mit dem Kopf gegen die Stahltrossen an der Reling, wurde von einer wuchtigen Woge wieder zurückgerissen, quer über das quatschnasse Deck und rücklings über die Backbordreling hinweg in die tobende See. Um mich glasgrüne Wasserwände. Ich spucke die salzige Brühe aus, kann kaum gucken, versuche zu schwimmen — und da sehe ich ihn : ein Rachen wie ein Krokodil. Zähne so groß wie Backsteine und so scharf wie Schlachtermesser. Ein Haifisch! Mich überlief eine Gänsehaut so dick wie Kopfsteinpflaster[6]. In diesem Augenblick...

Und in solchem Augenblick brachte Bombe es fertig[7], mit seiner Geschichte aufzuhören und zu sagen :

— So, Kai, jetzt ist dein Schuh wieder heil und hält mindestens noch zwei Jahre.

— Und wie ging's weiter? riefen die Kinder atemlos[8], wie ging die Geschichte weiter?

Meistens schüttelte Bombe daraufhin seinen kurzgeschorenen, grauen Kopf, starrte trübselig durch sein viel zu kleines Fenster in Regen oder Nebel und sagte traurig :

— Laßt nur, ich möchte daran doch lieber nicht erinnert werden. Es war zu schrecklich. Es muß euch genügen, daß ihr mich hier vor euch seht.

Und da sagten sich Kai und Tina : wenn er mit Tigern und Haifischen, mit Seeräubern und Riesenschlangen, mit Menschenfressern und Heuschreckenschwärmen fertig geworden ist, muß er ein Held sein, ein ganz großer Held.

EVA RECHLIN, (Das Schiff in den Wolken)
Schwabenverlag, Stuttgart

6. *das Pflaster* (-), le pavé; *der Kopfstein,* le pavé (la pierre).
7. *fertig,* prêt, fini. *Etwas fertig-bringen,* achever quelque chose, réussir quelque chose. Nous trouvons plus loin : *fertig werden mit,* venir à bout de... *Ich werde mit ihm fertig,* j'aurai raison de lui.
8. *atemlos,* hors d'haleine, essoufflé. Le suffixe -los marque la privation : *arbeitslos,* sans travail, en chômage.

ses requins. Je me cognais la tête contre les haussières d'acier du bastingage, je fus rejeté en arrière par une puissante vague, en travers du pont mouillé et glissant, et fus projeté à la renverse par-dessus le bastingage de babord, dans la mer en furie. Autour de moi, des murs d'eau, glauques. Je crache le bouillon salé, je peux à peine voir, j'essaie de nager — et voici que je l'aperçois : une gueule comme (celle d') un crocodile. Des dents aussi grandes que des briques et aussi tranchantes que des couteaux de boucher. Un requin! J'ai la chair de poule, une chair de poule épaisse comme du pavé. A cet instant... »

Et à cet instant, « Bombe » trouvait le moyen d'arrêter son histoire et de dire : « Voilà, Kai, ta chaussure est de nouveau en bon état et tiendra encore au moins deux ans. »

« Et comment est-ce que ça continuait? » s'écriaient les enfants, le souffle coupé, « comment l'histoire continuait-elle? »

Le plus souvent, « Bombe » secouait alors sa tête grise, tondue à ras, il regardait fixement et d'un air morose par sa fenêtre beaucoup trop petite, dans la pluie ou dans le brouillard, et il disait tristement :

— Laissez donc, j'aimerais mieux qu'on ne me le rappelle plus. C'était trop horrible. Cela doit vous suffire de me voir ici, devant vous.

Et alors, Kai et Tina se disaient : s'il est venu à bout des tigres et des requins, des pirates et des boas, des cannibales et des nuages de sauterelles, alors il faut que ce soit un héros, un très grand héros.

D'après EVA RECHLIN
(Le bateau dans les nuages)

81 Die Zwillingstaufe in Köln

— Du willst nach Köln, Christian? Sieh mal[1] einer an.
— Ich will nicht. Ich muß. Leiderleider.
— Das ist aber komisch, daß du mußt. Warum fährt denn die Hedwig[2] nicht mit?
Warum? Daran hatte er offengestanden noch gar nicht gedacht. Hedwig auch nicht. Eigentlich merkwürdig, daß er daran noch nicht gedacht hatte.
— Ja, Hedwig, wenn du Lust hast?
Natürlich hat sie Lust. Zum Reisen hat man immer Lust. Es wird ganz gut gehen. Mit dem Schlafen in Köln kann man sich einrichten. Die Maria muß das Haus verwahren. Maria ist aus der Eifel[3] und erst vier Monate in Stellung; vor ein paar Tagen hat sie nachts die Haustür offen gelassen, und im Februar, als das Wasserrohr platzte, ist sie vor dem Wasserstrahl ausgerissen und auf den Söller[4] geflüchtet. Und ein bißchen vergeßlich ist sie auch — nein, eigentlich kann man ihr das Haus doch nicht anvertrauen.
So kam es, daß der Kanzleivorsteher Christian Kempenich allein nach Köln fuhr.

Die Kölner sind eigentlich beklagenswerte Leute : Sie können nicht nach Köln fahren. Sie können höchstens[5] ins Siebengebirge oder an die Mosel[6]. Aber was will das schon besagen gegen Köln? Mit diesen und ähnlichen Gedanken kam Kempenich in Köln an, wurde am Bahnhof zahlreich abgeholt und sogleich in den Schoß der Familie aufgenommen.

1. *mal,* terme familier, employé à la place de *einmal,* une fois, un jour. Souvent, il n'est pas nécessaire au sens de la phrase : *Denken Sie mal!* pensez donc!
2. ***die*** *Hedwig,* emploi familier de l'article devant un nom propre; fréquent en Allemagne du Sud.
3. l'Eifel est un massif d'altitude moyenne entre le Rhin, la Moselle et l'Ardenne.
4. *der Söller* (-), le grenier; on dit aussi, dans le même sens : *der Dachboden* (*″̲ e*), *der Boden* (*″̲*), *der Dachraum* (*″̲ e*).
5. *höchstens,* tout au plus. Rappelez-vous les degrés de *hoch,* haut : *höher,* plus haut, *der höchste, am höchsten,* le plus haut.
6. *Sie können... an die Mosel :* on sous-entend le verbe de mouvement : *fahren, gehen,* aller.

Le baptême des jumeaux à Cologne

— Tu veux aller à Cologne, Christian? Voyez-moi cela!
— Je ne veux pas. Il faut que j'y aille! Hélas, hélas!
— Mais c'est curieux que tu y sois obligé! Pourquoi Edwige ne t'accompagne-t-elle donc pas?
Pourquoi? Très franchement, il n'y avait pas du tout pensé encore. Hedwige non plus. A vrai dire, c'est curieux qu'il n'y eût pas encore pensé.
— A propos, Hedwige, si tu en as envie?
Bien sûr, elle en a envie. On a toujours envie de voyager. Cela s'arrangera très bien. Pour ce qui est de passer la nuit à Cologne, on pourra s'organiser. Il faudra que Marie garde la maison. Marie est originaire de l'Eifel et elle n'est en service que depuis quatre mois; il y a quelques jours, elle a laissé la porte de la maison ouverte, la nuit, et en février, lorsque la tuyauterie a crevé, elle s'est sauvée à toutes jambes devant l'eau qui s'échappait et s'est réfugiée au grenier. Et elle est un peu distraite aussi — non, en vérité, on ne peut pas lui confier la maison.
C'est ainsi qu'il advint que Christian Kempenich, chef de bureau, se rendit seul à Cologne.
A vrai dire, les habitants de Cologne sont à plaindre : Ils ne peuvent pas, eux, se rendre à Cologne. Ils peuvent tout au plus aller dans le Massif des Sept Montagnes ou bien au bord de la Moselle. Mais qu'est-ce que cela peut bien signifier, comparé à un voyage à Cologne? C'est en ruminant de telles pensées que Kempenich arriva à Cologne; on alla le chercher en masse à la gare et il fut aussitôt reçu dans le sein de la famille.

Er war noch nie hier gewesen. Man gab ihm einige Erklärung : Das ist der Bahnhof. Das ist der Dom. Das ist die Brücke. Das ist der Rhein. Er nahm alles gewissenhaft zur Kenntnis, fuhr dann mit der Trambahn durch endlose Straßen bis in eine Gegend, wo alle Häuser gleich aussahen, und widmete sich dort mit Inbrunst der Zwillingstaufe und den damit verbundenen Feierlichkeiten.

Feierlichkeiten bestehen in der ganzen Welt und seit Urbeginn der menschlichen Gesittung aus Essen. Kempenich fraß sich drei Tage lang tapfer durch Filetbraten und junge Erbsen, durch Kalbsbrust und Mandelpudding und Kirschkuchen und Schlagsahne und bewunderte gebührend die sichtbaren und verborgenen Schönheiten der Zwillingssäuglinge und stellte tiefgründige Ähnlichkeiten fest. Er legte sich auf die Lauer, um das erste Lächeln zu erspähen; er baumelte mit der Uhr, schnitt Gesichter und quakte wie ein Frosch, ohne irgendwelchen Eindruck auf das Zwillingspaar zu machen. Lachen taten nur die andern[7].

Der Höhepunkt des Festes aber war die Blitzlichtaufnahme[8]. Kempenich bekommt zu diesem Zwecke die Säuglinge gereicht und ordnet sie malerisch auf seinen Knien an, allerdings nicht ohne vorher aus der Brusttasche ein Wachstuch zu entfalten und sorgsam über die Knie zu breiten. Dann wird das Zimmer verdunkelt. Bitte recht freundlich! Auf dieses Stichwort hin erheben die Zwillinge ein mörderisches zweistimmiges Gebrüll. Die Lunte brennt schon. Pff! Wieder hell. Ein kleines Fräulein jammert; sie hat sich gerade ihr Strumpfband festgemacht. Weißer Staub senkt sich auf Möbel und Menschen. Man lüftet. Es zieht. Die Gemütlichkeit ist zum Teufel. Aber das Ereignis ist der Nachwelt erhalten.

HEINRICH SPOERL, (Wenn wir alle Engel wären)
R. Piper & Co Verlag, München

7. *lachen taten nur...* m. à m. : Rire, seuls les autres le faisaient. Le verbe *tun,* faire (de façon générale), se distingue de *machen,* faire, avec, à l'origine, l'idée de fabriquer.
8. *das Blitzlicht (-er),* la lumière au magnésium (photo); *der Blitz (-e),* la foudre, l'éclair.

Jamais encore il n'était venu ici. On lui donna quelques explications : voici la gare. Voici la cathédrale. Voici le pont. Voici le Rhin. Il prit scrupuleusement connaissance de tout cela; il alla ensuite, en tramway, à travers des rues interminables, pour arriver à un quartier où toutes les maisons se ressemblaient et là, il se consacra avec ferveur au baptême des jumeaux et aux cérémonies qui s'y rattachaient.
Dans le monde entier et depuis les origines de la civilisation de l'homme, les cérémonies consistent en des repas. Durant trois journées, Kempenich s'attaqua avec bravoure (m. à m. : dévora bravement) aux filets rôtis et aux petits pois, à la poitrine de veau, au pudding aux amandes, à la tarte aux cerises, à la crème fouettée, et il admira dûment les beautés visibles et les beautés cachées des petits (m. à m. : nourrissons) jumeaux, et il détecta des ressemblances profondes. Il se mit aux aguets pour épier le premier sourire; il fit pendiller sa montre, fit des grimaces, et coassa comme une grenouille, sans faire la moindre impression sur le couple de jumeaux. Seuls les autres riaient.
Mais le point culminant de la fête, ce fut la photo au flasch. A cet effet, on tend les jumeaux à Kempenich (m. à m. : il reçoit tendus...) et il les dispose de façon photogénique sur ses genoux, non sans avoir tiré auparavant, il est vrai, une toile cirée de la poche intérieure de son veston; l'ayant dépliée, il l'étend soigneusement sur ses genoux. Ensuite, on fait l'obscurité dans la pièce. Souriez, s'il vous plaît! (m. à m. : très aimables, s.v.p.). Sur ce mot d'ordre, les deux jumeaux entonnent de terribles clameurs à deux voix.
Déjà, la mèche brûle. Pfft! Voici de nouveau la lumière. Une jeune fille se lamente; elle venait justement de fixer sa jarretière.
Une poussière blanche se pose sur les meubles et sur les convives. On aère. Il y a un courant d'air. Le bien-être est au diable. Mais l'événement est conservé pour la prospérité.

D'après HEINRICH SPOERL,
(Si nous étions tous des anges)

82 Aus den Memoiren des Herrn von Schnabelewopski

Mein Vater hieß Schnabelewopski, meine Mutter hieß Schnabelewopska; als[1] beider ehelicher Sohn wurde ich geboren den ersten April 1795 zu Schnabelewops. Meine Großtante, die alte Frau von Pipitzka, pflegte meine erste Kindheit und erzählte mir viele schöne Märchen und sang mich oft in den Schlaf mit einem Liede, dessen Worte und Melodie meinem Gedächtnisse entfallen. Ich vergesse aber nie die geheimnisvolle Art, wie sie mit dem zitternden Kopfe nickte, wenn sie es sang, und wie wehmütig ihr großer einziger Zahn, der Einsiedler ihres Mundes, alsdann zum Vorschein kam[2]. Auch erinnere ich mich noch manchmal des Papageis, über dessen Tod sie oft bitterlich weinte. Die alte Großtante ist jetzt ebenfalls tot, und ich bin in der ganzen Welt wohl der einzige Mensch, der an ihren lieben Papagei noch denkt. Unsere Katze hieß Mimi, und unser Hund hieß Joli. Er hatte viel Menschenkenntnis und ging mir immer aus dem Wege[3], wenn ich zur Peitsche griff. Eines Morgens sagte unser Bedienter, der Hund trage den Schwanz etwas eingekniffen zwischen den Beinen und lasse die Zunge länger als gewöhnlich hervorhängen; und der arme Joli wurde, nebst einigen Steinen, die man ihm an den Hals festband, ins Wasser geworfen. Bei dieser Gelegenheit ertrank er. Unser Bedienter hieß Prrschtzztwitsch. Man muß dabei niesen, wenn man diesen Namen richtig aussprechen will. Unsere Magd hieß Swurtszska, welches im Deutschen etwas rauh, im Polnischen aber äußerst melodisch klingt. Es war eine dicke, untersetzte Person mit weißen Haaren und blonden Zähnen. Außerdem liefen noch zwei schöne schwarze Augen im Hause herum, welche man Seraphine nannte. Es war mein schönes herzliebes Mühmelein[4], und wir spielten zusammen im Garten und belauschten die Haushaltung der Ameisen und haschten Schmetterlinge und pflanzten Blumen. Sie lachte einst wie toll, als ich meine kleinen Strümpfchen in die Erde pflanzte,

1. *Als* signifie ici comme, en qualité de. Nous trouvons plus loin *als* dans le sens de quand, au moment où.
2. *zum Vorschein kommen,* paraître, se montrer.
3. m. à m. : il allait toujours hors de mon chemin.
4. *die Muhme (n),* peu fréquent, signifie : la tante, la cousine, la bonne femme. Les termes courants sont : *die Tante (n),* la tante; *die Kusine (n),* la cousine.

Extrait des Mémoires de Monsieur de Schnabelewopski

Mon père s'appelait Schnabelewopski, ma mère s'appelait Schnabelewopska; je suis né comme fils légitime de tous les deux, le 1er Avril 1795 à Schnabelewops. Ma grand'tante, la vieille dame de Pipitzka, eut soin de ma première enfance et me racontait nombre de beaux contes et m'endormait souvent en chantant une chanson dont les paroles et la mélodie échappent à ma mémoire. Mais je n'oublie jamais la manière mystérieuse avec laquelle elle balançait sa tête tremblotante quand elle la chantait, et avec quelle mélancolie apparaissait alors sa grande et unique dent, ermite dans le désert de sa bouche. Quelquefois encore, je me souviens aussi du perroquet dont elle pleurait souvent la mort à chaudes larmes. Ma vieille grand'tante est morte aussi, à présent, et je suis probablement le seul homme dans le monde entier qui pense encore à son cher perroquet. Notre chat s'appelait Mimi, et notre chien Joli. Celui-ci avait une grande connaissance des hommes et m'évitait toujours quand je prenais le fouet. Un matin, notre domestique dit que le chien portait la queue un peu serrée entre les jambes et laissait pendre une langue plus longue qu'à l'ordinaire; et le pauvre Joli fut jeté à l'eau, avec quelques pierres qu'on lui avait attachées au cou. Ce fut dans cette circonstance qu'il se noya. Notre domestique s'appelait Prrschtzzwitsch. Il faut éternuer, quand on veut prononcer ce nom correctement. Notre servante s'appelait Swurtszska, ce qui rend un son un peu dur en allemand, mais tout à fait mélodieux en polonais. C'était une personne forte, ramassée, avec des cheveux blancs et des dents blondes. En outre, deux beaux yeux noirs couraient par la maison; on les appelait Séraphine. C'était ma belle petite cousine chérie, et nous jouions ensemble dans le jardin et nous observions le ménage des fourmis, nous attrapions des papillons et plantions des fleurs. Elle rit un jour comme une folle, quand je plantai mes

in der Meinung, daß ein Paar große Hosen für meinen Vater daraus hervorwachsen würden.
Wie oft als Knabe versäumte ich die Schule, um auf den schönen Wiesen von Schnabelewops einsam darüber nachzudenken, wie man die ganze Menschheit beglücken könnte. Man hat mich deshalb oft einen Müßiggänger gescholten und als solchen bestraft; und für meine Weltbeglückungsgedanken mußte ich schon damals viel Leid und Not erdulden. Die Gegend um Schnabelewops ist übrigens sehr schön, es fließt dort ein Flüßchen, worin man des Sommers sehr angenehm badet, auch gibt es allerliebste Vogelnester in den Gehölzen des Ufers. Das alte Gnesen, die ehemalige Hauptstadt von Polen, ist nur drei Meilen davon entfernt. Dort im Dom ist der heilige Adalbert begraben. Dort steht sein silberner Sarkophag, und darauf liegt sein eignes Konterfei in Lebensgröße, mit Bischofsmütze und Krummstab[5], die Hände fromm gefaltet, und alles von gegossenem Silber. Wie oft muß ich deiner gedenken[6], du silberner Heiliger! Ach, wie oft schleichen meine Gedanken nach Polen zurück, und ich stehe wieder in dem Dome von Gnesen, an den Pfeiler gelehnt, bei dem Grabmal Adalberts! Dann rauscht auch wieder die Orgel, als probiere[7] der Organist ein Stück aus Allegris Miserere; in einer fernen Kapelle wird eine Messe gemurmelt; die letzten Sonnenlichter fallen durch die bunten Fensterscheiben; die Kirche ist leer; nur vor dem silbernen Grabmal des Heiligen liegt eine betende Gestalt, ein wunderholdes Frauenbild, das mir einen raschen Seitenblick zuwirft, aber ebenso rasch sich wieder gegen den Heiligen wendet und mit ihren sehnsüchtig schlauen Lippen die Worte flüstert : « Ich bete dich an. »
« Ich bete dich an. » Galten diese Worte mir oder dem silbernen Adalbert?

HEINRICH HEINE, (Ausgewählte Prosa)
Wilhelm Goldmann Verlag AG. München

5. *der Krummstab (¨ e),* la crosse, vient de *der Stab (¨ e),* le bâton, la barre et *krumm,* courbé, tordu.
6. Le verbe *gedenken,* se souvenir de, se construit avec le génitif *(deiner);* dans la langue courante, on emploie plutôt : *denken an* (+ accusatif); *sich erinnern an* (+ accusatif).
7. On doit sous-entendre ici, *als ob* ou *als wenn,* comme si, suivi du subjonctif.

petits bas dans la terre, dans la pensée, qu'il en pousserait une paire de grands pantalons pour mon père.
Combien de fois, dans mon enfance, n'ai-je pas manqué l'école, pour aller réfléchir solitairement, dans les belles prairies de Schnabelewops, aux moyens de faire le bonheur de l'humanité tout entière. Souvent on m'a traité d'oisif à cause de cela et l'on m'a puni comme tel; et à l'époque déjà, il m'a fallu endurer beaucoup de peines et de souffrances pour mes pensées de bonheur universel. Les environs de Schnabelewops sont du reste fort beaux; il y coule une petite rivière où l'on se baigne agréablement pendant l'été, il y a aussi de charmants nids d'oiseaux dans les bosquets du rivage. La vieille-ville de Gnesen, ancienne capitale de la Pologne, n'en est éloignée que de trois lieues. Là, dans la cathédrale est enterré Saint Albert. On y voit son sarcophage d'argent et dessus, son propre portrait, de grandeur naturelle, avec mitre d'évêque et crosse, les mains pieusement jointes, et le tout en argent fondu. Que de fois il me faut penser à toi, Saint d'argent! Hélas! que de fois mes pensées retournent secrètement en Pologne, et je me retrouve dans la cathédrale de Gnesen, appuyé contre le pilier, près du tombeau d'Albert! Alors, j'entends de nouveau retentir l'orgue, comme si l'organiste répétait un morceau du *miserere* d'Allegri; dans une chapelle lointaine, on murmure une messe; les dernières lueurs du soleil tombent à travers les vitraux multicolores; l'église est vide; devant le tombeau d'argent du Saint, seulement, est agenouillée une personne en prière, une ravissante figure de femme qui me jette vivement un regard oblique, mais se retourne aussi vivement vers le Saint, et de ses lèvres consumées de désir et malignes, murmure ces mots : « Je t'adore. »
« Je t'adore. » Ces mots étaient-ils pour moi ou pour l'Albert d'argent?

D'après HEINRICH HEINÉ,
(Prose choisie)

83 Ein Städtchen namens Lugano

Eigentlich wollte ich Lugano zu einer Zeit erreichen, wo Hotelportiers unangemeldete Ankömmlinge noch nicht kritisch (was treibt der sich jetzt noch herum!) oder mitleidig (alles besetzt!) mustern. Aber der Uhrzeiger hatte Mitternacht schon überschritten, als vorm[1] Scheinwerfer das Schild erschien : *à Lugano 15 km.* Mir war nicht ganz wohl. Wo würde ich unterkommen? Freilich — noch hat die Saison ja nicht begonnen. Ich hielt vor einem Hotel, das in den Prospekten unter Luxusklasse rangiert. Es ist ratsam, zu so später Nachtstunde solch ein Hotel zu betreten. Ich habe es nicht bereut.
Der freundliche Empfangschef bot mir ein Zimmer mit Bad und Seeblick und nannte auch gleich den Preis. Sehr nett von ihm; denn manch einen bringt die Frage nach dem Preis[2] in dieser Umgebung in Verlegenheit. Da aber sagte der sympathische Mensch :
— Sie können es auch billiger haben. Ich hätte da noch ein kleines Zimmer zum Hof.
Gemacht. Und dieses « kleine Zimmer zum Hof » bot die Behaglichkeit einer erstklassigen Schiffskabine, klein, aber mit allem Komfort : eingebauter Schrank, Waschnische mit fließend kaltem und warmem Wasser, im Nachttisch eingebaut ein Radio.
Der Empfangschef hatte es wirklich gut mit mir gemeint. Vom Zimmer mit Blick über'n[3] See hätte ich nicht viel gehabt : Lugano lag in dichtem Nebel — enttäuschend für einen, der aus dem nebligen Hamburg auszog, den Frühling an der Schweizer Riviera zu suchen, in Lugano, welches verspricht, 2248 Sonnenstunden im Jahr zu haben, einer der sonnenreichsten Orte Mitteleuropas zu sein. Trotzdem braucht man in diesem idyllischen Städtchen nicht zu verzagen. Wallt auch der Nebel[4] über See und Gassen, zu frösteln braucht man nicht, denn die Luft ist milde.
An so einem Tage fährt man am besten nach Castagnola zwischen Lugano und dem malerischen Gandria. Dort bietet nämlich die Pinakothek in der Villa Favorita Kunstfreunden einen seltenen

1. *vorm* est la contraction de *vor dem.*
2. *die Frage nach dem Preis,* m. à m. : la question concernant le prix. Notez l'emploi du verbe : *Ich frage* ***den*** *Kellner* ***nach*** *dem Preis,* je demande le prix au garçon.
3. *über'n,* contraction de *über den.*
4. *Wallt auch...* Remarquez la construction de cette phrase; le verbe en tête nous indique qu'il faut sous-entendre *wenn,* si, quand, que (Mémento, n° 66).

Une petite ville du nom de Lugano

A vrai dire, je voulais atteindre Lugano à une heure où les portiers d'hôtels n'examinent pas encore ceux qui arrivent sans s'être annoncés, ou bien avec méfiance (qu'a-t-il à traîner encore sur les routes, à pareille heure!) ou bien avec pitié (tout est occupé!). Mais l'aiguille de ma montre avait déjà dépassé minuit lorsque, dans la lumière de mes phares, apparut le poteau indicateur : Lugano, 15 km. Je ne me sentais pas très à l'aise. Où trouverai-je à me loger? Certes, la saison n'a pas encore commencé. Je m'arrêtai devant un hôtel qui, dans les prospectus, était classé parmi les hôtels de luxe. A une heure aussi avancée de la nuit, il est conseillé d'entrer dans un hôtel de cette catégorie (m. à m. : dans un tel hôtel). Je ne l'ai pas regretté.
Le chef de réception, aimable, me proposa une chambre avec salle de bain et vue sur le lac et me fit connaître aussitôt le prix. Très gentil de sa part; car plus d'un (voyageur) est dans l'embarras quand, dans un tel endroit, il s'agit de demander les prix. Mais voilà que mon sympathique interlocuteur (m. à m. : l'homme sympathique) me dit :
— Vous pouvez également avoir quelque chose à meilleur marché. J'aurais encore une petite chambre sur la cour.
Marché conclu. Et cette « petite chambre sur la cour » présentait l'agrément d'une cabine de première classe de bateau; elle était petite, mais possédait tout le confort : une armoire encastrée dans le mur, une niche avec un lavabo, avec l'eau courante, chaude et froide, un poste de radio encastré dans la table de nuit.
Le chef de réception, vraiment, avait eu de bonnes intentions à mon égard. La chambre avec vue sur le lac, je n'en aurais pas beaucoup profité : Lugano était plongé dans un épais brouillard — chose décevante pour celui qui a quitté le brumeux Hambourg à la recherche du printemps sur la Riviera Suisse, à Lugano qui promet de nous offrir 2 248 heures de soleil par an et d'être une des localités les plus ensoleillées de l'Europe Centrale. Cependant, on ne doit pas se laisser décourager dans cette charmante petite ville. Même si le brouillard flotte sur le lac et dans les ruelles, il n'y a pas de quoi grelotter, car l'air est doux.
Par une telle journée, le mieux c'est d'aller à Castagnola, situé entre Lugano et le pittoresque Gandria. En effet, là-bas, la pinacothèque de la Villa Favorita offre un rare plaisir aux amateurs

Genuß : Gemälde von italienischen, spanischen, französischen, holländisch-flämischen und deutschen Meistern vom Mittelalter bis ins 18. Jahrhundert. Hier hängen Werke von Tizian, Rembrandt, Dürer, Rubens, Murillo, Gainsborough, um nur die berühmtesten zu nennen. Ich hätte nicht gedacht, hier solchen Schätzen zu[5] begegnen. Sie erschließen sich dem Touristen eigentlich nur, wenn Lugano einmal einen Nebelvorhang vor seine zauberhafte landschaftliche Umgebung zieht.

Indessen hält es[6] den Nebel nicht lange. Kommt der felsige Katzenbuckel des Monte San Salvatore, des Wahrzeichens Luganos, wieder zum Vorschein, läßt auch die Sonne nicht mehr lange auf sich warten, und dann breitet sich vor dem Betrachter die Postkarten-Landschaft des Lago di Lugano aus. Lieblich anzuschaun. Wer aber weiß, daß nur wenige Meter abseits von dieser Urlaubs-Idylle einsame, zerklüftete Hochtäler in die Berge führen? Daß weit von den großen Tempelpfaden[7] des Tourismus Straßen ans Ende der Welt führen, die auch heute noch kaum auf einer Autokarte eingetragen sind?

PETER WESTPHAL,
aus der Wochenzeitung « Die Zeit », Hamburg

5. Notez l'emploi de *zu,* après *denken.*
   Ich denke, länger hier zu bleiben, je pense rester assez longtemps ici.
6. Tournure impersonnelle. *Es hält uns nicht lange hier,* nous ne resterons pas longtemps ici (m. à m. : cela ne nous tient pas...).
7. *der Tempelpfad (-e),* m. à m. : le sentier du temple.

d'art : des tableaux de maîtres italiens, espagnols, français, hollandais – flamands et allemands, du Moyen-Age au XVIIIe siècle. Là sont accrochées des œuvres du Titien, de Rembrandt, de Durer, de Rubens, de Murillo, de Gainsborough, pour ne citer que les plus célèbres. Je n'aurais pas cru trouver (m. à m. : rencontrer) ici de tels trésors. A vrai dire, ils ne se révèlent au touriste que le jour où Lugano cache le paysage féerique de ses environs derrière un rideau de brouillard (m. à m. : tire un rideau de brouillard devant...).

Toutefois, le brouillard ne dure guère. Que reparaisse le gros dos (m. à m. : le dos de chat) du Monte San Salvatore, signe distinctif de Lugano, et le soleil non plus ne se fait guère attendre, et alors, le paysage du Lac de Lugano, paysage de carte postale, s'étend sous les yeux du spectateur. C'est un tableau plein de grâce (m. à m. : gracieux à regarder). Mais qui donc sait qu'à l'écart, à quelques mètres seulement de ce paradis de nos vacances, il y a de hautes vallées, solitaires et crevassées, qui conduisent dans les montagnes? Que loin des sentiers consacrés du tourisme, des routes mènent au bout du monde, qui, de nos jours encore, sont à peine portées sur les cartes routières (m. à m. : sur une carte pour autos)?

Leçon

84 Gespräch bei der Fondue

Die Fondue entsteht dadurch, daß man in einem tiegelartigen[1] Gefäß von feuerfestem Ton feinblättrig geschnittenen Emmentaler Käse zum Schmelzen bringt. Der Tiegel wird, bevor man ihm den Käse anvertraut, mit Schnaps ausgewischt[2]. Welcher sich hierzu vor jedem anderen eigne, darüber herrschen differierende Auffassungen. Oft wird Kirsch bevorzugt, doch möchte ich aus Gründen dem Gebirgswachholder oder dem Grappa das Wort reden. Ein Hauch von Aroma teilt sich dem Käse mit und vereinigt sich mit jenem kleinen Quantum neuenburgischen Weißweins, das während der Schmelzprozedur langsam dazugegossen wird; hier gibt es keinen Zweifel: selbst im Tessin ist Neuenburger in solchen Fällen *de rigueur.* Von sonstigen Zutaten, die sämtlich mit Sparsamkeit, ja mit Geiz verwandt werden wollen, verdienen Mehl, Pfeffer und eine Winzigkeit Knoblauch ihre Erwähnung. Es gibt auch Leute, die den Tiegel nicht mit Schnaps auswischen, sondern mit Knoblauch ausreiben und den Schnaps erst unmittelbar vor dem Essen hineinrühren. Hier muß man tolerant sein, ebenso wie gegen diejenigen, welche das göttliche Gericht, der Vernunft und dem Geist der französischen Sprache zuwider[3], neutralisierend « das Fondue » nennen. (Sie sind in der Mehrzahl). Solche Dinge gehören in die Neutralität und sind keine Kriege wert.

Der Rittmeister und ich sprachen nun eine Weile über die Fondue und waren uns einig, daß sie ein menschenverbindendes Gericht ist. Die miteinander Fondue essen, bilden eine wahrhafte Tischgemeinschaft. Denn wie viele sich auch zusammenfinden, ob zwei oder zwölf, sie fahren alle mit ihren Gabeln in den nämlichen Tiegel. Es ist der gleiche, in welchem das Gericht zubereitet wurde; und so lange die Mahlzeit währt, steht er über dem Feuer. Man setzt sich so, daß jeder der Conviven

1. *tiegelartig :* le terme *...artig,* en composition, signifie : de la nature de, semblable à.
2. *Der Tiegel wird ausgewischt :* m. à m. : le poêlon est essuyé, donc : on essuie le poêlon... C'est la voix passive, très fréquente en allemand.
3. ... *zuwider* (+ datif), contrairement à; remarquez la place de ce mot, qui vient après ses compléments (*der Vernunft, dem Geist...*).

Tête à tête auprès de la fondue

La fondue s'obtient en faisant fondre du fromage d'Emmental, coupé en fines lamelles, dans un récipient du genre d'un creuset, en terre à feu. Dans le poêlon, on passe de l'eau-de-vie, avant de lui confier le fromage. Quelle eau-de-vie convient plus que toute autre? Là-dessus, les avis sont partagés (m. à m. : là-dessus règnent des conceptions différentes). Souvent, on préfère le kirsch; pourtant je voudrais, moi, et pour cause, plaider pour le genièvre de montagne ou le Grappa. Un léger arome (m. à m. : un souffle d'arome) se communique et se mêle à la petite quantité de vin blanc de Neuchâtel, que l'on y verse lentement, pendant que le fromage fond (m. à m. : pendant la procédure de la fonte); il n'y a ici aucune hésitation (possible) : même au Tessin, c'est le vin de Neuchâtel qui est de rigueur dans de telles circonstances. En ce qui concerne les autres ingrédients, qui tous demandent à être employés avec parcimonie, avec avarice même, la farine, le poivre et une infime quantité d'ail méritent d'être mentionnés (m. à m. : ... leur mention). Il est aussi des personnes qui ne passent pas d'eau-de-vie dans leur poêlon, mais qui le frottent avec de l'ail et n'y ajoutent l'eau-de-vie qu'immédiatement avant le repas, tout en remuant. Sur ce point (m. à m. : ici), il faut être tolérant, tout comme vis-à-vis de ceux qui, au mépris du bon sens et de l'esprit de la langue française, appellent ce plat divin « das Fondue », en employant le neutre. (Ils sont en majorité). On doit rester neutre, dans ce genre d'affaires; elles ne valent pas une querelle (m. à m. : de telles choses appartiennent à la neutralité et ne valent pas des guerres.)
Depuis un moment déjà, nous étions en train de parler de la fondue, le capitaine de cavalerie et moi, et nous nous accordions (à trouver) que la fondue est un plat qui unit les hommes. Ceux qui mangent ensemble une fondue, forment une véritable communauté de table. En effet, quel que soit le nombre (de ceux) qui se réunissent, qu'ils soient deux ou douze, ils plongent tous leur fourchette dans le même poêlon. C'est celui-là même (m. à m. : le même qui...) dans lequel on a préparé le mets, et aussi longtemps que dure le repas, il est placé sur le feu. On s'assied de telle sorte que chacun des convives est aussi éloigné,

gleich weit vom Mittelpunkt, nämlich vom Fondue-Tiegel entfernt, jeder ihm gleich nahe ist. Ist es eine größere Tischgesellschaft, so erfordert die Anordnung viel Umsicht. Runde Tische empfehlen sich. Die Fondue, so ließ der Rittmeister mich wissen, gehört wie die Artischocke und der Spargel zu den nicht sehr zahleichen fleischlosen Gerichten, die auch der Nichtvegetarier ohne Bedenken zu sich nehmen kann. Insbesondere ist sie gänzlich frei von Vitaminen.

– Selbst wer von Vitaminen hoch denkt, meist also Frauenzimmer[4] und Ärzte, sagte er, kann schwerlich leugnen, daß sie vorwiegend an rohe, saure, kältende, kurz, an feindselige Stoffe gebunden sind, die sich wenig zur menschlichen Ernährung schicken. Für Kinder mögen sie unschädlich sein; bejahrten Eingeweiden sagt die milde Wärme des Beaujolais, die Kräftigkeit des halbroten Beefsteaks und das den Bauch in Erstaunen verzetzende Geprickel des mittelreifen Gorgonzola freundlicher zu. Natürlich, nichts gegen Früchte! Nichts gegen Erdbeeren, Pfirsiche, Ananas – aber in unseren Jahren tut man doch gut, sich mehr an das Rezente zu halten, an das in Wahrheit Stomachale. Übrigens sind die schätzenswertesten Früchte die, deren Geist dem Weine hold und gewärtig ist, das heißt : die sich zur Bowle eignen[6].

Dieser Text wurde dem Band entnommen :
WERNER BERGENGRUEN, der letzte Rittmeister, Roman, 344 Seiten, erschienen im Verlag der Arche, Peter Schifferli, Zürich (alle Rechte beim Verlag).

4. *das Frauenzimmer* (-), terme un peu péjoratif : femme, fille.
5. *das Rezente* est un adjectif pris comme nom : *rezent,* fort, piquant, picotant.
6. Notez dans ce texte qui a été écrit en Suisse, l'emploi fréquent de mots étrangers : *differieren – das Aroma – die Prozedur – tolerant,* etc.

aussi proche du centre, c'est-à-dire du poêlon à fondue, (que l'autre). Si c'est une tablée assez nombreuse, la manière de placer (les hôtes) exige beaucoup de circonspection. Les tables rondes sont recommandées.

La fondue, me fit savoir le capitaine, tout comme les artichauts et les asperges, compte au nombre des mets sans viande que même le non-végétarien peut manger sans hésiter. De plus, elle ne contient absolument pas de vitamines (m. à m. : est tout à fait libre de...).

— Même ceux qui font grand cas des vitamines, donc avant tout les femmes et les médecins, dit-il, peuvent difficilement nier qu'elles sont attachées surtout à des matières crues, acides, qui vous font frissonner, bref, des matières hostiles qui conviennent peu à l'alimentation de l'homme. Il est possible que, pour les enfants, elles soient inoffensives; mais quand on a un certain âge, l'estomac (m. à m. : les intestins d'un certain âge) trouve bien plus de charme (m. à m. : il leur plaît plus agréablement) à la douce chaleur du Beaujolais, à la vigueur du bifteck saignant (m. à m. : demi-rouge) et au picotement du Gorgonzola à demi-fait, qui frappe le ventre d'étonnement.

Naturellement (je n'ai) rien contre les fruits. Rien contre les fraises, les pêches, les ananas, — mais à notre âge (m. à m. : dans nos années) on fait bien mieux de s'en tenir à ce qui est fort, à ce qui est véritablement stomachique. Au demeurant, les fruits les plus estimables sont ceux dont l'esprit s'accorde au vin et qui sont tout à son service : c'est-à-dire ceux qui se prêtent à la préparation du punch.

D'après WERNER BERGENGRUEN
(Le dernier capitaine de cavalerie)

85 Stilmöbel dringen weiter vor

Schlichte Formen und einfache Linien beherrschten das Bild auf der Kölner Möbelmesse. Die Möbelindustrie spricht von einer « Beruhigung der Möbelformen », einer Beruhigung, die freilich die Gefahr einer Uniformierung des Geschmacks einschließt. Die Zeit der Stilexperimente scheint vorbei zu sein. Allzu viele Experimente liegen ohnehin weder im Interesse der Industrie noch[1] des Handels. Die Entwicklung neuer Modelle erfordert bis zu ihrer Herstellungsreife viel Zeit, Geld und Arbeit. Sie birgt außerdem ein ständiges Risiko, das oft in keinem Verhältnis zum Erfolg steht. Nicht minder[2] groß ist das Risiko eines raschen Modellwechsels für den Möbelhandel, besonders wenn die eingekauften Modelle schon nach kurzer Zeit wieder als veraltet gelten. Das geringe Interesse der Möbelwirtschaft an einem zu schnellen[3] Modellwechsel wird schon durch die nur alle zwei Jahre stattfindende[4] Möbelmesse dokumentiert.
Auf der Ausstellung dominieren wieder Nußbaum- und Teakholz. Auch Palisander wurde stärker beachtet. Die sogenannte Teakholzwelle scheint allerdings zumindest zum Stillstand gekommen[5] zu sein. Auffallend ist die Verwendung von Kunststoffen[6] für Furniere, wobei aber jede Nachahmung von echtem Holz durch Kunststoffe als verpönt gilt.

1. *weder... noch...,* ni... ni... (Leçon 73).
2. *minder* est le comparatif de *wenig,* peu. On emploie plus fréquemment *geringer,* moindre et *weniger,* moins (de).
3. *zu schnell,* trop rapide; *zu,* placé devant un adjectif ou un adverbe, marque l'excès.
4. *die nur alle zwei Jahre...* Remarquez la proposition qualificative. (Leçon 54).
5. *zum Stillstand kommen,* s'arrêter, marquer un temps d'arrêt (m. à m. : venir à l'arrêt). Le verbe correspondant est : *still/stehen,* s'arrêter.
6. *der Kunststoff(e),* le produit de synthèse; *Kunst* a ici le sens d'artificiel, faux. Nous le retrouvons p. ex. dans *das Kunstmittel* le moyen artificiel; *die Kunstseide,* la soie artificielle; *künstlich,* artificiel. – Par contre : *künstlerisch,* artistique : *der Kunstliebhaber,* l'amateur d'art; *der Kunstsinn,* le sens artistique.

Les meubles de style continuent à progresser

Les formes droites et les lignes simples ont commandé l'aspect général de la Foire aux Meubles de Cologne. L'industrie du meuble parle d'un « apaisement des formes du meuble », un apaisement qui, assurément, implique le danger d'une uniformisation du goût. L'ère des expériences de style semble être révolue. Trop d'expériences ne sont d'ailleurs ni dans l'intérêt de l'industrie, ni dans celui du commerce. La réalisation de nouveaux modèles exige beaucoup de temps, d'argent et de travail, avant qu'elle n'arrive au stade de production. Elle renferme en outre un risque constant qui souvent n'a pas de rapport avec le succès. Le risque d'un changement accéléré des modèles n'est pas moins grand pour le commerce du meuble, surtout si les modèles achetés sont considérés déjà peu de temps après comme démodés. Le peu d'intérêt que l'industrie du meuble apporte à un changement trop rapide des modèles apparaît dans le fait que cette Foire aux Meubles n'a lieu que tous les deux ans.

Le noyer et le teck dominent de nouveau à l'exposition. On a accordé également une attention plus grande au palissandre. Ce qu'on est convenu d'appeler la vague du teck semble pour le moins être stationnaire. On est frappé par l'emploi de matières plastiques pour les feuilles de placage, cependant toute imitation du bois véritable par des matières plastiques est considérée comme prohibée.

Stilmöbel erfreuen sich[7] offenbar wachsender Popularität. Entsprechend groß war das Angebot. Man will darin eine « Abwehrreaktion » der Käufer gegen die Uniformierung durch die « nüchternen » Möbel sehen. Doch kann auch das Stilmöbel zur Uniformierung führen. Die Qualität des Kölner Möbelangebots war insgesamt höher als auf der letzten Messe vor zwei Jahren. Darin kommt nach Ansicht der Möbelindustrie der Drang immer breiter werdender Käuferschichten zur höheren Qualität zum Ausdruck[8]. Gefragt werden heute Möbel, deren Qualität und Stil auf eine längere Lebensdauer angelegt sind. Zwar gibt es auch Kreise, die ihre Schlaf- und Wohnzimmer-Ausstattung[9] alle paar Jahre wechseln wie das Auto. Aber sie sind nicht repräsentativ.

Die Möbel werden aber nicht nur solider in ihrer Qualität, sondern auch größer in ihren Dimensionen, sie werden höher, länger und breiter. Auch Inhaber kleiner Wohnungen wünschen sich große Schränke. Das ist ein echtes Wohlstandssystem, denn die Schränke, Truhen und Kommoden sollen die zunehmenden Schätze an Haushaltgerät aufnehmen und zugleich das Prestigebedürfnis befriedigen. Man repräsentiert nicht nur mit dem Auto, sondern auch mit dem Schlafzimmer und dem altdeutschen[10] Wohnzimmerschrank, man repräsentiert sogar mit dem Holz, aus dem dieser Schrank besteht[11]. Palisander und Nußbaum gelten als ausgesprochen « vornehme » Hölzer. Die meisten Aussteller waren mit dem Erfolg der Möbelmesse zufrieden. Die Preise blieben zum großen Teil konstant. Nur bei neuen Modellen wurden sie angehoben. Auch Polstermöbel verzeichneten einen leichten Preisauftrieb. Küchenmöbel blieben stabil, Serienfabrikate wurden sogar zum Teil billiger angeboten.

H. RIEKER, (Rheinischer Merkur)

7. *...erfreuen sich...* Notez que le verbe *sich erfreuen* prend un complément de la chose au génitif. (Leçon 74).
8. *zum Ausdruck kommen,* s'exprimer (chose), m. à m. : venir à expression.
9. Il faut comprendre : *Schlafzimmerausstattung und Wohnzimmer-ausstattung;* le tiret indique les termes sous-entendus.
10. *altdeutsch,* m. à m. : ancien allemand; teuton; tudesque.
11. Notez la construction : *bestehen aus* (+ datif), se composer de, consister en. (Mémento, n° 76).

Les meubles de style jouissent manifestement d'une popularité croissante. Aussi, l'offre en était-elle importante. On veut y voir une « réaction de défense » des acheteurs contre l'uniformisation par les meubles « sobres ». Pourtant, le meuble de style lui aussi peut conduire à l'uniformisation. La qualité des meubles présentés à Cologne était dans l'ensemble supérieure à celle de la dernière foire, il y a deux ans.
Par là — c'est l'avis de l'industrie du meuble — des couches de plus en plus vastes d'acheteurs expriment leur désir d'une qualité meilleure. On demande aujourd'hui des meubles dont la qualité et le style sont conçus en vue d'une durée plus longue. Il est vrai qu'il existe également des milieux où l'on change régulièrement au bout de quelques années le mobilier de la chambre à coucher et de la salle de séjour, tout comme la voiture. Mais ils ne sont pas représentatifs.
Or, les meubles sont non seulement plus sérieux dans leur qualité, mais aussi plus grands dans leurs dimensions, ils deviennent plus hauts, plus longs et plus larges. Même les propriétaires de petits appartements désirent de grandes armoires. C'est un véritable système de prospérité, car les armoires, les bahuts et les commodes doivent contenir les richesses croissantes en équipement ménager, et en même temps assouvir la soif de prestige. On est quelqu'un non seulement par sa voiture, mais aussi par sa chambre et par son buffet ancien, et même par le bois dont il est fait.
Le palissandre et le noyer sont considérés comme des essences tout à fait « distinguées ». La plupart des exposants étaient satisfaits du résultat de la Foire aux Meubles. En grande partie, les prix sont restés stables. Ce n'est que pour les modèles nouveaux qu'ils furent relevés. Les meubles capitonnés, eux aussi, ont enregistré une légère hausse. Les prix des meubles de cuisine n'ont pas varié, les fabrications en série ont même été, en partie, offertes à meilleur marché.

D'après H. RIEKER (Rheinischer Merkur)

86 Eine Stunde Aufenthalt

(Die Szene spielt in der abgelegenen Ecke eines großen Bahnhofs, vor dem Gepäckschalter; hin und wieder hört man entfernt einen aus- oder einfahrenden[1] Zug, die Stimme eines Ansagers, Schritte, das Geräusch auf-[2] und zugeschobener Schalter).

Träger. — Soll ich das Gepäck nun abgeben, oder...?
Chrantox. — Warten Sie.
Träger. — Noch nicht entschlossen, Herr?
Chrantox. — Nein.
Träger. — Der nächste Zug fährt erst dreizehn Uhr neun. Die Stunde Aufenthalt müssen Sie schon hinnehmen.
Chrantox. — Ich habe nicht damit gerechnet, daß der Zug hier hält, sonst hätte ich eine andere Route gewählt. Nun mußte ich hier umsteigen.
Träger. — Ist es wirklich so schlimm, Herr? Bis Athen werden Sie bestimmt drei Tage brauchen. Kommt es da auf eine Stunde an[3]?
Chrantox. — Nicht auf die Stunde, aber auf die Stadt.
Träger. — Vielleicht schauen Sie sich die Stadt an. Gar nicht so übel. Sehenswürdigkeiten, Ruinen, Neubauten, Kirchen, Denkmäler — und nette Leute. Fast könnte ich gekränkt sein, aber *(müde)* ich bin nicht mehr so leicht zu kränken.
Chrantox. — Ich kenne die Stadt.
Träger. — Ach, sind Sie schon hier gewesen?
Chrantox. — Ja.
Träger. — Länger?
Chrantox. — Siebzehn Jahre lang.
Träger. — Nein.
Chrantox. — Ich sage Ihnen : siebzehn Jahre lebte ich hier. Sie glauben nicht?
Träger. — Natürlich glaube ich Ihnen, aber es kommt mir so unwahrscheinlich vor. Siebzehn Jahre, das ist eine lange Zeit, und älter als — (zögert) älter als vierzig würde ich Sie nicht schätzen.

1. Il faut comprendre : *einen ausfahrenden oder einfahrenden.* En cas de répétition, on sous-entend le 2ᵉ élément du premier terme.
2. *aufgeschobener Schalter :* m. à m. : des guichets que l'on ouvre en les faisant glisser — *schieben (o, o),* faire glisser.
3. *an/kommen auf* (accusatif), dépendre de.

Une heure d'attente

(La scène se passe dans un coin solitaire d'une grande gare, devant le guichet des bagages; de temps à autre, on entend au loin un train qui arrive ou qui part, la voix d'un annonceur, des pas, le bruit de guichets que l'on ouvre et referme).

Porteur. — Alors, dois-je mettre les bagages à la consigne, ou bien...?
Chrantox. — Attendez.
Porteur. — Vous n'êtes pas encore décidé, Monsieur?
Chrantox. — Non.
P. — Le prochain train ne part qu'à treize heures neuf. De cette heure d'attente, il faut bien que vous preniez votre parti.
C. — Je n'avais pas compté que le train n'allait pas plus loin qu'ici, sinon, j'aurais choisi un autre itinéraire. Or, il a fallu que je change ici.
P. — Est-ce vraiment si grave, Monsieur? Jusqu'à Athènes, vous allez mettre sûrement trois jours. Alors, faut-il en être à une heure près?
C. — Il ne s'agit pas de l'heure, mais de la ville.
P. — Vous pourriez la visiter, la ville (m. à m. : peut-être regarderez-vous la ville). Elle n'est pas si mal. (On y voit) des curiosités, des ruines, des immeubles neufs, des églises, des monuments — et des gens aimables. Je pourrais presque me sentir offensé, mais (sur un ton las) on ne peut plus m'offenser aussi facilement.
C. — Je connais la ville.
P. — Ah, vous êtes donc déjà venu ici?
C. — Oui.
P. — Vous êtes resté longtemps?
C. — Dix sept ans.
P. — Non!
C. — Je vous le dis. J'ai vécu ici dix-sept ans. Vous ne le croyez pas?
P. — Bien sûr, je vous crois, mais cela me paraît si invraisemblable. Dix-sept années, c'est une longue période, et je ne vous donnerais pas plus de... (il hésite), pas plus de quarante ans (m. à m. : je ne vous estimerais pas plus âgé que...).

Chrantox. — Ihre Schätzung stimmt fast, ich bin dreiundvierzig alt. Warum sollte ich nicht siebzehn Jahre hier gelebt haben?
Träger. — Sie sehen wie ein Ausländer aus.
Chrantox. — Ich bin einer.
Träger. — Sie sprechen gut deutsch, fast... ich meine... nun... (bricht ab).
Chrantox. — Was meinten Sie?
Träger. — Ich meine, daß Sie fast ein wenig unseren Dialekt sprechen, aber das bilde ich mir wohl nur ein.
Chrantox. — Vielleicht stimmt es.
Träger. — Nun, wie ist es, soll ich Ihr Gepäck bei der Aufbewahrung abgeben, oder wollen Sie lieber auf dem Bahnsteig den Anschluß abwarten?
Chrantox. — Am liebsten würde ich mit dem nächsten Zug weiterfahren und auf einer anderen Station den Anschluß nach Athen abwarten.
Träger. — So böse Erinnerungen an unsere Stadt?
Chrantox. — Böse und gute.
Träger. — Frischen Sie die guten auf, Herr.
Chrantox. — Es ist jetzt (kurze Pause) elf Uhr siebenundfünfzig; bis dreizehn Uhr neun, also mehr als eine Stunde noch. (Mit veränderter, weniger kalter Stimme) Sie hatten Krieg hier?
Träger. — Ja. Vor zwölf Jahren war er zu Ende. Der letzte; (müde) manchmal werf ich die Kriege schon durcheinander.
Chrantox. — Ich war so weit weg, daß er nur als Gerücht zu mir drang : Bomben — Hunger — Tod — Mord. Viel zerstört hier?
Träger. — Ziemlich. Doch Sie würden nicht mehr viel von der Zerstörung sehen. Wo wohnten Sie damals, als Sie hier lebten?
Chrantox. — Sophienstraße.
Träger. — Oh, feine Leute. Da war nicht viel zerstört. Am Sophienpark, nicht wahr?
Chrantox. — Gibt es den Park noch?
Träger. — Natürlich. Man hat ihn erweitert.
Chrantox. — Ach, auch das Café noch da und die Tanzterrasse?
Träger. — Ja, möchten Sie es sich nicht ansehen? (Da Chrantox schweigt, weiter[4] nach kurzer Pause) Zwölf Jahre ist der Krieg vorüber, sechs Jahre hat er gedauert. Siebzehn Jahre haben Sie hier gelebt. Wann war das?
Chrantox. — Ich bin hier geboren.

HEINRICH BÖLL (Erzählungen, Hörspiele, Aufsätze)
Verlag Kiepenheuer u. Witsch.

4. *weiter,* comparatif de *weit,* loin, souvent idée de continuer, d'avancer; on sous-entend le verbe parler : *er spricht weiter.*

C. — Votre estimation est presque juste, j'ai quarante trois ans. Pourquoi n'aurais-je pas vécu ici pendant dix-sept ans?
P. — Vous avez l'air d'un étranger.
C. — J'en suis un.
P. — Vous parlez bien l'allemand, presque... je veux dire... eh bien... (il s'interrompt).
C. — Que vouliez-vous dire?
P. — Je veux dire que vous parlez presque un peu notre dialecte, mais sans doute je me l'imagine seulement.
C. — Peut-être est-ce juste.
P. — Eh bien! quoi qu'il en soit, dois-je mettre vos bagages à la consigne, ou bien préférez-vous attendre la correspondance sur le quai?
C. — Ce que je préférerais, c'est partir par le prochain train, et attendre dans une autre gare ma correspondance pour Athènes.
P. — Avez-vous conservé de si mauvais souvenirs de notre ville?
C. — Des mauvais et des bons.
P. — Ravivez les bons, Monsieur.
C. — Il est maintenant (court silence) onze heures cinquante-sept; jusqu'à treize heures neuf... donc plus d'une heure encore. (D'une voix altérée, moins froide.) Vous avez eu la guerre, ici?
P. — Oui. Elle s'est terminée il y a douze ans. La dernière : (d'une voix fatiguée) parfois, je confonds les guerres l'une avec l'autre (m. à m. : parfois je jette les guerres pêle-mêle).
C. — J'étais si loin, moi, que seule une rumeur m'en est parvenue : les bombes — la faim — la mort — le massacre. Beaucoup de destructions, ici?
P. — Assez. Pourtant, vous ne verriez plus grand chose des destructions. Où habitiez-vous autrefois quand vous viviez ici?
C. — Rue Sophie.
P. — Oh, des gens bien. Là, il n'y a pas eu beaucoup de choses de détruites. Près du Parc Sophie, n'est-ce pas?
C. — Ce parc existe encore?
P. — Naturellement. On l'a agrandi.
C. — Ah! et le café, existe-t-il encore, et la terrasse de bal?
P. — Oui, ne voudriez-vous pas le voir? (Comme Chrantox se tait, il poursuit après un court silence). Voilà douze ans que la guerre est finie, elle a duré six années. Vous, vous avez vécu ici pendant dix-sept années. Quand était-ce?
C. — Je suis né ici.

D'après HEINRICH BÖLL

87 Ratschläge[1] für Totschläger

Meinungsforscher, Aerzte und Soziologen erklären übereinstimmend, daß die Zahl der untrainierten Totschläger immer mehr zunimmt, nämlich der Menschen, die nicht wissen, was sie mit sich und anderen anfangen sollen, und daher versuchen die Zeit totzuschlagen. Leider lehrt bisher keine Schule die Zeittotschlägerei, nicht einmal Oxford oder Harvard. Aber alles will gelernt sein. Die Leute, die keine Ahnung haben, wie man richtig die Zeit totschlägt, kommen auf allerhand schlechte Gedanken. Sie trinken zu viel, prozessieren, kümmern sich um Politik, kaufen neue Autos, probieren Rauschgifte. Und alles, weil sie nicht wissen, was sie mit der Zeit anfangen sollen.
Wer das Zeittotschlagen lernen will, muss vor allem verstehen, daß er nichts tun darf, was irgendwie konstruktiv, produktiv, positiv, aktiv oder subjektiv ist. Er darf daher keine Bücher lesen — das wäre schon eine Beschäftigung, wenn auch nicht immer eine geistige. Aber er müßte umblättern, das Buch aufheben, das ihm aus dem Bett fällt usw[2]. Alles zu mühsam. Er darf allerdings gewisse Zeitungen lesen, die nichts Lesenswertes[3] enthalten, und Illustrierte anschauen. Manche blättern sich gewissermaßen von selbst um[4], und man muß höchstens die Namen unter den Bildern lesen. Der Text ist auf den tiefsten gemeinsamen Nenner gebracht. Ein Achtel der Leser versteht ihn trotzdem nicht.
Der gewandte Zeittotschläger unternimmt Dinge, die zu nichts führen. Konferenzen mit Geschäftsfreunden, mit denen man gar kein Geschäft zu machen beabsichtigt. Damit kann man leicht zwei Stunden totschlagen. Ein anschliessendes Mittagessen auf Geschäftskosten (mit Vorspeise und Dessert) bedeutet zwei weitere Stunden gekillt[5].
In gewissen Kreisen sind Cocktail-Parties das beliebteste Mittel, die Zeit totzuschlagen. Nur hüte man sich, etwas zu sagen, was

1. *die Ratschläge,* les conseils (donnés à quelqu'un) : *die Räte,* les conseillers, les Conseils; singulier commun : *der Rat.* (voir Mémento, n° 17).
2. *usw : und so weiter :* etc.
3. *wert* (+ gén.), digne de; *sehenswert,* qui vaut la peine d'être vu; *lobenswert,* louable;
4. *umblättern; blättern,* feuilleter, vient de *das Blatt (¨ er)* la feuille; *um* donne ici l'idée de tourner.
5. *killen,* tuer, est un terme très familier (anglais : *to kill,* tuer, abattre).

Conseils pour tueurs

Les sondeurs d'opinion publique, les médecins et les sociologues s'accordent pour expliquer que le nombre des tueurs non entraînés augmente sans cesse, c. à d. (le nombre) de ces personnes qui ne savent ce qu'elles doivent faire d'elles-mêmes et de leurs semblables (m. à m. : ... commencer d'elles et des autres) et qui, pour cette raison, essaient de tuer le temps. Malheureusement, aucune école n'enseigne à ce jour l'art de tuer le temps, ni même Oxford ou Harvard. Mais tout demande à être appris. Les gens qui n'ont aucune idée sur la façon de tuer le temps correctement, en arrivent à toutes sortes de mauvaises pensées. Ils boivent trop, engagent des procès, se mêlent de politique, achètent de nouvelles voitures, goûtent des drogues. Et tout cela parce qu'ils ne savent ce qu'ils doivent faire de leur temps.
Quiconque veut apprendre à tuer le temps doit comprendre, avant toute chose, qu'il ne doit rien faire qui, d'une manière ou d'une autre, soit constructif, productif, positif, actif, ou subjectif. Aussi ne doit-il pas lire de livres — ce serait déjà une occupation, encore qu'(elle ne soit) pas toujours intellectuelle. Mais il lui faudrait tourner les pages, ramasser le livre qui lui tombe du lit, etc. Trop pénible, tout cela. Il a le droit, assurément, de lire certains journaux qui ne contiennent rien méritant d'être lu, et de regarder des illustrés. Il en est (m. à m. : certains) dont les pages se tournent pour ainsi dire d'elles-mêmes, et tout au plus doit-on lire les noms sous les illustrations. Le texte est réduit au plus petit (m. à m. : bas) dénominateur commun. Un lecteur sur huit (m. à m. : le huitième des lecteurs) ne le comprend quand même pas.
Celui qui sait habilement tuer le temps (m. à m. : l'habile tueur de temps) entreprend des choses qui ne mènent à rien. Des conférences avec des relations d'affaire, avec qui on n'envisage nullement de traiter le moindre négoce. Ainsi, on peut facilement tuer deux heures. S'enchaînant là-dessus, un déjeuner sur les frais généraux de l'entreprise (avec hors-d'œuvre et dessert), cela représente encore deux autres heures de supprimées.
Dans certains milieux, les cocktails sont le moyen préféré pour tuer le temps. Mais que l'on se garde bien de dire quoi que ce

ernst genommen werden könnte[6]. Man sagt zwanglose Banalitäten und stellt rhetorische Fragen, die unbeantwortet bleiben. Nachher gehen unmusikalische Leute zu Wagner. Wenn man Glück hat, bei « Siegfried », kann man fünf Stunden herrlich totschlagen. Andere tun es mit Hilfe von Sartre oder Genet.
Besuche von kunstlosen Kunstausstellungen sind ebenfalls zu empfehlen. Man starrt verständnislos[7] auf leere russische Kaviardosen, auf brasilianische Büstenhalter oder Blechmodelle des Schiefen Turms von Pisa. Auch die Bilderausstellungen gewisser Damen der Gesellschaft, die glauben « malen » zu können, gehören dazu. Nicht zu empfehlen ist der Besuch von Sportveranstaltungen, da die Zuschauer dabei meist mehr mitmachen als die Sportler.
Ideal sind Besuche bei Behörden, von denen es glücklicherweise immer mehr gibt. Vor Jahren, als wir noch nicht nach Bulgarien durften[8], bemühte ich mich einmal zwei Wochen lang, ein Visum zu bekommen, obwohl ich von der Zwecklosigkeit meines Nichtstuns überzeugt war. Zum Schluß versank ich in einem Vakuum von Gleichgültigkeit, wobei ich kaum wußte, ob ich noch mit beiden Füßen auf dem Boden stand oder vom Plafond hing. Es war die ideale, totale Zeittotschlägerei.

JOSEPH WECHSBERG, (Die Weltwoche, Zürich)

6. Notez la forme passive *genommen werden,* être pris (Mémento, n° 46).
7. verständnislos, qui ne comprend pas, vient de *verstehen (verstand, verstanden),* comprendre. — *das Verständnis (se),* la compréhension, l'intelligence.
8. *nach Bulgarien durften :* le verbe *gehen,* aller, est sous-entendu.

soit qui pourrait être pris au sérieux. On dit des banalités désinvoltes et l'on soulève des questions de rhétorique qui restent sans réponse. Ensuite, les gens qui ne comprennent rien à la musique vont écouter du Wagner. Si l'on a de la chance, avec « Siegfried », on peut magnifiquement tuer cinq heures de temps. D'autres le font à l'aide de Sartre ou de Genet.

La fréquentation d'expositions artistiques dénuées de tout art est également à recommander. On regarde fixement, sans rien y comprendre, des boîtes vides de caviar russe, des soutien-gorge brésiliens ou bien des maquettes en fer-blanc de la Tour penchée de Pise. Il faut y inclure les expositions de tableaux de certaines dames de la société, qui croient savoir « peindre ». La fréquentation de jeux sportifs n'est pas à recommander, vu que les spectateurs y participent la plupart du temps plus que les joueurs.

Rien ne vaut les démarches auprès des services officiels; il en existe heureusement de plus en plus. Il y a quelques années, alors que nous n'avions pas encore le droit de nous rendre en Bulgarie, il m'est arrivé de me donner du mal pendant deux semaines pour obtenir un visa, bien que je fusse convaincu de l'inanité de mon farniente. Finalement, j'ai sombré dans un vide d'indifférence où je savais à peine si j'avais encore les deux pieds sur terre ou si j'étais suspendu au plafond. C'était là la façon idéale et intégrale de tuer le temps.

D'après J. WECHSBERG, (Die Weltwoche)

Leçon

88 Beispiel

An einem Samstagabend, zwanzig Minuten vor neun Uhr, stießen zwei Autos vor dem Bahnhof zusammen. Die Bremsen quietschten, aber zu spät. Die beiden Wagen verbeulten[1] sich ineinander. Die Passanten schrien auf, blieben aber stehen oder rannten herbei[2], um besser zu sehen. Keine Toten – nicht einmal Schwerverletzte, aber sonst, alles dran, wie der Jargon sagt : heftige Diskussionen, wer die Schuld trägt. Gespannte[3] Erwartung, wie die interessante Sache weitergehen wird. Die Sensation der vom Todesschrecken gezeichneten Gesichter – und da heult ja auch schon der Polizeiwagen heran.
Die Neugierigen stehen wie die Mauern. Die Beamten messen, protokollieren. Andere bemühen sich, den Verkehr durch die fast ganz blockierte Fahrbahn zu schleusen[4]. Wahrhaftig, es gibt etwas zu sehen. Aber einer der Zuschauer, ein gutgekleideter Herr, sieht mehr als alle anderen. Er geht zu dem Polizeiwagen, läßt sich einen Besen geben, und tut, wozu die Beamten noch nicht gekommen sind, weil so viel zu erledigen ist : der Herr fegt die Glassplitter zusammen, mit denen die Fahrbahn übersät ist und die sich in die Reifen der vorüberfahrenden Wagen bohren[5]. Die Neugierigen machen ihre Witze[6] über den feinen Straßenfeger.

*
* *

Ein junger Mann, ein Landarbeiter, überholte auf seinem Motorroller einen Personenwagen, den eine Dame steuerte[7], die allein in ihrem Wagen saß. Wenig später prallte der Mann auf dem

1. *die Beule (n),* la bosse, *verbeulen,* cabosser; *ineinander,* l'un(e) dans l'autre (leçon 70).
2. *herbei* et, plus loin, *heran,* marquent le rapprochement vers quelqu'un ou quelque chose.
3. *gespannt,* participe passé de *spannen,* tendre; atteler; intéresser vivement.
4. *schleusen,* m. à m. : écluser; *die Schleuse (n),* l'écluse.
5. *bohren,* percer, forer; *der Bohrer* (-), le forêt, la chignolle; *der Bohrhammer* ( ), le marteau-piqueur.
6. *der Witz (-e),* l'esprit, le trait d'esprit, *das Witzblatt,* le journal satirique; *witzig,* spirituel.
7. *steuern,* conduire; *das Steuer* (-), le gouvernail, le volant; ***die*** *Steuer* (n), l'impôt. (Mémento, n° 17).

L'exemple

Un samedi après-midi, à neuf heures moins vingt, deux voitures entraient en collision devant la gare. Les freins grincèrent, mais trop tard. Les deux voitures s'emboutirent violemment. Les passants poussèrent des cris, mais demeurèrent sur place, où accoururent pour mieux voir. Pas de morts — même pas de blessés graves, mais pour le reste, « le grand jeu », comme l'on dit : Discussions passionnées — qui est-ce qui est responsable? Attente fiévreuse — quelle sera la suite de cette affaire intéressante? Sensation de ces visages marqués par une frayeur mortelle — et voilà que, déjà, hurle la voiture de la police qui arrive. Les badauds sont là comme des murs. Les agents prennent des mesures, rédigent le procès-verbal. D'autres s'efforcent de régler la circulation sur la voie presque entièrement bloquée. Vraiment, il y a quelque chose à voir. Mais l'un des spectateurs, un monsieur bien mis, en voit plus que tous les autres. Il s'approche de la voiture de police, se fait remettre un balai, et fait ce à quoi les agents n'en sont pas encore parvenus, parce qu'il y a tellement de choses à régler : le monsieur balaie les éclats de verre dont la chaussée est parsemée et qui s'enfoncent dans les pneus au passage des voitures.
Les badauds, eux, font leurs plaisanteries à propos de ce balayeur distingué.

Un jeune homme, ouvrier agricole, dépassait avec son scooter une voiture de tourisme conduite par une dame qui était seule dans sa voiture. Un peu plus tard, le conducteur du scooter

Motorroller mit einem anderen Fahrzeug zusammen[8] und wurde auf die Fahrbahn geschleudert. Da lag er blutend[9]. Die Wagen stauten sich zu beiden Seiten. Die Menschen stiegen aus. Sie sahen zu, wie der junge Mann hilflos in seinem Blute lag.
Auch die Dame war ausgestiegen. « Er verblutet ja! » rief sie. Die Schlagader war verletzt. Ohne sich um die Zuschauer zu kümmern, riß sie sich die Bluse vom Leibe, zerteilte sie in Streifen[10], kniete sich in die Blutlache und band das Bein des Schwerverletzten ab[11]. « Sie müssen ganz ruhig bleiben », sagte sie zu ihm und strich ihm über das Haar. Das Blut floß nicht mehr. Fünf Minuten später war der Streifenwagen da, nach einer Viertelstunde der Krankenwagen. Die Ärzte konnten den Verletzten durchbringen, aber ohne die Hilfe der Dame wäre er nicht zu retten gewesen[12].
Sie hatte noch die Ankunft des Krankenwagens abgewartet, dann das Nötige zu Protokoll gegeben und war ohne viel Worte weitergefahren.

HERBERT KRANZ, (Der Engel schreibt's auf)
Verlag Joseph KNECHT, Frankfurt/Main

8. *zusammen,* ensemble, l'un contre l'autre; *prallen,* se heurter.
9. *das Blut,* le sang; *bluten,* saigner; *verbluten,* perdre tout son sang; *ver* exprime ici l'idée de perte, de mort.
10. *der Streifen (-),* la raie, la bande; plus loin, dans *Streifenwagen,* nous avons le féminin *die Streife (n),* la patrouille, le raid.
11. *binden* (a, u), lier; *ab/binden,* ligaturer.
12. m. à m. : il n'aurait pas été à sauver; après *sein* (ici, au subjonctif 2 passé.) *zu* + infinitif *(retten)* exprime soit une nécessité, soit une possibilité.

heurta violemment un autre véhicule et fut projeté sur la chaussée. Il était étendu, perdant son sang. Les voitures se serraient des deux côtés. Les passagers en descendaient. Ils regardaient le jeune homme privé de secours et gisant dans son sang.

La dame aussi était descendue.

— Mais il va mourir d'hémorragie! s'écria-t-elle.

L'artère (fémorale) était touchée. Sans s'occuper des spectateurs, elle arracha son chemisier (m. à m. : du corps), en fit des bandes, s'agenouilla dans la mare de sang et mit un garrot autour de la jambe du jeune homme grièvement blessé.

— Il faut absolument que vous restiez sans bouger, lui dit-elle en lui passant la main sur les cheveux.

Le sang ne coulait plus.

Cinq minutes plus tard, la voiture-patrouille était sur place et, au bout d'un quart d'heure, l'ambulance. Les médecins réussirent à tirer d'affaire le blessé, mais sans le secours de cette dame, il n'aurait pu être sauvé.

Elle avait encore attendu l'arrivée de l'ambulance et fait les déclarations nécessaires au procès-verbal; puis, discrètement (m. à m. : sans beaucoup de paroles), elle était repartie.

D'après HERBERT KRANZ

Leçon

89 Sterne über der Ruinenwelt

— Junge, Junge[1], wenn das man gut geht!
— So was habe ich doch schon mal gesehen!
Sanitätsfeldwebel Wustmann und der Fahrer Stroh tauschten Erinnerungen aus. Die anderen hockten hinter ihnen im Wagen zusammengesunken zwischen Kisten. Auch in Weißensee hatten sie, wie vorher in Werneuchen, nur eine zurückgelassene Weisung vorgefunden, nach der sie weiterzufahren hatten, da der Feldverbandplatz jetzt in Berlin-Mitte, im Reichstagsgebäude, eingerichtet werden sollte. Bis zum Güterbahnhof Weißensee waren sie gekommen und hier in marschierende Truppen geraten und in eine Nebenstraße abgedrängt.
Panzer, Flakgeschütze, Artillerie, Soldaten, Gewehrläufe, Fahrzeuge. Der Zug bewegte sich zur Panzersperre und weiter in Richtung Werneuchen-Tiefensee-Semmelberg.
— Wenn das man gut geht!
— In Odessa, 1944, sah es ebenso aus, und als sie vor die Stellungen kamen, die sie besetzen sollten, saß schon der Russe drin[2]!
— Damals hat es Schnaps gegeben.
— Ja, damals wurde noch gesoffen[3] und laut gegrölt.
Schweigende Kolonnen trieben zum Stadtrand. Der Schein aus brennenden Häusern flackerte auf den Gesichtern. In den Geruch von Brand und Kalkstaub mischte sich die Ausdünstung ungewaschener Leiber[4], von Leder, von verschwitzten[5] Uniformen.
— Aber das gab es damals nicht!
Der Volkssturm zog vorbei, alte Männer mit Schirmmützen und in belgischen Militärmänteln. Die Hitlerjugend — sogar Vierzehn-, Fünfzehn- und Sechzehnjährige in Wehrmachtsuniformen[6], die viel zu groß waren und lose an den mageren, halbwüchsigen Körpern hingen. Langsam rollende Räder und schlurfende Füße. Flieger mit Infanteriegewehren, Flakeinheiten und Teile von Bauregimentern, Offiziersschüler, Polizei mit Karabinern, die Berliner Feuerwehr, Straßenbahner.

1. *Junge, Junge...* Expression familière.
2. *drin* = *darin,* y, dedans.
3. *gesoffen,* participe passé de *saufen (soff, gesoffen),* boire (en parlant des animaux).
4. *der Leib (-er)* = *der Körper,* le corps.
5. *schwitzen,* transpirer, suer.
6. *die Wehrmacht,* la force militaire, l'armée.

Des étoiles sur le monde en ruines

— Diantre, (ça m'étonnerait) que tout cela finisse bien!
— Mais, j'ai déjà vu cela un jour!
Wustmann, l'adjudant de la compagnie sanitaire et Stroh, le chauffeur, échangeaient des souvenirs. Les autres étaient accroupis derrière eux, dans la voiture, parmi des caisses. A Weißensee également, comme précédemment à Werneuchen, ils n'avaient trouvé qu'une consigne laissée à leur intention et selon laquelle ils devaient poursuivre leur route, puisque l'infirmerie de campagne allait être installée, à présent, au cœur de Berlin dans le bâtiment du Reichstag. Ils étaient arrivés jusqu'à la gare de marchandises de Weißensee; là, ils étaient tombés sur des troupes en marche et avaient été refoulés sur une route secondaire.
Des blindés, des batteries anti-aériennes, de l'artillerie, des soldats, des canons de fusils, des véhicules. Le cortège avança jusqu'au barrage antichars et continua en direction de Werneuchen-Tiefensee-Semmelberg.
(Ça m'étonnerait) que tout cela finisse bien!
— A Odessa, en 1944, c'était pareil, et quand ils sont arrivés devant les positions qu'ils devaient occuper, les Russes y étaient déjà installés!
— En ce temps-là, il y avait de l'eau-de-vie.
— Oui, alors, on avait encore de quoi lamper, on braillait.
Des colonnes silencieuses avançaient vers les abords de la ville. La lueur qui venait de maisons en flammes, vacillait sur les visages. A l'odeur d'incendie et de poussière de chaux se mêlait l'exhalaison de corps non lavés, de cuir, d'uniformes trempés de sueur.
— Oui, mais alors, ça, ça n'existait pas!
C'était la Garde territoriale qui passait, des hommes âgés en casquettes à visière et portant des manteaux militaires belges. La Jeunesse hitlérienne — même des garçons de quatorze, quinze et seize ans, dans des uniformes de la Wehrmacht qui étaient bien trop grands et qui flottaient sur leurs corps maigres d'adolescents. Des roues qui tournaient lentement et des pieds qui traînaient. Des aviateurs portant des fusils d'infanterie, des unités anti-aériennes et des groupes appartenant à des régiments du génie, des élèves officiers, des policiers avec des mousquetons, le corps des sapeurs-pompiers de Berlin, des employés du tramway.

Die Straße war von einer Kette aus Feldgendarmen abgesperrt, damit sich keiner auf die Seite drücken konnte. Ein Mann wurde durchgelassen. Ein Oberleutnant, er blieb neben dem LKW[7] stehen und fragte, ob er mitfahren könnte.
— Guten Tag, Herr Splüge! wurde er von dem Sanitätshelfer Wittstock begrüßt.
— Du, Günther? Wo kommst du denn her?
— Aus Buckow, wir sind getürmt.
— Da habt ihr Glück gehabt, und wo soll es hingehen?
— Zum Reichstag[8]!
— Ausgezeichnet, da muß ich auch hin! Na, Herr Feldwebel?
— Meinetwegen schon, fragen Sie unsern Oberarzt.
Oberarzt Heide hatte nichts dagegen, und Splüge durfte aufsteigen und mitfahren.
Bis zum Reichstag waren es acht Kilometer, und unter normalen Umständen hätte es eine halbe Stunde Fahrt bedeutet. Jetzt standen sie bereits Stunden neben dem Güterbahnhof, und als sie sich endlich in Bewegung setzten, um auf Umwegen und auf Nebenstraßen zu ihrem Ziel zu gelangen, kamen sie nur langsam vorwärts. Trümmerstücke lagen im Wege. Sie sahen einen ganzen Straßenzug in Flammen — es gab kein Wasser zum Löschen[9], und das Feuer konnte sich ungehindert ausbreiten. Im Schrittempo ging es weiter. Der Mond stand am Himmel. Sterne hingen über der Ruinenwelt.

THEODOR PLIEVIER (Berlin)
Verlag Kurt Desch, München

7. *der LKW* (prononcez : [èlkavé] = *der Lastkraftwagen,* le camion; *die Last (en),* la charge; *die Kraft (¨ e),* la force, l'énergie.
8. *der Reichstag,* le Parlement.
9. *löschen,* éteindre, employé ici comme infinitif substantivé.

La route était barrée par un cordon de police militaire afin que personne ne puisse se défiler. On laissa passer un homme. C'était un lieutenant; il s'arrêta près du camion et demanda si on pouvait l'emmener.
L'infirmier auxiliaire Wittstock le salua :
— Bonjour, Monsieur Splüge.
— Toi, Gunther? D'où viens-tu donc?
— De Buckow, nous avons décampé.
— Eh bien, vous avez eu de la chance, et où allez-vous?
— Au Reichstag.
— Épatant! il faut que je m'y rende aussi! Alors, mon adjudant?
— Moi, je n'y vois pas d'inconvénient; demandez à notre médecin-lieutenant.
Heide, le médecin-lieutenant, ne s'y opposa pas et Splüge put monter et partir avec eux.
Il y avait huit kilomètres jusqu'au Reichstag et, dans des circontances normales, le trajet aurait pris une demi-heure. A présent, ils attendaient depuis des heures déjà, près de la gare de marchandises et lorsqu'ils se mirent enfin en mouvement pour atteindre leur but par des détours et des routes secondaires, ils n'avancèrent que lentement. Des éboulis jonchaient la route. Ils virent toute une enfilade de maisons en flammes — il n'y avait pas d'eau pour éteindre le feu, et celui-ci pouvait se propager librement. On continua au pas. La lune brillait dans le ciel. Des étoiles scintillaient sur ce monde de ruines.

D'après TH. PLIEVIER *(Berlin)*
Version française : Flammarion, Éditeur, Paris
(Traduction M. Laval, R. et F. Chenevrard)

90 Eine neue Welt bringst du uns...

— Wir haben einen Neuen, Herr Oberlehrer, sagte der Primus und lächelte vertraulich, einen aus dem Walde.
— So? Aus was für einem Walde? Wie heißt er?
— Josua Ehrwürden[1] Jeromin, Herr Oberlehrer.
— Nun, keine Dummheiten, bitte. Wo ist er?
Jons stand auf. Er trug den selbstgewebten Anzug und das Haar über der breiten Stirn sauber gescheitelt[2]. Seine Augen waren verstört, aber er hatte die Lippen fest geschlossen wie seine Mutter, wenn sie den Steuerbescheid in der Hand hielt.
— Ah, mein Lieber, da bist du ja, sagte der Ordinarius. Laßt eure Witze unterwegs[3]. Dieser kleine Mann aus dem Walde wird euch alle schlagen. Und wie heißt du, mein Sohn?
— Jons Ehrenreich Jeromin.
— Richtig, ich erinnere mich. Ein litauischer Vorname und ein Wunschvorname. Und bist du nun auch an Ehren reich[4], Jeromin?
— Nein, Herr Oberlehrer. Mein Vater sagt, vielleicht ist man[5] bei seinem Tode an Ehren reich.
— So... das ist recht von deinem Vater. Und was ist dein Vater?
— Mein Vater ist Fischer und hat einen Meiler für den Herrn von Balk.
— Einen Meiler, sieh mal an! Und wer ist der Herr von Balk?
— Der Herr von Balk hat ein Schloß hinter dem Walde, und ihm gehört alles, was wir haben, der See und der Wald und das ganze Dorf.
— So, und ist er ein guter Herr, der Herr von Balk?
— Ja, er ist ein guter Herr, aber er ist traurig, und er hat einen Affen, der Pferdeäpfel[6] wirft, und einen Papagei, der sprechen kann. Otto, sei doch nicht komisch sagt er.

1. *Ehrwürden.* L'élève se moque du nouveau, dont il transforme le prénom *« Ehrenreich »,* riche en honneur, en *« Ehrwürden »,* Votre Révérence.
2. *Das Haar scheiteln,* faire la raie. *das Haar,* le cheveu, la chevelure.
3. *Laßt eure Witze unterwegs,* m. à m. : laissez vos traits d'esprit en cours de route.
4. *an Ehren reich.* L'adjectif *reich* gouverne la préposition *an. Er ist reich an Erfahrung,* il est riche en expérience.
5. *Mein Vater sagt, vielleicht ist man...* suppression de *daß,* que, donc le verbe en 2e place.
6. *der Pferdeapfel* (⁼), m. à m. : la pomme de cheval.

Tu nous apportes un monde nouveau...

— Monsieur le professeur, il y a un nouveau, dit le premier de la classe avec un sourire familier, un gars de la forêt.
— Ah! de quelle forêt? Comment s'appelle-t-il?
— Josué Ehrwürden Jeromin, monsieur le Professeur.
— Allons, pas de bêtises, je vous prie. Où est-il?
Jons se leva. Il portait son costume tissé à la maison et sur son front large, une raie soigneusement tirée partageait ses cheveux. Ses yeux étaient inquiets, mais il fermait les lèvres aussi étroitement que sa mère quand elle tenait en ses mains la feuille des contributions.
— Ah, mon cher ami, te voilà donc! dit le professeur principal; Retenez vos plaisanteries : ce petit bonhomme de la forêt vous damera le pion à tous. Et comment t'appelles-tu, mon garçon?
— Jons Ehrenreich Jéromine.
— Parfaitement, je me souviens; un prénom lithuanien et un prénom porte-chance. Et es-tu déjà riche en honneurs, Jéromine?
— Non, monsieur le professeur. Mon père dit que peut-être à l'heure de la mort on est riche en honneurs.
— Tiens! C'est très bien de la part de ton père. Et que fait-il, ton papa?
— Mon papa est pêcheur et il entretient une meule à charbon pour le seigneur von Balk.
— Une meule! voyez-moi cela. Et qui est le seigneur von Balk?
— Le seigneur von Balk a un château au-delà de la forêt et tout ce que nous avons lui appartient, le lac et la forêt, et le village tout entier.
— Ah! Et est-ce un bon maître, le seigneur von Balk?
— Oui, c'est un bon maître, mais il est triste, et il a un singe qui vous lance du crottin de cheval et un perroquet qui sait parler. Otto, ne fais donc pas de blagues, dit-il.

Die Klasse wand sich vor Vergnügen, aber Oberlehrer Carl, genannt « Charlemagne », sah ihn nachdenklich an.
– Eine neue Welt bringst du uns, Jons, sagte er, und wir können sie brauchen... wir sind ein bißchen[7] versteinert[8] hier...
So begann der erste Tag in der Schule für Jons, aber nur in der Schule, denn das andre hatte lange vorher begonnen. In der Dämmerung[9] schon, als er erwacht war und die graue Mauer vor seinem Kammerfenster gestanden hatte. Er hatte die Vorhänge nicht zugezogen, weil er Vorhänge nicht kannte und an den Seiten des Fensters so viele Schnüre herunterhingen, daß er Angst hatte, sie anzufassen.
Zuerst glaubte er, daß er träume und daß Nebel über dem Walde liege, so daß die Fichten wie eine graue Mauer aussähen. Aber dann erinnerte er sich, und die Erinnerung stürzte wie ein Stein auf seine Brust. Herr Stilling hatte ihn hierher gebracht und war wieder abgefahren, und nun war er allein, so allein wie der Vogel über einem fremden Wald. Nur daß er keine Flügel hatte. Sein Herz brannte[10] ihm, aber immer wenn die Tränen kommen wollten[11], dachte[10] er an seinen Vater, wie er am Meiler zu ihm gesprochen hatte.

ERNST WIECHERT (Die Jeromin-Kinder)
Verlag Kurt Desch, München

7. *ein bißchen = ein wenig,* un peu.
8. *versteinert < der Stein,* la pierre; *versteinern,* pétrifier.
9. *die Dämmerung* a) le crépuscule b) l'aube.
10. Remarquez ces verbes mixtes : *brennen, brannte, gebrannt,* brûler; *denken, dachte, gedacht,* penser (Mémento, n° 53).
11. *Wenn die Tränen kommen wollten* – le verbe *wollen* est ici un auxiliaire du futur : aller + infinitif (Mémento, n° 51).

La classe se tordait de plaisir, mais le professeur Carl, surnommé Charlemagne, regardait Jons d'un air pensif.
— Tu nous apportes un monde nouveau, Jons, dit-il, et nous en avons besoin; nous sommes un peu sclérosés, ici.
C'est ainsi que commença, pour Jons, le premier jour de classe, en classe seulement, car le reste avait commencé depuis longtemps : dès l'aube, lorsqu'il s'était réveillé et avait vu le mur gris devant la fenêtre de sa chambrette. Il n'avait pas tiré les rideaux parce qu'il ne savait pas ce que c'était, et parce que des deux côtés de la fenêtre il pendait tant de cordons qu'il n'osait pas les saisir.
Tout d'abord il crut qu'il rêvait, et qu'un brouillard couvrait la forêt, de sorte que les pins avaient l'air de former une muraille grise. Mais ensuite il se souvint et ce souvenir tomba comme une peine sur son cœur. M. Stilling l'avait amené ici, et il était reparti, et maintenant il était seul, aussi seul que l'oiseau audessus d'une forêt étrangère. Avec cette différence qu'il n'avait pas d'ailes. Son cœur le faisait souffrir, mais lorsque les larmes voulaient lui monter aux yeux, il pensait à son père, lui parlant auprès de la meule.

ERNST WIECHERT (Les enfants Jéromine)
Paru chez Calmann-Lévy, Éditeurs
Traduction F. Bertaux et E. Lepointe

MÉMENTO

LA PRONONCIATION

En principe, toutes les lettres se prononcent en allemand. Nous indiquons entre crochets la prononciation en orthographe française, avec quelques rares signes conventionnels.

1. Les sons

■ Les voyelles

a, i, o se prononcent à peu près comme en français.

La lettre **u** correspond à notre « ou ».
Ex. : *Luft,* prononcez : [louft], *du* [dou].

e long se prononce [é] comme dans « léger ».
Ex. : *Weg,* prononcez [vék], *sehr* [zér].

e bref se prononce [è] comme dans « lettre ».
Ex. : *Erbe* [èrbe] *selten* [zèlten], *Welt* [vèlt].

Enfin, dans la syllabe finale, **e** est atone, c'est-à-dire non accentué, mais il se prononce toujours, comme dans « je, me, te, le ».

Les voyelles surmontées d'un tréma (dites « infléchies ») :
ä correspond à [è] dans « bête » : *Bär* [bèr].
ö correspond à [eu] dans « beurre »; *können* [keunen].
ü se prononce comme [u] dans « lune »; *Tür* [tur].

L'allemand a trois diphtongues qui se prononcent en une seule émission de voix, en accentuant la première des voyelles indiquées entre crochets.
au [**a**o] : *Maus* [m**a**oç], *laufen* [l**a**ofen].
ei, ai [**a**é] : *Seife* [z**a**éfe], *Kaiser* [k**a**ézer].
eu, äu [**o**eu] : *Leute* [l**o**eute], *Käufer* [k**o**eufer].

Durée des voyelles :
Elles peuvent être longues ou brèves. Leur durée est plus différenciée qu'en français. Pour indiquer la longueur d'une voyelle, la langue écrite peut redoubler celle-ci ou lui ajouter **h**, ou — pour le i seulement — ajouter un **e** qui ne se prononcera pas. Sont longues également les voyelles suivies d'une seule consonne. Nous placerons une flèche sous la voyelle longue.

Haar [har], *Sohn* [zon'], *Liebe* [libe], *legen* [légen'], *holen* [holen'].

Par contre les voyelles suivies de deux ou plusieurs consonnes sont brèves.

Garten [g**a**rten'], *Sonne* [z**o**ne].

■ Les consonnes

Beaucoup de consonnes ont un son analogue au son français. Cependant **b, d, g,** placés à la fin d'un mot se prononcent comme **p, t, k.**

Laub [l**a**op], *Rad* [rat], *klug* [klouk].

g se prononce toujours [g] comme dans « gare ».

geben [gében'], *Gift* [gift].

p, t, k sont prononcés sèchement et durement, avec un souffle.

ch a deux sons différents :
1. Après a, o, u, au, il a un son guttural, obtenu en émettant un râclement au fond de la gorge. Nous le transcrivons ainsi : [ṛ].

Buch [bouṛ], *Loch* [loṛ], *auch* [**a**oṛ].

2. Après e, i, ä, ö, ü, ei, eu, il a un son chuinté qu'on peut obtenir en partant de notre « ail »; on laissera la langue dans la position finale et l'on fera suivre le mot d'une expiration : c'est ce souffle chuinté que nous représentons par [cḥ].

ich [icḥ], *Mädchen* [m**è**tcḥen'], *schlecht* [chlècḥt].

h, quand il se trouve au début d'un mot, est fortement expiré, comme pour couvrir une glace de buée.

haben [h**a**ben'], *Hund* [houn't].

Mais il ne se prononce pas à l'intérieur ou à la fin du mot.

j se prononce comme y dans « balayer », ou comme « ille » dans « travailler ».

ja [ya], *jeder* [y**é**der].

ng se prononce comme dans « camping, parking ».

Zeitung [tç**a**étou^{ng}], *lang* [la^{ng}].

nk ajoute au son précédent [^{ng}] un k.

Bank [ba^{ng}k], *trinken* [tr**i**^{ng}ken'].

qu se prononce [kv].

Quelle [kv**è**le].

l'**r** final se prononce faiblement.

s est sonore devant une voyelle, au début ou à l'intérieur du mot, comme dans « maison ». Nous le représentons par [z]. A la fin du mot ou devant une consonne finale, **s** est sourd, [ç], comme dans « savoir ».

sehen [z**é**en'], *Rose* [r**o**ze]; *los* [loç], *ist* [içt].

ss ou **ß** sont toujours durs.

Masse [maçe], *Grüßen* [gr**u**çen].

sch correspond à notre « ch » dans « cheval ».

Schuh [chou], *Tisch* [tich].

st et **sp** en tête de mot se prononcent [cht] et [chp].

stellen [cht**è**len']; *spielen* [chp**i**len'].

v a le son de notre « f ».

Vater [fater], *viel* [fil], sauf dans quelques mots d'origine étrangère : *Vase* [v**a**ze].

w correspond à notre « v ».

was [vaç], *wo* [vo].

x se prononce [kç].

Axt [akçt], *Hexe* [h**è**kçe].

z ou **tz** ont le son dur de [tç] dans le mot « tsé-tsé ».

Zeigen [tç**a**égen].

Enfin, retenez qu'il ne faut pas faire de liaison entre les mots.

Er ist alt, il est âgé [ér/ içt/ alt].

■ L'accentuation

Il est essentiel de bien accentuer les mots, c'est-à-dire de prononcer plus fortement la syllabe accentuée, tout en élevant la voix. Les voyelles accentuées seront imprimées en caractères gras. C'est la voyelle radicale (le plus souvent l'avant-dernière syllabe) qui porte l'accent principal. Les autres syllabes se prononcent plus faiblement, mais ne sont jamais muettes.

Tanne [t**a**ne], *lernen* [l**e**rnen'].

Certains préfixes ne sont pas accentués :

Bekommen [bek**o**men].

Les mots composés et les verbes à particule séparable ont deux accents, un accent principal (le premier) et un accent secondaire, moins fort.

Wagentür [v**a**'gent**u**r], *aufmachen* [**a**'ofm**a**chen].

L'accent d'intonation qui consiste à mettre en relief les mots importants de la phrase, se superpose à l'accent des mots.

LA DÉCLINAISON

2. Les quatre cas

Der Fremdenführer zeigt dem Touristen den Garten des Schlosses, le guide montre au touriste le jardin du château.
Er zeigt ihn ihm, il le lui montre.

La langue allemande comprend quatre cas :

- Le **nominatif,** cas du sujet ou de son attribut (*der Fremdenführer,* le guide; *er,* il)
- Le **génitif,** cas du complément du nom, marquant la possession (*des Schlosses,* du château).
- Le **datif,** cas du complément d'objet indirect ou d'attribution (*dem Touristen,* au touriste; *ihm* à lui).
- L'**accusatif,** cas du complément d'objet direct (*den Garten,* le jardin; *ihn,* le, lui).

Ces cas sont surtout marqués par les articles ou autres déterminatifs, et moins souvent par le nom lui-même.

L'ARTICLE

3. L'article défini

	Singulier			Pluriel
	Masculin	Féminin	Neutre	Les trois genres
Nominatif	der, *le*	die, *la*	das, *le*	die, *les*
Génitif	des, *du*	der, *de la*	des, *du*	der, *des*
Datif	dem, *au*	der, *à la*	dem, *au*	den, *aux*
Accusatif	den, *le*	die, *la*	das, *le*	die, *les*

Les adjectifs ou pronoms suivants ont la même déclinaison que l'article défini :

dieser, -e, -es; -e, *ce, celui-ci*
jener, -e, -es; -e, *ce, celui-là*
jeder, -e, -es; *chaque, chacun*
mancher,-e,-es;e,*maint,plusd'un*
solcher, -e, -es; -e, *tel*

welcher, -e, -es; -e, *quel? lequel?*
alles (neutre) alle (plur.), *tout, tous*
einige (pluriel), *quelques, quelques-uns*
mehrere (pluriel), *plusieurs*

4. L'article indéfini

	Masculin	Féminin	Neutre
N.	ein, *un*	eine, *une*	ein, *un*
G.	eines, *d'un*	einer, *d'une*	eines, *d'un*
D.	einem, *à un*	einer, *à une*	einem, *à un*
A.	einen, *un*	eine, *une*	ein, *un*

Remarques :

● L'article indéfini n'a pas de pluriel.

Ein Tag, un jour; *Tage,* des jours.

● L'article négatif **kein,** ne pas un, ne pas de, suit la même déclinaison au singulier; au pluriel, il se décline sur l'article défini.

● Il en est de même des possessifs :

mein, *mon*	unser, *notre*
dein, *ton*	euer, *votre*
sein, *son (à lui)*	ihr, *leur*
ihr, *son (à elle)*	Ihr, *votre (forme de politesse)*

● A notre partitif « du, de la » correspond l'absence d'article.

Wein, du vin; *Bier,* de la bière.

LE NOM

LES NOMS MASCULINS

5. Règle générale

En règle générale, les noms masculins font leur pluriel avec la terminaison **-e** et l'inflexion sur le radical, si c'est possible, c'est-à-dire si la voyelle du radical est **a, o, u** ou **au** (voir leçon 4).

N.	der Sohn, *le fils*	die Söhne, *les fils*
G.	des Sohns, *du fils*	der Söhne, *des fils*
D.	dem Sohn, *au fils*	den Söhnen, *aux fils*
A.	den Sohn, *le fils*	die Söhne, *les fils*

De même :

der Arzt (¨ e), *le médecin*
der Baum (¨ e), *l'arbre*
der Berg (-e), *la montagne*
der Fisch (-e), *le poisson*
der Fluß (¨ sse), *la rivière*
der Freund (-e), *l'ami*
der Hof (¨ e), *la cour*
der Hut (¨ e), *le chapeau*
der Knopf (¨ e), *le bouton*
der Kopf (¨ e), *la tête*
der Markt (¨ e), *le marché*
der Offiz**ie**r (-e), *l'officier*
der Platz (¨ e), *la place*
der Rock (¨ e), *la jupe, l'habit*
der Schatz (¨ e), *le trésor*
der Schritt (-e), *le pas*
der Stock (¨ e), *la canne : l'étage (les étages :* die Stockwerke)
der Strauß (¨ e), *le bouquet*
der Strom (¨ e), *le fleuve, le courant*
der Strumpf (¨ e), *le bas*
der Stuhl (¨ e), *la chaise*
der Turm (¨ e), *la tour*
der Traum (¨ e), *le rêve*
der Wolf (¨ e), *le loup*
der Wunsch (¨ e), *le souhait*
der Zahn (¨ e), *la dent*

Remarque : Au génitif sing. des noms masc. forts ainsi que des noms neutres, on ajoute parfois **es** et non simplement **s,** pour faciliter la prononciation.

6. Les noms masculins — Pluriel en *-e,* sans inflexion

N.	der Tag, *le jour*	die Tage, *les jours*
G.	des Tag (e)s, *du jour*	der Tage, *des jours*
D.	dem Tag, *au jour*	den Tagen, *aux jours*
A.	den Tag, *le jour*	die Tage, *les jours*

De même :

der Abend (-e), *le soir*
der Arm (-e), *le bras*
der Aufenthalt (-e), *le séjour*
der Beruf (-e), *la profession*
der Besuch (-e), *la visite*
der Dom (-e), *la cathédrale*
der Erfolg (-e), *le succès*
der Hund (-e), *le chien*
der Laut (-e), *le son (bruit)*
der Monat (-e), *le mois*
der Mond (-e), *la lune*
der Mord (-e), *le meurtre*
der Mund (-e), *la bouche*
der Ort (-e), *l'endroit*
der Park (-e), *le parc*
der Pfad (-e), *le sentier*
der Punkt (-e), *le point*
der Ruf (-e), *l'appel*
der Schuh (-e), *le soulier*
der Stoff (-e), *l'étoffe*
der Verlust (-e), *la perte*
der Versuch (-e), *l'essai*

7. Les noms masculins – Pluriel en ¨ *er*

N.	der Mann, *l'homme*	die Männer, *les hommes*
G.	des Manns, *de l'homme*	der Männer, *des hommes*
D.	dem Mann, *à l'homme*	den Männern, *aux hommes*
A.	den Mann, *l'homme*	die Männer, *les hommes*

De même une dizaine d'autres :

der Geist (-er), *l'esprit*
der Gott (¨ er), *le dieu*
der Irrtum (¨ er), *l'erreur*
der Leib (-er), *le corps*
der Rand (¨ er), *le bord*
der Reichtum (¨ er), *la richesse*
der Strauch (¨ er), *le buisson*
der Wald (¨ er), *la forêt*
der Wurm (¨ er), *le ver*

8. Les noms masculins – Pluriel sans terminaison.

Les masculins terminés en **-el, -en, -er,** ne prennent pas de terminaison au nominatif pluriel. Comme les masculins des §§ 5, 6 et 7 ils ont la terminaison **s** au génitif singulier, et **-n** au datif pluriel.

● Certains ne varient pas au pluriel :

N.	der Wagen, *la voiture*	die Wagen, *les voitures*
G.	des Wagens, *de la voiture*	der Wagen, *des voitures*
D.	dem Wagen, *à la voiture*	den Wagen, *aux voitures*
A.	den Wagen, *la voiture*	die Wagen, *les voitures*

De même :

der Haken (-), *le crochet*
der Maler (-), *le peintre*
der Schlüssel (-), *la cité*
der Spiegel (-), *le miroir*

ainsi que quelques noms masculins en **-en,** qui peuvent aussi s'employer sans **n** au nominatif singulier :

der Frieden (-), *ou* der Friede, *la paix*
der Gedanken (-), *ou* der Gedanke, *la pensée*
der Glauben (-), *ou* der Glaube, *la foi, la croyance*
der Namen (-), *ou* der Name, *le nom*
der Willen (-), *ou* der Wille, *la volonté*

● Une vingtaine de masculins en **-el, -en, -er,** prennent au pluriel l'inflexion. Retenez :

der Apfel (¨), *la pomme*
der Bruder (¨), *le frère*
der Faden (¨), *le fil*
der Garten (¨), *le jardin*
der Hafen (¨), *le port*
der Hammer (¨), *le marteau*
der Laden (¨), *la boutique, le volet*
der Mangel (¨), *le défaut*
der Mantel (¨), *le manteau*
der Nagel (¨), *le clou, l'ongle*
der Ofen (¨), *le poêle*
der Schaden (¨), *le dommage*
der Vater (¨), *le père*
der Vogel (¨), *l'oiseau*

9. Les noms masculins dits « faibles »

Ils prennent **-n** ou **-en** à tous les cas, sauf au nominatif singulier. Ils désignent des êtres animés. Certains sont des noms d'origine étrangère, accentués sur la dernière syllabe.

N.	der Bär, *l'ours*	die Bären, *les ours*
G.	des Bären, *de l'ours*	der Bären, *des ours*
D.	dem Bären, *à l'ours*	den Bären, *aux ours*
A.	den Bären, *l'ours*	die Bären, *les ours*

De même :

der Bauer (n, n), *le paysan*
der Christ (en, en), *le chrétien*
der Fels (en, en), *le rocher*
der Fürst (en, en), *le prince régnant*
der Graf (en, en), *le comte*
der Held (en, en), *le héros*
der Herr (n, en), *le monsieur, le maître*
der Nachbar (n, n), *le voisin*
der Narr (en, en), *le fou*
der Ochs (en, en), *le bœuf*
der Philos**o**ph (en, en), *le philosophe*
der Sold**a**t (en, en), *le soldat*
der Spatz (en, en), *le moineau*
der Stud**e**nt (en, en), *l'étudiant*
der Vagab**u**nd (en, en), *le vagabond*

Remarque : Der Nachbar peut également être « mixte ». Voir p. 50, et n° 10 du Mémento.

10. Les noms masculins de la déclinaison dite « mixte »

Ils prennent (e)**s** au génitif singulier, et (e)**n** à tous les cas du pluriel.

N.	der Staat, *l'État*	die Staaten, *les États*
G.	des Staats, *de l'État*	der Staaten, *des États*
D.	dem Staat, *à l'État*	den Staaten, *aux États*
A.	den Staat, *l'État*	die Staaten, *les États*

Retenez aussi :

der Doktor (s, en), *le docteur*
der Dorn (s, en), *l'épine*
der Schmerz (es, en), *la douleur*
der Strahl (es, n), *le rayon*
der Vetter (s, n), *le cousin*
der Zins (es, en), *l'intérêt (argent)*

LES NOMS NEUTRES

11. Règle générale

Le pluriel de la majorité des noms neutres se forme en **-e,** sans inflexion. Au datif pluriel, on ajoute en plus **-n.** D'autre part, tous les neutres prennent **-s** au génitif singulier.

N.	das Paar, *la paire*	die Paare, *les paires*
G.	des Paars, *de la paire*	der Paare, *des paires*
D.	dem Paar, *à la paire*	den Paaren, *aux paires*
A.	das Paar, *la paire*	die Paare, *les paires*

De même :

das Bein (-e), *la jambe*
das Boot (-e), *la barque*
das Brot (-e), *le pain*
das Ding (-e), *la chose*
das Fest (-e), *la fête*
das Haar (-e), *le cheveu*
das Heer (-e), *l'armée*
das Heft (-e), *le cahier*
das Jahr (-e), *l'année*
das Kreuz (-e), *la croix*
das Los (-e), *le sort*
das Meer (-e), *la mer*
das Netz (-e), *le filet*
das Pferd (-e), *le cheval*
das Recht (-e), *le droit*
das Reh (-e), *le chevreuil*
das Reich (-e), *l'empire*
das Schaf (-e), *le mouton*
das Schiff (-e), *le bateau*
das Schwein (-e), *le porc*
das Seil (-e), *la corde*
das Spiel (-e), *le jeu*
das Stück (-e), *la pièce*
das Tier (-e), *l'animal*
das Tor (-e), *le portail*
das Werk (-e), *l'ouvrage*
das Wort (-e), *la parole*
das Zelt (-e), *la tente*
das Ziel (-e), *le but*

(Voir n° 5, remarque).

12. Les noms neutres – Pluriel en ̈ *er*

Une soixantaine de neutres font leur pluriel avec l'inflexion (si possible) et la terminaison **-er.**
Voici quelques-uns parmi les plus usuels :

das Bad (¨ er), *le bain*
das Band (¨ er), *le ruban*
das Bild (-er), *l'image*
das Blatt (¨ er), *la feuille*
das Buch (¨ er), *le livre*
das Dach (¨ er), *le toît*
das Denkmal (¨ er), *le monument*
das Dorf (¨ er), *le village*
das Ei (-er), *l'œuf*
das Fach (¨ er), *le casier*
das Feld (-er), *le champ*
das Geld (-er), *l'argent*
das Gesicht (-er), *le visage*
das Glas (¨ er), *le verre*
das Glied (-er), *le membre*
das Grab (¨ er), *la tombe*
das Gras (¨ er), *l'herbe*
das Gut (¨ er), *le bien, la propriété*
das Haus (¨ er), *la maison*
das Holz (¨ er), *le bois*
das Huhn (¨ er), *la poule*
das Kalb (¨ er), *le veau*
das Kind (-er), *l'enfant*
das Kleid (-er), *le vêtement, la robe*
das Land (¨ er), *le pays*
das Licht (-er), *la lumière*
das Lied (-er), *la chanson*
das Loch (¨ er), *le trou*
das Nest (-er), *le nid*
das Rad (¨ er), *la roue*
das Rind (-er), *la bête à cornes*
das Schild (-er), *l'enseigne*
das Schloß (¨ sser), *le château, la serrure*
das Tal (¨ er), *la vallée*
das Tuch (¨ er), *le drap*
das Volk (¨ er), *le peuple*
das Weib (-er), *la femme*
das Wort (¨ er), *le mot (isolé)*

13. Les noms neutres invariables au pluriel

Les neutres en **-el, -en, -er** ne changent pas au pluriel. Ils ne prennent que la terminaison **(e)s** au génitif singulier et **(e)n** au datif pluriel (sauf s'ils se terminent déjà par **n**). Il en est de même des diminutifs, que l'on forme avec la terminaison **-chen** ou **-lein.**

N.	das Fenster, *la fenêtre*	die Fenster, *les fenêtres*
G.	des Fensters, *de la fenêtre*	der Fenster, *des fenêtres*
D.	dem Fenster, *à la fenêtre*	den Fenstern, *aux fenêtres*
A.	das Fenster, *la fenêtre*	die Fenster, *les fenêtres*

De même :

das B**ü**blein (-), *le garçonnet*
das Fr**äu**lein (-), *la demoiselle*
das H**äu**schen (-), *la maisonnette*
das L**a**ger (-), *le dépôt*
das T**i**schlein (-), *la petite table*
das M**ö**bel (-), *le meuble*
das Z**i**mmer (-), *la chambre*
das W**e**sen (-), *l'être*

Ne varient pas non plus au pluriel :

das Geb**äu**de (-), *le bâtiment*
das Geb**i**rge (-), *la chaîne de montagnes*
das Gem**ä**lde (-), *le tableau*
das Gew**e**rbe (-), *l'industrie*

14. Les noms neutres « mixtes »

Comme les masculins « mixtes » (n° 8), ces neutres prennent **(e)s** au génitif singulier et **(e)n** à tous les cas du pluriel. Se déclinent ainsi :

das Auge (s, n), *l'œil*
das Bett (es, en), *le lit*
das Ende (s, n), *la fin*
das Hemd (es, en), *la chemise*
das Leid (es, en), *la souffrance*
das Ohr (s, en), *l'oreille*

Voir aussi la leçon n° 50 pour : das Herz, *le cœur.*

LES NOMS FÉMININS

15. Règle générale

Tous les féminins sont invariables au singulier. Au pluriel, ils prennent en majorité la terminaison **(e)n** à tous les cas.

N.	die Frau, *la femme*	die Frauen, *les femmes*
G.	der Frau, *de la femme*	der Frauen, *des femmes*
D.	der Frau, *à la femme*	den Frauen, *aux femmes*
A.	die Frau, *la femme*	die Frauen, *les femmes*

De même :

die Arbeit (-en), *le travail*
die Art (-en), *la manière*
die Blume (n), *la fleur*
die Erde (n), *la terre*
die Farbe (n), *la couleur*
die Feier (n), *la solennité*
die Freude (n), *la joie*
die Höhe (n), *la hauteur*
die Kirche (n), *l'église*
die Reise (n), *le voyage*
die Ruhe (n), *le repos*
die Schule (n), *l'école*
die Stimme (n), *la voix*
die Straße (n), *la rue*
die Stube (n), *la chambre, la pièce*
die Stunde (n), *l'heure*
die Tanne (n), *le sapin*
die Tür (-en), *la porte*
die Welt (-en), *le monde*
die Wiese (n), *le pré*
die Wolke (n), *le nuage*

Remarque : Les noms féminins en **-in** doublent l'**n** avant la terminaison du pluriel. Ex. : *die Ärztin, die Ärztinnen,* la doctoresse.

16. Les noms féminins — Pluriel en ¨ *e*

Un certain nombre de féminins (une quarantaine) d'une seule syllabe font leur pluriel avec l'inflexion et la terminaison **e**.

N.	die Nacht, *la nuit*	die Nächte, *les nuits*
G.	der Nacht, *de la nuit*	der Nächte, *des nuits*
D.	der Nacht, *à la nuit*	den Nächten, *aux nuits*
A.	die Nacht, *la nuit*	die Nächte, *les nuits*

Retenez :

die Bank (¨ e), *le banc*
die Braut (¨ e), *la fiancée*
die Brust (¨ e), *la poitrine*
die Frucht (¨ e), *le fruit*
die Hand (¨ e), *la main*
die Haut (¨ e), *la peau*
die Kraft (¨ e), *la force*
die Kuh (¨ e), *la vache*
die Kunst (¨ e), *l'art*
die Luft (¨ e), *l'air*
die Macht (¨ e), *la puissance*
die Nuß (¨ sse), *la noix*
die Schnur (¨ e), *le cordon*
die Stadt (¨ e), *la ville*
die Wand (¨ e), *la cloison*
die Wurst (¨ e), *la saucisse*

Notez également ces deux pluriels particuliers :

die M**u**tter, *la mère* — die M**ü**tter
die T**o**chter, *la fille* — die T**ö**chter

REMARQUES PARTICULIÈRES

17. Genres ou pluriels différents

der Band (¨ e), *le volume*	das Band (¨ er), *le ruban*
die Bank (¨ e), *le banc*	die Bank (en), *la banque*
der Kunde (n), *le client*	die Kunde (n), *la nouvelle*
der Leiter (-), *le directeur*	die Leiter (n), *l'échelle*
die Mark, *le mark*	das Mark, *la moëlle*
der Rat (¨ e), *le conseil (assemblée)*	der Rat, die Ratschläge, *le conseil, l'avis*
der See (n), *le lac*	die See (n), *la mer*
die Steuer (n), *l'impôt*	das Steuer (-), *le volant, le gouvernail*
der Stock (¨ e), *le bâton*	der Stock (-werke), *l'étage*
das Wort (¨ er), *le mot*	das Wort (-e), *la parole*

18. Les noms propres de personnes

N.	Karl, *Charles*	Eva, *Eve*
G.	Karls, *de Charles*	Evas, *d'Eve*
D.	Karl, *à Charles*	Eva, *à Eve*
A.	Karl, *Charles*	Eva, *Eve*

Les noms de personnes masculins et féminins prennent **-s** au génitif. Dans la langue courante, ce génitif est souvent remplacé par **von,** de, surtout quand le nom se termine par **-s.**

Ein Buch Karls, un livre de Charles; *ein Buch von Hans,* un livre de Jean.

Après un article au génitif, le nom propre reste invariable.

Die Gedichte des jungen Goethe, les poésies du jeune Goethe.

19. Le génitif saxon

Das Buch Karls, le livre de Charles, peut se remplacer par : *Karls Buch.* Dans ce cas, le nom déterminé *(das Buch)* perd son article. Cette construction n'est fréquente qu'avec les noms propres. Elle n'est pas possible quand l'article du nom déterminé est l'article indéfini, par exemple :

Ein Buch Karls.

20. Les noms géographiques

Les noms de ville ainsi que la plupart des noms de pays sont neutres. Ils s'emploient sans article et prennent **s** au génitif.

Die Industrie Deutschlands, l'industrie de l'Allemagne.

Mais on emploie l'article quand ces noms sont précédés d'un adjectif.

Österreich, l'Autriche; *das malerische Österreich,* l'Autriche pittoresque.

Quelques noms de pays sont féminins et s'emploient toujours avec l'article.

die Schweiz, la Suisse; *die Türkei,* la Turquie; *die Pfalz,* le Palatinat.

Exception : On emploie toujours avec son article le neutre *das Elsaß,* l'Alsace.

21. Les noms de poids et de mesure

S'ils sont du masculin ou du neutre, précédés d'un nombre, ces noms restent invariables au pluriel :

das Pfund : zwei Pfund Fleisch, *2 livres de viande*
das Kilo : fünf Kilo Zucker, *5 kilogrammes de sucre*
das Dutzend : drei Dutzend Eier, *3 douzaines d'œufs*
das Glas : vier Glas Wein, *4 verres de vin*
das Stück : sechs Stück Torte, *6 morceaux de tarte.*

22. Le complément de temps

● Il se met au génitif quand il exprime un moment imprécis :

Eines Tages, un jour; *eines Abends,* un soir.

On peut aussi employer une préposition :

Am Tage, le jour; *am Sonntag,* le dimanche.

● Quand il exprime un moment précis ou une durée, il se met à l'accusatif :

Diesen Monat, ce mois-ci; *nächsten Montag,* lundi prochain; *den ganzen Tag,* toute la journée (durant); *letztes Jahr,* l'année dernière.

L'ADJECTIF

23. L'adjectif attribut

L'adjectif attribut est invariable.

Der Dom (ou : *das Museum* ou *die Kirche) ist* **alt,** la cathédrale (ou le musée ou l'église) est ancienne.
Diese Häuser sind ***alt,*** ces maisons sont anciennes.

24. L'adjectif épithète — Déclinaison faible

Après un article défini, ou un déterminatif du même groupe (voir n° 1) :

	Masculin	Féminin	Neutre	Pluriel
N.	der gute	die gute	das gute	die guten
G.	des guten	der guten	des guten	der guten
D.	dem guten	der guten	dem guten	den guten
A.	den guten	die gute	das gute	die guten

25. L'adjectif épithète — Déclinaison forte

Employé sans article ni déterminatif, l'adjectif épithète prend les terminaisons de l'article défini, sauf au génitif singulier masculin et neutre, où il prend **-en.**

	Masculin	Féminin	Neutre	Pluriel
N.	guter	gute	gutes	gute
G.	gut**en**	guter	gut**en**	guter
D.	gutem	guter	gutem	guten
A.	guten	gute	gutes	gute

26. L'adjectif épithète — Déclinaison mixte

C'est la déclinaison de l'adjectif employé avec **ein, kein,** ou un adjectif possessif (voir n° 2).

	Masculin	Féminin	Neutre
N.	ein guter	eine gute	ein gutes
G.	eines guten	einer guten	eines guten
D.	einem guten	einer guten	einem guten
A.	einen guten	eine gute	ein gutes

Au pluriel, il suit la déclinaison forte (n° 25) dans le sens indéfini, **ein** n'ayant pas de pluriel. Après **kein** ou un possessif, il suit au pluriel la déclinaison faible (n° 24).

27. La comparaison — Règle générale

- L'égalité et l'infériorité :
  *Ich bin **so** flink **wie** du,* je suis aussi leste que toi.
  *Er ist **nicht so** flink **wie** ich,* il n'est pas aussi leste que moi.
- La supériorité :
  *Ich bin flink**er als** er,* je suis plus leste que lui.

● Le superlatif :

*Ich bin **der** flink**ste** von allen,* je suis le plus leste de tous. *Er ist **der** schlecht**este** Spieler,* il est le joueur le plus mauvais.

● Quelques adjectifs, presque tous à une seule syllabe, prennent l'inflexion au comparatif de supériorité et au superlatif.

kalt, froid; *kälter,* plus froid; *der kälteste,* le plus froid.

De même :

alt, vieux	*klug,* ingénieux	*krank,* malade
jung, jeune	*stark,* fort	*gesund,* bien portant
lang, long	*schwach,* faible	*schwarz,* noir
kurz, court	*kalt,* froid	*rot,* rouge
dumm, sot	*warm,* chaud	

(voir leçons 15 et 16).

28. Comparatifs et superlatifs irréguliers

groß, grand; *größer,* plus grand; *der größte,* le plus grand;
gut, bon; *besser,* meilleur; *der beste,* le meilleur;
hoch, haut; *höher,* plus haut; *der höchste,* le plus haut;
nah, proche; *näher,* plus proche; *der nächste,* le plus proche.

LE NOMBRE

29. Le nombre cardinal

1 eins	11 elf	21 einundzwanzig
2 zwei	12 zwölf	22 zweiundzwanzig
3 drei	13 dreizehn	23 dreiundzwanzig
4 vier	14 vierzehn	24 vierundzwanzig
5 fünf	15 fünfzehn	25 fünfundzwanzig
6 sechs	16 sechzehn	26 sechsundzwanzig
7 sieben	17 siebzehn	27 siebenundzwanzig
8 acht	18 achtzehn	28 achtundzwanzig
9 neun	19 neunzehn	29 neunundzwanzig
10 zehn	20 zwanzig	30 dreißig

40 vierzig	200 zweihundert
50 fünfzig	347 dreihundertsiebenundvierzig
60 sechzig	1 000 tausend
70 siebzig	4 000 viertausend
80 achtzig	100 000 hunderttausend
90 neunzig	1 000 000 eine Milli**o**n
100 hundert	1 000 000 000 eine Milli**a**rde

30. Le nombre ordinal (le rang)

1. der erste, *le 1*[er]	20. der zwanzigste, *le 20*[e]
2. der zweite, *le 2*[e]	21. der einundzwanzigste, *le 21*[e]
3. der dritte, *le 3*[e]	35. der fünfunddreißigste, *le 35*[e]
4. der vierte, *le 4*[e]	93. der dreiundneunzigste, *le 93*[e]
5. der fünfte, *le 5*[e]	100. der hundertste, *le 100*[e]
etc...	150. der hundertfünfzigste, *le 150*[e]
19. der neunzehnte, *le 19*[e]	1000. der tausendste, *le 1 000*[e]

(voir leçon 22)

31. Dérivés des noms de nombre

einmal, *une fois*
zweimal, *deux fois*

zehnmal, *dix fois*
hundertmal, *cent fois, etc.*

einfach, *simple*
zweifach, *double*

dreifach, *triple*
vierfach, *quadruple, etc.*

einerlei, *d'une sorte*
zweierlei, *de deux sortes*

dreierlei, *de trois sortes, etc.*

erstens, *premièrement*
zweitens, *deuxièmement*

drittens, *troisièmement, etc.*

das Drittel, *le tiers*
das Viertel, *le quart*

das Fünftel, *le cinquième, etc.*
exception : die Hälfte, *la moitié*

LE PRONOM

32. Le pronom personnel

1re personne

Sing.	N.	ich, *je, moi*	Plur	N.	wir, *nous*
	D.	mir, *me, à moi*		D.	uns, *nous, à nous*
	A.	mich, *me, moi*		A.	uns, *nous*

2e personne

Sing.	N.	du, *tu, toi*	Plur.	N.	ihr, Sie, *vous*
	D.	dir, *te, à toi*		D.	euch, Ihnen, *vous, à vous*
	A.	dich, *te, toi*		A.	euch, Sie, *vous*

3e personne

		Masculin	Féminin	Neutre
Sing.	N.	er, *il, lui*	sie, *elle*	es, *il; cela*
	D.	ihm, *lui, à lui*	ihr, *à elle*	ihm, *lui, à lui*
	A.	ihn *le, lui*	sie, *elle*	es, *le*

Pluriel pour les trois genres :	N.	sie, *ils, eux, elles*
	D.	ihnen, *leur, à eux, à elles*
	A.	sie, *les, eux, elles.*

Remarque : le génitif du pronom personnel est d'un emploi de plus en plus rare (leçon 74).
Voir les exemples dans les leçons 13, 14 et 74.

33. Le pronom réfléchi et le pronom réciproque

● A la 1re et à la 2e personne, le pronom réfléchi a la même forme que le pronom personnel, au datif et à l'accusatif. Mais à la 3e personne, singulier et pluriel, toutes les formes du pronom réfléchi sont **sich.**

Er wäscht sich, il se lave.
Sie kauft sich ein Kleid, elle s'achète une robe.

● Quand l'action est réciproque, on emploie **einander,** l'un l'autre, qui est invariable, mais qui peut être précédé d'une préposition : *miteinander,* l'un avec l'autre; *nacheinander,* l'un après l'autre.

Sie helfen einander, ils s'entre-aident.

Mais :

Sie wissen sich zu helfen, ils savent se débrouiller (m. à m. : s'aider eux-mêmes).

(Voir leçons 13 et 14).

34. Le pronom possessif

● meiner, *le mien* — unsrer, *le nôtre*
deiner, *le tien* — eurer, *le vôtre*
seiner, *le sien (à lui)* — ihrer, *le leur*
ihrer, *le sien (à elle)* — Ihrer, *le vôtre (politesse)*
seiner, *le sien (neutre)*

Ce pronom se décline comme l'article **der** (n° 3).

● Autres formes : *der meine,* ou *der meinige,* le mien; etc. (déclinaison : n° 24).

35. Le pronom démonstratif

● *dieser,* celui-ci; *jener,* celui-là (voir n° 3).

● *derselbe,* le même.
On décline séparément les deux termes :
G. *desselben,* du même; D. *demselben,* au même; A. *denselben,* le même (n° 24).
Féminin : *dieselbe,* la même
Neutre : *dasselbe,* le même
Pluriel commun : *dieselben,* les mêmes.

● Retenez aussi :

ein solcher, un tel (déclinaison, voir n° 26)
derjenige, der, celui qui (déclinaison n° 24)
was, ce qui, ce que.

36. Le pronom interrogatif

N.	Wer? *qui?*	Was? *quoi?*
G.	Wessen? *de qui?*	—
D.	Wem? *à qui?*	—
A.	Wen? *qui?*	Was? *que? quoi?*

Wer? se rapporte toujours aux personnes (singulier et pluriel).
Was? se rapporte aux choses.
(Voir leçons 3, 9, 10).

37. Le pronom relatif

	Masculin	Féminin	Neutre	Pluriel	
N.	der	die	das	die,	*qui, lequel, laquelle*
G.	dessen	deren	dessen	deren,	*de qui, dont*
D.	dem	der	dem	denen,	*à qui*
A.	den	die	das	die,	*que*

Remarque : Un autre pronom relatif, **welcher,** qui, se décline comme l'article défini; il n'existe pas au génitif et s'emploie moins fréquemment que **der.**
(Voir leçons 31, 32, 33).

38. Les pronoms indéfinis

man, *on*
etwas, *quelque chose*
nichts, *rien*
einer, *un, l'un*
keiner, *aucun*
irgend einer, *n'importe lequel*

jeder, *chacun*
mancher, *plus d'un*
jemand, *quelqu'un*
niemand, *personne*
viel, *beaucoup*
wenig, *peu*

Remarque : man est toujours sujet; autrement, on le remplace par les formes du pronom *einer;* au datif : *einem,* à vous; à l'accusatif : *einen,* vous.

> *Man freut sich, wenn einem ein guter Rat gegeben wird,* on se réjouit, quand un bon conseil vous est donné (quand on vous donne...).
> *Es freut einen,* cela vous réjouit.

LES PRÉPOSITIONS

39. Les prépositions gouvernant l'accusatif

durch, par, à travers
für, pour
gegen, contre, vers, envers
(voir leçon 8).
ohne, sans
um, autour de
wider, contre (rare)

40. Les prépositions gouvernant le datif

aus, (hors) de, en
bei, auprès de; chez (état)
mit, avec
nach, après; vers
seit, depuis
von, de
zu, à; chez (direction)

Retenez : *Ich gehe zu Herrn Fischer,* je vais chez Monsieur Fischer (direction).
Ich bin bei Herrn Fischer, je suis chez Monsieur Fischer (position). (Voir leçon 9).

41. Les prépositions gouvernant tantôt le datif, tantôt l'accusatif

in, dans
an, à, au bord de
auf, sur
vor, devant, avant
hinter, derrière
neben, à côté de
zwischen, entre
über, au-dessus de
unter, sous; parmi

Datif : lieu où l'on est.
Wo ist er? Er ist in dem Park.
Où est-il? Il est dans le parc.
Accusatif : lieu où l'on va.
Wohin geht er? Er geht in den Park.
Où va-t-il? Il va dans le parc.
(Voir leçon 12).

42. Les prépositions gouvernant le génitif

anstatt, *au lieu de*
längs, *le long de*
trotz, *malgré*
während, *pendant*
wegen, *à cause de*
außerhalb, *à l'extérieur*
innerhalb, *à l'intérieur*
oberhalb, *en haut de*
unterhalb, *en bas de*
jenseits, *au-delà de*
(Voir leçon 35).

LE VERBE

43. **Sein,** être

Indicatif		
Présent	*Prétérit*	*Futur*
ich bin	ich war	ich werde ... sein
je suis	j'étais, je fus	je serai
du bist	du warst	du wirst... sein
er (sie, es) ist	er war	er wird... sein
wir sind	wir waren	wir werden... sein
ihr seid	ihr wart	ihr werdet... sein
sie (Sie) sind	sie (Sie) waren	sie werden... sein

Passé composé	*Plus-que-parfait*
ich bin... gewesen	ich war... gewesen
j'ai été	j'avais été
du bist... gewesen	du warst... gewesen

Subjonctif I	**Subjonctif II**
Présent	*Présent*
ich sei	ich wäre
du seist	du wärest
Passé	*Passé*
ich sei... gewesen	ich wäre... gewesen
du seist... gewesen	du wärest... gewesen
Futur	*Futur*
ich werde... sein	ich würde... sein
du werdest... sein	du würdest... sein

Impératif		**Participes**	
sei!	seid!	*Présent*	*Passé*
sois	soyez (tutoiement)	seiend	gewesen
seien wir!	seien Sie!	étant	été
soyons	soyez (vouvoiement)		

● Voir § 49 Remarque n°1, et pour le subjonctif, Leçons 40 et 42.

44. **Haben,** avoir

Indicatif		
Présent • ich habe j'ai du hást er (sie, es) hat wir haben ihr habt sie (Sie) haben	*Prétérit* ich hatte j'avais, j'eus du hattest er hatte wir hatten ihr hattet sie hatten	*Futur* ich werde... haben j'aurai du wirst... haben er wird... haben wir werden... haben ihr werdet... haben sie werden... haben

Passé composé ich habe... gehabt j'ai eu du hast... gehabt	*Plus-que-parfait* ich hatte... gehabt j'avais eu du hattest... gehabt

Subjonctif I	**Subjonctif II**
Présent ich habe du habest *Passé* ich habe... gehabt du habest... gehabt *Futur* ich werde... haben du werdest... haben	*Présent* ich hätte du hättest *Passé* ich hätte... gehabt du hättest... gehabt *Futur* ich würde... haben du würdest... haben

Impératif		**Participes**	
habe! aie haben wir! ayons	habt! ayez (tutoiement) haben Sie! ayez (vouvoiement)	*Présent* habend ayant	*Passé* gehabt eu

● Voir § 49 Remarque n° 2, et pour le subjonctif, Leçons 40 et 42.

45. **Werden,** devenir

Indicatif		
Présent	*Prétérit*	*Futur*
ich werde	ich wurde	ich werde... werden
je deviens	je devenais, je devins	je deviendrai
du wirst	du wurdest	du wirst... werden
er (sie, es) wird	er wurde	er wird... werden
wir werden	wir wurden	wir werden... werden
ihr werdet	ihr wurdet	ihr werdet... werden
sie (Sie) werden	sie wurden	sie werden... werden

Passé composé	*Plus-que-parfait*
ich bin... geworden	ich war... geworden
je suis devenu	j'étais devenu
du bist... geworden	du warst... geworden

Subjonctif I	**Subjonctif II**
Présent	*Présent*
ich werde	ich würde
du werdest	du würdest
Passé	*Passé*
ich sei... geworden	ich wäre... geworden
du seist... geworden	du wärest... geworden
Futur	*Futur*
ich werde... werden	ich würde... werden
du werdest... werden	du würdest... werden

Impératif		**Participes**	
werde!	werdet!	*Présent*	*Passé*
deviens	devenez (tutoiement)	werdend	geworden
werden wir!	werden Sie!	devenant	devenu
devenons	devenez (vouvoiement)		worden (passif)

● Voir § 49 Remarque, n° 3, et pour le subjonctif, Leçons 40 et 42.

46. **Fragen,** demander *(verbe régulier)*

Indicatif		
Présent	*Prétérit*	*Futur*
ich frag e	ich frag te	ich werde... fragen
je demande	je demandais, je demandai	je demanderai
du frag st	du frag test	du wirst... fragen
er (sie, es) frag t	er frag te	er wird... fragen
wir frag en	wir frag ten	wir werden... fragen
ihr frag t	ihr frag tet	ihr werdet... fragen
sie frag en	sie frag ten	sie werden... fragen

Passé composé	*Plus-que-parfait*
ich habe... ge frag t	ich hatte... ge frag t
j'ai demandé	*j'avais demandé*
du hast... ge frag t	du hattest... ge frag t

Subjonctif I	**Subjonctif II**
Présent	*Présent*
ich frag e	ich frag te
du frag est	du frag test
Passé	*Passé*
ich habe... ge frag t	ich hätte... ge frag t
du habest... ge frag t	du hättest... ge frag t
Futur	*Futur*
ich werde... fragen	ich würde... fragen
du werdest... fragen	du würdest... fragen

Impératif		**Participes**	
frage	fragt	*Présent*	*Passé*
demande	demandez (tutoiement)	frag end	ge fragt
frag en wir!	frag en Sie!	demandant	demandé
demandons	demandez (vouvoiement)		

● Voir § 49 Remarque n° 4, et pour le subjonctif, Leçons 40 et 42.

47. **Geben,** donner *(verbe irrégulier)*

Indicatif		
Présent	*Prétérit*	*Futur*
ich geb e	ich gab	ich werde... geben
je donne	je donnais, je donnai	je donnerai
du gib st	du gab st	du wirst... geben
er (sie, es) gib t	er (sie, es) gab	er wird... geben
wir geb en	wir gab en	wir werden... geben
ihr geb t	ihr gab t	ihr werdet... geben
sie (Sie) geb en	sie (Sie) gab en	sie werden... geben

Passé composé	*Plus-que-parfait*
ich habe... gegeben	ich hatte... gegeben
j'ai donné	j'avais donné
du hast... gegeben	du hattest... gegeben

Subjonctif I	**Subjonctif II**
Présent	*Présent*
ich gebe	ich gäb e
du geb est	du gäb est
Passé	*Passé*
ich habe... gegeben	ich hätte... gegeben
du habest... gegeben	du hättest... gegeben
Futur	*Futur*
ich werde... geben	ich würde... geben
du werdest... geben	du würdest... geben

Impératif		**Participes**	
gib!	gebt	*Présent*	*Passé*
donne	donnez (tutoiement)	gebend	gegeben
geben wir!	geben Sie!	donnant	donné
donnons	donnez (vouvoiement)		

● Voir § 49 Remarque n° 5, et pour le subjonctif, Leçons 40 et 42.

48. **Sich freuen,** se réjouir *(verbe réfléchi)*

Indicatif

Présent	*Prétérit*	*Futur*
ich freue mich	ich freute mich	ich werde mich... freuen
je me réjouis	je me réjouissais	je me réjouirai
du freust dich	du freutest dich	du wirst dich... freuen
er (sie, es) freut sich	er freute sich	er wird sich... freuen
wir freuen uns	wir freuten uns	wir werden uns... freuen
ihr freut euch	ihr freutet euch	ihr werdet euch... freuen
sie (Sie) freuen sich	sie freuten sich	sie werden sich... freuen

Passé composé	*Plus-que-parfait*
ich habe mich... gefreut	ich hatte mich... gefreut
je me suis réjoui	je m'étais réjoui
du hast dich... gefreut	du hattest dich gefreut

Subjonctif I	**Subjonctif II**
Présent	*Présent*
ich freue mich	ich freute mich
du freuest dich	du freutest dich
Passé	*Passé*
ich habe mich... gefreut	ich hätte mich... gefreut
du habest dich... gefreut	du hättest dich... gefreut
Futur	*Futur*
ich werde mich... freuen	ich würde mich... freuen
du werdest dich... freuen	du würdest dich... freuen

Impératif		**Participes**	
freue dich!	freut euch!	*Présent*	*Passé*
réjouis-toi	réjouissez-vous (tutoiement)	sich freuend	sich gefreut
freuen wir uns!	freuen Sie sich!	se réjouissant	(se) réjoui
réjouissons-nous	réjouissez-vous (vouvoiement)		

● Voir § 49 Remarque n° 6.

49. **Gefragt werden,** être interrogé *(verbe passif)*

Indicatif

Présent	*Prétérit*	*Futur*
ich werde... gefragt	ich wurde gefragt	ich werde... gefragt werden
je suis interrogé	j'étais interrogé (je fus)	je serai interrogé
du wirst... gefragt	du wurdest... gefragt	du wirst... gefragt werden
er (sie, es) wird... gefragt	er wurde... gefragt	er wird... gefragt werden
wir werden... gefragt	wir wurden... gefragt	wir werden... gefragtwerden
ihr werdet... gefragt	ihr wurdet... gefragt	ihr werdet... gefragt werden
sie (Sie) werden... gefragt	sie wurden... gefragt	sie werden... gefragt werden

Passé composé	*Plus-que-parfait*
ich bin... gefragt worden	ich war... gefragt worden
j'ai été interrogé, on m'a...	j'étais interrogé (je fus...), on m'avait
du bist... gefragt worden	du warst... gefragt worden

Subjonctif I	**Subjonctif II**
Présent	Présent
ich werde... gefragt	ich würde... gefragt
du werdest... gefragt	du würdest... gefragt
Passé	*Passé*
ich sei... gefragt worden	ich wäre... gefragt worden
du seist... gefragt worden	du wärest... gefragt worden
Futur	*Futur*
ich werde... gefragt werden	ich würde... gefragt werden
du werdest... gefragt werden	du würdest... gefragt werden

	Participe passé
	gefragt werden être interrogé

● Voir § 49 Remarque n° 7.

Remarques :

1. On emploi *sein* pour former le passé composé et le plus-que-parfait des verbes intransitifs qui expriment un mouvement (*ich bin gesprungen,* j'ai sauté), ou un changement d'état (*ich bin... gewachsen,* j'ai grandi).

2. avec *haben,* on forme le passé composé et le plus-que-parfait des verbes transitifs (*ich habe... gefragt,* j'ai demandé), des verbes réfléchis (*ich habe mich gefreut,* je me suis réjoui) et des verbes intransitifs qui marquent un état (*ich habe... geschlafen,* j'ai dormi).

Exceptions : *Ich bin... geblieben,* je suis resté; *ich bin... gewesen,* j'ai été.

3. On emploie *werden* avec les autres verbes pour former le futur (*ich werde... fragen,* je demanderai), le conditionnel (*ich würde... fragen,* je demanderais) et le passif (*ich werde... gefragt,* je suis demandé, on me demande).

4. Quand le radical du verbe est terminé en *d, t* ou par un groupe de consonnes difficiles à prononcer, on place un *e* devant les terminaisons *st, t, te.*

> *Er arbeitet,* il travaille; *du zeichnest,* tu dessines; *er redete,* il parlait; *es regnete,* il pleuvait.

5. Au présent, les verbes irréguliers en *a* prennent l'inflexion aux 2e et 3e personnes du singulier. (*ich schlage,* je frappe, *du schlägst, er schlägt.*) Mais leur radical ne varie pas à l'impératif : *schlage!* frappe.
Il faut retenir l'infinitif, le prétérit et le participe passé de ces verbes irréguliers (voir leçons 4, 5, 15, 19, 20, 59 et suivantes, ainsi que le § 78 du mémento).

6. Notez l'emploi de ***haben,*** au passé composé et au plus-que-parfait. (Voir leçons 13, 14, 21).

7. L'emploi du passif est fréquent en allemand. On conjugue le verbe au passif avec l'auxiliaire *werden,* qui prend alors au participe passé la forme *worden* au lieu de *geworden* (voir leçons 36 et 39).

50. Cas particuliers

Les 6 verbes auxiliaires de mode :

POUVOIR	VOULOIR	DEVOIR
können	**wollen**	**müssen**
pouvoir, être capable de	vouloir (fermement)	devoir (nécessité)
dürfen	**mögen**	**sollen**
avoir le droit de	avoir envie de	devoir (obligation morale)

Présent		
ich kann du kannst er kann wir können ihr könnt sie können	ich will du willst er will wir wollen ihr wollt sie wollen	ich muß du mußt er muß wir müssen ihr müßt sie müssen
ich darf du darfst er darf wir dürfen ihr dürft sie dürfen	ich mag du magst er mag wir mogen ihr mog sie mogen	ich soll du sollst er soll wir sollen ihr sollt sie sollen
Prétérit		
ich konnte du konntest, etc	ich wollte du wolltest, etc	ich mußte du mußtest, etc
ich durfte. du durftest, etc	ich mochte du mochtest, etc	ich sollte du solltest, etc
Participe passé		
gekonnt	gewollt	gemußt
gedurft	gemocht	gesollt
Présent du subjonctif I		
ich könne	ich wolle	ich müsse
ich dürfe	ich möge	ich solle
Présent du subjonctif II		
ich könnte	ich wollte	ich müßte
ich dürfte	ich möchte	ich sollte

Remarques :

- Pour exprimer le conditionnel, on emploie le présent ou le passé du subjonctif II :

  Ich möchte, je voudrais; *ich hätte... gemocht,* j'aurais voulu.

- Le futur se remplace le plus souvent par le présent.

  Er kann bald schwimmen, il saura (= pourra) bientôt nager.

- Le passé composé a deux formes :

  Ich **habe** *es* **gewollt,** je l'ai voulu.

Mais :

  Ich **habe** *es kaufen* **wollen,** j'ai voulu l'acheter.

(Voir leçons 18, 19, 20, 46, 52)

51. Nuances des auxiliaires de mode

können
savoir faire : *Er kann gut englisch,* il sait bien (parler) l'anglais.
supposition : *Es kann möglich sein,* il se peut que ce soit possible.
wollen
futur proche : *Wir wollen nun etwas essen,* nous allons manger quelque chose maintenant.
mögen
concession, éventualité : *Es mag wohl sein,* c'est bien possible.
(souhait) : *Möge er glücklich sein,* puisse-t-il être heureux.
müssen
probabilité ou déduction : *Warum kommt er nicht? er muß krank sein,* pourquoi ne vient-il pas? il doit être malade.
sollen
futur : *Das Paket soll morgen ankommen,* le paquet arrivera demain.
On dit que... : *Seine Küche soll sehr gepflegt sein,* on dit que sa cuisine est très soignée.

52. Le verbe wissen

Le verbe **wissen,** savoir, se conjugue comme un auxiliaire de mode. Cependant, son passé composé est toujours : *ich habe... gewußt,* j'ai su. Et l'on dira : *er weiß* **zu** *leben,* il sait vivre.

Présent	
ich weiß, *je sais* du weißt, *tu sais,* er weiß, *il sait,*	wir wissen, *nous savons* ihr wißt, *vous savez* sie wissen, *ils (elles) savent*
Prétérit ich wußte, *je savais, je sus*	*Passé composé* ich habe... gewußt, *j'ai su*
Subjonctif I présent ich wisse, *que je sache*	*Subjonctif II présent* ich wüßte, *je saurais*

(Voir leçon 24).

53. Les verbes mixtes

brennen,	brannte	gebrannt	*brûler*
kennen,	kannte	gekannt	*connaître*
nennen,	nannte	genannt	*nommer*
rennen,	rannte	gerannt	*courir*
senden,	sandte	gesandt	*envoyer*
wenden,	wandte	gewandt	*tourner*
bringen,	brachte	gebracht	*apporter*
denken,	dachte	gedacht	*penser*

(Voir leçon 44).

L'ADVERBE

54. Notions générales

- La plupart des adjectifs allemands s'emploient comme adverbes de manière, sans changement :

  Er ist reich, il est riche (adjectif).
  Er hat mich reich belohnt, il m'a récompensé richement (adverbe).

- Le comparatif se forme en **-er,** comme celui de l'adjectif.

  Du fährst schneller als ich, tu roules plus vite que moi.

- Le superlatif se forme avec **am... sten.**

  Karl fährt am schnellsten, Charles roule le plus vite. (Voir leçons 16 et 49).

55. Comparatifs et superlatifs irréguliers

gut, bien; *besser,* mieux; *am besten,* le mieux;
viel, beaucoup; *mehr,* plus; *am meisten,* le plus;
gern, volontiers; *lieber,* plus volontiers; *am liebsten,* le plus volontiers.

Locutions :

Ich esse gern(e) Eis, j'aime la glace;
Ich esse lieber Torte, j'aime mieux la tarte;
Ich esse am liebsten Obst, j'aime le mieux (je préfère) les fruits.

(voir leçon 49).

56. Adverbes de manière

allmählich, *peu à peu*
anders, *autrement*
dennoch, *cependant*
leider, *malheureusement*
umsonst, *en vain*
wohl, *bien; sans doute*

Avec le nom : die Weise, *la manière,* on forme des adverbes composés : glücklicherweise, *heureusement;* möglicherweise, *il se peut que;* teilweise, *partiellement;* stückweise, *morceau par morceau.*

57. Adverbes de lieu

Position	*Direction vers...*	*Provenance de ...*
wo? *où?*	wohin? *où?*	woher? *d'où?*
da, *là, y*	dahin, *là, y*	daher, *de là, en*
dort, *là-bas*	dorthin, *(vers) là-bas*	dorther, *de là-bas*
hier, *ici*		hierher, *ici*
überall, *partout*	überallhin, *partout*	überallher, *de partout*
draußen, *dehors*	hinaus, *dehors*	heraus, *dehors*
drinnen, *là-dedans*	hinein, *dedans*	herein, *dedans*
oben, *en haut*	hinauf, *en haut*	herauf, *en haut*
unten, *en bas*	hinunter, *en bas*	herunter, *en bas*
daheim, *à la maison (être...)*	heim, *à la maison (aller...)*	von daheim, *de la maison*
vorn, *devant*		
hinten, *derrière*		

58. Adverbes de temps

wann? *quand*
jetzt, nun, *maintenant*
jemals, *jamais* (positif)
niemals, *ne ... jamais*
meistens, *le plus souvent*
sonst, *autrefois*
früher, *plus tôt*
nachher, *après cela*
einst, einmal, *un jour*
da, dann, *alors*
damals, *à cette époque*
immer, *toujours*
schon, *déjà*
noch, *encore*
noch nicht, *pas encore*
heute, *aujourd'hui*
gestern, *hier*
nicht einmal, *même pas*
vorgestern, *avant-hier*
morgen, *demain*
morgen früh, *demain matin*
übermorgen, *après-demain*
morgens, *le matin*
abends, *le soir*
nachts, *de nuit*
manchmal, *quelquefois*
oft, oftmals, *souvent*
bald, *bientôt*
gleich, *tout de suite*
zuerst, *d'abord*
zuletzt, *enfin*
lange, *longtemps*
täglich, *par jour*
monatlich, *par mois*
jährlich, *par an*

(voir leçon 8)

59. Adverbes de quantité

wieviel? *combien?*
beinahe, fast, *presque*
erstens, *premièrement*
zweitens, *deuxièmement*
etwa, *environ*
etwas, *un peu*
ganz, *tout-à-fait*
teils, *en partie*
genug, *assez (suffisamment)*
ziemlich, *assez (passablement)*
gleichfalls, *pareillement*
halb, *à moitié*
kaum, *à peine*
nur, *seulement*
erst, *seulement (temps)*
recht, *bien*
sehr, *très*
viel, *beaucoup*
wenig, *peu*
so, ebenso, *si*
sogar, *même*
ungefähr, *environ*
zu, zu sehr, *trop*

LA SYNTAXE

LA PROPOSITION PRINCIPALE OU INDÉPENDANTE

60. Notions générales

● Le verbe personnel est toujours à la deuxième place. Il n'est précédé que d'un seul membre de phrase.

Herr Müller ***fährt*** *oft nach München,* Monsieur Müller va souvent à Munich.

● Le verbe impersonnel (infinitif ou participe) se place après les compléments.

Herr Müller wird oft nach München ***fahren*** (... ira ...).
Herr Müller ist oft nach München ***gefahren*** (... est allé ...).

● La proposition principale peut commencer par un terme autre que le sujet. Dans ce cas, le verbe garde la 2e place, et le sujet se place après le verbe (Inversion).

Oft ***fährt*** *Herr Müller nach München. Nach München* ***fährt*** *Herr Müller oft.*

● ***Exceptions :*** Le verbe prend la première place dans la proposition interrogative (directe) ou impérative.

Fährt *Herr Müller oft nach München?* Monsieur Müller va-t-il souvent à Munich?
Nimm *diesen Koffer mit!* Emporte cette malle!

D'autre part, on ne fait pas l'inversion après les conjonctions de coordination : *und,* et; *oder,* ou; *aber,* mais; *sondern,* mais (au contraire); *denn,* car; ni après : *ja,* oui; *nein,* non; *doch,* si; ni après les exclamations telles que : *ach!* hélas! *mein Gott!* mon Dieu!

Donnerwetter! Er hat den Koffer vergessen, Mille tonnerres! Il a oublié la malle!

(voir leçons 2, 6, 11).

LA PROPOSITION SUBORDONNÉE

61. Construction

● Le verbe personnel occupe la dernière place dans la proposition introduite par un terme subordonnant (conjonction, relatif; interrogation indirecte). C'est la règle du **rejet du verbe.**

Man sagt, daß Herr Müller oft nach München fährt,
On dit que Monsieur Müller va souvent à Münich.

● L'infinitif ou le participe sont placés avant le verbe personnel.

*Ich glaube, daß er uns **besuchen** wird,* je crois qu'il nous rendra visite.

● ***Exceptions :*** L'auxiliaire précède le double infinitif :

*Er kam nicht, weil er gestern **hat** arbeiten müssen,*
Il ne vint pas, parce qu'il a dû travailler hier.

(voir leçon 22, ainsi que § 66 et § 67).

62. Conjonctions de subordination

als, *quand (au moment où)*
wenn, *quand (toutes les fois que)*
wenn, *si* (conditionnel)
ob, *si* (dubitatif)
wann, *quand* (interrogatif)
indem, *tandis que*
bevor, ehe, *avant que*
nachdem, *après que*
sobald, *aussitôt que*
daß, *que*
weil, *parce que*
da, *puisque, comme*
wie, *comme*
damit, *pour que*
falls, *au cas où*
obgleich, *quoique*
obschon, *bien que*
während, *pendant que*

63. *Wenn* et *ob*

● Notre « si » conditionnel se traduit par **wenn :**

Wenn ich Zeit hätte, würde ich dieses Buch sofort lesen,
Si j'avais le temps, je lirais ce livre immédiatement.

● Quand notre si exprime un doute ou une question, on le traduit par **ob** :

Ich weiß nicht, ob ich morgen kommen kann, je ne sais pas si je pourrai venir demain.

(voir leçons 25 et 30).

64. *Wenn* et *als*

● Pour traduire notre quand, lorsque, on emploie **wenn** avec un verbe au présent ou au futur :

Wenn er nach München fährt (ou : *fahren wird)...* quand il va (ira) à Munich...

● Avec un verbe au passé, on emploie **wenn** avec l'idée de « toutes les fois que » :

Wenn er nach München fuhr, nahm er oft seinen Freund mit, quand il allait à Munich, il emmenait souvent son ami.

Pour une action ou un état unique dans le passé, il faut traduire « quand » par ***als*** (au moment où) (voir leçon 27) :

Als er zum ersten Mal nach München fuhr,... quand il alla pour la première fois à Munich...

65. *Wenn* et *wann*

Wann, quand, à quel moment? s'emploie uniquement dans un sens interrogatif.

Ich frage mich, wann er kommen wird, je me demande quand il viendra.

66. *Wenn* sous-entendu

Dans la subordonnée qui précède la principale, on peut sous-entendre *wenn.* Dans ce cas, on commence par le verbe dans la subordonnée. La principale commence le plus souvent par **so,** (*ou* dann *ou* da), qui ne se traduit pas. Ainsi, on peut dire indifféremment :

Wenn das Wetter schön wäre, würde ich an den Rhein fahren.
ou : *Wäre das Wetter schön, so würde ich an den Rhein fahren,*
Si le temps était beau, j'irais au bord du Rhin.

(voir leçon 38).

67. *Daß* sous-entendu

Après un verbe d'opinion placé dans une proposition affirmative, on peut sous-entendre *daß,* que, qu'il faudra rendre dans la traduction; le verbe est alors à la 2e place :

Ich hoffe, daß es nicht schlimm ist.
ou : *Ich hoffe,* ***es ist*** *nicht schlimm,*
J'espère que ce n'est pas grave (voir leçon 35).

AUTRES RÈGLES DE CONSTRUCTION

68. La place de *nicht*

En général **nicht,** *ne pas,* se place après les compléments sans préposition :

Er möchte dieses Programm nicht sehen, il ne voudrait pas voir ce programme.

Mais la négation se place avant les compléments avec préposition :

Er möchte nicht vor dem Bildschirm sitzen, il ne voudrait pas être assis devant l'écran.

Nicht précède également le terme qu'il concerne en particulier :

Er möchte nicht den Film, sondern die Fernsehnachrichten sehen, ce n'est pas le film, mais les actualités télévisées qu'il voudrait voir.

69. L'ordre des compléments

Cet ordre peut varier selon l'importance que l'on accorde à tel ou tel complément; cependant, on suit en général l'ordre suivant :

- Le temps vient avant le lieu :

  Ich werde morgen früh nach Mainz abfahren, je partirai demain matin pour Mayence.

- Le complément d'attribution vient avant le complément direct d'objet :

  Ich werde deinem Freund das Paket übergeben, je remettrai le paquet à ton ami.

- Toutefois, les pronoms se mettent avant les autres compléments :

  Ich werde es deinem Freund übergeben, je le remettrai à ton ami.

- Dans le cas de deux pronoms compléments, l'accusatif précède le datif :

  Ich werde es ihm übergeben, je le lui remettrai.

70. L'infinitif complément

● En règle générale, l'infinitif complément est précédé de **zu** et se place à la fin de la proposition :

Ich habe keine Lust zu warten, je n'ai pas envie d'attendre.
Ich hoffe ihn zu sehen, j'espère le voir.

● Quand l'infinitif a une particule séparable, **zu** s'intercale entre la particule et le verbe.

Ich glaube, es ist Zeit abzufahren, je crois qu'il est temps de partir.

● De même qu'en français, certains verbes prennent un infinitif complément sans aucune préposition.

Er will eine Postkarte kaufen, il veut acheter une carte postale.

(voir leçon 26).

71. La subordonnée infinitive

Trois prépositions seulement peuvent introduire une subordonnée infinitive : *um ... zu,* pour ...; *ohne ... zu ...* sans ...; *anstatt ... zu ...* au lieu de...

Er setzte sich in die erste Reihe, um das Stück besser zu sehen, il prit une place dans la première rangée pour mieux voir la pièce.
Er ging an mir vorbei, ohne mich zu sehen, il passa près de moi sans me voir.
Er hat seinen Mantel anbehalten, anstatt ihn in der Garderobe abzugeben, il a gardé son manteau, au lieu de le remettre au vestiaire.

Remarque. — Nos tournures : avant de (+ infinitif) et : après avoir (+ infinitif), doivent se rendre par *bevor,* avant que et *nachdem,* après que, suivis non d'un infinitif, mais d'un sujet et d'un verbe conjugué :

Avant de partir, il prend son chapeau, *bevor er weggeht, nimmt er seinen Hut.*
Après avoir acheté le journal, il alla au bureau, *nachdem er die Zeitung gekauft hatte, ging er ins Büro.*

(voir leçons 28, 29).

EMPLOI DU SUBJONCTIF

72. Le subjonctif, mode de l'irréel

- Affirmation :
  Ich käme oft hierher, je viendrais souvent ici.
- Souhait :
  Wenn er doch heute käme! si seulement il venait aujourd'hui.
- Condition :
  Wenn er reich wäre, würde er sich dieses Haus kaufen, s'il était riche, il s'achèterait cette maison.

73. Le style indirect

Quand on rapporte les paroles d'autrui (il dit que...), on emploie en général le subjonctif; l'indicatif peut s'employer pour un fait absolument certain. Souvent, on supprime *daß,* que.

Choix du temps (il dépend de celui qu'on aurait dans le style direct) :

- Style direct :
  Er sagt : « Ich bin krank » **(présent),** il dit : « Je suis malade ».
  Style indirect :
  Er sagt, er sei krank (subj. I présent).
  Er sagt, er wäre krank (subj. II présent).
  Il dit qu'il est (qu'il était) malade.
- Style direct :
  Er sagt : « Ich war krank » **(passé),** il dit : « J'étais malade ».
  Style indirect :
  Er sagt, er sei krank gewesen (subj. I passé).
  Er sagt, er wäre krank gewesen (subj. II passé).
  Il dit qu'il avait été malade.
- Style direct :
  Er sagt : « Ich werde krank sein » **(futur).**
  Il dit : « Je serai malade ».
  Style indirect :
  Er sagt, er werde krank sein (subj. I futur).
  Er sagt, er würde krank sein (subj. II futur).
  Il dit qu'il serait malade.

Note : On emploie en général le subjonctif I. Cependant, si le subjonctif I ne se distingue pas de l'indicatif, ou si l'on veut insister sur le fait qu'on n'adhère pas aux paroles rapportées, on emploie les temps du subjonctif II.

LE RÉGIME DES VERBES

74. Verbes demandant le datif

beg**e**gnen, *rencontrer*
danken, *remercier*
dienen, *servir*
folgen, *suivre*
glauben, *croire*
gratul**ie**ren, *féliciter*
helfen, *aider*
sich nähern, *s'approcher*
schmeicheln, *flatter*

Ich begegnete ***meinem*** *Freund,* je rencontrai mon ami.

75. Verbes gouvernant l'accusatif

aus/lachen, *se moquer de*
ben**u**tzen, *profiter de*
fragen, *demander à*
heißen (ie, ei), *ordonner à q. q.*
kosten, *coûter*
lehren, *enseigner à*
schelten (a, o; i), *traiter de*

Ich fragte ***meinen*** *Freund, ob...,* Je demandai à mon ami, si...

(Verbes gouvernant le génitif : leçon 74).

76. Verbes suivis d'une préposition et du datif

sich freuen an, *se réjouir de*
hindern an, *empêcher de*
teil/nehmen (a, o; i) an, *participer à*
zweifeln an, *douter de*
best**e**hen (a, a), aus, *se composer de*
trinken (a, u) aus, *boire dans*
beg**i**nnen (a, o) mit, *commencer par*
enden mit, *finir par*
bed**e**cken mit, *couvrir de*
sich begn**ü**gen mit, *se contenter de*
sich besch**ä**ftigen mit, *s'occuper de*
füllen mit, *remplir de*
vergleichen (i, i) mit, *comparer à*
fragen nach, *s'informer de*
sich sehnen nach, *aspirer à*
erz**ä**hlen von, *parler de*
sich fürchten vor, *avoir peur de*
schützen vor, *protéger contre*
warnen vor, *mettre en garde*
dienen zu, *servir à*
ein/laden (u, a) zu, *inviter à*
ern**e**nnen zu, *nommer*
geh**ö**ren zu, *faire partie de*
zwingen (a, u) zu, *forcer à*

77. Verbes suivis d'une préposition et de l'accusatif

denken an, *penser à*
glauben an, *croire en*
sich er**i**nnern an, *se souvenir de*
klagen über, *se plaindre de*
sich richten an, *s'adresser à*

antworten auf, *répondre à*
sich vorbereiten auf, *se préparer à*
warten auf, *attendre*
zählen auf, *compter sur*
vertr**au**en auf, *avoir confiance en*

danken für, *remercier de*
gelten für, *passer pour*

halten für, *tenir pour*
sorgen für, *veiller à*
sich ärgen über, *s'irriter de*
sich gew**ö**hnen an, *s'habituer à*
lachen über, *rire de*
nach/denken über, *réfléchir à*
spotten über, *se moquer de*

sich wundern über, *s'étonner de*

ben**ei**den um, *envier q. ch. à q. q.*
bitten (a, e) um, *demander q. ch.*

es handelt sich um, *il s'agit de*
sich kümmern um, *se soucier de*

LES VERBES IRRÉGULIERS

78. Liste alphabétique.

L'astérisque indique que le passé composé se forme avec l'auxiliaire **sein.** Nous indiquons, en bas de page, la 3ᵉ personne du singulier, au présent, si le radical est modifié.

Infinitif	Prétérit	Part. passé	
backen[1]	buk	gebacken	*cuire au four*
befehlen[2]	befahl	befohlen	*ordonner*
sich befleißen	befliß	beflissen	*s'appliquer*
beginnen	begann	begonnen	*commencer*
beißen	biß	gebissen	*mordre*
bergen[3]	barg	geborgen	*abriter*
*bersten[4]	barst	geborsten	*éclater*
bewegen	bewog	bewogen	*engager à...*
biegen	bog	gebogen	*courber*

1. er bäckt. — 2. er befiehlt. — 3. er birgt. — 4. er birst.

bieten	bot	geboten	*offrir*
binden	band	gebunden	*lier*
bitten	bat	gebeten	*prier (de faire)*
blasen[5]	blies	geblasen	*souffler*
*bleiben	blieb	geblieben	*rester*
braten[6]	briet	gebraten	*faire rôtir*
brechen[7]	brach	gebrochen	*briser*
brennen	brannte	gebrannt	*brûler*
bringen	brachte	gebracht	*apporter*
denken	dachte	gedacht	*penser*
dreschen[8]	drosch	gedroschen	*battre (au fléau)*
*dringen	drang	gedrungen	*pénétrer*
dürfen[9]	durfte	gedurft	*pouvoir*
empfehlen[10]	empfahl	empfohlen	*recommander*
*erlöschen[11]	erlosch	erloschen	*s'éteindre*
*erschrecken[12]	erschrak	erschrocken	*s'effrayer*
erwägen	erwog	erwogen	*considérer*
essen[13]	aß	gegessen	*manger*
*fahren[14]	fuhr	gefahren	*aller (véhicule)*
*fallen[15]	fiel	gefallen	*tomber*
fangen[16]	fing	gefangen	*attraper*
fechten[17]	focht	gefochten	*combattre*
*fliegen	flog	geflogen	*voler (en l'air)*
*fliehen	floh	geflohen	*fuir*
*fließen	floß	geflossen	*couler*
fressen[18]	fraß	gefressen	*manger (animaux)*
frieren	fror	gefroren	*geler*
gebären	gebar	geboren	*enfanter*
geben[19]	gab	gegeben	*donner*
gedeihen	gedieh	gediehen	*prospérer*
*gehen	ging	gegangen	*aller*
*gelingen[20]	gelang	gelungen	*réussir*
gelten[21]	galt	gegolten	*valoir*
genesen[22]	genas	genesen	*guérir*
genießen (acc.)	genoß	genossen	*jouir de*
*geschehen[23]	geschah	geschehen	*arriver (impersonnel)*
gewinnen	gewann	gewonnen	*gagner*
gießen	goß	gegossen	*verser*
gleichen	glich	geglichen	*ressembler*

5. er bläst. — 6. er brät. — 7. er bricht. — 8. er drischt. — 9. er darf. — 10. er empfiehlt. — 11. er erlischt. — 12. er erschrickt. — 13. er ißt. — 14. er fährt. — 15. er fällt. — 16. er fängt. — 17. er ficht. — 18. er frißt. — 19. er gibt. — 20. es gelingt ihm. — 21. es gilt. — 22. er genest. — 23. es geschieht.

*gleiten	glitt	geglitten	*glisser*
glimmen	glomm	geglommen	*se consummer*
graben[24]	grub	gegraben	*creuser*
greifen	griff	gegriffen	*saisir*
halten[25]	hielt	gehalten	*tenir*
hängen[26]	hing	gehangen	*être suspendu*
hauen	hieb	gehauen	*donner un coup*
heben	hob	gehoben	*lever, tailler*
heißen	hieß	geheißen	*s'appeler, dire de...*
helfen[27]	half	geholfen	*aider*
kennen	kannte	gekannt	*connaître*
*klimmen	klomm	geklommen	*grimper*
klingen	klang	geklungen	*tinter, sonner*
kneifen	kniff	gekniffen	*pincer*
können[28]	konnte	gekonnt	*pouvoir*
*kommen	kam	gekommen	*venir*
*kriechen	kroch	gekrochen	*ramper*
laden[29]	lud (ladete)	geladen	*inviter, charger*
lassen[30]	ließ	gelassen	*laisser*
*laufen[31]	lief	gelaufen	*courir*
leiden	litt	gelitten	*souffrir*
leihen	lieh	geliehen	*prêter*
lesen[32]	las	gelesen	*lire, ramasser*
liegen	lag	gelegen	*être couché*
lügen	log	gelogen	*mentir*
meiden	mied	gemieden	*éviter*
messen[33]	maß	gemessen	*mesurer*
mögen[34]	mochte	gemocht	*pouvoir*
müssen[35]	mußte	gemußt	*devoir*
nehmen[36]	nahm	genommen	*prendre*
nennen	nannte	genannt	*nommer*
pfeifen	pfiff	gepfiffen	*siffler*
preisen	pries	gepriesen	*priser, louer*
quellen[37]	quoll	gequollen	*jaillir, sourdre*
raten[38]	riet	geraten	*conseiller, deviner*
reiben	rieb	gerieben	*frotter*
reißen	riß	gerissen	*arracher*
reiten	ritt	geritten	*aller à cheval*

24. er gräbt. — 25. er hält. — 26. er hängt. — 27. er hilft. — 28. er kann. — 29. er lädt (ladet). — 30. er läßt. — 31. er läuft. — 32. er liest. — 33. er mißt. — 34. er mag. — 35. er muß. — 36. er nimmt. — 37. er quillt. — 38. er rät.

*rennen	rannte	gerannt	*faire la course*
riechen	roch	gerochen	*sentir, flairer*
ringen	rang	gerungen	*lutter*
*rinnen	rann	geronnen	*couler*
rufen	rief	gerufen	*appeler*
saufen[39]	soff	gesoffen	*boire (animaux)*
saugen[40]	sog (saugte)	gesogen (gesaugt)	*sucer*
schaffen[47b]	schuf	geschaffen	*créer*
*scheiden	schied	geschieden	*(se) séparer*
scheinen	schien	geschienen	*briller, sembler*
schelten[41]	schalt	gescholten	*traiter de, gronder*
scheren	schor	geschoren	*tondre*
schieben	schob	geschoben	*pousser déplacer*
schießen	schoß	geschossen	*tirer (arme)*
schlafen[42]	schlief	geschlafen	*dormir*
schlagen[43]	schlug	geschlagen	*battre*
*schleichen	schlich	geschlichen	*se glisser*
schleifen	schliff	geschliffen	*aiguiser*
schließen	schloß	geschlossen	*fermer*
schlingen	schlang	geschlungen	*enlacer*
schmeißen	schmiß	geschmissen	*jeter*
schmelzen[44]	schmolz	geschmolzen	*fondre (intr.)*
schnauben[45]	schnob	geschnoben	*souffler fort*
schneiden	schnitt	geschnitten	*couper*
schreiben	schrieb	geschrieben	*écrire*
schreien	schrie	geschrieen	*crier*
schreiten	schritt	geschritten	*marcher*
schweigen	schwieg	geschwiegen	*se taire*
*schwellen[46]	schwoll	geschwollen	*se gonfler*
*schwimmen	schwamm	geschwommen	*nager*
*schwinden	schwand	geschwunden	*disparaître*
schwingen	schwang	geschwungen	*brandir, osciller*
schwören	schwor	geschworen	*jurer*
sehen[47]	sah	gesehen	*voir*
senden[47c]	sandte	gesandt	*envoyer*
sieden	sott	gesotten	*bouillir*
singen	sang	gesungen	*chanter*
*sinken	sank	gesunken	*s'affaisser*
sinnen	sann	gesonnen	*réfléchir*

39. er säuft. – 40. er saugt. – 41. er schilt. – 42. er schläft. – 43. er schlägt. – 44. er schmilzt. – 45. (égalt, faible). – 46. es schwillt. – 47. er sieht. – 47b. er schafft. – 47c. (égalt, faible).

sitzen	saß	gesessen	*être assis*
sollen[48]	sollte	gesollt	*devoir*
speien	spie	gespieen	*cracher*
spinnen	spann	gesponnen	*filer*
sprechen[49]	sprach	gesprochen	*parler*
*sprießen	sproß	gesprossen	*bourgeonner*
*springen	sprang	gesprungen	*sauter*
stechen[50]	stach	gestochen	*piquer*
stehen	stand	gestanden	*être debout*
stehlen[51]	stahl	gestohlen	*dérober*
*steigen	stieg	gestiegen	*monter*
*sterben	starb	gestorben	*mourir*
stinken	stank	gestunken	*puer*
stoßen[52]	stieß	gestoßen	*heurter, pousser*
streichen	strich	gestrichen	*frotter légèrement*
streiten	stritt	gestritten	*lutter*
tragen[53]	trug	getragen	*porter*
treffen[54]	traf	getroffen	*atteindre*
treiben	trieb	getrieben	*pousser (devant soi)*
*treten[55]	trat	getreten	*mettre le pied*
trinken	trank	getrunken	*boire*
trügen	trog	getrogen	*tromper*
tun[56]	tat	getan	*faire, agir*
verbieten	verbot	verboten	*interdire*
*verderben[57]	verdarb	verdorben	*se gâter*
verdrießen	verdroß	verdrossen	*contrarier*
vergessen[58]	vergaß	vergessen	*oublier*
verlieren	verlor	verloren	*perdre*
*wachsen[59]	wuchs	gewachsen	*croître*
waschen[60]	wusch	gewaschen	*laver*
weben	wob	gewoben	*tisser*
*weichen	wich	gewichen	*céder*
weisen	wies	gewiesen	*indiquer*
wenden[64]	wandte	gewandt	*tourner*
werben[61]	warb	geworben	*rechercher, briguer*
werfen[62]	warf	geworfen	*lancer*
winden	wand	gewunden	*tordre*
wollen[63]	wollte	gewollt	*vouloir*
*ziehen	zog	gezogen	*tirer, aller*
zwingen	zwang	gezwungen	*forcer à*

48. er soll. — 49. er spricht. — 50. er sticht. — 51. er stiehlt. — 52. er stößt. — 53. er trägt. — 54. er trifft. — 55. er tritt. — 56. er tut. — 57. es verdirbt. — 58. er vergißt. — 59. er wächst. — 60. er wäscht. — 61. er wirbt. — 62. er wirft. — 63. er will. — 64. (égalt. faible).

TABLE DES MATIÈRES DU MÉMENTO

Les chiffres renvoient aux articles 1 à 78

INDEX GRAMMATICAL

Les chiffres en romain renvoient aux leçons, ceux en italique, au mémento.

Index des sujets

(Les chiffres renvoient aux pages)

Version sonore Méthode 90

I. Présentation

Pour l'enregistrement sonore de la **Méthode 90** d'allemand, nous avons fait appel à des voix de diverses provenances. Vous pourrez ainsi vous familiariser avec des intonations différentes.

Le rythme des voix est naturel pour que vous puissiez vous accoutumer à la communication orale courante.

Comme dans le livre, vous retrouverez le découpage en trois parties :

1. Éléments de base (leçons 1 à 25) ;
2. Allemand de la vie quotidienne (leçons 26 à 75) ;
3. Textes d'écrivains contemporains (leçons 76 à 90).

Les 25 premières leçons s'adressent aux débutants ou aux personnes qui désirent se recycler.

Les **cinq cassettes** qui composent la **version sonore** de la **Méthode 90** comportent chacune, en moyenne, 70 minutes d'enregistrement (35 minutes environ par face) ; vous disposez donc de près de 6 heures d'écoute.

Chaque cassette débute et se termine par quelques mesures de musique. Les leçons sont annoncées par un top sonore.

II. Conseils d'utilisation

Nous vous conseillons d'utiliser la version sonore de la **Méthode 90** en vous conformant au programme suivant :

1. Familiarisez-vous avec la sonorité, avec l'enchaînement sonore de la phrase allemande. Après l'énoncé du numéro de chaque leçon et de son titre, vous entendrez la rubrique : **Wiederholen Sie** (Répétez) ou **Wiederholen Sie bitte** (Répétez s'il vous plaît). Chaque paragraphe est précédé du numéro correspondant. Écoutez chaque phrase, efforcez-vous de la répéter mentalement. Puis écoutez de nouveau et répétez à haute voix. Si l'intervalle laissé après chaque phrase ne vous suffit pas, arrêtez votre lecteur de cassette.

Vous écouterez ensuite l'ensemble de ce texte enregistré continûment, sans arrêt entre les phrases: **Hören Sie zu** (Écoutez) ou bien **Hören Sie bitte zu** (Écoutez s'il vous plaît).

2. Familiarisez-vous avec le sens du texte. Vous avez entendu, vous avez répété ; comprenez le sens. Aidez-vous de la traduction. Étudiez nos explications (prononciation, vocabulaire, grammaire). À partir de la traduction, faites un thème, c'est-à-dire retrouvez le texte allemand (par écrit ou par oral ; dans ce cas, dites la phrase avant de l'entendre prononcée par la voix allemande).

3. Faites, par écrit, les exercices. Étudiez-en le corrigé. Écoutez ensuite l'enregistrement des exercices et parlez.

Considérez que vous ne perdez jamais de temps en écoutant et en parlant, même si vous avez l'impression de savoir. N'oubliez pas que, dans votre langue maternelle, vous répétez chaque jour les mêmes tournures et les mêmes mots, ou presque.

- Nous vous guiderons, au cours de la **première leçon**, en vous répétant quelques-uns des conseils qui précèdent.

- À partir de la **septième leçon,** vous entendrez d'abord tout le texte de la première page de chaque leçon avant de l'entendre paragraphe par paragraphe. Écoutez la leçon dans son intégralité (première page) d'abord livre fermé. C'est un excellent exercice d'accoutumance au rythme et à la musique de la langue ; et peut-être reconnaîtrez-vous des mots que vous savez déjà. Après cette phase de découverte, suivez le même programme que celui précédemment indiqué.

• Terminez **toujours** votre séance de travail par l'écoute et la répétition ou la traduction **livre fermé** pour vous assurer que vous avez assimilé la matière de la leçon.

• Les **leçons 76 à 90** comportent uniquement des textes d'écrivains et de journalistes contemporains. Vous avez avantage à aborder ces leçons par voie d'écoute, livre fermé. Puis à les lire en écoutant de nouveau. Étudiez la traduction. Lorsque vous avez compris le sens, revenez à l'écoute livre fermé, comme précédemment.

III. Contenu des cinq cassettes

Cassette 1A

■ **Présentation**

Leçon 1. Il apprend dans le parc.
Leçon 2. Le Congrès de Cologne.
Leçon 3. L'hôtel.
Leçon 4. Des lettres aux amis.
Leçon 5. Monsieur Beckmann, l'interprète.
Leçon 6. Ce langage est international.
Leçon 7. Dans la salle de congrès.

Cassette 1B

Leçon 8. Une journée à Cologne.
Leçon 9. Dans la famille Müller (1).
Leçon 10. Dans la famille Müller (2).
Leçon 11. Notes du congrès.
Leçon 12. Le grand magasin.

Leçon 13. Le matin à l'hôtel.
Leçon 14. Une petite excursion (1).

Cassette 2A

Leçon 15. Une petite excursion (2).
Leçon 16. Un accident de circulation.
Leçon 17. Un orage.
Leçon 18. Camping.
Leçon 19. La visite d'une filature.
Leçon 20. L'artisanat et l'industrie.
Leçon 21. Délassement entre les fleurs et les légumes.

Cassette 2B

Leçon 22. La grande fête d'automne.
Leçon 23. La télévision.
Leçon 24. Nouvelles brèves.
Leçon 25. Une surprise agréable.
Leçon 26. La voiture.
Leçon 27. Au poste à essence.
Leçon 28. L'avion.
Leçon 29. Nous voyageons par avion.

Cassette 3A

Leçon 30. Le chemin de fer.
Leçon 31. Vous allez prendre le train.
Leçon 32. Le bateau.
Leçon 33. L'arrivée à bord.
Leçon 34. Le passeport.
Leçon 35. Douane et change.
Leçon 36. L'hôtel.
Leçon 37. Nous réservons une chambre à l'hôtel.
Leçon 38. Arrivée à l'hôtel.
Leçon 39. Les repas.
Leçon 40. Le petit déjeuner.

Cassette 3B

Leçon 41. Un déjeuner expédié.
Leçon 42. Le dîner.
Leçon 43. Circulation en ville.
Leçon 44. Comment demander son chemin.

Leçon 45. La banque ; la poste.
Leçon 46. À la banque.
Leçon 47. À la poste.
Leçon 48. Le téléphone.
Leçon 49. Le médecin.

Cassette 4A

Leçon 50. Chez le médecin, chez le dentiste.
Leçon 51. Les monuments.
Leçon 52. Au musée.
Leçon 53. Au théâtre.
Leçon 54. La fête d'octobre à Munich et le carnaval rhénan.
Leçon 55. Politesse.
Leçon 56. Nous rendons visite à des amis communs.
Leçon 57. À la campagne.
Leçon 58. Excursions.
Leçon 59. Nous achetons des souvenirs pour nos amis.
Leçon 60. En flânant dans le quartier des affaires.

Cassette 4B

Leçon 61. Achats dans un magasin d'alimentation.
Leçon 62. Livres, papiers, journaux.
Leçon 63. Vêtements d'homme.
Leçon 64. Vêtements de femme.
Leçon 65. Dans le magasin de chaussures et chez le cordonnier.
Leçon 66. Chez le coiffeur.
Leçon 67. Entretien, propreté.
Leçon 68. La maison de campagne
Leçon 69. L'appartement.

Cassette 5A

Leçon 70. Des amis mettent leur appartement à votre disposition.
Leçon 71. La famille.
Leçon 72. Les enfants et l'école.
Leçon 73. Le corps humain.
Leçon 74. Qu'aimez-vous lire ?
Leçon 75. Qu'aimez-vous voir ? Qu'aimez-vous entendre ?
Leçon 76. Vacances en Allemagne (M. Schiff).

Leçon 77. La ville et la campagne (M. Schiff).
Leçons 78 et 79. La Mort marraine (Grimm).
Leçon 80. Un héros, un très grand héros (E. Rechlin).

Cassette 5B

Leçon 81. Le baptême des jumeaux à Cologne (H. Spoerl).
Leçon 82. Extraits des Mémoires de Monsieur de Schnabelewopski (H. Heine).
Leçon 83. Une petite ville du nom de Lugano (P. Westphal).
Leçon 84. Tête-à-tête auprès de la Fondue (W. Bergengruen).
Leçon 85. Les meubles de style continuent à progresser (H. Rieker).
Leçon 86. Une heure d'attente (H. Böll).
Leçon 87. Conseils pour tueurs (J. Wechsberg).
Leçon 88. L'exemple (H. Kranz).
Leçon 89. Des étoiles sur le monde en ruines (Th. Plievier).
Leçon 90. Tu nous apportes un monde nouveau (E. Wiechert).

IMPRIMÉ EN FRANCE PAR BRODARD ET TAUPIN
Usine de La Flèche (Sarthe).
LIBRAIRIE GÉNÉRALE FRANÇAISE - 6, rue Pierre-Sarrazin - 75006 Paris.

ISBN : 2 - 253 - 00439 - 1 30/2298/5